PEN
A DAUGHTER

Born in Paris and educated in Europe and America, poet and novelist Natasha Borovsky is the daughter of Alexander Borovsky, the late concert pianist and former music tutor to the nephews of Tsar Nicholas II. Ms Borovsky's mother was descended of Russian and Polish nobility. Her maternal grandfather, General Sila-Nowicki, Grand-Duke Constantine's aide-de-camp, was murdered by deserters in 1917. Her uncle Julian, an army cadet when the Russian Revolution erupted, died in a Soviet prison. Both branches of her family were intimately involved in the historical events she describes.

Ms Borovsky and her British husband, a journalist, live in Berkeley, California.

NATASHA BOROVSKY

* * *

A DAUGHTER OF THE NOBILITY

*

PENGUIN BOOKS

Penguin Books Ltd, Harmondsworth, Middlesex, England
Viking Penguin Inc., 40 West 23rd Street, New York, New York 10010, U.S.A.
Penguin Books Australia Ltd, Ringwood, Victoria, Australia
Penguin Books Canada Limited, 2801 John Street, Markham, Ontario, Canada L3R 1B4
Penguin Books (N.Z.) Ltd, 182–190 Wairau Road, Auckland 10, New Zealand

First published in the U.S.A. by Holt Rinehart Winston 1985
First published in Great Britain by Viking 1986
Published in Penguin Books 1986

Made and printed in Great Britain by
Richard Clay (The Chaucer Press) Ltd,
Bungay, Suffolk
Filmset in Monophoto Times by
Northumberland Press Ltd, Gateshead,
Tyne and Wear

To the memory of my mother and father
and their generation

AUTHOR'S NOTE

This is a novel, not a memoir. Any resemblance it may bear to the memoirs of real persons, living or dead, is coincidental.

The daughters of Tsar Nicholas II did not have even the single friend my story attributes to them.

The Silomirsky Foundation is not meant to detract from the merits or achievements of existing institutions of its kind.

Russian dates before 1918 are given in the Old Style (the Julian Calendar). Events of international scope, like the First World War, are dated in New Style (Gregorian).

I am indebted to members of the Russian colonies in San Francisco, New York, London and Paris for their advice on points of authenticity. And I cannot thank my husband enough for his invaluable assistance and support.

THE SILOMIRSKY FAMILY

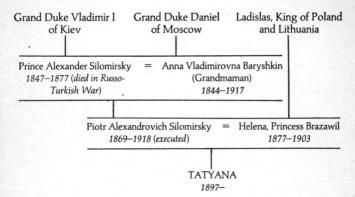

RURIK DYNASTY
(800–1500)

JAGIELLON DYNASTY
(1300–1500)

Grand Duke Vladimir I of Kiev

Grand Duke Daniel of Moscow

Ladislas, King of Poland and Lithuania

Prince Alexander Silomirsky = Anna Vladimirovna Baryshkin (Grandmaman)
1847–1877 (died in Russo-Turkish War) — *1844–1917*

Piotr Alexandrovich Silomirsky = Helena, Princess Brazawil
1869–1918 (executed) — *1877–1903*

TATYANA
1897–

THE VESLAWSKI FAMILY

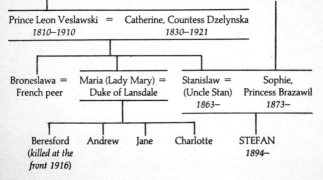

PIAST DYNASTY
(900–1300)

JAGIELLON DYNASTY
(1300–1500)

Boleslas III

Ladislas, King of Poland and Lithuania

Prince Leon Veslawski = Catherine, Countess Dzelynska
1810–1910 — *1830–1921*

Broneslawa = French peer

Maria (Lady Mary) = Duke of Lansdale

Stanislaw (Uncle Stan) = Sophie, Princess Brazawil
1863– — *1873–*

Beresford *(killed at the front 1916)*

Andrew

Jane

Charlotte

STEFAN
1894–

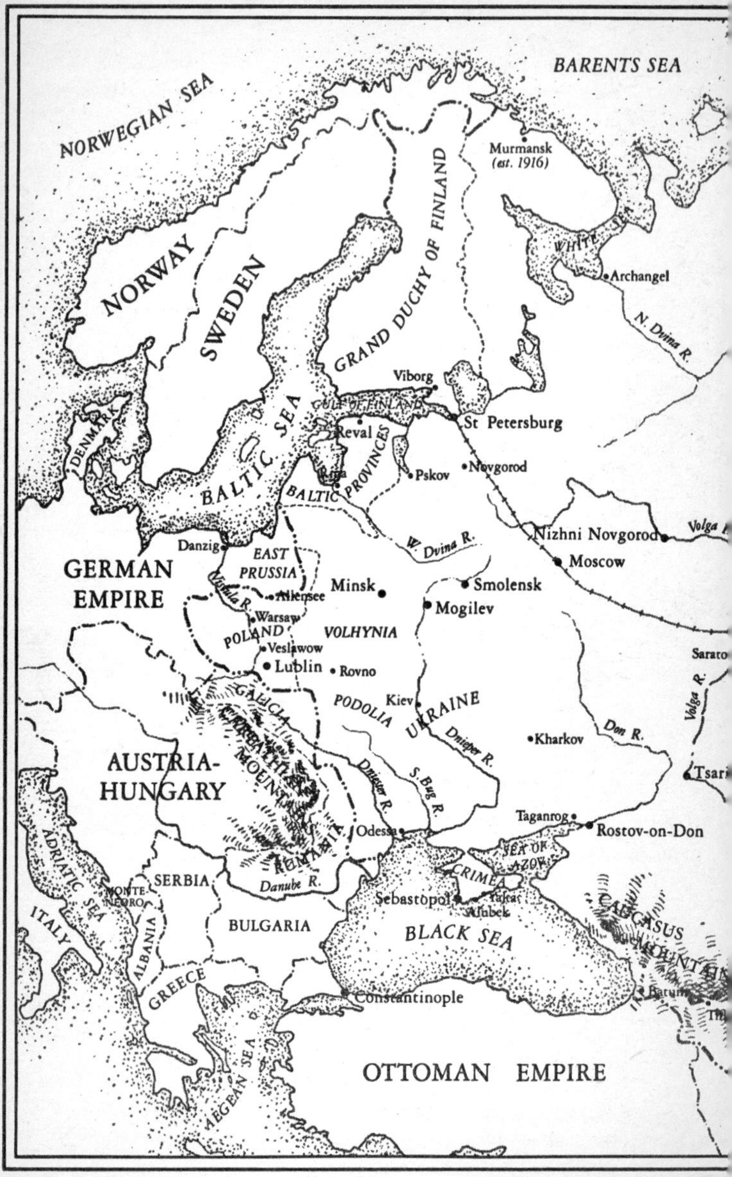
BARENTS SEA
NORWEGIAN SEA
Murmansk (est. 1916)
WHITE SEA
Archangel
N. Dvina R.
NORWAY
SWEDEN
GRAND DUCHY OF FINLAND
Viborg
GULF OF FINLAND
St Petersburg
DENMARK
BALTIC SEA
Reval
BALTIC PROVINCES
Riga
Pskov
Novgorod
Nizhni Novgorod
Volga R.
W. Dvina R.
Moscow
Danzig
EAST PRUSSIA
GERMAN EMPIRE
Vistula R.
Allensee
Minsk
Smolensk
Mogilev
Warsaw
POLAND
VOLHYNIA
Veslawow
Lublin
Rovno
GALICIA
CARPATHIAN MOUNTS
PODOLIA
Kiev
UKRAINE
Dnieper R.
Kharkov
Don R.
Volga R.
AUSTRIA-HUNGARY
Dniester R.
S. Bug R.
Taganrog
Rostov-on-Don
Odessa
RUMANIA
SEA OF AZOV
CRIMEA
ADRIATIC SEA
MONTENEGRO
SERBIA
Danube R.
Sebastopol
Yalta
Alubek
CAUCASUS MOUNTAINS
ITALY
BULGARIA
BLACK SEA
ALBANIA
GREECE
Constantinople
Batum
AEGEAN SEA
OTTOMAN EMPIRE

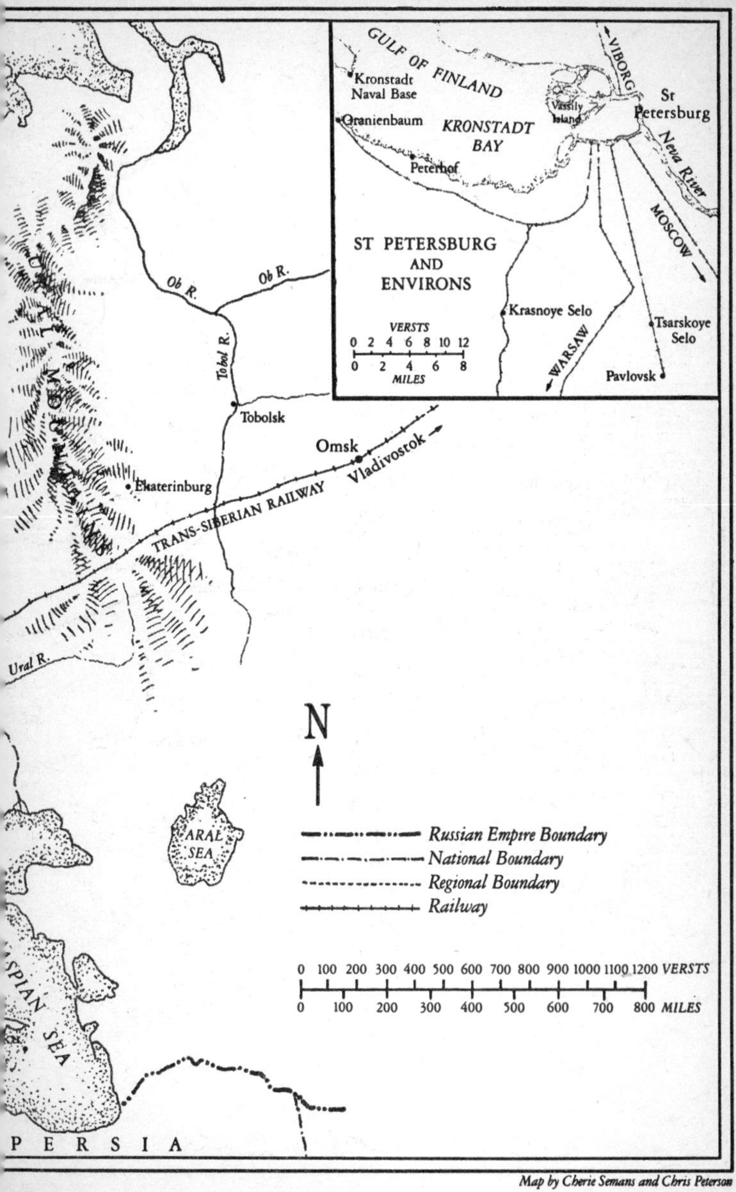

GULF OF FINLAND
Kronstadt Naval Base
Oranienbaum
KRONSTADT BAY
Peterhof
Vassily Island
St Petersburg
VIBORG
Neva River
MOSCOW
ST PETERSBURG AND ENVIRONS
Krasnoye Selo
WARSAW
Tsarskoye Selo
Pavlovsk
VERSTS
0 2 4 6 8 10 12
0 2 4 6 8
MILES
Ob R.
Ob R.
Tobol R.
Tobolsk
Omsk
Vladivostok
Ekaterinburg
TRANS-SIBERIAN RAILWAY
Ural R.
N
ARAL SEA
Russian Empire Boundary
National Boundary
Regional Boundary
Railway
0 100 200 300 400 500 600 700 800 900 1000 1100 1200 VERSTS
0 100 200 300 400 500 600 700 800 MILES
SEA
P E R S I A

Map by Cherie Semans and Chris Peterson

PART ONE

GIRLHOOD

1897–1914

1

I was born in a great colonnaded house on the Quai Anglais in Petersburg on the same day as the Tsar's daughter, Grand Duchess Tatyana, and named Tatyana in her honour. Cathedral bells pealed; the Fortress of Petropavlovsk fired a twenty-one-gun salute to the imperial birth. The date was 28 May 1897, three years after the accession of Nicholas II and eight years before the Revolution of 1905, which was the beginning of the end for both our families.

Our fathers had grown up together. They served together in the Guard Hussars. A favourite of Alexander III's, my father had been intended for a Romanov princess. But he married a Polish one instead, incurring the Court's displeasure. In later years my father told me how the happy coincidence of their daughters' arrival had moved the Tsar to a reconciliation.

'I hope, Pierre,' our sovereign had said graciously when my father presented his congratulations the day after our birth, 'our Tatyanas will be as close friends as we.'

'It is also my fondest wish, Your Majesty,' my father replied.

The same afternoon, he accompanied the Tsar on a walk with his collies through the grounds of Peterhof, a Russian Versailles on the Finnish gulf. Later that month, he was invited back to Peterhof to have tea in the Alexandria Cottage, the modest summer residence of Nicholas and Alexandra more suited to their taste than the proud palace over the sea. The conversation, in English, was banal and bland as usual. One remark of the Tsar's, however, was worth reporting and came to be associated with my image of our sovereign.

The Empress had criticized the custom of granting amnesty when a child was born to the Emperor. 'These political prisoners are such rabble, Nicky,' she said. 'They only want to destroy you and Russia.'

'God has been good to us,' the Tsar rejoined. 'One must be merciful.'

From the time I said my first word, which was *Pa-pa*, I was in love with my father. I thought him the handsomest man in the world, the bravest and the kindest. He called me his beauty and his joy, took me swimming on his broad back and riding behind his saddle, carried me to bed when I fell asleep on an outing, and sat by my bed when I was ill.

In 1901, the Tsar made him commander of the Guard Hussars. To watch him review his regiment was the most exciting event in my early life and I knew parade drill by heart before I learned nursery rhymes.

When Father was gone, I was disconsolate and asked everyone, 'Where did Papa go? When will Papa be back?'

In his presence I was ecstatic. But the moment my mother appeared, bliss vanished. For even though Father remained just as tender, his attention was no longer totally on me. I also noticed that my mother, who often looked languid and distant, grew strangely rapt and absorbed under Father's gaze. I became aware of powerful emotions between my parents, which disturbed and angered me. I wanted to surprise them alone together, to get at the source of the puzzle, but this was not easy.

In Petersburg in winter, I was restricted to my nursery suite on the third floor of the private wing of our *osobnyak* overlooking the Neva. In charge of my world were Nanny Bailey, an amiable young Scotswoman, and Nyanya. Born a family serf, Nyanya, black-haired, black-eyed, lithe and little, had been my father's wet nurse. She still wore the *kakoshnik* and *sarafan* – the national headdress and pinafore – blue, in this instance, to designate her calling. A bevy of peasant maids in scarlet pinafores and wide-sleeved embroidered blouses served as Nyanya's minions and officiated at my toilette.

There was also my footman, the blond, snub-nosed giant, Fyodor, a *bogatyr* – a mighty warrior out of the pages of my storybooks. Childishly simple and as imperturbable as he was huge, Fyodor strummed the balalaika for me. He rode on the running board of my sleigh, and carried me out of forbidden places like the stables, cellars and kitchens. On my daily promenade along the quay, Fyodor also frustrated my attempts to straddle the stone lions at the head of the steps going down to the frozen river.

My other thwarted desire was to take part in snowball battles with our yard porter's male brood. Instead I was taken to play at

the Marble Palace of Grand Duke Constantine or the Tsar's Winter Palace. At the latter I attended dancing class with Olga and Tatyana, the Tsar's oldest daughters – two more had arrived since the birth of my imperial namesake.

At our first dancing lesson, when we were four, I took the Grand Duchess Tatyana Nikolayevna by the neck, rather than by the hand as instructed, and proceeded to choke her. In response, Tatyana Nikolayevna seized me by the neck. We circled in silent fury until pulled apart.

'That child is a horror,' said my mother to Their Majesties.

The Tsar only laughed and remarked in his soft voice, '*Elle sera une maîtresse-femme, cette petite!* She'll be a woman to reckon with!'

Father also laughed, but Grandmother was not amused.

The Dowager Princess Silomirskaya – Anna Vladimirovna to her friends, Grandmaman to me – was a tall, vigorous and stately lady with a voice like a man's, a manner disconcertingly direct, and expressive brown eyes, typically Russian. In contrast to Father, who liked to wear jewels and furs and to surround himself with *objets d'art*, she affected a spartan simplicity. Except at court functions, where black was forbidden, she had worn mourning since the death of my grandfather in 1877 in the Russo-Turkish War. She usually had about her a black French poodle and always carried an ebony cane. Autocrat of Petersburg high society and of the Silomirsky household, she was the only person of whom I stood in awe.

The winter I was five, on the day of the Palm Ball at the Winter Palace, I was playing horse in the nursery after tea when a maid came up to say my mother was resting and was not to be disturbed. Sulkily, I went to the window and blew on the frosted double pane. Two mounted hussars appeared on the quay at a fast trot, escorting a small sledge in which my father sat, dressed in a white greatcoat with a mink collar and a flowing half-cape. Behind him on the running board stood his Cossack orderly in black fur bonnet.

Sledge and escort disappeared under the arcades of our carriage entrance – the *podiezd* – and I knew that in a few seconds Father would be going up to Mother's apartment. Now might be the moment to surprise them alone together! I ran out of the nursery, down a stairway, past my mother's startled Polish page, and through her empty sitting room and study. The door of her boudoir was slightly ajar. I pushed it and stood quietly in the opening.

Mother in a white flounced dressing gown, her chestnut hair loose and thick, reclined on a chaise longue. Father sat by her, his hands about her small waist. I was struck by the expression on Mother's face. Father's back was turned to me. As he bent over Mother, her large lids closed, while her slender hands clasped Father's sandy head. I must have gasped, for she opened her eyes.

'Pierre, your daughter is watching us,' she said, and Father turned abruptly. His face was flushed, its expression strange and terrible. I fled.

All evening I brooded over Father's betrayal. I did not eat supper. I did not hold a towel to my eyes after the bath and play Moslem princess. I did not even screech when Nyanya brushed my hair and wound it painfully tight in paper curlers. The more concerned Nyanya was, the harder she pulled.

At bedtime prayers, Father entered, wearing the white gold-laced tunic of his dress uniform. Elegantly fastened to one shoulder was a red velvet capelet with mink border – a *mentik*.

I gazed up as though at God the Father. Mine did in fact resemble His image in Grandmaman's Bible illustrated by Gustave Doré.

After hearing from Nyanya how I was not quite myself that night, he dismissed her and said in English, 'If you wish to see your mother, Tanichka, you know you must ask permission, don't you?'

'Mama never wants to see me.'

Father was silent. Then, 'You don't feel you've done anything wrong?'

'I'm sorry, Papa.' I hung my head.

'All right. Now will you forgive me for frightening you?'

'Will you pay a penalty?'

'I don't have to crawl under the bed or through a chair, do I? I'm dressed for the ball.'

I extended my hand. 'Kiss it. No' – as he ceremoniously took it – 'I am Catherine the Great. Kneel.'

So Father bent his knee and kissed my hand respectfully. Then, seizing me about the waist, he asked, still kneeling, 'What else does my Empress command?'

I hadn't the heart to send him to the torture. Placing my hands on his hair in a domineering gesture, I ordered, 'Put me to bed and tell me a story.'

Which story did I want to hear tonight? 'Tsar Saltan'? 'Baba Yaga'? 'The Snow Maiden'?

'You know,' I fairly screamed.

'Ah yes, "The Little Mermaid"!'

Many were the nights my own legs had ached and I had been that mute little mermaid who loved an indifferent prince.

'Papa,' I asked when his beautiful, deep voice was still, 'who do you love the most in the whole world?'

'You' – he kissed me on the cheek – 'and your mama' – he kissed me on the other.

'But who do you love the most?' I persisted.

'You, and your mama.' Again, he kissed and tickled me with his silky, scented beard. 'Each in a different way but both equally well.'

'Papa ... I love *you* more than anybody in the whole world.'

Father looked at me long and thoughtfully. 'How would you like Mama to come and kiss you goodnight?'

'Mama wouldn't!'

'Shall we see?' He sent to ask Princess Helena to come up. My mother's favourite Polish maid reported that Her Serene Ladyship was ready and awaiting His Mighty Lordship downstairs.

'Tell Her Ladyship I expect her *here*.'

While his request was conveyed, Father sat tapping a hand covered with precious rings.

Will Mama come? Will she be angry at Papa? I thought, feeling both alarm and delight.

Mother came.

I sat up in dumb wonder. She wore a court dress of white brocade with jewelled buttons down the front. From her shoulders fell a train of scarlet velvet bordered with sable. A diamond necklace with a ruby pendant clasped her slender neck. Ropes of pearls reached to her knees. Her hair was crowned by a pearl-studded *kakoshnik* of scarlet velvet with a floor-length veil sewn with gems. The blue ribbon of the Polish Order of the White Eagle crossed her breast. She was a fairy queen, but a cold queen, a snow queen, a queen of the night.

'Am I to be summoned like a servant, my lord?' she demanded.

Father had risen. If Mother was Snow Queen, he was Ice King. 'Is it too much to ask a mother to kiss her only daughter goodnight?'

I watched, wide-eyed, this clash of wills.

Mother broke first. 'Don't be cross with me tonight, Pierre,' she said with musical Polish intonation. 'It's difficult for me to come upstairs. The train is so heavy.'

'Difficult?' Father looked at her intently. 'You're not well?'

'I'm not . . . ill.' Her expression, under his gaze, grew sweet and suggestive, as it had earlier during his kiss. Gracefully, she extended a pleading hand.

He took it in both of his. 'Helena, my dearest, really? Are you quite sure?'

'Quite. I was about to tell you this afternoon, when Tanya interrupted.'

'Dearest, beloved, I'm so grateful.' He kissed her hand repeatedly. 'Forgive me. Would you rather we stayed home?'

'No. We must go. But after tonight' – Mother came to the bedside – 'I will stay home more – with *our* daughter.'

Mother's expression was so tender I wondered if she might not love me, at least a little.

Father guessed my question. 'You see, Tanichka, Mama loves you so much she's going to give you the most wonderful present of all, a baby sister or brother so you won't be lonely any more.'

I wasn't lonely as long as I had Father. And I was not sure I wanted that sort of present. Still, if it made Mother look at me that way . . . 'Shall I get one for my birthday?'

'Not quite so soon. In the summer. Goodnight, my darling.' Mother bent over me.

Could she really be about to kiss me? I closed my eyes. A cheek softer than any I had imagined touched mine. I kept my eyes blissfully shut until the rustle of Mother's pearls and brocade gown had faded. I opened them to see her go out the door, her hand over Father's as in a polonaise. And no fairy-tale prince and princess in my world of make-believe were as stately and splendid as these – my own parents.

After the Palm Ball, I saw a good deal more of Mother. She took me driving, had me brought down to her apartment for a kiss at bedtime and sometimes when she was resting in the afternoon as well.

Sitting on the floor beside her chaise longue, I prattled as I built a castle of cards or dominoes. From time to time I would say, 'Yes, Mama, yes?' and she would answer, 'Mmm-hmm', very sweetly.

I looked up suspiciously. Clearly, she had not heard a word. The novel she had been reading dangled from listless fingers. I saw she was not thinking about me or even about Father. What did she dream about?

I noticed that Mother's waist was no longer slender. Her hands often strayed to the new roundness beneath her dress, and she had, at such moments, a soft and dreamy look.

I began to tuck a small pillow under my skirt, imitating my mother's expression.

'What is it you've got under there, my love?' Nyanya would ask.

'A baby brother,' I would answer.

Who had put the baby brother in Mother's tummy? I wondered.

Nanny Bailey would turn red at the question and stammer unintelligibly.

Nyanya would reply, God had. But when I wanted to know how, she brushed me off with, 'In the way it was meant to be.'

I finally asked Grandmaman, who was very frank. 'Your papa did,' she answered in her deep voice. 'And about time, too.'

'But how did Papa do it?' I persisted.

'In the way God meant him to,' said she, and I was left to my conjectures.

I stuffed my dolls' skirts with rags, drew ladies with protuberant tummies, and played house instead of horses with the Tsar's daughters. I even became maternal towards plump and clumsy Grand Duchess Marie, who was relegated to the role of footman by her older sisters Olga and Tatyana. Anastasia – fourth and last of the dynastically superfluous daughters, in Grandmaman's phrase – was still a baby, and Marie had no ally as yet.

Like me, little Marie doted on her father. The Tsar was as patient and affectionate with her as with his other girls. But he lavished more tenderness and adoration on his beautiful, frail empress, the former Princess Alix of Hesse, raised at Queen Victoria's court and transplanted to exotic, alien soil.

As Mother drew near her term, I, too, moved slowly, with a new dignity. I even sat still long enough to pose with Mother for the portrait Father was painting. Done with the light brushwork inspired by his friend and teacher, Valentin Serov, the portrait was his best work.

It prompted Grandmaman to say, 'What does a man of your artistic sensibility, Pierre, find in lurid trash?' She disapproved of Father's Fauvist and Expressionist acquisitions.

In June 1903, after my sixth birthday, we did not go to the Crimea. In expectation of Mother's confinement, we moved instead to our suburban dacha on the Gulf of Finland. It was here we usually stayed while the Court was in residence at Peterhof. The land was marshy and wooded, abounding in polecat and wild duck, with hidden coves and a bridle path along the shore. Secluded among conifers, the main villa faced the sea. Terraced gardens with fountains only slightly less magnificent than those at Peterhof descended to the granite quay where our yacht, the *Helena*, was berthed. I had my own sailboat and rowboat, a pack of dogs, and a pony cart that I drove, followed by a mounted groom. I ate my meals on the upper terrace with Bailey and, once again, saw little of Mother.

A change had come over her. She grew not only round but puffy. Her fingers were swollen, her fine features distorted. She was put to bed with an English doctor and nurse in attendance. The villa grew strangely still, and I was repeatedly told to be quiet. Father was never sharp with me, but his fine grey eyes expressed a mortal anguish. Grandmaman looked very stern, and Nyanya jerked my hair as she curled it, in a perfect frenzy of concern.

One morning in mid-July, as I was breakfasting in the nursery, Mother walked in, a white-and-gold silk kimono about her large figure. Her hair fell in a thick braid down one shoulder. Her puffy face was sallow. Her eyes had a feverish glitter.

Dismissing Bailey, she sat down across the table. She asked absently what I had done the previous day, then interrupted my answer. 'Tanya, don't judge me too harshly when you're grown. I was only eighteen when I married, spoiled and foolish. If I survive this ... this awful illness, I promise I'll be a better mother to you. If I don't ... be good to your father. Stay with him always. Promise.'

I thought this strange. Why should I ever want to leave Father?

'Promise. Swear it on the cross.' Mother spoke with growing agitation. 'A cross.' She turned to Nyanya. 'Fetch a cross.'

'This very minute, Princess dear.'

Nyanya returned, not only with a cross but several maids and the medical nurse as well. They surrounded Mother and urged her to come to bed.

'Tatyana, swear,' Mother reiterated, 'that you will never leave your father as long as he lives.'

I could not understand the game she wanted to play. But I swore solemnly, crossing myself and kissing the crucifix she held out.

'She is feverish, delirious.' 'Fetch the doctor.' 'Come, Your Ladyship,' cooed the women, 'you'll feel better in bed.'

'I am coming. Leave me be.' Mother stood up with effort and raised a hand to her forehead. 'Mother of God,' she said in Polish and fell heavily to the floor.

For a moment I saw her body jerking about with terrifying violence. Then Father strode in with the doctor and both knelt beside her thrashing body, hiding it from sight. Nyanya lifted me up, pressing my head to her bosom, and carried me off.

Two days later I saw Mother for the last time. She lay amidst tall candles in the chapel of the villa, lilies at her head, her hands crossed on her breast, her large lids closed. The swelling had disappeared. In death she lay slender and beautiful once more. A secretive half-smile was on her lips, as though she had been witness to some awesome, marvellous event.

Nyanya lifted me up to the bier to kiss the round white forehead, smooth and cold as marble. I wondered why it was so cold and how was it Mother did not mind the cold. I saw that she did not mind anything, that she was well. I was not sad, but everyone else seemed to be, and so I grew sad too. I began to cry, and Nyanya led me away.

That evening, like the previous, I waited in vain for Father to come and kiss me goodnight. A tall, blonde and lovely lady in a black dress with a high neck and puffed sleeves entered instead. It was my mother's older married sister, Sophie Veslawska.

'Tanyussia' – her voice had a Polish inflection like Mother's – 'God has called your mama to Him. She has gone to heaven with her infant son. We will pray for them both this night and every night from now on.'

'Mama is dead?' I said without emotion.

Aunt Sophie bowed her head.

I thought I would now have Father all to myself. Oddly enough, this did not make me happy. 'Who'll be my mama now?'

'I will, if you'll let me. You see, the Lord blessed me with a son, your cousin Stevie. But I can never have another child. Will you be my daughter, Tanyussia?'

I looked into Aunt's gentle face. It was not as exquisite as Mother's, but still lovely, compassionate and wise. I climbed into her lap, clasping her neck with one hand and stroking her silk blouse with the other. And there, in Aunt Sophie's lap, without even a prayer for the dead, I fell asleep.

After memorial services in St Isaac's Cathedral and the Catholic church of St Stanislaw, the baby was buried in our family crypt in the Convent of Alexander Nevsky, and Mother's body was taken in state to Poland to be laid with the Brazawil princes.

Father did not accompany the funeral train. He locked himself in his apartment in our villa, refusing admittance to any but his orderly, Simyon. I hovered forlorn outside his room.

A week went by. Then one morning, as I was being dressed, Father entered. He wore the grey-blue uniform of an imperial aide-de-camp and carried cap and gloves. He had grown thin. I could scarcely believe my eyes – his hair had turned silver. His eyes held the beginning of an incurable melancholy.

I looked up at him, heartbroken.

Father lifted me and held me long and hard. 'Tanichka, the Tsar, our sovereign, is sending me on a mission to the Far East. You will be going to Veslawa to stay with Aunt Sophie and Uncle Stan until I come to fetch you.'

'I don't want to go to Veslawa! I want to go with you!'

'Someday you and I will take a long trip together. But now we must each go our way. The Lord keep you. Be brave.' He kissed me and handed me into Nyanya's arms.

'Mama said I must never leave you. Mama made me promise. Mama made me swear on the cross!' I beat on Nyanya's thin breast and strained to free myself.

Father's face grew unfamiliar and frightening. Rapidly, he blessed me, put on his cap, and was gone.

I refused to be dressed. I marched into the playroom where my dolls, gifts from foreign princes and ambassadors, were arrayed against the wall. I hurled them about. I kicked and stamped on them. Then I threw myself facedown, pounding the floor with feet and fists, and screamed, 'Papa, Papa, I want my papa!'

Suddenly a vigorous step was heard and in strode Grandmaman. 'Out with you!' She waved her cane at my distraught maids.

Curtsying, they pushed each other out of the door.

'And you?' Grandmaman challenged Nyanya. 'Haven't you heard?'

'Your Most Serene Highness, Anna Vladimirovna my love, have pity on a motherless child. Allow me to relieve you of your stick.' Craftily, Nyanya approached my imposing grandmother.

'Hold still.' With the tip of her cane, Grandmaman held her at bay. 'You, Tatyana Petrovna' – she gave two taps of her cane – 'be so good as to stand up.'

Pulling a handkerchief out of her long black sleeve, Grandmaman wiped my nose none too gently. 'There'll be no more tantrums in this house, my good lady, nor in any house, be it palace or hut that you find yourself in.' She spoke in forceful Russian for emphasis. 'You are a soldier's daughter. If you must cry, do it under your pillow, so no one will hear.'

'Yes, Grandmaman.'

'Now tidy this mess, and you may come and breakfast with me.' She extended a hand to be kissed. 'Well, Nyanya? Is your chick still alive?'

Nyanya beamed. 'I know you have a good heart, my love. It's just that your patience is a little short . . .'

'Well, see you don't make me lose it.' Grandmaman gave a rare smile and left.

I was driven to Petersburg and the Warsaw Station that same day. An adjutant on Father's staff escorted me. Fyodor, that child of Russia, could not be trusted to behave beyond her borders. Accompanied by Bailey, Nyanya and Bobby, my setter, I departed in a *wagon-lit* suite on the Warsaw express.

2

The town of Veslawow lies midway between Warsaw and Lublin on the east bank of the Vistula. There, in mid-afternoon, I arrived with my retinue, to the excitement of the townspeople drinking coffee with whipped cream in the station's dining room.

On the platform to greet me was Sir Casimir Paszek, the portly and imposing overseer of Veslawa, the princely domain. In the station square, flanked by mounted postillions, stood two black landaus with the Veslawski arms on the panels.

I demanded to sit on the box beside the coachman, Tomasz, and off we rattled on the cobblestones at a heedless pace, scattering the curious crowd. Down the main boulevard of Veslawow, between a double row of old limes, we clattered past the stone wall of the Russian garrison. (In the days of Polish independence, this had been the barracks of the Veslawski lancers.) As we thundered across the medieval City Hall Square, I was enchanted by the Renaissance arcades, the brilliantly painted baroque façades with animal and flower designs, the curving lines of attics, the white church of St Stanislaw with its slender gold cupola.

The square had been shelled by the Russians in 1830, when the Veslawskis had been in the forefront of the War of Rebellion against Nicholas I, the despotic tsar who abrogated the constitution granted the Polish kingdom by Alexander I. It was shelled again during the insurrection of 1863, which the banished Veslawskis endeavoured to lead from their Paris residence. In 1864, the Veslawski family having been granted amnesty by Alexander II, Great-Uncle Prince Leon had had the square restored upon his return from exile.

After following the Vistula north beyond the town, we turned inland along a sandy road lined with poplars that led straight to the crested gates of Veslawa. The road climbing through woods to the palace grounds was narrow, winding and full of the deepest ruts and puddles. My great-uncle wanted it left in its natural deplorable state, to impede the movement of Russian troops on that day of liberation he believed inevitable.

At the end of the rough ascent, the carriages rolled on to the smooth driveway of a formal French park. The Veslawski palace, with its medieval west towers and the Renaissance arcades of its central corps and east wing, loomed into view at the far end of a rectangular pond.

My aunt and uncle, with Cousin Stevie, were on the central portico to greet me. Uncle Stan was very tall and thin, with a drooping brown moustache and sad long face. He wore his summer whites with a weary, English sort of elegance, as though dressing, like speaking, were a bit of an effort and an imposition. He lifted me off the box, dishevelled and mud-spattered as I was, held me up for Aunt Sophie to kiss, then set me down in front of Stevie. 'Well, Stevie boy,' he said in English, 'say hello to Cousin Tanya.'

'Hello, Tanya,' Stevie responded without enthusiasm.

At eight and a half, Stefan was a strong, gap-toothed boy, with broad knees covered with scabs. Largest of all about this large boy were his ears, which stuck out comically. He observed me sulkily out of light brown eyes.

'I don't know why I had to get cleaned up for *you*,' he shot at me as we went up the steps.

I was made presentable and taken to supper with Stevie and Casimir, his faithful second and slavish imitator, son of Sir Casimir Paszek. Young Casimir was a good-looking, green-eyed boy of Stevie's age. They had been raised together like brothers after Casimir's mother had run off with a Frenchman. In the absence of the boys' Swiss tutor for the summer, the English governess, Poole, presided at the table. The boys called her Penguin, because of her striking resemblance to that bird. She also had a habit of flushing violently when angered, and before this meal was over she had suffered several flushes over Lord Stefan's behaviour.

When Poole wasn't looking, Lord Stefan reached over and pulled my long hair like a bellpull. I reached for a monkey ear and gave it a vicious tug. He kicked me under the table on the shin. I kicked back. His look promised dire retaliation. I was relieved to be called down to the Coronation Room immediately after supper to bid the grown-ups goodnight.

Under the vast fireplace surmounted by the Veslawski coat of arms, there stood a tall, gaunt, and fierce old gentleman with a white mane to the shoulders, a pair of greyhounds at his feet, and a pet falcon on his fist. This was Great-Uncle Leon, the despotic patriarch of Veslawa.

At one and ninety, Prince Leon, though nominally still head of the household, had been glad to leave the domain and district in his son's hands. The former insurrectionist hero was past forty when he acknowledged the need to continue the family line. Between two flights from Poland, he managed to woo and wed Princess Catherine, a grandee's daughter less than half his age. From the first, he mistreated her. While he could not do without them, he professed to despise women. They had three daughters. And when at last Princess Catherine bore him a son – Uncle Stan – in Paris, he took the boy from his mother at the age of seven and shipped him off to an English public school. He would not have the boy made a girl of, he declared.

Princess Catherine called her husband 'little angel', prepared for him nightly an infusion of lime that, he claimed, would drive him to an early grave, and bore his scorn, as she had his infidelities, with angelic meekness. She had a face of aged loveliness under a halo of fine-spun white hair. She always wore lilac or mauve.

'Tanyussia, poor dear child,' she said in Polish in a sweet quaver as I made my curtsy, 'your poor dear mother, so young, so beautiful!'

In my childish callousness, I thought her rather ridiculous. Next I was passed from hand to hand among the guests. Remarks were made by certain ladies that it was a pity I did not resemble my late beautiful mother. But I did have extraordinary eyes and lovely hair, and after all being a *good* girl was more important than being beautiful. I was, as usual, bitterly vexed.

Uncle Stan noticed my vexation. He lifted my drooping chin and said, 'Well, *I* think she's beautiful. She looks just like her Aunt Sophie at that age.'

After Aunt and Uncle had come to kiss me goodnight, and Nyanya had tucked me in, I had an unexpected visitor. Standing at the French window on the first-storey balcony was Cousin Stevie, in pyjamas, a brown lock of hair in his eye, bare feet nonchalantly crossed.

He looked at me long and steadfastly. Then, 'Papa thinks you're beautiful ... but *I* don't,' he observed, and vanished.

I burst into tears. I felt ugly, unwanted, abandoned and all alone. Remembering Grandmaman's injunction, I put a pillow over my head and sobbed myself to sleep.

I moped for a fortnight. Then came Harvest Festival Day, and sadness fled.

In the morning, preceded by choirboys bearing religious images, peasants from all over the domain marched in brilliant procession through the court of honour: girls in wool skirts in black and orange stripes, with rows of coloured beads about their necks, men in full-skirted tunics and plumed hats riding white horses with tasselled bridles. The girls placed a crown of wheat and field flowers on Aunt Sophie's head and a member of each passing family laid a sheaf of wheat before Prince Stanislaw, their lord.

There followed a feast on the turf at the foot of the rear terrace and, as the sun set, a muffled drumbeat announced the approach of the band. All of us children ran to meet the musicians. Led by the drummer came the Jewish fiddlers in their long black caftans with their trailing beards and curly sideburns. Skipping and whirling around the musicians like a swarm of butterflies about black beetles, we children in our brilliant costumes escorted the band to the turf where a wooden platform had been erected for the dance.

By the light of the Japanese lanterns strung in the great limes, the couple who had worked hardest during the harvest were elected king and queen of the festival by acclamation. After they had been crowned by Prince Stanislaw, the king and queen danced the *oberek* together, then Uncle Stan invited the queen to dance and the king stepped up proudly to Aunt Sophie, whirling her away. Soon the platform was a blur of flying tunics and skirts, as drum-beating, heel-stamping, hand-clapping, and cries of '*oj dana*' syncopated the frenzied rhythm of the strings. There were some dances in squares and threes, and again and again the favourite *mazur* – proud, martial, gay, and of a sudden whimsical, wistful and lilting, always ending in the *oberek*'s intoxicating whirl.

After dancing until I was exhausted with Stevie, Casimir and the peasant boys, I went to sit in the lap of Great-Uncle Leon. Children sprawled on the trampled turf. Old peasants sat nodding at the littered tables. Here and there snored a farmer overcome by slivovitz or vodka. I watched the glowworms in the glass signalling the stars above the palace towers and grew very sleepy. I came to with a start as Uncle Stan lifted me out of his father's lap.

Stevie stood beside Aunt Sophie, watching me. 'She's still a baby, Mummy, isn't she?' he said in a funny tone.

I thought him terribly attractive with his feather and cap, and made the wish, with eyes closed tight, that he call me beautiful.

After the festival the peasants returned to their villages, Uncle Stan and Aunt Sophie to their duties. Besides supervising her enormous household, placating her tyrannical father-in-law, and entertaining on a grand scale, Aunt Sophie saw to the health of the district as well as of Veslawa proper. On the palace grounds east of the gardens she had converted a guest pavilion into a forty-bed hospital with a maternity clinic and out-patient service.

I accompanied her on her daily visit to the hospital and was fascinated. I liked its stillness, austerity and cleanliness. I liked the shiny canisters and instruments that normally evoke distaste or dread in children. It seemed to me a place of peace and hope rather than of suffering.

The patients were always happy to talk, even to a child of six. I asked where they hurt and later I asked Aunt Sophie why. I was shocked to learn one could not always make them well. Aunt showed me simple bandaging. I practised it all day on my dolls and on Bobby, my long-suffering setter. Normally a bounding, helter-skelter young dog, Bobby understood the seriousness of my doctor game. I would have preferred a human patient, but Stevie and Casimir usually ignored me when they were not off somewhere on marvellous adventures that I burned to share.

On the first afternoon that I happened to be left alone, in the absence of Aunt and Uncle, I stole out of the palace down a side stair. Bobby was always ready for excitement. With him at my heel, I went through the gardens, hospital pavilion and stables and out of the east gate, which in peacetime was never closed.

To the right the road led to the cemetery on the edge of the Veslawa plateau, with a view of the valley and the river Vistula. To the left it led to the village. A few old women in white kerchiefs sat on the benches under the narrow windows of clean and roomy white-washed huts.

At my passage they rose and bowed. 'Jesus Christ be praised,

Your Serene Ladyship,' they said, and I answered, as was proper, in the little Polish I knew, '*Na wieki wekov*. Forever and ever.'

I went on my way through the half-empty village – most of the peasants had gone to market – and came to a pasture that served as parade ground and drill field for Stefan's company of village boys.

The men of the company were in town and their 'Sir Lieutenant' was alone. The fact that he had no men in the flesh did not bother him. He told a trumpeter of his creation, 'Officers to me.' Then, as trumpeter, he blew the officers to himself. Now colonel of the Veslawski lancers, he issued battle orders. Lastly, mounting his horse and drawing his sabre, he charged the enemy with such conviction that when he fell, mortally wounded, I rushed to him, crying, 'Stevie, Stevie, are you hurt?'

A lance had gone through his stomach and he writhed and groaned until I pulled it out. I suggested we play field hospital. We began carrying wounded off the battlefield into a tent made of a moth-eaten blanket. This served as our dressing station. Stevie was by turns stretcher-bearer and casualty, and I surgeon and nurse.

While we were thus absorbed, little Wanda, the youngest daughter of the village elder, had come quietly on the scene. She was about my age, but smaller, prettier and much dirtier. She watched us raptly, chewing on a strand of blonde hair. Our game soon palled. We grew listless and went into an abandoned old barn at the pasture's edge. Stiff old harnesses hung on rusty nails. The windowpanes were cracked, and wasps buzzed in the empty grain boxes. I decided it would make a better hospital than the tent and that we could have a better game if Wanda were our patient.

'This is the hospital, you're the patient, I'm the doctor, and Lord Stefan is the orderly,' I explained.

'Why do *I* have to be the orderly? Why can't I be the doctor?' Lord Stefan wanted to know.

'You're always *every*thing.'

'I'm the doctor or I don't play.'

'All *right*, he's the doctor and I'm the nurse, and I'm going to put you to bed here' – I spread some hay on the floor – 'and give you a hospital gown. But first you have to take off your clothes.' I said this softly and rapidly in English, holding the girl's hand and speaking closely into her face.

Stevie thoughtfully blew up his round cheeks. Then, casually, he translated my orders.

Wanda, still giggling, began to take off her clothes. Then she lay down naked on the hay, chewing on a hair strand and watching us aslant. Stevie observed her nervously. 'This isn't a jolly game. It's going to get me in horrible trouble.'

I was far too absorbed in a human patient to heed his warning. I felt my patient's forehead and stuck a stick of straw in her mouth in the guise of a thermometer. This for some reason set off an unrelated train of thought.

I sat back on my heels and pointed to the straw. 'Stevie, look, a mast. She's a steamship.'

'A steamship?' Stevie said. 'A steamship!' We both went off into spasms of laughter.

Steamship Wanda got to her knees, in her excitement chewing on a handful of hair.

In the midst of our merriment, the door opened slowly with a grinding squeak and a peasant woman put in her head. 'Wanda, where are you, just you wait till I catch you!' Then, catching sight of her daughter, who had leaped up in terror, she let out a scream and fell to beating her with both hands as though putting out flames.

'*Oy*, you good-for-nothing, so *that's* how you amuse yourself with Their Lordships! Just wait and see what you'll catch from your father when he comes home from market. And you, my Lord Prince' – she turned on Stevie – 'playing with little girls in this fashion! What will your saintly mother say and your noble father, so just to his people? This is one trick you won't get away with, as Jesus is my witness. Harming little girls at your age!' All this in a spate as she violently dressed the wailing child.

'Wanda's mother's going to raise a frightful row. I'm really in for it this time,' Stevie said after the elder's wife had dragged her daughter off.

I suggested we run away, but he said we'd be caught. We joined hands, ready to face retribution together, and went out into the blinding sunlight. The peasants were returning from market. A crowd of women stood about Wanda and her mother. They began pointing at us and the boys who started to run to their 'Sir Lieutenant' were called shrilly to their mothers' sides.

Stevie could not face the villagers and led me homeward through a side gate. In the court of honour, alongside the black landau with the armoried panels that had brought Uncle Stan and Aunt Sophie home, were several peasant carts. They had evidently preceded us with the report of our crime. We were taken forthwith to Uncle Stan's study.

From behind his desk Uncle Stan observed us impassively, stroking his drooping moustache with the index finger of his right hand. After ascertaining that the report brought him by the Lady Elder was true, he asked Stevie in English, with dreadful coldness. 'D'you realize, sir, what you've done?'

'I have committed . . . an offence against my people.'

'Yes. And that, as you know, is the most serious of offences. Our powers and privileges are not as great as they once were, but they are still too great to permit of abuse. We have tried to teach you this since you were old enough to learn anything. Apparently, you haven't learned it. You need a lesson you'll never forget.' Uncle Stan then bade 'Sir Elder' and his lady come to the armoury to witness his son's punishment. To me he said, 'You may come along too, miss, since you're the one who put Stevie up to it.'

Aunt Sophie, who had stood silently by a window during this scene, asked to speak to him alone a moment. Uncle looked at her with his air of languid official courtesy, as though she were an ordinary supplicant. 'As soon as I've attended to this matter. Your leave, my lady.'

Before we could pass through the doors of the study, Great-Aunt Catherine appeared. She joined her frail hands and pleaded in Polish, 'Little son . . . be merciful . . . in the name of Christ . . . Stefan is so little.'

Uncle Stan looked at his mother as he had at his wife, with weary official courtesy. Before she could kneel, he took her under the elbows and placed her gently on a settee.

'Sophie, look to Mother,' he said and went on.

Prince Leon joined us, panting from haste and excitement, and we proceeded to the armoury, where the village elder with his wife and daughter and a dozen or so peasants were gathered. By a praying stool stood a groom, riding crop in hand.

Stevie walked to the stool as if in a trance, took off his polo shirt, and handed it to his father's valet, Josef. He knelt on the stool, crossed his arms, and put his face down on them. Josef gave him a hard rubber mouthpiece to bite down on. Uncle, holding me by the shoulders, nodded to the groom to proceed.

An oppressive silence reigned as the crop fell rhythmically. I wanted to howl, kick and bite, but Uncle's fingers held me in a vice, and I could only blink and start at every whistling stroke. Angry red marks appeared on Stevie's back.

Little Wanda slowly turned the head she had hidden in her mother's skirt. 'Look, *Matka*, he's not crying,' she whispered.

'And what do you think he is, a peasant?' the mother said with pride. And pride, as well as pity, was reflected in the red and strained faces of all the peasants present.

After what seemed forever, Uncle Stan lifted his hand from my aching shoulder even as blood started to trickle down Stevie's back. The groom stepped aside. Josef washed off the blood and applied iodine to the broken skin. Then he sponged Stevie's head and helped him to his feet.

Uncle Stan's pale face was covered with perspiration but he spoke in his normal calm tone, in English. 'Apologize, sir.'

Stevie did not seem to hear or see very well. The order was repeated. He said tonelessly in Polish, 'I beg your forgiveness for having offended you . . . I will never . . . do it again.'

The peasants beamed, and, bowing, they withdrew.

Uncle Stan ordered us taken to the dungeon nearby and locked in adjoining cells.

I tapped on the wall of my cell. When I received no answer, I began to pound and kick on the iron door. Josef's friendly, clean-shaven face appeared inside the barred opening.

'Josef, let me in to see Lord Stefan, please Josef, oh please!'

Josef unlocked my cell, let me into Stevie's, and locked us in.

Stevie lay on his stomach on a pallet, his curly head on his arms.

I squatted beside him and whispered, 'Stevie, Stevie, are you ill?'

He let his head roll sideways and looked at me dully. 'I threw up after I drank. I'm thirsty.'

I poured water from a jug into a tin cup and held it to his lips. For lack of a handkerchief, I wet my petticoat and wiped his face.

'D'you feel better now, Stevie?' I asked as he lay with closed eyes. 'Does it still hurt awfully?'

'I don't mind the hurt. I'm glad it hurts. It makes it hurt less inside.' And putting his face down again, he burst into sobs.

I could not understand why Stevie should be ashamed. I had not acquired the notion of 'my people' in my anglicized Victorian nursery world, any more than had my imperial playmates, and I still could not see that we had done anything bad to Wanda.

'Stevie, don't be ashamed. It's all right. No one's angry at you any more. They like you awfully, Stevie, they really do. Don't cry,' I urged.

His sobs ceased. I stroked his hair. '*I* like you, Stevie, I like you awfully. I'm sorry I got you in trouble. I'm most awfully sorry.'

He tilted his head and showed his few teeth in a broad smile. 'I like you awfully too, Tanya. I'm sorry I said you weren't beautiful. You've got beautiful hair, just like Mummy's.' He stroked it tenderly in turn.

I put my face close to his. 'Stevie ... can we be blood brothers the way you and Casimir are, share secrets and die for each other?'

'You're a girl, silly, you can't be my *brother*.'

'I could be your blood sister, couldn't I, Stevie? Couldn't I?'

'We'd have to mix our blood. I'm too tired now.'

'I'll do it, Stevie. Tell me how to do it.'

Under his instructions, I took his pocket knife from his belt, gashed my forearm with the coolness of a surgeon, then – not quite so coolly – my cousin's. We sucked each other's wounds and rubbed them together to properly mix the blood, getting it all over the pallet and our clothes in the process. Recalling Aunt Sophie's lessons, I tore up my petticoat and we tightly bound up our wounds, which soon stopped bleeding.

Stevie then solemnly said, 'I, Stefan Stanislaw Leon Augustus, Prince Veslawski, swear before the Lord Jesus Christ to help my blood sister Tatyana no matter what trouble she's in wherever she is and wherever I am and keep no secrets from her and bear for her the most awfullest tortures and die for her, word of a Veslawski. Amen.'

I repeated the lengthy oath, adding, 'And if you're ill I'll be ill, and if you're punished I'll be punished, and if you go to war I'll go to war, and we'll do everything together, because we love each other and we'll love each other always, ha?'

I was not sure how he would take this declaration, but Stevie regarded me in that curious, intense way, as on the night of the Harvest Festival. Emboldened, I stretched out beside him and put a hand up to his neck. It was surprisingly warm and soft. He laid an arm across my shoulders. Thunder rolled and rain fell on the sand and gravel of the court of honour, spattering through the barred opening of the cell. Ants driven indoors scurried across the dirt floor. It grew dark and cool in the dungeon. I pressed myself close to Stevie and he held me tighter. So we fell asleep in each other's arms and so Aunt Sophie and Uncle Stan found us at nightfall. And even my stern uncle could not help relenting and reprieving us from all further punishment.

After the blood-brother ceremony, Stevie and I became inseparable. In the morning, once he recovered, he would pop into my room with his German shepherd and we would race down the gallery to Aunt Sophie's blue Regency bedroom, where we would have a grand romp with the dogs under Uncle Stan's wary eye.

'Don't be rough with your mother, sir,' his father would say occasionally. Or he might ask Aunt Sophie, 'Isn't the boy a bit old for that sort of thing?'

'Don't be cross, Stan. It'll pass,' she would smile.

Uncle, in his reserved British fashion, was very much in love with Aunt. He bore an unacknowledged resentment, however, towards the large son whose difficult birth had almost cost Sophie her life. This animosity was in good part responsible for Stevie's disobedience. Both were painful to my aunt. She never made scenes, but she did grow distant, and since Uncle could not easily express his feelings, their harmony and closeness were interrupted by periods of estrangement.

Such a period followed the unusually harsh whipping administered Stevie after our doctor game. The time Aunt Sophie usually spent with Uncle was spent with us. Wearing a black hat like a postillion's, with a chiffon veil, she accompanied us on horseback. She took us to the woods to gather mushrooms. When the storm bell by the east gate began to ring, we went to the chapel carved inside the trunk of a great oak, to pray with the peasants for the preservation of the crops.

In the stormy grey light, the candles before the images of St Stanislaw and St Casimir flickered in the wind. Thunder rolled over the murmur of prayer. As large drops fell, the peasants ran towards the village and we children, holding Aunt Sophie's hands, pulled her homeward, shrieking excitedly. Lightning lit up the galleries and ivied gables of the palace. Lime leaves and gravel rolled down the sandy path. The smooth surface of the pond was all rippled and the swans' feathers ruffled. A footman met us with a large green umbrella, and the moment we were indoors, sheets of rain came drumming down. We pressed ourselves to the windowpanes and played at being afraid.

3

After the happy Polish summer, the Petersburg winter that followed sorely curbed my independence and Bobby's. Grandmaman was stern in earnest and kept me to a strict schedule of lessons, sports and religious observances. Under the towering surveillance of Fyodor, I resumed my promenades on the frozen Neva and dancing lessons at the Winter Palace.

Alexandra, who was again expecting, was newly sweet to me, the motherless child.

In emulation of my namesake, I tried to mend my unruly ways, and offered loving obedience to this my second Russian family. Obedience did not come to me naturally; I felt the more keenly my namesake's superiority in that respect.

Tatyana Nikolayevna, for her part, never tired of hearing about my naughtiness at Veslawa.

'Tell us about the night in the dungeon, Tata,' she urged. 'Tell us again about the doctor game.'

My freedom fascinated her. I was, in her eyes and in Olga's, the heroine of an adventure tale.

The Empress's ready sympathy extended to my father, who continued to brood over Mother's death and shunned social life. In his normal, expansive state, Father found the royal family's ideal Victorian life stuffy and provincial. But he was grateful, in his low spirits, to be welcomed in the warm family ambience the sovereigns could create so well, the only ambience in which they themselves felt at ease. It was Father's last opportunity to take advantage of the Tsar's affection to plead the parliamentary cause.

Nicholas, for all his mildness, was enamoured of things military. Father's mission to the Far East had revealed to him the army's shocking lack of preparedness, this at a time when both Russia and Japan put forth claims on Manchuria that would lead to war. In the course of enlisting his sovereign's thoughts and opinions on the modernization of the Far Eastern command, Father tactfully advised the Tsar to liberalize his rule.

'What a pity,' Father observed to Grandmaman after eliciting only polite attention from His Majesty, 'that Nicholas, who would make an ideal constitutional monarch on the English model, should be obstinately committed to the role of autocrat!'

Father also begged the Tsar to put an end to the pogroms, which marred the image of a benevolent despot so dear to the sovereign. He urged the Tsar to prosecute the ultranationalists and give orders to local garrisons to protect the Jewish population. In this instance, Father encountered a curious indifference.

'There runs some streak of barbarous stupidity throughout our history, I swear!' Father exclaimed to Grandmaman. 'And our sovereign – in most respects a gentleman in the deepest sense – is not immune. I constantly marvel at his ability to dismiss whole categories of people. How is it he's not revolted by pogroms? How can he refer to the Japanese as "yellow monkeys"? How can he be deaf to the Poles' demands for autonomy?'

As Father had foreseen, the Russo-Japanese War did break out in February of 1904, with unrealistic expectations of an easy victory on the Russian side. It gave Father the opportunity he desired for a combat command. He resigned from the Guard Hussars to take a cavalry division to Manchuria.

Grandmaman had wanted to keep me during my father's second absence. But I grew so pale, thin and listless that she brought me in desperation to Veslawa. I improved so dramatically that she consented to leave me there for the war's duration.

This time Stevie was overjoyed to see me. He turned cartwheels for my benefit, stood on his head, walked along perilous ledges, swung monkey-wise from trees or trapeze, rode a bicycle without hands and a horse without bridle, pulled his scabs to make himself bleed, held his hand in the flame of a candle, wiggled his ears: all to prove his manhood and valour.

After I had proven my stoicism and valour in turn, I was enrolled as field surgeon in his company. I tramped with the boys through mud and brush and icy stream, showing up at the palace with bleeding arms and blistered feet, dress torn, hair full of burrs, snarls and twigs. Neither Bailey's 'Dear me!' nor Nyanya's '*Akh ty!*' nor Aunt Sophie's gentle remonstrances nor Uncle Stan's chilly warnings nor any form of persuasion or punishment could keep me from Stevie and his war games.

I also joined my cousin in the mischief no amount of persuasion or punishment could deter him from. Dressed up as ghosts and carrying phosphorescent cherry twigs, we appeared on stilts in the dead of night to the Jewish watchmen guarding the orchards and put them to flight; suspended under a carriage from the springs, we rode to Veslawow and roamed blissfully over the river harbour.

We spent many a night in separate dungeon cells in punishment, until the imposition of martial law narrowed our field of mischief. Cossacks armed with long whips tipped with steel appeared at potential trouble spots. The east gate on the village side was then closed and we were forbidden to leave the grounds unescorted.

The Russian army's defeat at Mukden in Manchuria in late winter 1905 was capped in the spring by naval disaster in the Korean Strait of Tsushima, where Russia's lumbering Baltic fleet was sunk after steaming for long months around the world. Mutinies and disorders spread throughout the empire. Spurred by the blatant weakness of a would-be autocratic regime and fanned by revolutionaries, discontent flared among the working class and peasantry.

A prelude to revolution was Petersburg's 'Bloody Sunday', when an unarmed crowd of workmen with their families converged on the Winter Palace. In the Tsar's absence, their petition for better working conditions was answered by gunfire. Over a hundred casualties were officially acknowledged. In actuality, there were many more.

'News of the massacre has shocked me beyond words,' wrote Father in a letter to Grandmaman.

What ill luck dogs this reign of Nicholas II, from the tragedy of the coronation – who knows how many thousands were crushed and trampled to death in the collapse of that hastily built stand – to this Bloody Sunday! True, the crowd did not obey the command to disperse. True, the Tsar did not give the order to fire. But why did he not drive back to Petersburg immediately on being informed of the situation and show himself to the people? Why did he hide in Tsarskoye? Why did he not forbid the use of violence against peaceful demonstrators bearing his picture and religious banners? It is our sovereign's lack of resolve, his numbness in the face of crisis, his retreat into passivity that gives our Rightist 'all-Russian' zealots a free hand. God only knows what the consequences of this latest outrage will be!

The outrage by the Petersburg authorities was countered in Moscow by a terrorist outrage on the Left: the assassination of the Tsar's uncle, Grand Duke Sergey. In the capital and other industrial centres, Red councils of workers' deputies, the newly born soviets, fomented mass marches, strikes and disorders. And in the countryside, the 'red rooster' – murder and arson – was unleashed on an unprecedented scale.

Meanwhile the liberal bourgeoisie and the more conservative nobility alike clamoured for representative government. The granting of a narrowly based constituent assembly – a duma – by the Tsar, could not calm the storm. Only the Tsar's October manifesto, proclaiming civil liberties and broadening the suffrage, defused the revolutionary ardour. By the end of 1905, the revolution was over. But the breach it had created between Russia and its sovereigns could not be mended.

Revolution in Russia had rallied Polish patriotic spirit, as divisive as it was flammable. Once again, Russian troops were stationed in Veslawow to forestall insurrection.

Uncle Stan was far too wise to lead yet another abortive uprising. He ordered Prince Leon's dentures hidden to prevent his father from making seditious speeches. Uncle exerted all his prestige and calm authority to cool the Polish hotheads, while putting pressure on the Russian authorities to relax their hateful control. He grew even more wan, as well as more short-tempered towards his son.

Stevie, not to be outdone by his grandfather in patriotism, now conceived with Casimir his secret organization of Royal Republicans, pledged to rid Poland of Russian, German and Austrian occupation and to elect him king. Over the signature S.R.P. for Stefan Rex Poloniae, he issued instructions to his supporters nationwide: Cut the cinches of Russian cavalry officers' saddles. Ambush and overturn carriages. Pop motor tyres. Create havoc at official functions by introducing a turkey or goose. Et cetera.

The governor general in Warsaw could not discover the source of the nuisance, nor did Uncle Stan suspect it came from his own palace. Prince Leon, a Royal Republican recruit, took a conspiratorial pleasure in helping the boys devise ways to exasperate the Russians in defiance of his prudent son. On Prince Leon's advice I was not let in on the secret, for fear I would betray it to my imperial playmates.

I knew Stevie was hiding something and was hurt. My glorious freedom was also over and, as the great limes of the park shed their leaves, I began to look wistfully out of the window for a mounted escort and sleigh bringing Father to fetch me home.

At last, in September 1905, thanks to the good offices of President Theodore Roosevelt, Russia and Japan signed a peace treaty at Portsmouth, New Hampshire, and renounced their claims on Manchuria. And, on a rainy October day, as I was coming down to tea on Bailey's hand, I saw below me in the vestibule between Aunt and Uncle a tall and splendid-looking Russian officer with silver hair. I tore down the grand staircase without ceremony and was swooped up into Father's arms.

Father had recovered fully from the shock of Mother's death. His prematurely silver hair, the only visible trace of ordeal, made his appearance even more striking, adding to the lofty beauty of a still youthful, rosy face.

But to one who knew him well, the fine grey eyes that had held since boyhood a predisposition to melancholy, now revealed the disease full-blown and incurable. The Russian resonance of his voice was in a minor tone and his vigorous and joyous manner was as much a mask as the languid sad-hound air of Uncle Stan. At times Father tired of his jocular role and an unfathomable distance would come into his gaze, as though he had left for some far-off waste where no one could join him. This wasteland I would then experience with my whole being, which ached like the mermaid's legs in my favourite fairy tale. Again, I felt excluded and doubted his love. His spiritual absences struck terror in my heart, as in the hearts of many women who were to imagine they could cure Father's melancholy and rekindle in him the missing spark of life.

After a happy fortnight at Veslawa, Father took me back to Petersburg. The better to devote himself to the reorganization of the army that had proved so inadequate in the test of war, he retired from active service. Already on the Imperial Council of Defence since 1904, he now sat on the Council of Empire. As chairman of its foreign-relations committee, he frequently went abroad. In the spring of 1906, we sailed to Southampton from the Crimea on our yacht the *Helena*.

While Father sought an Anglo-Russian *rapprochement*, my first visit to the British Isles is chiefly remembered for my new governess, Diana Yates. The young woman whom Father hired to replace Nanny Bailey was the daughter of a Welsh surgeon. Diana had an attractive face and figure, fair English skin with a few freckles, red hair and green eyes in pleasing combination. She had a discreet voice, a discreet sense of humour and perfect poise, of the rare sort that stems from the lack of consciousness of social caste. She had studied at Cambridge and been a suffragette. Those few people I cared for I did so passionately, and I soon became passionately fond of my governess.

From Scotland we sailed to France, arriving in Paris when chestnut trees were in bloom. Our formal visit to the presidential Elysée Palace was attended by more pomp than our calls at Buckingham Palace and Windsor Castle, and left me with the impression that a *président de la république* was more than a king but less than an emperor.

I liked chasing a hoop down the alleys of the Jardin des Tuileries. I dragged my feet on the tour of museums, which Father claimed was for my benefit but in fact entertained Miss Yates far more. More interesting were art dealers' shops where Father unearthed treasures he took home and cleaned himself with a paste of egg yolk, after rolling up his shirt sleeves and removing his rings.

The country I loved best, when we had sailed from Nice to Naples, was Italy, and Italy loved us. Whether in the south or north, at Ischia or Lago Maggiore, Florence, Rome, or Venice, '*Il signor principe russo e la sua figliola*' were fêted. I wanted to learn Italian, Father's favourite language after Russian, and he at once began teaching it to me and my governess. I was the faster pupil, which made me like her even more.

At first we were Miss Yates and Lady Tatyana to one another. But one day, as we were sailing homeward along the Greek coast, I rushed up to Father, sitting lost in melancholy at the stern, his eyes on the ship's wake, his hand tapping the arm of his deck-chair.

'I may call Miss Yates Diana, Papa, may I not?' I cried.

He roused himself and looked up at her with half-closed eyes as though she were a landscape he wished to paint. 'To know what colours to choose, one must close one's eyes a little, to see the ensemble rather than the detail,' he would instruct me when we anchored in some idyllic Aegean bay and set up art school ashore.

'It's quite all right with me,' he said now to my request. 'I wouldn't mind calling Miss Yates Diana myself. It's such a pretty name.'

'You may call me Diana if you wish, my lord,' my governess said, with a becoming flush.

She was Diana to us thereafter and I saw nothing suspicious in her new shyness towards Father. We were more like sisters than like pupil and teacher.

In Petersburg, where we returned for the winter season, her rooms were across the hall from my apartment. Often, after Nyanya had tucked me into bed, I would burst in on my governess, crying, 'Diana, Diana darling, I'm not a bit sleepy. Let's talk!'

'Oh all right . . . but not for long,' she would say.

I would press myself close to her and she would tell me about her father, who was such a fine surgeon and had such a struggle of it, and about the great men of medicine, Sir Osler and Lord Lister, Pasteur, Zemmelweiss and Koch. She had completed her pre-medical studies and had taken a position as governess to save money to go to medical school and buy a practice.

I thought it exciting that we should both want to be doctors. Lying in bed after these chats, I imagined myself a medical heroine, stopping epidemics, operating in a field hospital under fire, rendering assistance to victims of cave-ins or railroad wrecks – all rather gory visions in which a part of childish sadism was mixed with humanitarian instinct. The mornings after, I would study with Diana all the harder, especially the arithmetic, for which I did not have Cousin Stevie's facility. Because, Diana said, with her quiet smile, if one wanted to be a doctor, one must learn a lot of mathematics.

Sometimes Father would sit in on the lesson, and suddenly striking the table he had been tapping, propose that we go for a drive. A troika would be ordered and we would go tearing about the flat, wooded countryside. I sat between Father and Diana, looking in delight from one to the other, happy to be close to the two people I loved best – in childhood the last loved is always the best loved – happy with the speed, the white spaces, the cold, the squeak of runners, the jangling sleigh bells, the coachman's cries, and above all with the nearness of my splendid father in his caped greatcoat with a collar of mink. He would put an arm against the seat in an attitude of elegant relaxation and when the sleigh gave a jolt, he would steady Diana's shoulder with his gloved hand. At first he released her right away but soon he began to keep his arm about her as well, and this, too, I thought quite natural.

In early 1907 Father decided on the spur of the moment, as he liked to do things, to spend a few days at our suburban dacha. The main villa was closed but a hunting lodge where the gamekeeper and his wife lived was always in readiness. It was a large two-storey log cabin in the middle of a fir wood a quarter-mile from the shore. It had modern plumbing but was native-looking enough to serve as decor for the 'Russian' parties Father threw for his foreign guests.

When we drove up to the lodge at nightfall – Father, his orderly Simyon, Diana, Nyanya, and I – the tile stove glowed in the large central room. *Zakusky*, Russian hors d'oeuvres, were spread on the table. Water boiled in the samovar. It was warm, bright and cosy after the cold drive. The pine floor was painted red. The wooden chairs and chests were gaily decorated. A *lampada*, a small red lamp, burned in front of the icons on a high corner shelf. A built-in bench ran the length of one wall.

After supper, Father lay back against the bright pillows on the bench, and drawing me to his chest, called for songs. The gamekeeper brought out his accordion, Simyon his balalaika, and everyone except Diana joined in. She sat apart at the table, discreetly smiling. Her suit of dark green velvet with beaver trim became her red hair.

The songs over, Father asked Nyanya to dance. She put on a perfunctory show of bashfulness, then she stepped out, hands on her hips. She circled the room slowly and majestically at first, then faster and faster as the tempo speeded to a frenzied close.

'Well done, my darling!' Father pulled the little woman on to his knees and fell to kissing her.

'Aren't you ashamed, my Prince, at my age! Let me go! What kind of doings are these?' she protested and struggled delightedly.

'Me too, Nyanya, I want to kiss you too,' I demanded. Annoyed that Father should kiss her instead of me, I fell on her none too gently.

At last she escaped us, pretending injured dignity, and Father called, 'Diana, why are you sitting over there all alone? Come and join us.'

'Yes, do, Diana, come and sit here, next to me,' I cried.

Diana smilingly complied.

Father told Simyon to serve champagne and the gamekeeper to play on. 'Is the atmosphere Russian enough for you, Miss Yates? Shall we send for a dancing bear and gypsies?' And he handed Diana a cup of champagne.

I asked for some, too, and received half a cup. We drank each other's health and Father smashed his empty cup against the stove – it was our finest monogrammed crystal. 'Russians are supposed to smash their glasses after they drink, aren't they, Miss Yates?' he said. 'Go ahead, smash yours.'

Diana lifted her cup. 'It seems a pity to smash such pretty crystal,' she said, and flung it at the stove.

'Done like a true Russian!' Father cried and tilted his head admiringly.

I drank up my champagne and smashed my glass in turn. Then, on a wild impulse, I ran to the table and began flinging all the glasses within reach.

Father's 'Tanya, that will do' brought me back to my senses. While the gamekeeper's wife stolidly swept up the damage with a broom made of twigs, I returned, head low, to the bench. But when I raised my eyes to Father anxiously, I saw that his face reflected not displeasure, but that unfathomable distance into which he departed.

Father's change of mood had produced a general malaise.

Diana rose. 'I think Tanya's a bit excited. I'd better take her up to bed.'

Without stirring, Father seized her wrist. 'Nyanya can put the child to bed. You're not going to leave me here alone, are you?'

Diana blushed and slowly sat down again.

They had both forgotten me. It was now Diana Father wanted to be with. I was in the way. Nyanya took me up to bed. In vain I waited for Father to come and kiss me goodnight. I waited long after all sounds of accordion and balalaika had died down. And my last wish, before I fell asleep, was, 'God, make Diana wake up crooked and cross-eyed. Make Papa hate her as much as I do.'

*

In the morning, Father was again gay and tender. Towards Diana he was particularly kind and thoughtful, almost as though he were sorry that he must hurt her. She did not avoid his gaze as before. Rather, she seemed irresistibly drawn, returning it with a look of helplessness, hopelessness, submission and trust. Our former cosy comradeship was quite spoiled. I was coldly polite towards my governess. She was formal and ill at ease with me.

None of this escaped Grandmaman upon our return, and she demanded an explanation. The upshot of her row with Father was the opposite of the one she intended.

When Father came to kiss me goodnight, he sat down on my bed and said, 'Tanichka, you're almost ten years old, old enough for me to talk to you about something very important for us both. Your mother has now been dead four years. I could never love another woman as I loved her. But a man needs companionship and tenderness, someone to share his troubles –'

'I'll share your troubles, Papa.'

'I know you would, darling, but it's not quite the same. Then, too, I must think of you. It's difficult for a man to bring up a girl. She needs a mother, to be an example, to love and teach her.'

'I don't *need* a mother. I don't *want* a mother. I want only you!'

'Not even if it were someone you already knew and loved? Someone you were very good friends with, like Diana?'

'I'm not friends with Diana. I don't love her, I hate her! She's . . . she's *common*!' I found the most spiteful epithet.

'Diana is not common in the least. She is beautifully brought up and educated. She is as much a lady as any woman I know.'

'She is not a lady, not a *born* lady, like Mama, or Aunt Sophie.'

Father looked at me gravely. 'That's a very foolish thing to say. Nobility is in the heart, not in the name. I would not be at all ashamed to make Diana Princess Silomirskaya. But I am ashamed of you, Princess Tatyana, for those words. We won't talk about it any more. Diana will be going to live in her own flat. In a few days, we'll call on her and I'm sure you'll soon love her as much as ever.'

I understood mainly that Father loved Diana better than me.

'I won't call on her. I'll never call on her. And if you marry her,' I screamed, 'I'll never never speak to her!'

Too late I noticed Diana standing in the door with a look of hurt and disbelief. My cheeks burned and I felt a twinge of remorse. But I merely stared spitefully until she averted her eyes.

Father went to her and took her hand. 'Diana dearest, you mustn't mind the child. She's upset. We must give her time.'

Diana looked at him long. Then she said softly, 'Oh Peter, what's the use?'

Father followed her out.

Diana moved out the next day, and soon after, I learned she had gone back to England. Father had gone there also. I was certain he'd joined Diana, that he would marry her and have a son he would love more than me. I hated her for stealing Father. Yet I missed her too, and remembered wistfully the good times we three had together, before I had spoiled it all.

To replace Diana until another English governess could be hired, Grandmaman appointed as my *éducatrice* her poor but socially prominent spinster relation, Countess Vera Kirilovna Liline.

Vera Kirilovna was then in her late forties and a still-handsome woman. Her somewhat overpowering, fulsome femininity was tempered by a courtier's circumspection and compunction. She had thick amber-brown hair, and a preference for amber and beige. Descended of sixteenth-century boyars, she had been a lady-in-waiting to the Tsar's mother, the Dowager Empress Marie Fyodorovna. She carried her bust as though she still wore the medallion portrait of Her Imperial Majesty, a privilege she had enjoyed in her capacity of *dame d'honneur à portrait*.

She taught me how to stand, sit and walk, how to eat holding rolled newspapers under the arms, how low to curtsy and to whom. She was forever reminding me that my association with our sovereign's daughters was a rare, indeed a unique privilege – the Grand Duchesses barely associated with their Romanov relatives, and with the children of courtiers not at all.

This exceptional friendship, more than ever after Father's departure, became my only escape from the discipline and decorum that Grandmaman and my *éducatrice* now dispensed in increasing doses.

I envied the Grand Duchesses their cosy and tender family life far more than their imperial rank, of which they themselves were so little conscious. 'Oh, you're so stuck-up, you think you're a baroness,' Olga Nikolayevna chided her sister Tatyana.

That such an ideal bourgeois existence could only be led in isolation from social and political reality; that it left the Empress, who felt eclipsed by her peers, free to surround herself with mediocrities, and the shy Emperor to follow, increasingly, her example; that it enabled the imperial couple to regard matters of state as private family affairs, to be settled like household problems over breakfast or tea – all this, and much more, escaped me.

I loved all four girls uncritically. I delighted in the antics of Schwibzik (Anastasia), the youngest. Marie's good nature put my impatience to shame. I admired Olga's quick mind and repartee. I worshipped my poised and pretty namesake. I shared in the Grand Duchesses' adoration of the long-awaited little brother, the beautiful and ailing Aleksey Nikolayevich. His birth had been greeted by a hundred-and-one-gun salute! Yet, barely six weeks later, he had suffered his first haemorrhage.

How serious the illness of the Tsarevich was, I had no idea then. I had never heard of haemophilia, a word that was whispered low in court circles, and outside them not at all. I did not know that the rings under Alexandra's beautiful haunted eyes were from sleepless vigils at the heir's bedside. Nor could I suspect that a half-literate 'holy man' from Siberia, whom she believed to be a healer, was to acquire such a disastrous influence over the Empress's naïvely impressionable, mystically coloured mind.

Early in the spring – I was not quite ten – I was invited to spend the weekend at Tsarskoye Selo. Here, in the outskirts of Petersburg, the Grand Court had taken refuge since the infamous 'Bloody Sunday' of 1905, as if haunted by the scene of carnage on the Winter Palace Square.

A carriage with a coachman and footman in scarlet coats drove Vera Kirilovna and me the short distance from Alexandrovsk Station to the Alexander Palace, a graceful white building with a green roof and a frontal colonnade by Rastrelli, facing an informal English park with several ponds and islands. Countess Liline and I were given rooms opposite the wing of imperial apartments. In the evening, after Trina – Mlle Schneider, the court reader, the world's gentlest soul – had read us a Kipling story aloud, and before Alexandra had tucked her daughters into their camp beds in their sparse dormitory upstairs, I managed to suggest to my namesake a midnight rendezvous. The Grand Duchess agreed to meet me in the audience chamber so we could really talk.

I kept awake by reading *Treasure Island*, setting my lamp on the floor as I did at home when I wanted to stay up half the night. At the stroke of one I put on a dressing gown and slippers and made my way down the oak staircase. It creaked to my guilty ears like the good ship *Hispaniola* in the storm. The palace was dark and silent, the sovereigns setting the example of retiring early. A single guard was on duty in the entrance semicircle – the Tsar could not bear surveillance and despised the secret policemen who followed him about in various ridiculous disguises.

In the audience chamber I met my friend, and we embraced in a passion of exquisite fright. Our arms about each other, we sank down behind a heavy velvet drapery.

'My Tanik, my blood sister' – we, too, had taken an oath, without the blood-mixing part, and sworn to endure for each other the most awful tortures – 'I love you as much as I do Stevie, I'll be your lady-in-waiting and never marry and follow you everywhere.' I had transferred my former passion for Diana to my imperial namesake.

'I love you, Tata, I love you as much as my sisters, and if you won't marry I won't either,' murmured the Grand Duchess. Then, as she was already reasonable – her sisters were to call her 'governess' – 'But how're you going to be my lady-in-waiting if you're going to be a physician?'

'I could be your lady-in-waiting *and* court physician.'

The Grand Duchess thought this a colossal idea. 'Colossal' was a pet word in the family.

To test our blood-sister kinship, we guessed each other's thoughts. We related our dreams and exchanged cabalistic beliefs. We imposed penances on each other for our sins.

'I wonder,' I mused, 'if one shouldn't give up one's home and all one's toys and belongings and go begging on the roads barefoot.' The idea had begun to appeal to me strongly of late. 'Jesus asked His disciples to leave father and mother and everything in order to follow Him.'

'We'd be caught,' my sensible friend responded, 'and people mightn't understand. Papa and Mummy'd be awfully angry, and if we make our parents angry, that wouldn't be pleasing God, would it?'

I discarded the idea for the moment, and we recited *Alice in Wonderland* between bursts of smothered laughter. At dawn, feeling chilled, achy and unsteady on our feet, we parted after a long embrace.

A few hours later, a footman discovered the belt of the Grand Duchess's dressing gown in the audience chamber. There was no mistaking Tatyana Nikolayevna's dressing gown in the colours of the lancers of Voznisensk, whose honorary colonel she was. A confrontation with Their Majesties followed under the portrait of Marie-Antoinette in Alexandra's boudoir, and I was brought home in disgrace.

Grandmaman was giving a *déjeuner intime* for my godmother, Grand Duchess Marie Pavlovna.

The wife of the Emperor's uncle, Grand Duke Vladimir, Marie Pavlovna ranked high in the imperial hierarchy. A patron of the arts and favourite of foreign ambassadors, this witty and brilliant German princess, unlike the former Alix of Hesse, had shown the tact and astuteness wanting in her reigning countrywoman. It had been her thankless task to tutor the young Empress in the ways of the Russian court. Feared and detested by the Empress ever since, she had become the focus of a growing opposition to Alexandra among the members of the dynasty and their friends.

Also the mother of five, Marie Pavlovna did not have the tall and slender figure or the chiselled features of the Empress. But her carriage and self-assurance, like that of the Dowager Empress, Marie Fyodorovna, the Tsar's mother, were a reminder of the grandeur of the former reign and a reproof to the mediocrity of the present one. I thought her rather homely in a nice way.

She drew me to her after hearing Vera Kirilovna's account of our escapade. 'You naughty girls! And weren't you afraid of being caught?'

'Awfully!'

'And that made it all the more exciting.' Marie Pavlovna understood perfectly. 'I find it a charming story.' And she laughed handsomely.

'Your Imperial Highness may be amused, but I'm not.' Grandmaman spoke with customary directness and sarcasm. 'If Her Majesty chooses to raise her daughter any old way, *n'importe comment*, I won't have my grand-daughter running about palaces in *déshabillé* in the middle of the night.'

'Come, dear friend, don't be so severe,' Marie Pavlovna said. 'Tanya's spirit can only do my grand-nieces good. They lead such dull lives!'

'Their Majesties lead a life of piety and propriety,' Grandmaman roguishly rejoined. 'We would do well to follow their example.'

'Oh, quite!' Marie Pavlovna lifted the back of her hand to her mouth to stifle a yawn.

The Grand Duchess gone, Grandmaman read me a sermon on my Role and Responsibilities. In conclusion, I was informed that I was not to see the Grand Duchess Tatyana Nikolayevna until Father's return.

I was deprived of all things. I wrote daily to my imperial namesake but my letters remained unanswered. I suspected our correspondence was intercepted. I began to think I must be truly bad and sinful. Should I do something extraordinary to redeem myself, give up my toys and go barefoot on the roads? I might become a saint, another Joan of Arc. (Then at least I would not have to give up horseback riding.) In the vain hope of seeing visions, I fasted and knelt for hours. I suspected the Silomirsky *osobnyak* was not the place for sainthood and I watched for the opportunity to run away.

When Grandmaman gave a reception after Easter, I waited until the guests began to arrive, got out of bed and dressed without the help of my officious maids. To my pillow I pinned a note: 'Please forgive me Grandmaman I am no use to anybody here I am going to live with the poor.'

Fyodor no longer slept outside my door. With Bobby, my adventurous setter, at heel, I stole down the back stairs to the cellars and crossed the length of the central corps. In the stable, I opened a box stall and turned a trotting stallion loose. While the grooms were giving chase, I slipped unnoticed out of the service gate.

I walked quickly, ducking under the arcade of a carriage entrance to avoid being seen by a block watchman and darting out again.

After I had passed the gasworks, I found myself in an unknown quarter of low wooden houses. Here the 'poor' I was looking for must live. The wide unpaved street without sidewalks was muddy, unlit and seemingly endless. The only traffic was a string of dray carts in somnolent and shabby procession. Three workmen came out of a *traktir*, weaving and singing. Bobby growled, and the men, mistaking me, perhaps, for a drunken apparition, lurched on. As I prayed for some officer of the Guard to give me a lift, an empty horsecab pulled alongside instead.

Getting down, the driver bowed low, hat in hand. 'It's not safe to walk the streets at this hour. Allow me to drive Your Excellency home.'

His beard fell unkempt on his collarless blue coat, his bushy red eyebrows almost covered his eyes. But his wide nose was harmless-looking enough.

I decided to trust him. 'I have no home, but if you will drive me into the country, I will find some kind peasant family who will take me in.'

He looked at me a long while, scratching his middle part, then said to his horse, 'We'll take the young lady home. Maybe the wife will understand what this is about.'

In front of a huddle of shacks, a sallow woman in a shabby brown shawl answered the cabman's knock.

She examined me by the feeble light of a bottle with a lighted kerosene wick. Then, 'Have you gone out of your mind?' she addressed my rescuer. 'What do you mean bringing a young lady here?'

'I found her on the street. She wouldn't say where she lives.'

'She comes from a rich family, that's clear. Tell us, miss, where you live.' She turned to me unctuously. 'Your parents must be sick with worry.'

'I haven't any parents. Will you let me live with you?'

'Lord God of mine, as if I hadn't enough children of my own already, and no money to clothe or feed them.' My hostess held up her crude lamp, and I made out a low room of logs with small windows half nailed shut, a rough table and stools in the middle, and, in one corner, a large iron bed. Four towheads, from a toddler to a girl my age, sat up fully dressed on the bed and peered at me in silence. On a bench under blankets a fifth child lay asleep, his head turned to the wall. A disagreeable sour odour came from this corner.

'Should we go to the police?' asked the cabdriver, who had been scratching his head all this time.

'They'll say you kidnapped her, stupid, and send you to Siberia without even a trial. Never fear, she'll tell us where she lives soon enough.'

My hostess now poured me some tea into a cracked saucer. She served her husband a bowl of cabbage soup with kasha cooked on an iron box filled with boiling water from the samovar. Then she pressed on me a dry herring on a slice of black bread. The herring made me thirsty but I would not drink tea out of a saucer like a peasant and asked for a glass of water. It did not occur to me that the water might not be boiled.

Four of the children, meanwhile, had drawn near. They reached out furtively to touch my hair, the sable collar of my coat, the English leather of my boots. To my horror, the mother, with screams and cuffs, drove them back to bed.

I asked where I could brush my teeth and learned there was no running water or toilet.

'When there's money, I take them to the public bath,' my hostess said.

She showed me the toilet facilities in a miserable pitch-dark and muddy courtyard. I declined to use them. She would have moved the sleeping child from the bench to the bed so I could lie down, but the girl's flushed face and shallow breathing aroused my medical instinct.

'She's ill,' I said. 'You must call a doctor.'

'Ah, what for? The doctor will prescribe medicines we can't pay for. It's only a fever. Children are always having them.'

'Grandmother will send a doctor and the money for medicine,' said I unthinkingly.

'And where does your grandmother live?' the woman asked with cunning.

'In the Silomirsky *osobnyak* on the English Embankment.' I had decided I must tell Grandmaman about the sick child.

I would like to be able to say this was my chief reason for wanting to go home, but to be perfectly honest an even stronger one was the lack of an inside toilet.

The cabdriver drove me home. He roused our yard porter, who roused the entire household. I thought my maids would never be done with their exclamations, or Nyanya with her scolding. To my astonishment and relief, Grandmaman listened carefully to my report about the sick child and said not one cross word. After she had dismissed the cabdriver with a generous sum of money and the promise to have the child taken to the hospital under her patronage if necessary, she had me bathed with disinfectant and put to bed. In the morning Dr Botkin, who was soon to be appointed court physician, examined me and found nothing more serious than a cold. But a week later I came down with typhoid fever.

Father was recalled from Great Britain. I was delirious when he returned and I could not be sure that the face above the silver beard bending over my bed was not a dream; that the fine grey eyes holding the depths of anxiety and love were really my father's; that he had come back to me; that he was not going away any more; that he was here with me, his adored Tanichka, his very own, whom he loved more than anybody in the world. So his beautiful resonant voice assured me each time I asked was it really he.

When the fever had run its course, my first question was, 'Papa, how soon will you be going back to England and Diana?'

Father answered that he was not going anywhere until I was well and not to think about Diana any more. But I could not stop thinking about her and remembering the awful look she had given me when I had screamed out my spite and hatred. Added to my guilt towards Diana was my guilt towards the cabdriver's children, who had no money for medicine, no place to wash, who liked to touch soft fur and leather they had never worn.

'Grandmaman,' I asked when she was relieving Father at the bedside, 'why must some people live like the cabdriver's family, like . . . like animals?'

Grandmaman sighed. The world was full of injustice and misery, she said, and there was more of it in Russia than anywhere because there was more of everything both good and bad in Russia.

I did not quite understand and persisted. 'But Grandmaman, is it right for us to have what we have, when other people don't have enough to eat and no place to wash?' This seemed the worst part of being poor.

'From a Christian point of view, it's not right,' Grandmaman agreed. 'But if we gave away all we have, there would not be fewer cold, dirty and hungry people. If all the wealthy gave their wealth away, very soon there would be again rich and poor, because that is the way of the world. If those children you feel so sorry for had what you have and you were in their place, they would not feel sorry for you. We run hospitals and schools for the poor and take care of anyone who comes to us in need. But if half the poor in Russia became rich they would not take care of the remaining poor; they would take advantage of them. The people need to become educated first, to learn Responsibility. I trust, after this experience, you will begin to learn it, too.'

I pondered a great deal on this conversation. I saw there was a gulf between the way of God and the way of the world; nor could the wrongs of this world be remedied by the laws of God. The earth seemed a place full of injustice and misery in which it was impossible to be good. The less appealing this world, the more tempting the world beyond.

I asked Father to read me the New Testament. I puzzled over the story of Martha and Mary. I imagined myself Mary sitting at the feet of the Saviour. The Lord appeared to me in a dream, on either side of Him an angel with the features and expression of my mother, who had known, in death, an awesome and marvellous event.

So poignant was my longing that, as I awakened, I wished myself back to sleep, never to wake again. Death seemed the solution to all my problems. Father could marry Diana. Everyone would be sorry I had died and remember me with love only. If I wished hard enough, it must happen! I concentrated on my wish. My recovery was arrested, my temperature remained subnormal, and I grew progressively weaker.

One morning, I grew so exasperated with Nyanya for pressing me to drink my hot chocolate that I blurted out, 'I don't want it. I don't *need* it. You're in my way. I've been wishing so hard and I feel . . . He is coming.'

'Who is coming, my love?'

'Christ is . . . to take me away.'

'Lord God of mine, *now* what is it she's dreamed up!' cried Nyanya and marched out to return with Father.

He sat down by my bed in his dressing gown of Bukharan silk, lifted a spoonful of chocolate to my lips – I could not refuse it from his hand – and asked: why did I want Christ to take me away?

I told Father all, including the part about his being happier with Diana if I were out of the way.

He watched me with a strangely troubled intensity. Then he

smiled and said in his resonant voice, 'Instead of a trip to heaven, how would you like to go to Veslawa?'

'Will you come too?'

'Yes. If you want me to.'

The façade of the Veslawski palace looming at the far end of the pond between the towering limes was a more vivid vision than that of Judgement Day.

'Oh Papa!' I said, and promised to eat to be strong enough for the trip.

4

On my tenth birthday, I was judged strong enough to travel, and a week later, Father and I arrived in Veslawow with our retinue. This time we were met by motorcars instead of carriages.

To stop his incorrigible father from stirring up anti-Russian sentiment and thwarting his own patient efforts towards liberation, Uncle Stan had bought Prince Leon a Clément-Bayard automobile, and for himself and Aunt a Belville coupé. The ninety-seven-year-old gentleman developed a passion for motoring and suddenly demanded a 'civilized' road to Veslawa. Uncle Stan was only too glad to pave the road at long last.

Besides earning him a respite from paternal nationalism, the introduction of motorcars put a stop to the rascality of Tomasz, his father's favourite coachman. Tomasz could sideswipe a Jew so skilfully that the carriage wheels just passed over the hem of his caftan. This would earn him a rap on the back from Prince Leon's cane and a severe reprimand from Uncle Stan. (A friend of the Rothschilds' and admirer of Disraeli, Uncle prided himself on his lack of prejudice.) Tomasz was now kept busy driving Uncle on his rounds as district marshal of the nobility and no longer dared show off.

Motorcars were no novelty to me. Had I been well, I would have missed the brazen little coachman, the rollicking ride, the postillions sounding the horn as if Poland's freedom were at hand. In my convalescent state, however, I was glad to doze on Father's shoulder after the long journey, until the road levelled and the beautiful palace, familiar yet always startling, came into view.

Stevie was in the portico with his parents when Father lifted me out of the car. Although it was a hot day in June, I was wrapped in a plaid. At twelve and a half, Stevie was still the same large and strong-looking boy with a lock of brown hair in his light brown eye and the funny monkey ears. I thought him as magnificent as ever.

He said, 'Hello, Tanya,' in a moved voice, and I put out my left index finger in blood-brother greeting.

I waited for him to appear at the French window of the balcony and, early the next morning, before Nurse had taken my temperature, there he was with Krak, his German shepherd.

He bounded in, plopped down on the floor, the faster to hide under the bed should Nurse enter, and said, 'I'm awfully glad you're alive, Skinny-ninny. You gave us an awful scare. How d'you catch the typhoid anyway?'

I told him the whole story.

'Running away's awfully childish, old girl,' he remarked loftily. 'You really ought to know better.'

'I do now. Stevie, did you know there were people who live like that cabdriver, like ... like animals?'

'I've been taken to poor districts. It's supposed to be part of my education.'

'But don't you think it shocking?'

'It's bad government. When I'm S.R.P., nobody'll be poor.'

'S.R.P.?'

'Stefan Rex Poloniae.' And, as I continued to look perplexed, 'King of Poland, silly. Don't you know Latin?'

I might not know much Latin but I knew the Tsar was King of Poland. Stevie then revealed to me the secret of the Royal Republicans.

'When I grow up, I'm going to be court physician to Tatyana Nikolayevna,' I said haughtily. I might be a poor patriot beside Stevie but I could not sympathize with an anti-Russian organization.

'A court physician!' said Stefan Rex Poloniae. 'That's being a toady.'

'Dr Botkin's not a toady. And that way I can make sure the poor are taken care of. Unless God still decides to call me.'

It was Stevie's turn to look perplexed, and I explained my wish to leave this earth full of injustice and misery.

Stevie watched me uneasily. Then, 'D'you still wake up and wish you could go back to sleep and die?' he asked.

I hung my head over the edge of the bed so that my hair fell on his shoulders. The attempt to cut it during my illness had met with such violent resistance that it had been abandoned. 'If I did, would you be sad?'

'Awfully!' He seized my hair in both hands. 'I wish you'd stop this dying business!'

'Let go my hair first.'

He did, and I fell back on my pillow. 'I suppose a lot of people'd be sad if I died,' I mused. 'Nyanya, and Tatyana Nikolayevna, and Aunt Sophie and Grandmaman, and ever so many others. And Papa'd be most horribly sad. You know, Stevie, I thought for a while he didn't love me, but he does. He loves me more than anybody in the world. So I don't think I'll wish to die any more. Stevie,' I added as he bounded up, 'when I'm well ... let's do something naughty.'

With a laugh, he was gone out of one door just as Nurse came in through the other.

I recovered so fast that at the end of June 1907, Father felt it safe to leave me in Aunt's maternal care. I remembered his remark about needing someone to share his troubles and look after him if he were ill, and I said, 'Papa ... if you want to remarry I won't mind ... I'll understand.' When he did not respond, I added, 'I'll never marry, Papa. I'll stay with you always!'

Father smiled wistfully. 'It's too soon for you to worry about that now. Have a good time and be good to Aunt and Uncle.' And he kissed me goodbye.

Remorse over Diana was to remain with me in other forms. But that summer I felt relieved of it.

I spent my days, accompanied by an ecstatic Bobby, with Stevie and his echo, Casimir. We tramped the narrow paths between the fields; lunched in the shade of a haystack in the heat of noon; galloped over the moors, flushing out the heathcock with whirring wings; hunted, fished and rocketed down the rutted roads to a fire, riding at the back of the engine with its gleaming brass tanks. I outdid Casimir as Stevie's worshipful flunkey. I never missed a fencing or jumping lesson, held a stopwatch for Stevie at track, walked his horse when he brought it in hot against the rules, brushed his dog, cleaned his gun, unravelled his fishing line and fed his reptilian pets.

I would have liked to express my affection and worship physically, as I could when we were small. But I sensed this would now be taboo. I had to be content to play with Stevie's shoelaces or the buttons of his jacket. In turn, he was more than ever attracted by my long blonde hair, and was forever touching and playing with it, but in ways acceptably boyish, like making bridle reins, or tying me up.

When I was tied up, 'I'll help you be a boy by cutting off your hair,' he offered and approached with a pair of scissors.

'I don't want to be a boy! Boys are revulsive.' I meant revolting and repulsive. 'And you're the most revulsive. You're a monstro!'

At other times Stevie would ask why God couldn't make my hair curl if He could do everything? This touched my two most sensitive points, my vanity and my religiosity, at one stroke.

Though he made fiendish fun of the latter, Catholicism was part and parcel of Stevie's upbringing as a Veslawski prince, which he did not question, whereas I neither accepted nor fully understood my upbringing as Princess Silomirskaya.

In midsummer Stevie came down with the measles and I had the chance to do something naughty and express my affection physically. Early one morning, while Nurse was out of the room, I appeared at his bedside.

'Let me get into bed with you, Stevie, so I can catch the measles too,' I begged.

'Measles aren't any fun,' he said as he made room for me.

I pressed myself to his hot body. 'Stevie-levie, monkey ears, you old lobster, I love you so much I love you almost as much as Papa.'

'Tanya-panya, skinny-ninny, freckle nose and ice toes,' he responded. 'When I'm S.R.P. I'll make you my queen.'

'If I'm queen of Poland, will you promise not to fight the Russians?'

'No.'

'Then I shan't marry you. Anyway I'd much rather be a surgeon. Wouldn't you like to be a surgeon too, Stevie, and we could do operations together?'

'A surgeon, pooah!' said the future Rex Poloniae, drawing me close.

We lay in sweet communion in that sticky sickbed, as we had four years earlier on the pallet of a dungeon cell.

When Nurse, shortly after, saw us lying there embraced, she

clapped her hands to her head, ran out and returned with Aunt Sophie.

'We're not doing anything *wrong*, Mummy,' Stevie said hotly as she stood over the bedside in a wise and grave way without anger.

'Perhaps not wrong, but very silly,' she said. 'Go back to your apartment, Tanya, right away.'

I was laid up with the measles in due course. My case was lighter than Stevie's and we were allowed to spend most of our convalescence together.

Casimir brought Stevie news of the Royal Republicans and tribal offerings in the form of curious bugs in smelly jars. Poole read us *Through the Looking Glass* and when his lordship graciously told her she read awfully well, she flushed with pleasure to the tip of her penguin nose.

I admired my cousin's ability to twist people around his little finger as much as I did his aptitude for bareback riding and arithmetic. He could also sing like an angel, whereas my musical gifts were on a par with my mathematical facility. I felt utterly mediocre beside him, as I felt unattractive and gauche beside the Grand Duchess Tatyana Nikolayevna. This only made me the more determined to do something extraordinary when I grew up, something *on my own*.

In the autumn after our recovery, Stevie and Casimir were enrolled at Eton, Uncle Stan's school, and Father and I accompanied the Veslawskis to England. Father resumed the goodwill mission undertaken on behalf of the Council of Empire the previous year. Anglo-Russian relations, already cool when the Russo-Japanese war broke out, had not been improved by the ridiculous Dogger Bank incident: Russian warships, firing at each other in the North Sea fog in the belief they were under enemy attack, inadvertently sank a British fishing boat and killed eighteen men.

While Father successfully plied his diplomatic charm in London, I spent two happy months with Aunt and Uncle in Kent, in the castle of the Duke of Lansdale, husband of Uncle Stan's sister, Lady Mary. Poole-Penguin, Stevie's emotive governess, found a position educating his English cousins and at once proceeded to hold up Lord Stefan as a model gentleman.

Life at Lansdale revolved about horses and dogs, which suited me, in my eleventh year, well enough. I liked the lofty copper beeches, the rooks cawing in the mist, the white fences and many hedges that made ideal hurdles during the hunt. In appearance, speech and manners I could have been mistaken for an English peer's daughter, and often was. But I was more competitive and intense than my hosts. I was genuinely religious, while they went to chapel perfunctorily – the Duke had embraced Catholicism in order to wed a princess Veslawska. I read a great deal more. I devoured *Jane Eyre*, *Vanity Fair* and *David Copperfield.*

'Oh, Dickens!' said Stevie's fellow Etonian, Lord Beresford, eldest son and heir, who was as long as Stevie was large, when they arrived for a weekend. 'How old hat!' And he added, 'If you weren't superb on horseback, Tanya, you'd be a bore!'

The children were also critical of my conversations with grooms, cooks, scullery maids, tenant farmers and the postman, with whom, once I understood their peculiar speech, I got on as well as with their Russian and Polish counterparts. The servants at Lansdale did not talk back like Russians or Poles. They were polite and efficient. But one could not imagine the Duke of Lansdale taking Nanny on his knee as Father did Nyanya. The difference between classes might not be so apparent. But the distance was greater.

Disapproval of my egalitarian ways left me indifferent. But I was hard put to reply when Lord Beresford once, with un-English rudeness, posed the humiliating question, 'How d'you explain that the Japanese, those little chaps, beat the Russians, those strapping fellows, with one hand tied behind their back?'

Every Russian had asked himself the same question.

'Russian supply lines were too long.' Stevie's defence of Russia surprised me all the more since he had formed a committee in support of Royal Republicans among his anti-Russian class-mates.

'And Russian warships obsolete,' scoffed Lord Beresford, whose father was in the navy. 'Not to mention they were commanded by landlubbers.' The Dogger Bank incident had not been forgotten in that family.

'What's that got to do with Tanya?' Stevie said. 'Her father is cavalry.'

That closed the discussion, and Lord Beresford vouchsafed me a smile.

I was in no danger of being challenged by his two sisters and younger brother, Andrew. They were as limited and apolitical as my imperial namesake and her siblings.

Father came for me just as I began to be tired of rain and homesick for snow. To replace Diana – with Father's help, she had realized her earlier ambition to study medicine – Father hired middle-aged and sporty Nancy Radford.

'Radfie' had strong notions of hygiene, and from the moment we returned to Petersburg she disapproved of Russian overheating, overeating and wild driving habits. Countess Liline remained as my social *éducatrice* and continued to accompany me on my visits to Tsarskoye.

The next five summers saw me back at Veslawa, but my childhood intimacy with Stevie was not to be renewed. As we grew self-conscious about our sexual identities, we began to draw apart. My admiration of Stevie's masculine splendour was to be tempered henceforth by the sense of my greater feminine maturity. For all my feelings of inferiority, I was glad to be a girl; a son would not have had the same hold on Father. Thanks to my enlightened aunt, I was psychologically prepared for puberty. I could not imagine having children, since that would involve marriage and interference with my freedom. But the ability to have them, I sensed, gave me a power no man could match. I meant to stay as resourceful and athletic as a boy. By the standards of the age, I was a tomboy still. But I began insensibly to copy Aunt's tranquil graciousness. As I returned little by little to the femininity of early childhood, the first passion of childhood proved stronger than the second, and my love for Father returned in all its painful intensity.

I resigned myself to the fact that I could not have Father all to myself and accepted his mistresses, as did Grandmaman, as the lesser of two evils – since the Diana episode, Grandmaman lived in dread that Father might commit a *mésalliance*. As for Radfie, since Father's affairs were not a matter of hygiene, she could not get excited about them.

So there was always present some lovely lady of one nationality or another during our yearly cruise and stay abroad. And when Father grew particularly kind and thoughtful, as if he were sorry for her, I knew he would soon leave this paramour for another. I was so pleased at the knowledge that I accepted the advances the poor women invariably made me. The more perfidious my behaviour, the more earnest were my prayers, the more severe my self-imposed penances, the greater my determination to *do* good, if I could not *be* good, and devote my life, at Father's side, to the sick and the poor.

In the summer of 1910, Great-Uncle Prince Leon died at one hundred years of age, after complaining with his dying breath that his wife had driven him to an early grave. He was buried with royal pomp and laid to rest, according to his wish, not in the family crypt but in the cemetery overlooking the valley of the Vistula he had so loved. There, between the birch and aspen, a marble cenotaph was erected and there his sweet widow Catherine, whom he had cruelly mistreated and deceived, came every day for the remainder of her life to lay fresh flowers on her 'little angel's' grave.

In September of 1911, another fanatical patriot died, in the person of Russia's prime minister, Stolypin. Father was in attendance on the Tsar at the Kiev Opera House when the Premier was fatally shot. Olga and Tatyana Nikolayevna were also present.

'It was such a shock to the Grand Duchesses,' Father told us when he came for me at Veslawa directly from Kiev. 'Tatyana Nikolayevna turned to stone. Olga wanted to rush to the aid of Stolypin's daughter – the child was gravely wounded. The Empress had to reprimand her sharply. Her Majesty herself was very agitated. Only the Tsar remained perfectly composed.'

'How awful!' I cried.

I pictured the scene, the shots, the screams, the swarming security police. And the victim could have been our sovereign, the wounded girl Tatyana Nikolayevna or Olga!

'The assassin was also in the pay of the Okhrana – ironic, isn't it, that this same secret police should be charged with the task of protecting high personages. The crime is as sordid as it is tragic,' Father continued.

'How can a Social Revolutionary be a double agent?' Aunt wondered.

'It's rather common in Russia, isn't it, Peter?' Uncle said.

'Yes,' Father rejoined. 'The connection between terrorists, criminals and the police seems curiously close. It makes one think of Dostoevsky's *Possessed*: men so warped by their vocation of terror that their actions are a mystery to the rest of us.'

'Stolypin was high-handed and narrowly nationalistic. He was no friend of Poland,' Uncle remarked.

'Granted,' Father was quick to agree. 'Nevertheless, his assassination is a blow to parliamentary government. Tell me what leader of calibre and integrity will come forward now?'

'Stolypin's successor, Kokovtsvov, is no blazing liberal either, but he's been a capable finance minister. Why shouldn't he be adequate as prime minister as well?' asked Uncle.

'Adequate's not good enough.' Father's voice remained calm, but I felt his emotion. 'On the one hand, you have a duma embittered by repeated dissolutions, on the other a sovereign who clings to autocratic prerogative. Who'll reconcile the two? Who'll control the extremists on the Left?'

'And on the Right,' Uncle interjected.

'Quite so. Who'll reverse Their Majesties' growing dependence on pernicious occult influences? Who'll reform the army in the face of Prussian belligerence? Who, dear God, will save Russia?'

It was the first time Father had spoken of his fears in my presence.

I was now a serious fourteen-year-old encumbered by my too-tall body and weighted with the sense of the rift between Christian ideal and practice. I had no interest in world affairs. That my world was corrupt I well knew. I would take care not to be sullied by it. That it should be threatened had meant little to me until now. Through the eyes of Tatyana Nikolayevna at the Kiev Opera House, I suddenly saw its precariousness. I saw too that Father was unhappy, and was unhappy for him.

In a few days, however, I had relegated it to the mental back closet where the incomprehensible and cruel were stored. Once again, nothing was as important and absorbing as myself.

With the help of Aunt Sophie, I had persuaded Father to let me attend school. That autumn on my return to Petersburg, I was enrolled at the Smolny Institute for Daughters of the Nobility.

5

The winter day is short in northern Russia, and at eight in the morning the courtyard of our *osobnyak* was still pitch-dark when I got into my sleigh to drive to the Smolny Institute after a cosy breakfast with Father. Heads tucked in, tails sweeping the snow from under the blue netting that covered them, the black pair of Orlov trotters followed the Neva at a racing trot. The broad padded bulk of Gerazim, the coachman, sheltered us from the front and Fyodor's giant figure from behind. Radfie kept her narrow English face inside the sealskin collar of her fur *shuba* in silent disapproval of the barbarous Russian cold and the still more barbarous driving habits of Russian coachmen. An ermine cape over my school uniform, my ermine bonnet low over my ears, I looked with pleasure down the stately quays, at the illumined arc of the Nicholas Bridge, the long straight span of the Alexander Bridge shimmering with lights, and the golden spire of the Cathedral of Petropavlovsk Fortress gleaming in the dark.

On still days, the city at this hour appeared to me infinitely vast, majestic and mysterious. On windy days the wind whistled above the frozen river, sending up clouds of fine snow, lifting the manes of the shaggy ponies pulling the low sledges with round yokes across the ice and ruffling the white beard of the veteran guarding the Alexander Column in the Winter Palace Square. Stony and forbidding then were the colonnaded façades along the quays, the apartment and office buildings I glimpsed as we crossed the broad rectilinear *prospekts* stretching out of sight. The cold cut the breath and stopped up the nose, and it was a relief to round the wide bend of the river and see the three blue cupolas of Rastrelli's cathedral rising on the Smolny heights.

The white halls of the institute were brightly lit and warm as we fell in silently two by two behind our *klasnaya dama* – the class matron – and followed her first to chapel, then to class. An earnest student, I sat on a window ledge during recess, reading or studying.

My classmates whispered that Her Serene Highness was too good to associate with anybody but Grand Duchesses. I ignored their early attempts to ridicule me as I did their subsequent advances. I managed, as a point of pride, to be at the head of my class and, judging by their attitude, gladdened equally the snobbish and pedagogical hearts of my professors.

At three o'clock in the afternoon the sleigh returned for me, bringing Countess Liline instead of Radfie, if the weather was good. My handsome *éducatrice* bloomed in her white fox collar like some opulent northern flower, looking as much at ease in furs as Radfie did in a macintosh. In the heart of winter the streets were already dark and streetlights on. Maintenance crews sprinkled saffron-coloured sand on the sidewalks. The high yellow trams were full. Street vendors hawked their wares. Cabdrivers' tea stands did a brisk trade. Ladies in furs went shopping accompanied by their footmen. Cossacks of the guard trotted by in pairs.

Better than the animated scene on the Nevsky Prospekt, I loved the spectacle, on a sparkling sunny day, of the winter boulevard of the Neva River proper. From the quays of rose granite on its southern bank to the islands linked by arching bridges, the frozen river, vast as a lake, was crisscrossed with flying sledges. The sledges and padded coachmen alike appeared diminutive and delicate against the prodigious scale of land and sky, which lent the monumental architecture of Peter's city an Italianate grace.

The rose and yellow façades of the imperial palaces and aristocratic residences had a particular gay splendour on such a day. And the motley crowd walking past, the brilliant tunics of the Guard, the scarlet livery of an imperial house, a peasant woman's quilted blue coat, the bonnets of mink, beaver, sheepskin and astrakhan, bespoke a richness and diversity, an exuberance and opulence, that belied the misery and monotony of life for the majority of Petersburg's inhabitants – those who made their livelihood by ministering to the needs and pleasures of the fortunate few in the palaces and *osobnyaks*.

On alternate days I was taken to the Michael Riding School for a dressage and jumping lesson and to the skating rink in the gardens of the Palais Tauride. Bent over like a boy, hands clasped behind my back, I raced around the rink with boys from the Guryevsky School or Corps des Pages. I loved to pull up with a shattering stop before some startled young thing clinging to the arm of a Guard Officer. And it was in vain that my *éducatrice* reproached me, when I returned with false demureness to her side. '*Princesse, ce ne sont pas des façons*. This isn't done.'

Less amusing were piano and dancing lessons and weekly visits with Grandmaman to the charitable institutions under her patronage. I also had the duty of standing beside her chair on her 'at home' day, and of saying all afternoon long in English, or French, to the guests, 'D'you take cream or lemon in your tea, Your Highness? Your Excellency?' – a phrase that earned me the compliment of being a very intelligent girl.

This period was marked by two parallel and inevitably conflicting developments – my education and expectations as a daughter of the nobility and my secret aspirations and preparations for a career in medicine. In these latter, I was aided and abetted by the famous scientist Alexis Holveg.

It was Igor Constantinovich, the son of our great family friend Grand Duke Constantine and my comrade since my childhood visits to the Marble Palace, who first drew my attention to Professor Holveg.

Alexis Holveg, then already a full professor of chemistry at the University of Petersburg, had spent two summers at Pavlovsk in the Grand Duke's summer palace as tutor to Prince Igor and his brother Costia. Even after Igor was enrolled in the Corps des Pages, Professor Holveg remained on good terms with his pupils' family. The Grand Duchess liked him because he was a German Lutheran like herself and the Grand Duke, as president of the Academy of Sciences, had followed closely his discoveries in the new field of radium research and his scientific honours – at twenty-eight, Alexis Holveg was a member of the Academy of Sciences and the prestigious Chemico-Physical Society.

Prince Igor was no intellect. Horses were his passion. But he was an extremely likeable and unpretentious young man, with a self-assurance so often wanting in royal princes because of their restricted upbringing. His brothers thought him brash, and would remind him to keep down his loud voice. He was very fond of Professor Holveg and never failed to relay his caustic tutor's latest sally. There was also, I learned from Igor, an aura of mystery about the scientist.

'His mother is Jewish,' said he, 'but his father was a prince. *On dit qu'il est fils naturel d'un grand-duc allemand.*'

We were rehearsing, in the private theatre of the Marble Palace, a religious play written by Grand Duke Constantine, when Igor chose this moment to confide his tutor's alleged bastard birth in a whisper heard all over the stage.

There were dire looks from his brothers, and I had to master my curiosity until I could catch Igor's sleeve in the wings and demand, '*What* German grand duke is Professor Holveg's natural father? *How* does he have a Jewish mother?'

'Oh, it was a proper scandal.' Igor rolled his eyes theatrically. 'But you're a young vestal. *Ce genre d'histoire*, this type of story can't be of interest to you.'

I could have kicked Igor. But we were summoned back on stage and my curiosity had to wait.

I was the more pleased the next day when Father, after dinner, told Grandmaman that he would like to ask Alexis Holveg to our next evening of chamber music.

'I'm curious to learn Professor Holveg's reaction to his audience with His Majesty, which I arranged,' Father said. 'You know it's always been my idea that instead of persecuting the intelligentsia, our government ought to exploit its vanity, which, I believe, is even greater than that of any other class of people. The best way to make a monarchist out of a republican is to present him with a monarchist order. Young Holveg has an immense following in university circles. He made a good impression on His Majesty, and I think you'd like him too, Maman, if you'd permit me to invite him.'

'As if you'd ever asked permission to bring home all sorts of Bohemians and misfits' – Grandmaman referred to Father's patronage of needy artists. 'But you're welcome, of course, to ask your young Jewish protégé. My son has always had a weakness for oppressed minorities.' This last observation, in French, was made to Zinaida Mikhailovna, Grandmother's timorous, plump companion, who clearly did not know what to make of it. It was followed, in Russian, with, 'The devil! It's not coming out' – a reference to her game of solitaire.

Father exchanged with me a little smile and shifted Grandmaman's cards. 'Try this, Maman. As for my little Jewish protégé, he is one of our most promising scientists, by way of becoming another

Mendeleyev. Besides, he's only half Jewish, baptized a Lutheran and on the paternal side not only well- but high-born.' And he related with the subtle pleasure of the raconteur the story of Alexis Holveg's curious origin.

I listened avidly and thought it cruel of the Grand Duchess Margareta of Allensee to have disowned her son and heir for secretly marrying a beautiful Jewish girl from the neighbouring Polish town of Bialla. I now burned to meet Professor Holveg and I asked Father to introduce him.

The chamber concert over, Father beckoned me with a finger to the drawing-room corner in which he stood towering over a scholarly looking young man with spectacles and a very trim and black goatee.

'Tatyana Petrovna, my daughter, has been most anxious to meet you, Professor. She's very interested in scientific subjects,' Father said, in the same tone he'd use to call me Florence Nightingale.

'That's always encouraging to hear.' Professor Holveg flashed his black eyes on me in a way I thought rather bold, and drily shook the hand I proffered to be kissed.

Father resumed his interrupted conversation. 'I'm happy His Majesty's real sympathy for you was reciprocated, Professor. I hope your meeting will have had some effect on your political views?'

'Not in the least,' Professor Holveg burst out. 'I'll admit that, as a man, I found Nicholas II simple and unassuming. But I cannot forget that he is an autocrat.'

'But is he really?' Father rejoined. 'We have a parliament and a proliferation of political parties. We have a virtually free press. Oh, I know there is censorship' – Father anticipated the Professor's objection – 'but it is ignored. The newspaper publisher pays a fine, and goes right on excoriating the government. Theatre and the arts flourish. Every form of religious worship is openly practised and every kind of occultism indulged in. As for our sexual mores' – Father glanced at me – 'the less said the better.'

'And discrimination against the minorities?' Professor Holveg came back quickly, to my disappointment. 'Sexual mores', as Father so elegantly put it, interested me much more. 'Are there not Jewish quotas for secondary schools and universities, and many similar statutes that deprive Jews of their full and just civic rights? Aren't Ukrainians considered second-class citizens? Isn't it a fact that the Baltic peoples, like the Finns and the Poles, are under Russian rule?'

'Granted, and I deplore all these injustices. But their roots lie in Russian nationalism, which harks back to the Mongol occupation – two centuries of it, Professor, don't forget. Nationalism goes deeper than political colouring. You cannot put all the blame for it on "autocracy".'

'You may be right.' Professor Holveg's lively gaze was riveted on Father's, as if he were trying to understand and solve all questions at once. 'Nationalism is a universal phenomenon, as ugly as it is puzzling to a scientific mind. But that does not absolve the Tsar-Autocrat of all the Russias. Whether in name only or in fact, autocracy has no place in the twentieth century, Prince.'

'Quite.' Father faintly smiled at beliefs so earnestly held and heatedly expressed. 'Neither am I a champion of autocracy, Professor. But unlike your vociferous liberals I would like to see the monarchy modified even more along constitutional lines, not overthrown. What liberals don't seem to realize is that the Left is a far greater danger to them than the Right and much closer to the Right in its extreme.'

'I don't belong to the Left, properly speaking,' Professor Holveg retorted defensively, as though compelled to state the obvious. 'I'm not in sympathy with Karl Marx. But I can't help feeling, as any intelligent person must, that monarchy is a childish concept, one the human race must outgrow as children outgrow fairy tales. Hereditary rule, like the criterion of birth, has no place in a modern society.'

'What criterion would you substitute for it, Professor? That of intelligence? How would you determine it? As Pushkin observed, "How taxed would our poor butlers be if they had to serve the dinner guests according to precedence of brains rather than of rank."' Father asked me to see that Professor Holveg had some tea, and excused himself to join his other guests.

I led the Professor to the table at which Grandmaman presided behind the eagle-crested silver samovar with our monogram. While she poured his tea, measuring him with her most direct and disconcerting look, a thought took form in my mind.

'Professor' – I took him to a Tiepolo that had caught his attention on a far wall – 'you attended a German university. You must speak German very well.'

'I am fluent in it, yes.'

'Would you teach it to me?'

'I should be happy to, but languages are hardly my field. I'm certain you could find someone better qualified.'

'Professor' – I looked round to make sure I was not overheard – 'I don't really want to learn German. It would only be a pretext, so that you could help me with physics and chemistry and biology. They don't teach enough of it at Smolny and it's so terribly important to me!'

Professor Holveg's perceptive look was almost as disconcerting as Grandmaman's. 'Why should those subjects be so terribly important, Tatyana Petrovna?'

'Because' – I lowered my voice even more – 'I'm going to be a doctor.'

'You . . . a doctor, Tatyana Petrovna?'

'Please, Professor, speak softly. Nobody must know, not even Papa. He wouldn't understand.'

'But, excuse me, Tatyana Petrovna, I don't understand very well either. For a person of your rank and fortune and position, a medical career is out of the question.'

'I don't care about rank and position. I don't consider those things important. But to save a human life, to cure a sick child, to deliver a baby, I think that's important . . . and *real* . . . and the Grand Duchess Tatyana Nikolayevna thinks so too!'

'Does she indeed? And does Her Imperial Highness plan to be your assistant?'

I was vexed at the Professor's irony. 'Oh, you don't take me seriously either! Nobody takes me seriously, just because I'm only fourteen. I've wanted to be a doctor since I was six years old. It's something I can't help, and nothing, or no one, can prevent!'

Professor Holveg observed me with new interest. 'I knew I was going to be a scientist when I was six years old, and that nothing, or no one could prevent me. I believe I do understand, Tatyana Petrovna.'

'Then you *will* help me? On top of the German? Just between us?'

'Tatyana Petrovna, I must warn you, I'm not a biologist, or even a biochemist. My main field is the investigation of radioactive elements and their properties. And in its present primitive state, medicine hardly deserves to be called a science, especially not in the clinical aspects which interest you.'

'Yes but those come last. First one must have some knowledge of . . . knowledge of . . .'

'The basic sciences?'

'Exactly.' I smiled and the Professor smiled back. His teeth were white and straight, his smile unexpectedly frank and attractive. 'You will do it, Professor?'

'I'll think about it, Tatyana Petrovna,' he said in his dry way. And at this moment Vera Kirilovna glided up to suggest it was time I retired.

A half-hour later I was saying to Nyanya while she brushed my hair, 'Professor Holveg's hands are small and fine and his teeth are nice, and his eyes, they're so intelligent, he has such a look in them! And he's so funny and touchy, Nyanya, he's all prickly like a porcupine, but inside, I'm sure he's very soft. He couldn't really hurt anybody. Just think, Nyanya, knowing a genius! He is a genius, Papa says so. And he understands me, I'm sure.'

'A person would have to be a genius to understand you, my love.'

I ignored her sarcasm. 'D'you think, Nyanya, Papa would engage him to tutor me in mathematics and science, as Grand Duke Constantine did for Igor Constantinovich and Costia?'

'And what do you want with mathematics and science, my love? The Lord hasn't made a woman's mind for such things, and with good reason. It's not learning in mathematics and science your babies will want from you, nor will your husband love you better for it.'

This traditional view of women made me boil. 'I'm not going to marry! I'm not going to have children! I'm going to live with Papa and be a doctor!'

'That's something I'd like to see, a Serene Princess Silomirskaya a doctor! You'd best not mention it to your papa, my love. Good as he is, it will make him lose his patience.'

I was afraid it might. I only asked Father to engage Professor Holveg to tutor me in German, if he was willing. To Father's surprise, Professor Holveg was.

Once a week thereafter, from mid-September to the end of May and until the eve of my graduation in 1914, the majordomo escorted the Professor to my study on the third storey of the wing of private apartments overlooking the Neva. I poured him a cup of tea and we sat down on either side of my large desk of Karelian birch under the window, Bobby, now chastened by the years, snoozing at my feet. Radfie stayed with us awhile. But as I closed the ventilating pane in the upper corner of the double window, on the pretext that Professor Holveg caught cold awfully easily, my sporty governess soon suffered from the heat generated by the stove of Delft tile and retreated to an adjoining room, leaving the field clear for physics.

I made rapid progress in German. I was not so confident about physics.

'Professor,' I asked at the end of our first winter of clandestine instruction, 'd'you really think I'll ever learn all I need to become a doctor? I'm not frightfully intelligent like you, or like my cousin Stefan Veslawski. Things just come to him.'

'Your intelligence is adequate, Tatyana Petrovna. Your comprehension is good, your memory excellent, your tenacity . . . remarkable. I believe you'd achieve anything you'd set your mind to.' The Professor held the point of his little beard as he observed me across the desk, and although I was not absolutely sure he took me absolutely seriously, I was heartened by his words.

Professor Holveg soon became a favourite visitor. His frankness and sarcasm delighted my frank and sarcastic grandmother. My tutor, I saw, rejected the beliefs the majority of people took for granted and I was beginning to take for inevitable, as long as they did not interfere with my ambitions. Professor Holveg said nothing was inevitable or immutable; every concept must be examined afresh. Even a scientific law must not be accepted until the student had proved its validity by repeated experiments. But when I questioned the Professor on his solution to those social ills that so incensed him, he claimed this was outside his competence.

'I'm already overstepping my province by helping you with your little science problems,' he said. 'I would like to see you acquire a healthy scepticism but I would not want to see you apply it as a philosophy of life. It's not my intention to make you dissatisfied with your position in society.'

'But I know there is very much wrong with our society, Professor. I've seen for myself how the poor live. When I'm grown up, I'll do something about it. But it seems to me society will only change when people themselves change, in their hearts – when they become real Christians.' I fell silent as Professor Holveg fingered his little beard uneasily. Then, 'Professor,' I shot at him, 'd'you believe in God?'

'Tatyana Petrovna, that's another topic I'd rather not discuss. I hope you can reconcile your very real scientific curiosity with your religious beliefs. I would be the last person to wish to create a conflict between them.'

'But you see, Professor, for me, there can be no conflict. Because science is something I must learn about, with my mind. Faith is something I feel. I know it, deep inside.' I pressed my hands to my waist. 'I understand evolution very well. I know the Bible is not to be taken literally. I believe Man evolved from a unicellular organism, as you told me, to a creature with a brain, which is a very complex structure with millions of cells. And only a creature with a brain that can think can be aware of the existence of God and that was the whole purpose of it.' A creature capable of perceiving God being the purpose of evolution, I meant. I stopped, exhausted by my philosophical effort.

'I'm not sure Man is the purpose of evolution, or that evolution has any purpose.' Tapping his pencil on the desk, the Professor asked me to define osmotic pressure once more.

On another occasion, I embarrassed my tutor even more by asking, 'What d'you suppose Father referred to, Professor, when he spoke of our sexual mores? It was at our very first meeting. Do you remember?'

'How could I forget? But your question, Tatyana Petrovna, is . . . is . . .'

'Outside your competence?'

'How well you recall my every word! I was going to say, outside my province.'

'But I must learn about these things if I'm going to be a doctor!'

'In time, in time you will learn more than you will care to know. But for the present, why not ask your father?'

I did, when we had our breakfast *à deux*.

Father was neither surprised nor confused. He thought awhile, tapping the table with manicured fingertips, then said, 'You see, Tanichka, sexual pleasure is the greatest pleasure a human being can experience. In a sensitive person, when it accompanies love, it brings bliss – without love, self-disgust.' He looked at his rings, as if to avoid my gaze, and I thought, Poor Papa! He is talking about himself. How unhappy he must be!

'Marriage,' Father continued, 'when it is a love match, is the ideal form of sexual expression.' He spoke with longing.

He is thinking of Mother, I thought. Why did I bring this up?

'But there are many other forms,' he went on. 'Adultery – you've read *Anna Karenina* – illegitimate or free love –'

'I know about that too.' It did not seem very terrible. And as much as I adored *War and Peace*, I could not see what the fuss in *Anna Karenina* was about.

'Sex which is bought –'

'Prostitution,' I said. That I found awful.

'Yes. When it's bought cheap, it's called prostitution. When it's bought dear, it may even be called marriage. Then there is sex obtained by force.' Father waited for my reaction again.

I nodded wordlessly. Rape was not only ghastly, it was my one acknowledged terror.

'You know to be on your guard against it,' Father said. 'You know quite a bit. Quite enough, I should say.' He smiled. Then, as I still waited for more, 'There are also men and women, homosexuals,' he added, 'who can only find pleasure with a partner of their own sex. The practice is as old as Sodom and Gomorrah. In big cities like Paris, London or Petersburg it is not uncommon.'

Like most adult explanations, it left the mechanics to the imagination. I was no longer so slow to grasp them as I had been when I wanted to know how Papa had put a baby in Mother's tummy.

'Heard enough?' Father guessed my reaction.

'Papa,' I asked at the end of breakfast, as I leant over his chair to kiss him goodbye, 'isn't it a sin?'

'Homosexual love? It is. But that only makes it all the more attractive. One must be careful, Tanichka' – Father turned in his chair and took me by the arms – 'not to judge or condemn. Righteousness is a greater sin than the transgression of the flesh. Don't look so stern. It's not becoming. You are too young and inexperienced to understand these matters. And you are far too young to judge them.'

A hint of rebuke on Father's part was enough. 'I'll try not to,' I promised.

I controlled the natural impulse to share my discoveries with my namesake. I had the sense to suspect that, were Tatyana Nikolayevna to question her parents in turn, I would be banished from her presence. Then, too, I liked to think of her as pure and innocent in contrast to me. I wanted her to remain my ideal of girlish goodness, as she was of beauty and royal grace.

Having satisfied my curiosity about sexual mores for the time being, I then became curious about university life. I pictured it as free and gay. But the Professor, whom I questioned, said that in tsarist Russia it was neither. The students were mostly poor, the professors too few, and the lecture halls so crowded that he could hardly attend courses for fear of fainting in the foul air. Nevertheless I burned to visit the university quarter and, just before the thaw, I received permission to drop my tutor off after our lesson at his flat on Vassily Island.

My *éducatrice* accompanied me on this exceptional outing and allowed me to walk with the Professor down the quay of the Big Neva, while she followed in an open carriage at a walking pace. We passed a group of students in long greatcoats or tunics of military cut and long, motley scarves. Their visored caps in the colour of their particular faculty sat askew on their uncombed hair. They greeted Professor Holveg respectfully but stared at me with undisguised hostility.

On my visits to Grandmaman's philanthropic institutions, I was used to being met by smiles and bows. 'Professor,' I asked, 'why do the students glare at me?'

'Because you are the Serene Princess Silomirskaya and the closest friend of the daughters of the Tsar, who is not very well liked on this island. Because you are immensely rich, and most of these young people are poor.'

'But why should it matter so much, Professor, whether one is rich or poor?'

We had rounded the point of Vassily Island and as we stopped before the Doric *fronton* of the Exchange to admire the view, he answered this naïve question. 'It doesn't matter to you, Tatyana Petrovna, because you have never been poor. For you, the struggle for daily existence has no reality. But for the majority of mankind, it is still the main reality besides birth and death. Hunger and cold, *cholod i golod, Kalt und Hunger, le froid et la faim,*' he repeated in Russian, German and French, 'they fill the minds of thousands in this city which spreads so splendidly before us. I knew them firsthand during the first twenty years of my life. I will never forget them.'

I was reminded of my tutor's romantically unhappy history. 'Oh, it's so unfair. But didn't ... couldn't your father do anything for you and your mother?'

'I never had the honour of knowing my princely father,' the Professor replied drily. 'Margareta of Allensee had him banished to Japan for refusing to renounce his Jewish bride. As an officer in the Japanese army, he was killed in the war with Russia. My mother was offered a comfortable income for life if she would agree not to use my father's name – Holveg is the name of our Swedish forbears. She preferred to raise me a pauper rather than a bastard ... excuse me, Tatyana Petrovna. I quite forgot myself.'

I was afraid I had been tactless and kept silent. We walked on down the quay of the Small Neva and passed a chattering group of girls from the Kursy – the Women's University. With their short hair and brusque gestures, they were even more sloppy and angry-looking than the men.

'There you see several future doctors, Tatyana Petrovna,' said the Professor – Russian girls were already then entering the medical profession in numbers – 'and possibly a few terrorists.'

Women, I knew, had taken part in terrorist acts as long ago as the assassination of Alexander II, liberator of the serfs. A young girl had been one of the assassins of the minister of the interior, von Plehve, in 1904. I thought I was as rebellious as any woman. I could kill without a qualm in my own defence or that of my loved ones. But I could never throw a bomb. 'What kind of woman becomes a terrorist?' I asked.

'Daughters of the intelligentsia and the professional bourgeoisie. The same combination of anger and idealism motivates revolutionaries of both sexes. There are even those, like Vladimir Lenin, the Bolshevik leader in exile in Switzerland, who come from the landed gentry. And, of course, there will be Jews. They have suffered most under tsarist oppression.'

'You're quite bitter about the treatment of Jews, Professor, aren't you?'

'Anti-semitism, Tatyana Petrovna, is a manifestation of stupidity and ignorance. Prejudice in one form or another, is universal. In North America, they lynch Negroes. In India, there are millions of untouchables. And women everywhere are treated as inferiors.'

'It makes me furious!' I looked with new sympathy at my ill-kempt university sisters. 'If I can't go to the university here, I'll go to England or Switzerland for my pre-medical studies. And when I come into Mother's inheritance, I'll found a medical college for girls of the nobility. Professor, next year, will you take me through the Zoology Museum and the Museum of Anatomy?'

'Tatyana Petrovna, please. I can't become involved in your scheme any more than I am already. After all, it is entirely hypothetical.'

'If it's hypothetical, it can do no harm.' I could not help laughing.

At once the carriage bearing my *éducatrice*, opulently blooming in her fox collar, stopped alongside, and Vera Kirilovna bent on me a look I understood to signify that open hilarity in the streets was not *comme il faut*. My short promenade with Professor Holveg was at an end.

Winter had ended too. Like a paved road in an earthquake, the Neva split into jagged chunks, which icebreakers pushed out to sea. On the way to Smolny, bonfires were lit on street corners to hasten the thaw of dirty old snow. Gutter spouts hung with icicles made a continuous drip. Packets of snow slid from red metal roofs now gleaming as though freshly painted. Soon, to the boom of cannon, the port admiral and the governor of Petropavlovsk Fortress met on their yawls in midstream: the Neva was open to navigation again.

The white immensity of the frozen river came alive with steamships, rowboats, patrol boats, tugs, barges, and pleasure yachts. Sleighs gave way to open carriages and motorcars. Ostrich plumes reappeared on ladies' hats, fluffy boas instead of furs about their necks and parasols in their hands. The Summer Garden and the elms along the Neva burst into bloom, the air was light and balmy, the imperial standard billowed yellow above the red roof of the Winter Palace.

The northern spring comes swiftly, riotously, and is as swiftly gone. Summer brought Petersburg the heat and the smells. The sea-green waters of the Neva grew murky and leaden-looking. Bad odours rose from the picturesque canals. The flags above the imperial palaces drooped. On Sundays the lower classes took to the pleasure islands in the Neva or to the suburban woods. The well-to-do left for their summer dachas. The daughters of the nobility on holiday from the Smolny Institute departed to the seashore or their country estates. After celebrating my fifteenth birthday, Father left for Florence to paint and enjoy his latest love affair. Grandmaman moved to our seaside dacha north of Petersburg, and I boarded our private railway car bound for Veslawa.

Professor Holvég happened to be going to visit his mother in Warsaw by the same train. I invited him to my drawing room and we managed, in spite of Radfie's unsmiling presence, to enjoy ourselves thoroughly.

6

The cousin who greeted me on the portico of the Veslawski palace in July 1912 was a tall and strong seventeen-and-a-half-year-old with a deep and resonant voice. We shook left-hand forefingers in blood-brother greeting, out of childhood habit. But we were now strangers.

When Stevie and Casimir were not primping or stuffing themselves, they would tear about the countryside in an open car or ride off to secret meetings of Royal Republicans in the woods. They had other business too, as I discovered one day riding past an arbour where Stevie sat kissing a peasant girl.

I reined in and flushed with inexplicable fury. Stevie regarded me mockingly. As I cantered on, I heard behind my back the giggle of the girl in Stevie's arms – who was none other than Wanda.

Another trial for me was the weekly Saturday night dance at the palace.

'Oh, what a stick!' or, 'What little talent for the dance!' Stevie, in the quadrille, would make some barbed remark.

Casimir tried to console me. 'Never mind Stevie. Why don't you twit him about his voice studies? He was awfully sensitive about them at Eton.'

I did so, and scored. Yet I continued to feel gauche and graceless.

'It's no use, Kim,' I said to kind, thoughtful Casimir – he was more than just an echo of Stefan. 'I know I'm not pretty or attractive. But I, at least, will do something worthwhile.'

I would compel the world's admiration as a surgeon.

Casimir was ready to admire me now. He shared my contempt for girls whose only goal was to catch the most eligible husband. They'd never catch him, he swore.

To compensate for my deficiencies, I practised tirelessly with the Männlicher .256-calibre sporting rifle Father had given me on my fifteenth birthday, hurled myself at ever-bigger obstacles in the jumping paddock, and was as ready to challenge any young man on the hunting field as I was unfit to meet him on the dance floor.

I read a great deal that summer, taking advantage of the French collection in the palace library. I was interested anew in sexual behaviour. English novelists shed no light on the subject, Russian ones only a little more. What I knew about prostitution I had learned from Tolstoy and Dostoevsky. Emile Zola's *Nana* vastly broadened my knowledge, not only of prostitution but of sexual mores generally. Was European society really riddled with perverts, and, if so, how could one tell them from the others?

I screwed up enough courage to ask Stevie, offhand, if 'that sort of thing, you know', went on at Eton.

'Of course,' he said, 'to some extent. But no one bothers about it. You've been reading too many books.'

'No more than you have.'

'Yes, but I didn't take everything in such earnest.'

I could only take literature, like life, in dead earnest. I was inclined to believe literature the more truthful and trustworthy of the two. The ordered, elegant and complacent existence led by those of my circle blossomed over a cesspool. Lust in all its variety secretly possessed the powerful. I forgot my promise to Father not to judge and condemn what I did not understand.

In September, Stevie and Casimir got ready to leave for Oxford – they had been accepted at Magdalen. I prepared to resume school at Smolny. Instead, Father came to take me away, not to Petersburg, but to Bialowieza, where the Tsar and his family were vacationing.

The Bialowieza *puszcza*, the immense wild forest not far from my maternal family's Podlesian domains, had once been a hunting preserve of Polish kings. For all his patience and diplomacy, Uncle Stan's gorge rose at the thought of a Russian tsar disporting himself in the Veslawskis' ancestral preserve. He declined the Tsar's invitation, which Father extended, to join the imperial hunting party.

I was happy to see the Grand Duchesses and their brother, who was active and jolly for the time being. Aleksey, the Tsarevich, was a handsome, chestnut-haired eight-year-old, as winsome as he was spoiled. As a sick child, he had for me a special appeal. He reciprocated my affection, casually though I expressed it. When he was well, his mother became quite amiable and concealed the dislike she had taken to Father. But neither Alexandra's amiability nor Aleksey's apparent health lasted long.

The Bialowieza forest was not only the last bison preserve in Europe but it abounded in game, big and small. As a result, the carnage was prodigious.

I was as keen a sportsman as Stevie. Riding to hounds, whether after fox in England, stag in France, lynx, wolf or boar in Poland and Russia, was always an unforgettable thrill. But shooting from the safety of a stand at animals driven by beaters to the slaughter was not my idea of sport. It saddened me as well to see the lovely pheasants, heath cocks, pigeons and other game birds piled by the thousands on the perron of the castle, while the hunting horns saluting the Tsar by torchlight at the end of each day sounded more like a dirge than a fanfare.

Then, too, my Polish half told me Uncle Stan was right: a Russian emperor had no business hunting on the ancient preserve of our royal ancestors. The Russian custom of kissing the sovereigns' hands, which Polish ladies did not observe, struck me as servile. And, to make matters worse, I would incur Alexandra's displeasure!

Father thought it would amuse the Tsar, himself an ardent sportsman, to see what a crack shot I was. Calling me out from the stand where I stood with the Empress and the two eldest Grand Duchesses politely applauding the gentlemen sportsmen, he handed me his rifle, which a keeper had reloaded. It was a bigger calibre than mine. And even though I had used Stevie's rifle, the recoil rattled my teeth. I was lucky to shoot an elk through the heart. The gentlemen applauded this time, and the Tsar caressed me, calling me *amazonka* – little amazon. Olga and Tatyana Nikolayevna did not disguise their admiration.

'Don't you wish, Olichka, we could shoot as well as Tata?' whispered my namesake to her sister as we walked back to the castle behind the Empress.

'I'm not the sporty type,' Olga retorted. 'But you can practise marksmanship with Tata all you like.'

'As if I could do something on my own, just with Tata!'

'Don't let *me* prevent you!' Olga lengthened her stride.

'I didn't mean you, silly!' Her sister caught her arm. 'But you must admit, it gets to be such a bore, presenting at all times this united family front to the world.'

'A happily united front,' Olga agreed good-naturedly. '*A qui le dis-tu?*'

'You are exemplary, both of you,' I said.

If the Grand Duchesses were delighted to see me in the limelight, the Empress Alexandra could not permit anyone to draw away attention from her daughters. The girls were to perform some scenes from *Le Bourgeois Gentilhomme* during their stay in Poland.

The evening after my exploit, after I had helped them rehearse, the Empress addressed Father with a cool, 'Is it not time, Prince, that Tata were back in school?'

Stung by the unspoken rebuff, I was eager to be gone. Yet, when Aleksey injured himself, it was none other than Alexandra who detained me another week.

The accident occurred on the eve of my expected departure. The imperial children and I went boating on one of the two lakes formed by the Narewka river in its course through the forest. Aleksey Nikolayevich, in climbing out of the boat, hit his thigh, which began to bleed. Immediately, he was put to bed.

The Tsarevich had to be watched around the clock. His mother asked for me at his request, and for five days I spent many hours at the bedside. To keep the patient quiet, and control my own restlessness, I read to him, recited comical verses, and made up stories: about the poor little shark caught by the cruel fisherman or the baby crocodile who lost his mummy and cried till he flooded the Amazon. My fantastic tales and horrid faces could always bring a smile to Aleksey's pale and pained little face. I could also arrange his pillows, he claimed, better than anyone. Nor would he eat unless I was by. He cried when he heard I must go back to school. The Tsar himself told him not to act spoiled.

Fortunately, the episode did not seem too serious and Aleksey was able to be carried out to the palace portico by his sailor-nurse to see me off.

Father remained with the Tsar, whose favourite hunting companion he had been since boyhood, and Radfie accompanied me back to Petersburg. Before I left, Father again pledged me to strict secrecy about Aleksey's latest bout of illness. I knew that haemophilia was a forbidden topic. If it was talked about increasingly in dynastic and society circles, the fault was not mine. Yet, before a month had passed, the secret was out.

From Bialowieza, the imperial party went on to Spala, another royal Polish hunting preserve. There, the Tsarevich's condition took a sudden turn for the worse. He was in great pain from a mass of collected blood in the groin and infection set in. As the fever rose alarmingly, the Minister of the Court, Count Friedrichs, strongly seconded by Father, persuaded the Tsar to issue a health bulletin.

Alexandra, meanwhile, cabled her 'holy man', who had prudently gone home to Siberia to allow the wrath of his enemies to cool. Rasputin's answer, variously quoted, assured the Empress that God had heard her prayers and her son would recover. And the next day, indeed, the boy's temperature fell and the pain subsided. He was pronounced out of danger.

'Considering the force of superstition in our exalted circles, even in this scientific day,' Father reported to Grandmaman on his return from Spala, 'it's not surprising that Her Majesty should prefer a miraculous explanation of the Tsarevich's improvement to a medical one. But I commented that even the miracles of Lourdes are performed on the spot and not by telegraph at a distance of several thousand miles.

'At our next meeting, Alexandra Fyodorovna turned red as a crab and could barely speak. Evidently, my innocent statement had been kindly passed on to her. I'm already in Her Majesty's bad graces because of my constitutionalist views. And you know she's never forgiven me, Maman,' added Father with his fine little smile, 'for declining a match with one of her ladies-in-waiting.'

'Your private life is a disgrace, Pierre,' said Grandmaman gruffly, but with a note of amusement. She ignored Father's cautionary look. 'I can speak in front of Tatyana. She is *au courant*. Her Majesty, who is a virtuous wife and mother, is perfectly right to disapprove.'

The conversation made me squirm. Where Father's love life was concerned, I could be as much a puritan as Alexandra. His *libertinage*, which was alluded to so lightly in high society, pained me. Only his marrying again could have pained me more.

That subject was to come up again six weeks later in Paris, where we were invited to spend the Christmas holiday with the Veslawskis, Stevie and Casimir.

Since our first visit with Diana, our subsequent trips to Paris had been a mixed joy due to the presence of Father's mistress of the day. This time, we were guests of the Veslawskis', and if Father had a mistress waiting for him, he did not parade her before his kin. We stayed in the seventeenth-century town residence in the Faubourg St Germain that had served as Polish insurrectionist headquarters in the previous century and was now tenanted by the French branch of the family – Uncle Stan's middle sister had married a French peer. There Stevie and Casimir had preceded us from England.

'Seriously, old boy, when are you going to settle down?' Uncle Stan asked Father in his languid tone at the first opportunity for an intimate talk. Christmas was over, and our French hosts had tactfully gone out, leaving us with the Veslawskis, Stevie, and Casimir. 'These rumours one hears about your impending marriages are rather hard on one's nerves.'

We sat drinking coffee after lunch, about the fireplace in a *petit salon* hung with Gobelin tapestries, which overlooked the soggy garden. I seldom was in Paris when it did not pour.

Father turned on Aunt Sophie that kind and caressing gaze he reserved for attractive women and said, 'When I find someone who is beautiful, gracious, intelligent and kind, I shall marry. But so far the only woman who fits this description is already married to my brother-in-law.'

Aunt smiled placatingly at my jealous uncle. Then she asked if the tales about the growing influence of Rasputin – that ignoble Siberian monk – on the Empress Alexandra, were true.

'Alas,' answered Father, 'they are all too true, especially since his prescient telegram to Spala this autumn.' He related from personal experience the episode, which had become distorted through notoriety. 'Alexandra not only believes that the *starets* – he is a village seer, by the way, not a monk – can intercede with God on behalf of her sick son, but that he speaks with the voice of the Russian people.'

'And the Tsar?' Uncle Stan asked. 'Is he also taken in by this charlatan?'

'It's difficult to say. One thing is sure. Whoever criticizes Alexandra earns His Majesty's displeasure and mistrust, just as whoever criticizes her "holy man" earns the displeasure and mistrust of the Empress. For example, Mlle Tchiucheva, the Grand Duchesses' governess, who insisted Rasputin be barred from the children's floor at Tsarskoye, was eventually forced to leave.'

'Imagine allowing such a notorious lecher to visit the imperial children! I wonder, Pierre' – Aunt Sophie looked at me – 'if it's wise to let Tanya continue her association.'

'I have never seen him,' I hastened to interject – I did not want to be cut off from my friends. 'I never even hear him mentioned. I don't think he comes to the palace.'

'Tanya's right,' Father acknowledged. 'Alexandra has had to yield on that point. She communicates with him through her bosom friend and confidante, her former maid-of-honour, Anya Vyrubova, who has a little house at Tsarskoye Selo near the Alexander Palace. The Empress visits her every day. Sometimes she meets Rasputin there. More often, Anya transmits his verbal messages – the man can barely write.'

'She is a fat fool, Vyrubova,' I said. I disliked her coyness and sentimentality, and her doting on the imperial children, which embarrassed Aleksey Nikolayevich. 'We all make fun of her.' The Grand Duchess and I, I meant.

'It's simply unbelievable!' Aunt Sophie shook her head.

'Oh, why?' said Uncle Stan. 'They say Queen Victoria was ruled by her Scottish footman after Prince Albert died. Monarchs are a ready prey to servile, low creatures.'

'One more reason why their powers should be constitutionally limited,' Father said.

He was silent and his eyes, gazing into some unfathomable distance beyond the fire, reflected the relentless progress of his melancholy. The familiar pang shot through me and I moved to the back of his armchair to put my arms about his neck.

'In any case, whatever happens, you'll be the comfort of my old age.' He clasped my arms and smiled up at me.

I noticed Stevie watching me in that intent and curious way of his. Why does he look at me like that? I wondered. I know he thinks me plain and dull, but why should I care? As our eyes met, I felt myself stiffening and his expression changed. Once again everything between us was the same as before, but not as it had once been.

From Paris, we went on to England, returning home via Scandinavia. After six weeks of travel, my rigorous Petersburg routine required painful readjustment, and I was glad, as always, to escape to the laxer life at Tsarskoye Selo.

Olga and Tatyana fell upon me. 'Tell us everything from the beginning, Tata.'

I related my impressions of Paris, London and Stockholm, but did not offer my more mature reflections. I had seen *A Doll's House* and *Miss Julie* in Stockholm, and concluded that in Scandinavia, too, hypocrisy and morality went hand in hand.

'And Oxford?' asked my namesake as I glossed over my visit with the Veslawskis and their Lansdale cousins to that masculine stronghold of scholarship so different from our own revolutionary hotbed, the University of Petersburg. 'Did you meet any attractive boys there?' she prodded.

'Tata's a bluestocking, don't you know?' Olga laughed as I looked blank. 'She's not interested in boys.'

'They're not interested in me,' I retorted, 'so why should I care about them?'

'That's because you act like a boy yourself.' Olga imitated my long-legged strut.

'I won't have you making fun of Tata!' Tatyana Nikolayevna said haughtily. 'She's splendid, just as she is!'

Darling Tanik! The truth was, I was even more unpopular with girls than with boys. I was all the more grateful to my namesake.

While I continued to be welcome at the Alexander Palace and treated graciously by the sovereigns, Alexandra did not forgive Father.

But the Tsar was as warm towards him as ever. He made him a full general *à la suite* and appointed him to head a special commission for the modernization of the army. But whatever political influence he still had on the Tsar was at an end. For the next two years, outside of the Council of Empire, he was limited to the military sphere, where he clashed with another favourite of the Tsar's, the inept war minister, General Sukhomlinov.

In March of 1913, the Romanov tercentenary celebrations were held in an atmosphere of mistrust in the government, disaffection in the duma, discontent in society circles, and public apathy. The crowds were thin, the cheers few. During the ceremonies in the Kremlin, it was painful to see the heir to the House of Romanov borne in the arms of a Cossack of the Guard.

I attended the functions and church services in Moscow as well as Petersburg.

In the Kremlin's Cathedral of the Assumption – Ouspensky Sabor – a chair had been placed for the Empress on the Tsar's right. Alexandra never could stand throughout the lengthy Russian service, especially wearing heavy court dress. After she sat down, the proud, immobile stance of the Tsar's mother and aunt, Marie Fyodorovna and Marie Pavlovna, was the more remarkable in contrast. It was also duly remarked upon.

I was too moved by the service to be ruffled at this breach with centuries of tradition. The clergy was present *en masse*, from the Patriarch to the bishops to the priests and a phalanx of deacons, every one of them tall and broad, with a long beard and powerful basso. When, in response to the prelates, the priests and deacons intoned 'God have mercy' in unison, the vast dome that had witnessed the coronation of tsars for five centuries reverberated with their Gregorian chant. I understood why the Greek-Orthodox Church held the human voice the only instrument fit to sing the praise of the Almighty.

The gold mantles, jewelled mitres, and crucifixes shimmered in the light of thousands of candles. Through the haze of incense, the brown Byzantine faces of the Holy Family, apostles and saints gazed enigmatically out of gilt frames. And the ancient magnificence of Holy Russia, heir of Byzantium, seemed a reality still.

On their return to Petersburg, the sovereigns were given a grand ball in the Hall of the Nobility. While Olga Nikolayevna was the star of the evening, Tatyana and I were too young to attend. But I did accompany Grandmaman to the command performance of Glinka's opera *A Life for the Tsar* at the Marinsky Theatre.

Alexandra stood stiffly throughout 'God Keep the Tsar', the national hymn. It was sung three times by the operatic chorus on its knees – a survival of Mongol custom I thought repellent. Then she bowed without a smile and withdrew at once behind the curtain of the imperial box, arousing a storm of criticism.

In our box, adjoining the imperial boxes and opposite those reserved for the diplomatic corps and the Emir of Bukhara, Vera Kirilovna expressed the opinions being heard on all sides.

'What lack of presence! What provincialism! What a contrast with the Dowager Empress! Now, Marie Fyodorovna, there's a real majesty.' Vera Kirilovna spoke with reverence of her imperial patroness. 'Small wonder Alexandra is jealous of the Tsar's mother and keeps them apart. She would isolate our sovereign from his entire family, not to mention us of the old Russian nobility. Alexandra a bad heart?' she countered a timid defence of the Empress by Grandmaman's companion. '*Chère* Zinaid, it's nothing but hysteria. Doctor C., who attended Her Majesty at Baden-Baden, told me so personally. It is familial. The Grand Duke of Hesse, her brother, is notoriously odd.'

'Even so, with a sick boy, and knowing that she has transmitted to him that terrible disease, Her Majesty's nervous condition would be excusable,' said Zinaida Mikhailovna, herself the doting mother of an only son.

'Since when have queens had an easy lot?' Vera Kirilovna quickly came back. 'If a queen does not set the example of courage and self-control, who will? To say nothing of an empress!'

'Vera Kirilovna' – Grandmaman rounded on her talkative kinswoman in Russian – 'be so good as to shut up.'

To criticize her sovereigns was Grandmaman's prerogative; on the part of her social inferiors, it was *lèse majesté*.

To hide my mirth, I looked down on the parterre, filled with court officials in scarlet coats and officers of the Guard in bright tunics and silver breastplates.

Everyone's all dressed up tonight, with chests full of orders and medals, and do medals really make people happy? I mused.

Then, looking about the magnificent blue-and-silver theatre with the yellow escutcheons of the Romanovs above the imperial boxes, I thought, Still, *dans l'ensemble*, it's rather handsome. But how beastly hot it is, and poor Alexandra Fyodorovna is like Radfie, she can't bear our Russian heat. I wonder what causes her to flush in patches? It must be a chemical discharge, but how do nerves make us react chemically? I must ask Professor Holveg, even though he's not interested in clinical phenomena. I smiled at the Professor's long words.

In response to the smile, Igor Constantinovich, sitting among his brothers in Grand Duke Constantine's box, smiled at me cockily, as if we were sharing a secret joke.

Is Igor also thinking of Professor Holveg? I wondered. Did I communicate my thoughts? The Professor would say that was unscientific. If he were here tonight, he'd think it all ridiculous. He doesn't like opera, and it is artificial and unnatural. But Nejdanova sings beautifully. One must close one's eyes to enjoy it.

I closed my eyes and felt someone looking at me. I opened them. It was Igor Constantinovich again. Why does Igor look at me like that, as if I were a beautiful filly? I wonder what Tatyana Nikolayevna is thinking about. She doesn't look at all happy. But how pretty she is tonight, how regal. Does she find it all a bit silly also, or is it just me? Probably when I'm old, it will seem perfectly natural. I meant, when I was twenty or so. Professor Holveg is always criticizing everything and everybody. And yet, he's really a happy person.

I smiled again, and absently turned my head towards the box of Grand Duke Constantine. An exchange of merry glances between his brothers made Igor redden and look angry. Everyone in our box began to smile too, even Grandmaman, who rarely did. Vera Kirilovna smiled with particular significance. I disliked being the object of so much smiling solicitude and lowered my eyes to the stage. Nor did I lift them again until intermission, when Father, who was in attendance on the Tsar, fetched me to make my obeisance.

In the drawing room at the back of the imperial box, the Tsar – in the white uniform of the Chevaliers Gardes and the blue ribbon of St Andrew – held an informal circle, puffing on the cherrywood cigarette holder in his left hand. In contrast to the stiff compunction of the bemedalled and beribboned functionaries, his manner was soft-spoken and natural. Tea was being served in a monogrammed silver service from the Winter Palace.

Alexandra, in a tiara, sat fanning herself with a large fan of white eagle's feathers. I noticed how her necklace of turquoise and diamonds rose to her laboured breathing. Her magnificent jewels, the silver embroidery on her white velvet *sarafan*, enhanced the morose and pinched expression of her chiselled features – the expression of a victim rather than an empress.

At the end of the intermission, she said she was tired and told the Emperor to go on without her, she would show herself at the finale. He kissed her hand tenderly and went to the front of the box with the Dowager Empress Marie Fyodorovna and Olga.

Tatyana Nikolayevna, who stayed by her mother, anxiously asked, 'Are you ill, Mummsy dear? Should we send for Botkin?'

'No, no, it won't be necessary. I'm not ill, just *ramolie*. I'll be all right after I rest a bit. I'm sure no one'll miss me,' added Alexandra with a bitter smile. '*Tout Pétersbourg me déteste*.' And she looked directly at Father, as if he represented all Petersburg.

Father's features remained unmoved. He bent his head slightly and asked permission to check on the security measures in the foyer. Alexandra made a stiff nod of assent.

I also asked permission to withdraw, but my namesake looked unhappy, and the Empress said, 'Why don't you go out in the corridor, Tatyana, and walk about with Tata a bit? I know you've been very dull these days. I should like to be by myself.' And, as her ladies-in-waiting looked astonished, 'Yes, all by myself. Is that so much to ask?'

We all followed Tatyana Nikolayevna into the corridor, which Father ordered cleared for Her Imperial Highness.

'I don't know why people should be locked up in their boxes on my account,' my thoughtful friend remarked, as we walked slowly between the rows of Chevaliers Gardes standing immobile at attention in their eagle-crested silver helmets.

'Kshesinskaya and Pavlova are dancing in the ballet. Nobody will want to miss them,' I said and at once feared I had committed a faux pas: Kshesinskaya had been the Tsar's mistress before his marriage.

Such family skeletons were supposed to be kept from the Grand Duchesses. But my namesake assumed her haughty little air of displeasure, which confirmed me in my supposition and made me keep silent.

'Poor Mummsy,' Tatyana Nikolayevna said softly at last, voicing her real preoccupation, 'she's been under such a strain. The reception at the Winter Palace was interminable, and she hates going to the opera so, ever since Stolypin was shot under our very eyes, in Kiev, you remember.'

'Papa told me about it,' I said.

The thought of the assassinated prime minister and of his daughter, crippled for life by a terrorist bomb, the omnipresent guard, the heavy security measures throughout the theatre passed like a fearful shadow over me. And as I gazed admiringly at my friend, so tall and slender in a Russian court dress of white satin with a train, this shadow took the shape of a vulture that had attacked the swan princess of Pushkin's fairy tale. The Grand Duchess had played the part as a child at Pavlovsk. In an effort to shake my dark thoughts, I said, 'Your Imperial Highness is a true swan princess tonight.'

'You promised never to highness me when we were alone.' Tatyana Nikolayevna's sloe eyes rested on me caressingly. 'You're much more of a swan princess than I.' Then, her pretty face growing pixie and mysterious, 'I know someone else who finds you beautiful tonight,' she added.

'Me, beautiful? Tanik, you're being a tease again. Can't you ever be serious?'

'But I am! Didn't you notice that Igor never took his eyes off you during the first act? Everyone else did.'

I had indeed noticed. But I said, offhand, 'His brothers probably put him up to it. Why should Igor Constantinovich look at me particularly?'

'Can't you guess?'

'Guess what? Tanik, why are you so odd?'

'That Igor is in love with you. The whole family knows it, even Anmama. She quite approves.'

I pretended not to understand what the Dowager Empress approved of, though I was beginning to understand not only this, but all the significant smiles in our box and Grand Duke Constantine's.

'Her Imperial Majesty approves . . . of what?' I asked.

'Of your marrying into the family. After all, Igor's sister married Prince Bagration and your family is older and higher-ranking than his. Papa thinks it'd be splendid and, I'm sure, so would Prince Silomirsky. I probably shouldn't speak of it, but we did promise not to have secrets from each other. How do you feel about it, Tata?' Tatyana Nikolayevna stopped and looked at me in happy expectation.

'It's most gracious of His Majesty. I know that marrying a prince of the blood, His Majesty's second cousin, is a very great honour,' I said in an agitated whisper. 'But you know I've always wanted to study medicine. I don't want to just *be* somebody, I want to *do* something, something *real*, and important, and *use*ful . . . Tanik . . . say *you* understand.'

'Yes, I think I do.' The Grand Duchess resumed her stately promenade. 'I sometimes wonder too if our life is truly useful and important. We're so childish and sheltered. We never read a newspaper. Politics are never discussed in front of us. Oh, I know we knit things for the poor at Christmas and visit the sick, but still, we see nothing outside our own little world. You know how you can think of a certain word, which is perfectly familiar and ordinary, and suddenly it seems absurd, and you don't even know how to spell it any more? At times I've this same feeling about the fuss that's made over us, and it all seems absurd for a moment, but then it passes right away. D'you know what I mean, Tata?'

'Yes, I do, that's just the way I feel!' I looked radiantly at my friend. I had underestimated her. 'Tanik, you will help me? If you could speak to your father, I'm sure His Majesty could persuade Papa to consent to my studying medicine . . .'

'I'll speak to Mummsy, that's even better,' Tatyana Nikolayevna promised. 'Although,' she added with an elfin smile, 'I'm not at all sure it's a good idea.'

We parted at the doors of the imperial box, and Father took me back to our box with a warning not to say a word of Alexandra's indisposition.

At midnight the performance ended. The anthem was again sung three times by the chorus on its knees. Their Imperial Majesties bowed and departed. The theatre began to empty and we left.

'His Highness Prince Igor Constantinovich is very handsome, *ne trouvez-vous pas, chère enfant?*' Vera Kirilovna asked as she escorted me to my apartment.

'I hadn't thought about it,' was the sleepy answer. 'Goodnight, Vera Kirilovna.'

When I was in bed, Father came as always to bless and kiss me. I put my arms about his neck and asked, 'Papa, would you ever make me marry someone I didn't love?'

'My dearest daughter, how could I *make* you do anything?'

'But if it were someone His Majesty had chosen for me, someone of his own family?'

'My darling, you know that our good sovereign would not even ask his own daughters to marry anyone against their wishes,' Father replied. After a pause, he added, 'But I also think his daughters would put his wishes above their own, if the good of Russia required it, and so would you.'

I refused to see how my marriage to a prince of the blood could do Russia good.

'Because it would please our old aristocracy, which you represent' – Father was patient with my obduracy – 'and help to arrest, to some extent, the deterioration of its relations with the court. You see, my darling girl, our sovereigns are not as close to the Russian people as they think they are. If they completely alienate the nobility too, they'll have no one to stand by them in a crisis. That is what I'm trying at all costs to prevent. I had always hoped you would help me, when the time came.'

'But what if ... if I had my own plans?' I persisted. 'What if I should want to study medicine?'

Father took my face in his hands. 'My little girl still wants to play doctor, ah?'

'Papa, please, I'm not a child any more. I'm being serious.'

'I know you are, dearest, and so am I. And I tell you right now to put such a wish out of your mind, for it can only bring you disappointment. And any disappointment my darling daughter suffers, no matter how unreasonable, causes her poor father pain.'

I did not want to cause Father pain. But I still did not believe he took my ambition to be a doctor seriously and I was confident that, when he did, he would not stand in its way.

During her stay at the Winter Palace for the tercentenary festivities, Tatyana Nikolayevna contracted typhoid fever, as I had six years previously. I spent every free hour at her bedside and Alexandra, ever a devoted nurse, included me in her maternal tenderness.

Surprised to see me busy with needlework, the Empress one day asked to examine my progress. I handed over my embroidery in some confusion. Alexandra looked puzzled and I confessed I had been making surgical stitches.

'Ah yes,' she said calmly while her daughter gave a rare giggle. 'Tatyana has told me about your passion for medicine.'

As she did not seem to ridicule it, I was moved to open my heart. 'Medicine seems such a high calling, Your Majesty. I can't believe it's wrong of me to want to be a doctor.'

'I think it splendid of Tata, don't you, Mummsy?' Tatyana Nikolayevna interposed as her mother remained silent. Then she shot me a look that I read to mean, 'Splendid, if not sensible.'

Alexandra spoke at last. 'I also think medicine a high calling. And I know you have a way with the sick. It is God's gift.' She reflected again and added, 'If my influence can help you to achieve your goal, I will gladly lend it.'

I did not stop to think how Father might react to Alexandra's influence. 'Your Majesty!' I kissed the hands that gave back my surgical needlework. 'If I'm able to found a medical college for girls of the nobility, I should like to name it after Your Majesty.'

'Well, we shall see. We'll talk about this again in a year or so. But in the meantime,' said Alexandra, 'I still think you should learn to embroider properly.' And she smiled with a charm and humour unknown and even unsuspected outside the family circle.

'Mummsy, you're wonderful!' her sick daughter cried, her expressive sloe eyes going from the Empress to me as if to say, 'You see, I told you so.'

Needless to say, I thought so too.

Tatyana Nikolayevna was much improved for her sixteenth birthday, which passed with little public notice. At the garden party Father gave for my birthday a few days later at our suburban dacha, the press turned out in force, and I had to spend hours posing for photographers.

In a white organdie dress with a pale blue sash and a wide organdie hat with blue streamers to match, I stood hours more receiving the congratulations of the guests, among them Professor Holveg, looking stiff and bothered in his top hat and cutaway. He flashed his black eyes at me ironically.

At sixteen I was beginning to acquire at last the accomplishments expected of me as a daughter of the nobility, chief of which was the ability to stand hours on my feet under the dullest possible circumstances. I spoke six languages fluently. I played a Beethoven sonata adequately and a Chopin nocturne nicely and took blue ribbons in horse shows. To satisfy the Empress, I had even learned some embroidery. I was, to all appearances, the successful product of thoroughbred breeding and training. Ready to be entered, along with the other filly-debutantes in the marriage race, I was expected to come out the winner, with an imperial prince.

7

In the summer of 1913, instead of going to Veslawa, I accompanied Grandmaman on her annual inspection tour of our family lands and industries. I saw my native Russia in its far-flung monotony, its diversity, grandeur, shoddiness, colour and crudity. In the provincial towns, churches with blue bulbous cupolas rose above the houses of green clapboard or pink and yellow stucco. The dust was thick in the wide, straight streets, the flies aswarm and the heat fierce.

Grandmaman never mentioned the flies or the heat. Buttoned up in black silk, wearing black hat and gloves, ebony cane in hand, she went into the fields, the villages, hospitals and schools of our estates, tasted the food in the kitchens, heard the schoolchildren read and count, listened to the superintendents and village elders, to factory managers and foremen. She saw instantly through evasions and excuses.

'Never take anyone's word without checking it personally,' she instructed me. 'The Russian people are an impossible people, the most stubborn, the most perverse, the laziest, the most disorganized and undisciplined in the world. They think a rule is made to be broken. Foreigners picture them as meek and downtrodden, crushed by a tyrannical government. I would like to see them try to get things done by Russians! "Everything will come out, don't upset yourself, Your Serene Highness dear," they tell me. Well, I'll show them it'll come out. I'll make order around here,' said Grandmaman in a burst of forceful Russian.

'This' – shaking her cane – '*vlast* – power, might, this is what they understand. If our present government is overthrown it will not be because of its so-called tyranny, but because of its weakness and ineptitude. People will gladly be dominated by a strong hand they can respect, never by a weak and fumbling one. Remember that. Be strong, be sure of what you do. God willing, all that we have will be yours to manage someday, yours, not your husband's –

Russian men are weaklings – when they're not drunkards they're dreamers, like your father. *I've* saved his possessions for him, and for you and your children.'

'But Grandmaman,' I naïvely ventured, 'is it necessary for us .. for me . . . to have . . . so much?'

'Ne-ces-sa-ry? No, it's not ne-ces-sa-ry. We could live on a fraction of our income. We've distributed more than half our lands among our peasants since 1905 and we're continuing to do so. But it's not a matter of *our need.* It's a matter of re-spon-si-bi-li-ty – the responsibility our family has had for ten centuries, since our ancestors founded Russia.

'If we all sell our factories, can we be certain our people will find work under another owner? If we give away our land without retaining some control over it, do we know it will be well used?

'The Communists have been poisoning everyone's mind with their twaddle, even our landowners have been infected. Is it right to own so much? they begin to wonder, even as you do. And if we don't own it, who will? The peasants? No, my sweetheart. The state. And how much better off will the peasants be then? Ah?'

I thought possibly neither the state nor the nobility might own most of the land and wealth but the people themselves. Grandmaman said that could never be in Russia, because it would be a sensible and moderate state of things, and there could never be a state of things moderate and sensible in Russia.

'Someday, you'll know what I mean. When you find that all your efforts, all your worries, are for nothing. Next year, everything will again be a sublime mess. But if I didn't keep them stirred up, dear God preserve us!' And Grandmaman smiled her rare and startling smile of great humour, which expressed her maternal fondness for this lazy, undisciplined, perverse and impossible child of hers, the Russian people.

My education as an heiress continued apace during my last year at Smolny. Besides attendance at Grandmaman's 'at home' day and charity bazaars, I now stood by her chair at board meetings and when she received petitioners for her well-known largesse. The pitiful stories I heard broke my sixteen-year-old heart. I would have been ready to hand out inordinate sums, even as I could never resist a beggar, but Grandmaman said, 'Never give money outright.

Gratitude sticks in a human throat. Give people the means to help themselves and then check for yourself that they do.'

One of Grandmaman's means was to give scholarships to gifted students. One such recipient, a girl with honours in mathematics, suddenly began to fail her university courses. Grandmaman sent me to the girl's home to find out why.

I felt plunged in a Dostoevsky novel: the cramped flat smelling of penury, the bank-clerk father a tippler, the ailing mother sallow and sour, the younger brother a lout. The cause of the girl's lapse was apparent: she was pregnant. The family berated her cruelly for spoiling her golden opportunity. She was eighteen, and we were both ashamed and embarrassed. I was glad for Radfie's no-nonsense presence. I said haltingly that we would reopen the matter of the scholarship after the baby was born. In the meantime, the girl would receive a cheque for 500 roubles to tide her over. Don't get married and ruin your career, I wanted to say. But I merely shook her hand and wished her well. Then I fled from the parents' effusive thanks.

I went away discouraged. There was no hope for women as long as sex ruled their lives!

From this and other visits – to the home of an injured workman, of a musical prodigy with a blind father and eight siblings, of a former political prisoner returned from Siberia – I discovered that charity was not easy to practise. One must have no illusions about people, like Grandmaman, yet remain compassionate. For that, one needed understanding. But the more I came in contact with that world in which hunger and cold, or rather sex, hunger and cold, were the main reality, the less I felt I had in common with it. Yet there, among that humble humanity teeming about me, at once so near and so remote, there, I thought, was life.

I confided my social scruples to Professor Holveg. Radfie having come into an inheritance in the early spring of 1914 and gone to live sportily and hygienically in her Sussex manor, Zinaida Mikhailovna had been assigned to chaperone the lessons. She snoozed now as peacefully as Bobby – I regularly doctored her tea with rum – and I was able to speak freely.

'You see, Tatyana Petrovna,' the Professor said, 'you belong to a social unit which is self-contained and closed, like an exclusive club. Its members behave according to the rules of the club and care only for the approval of other members. Above this club of the Russian aristocracy is another, even more self-contained and exclusive club, that of the imperial family, which is even more out of touch with the rest of society. One can picture Russian society as a series of concentric circles, with the imperial family the smallest circle in the centre, next the nobility, the bureaucracy, the bourgeoisie and so forth, and, on the periphery, the huge mass of peasants and workers. These circles do not overlap. So long as society remains static, the circles revolve each in its orbit and the largest, the outer circle, slowest of all. But now, under the pressure of industrialization, the outer circle is beginning to speed up.'

He began stirring his tea around the edge of the cup. 'When it attains enough momentum, it will create a vortex, which will engulf all the other circles. And the ones closest to the centre will find themselves at the bottom.' He stirred the tea rapidly and I could see the liquid forming a hollow in the middle of the cup. The shadow of some formless dread passed over me again.

'Shall I be at the bottom then?' I asked.

'I hope not. It would be a great pity.' And my tutor recalled my attention to the optics problem before me.

As I reflected on this conversation, I felt all the more determined not to be confined to the two innermost circles of society, the aristocratic and the imperial. I had told Professor Holveg of Alexandra's faith in my medical vocation and her promise of support. Whatever his doubts, my illustrious tutor had not only taken me to the zoology and anatomy museums and introduced me to his colleagues at the faculty of medicine – including the great Pavlov – but he had also smuggled into the house a microscope, reagents, slides, a pocket surgical kit (with which I dissected dead mice in the attic), a pile of medical textbooks and finally, in a long box, a skeleton. That I stored with Fyodor's help at the back of my bedroom closet. At night I brought it out to draw anatomy sections. If discovered, I could always say I was studying anatomy for the sake of art. That Father would surely understand.

One May afternoon, as I came home from a game of tennis, I was summoned directly to Grandmaman's sitting room. Beside her chair stood the skeleton.

'My good lady,' she demanded in her manly voice, 'what kind of joke is this to play on the servants at your age?'

'I . . . I'm sorry, Grandmaman . . . it wasn't a joke. I was studying.' The lie about art would not come out.

'Studying? Hmmm, now I begin to see. You haven't a cadaver hidden about the house also by chance?'

'That wouldn't be practical, Grandmaman.'

'Don't jest with me, miss! What else have you been "studying"? Tell me this instant!'

I confessed the existence of my attic laboratory.

Grandmaman went to see for herself. 'Who brought this microscope here?' Her cane swept test tubes and reagents off the shelves. 'That little Jewish scientist, protégé of your father's, of course. I never trusted him. What else did Professor Holveg bring you?'

In my bedroom, the extent of my medical library was revealed.

'Have it all sent back,' Grandmaman said to Vera Kirilovna, who had lost her great facility of speech in the shock of these revelations. 'Ah, the cheat, the fraud, stuffing a young girl's mind with this trash, yes, for you trash,' as I started in shock. 'If you think for one moment you will be allowed to be a practitioner' – she used a contemptuous colloquial term for physician – 'it's you who need a doctor, my good girl, for your head!' And Grandmaman tapped my forehead with the handle of her cane.

The blow capped my rage.

'I hate Grandmaman!' When she had gone, I raged like a tigress through my apartment. 'I hate Vera Kirilovna! I hate them all! They won't let me be what I want to be, they don't care what I'm really like, not even Papa. I'm still his darling girl, to spoil and play with but he doesn't know *me*, the real me at all. He thinks I ought to marry Prince Igor for the good of Russia, but how will I help Russia by living in a palace and holding "at home" days and travelling abroad? Don't we have enough imperial princesses to do these things better than I, and what use are *they* to Russia, really? Even Tatyana Nikolayevna's life is useless and she herself knows it, it's even more shallow and sheltered than mine. But there's no help for her, the Tsar's daughter, and there's no help for me either. Oh, I'll die, I'll die, I'll die!'

Having reached a peak of impotent fury, I felt calmer. I rang for Dunya, my head maid, who was huddled with her assistants in the anteroom, and told her to prepare a bath. I summoned Fyodor. He was to warn me when Professor Holveg called on Father, as I was sure he shortly would. When I was dressed with care, Fyodor reported the Professor was in Father's study. I went down to the foyer and waited behind one of the columns.

Soon the Professor came hurrying along with furious little steps, like Alice's rabbit.

'Professor Holveg,' I said softly. He stopped and looked at me as though he were not sure it was I. Instead of my usual school uniform, I wore a dress of white lace and a string of pearls. 'Professor, forgive me all the trouble I've caused you. Was Father very angry?'

'The Prince was not pleased. He pointed out to me, quite rightly, that you had responsibilities towards your country incompatible with a medical career. He also accused me of teaching you deceit and that I denied. I have tried, on the contrary, to teach you intellectual honesty, to seek in the pursuit of intellectual excellence one of life's most rewarding pleasures. This I would like you to remember always, Tatyana Petrovna, even when you have forgotten me.'

'I shall never forget you, Professor, or what you taught me. Thank you for everything. *Adieu.*'

I gave him my hand, which he kissed this time, quickly, drily and not without elegance. He shot me a look, not only of extraordinary intelligence but of emotion. Then he hurried down the stairs and, so I thought, out of my life.

There was a second confrontation in Grandmaman's sitting room, this time in Father's presence. Indulgent parent that he was, he was ready to attribute my bad behaviour to bad influence, in this case Professor Holveg's.

But when Father heard that Alexandra Fyodorovna had given her gracious approval to my medical studies, he exploded. 'Ah no, that's too much! To be made a fool of by that little Professor I befriended is bad enough. But to have my authority undermined by Alexandra, to be made a laughing-stock by her and that sot and lecher who is disgracing our throne ... dear God, what a humiliation! And all because of you, my own daughter, of whom I was so proud, so proud!' And he looked at me so long and bitterly that I went down on my knees.

'Papa,' I pleaded, 'I did not know ... I did not understand ...'

'You did not understand! Is it possible you could be so naïve?

Don't you know that nothing could please Her Majesty more than to interfere with your proposed betrothal to a member of the imperial family, to spoil any attempt to reconcile the Tsar with the nobility? And you, by inviting her to meddle in your life, have given her that opportunity!'

'Papa, I hadn't thought!' I hadn't thought, when Alexandra so readily supported my vocation, that she might indeed have an ulterior motive.

'You hadn't a thought for your father or your country, only for yourself! I don't want to know you any more,' he said, and walked out.

Grandmaman made me get to my feet and I went to my room stupefied by Father's dreadful words.

'What is it, my love, why are you crying so?' Nyanya asked that night when she found me sobbing my heart out in bed.

'I've been bad, Nyanya. I lied, I cheated, and I was disloyal to Papa, and now he doesn't want to know me any more!'

'That'll be something new in this world when a father doesn't want to know his only daughter any more, and such a loving father too,' my nurse soothed. 'Now go to sleep and it will all come out all right tomorrow.'

But there was no going to sleep without Father's blessing and goodnight kiss. At one o'clock in the morning Nyanya came in, found me lying with staring eyes, marched out, and returned with Father. Poor Papa! I can imagine how perplexed he was to find in me a sudden stranger. To a man of his fastidious nature my sense of medical mission could only be distasteful and incomprehensible, as well as socially beneath me. He could no more understand my narrow and selfish ambition than I could understand his broad and selfless concern for his country.

On the other hand, he could no more remain angry at me than I could at him. He wiped my eyes with his scented batiste handkerchief and said tenderly, 'Forgive me for being so harsh, my darling girl. All this is my fault. I thought that a father could not know what a girl needed. I left your education to Grandmaman, to Aunt Sophie, to Vera Kirilovna, to Miss Radford. That education was the best, better than that of any of our imperial princesses, but I see it failed to prepare you for your proper role in life. Professor Holveg told me today I was trying to force you to conform to the standards of a dying society. Perhaps he is right. But it is precisely, you see, because our society is in danger that we, its leaders, must accept our responsibilities more seriously than we ever have before.'

I was prepared to accept anything not to lose my father's love. 'I'll marry Prince Igor, Papa. I'll do anything you say!'

'We won't talk of it now. There'll be time enough for you to make up your mind. Next month, Aunt Sophie will be coming from England with Stevie for your graduation ball. Perhaps they'll accompany us to Italy this summer on the *Helena*. There'll be a great many things before my little girl's debut to take her mind off skeletons and dead mice.' He kissed and blessed me and returned to his guests.

I graduated with a gold medal at the head of my class and had the honour of delivering the valedictory speech. The proper pious and patriotic sentiments were duly expressed without originality or brilliance; originality and brilliance in a daughter of the nobility would have been considered bad form. The noble families of the girls were present in force and the noble ladies of our staff were as moved as mothers on their daughters' wedding day. My classmates wrote poems and quotations in their memento books but I merely condescended to sign my name. I passed silent and aloof among the twittering girls, a mute cygnet in an aviary, Father said, as though my prospect in life were the nunnery rather than a royal match.

The prospect of my graduation ball did not cheer me either. I stood so unwillingly during the fittings of my ball gown that Grandmaman ordered a heavy book placed on my head and fifteen minutes of additional standing every time the book slipped. I stood much better after it had fallen off once or twice. But Father's tender repentance could not shake my listlessness all that hot June of 1914.

Father soon had more than my mood to worry about. On 28 June, he returned from the officers' races at Krasnoye, where he had been attending the Emperor, with news of the assassination at Sarajevo of Archduke Ferdinand of Austria. The tragic incident took on the appearance of a *casus belli* after Kaiser Wilhelm II called a council of war at Potsdam on 5 July.

At this juncture, the Tsar again placed his confidence in Father. By birth and character, Father was above the rivalries that divided branches of the government and the opportunism that debased them. Though he refused an official appointment, he became virtually a minister without portfolio. He was in close and constant touch with the Emperor at Peterhof, with the Tsar's uncle, Grand Duke Nikolay Nikolayevich, the commander of the Imperial Guard, at his summer headquarters at Krasnoye, with the general staff, the war ministry, the Foreign Minister, Sazonov, and the French and British ambassadors, Paléologue and Buchanan.

I did not grasp the gravity of the Austro-Serbian crisis. In this I was no different from the majority of people in Petersburg, Paris or London. Society girls talked about the handsome British naval officers at the ball on board Admiral Beatty's flagship; of Olga Nikolayevna's refusal of Prince Carol during the imperial family's visit to Rumania; about the nuisance of tubular skirts and silliness of turbans and jackets *à la turque* inspired by the Balkan Wars; and about my coming *bal blanc*, at which the Grand Duchesses Olga and Tatyana Nikolayevna were at last to be seen.

On the eve of the ball, as I stood in my study for my final fitting with – in Nyanya's words – the air of a Christian being readied for martyrdom, I heard Aunt Sophie's sweet and singing voice mingling with Vera Kirilovna's deeper and more affected tone.

'Aunt, Aunt Sophie, Auntie!' I ran to meet her and threw myself around her neck while the dressmaker pleaded, 'Your Serene Highness, Tatyana Petrovna dear, don't *crush* the dress.'

I continued crushing.

My aunt put a hand to her little hat of white ostrich feathers and tipped her head at me. 'What a little calf you are still, Tanyussia, even though you've grown up so!'

I was now taller than Aunt. My arms about her neck, I looked at her worshipfully. At forty Aunt Sophie was still slender and graceful, her lovely face even more gentle and wise. She wore a Parisian suit of Irish linen and her blonde hair in the high Edwardian hairdo that so became her.

'Oh Auntie, I'm so happy to see you, you don't know how I've missed you,' I cried. 'How is Princess Catherine, and Uncle Stan and Stevie? I want to know everything!'

'Mother's just the same, darling, taking care of her roses and going to Father's grave every day. Stan is having dinner with your father at the Yacht Club. You'll see him soon. Stevie's simply immense, six-feet-six like your father and almost as broad-shouldered. At the moment, he's at the Sikorsky factory, looking over aeroplanes. Horses and motors are no longer sufficiently fast or dangerous for him, I'm afraid.'

'An aeroplane!' I laughed at the vision of Stevie in leather cap and goggles. But then I remembered my problem, and joy vanished. 'Oh Auntie, I've been so wretched . . .'

'We'll have a talk,' said Aunt. 'But first, hadn't you better get on with your fitting?'

She sat down by the window in an erect yet relaxed pose, her head in the becoming feather hat a little to the side, the tip of her parasol playing against the pointed toe of her shoe.

Vera Kirilovna supervised the fitting, making suggestions in Russian in her high-society speech with a rasping French *r*. My *éducatrice* had reacted to my connivance with Professor Holveg under her very nose as though we had been carrying on a love affair, but no one seeing her decorous pose and fluent manner would have guessed her vexation.

At last she pronounced approval. I began to step out of the dress, but the dressmaker caught it up. 'Your Most Serene Highness my dove, one always takes off a dress *over* the head.' At last, with many smiles, inclinations and expressions of respect the good woman and her minions withdrew.

My *éducatrice* did not appear disposed to move, but Aunt Sophie said in her sweet way, 'We'll see you at dinner, dear Countess.' With a courtier's composure, Vera Kirilovna took the hint.

'Oh, she's such an old nosy, I thought we'd never be alone,' I cried. 'Oh Auntie, I've missed you so!' And dropping down beside my aunt, I pressed my head into her lap.

'Well, tell me all about it.' Aunt Sophie stroked my hair with the tips of her long fingers.

I poured out my tale of thwarted ambition.

When I was done, she said, 'I've already had a talk with your father, Tanyussia. He agrees you are still too young to think of marriage. I have persuaded him to let you enrol for two years in the Nursing Institute for noble girls I founded in Warsaw. There you will learn hospital administration, child nursing and midwifery as I did. I believe that will satisfy in good part your interest in doctoring, which is not unnatural, as your father believes, but feminine and maternal. And what will satisfy it even better, in time, will be having a child of your own. You see, my darling girl, a woman's deepest joy comes from giving of herself. And it is through her children that she achieves her power and authority.'

But I wanted to achieve power and authority on my own, so I was unmoved. All the same I gazed lovingly into Aunt's maternal visage. 'If only I could be like you, Auntie' – wise and serene, ever understanding and kind, strong without harshness, with gentle authority over all – 'but I'll never be, never!'

'It isn't easy, my darling. A woman's task demands continual self-discipline and self-sacrifice. Husbands are seldom as kind and considerate as my Stan, and even we have had our differences. Children grow up and leave. When they're small, they're forever ill, or hurting themselves. They fight us when we only want to guide and help them. If they are boys, they go to war and may be killed, or crippled.'

Aunt was silent, and I thought she must be thinking of the troubling international news. Then, taking my face in her hands, she said tenderly, 'Being a mother is difficult, Tanyussia, and being seventeen is difficult, I know. Life is difficult, my dearest, from the moment we can think for ourselves. It holds much, much pain, but also much joy. And you have most of it ahead still. Your first child, your first love . . . and your first ball.'

Yes, I saw it opening before me, this life that was difficult, painful and full of joy – not mean and narrow and dutiful but splendid and noble, beautiful and profound.

'Oh, Auntie, Mother, I've been so blind and ungrateful for all I have and all that's been given me,' I cried, kissing Aunt's hands. 'But now I see everything, everything is clear!'

It was not clear at all, this sudden vision of life. It lay in a golden haze that must lift at any moment on a spectacle of miraculous beauty.

Aunt Sophie smiled, kissed me on the tip of the nose, and told me to go and comb my hair.

We went downstairs together to fetch Grandmaman. She gave me a long look that apparently satisfied her, and not another word was said of my disgraceful conduct.

We dined by a fountain in the inner court among flower beds set in paths of marble mosaic. Then we went for a carriage drive to the islands.

The Finnish gulf lay in the golden haze of sunset. Guard officers with their elegant companions promenaded majestically on the esplanade. The sea air smelling of brine brought the lilting tunes of an accordion from an excursion boat. On the far shore of the Neva delta, still as a lagoon, the pink and yellow palaces had an Italianate grace. The angel soared on its golden spire above the low white walls of the fortress. All is well ordered and purposeful in God's world, I thought, and nowhere more than here in this capital of the Russian Empire. Only I, in my narrow self-centredness, had failed to perceive it until now.

My solemn mood remained with me all evening. After Uncle Stan had come to fetch Aunt home to his eldest sister, wife of a Russian diplomat, I undressed slowly, talked softly not to break the spell.

'Now what are you imagining?' asked Nyanya as she brushed my hair until it crackled and stood round my head. 'This morning you were going to die a martyr and tonight you're floating among the angels . . .'

'Don't joke. Brush more evenly . . . like this.' And, when I was in bed, 'Nyanya' – I put my arms about her neck – 'I've a feeling something unusual is going to happen tomorrow.'

'If it didn't, that would be unusual,' was her tart reply.

But I would not let her spoil my mood, and went to sleep in the expectation of an extraordinary event.

PART TWO

LOVE AND WAR

1914–1916

8

For days before the ball, a battalion of women in big felt slippers had been waxing the parquet floors in the grand ballroom and reception rooms of our Petersburg *osobnyak*. The windows and chandeliers, the Venetian mirrors and crystal appliqués on the walls had been washed until they sparkled, the gilt frames in the portrait gallery dusted, the Turkish carpets beaten, the footmen's royal-blue liveries pressed. On the day itself the great courtyard was swept, a rose carpet laid on the steps of the arcaded carriage entrance, and police stationed along the approaches to the quay.

Grandmaman went about cane in hand, reconciling Anatole, our Polish chef, and Agafia, the Russian head cook, over a flare-up of their running nationalistic feud that threatened to leave the guests without supper. She dried the tears of Zinaida Mikhailovna, her timorous companion, whose adored only son, the angelic Kolenka, had been arrested in a drunken brawl; settled a thorny point of protocol with the majordomo; and took in her stride the normal vicissitudes of a Russian household that would have driven any but a Russian hostess out of her mind.

My extraordinary mood of the previous evening had of course vanished and I was unusually peevish. At half past nine, after Grandmaman's French hairdresser had done my hair *à la grecque* on top of my head, I stood in my dressing room in my white ball gown, surrounded by dressmaker and maids, feeling sleepy and cross. Powder was applied to my bare shoulders, the tulle skirt fluffed up, white gloves buttoned to the elbow, and a fan placed in my hand.

'Press your lips together, *chère enfant*, it will make them redder,' Vera Kirilovna said.

I chewed on my lip so sullenly that my *éducatrice* despaired. But the moment Father was announced I came to life. He wore my favourite white-and-gold dress uniform of the Guard Hussars, with the mink-bordered scarlet *mentik*. Never had his rosy, fresh face, with its expression of noble kindliness and calm, seemed more beautiful to me.

'Well, my Prince, what do you say of your daughter now?' Nyanya asked.

Father wonderingly shook his head. 'I can't get over it. Our ugly duckling is going to be the loveliest swan in the pond.'

He placed on my head a circlet of diamonds and pearls made to his order by Fabergé. Then he offered me his arm to lead me to our places in the foyer above the parade staircase.

At the head of the stairs lined with footmen in powdered wigs, holding lighted candelabra, stood Grandmaman's Ethiopian head footman, who announced the guests in a stentorian voice. Girls came up with their chaperones, young men in pairs or with an elder escort. First they were greeted by Father and me in the foyer, where they made last-minute adjustments in front of the mirrors. Then they passed into the ballroom to be announced again and directed to Grandmaman and her dear friend, Grand Duchess Marie Pavlovna, that brilliant and caustic imperial lady so detested by Alexandra.

The Empress, we had been informed by Zizi Naryshkin, the Grand Mistress of the Court, had intended to chaperone her daughters. But to everyone's relief she was indisposed as usual and they came with a lady-in-waiting instead. I thought Tatyana Nikolayevna prettier than ever in a pink chiffon dress with a matching pink *bandeau* about her dark curls, and her sister Olga quite plain beside her. But if Olga Nikolayevna's round face lacked finesse, it reflected a lively intelligence that made a more agreeable first impression than her sister's haughty air of reserve.

There was no trace of this, however, as Tatyana Nikolayevna received my obeisance and said with feeling, 'Tata, you look beautiful!'

'Oh no, Your Imperial Highness does,' I said even more feelingly, and Father escorted the Grand Duchesses into the ballroom.

After he had returned to my side, I listened rather perfunctorily to the footman's calls, until I heard, 'The Most Serene Prince Stefan Veslawski and Sir Casimir Paszek.' I thought, Here comes Stevie-levie monkey ears, with his echo, Kim, and wanted to laugh. But as I looked at the young man in the plain black uniform of the nobility who was bearing down on me with a long and springy stride, I felt instead a novel and indescribable sensation. I could not see my cousin well. I knew only that he was immensely tall, strong and splendid, and that his physical presence overwhelmed me. Fearing I would fall before his onrush, I braced myself on my left heel, while my right hand, instead of going out in greeting, went protectively to my breast.

Stevie's eyes followed my gesture and rested for a moment on my breast. A high colour rose to his hair roots and he stood above me fiercely silent.

'Well, children,' Father said, as I too stood speechless. 'Have you forgotten each other?'

'Hello, Stevie,' I brought out, giving him my hand.

'Hello, Tanya,' he answered in a tone equally strained.

How nicely he kissed my hand, I thought, as I began to see him more clearly. His skin is rosy and fresh like Papa's, as if he'd just come out of a bath. His hair ... why, it isn't curly any more but smooth and so nicely shaped, like a helmet. His eyes, yes, they are still amber-brown, the exact colour of Bobby's, and they're no longer full of malice but of something ... something out of the ordinary. And what a straight, classical nose he has, almost as handsome as Papa's. But his ears, yes, they are still monkey ears.

I no longer felt intimidated. But then I noticed something new.

'You have a moustache,' I said in wonderment.

Stevie lifted a finger to the moustache in his father's characteristic gesture. 'You don't like it?'

'Oh yes, I do! And you have one also, Kim.'

Casimir's moustache was almost exactly like Stevie's, with fine little waved points. His brown hair lay almost as smooth and he wore the identical black uniform of the nobility. He too held a fingertip to his moustache and looked at Stevie questioningly, as if to ask whether I had been making fun of that manly attribute.

Father smiled subtly as he shook hands with the discomfited pair. 'You both look splendid, delighted to have you.'

Stefan and Casimir went on into the ballroom, where we joined them shortly.

Little gilt chairs with gilded straw seats for the dancers circled the ballroom along the colonnade of rose marble. Chaperones occupied the Empire chairs in rose-and-silver satin stripes. Next to Grandmaman, in the centre of the row of velvet armchairs, sat Grand Duchess Marie Pavlovna. Garlands of fresh roses hung from the fluted balustrade of the gallery. The frescoed dome of the ballroom was illumined by the blaze of two immense chandeliers, whose crystal prisms reflected all the colours of the rainbow. The orchestra tuned up on a marble platform in an alcove between rose velvet draperies surmounted by the family arms.

At our entrance the orchestra struck up the inevitable polonaise from Glinka's *A Life for the Tsar*. Father led the dance with Marie Pavlovna and I followed with Grand Duke Constantine. After the polonaise, the older guests sat down to watch. The younger dancers took their places on the little gilt chairs, girls facing their partners, and the calls for the first quadrille began. Because Grand Duchesses were dancing the chaperones remained standing, until Grandmaman again passed the word that court etiquette need not be observed and to please sit down.

Stevie was my partner opposite, my vis-à-vis.

'*Avancez!*' called the dance master.

As Stevie crossed the floor with his onrushing stride, I was seized with that same novel sensation of exquisite dread.

'*Balancez!*' came the call.

We swung together blissfully back and forth.

'*Chassez à droite . . . à gauche!*'

Off we galloped sideways down the slippery parquet, and my feet flew. When we changed partners, my eyes never left Stevie. And all the movement, glitter, faces, lights, sounds and scents merged into a blur out of which he alone emerged.

In the first break between the quadrilles I sought out my namesake. Tatyana Nikolayevna evidently had the same thought and we met behind a column, clasping hands and communicating by a long pressure our common excitement and joy at this our first grand ball.

'Well, what d'you think of him?' I could not wait to ask. There was no need to elaborate.

'I think,' said Tatyana Nikolayevna, 'he's very dashing.'

Dashing was not good enough. And was there mockery in my friend's sloe eyes? 'No, but don't you find him . . . find him . . .'

'Simply colossal?'

'But' – I grew hot – 'don't you think he's a marvellous dancer?'

'*Il sait danser*,' my friend conceded.

'No, but have you noticed how he kisses your hand? He holds it high a moment, so.' I tried to illustrate.

'*Son baise-main est remarquable*,' Tatyana Nikolayevna agreed, and resting her dark head against the column, she began to laugh exasperatingly.

Olga Nikolayevna now joined us with her quick step and inquired, 'What're you two laughing about?'

'I don't know what your sister finds so funny,' I answered furiously. 'If Your Imperial Highnesses will excuse me . . .'

My namesake caught me by the hand. 'We won't. I'm not laughing any more. Tata, I'm absolutely serious. Shall we ask Olichka what she thinks of . . . ?'

'Of whom?' said Olga Nikolayevna. 'Let me guess. The Polish prince, Tata's cousin. *Tout le monde en parle*. He's the talk of the ball.' And she added meaningfully, 'His reputation has preceded him.'

I faltered. 'What sort of . . . reputation?'

With the condescension of a nineteen-year-old, Olga Nikolayevna tapped my arm with her fan. 'Not the sort of reputation young girls should know about.'

Instead of coming to my defence, Tatyana Nikolayevna said, 'If Prince Veslawski is so fascinating, I'll ask him to dance the next waltz.'

'And I the next,' said Olga Nikolayevna.

'We'll keep him busy all evening, between the two of us,' said my namesake.

To be teased by both Grand Duchesses was too much! 'No court etiquette tonight. Your Imperial Highnesses will have to be asked to dance like anybody else. Oh, dance with him if you will, he means nothing to me,' I added in despair.

Just then the orchestra began a Strauss waltz, a departure from *bal blanc* tradition especially requested by Olga and Tatyana Nikolayevna, and the master of the dance called for the gentlemen to choose their partners. The Grand Duchesses and I were at once surrounded by five times our number of young men, Stevie among them. But instead of bowing to me, as I expected, he bowed to Tatyana Nikolayevna. In preference to two of her imperial cousins she placed her gloved hand on his shoulder, while giving me a sidelong look. In spite, I accepted the invitation of Prince Igor, my future intended.

Igor Constantinovich had just been commissioned a cornet in the Guard Hussars. He looked very dashing in his dress uniform with the scarlet *mentik* slung from one shoulder. He was, I suppose, almost as dashing as my cousin. In fact, he was not so different from Stefan, or any number of lusty young princes with their passion for fast horses and motorcars, their ambition for military glory and amorous conquests. But something in Stefan – I could not say what precisely – set him apart.

As I observed Stevie waltzing with Tatyana Nikolayevna, I thought: How well they look together. How superior they are to everyone else. How inevitable that they should fall in love. But even as I watched Stevie for signs of infatuation with the Grand Duchess, he seemed to watch me just as carefully.

Was he worried when I danced with Igor? I pondered during the next quadrille. Is it possible it is me he cares about? I tested this by assuming my most disdainful air when we met in the figures. Instantly, he looked abject. He looks like my setter when I scold him, and how could anyone with such a look have a 'reputation' and what sort of 'reputation' is it anyway? Suddenly I remembered him kissing Wanda. I lowered my lids haughtily as we swung together. He looked like a dog not only scolded but beaten. I was instantly sorry and smiled. At once, he looked joyful. He cares, yes, he cares, I decided.

During the very next break, when he took me to the buffet, I asked, to be certain, 'Isn't Tatyana Nikolayevna marvellous?'

'She's a splendid girl. She absolutely adores you.' This, clearly, made the Grand Duchess splendid. 'We talked about you all through the waltz.'

'Wouldn't you like to marry her?'

'Marry the Grand Duchess Tatyana?'

'Yes, and be crowned King of Poland by the Tsar.' And I would follow Tatyana Nikolayevna as her lady-in-waiting and watch their happiness with terrible pains in my legs, like the mermaid of the fairy tale.

'If I'm to be King of Poland, it will be by the free will of my people, not by the favour of the Tsar,' Stevie said fiercely.

No, he doesn't love her, I thought. And how fierce and proud he is! What a magnificent king he would make and how gladly I would make him a deep obeisance! So entranced was I by the vision that Stevie had to repeat his invitation to the next waltz. But even as I dreamed of curtsying low to him, I said, 'I already promised it to Prince Igor.'

'Tell him you promised me earlier.'

'I can't. And anyway, why should I?'

'Why should you indeed? You've only been amusing yourself with me all evening,' said he, looking a storm. He turned on his heel and left.

I sought out Father. 'Papa, Stevie's in a mood. I'm afraid he's going to do something wild.'

We found my cousin by the wrought-iron balustrade of the foyer, facing Igor Constantinovich. Both looked equally furious and haughty.

'The waltz has started. You'd better go in and choose your partners, gentlemen, or you'll be without,' Father said.

'I have something to settle with His Highness first, Uncle Peter,' Stevie rejoined.

'As soon as I receive His Majesty's permission, my seconds will get in touch with you, Prince,' Igor addressed his rival, in a voice loud with excitement.

Father spoke with calm. 'His Majesty does not care for duelling. Whatever the provocation, this is not time for cadet-school heroics. You both may soon be using your sabres against a common enemy. Please apologize and shake hands.'

'A Romanov does not apologize to a Veslawski.'

'A Veslawski does not apologize to a Romanov.'

'I ask you both to apologize to me, as your host, for quarrelling under my roof.' Father's tone did not admit of retort.

The young men made their apologies. But they still would not shake hands. I took their right hands and joined them. 'Shake!' I ordered and they shook. Then, in unison, 'May I have this dance?'

'I'll not dance with either of you,' said I. And turning to Father, I put my hand on his shoulder.

'*Désolé, Messieurs,*' Father said. 'But I see two young ladies over there who are still free.' He indicated two girls sitting primly side by side on the empty row of little gilt chairs. They were the twin Baronesses Norden, fearfully rich and homely. As Igor and Stevie dutifully started towards them, I saw by the look they exchanged that their sad lot had mended the quarrel.

'We'd better put you in nursing school in a hurry before you cause any more trouble,' Father remarked as we waltzed. 'A duel between a Veslawski and a Romanov could have repercussions almost as grave as the assassination of Archduke Ferdinand. If you stir up men like that at seventeen, what will it be later?'

'It's only Stevie, Papa,' I said with sisterly fondness. 'He's so absurd. He hasn't changed at all. He's still a boy.'

'Yes, hmmm. Quite a boy, though, quite a boy.'

This reminded me of my cousin's reputation. 'Papa, what have you heard about Stevie?'

'Nothing I haven't heard about other young men his age, my dearest,' he answered. And, as I stiffened, 'You should never have ugly thoughts, Tanichka. They spoil your lovely little face. And they make you difficult to dance with. Come, *un peu de souplesse*, head up, and a smile.'

I obeyed. Father was a superb dancer. Until that night I would rather have danced with him than with anyone. But that night it was only second best.

After another quadrille, a mazurka was announced, gentlemen dancing with their vis-à-vis. The Guard officers and cadets advanced in a line towards the seated girls and bowed. In delicious languor, I rose and leaned against Stevie's large hand. In spite of his size, Stevie was quick and light as a cat, even as a seventeen-hand hunter can be as handy as a polo pony. I was a much better horsewoman than a dancer but this night I felt as light and supple as the smaller, less angular girls.

Stevie, never averse to showing off, guided me towards the orchestra and called, 'Can you play the *mazur*, friends?'

There were no Jewish fiddlers in the band, ordinary Jews not being allowed to reside in the capital. But the first violin, with the black curls and white teeth of the tzigane, nodded affirmatively. The tempo grew fast and furious and Stevie began whirling me with gathering speed. The rest of the dancers fell back. We were alone in the centre of the ballroom. I saw, not marble columns and crystal chandeliers but towering limes hung with Japanese lanterns; not society girls and Guard officers but peasant girls in striped skirts and peasant boys in full tunics. Under my feet was not lustrous parquet but the rough planks of an outdoor platform, and in my ears the frenzied fiddling of the Jewish band on Harvest Festival night eleven years ago.

The dance over, we made our bow and curtsy before Marie Pavlovna.

My godmother smiled on us handsomely. '*Charmant, mes enfants, charmant.*' While Grandmaman shot us a perceptive look, which was not of satisfaction.

Olga and Tatyana Nikolayevna now came before their 'Aunt Miechen' to make their curtsies and to thank Grandmaman for the lovely evening.

'*Déjà, mes petites, quel dommage!*' Marie Pavlovna expressed the general regret that the Grand Duchesses should leave before the cotillion.

Olga Nikolayevna, always independent, had objected. But her reasonable sister reminded her that their mother was unwell, and begged her not to make a fuss.

'Tata, it's been the most marvellous fun,' the latter said as we had a moment aside in the foyer before parting, 'and I'm so glad you're not desperate any more. You know, I never really thought your medical school idea would work.'

I could not remember how desperate I had been. 'Yes, you were right, of course ... Tanik, I'm so worried. D'you think *he* feels the way I do?'

'Even more ... but Tata darling, he's your first cousin and a Pole. I don't think Papa'd like it at all. It'd be frightfully complicated. Don't let yourself be carried away again. You know how impulsive you are.'

My friend was being sensible, as usual, but I only thought, Tanik is marvellous but she's still so young. How can she give me advice when she hasn't experienced what I have tonight, the most important, the most *real* experience I have ever known? She doesn't know what life is about.

Tatyana Nikolayevna saw I was beyond reasoning. 'I do hope, for your sake, it'll work out. He *is* most dashing,' she said and joined her sister.

The Grand Duchesses gone, the ball continued at a more hectic pace. Girlish noses began to shine, trains to rip, hairdos to slide. At the end of the cotillion, the dancers passed under an arch of violets, roses and carnations to the adjoining reception rooms, where small tables had been set.

Stevie sat at my table and I listened spellbound to his verbal fireworks. Verse, quotation, anecdote and witticism in several languages exploded one upon the other. I knew this verbal extravagance was for my benefit, even as the boy Stevie had turned cartwheels, picked his scabs and held his hand in the flame of a candle to prove his manly valour. I was just as impressed at seventeen as I had been at seven. Stevie's elegant erudition capped the physical perfection that overwhelmed me. And this most dashing of all dashing young men was anxious to please me – plain-looking, intellectually mediocre and altogether commonplace beside him. I was afraid to believe it. Yet I did.

At dawn, the ball came to an end at last. Again I stood with Father in the foyer, now bidding the guests goodbye. Holding their wilted bouquets and their torn trains, the girls descended the stairs, listening sleepily to the parting admonitions of mamas and chaperones. Stevie and Casimir were among the last to leave. Once more I admired the way my cousin kissed my hand and the glossiness of his hair. He was sleek and strong like a fine hunter and surely as nice to stroke.

I felt desolate from the moment he was gone. The foyer and the vestibule below were empty. Only the musicians remained to eat their supper.

'Have we made our little girl happy tonight?' Father asked.

'Oh yes . . . thank you!' I flung myself about his neck.

Then, more decorously, I kissed Grandmaman's hand and drifted dreamily upstairs.

My waiting maids questioned me as they divested me of my finery, until Nyanya said crossly, 'Ey you, women, can't you see she's asleep on her feet, the darling, and here you bother her with your stupid questions! Be off with you!'

'Nyanya,' I said when I had slipped into bed after a short prayer, 'did you see *him*?'

'Who's that?' asked my nurse in her sly way.

'My brother, my only one, my Stefan, my sweet prince.'

'And what would I be doing at the ball with all kinds of Grand Princes and Grand Princesses there? No, I didn't see Prince Stefan. But I ought to know him well enough, since he came here with his parents for your birth . . . and such a devil he was at two years of age, even worse than your father, my nursling.'

'Nyanya' – I was delighted at the comparison – 'isn't he handsome?'

'Handsome I wouldn't say exactly, with those big ears that stick out.'

'But he's awfully strong!'

'Yes, that he would be, built like a warrior of old. He'll give a woman fine sons, I don't doubt.'

I remembered Aunt Sophie's words about a woman's most glorious experience. 'Nyanya, I would like to give him a son.'

'A son to a Pole, to fight against Russians, against your own father maybe?' Nyanya said. 'You'd best forget it, my soul. It can never be.'

'Why can't it? If our sovereign makes Uncle Stan viceroy of an autonomous Poland, the Poles will become our friends. And perhaps, someday, when his father is old, Stefan will be king, our two countries will be allies, and I will give my king an heir.'

'Now what is it you've thought up?' cried my nurse. 'What a strange girl you are, always so serious and your nose in books and now dreaming some kind of fairy tale. Well,' she sighed as she tucked me in, 'there's no harm in it for one night. Dream of your prince, my love, dream of him while you can.'

Eyes open in the northern light, I dreamed. Life, as Aunt Sophie had revealed it, unfolded before me beautiful as an old legend, profound and mysterious. And in the centre of the vision was *he* – my warrior-prince, my lord and king.

9

It was past noon when I awoke the day after the ball. Instead of jumping out of bed I lay in a delicious languor. What is *he* doing now? was my first thought. Does he really shave? And how does he make his curly hair lie so flat, like a glossy helmet?

Nyanya came into the room in blue pinafore and headdress, tucking up her wide sleeves. 'How you've slept, my soul! I had no orders to wake you, although your serene grandmother, Anna Vladimirovna, was on her knees in the chapel at eight o'clock the same as always. Well, time to get up.'

'Nyanya,' I announced, 'I want my chocolate in bed.'

'Chocolate in bed? And what else? Where did you learn such lazy habits, Princess mine? What are you, a spoiled merchant's daughter or some kind of ballerina?'

'Oh, all right, stop your scolding.' I swung my legs over the side of my camp bed. But as I stood up I let out a moan. 'My feet ... they hurt. I can't walk!'

'Now you'll start complaining of a little pain. I've heard everything! What will our women think?' declared my nurse.

The new me did not care what anybody thought. I remained in slippers even when fully dressed.

'And how is our dear child today?' inquired Vera Kirilovna, coming in after my breakfast tray had been taken down.

'No one would know her, Your Excellency. Sighing one minute and smiling the next and so lazy and empty-headed one would never guess she had a gold medal from the institute,' answered Nyanya.

My *éducatrice* smiled with fond indulgence. Then, sitting down beside me, she said with an air at once tender, excited, and significant, 'You're a success, dear child. Bouquets and candy from Ielisseyef's have been coming for you all morning. And several gentlemen have left cards. One, in particular ...'

It is from *him*, thought I. But as Vera Kirilovna handed me the card of Igor Constantinovich, with the lion rampant of the House of Romanov, I let it hang in listless fingers. 'Who were the other cards from, Vera Kirilovna?'

From everybody except *him.*

But had he sent flowers, candy, anything? Evidently not. Could something have happened to him, oh my God, that was it, he was hurt, ill! No, Vera Kirilovna said Father had taken Uncle Stan for a drive. She had heard nothing about young Prince Stefan.

'But what d'you think he could possibly be doing, Vera Kirilovna?' I persisted.

'Perhaps he's flying his new aeroplane, or he may have ... other interests.' Interests in keeping with his reputation, I understood. I looked at my *éducatrice* with hatred. 'If Prince Veslawski calls, Vera Kirilovna, I'm not at home.'

I bade her send the flowers and candy to the Hospital Marie and asked to be alone to study.

Instead of studying, I hobbled about, falling with deep sighs into a chair, picking up a book and dropping it, going to the window and looking out at the busy river traffic, finding all that busyness irritating and meaningless.

'What's the point?' I addressed Bobby, who had grown tired of watching my erratic movements and clearly wanted me to settle down. 'What's the use in living when *he* already has his own life in which I play no part; when at this very moment he may be taking a girl up in his new aeroplane to get her properly terrified and submissive ... for whatever it is he wants to do with her? I can't bear to think about it!'

At the thought I flamed with rage. I wished the aeroplane would crash with them both. But supposing it did crash, and he were hurt, or killed! I felt mortal anguish. I must telephone and find out ... But no, he was all right, he simply hadn't time to think of me, I had imagined everything at the ball. And I sank dejectedly at my desk.

Thus I sat, cheeks on my palms, Bobby's nose on my foot, when Nyanya entered and said curtly, 'Prince Stefan is downstairs.'

'Stevie? Here?' I flew to the door, remembered my slippers. 'My shoes! Give them to me, where *are* they? How slow you are! Bobby, stay! Oh my God, I'll miss him, he'll leave!' I flew out of the apartment and down the winding stairs.

'Her feet, her feet hurt her, she couldn't walk!' said Nyanya to the maids who had rushed to the head of the stairs at my passage.

'It must be her betrothed, it must be the imperial prince her betrothed, ah what a great day, our beloved Princess, so young, ah how sad, how wonderful!' the maids exclaimed.

'Betrothed! Imperial prince indeed! Idiots!' Nyanya's retort came to me on the landing below.

I continued my flight through the music room and portrait gallery. I only checked myself at the stately approach of Vera Kirilovna, who said, 'I've told the Prince your cousin you were too tired after the ball to receive him, dear child.'

'Vera Kirilovna, no, you didn't! Oh, call him back, oh!'

I would have rushed on but my *éducatrice* lifted her proud bust. 'Princess, control yourself.' Calling a footman, she told him to see if Prince Veslawski had not yet gone. 'Ask him into the blue drawing room if he hasn't.'

After what seemed an eternity, the footman returned to inform us Prince Veslawski was waiting.

'We will see Prince Stefan for a few minutes, *if* you can behave in a seemly manner, Mademoiselle,' Vera Kirilovna warned, and we proceeded down the enfilade of rococo and Empire drawing rooms to the Louis Quinze *petit salon* hung in blue damask.

Stevie looked rosy, rested and wonderfully elegant in a linen suit with a waistcoat, a pearl pin in his perfectly knotted blue-and-white dotted silk tie. I thought him even more magnificent than the previous night. I gave him my hand, said 'Hello, Stevie,' and lapsed into awkward silence.

For all his elegance my cousin also looked shy.

'Kim and I stayed up till morning talking ... about you,' he explained. 'We just woke up. I came directly. I left the flowers with the Swiss doorman when he said you weren't receiving.'

He had overslept! How touching! 'I thought ... you were flying your aeroplane.'

'Oh, that!' Something more exciting than an aeroplane had come into his life.

The roses were brought in a vase.

'Oh, how lovely,' I said, overcome. They were white and yellow and matched my white chiffon dress and yellow taffeta sash. 'They're my favourite.' They had become so as of that moment.

As I gazed up at my cousin in mute admiration, Vera Kirilovna suggested, 'Won't you ask the Prince your cousin to sit down?'

'Oh yes. Please be seated.'

Stevie did so, giving his trousers a slight tug so that their creases would lose none of their perfection. I sat down in a corner of the Regency couch facing him.

'It's gone,' I said suddenly.

'What's gone?'

'Your moustache.'

He touched a fingertip to his bare upper lip. 'I thought . . . you didn't like it.'

'Oh yes. But I like it this way too,' I quickly added as he looked upset. 'I like it even better.'

Vera Kirilovna lightly touched the rose of brown satin at her bosom, to signify disapproval of this intimate conversation. 'Won't you offer the Prince some tea, Mademoiselle?'

'No, not tea, coffee. Poles prefer coffee.'

Stevie looked touched.

My *éducatrice* rang for coffee.

'You may smoke if you like,' I continued. I was anxious to see him do it.

He would not pollute the air I breathed.

Conversational stalemate again.

Vera Kirilovna came to the rescue once more, questioning Stevie in her fluent manner about his friends at Magdalen and the young royal dukes said to be foremost amongst them. I was not the least bit interested in the Prince of Wales. I sat silent as coffee was served, watching my cousin and thinking, How nicely he holds his cup, how elegant his gestures, almost as elegant as Papa's. And what beautifully shaped and rosy nails he has. He must buff them. I wonderingly contemplated his nails.

'What're you looking at?' he asked nervously.

'Your nails . . . they're so clean.' In this smart young man sitting so staid and well behaved in a Petersburg salon I suddenly saw a grimy, messy, loud and overbearing boy who cut saddle cinches and put spiders in the beds of house guests.

He set down his cup, looked at his nails, then at me. He must have seen that same boy reflected in my eyes. He blew up his full cheeks and went 'p-p-p-p' so comically that I could no longer control myself. We exploded simultaneously into uproarious childish laughter.

Vera Kirilovna drew herself up in sign of censure. Then, as we took no notice, she rose, folding her hands downward significantly.

Stevie had immediately risen too, stone sober.

I did not need to stand for a mere countess. 'Please be seated a minute longer, Vera Kirilovna.' I returned her look very coolly. 'The Prince my cousin has not finished his coffee.'

Vera Kirilovna sat down.

We sipped our coffee silently, in perfect propriety. So intent were we on one another that we started at Aunt Sophie's singing tones. '*Comme c'est gentil.* How sweet,' she said from the door.

We rose and stood in confusion as the Veslawskis entered with Father and Grandmaman.

'I see your feet no longer trouble you,' Grandmaman remarked.

There followed gentle chiding of my fatigue after my first ball, which vexed me greatly. I did not want to be treated like a child in front of my cousin. I wanted to appear worldly and sophisticated, the sort of girl I thought would fascinate a young man who already had a reputation.

Vera Kirilovna withdrew from the family reunion. Grandmaman and Aunt Sophie sat down. Uncle and Stevie remained standing. Father sat down beside me, putting an arm about me.

'What d'you think of our ugly duckling?' he asked the Veslawskis in English. 'Would you believe the Swiss can't take in the cards of her admirers fast enough? What am I going to do with her, I ask you?'

'Marry her off and good riddance,' Grandmaman declared.

'Prince Igor Constantinovich of Russia has asked my permission to pay his court to my daughter,' Father continued. He took my hair in his hand and turned my head towards him. 'Will you give the young man some hope?'

I said I would not.

'Wha-at? You don't care for him even a little bit?'

I shook my head negatively.

'You don't care for anybody at all?'

I felt myself flushing.

'Aha! You've been keeping secrets from your papa again. Who is he?'

I glanced at my cousin, then back at Father.

'Yes, I was afraid of it,' he said in a wistful tone.

‘Afraid, why afraid, Uncle Peter?’ cried Stevie. ‘I too care for no one but Tanya. I’ve never cared for anyone else.’

‘You’ve a short memory, sir,’ Uncle Stan observed languidly, stroking his moustache.

‘I think that’s most unkind of you, sir,’ Stevie retorted with heat. ‘My feelings for Tanya are something ... something entirely different ... something sacred ... as yours were for Mother!’

‘How d’you know what your feelings for Tanya are when you’ve only seen her two days in two years?’

‘But, sir, it’s not something that just happened last night. I’ve known it for years, ever since I was eight years old, only I didn’t know it then. What I’m trying to say is ... I didn’t realize it was ... what I feel now.’ I understood he could not say ‘love’ in front of everybody. He looked to his mother to interpret his feelings.

Aunt Sophie inclined her head in response to his plea. ‘I saw it and understood it before either of you. And I must confess I was glad, because I hoped Tanya would always be my daughter.’

‘Auntie!’ I cried. And rushing from Father’s side, I fell to my knees beside her chair, clasping her waist and gazing up into her face as at a holy image.

Aunt Sophie smiled. ‘I still hope you can be our daughter, Tanyussia. But it’s not something that may be decided rashly. For one thing, I’m afraid it would not meet with His Majesty’s approval. Am I right, Pierre?’

‘It would undoubtedly end whatever influence I have regained,’ answered Father. ‘But who knows how long that will last? I myself married a Polish princess. If my daughter falls in love with a Pole, who am I to oppose it? I don’t know how you’d feel, Stanislaw, about the possible effect of His Majesty’s displeasure on the cause of Polish autonomy.’

‘It won’t advance it, that’s certain.’ Uncle Stan’s tone chilled me. ‘But in any case Stefan must do his military service before he can even think of marriage.’

‘But, sir, that’ll mean another two years! There may be war, I may be dead, anything might happen! Mother!’ Stevie appealed again to the one person who always understood.

‘Your father’s right, my Stevie boy.’ Aunt Sophie laid her hand over his. ‘You must wait a couple of years. If your feelings are strong and true, they will only grow stronger as you both mature a little. You're so very young.'

'We'll wait, won't we, Stevie?' I pleaded.

'I'll wait, if we can be formally engaged,' Stevie announced.

'You, sir, are in no position to make conditions of any kind,' his father reminded him frigidly.

'Uncle Stan' – I turned to Uncle – 'don't be angry with Stevie. He'll wait, as I will, as long as you want us to. Please ... give us your blessing.'

Uncle Stan looked long from me to Aunt Sophie. Then, putting one hand on my shoulder and another on her arm, he said, 'If you grow up to be like your Aunt Sophie in heart and deed, Tanyussia, as much as you are already like her in appearance, I could not wish for a better wife for my son.'

I looked up at him radiantly. Father seemed moved and a little saddened. My thoughtful aunt was the first to take notice of Grandmaman, turning impatient eyes on a scene of which she was not, for once, the focus. 'Anna Vladimirovna, do these plans meet with your approval?'

'Why ask me?' retorted Grandmaman. 'Since when have my wishes been taken into consideration?' This and 'You know I never interfere in anybody's affairs' were two of my autocratic grandmother's favourite statements and she believed them both sincerely. 'I had hoped my grand-daughter would take over the very great responsibilities I must soon lay down,' she continued. 'She is the last of our line, one of Russia's oldest and most honourable. But that has never meant anything to her. She would prefer to give herself to the sick ... or to the Poles. I wish her happiness in her new family,' she finished furiously and rose. 'Excuse me.'

The Veslawskis and Father followed Grandmaman to mollify and bring her back.

I remained on the floor. Stevie gave me his hand to help me up. But I liked being on my knees before him.

'If you won't come up, I'll come down,' he said comically, and went down on one knee.

How like a boy he still is, I thought, and how nice to be again like children, on the floor.

I felt a rush of childish tenderness and leaned towards him. But he held me off, his expression full of some fierce suffering. And as he gripped my arms until they ached, my feelings too became strangely fierce and painful and no longer childish. I dropped my head. Rising, he raised me up, avoiding my eyes. The Veslawskis now returned with Father and Grandmaman. Her vivid brown eyes rested on me perceptively.

Aunt also observed my flushed and uneasy countenance. 'I think the excitement has been too much for Tanya,' she said. 'The child needs a few days of peace and quiet.'

It was agreed I should go to our gulf-shore dacha, and the Veslawskis left.

10

At the dacha I rode horseback, accompanied by Father's favourite aide, Colonel Boris Maysky, played tennis, learned by heart pages of verse from *Pan Tadeusz* – the Polish classic as dear to Poles as *Eugene Onegin* is to Russians – and played only Chopin on the piano.

It was hot and I felt languid and lazy. At night, as I lay listening to the gulf waters lap against the granite landing at the foot of the tiered terraces below, I fell asleep thinking of *him*. In my sleep I dreamed of *him* and of Father, one often turning into the other and the other way around. And so I was not startled, when I opened my eyes one night, to see *him* standing at the foot of my bed, in the white light of the summer solstice that streamed through the French window open on the balcony.

How clearly I see him, what a good dream this is, I thought. But why is Stevie dressed like a sailor? And why is he carrying a cloak?

I sat bolt upright, holding my blanket to my chin. 'Stevie!' For it was he, in the flesh. 'What're you doing here?'

Bobby, who had not even barked, so accustomed was he to Stevie's intrusions in the past, was up on his feet, head cocked. He, too, was full of wonder.

Stevie sat down on my bed and, stroking the setter, he said, 'I've come for you. My cousin Beresford and some English friends are waiting on their yacht in the gulf. The captain will marry us.'

'Marry us? The captain?' The leap between fantasy and reality was too fast for my imagination.

'It'll be perfectly legal. Later on, when things settle down, you'll be converted to Catholicism and we'll be married in our palace chapel.'

'What if they don't settle down?'

'Of course they will. Father'll fume a bit, but Mother'll bring him around. Uncle Peter'll understand.'

'How long would we have to be . . . on the yacht?'

'As long as necessary. It'll be our honeymoon.'

I clasped my tucked-up legs and tried to envision this honeymoon on a yacht; sitting astern hand in hand after supper watching the ship's phosphorescent wake, as I had so often at Father's side on the *Helena*; going to our cabin for the night and . . . I took a deep breath. 'It won't do, Stevie.'

'Why not?'

'You'd be horribly seasick.' Prosaic reality now came to my aid.

Stevie was clearly not in the mood for it. 'Tanya, our future's at stake and you're being childish!'

I thought of what my imperial namesake would say to the scheme and took courage. 'It's you who are being childish, my sweet silly Stevie. We can't go climbing down balconies and running off at night as we used to. You're not a boy any more.'

'No, I'm a man. And a man can't wait two or three years for the woman he loves, and wants.'

I felt a delicious chill. What if he should kidnap me? But I summoned sense and propriety in time. 'You mustn't talk like that. You shouldn't be here at all. You shouldn't sit on my bed!'

He rose and ordered, 'Hurry up and dress.'

'My clothes are in the dressing room and Nyanya sleeps next door. Fyodor sleeps armed in the anteroom. If he finds you here, you're dead.'

Danger would not deter a Veslawski. 'I brought a cloak. Your dressing gown will do.' He handed me the dressing gown hanging over the back of a chair by the bed.

I thought I would be safer out of bed. 'Turn around.'

While he turned his back, I was up, tied into the gown and at the farthest end of the bedroom all in one moment. Stevie approached me, holding up the cloak.

I backed away, palms forward. 'Stevie, do be sensible, we can't! Think of your mother, your father, remember who you are. You might never be king of Poland any more. It wouldn't be a true marriage and His Majesty'd be simply furious! You might be sent to Siberia . . .' I spoke in a quick whisper, while my inner voice whispered, Nonsense! Be quiet, be still, and let him do with you what he wants.

'Never!' Stevie scoffed. 'The Poles would rise against Russian rule as one man. I tell you, I know, it's the only way. I feel, if you don't become mine now, you never will. Don't run away from me, my sweet, I'll not hurt you, I'll not let any harm come to you ever, dearest beloved,' he pleaded, stalking me about the room.

I stumbled against an armchair and the fear, not of being abducted, but of my cousin being discovered, paralysed me for a moment. Stevie was instantly upon me, looking at me tenderly, pleadingly, but also with determination.

'There, my beauty, don't be frightened.' He laid the cloak on my shoulders. 'How lovely you look in a hood! Come now, Kim's waiting in the boat below.'

I still could not move. 'If you don't leave this instant, I'll call out and you're dead,' I lied.

My cousin no longer looked pleading and tender. 'I thought you might not come willingly,' he said.

And with a catlike rapidity he turned me around, tied a silk kerchief about my mouth and another about my wrists behind my back, then lifted me up.

He *will* kidnap me, I thought with relief.

I felt entirely safe in his arms, which had lifted me with such ease. I closed my eyes in abandon.

But suddenly, I was set down in a chair and untied.

Falling to his knees, Stevie kissed my wrists. 'My sweet, forgive me, I must have been mad to use force! Did I hurt your beautiful hands? Call for help, I deserve to be shot!' And he pressed his large head into my lap.

I was cold, although my cheeks burned. 'It's all right,' I murmured. Oh, why didn't you carry me off? I added silently, even while I shuddered at the consequences of an abduction. Sweet, silly Stevie, so sophisticated yet so easily duped. How terrible you looked a moment ago, and how harmless now, I thought. How absurd and romantic you are, how fierce and yet how gentle! And your voice, it is as beautiful as Papa's.

I stroked the chestnut head in my lap, from which the funny sailor cap had slipped. It was even smoother and softer than I had imagined.

'Is it still curly?' I asked.

'Yes. I've an awful time keeping it flat.' He lifted a miserable, comical face. 'I wet it and wear a tight net over it every morning.'

I went on stroking his hair, his forehead, his full, baby-soft cheeks. Then I put my hands over his ears. They were cold, while his cheeks were warm. I held his head hard. I wanted to shower it with kisses. But I heard someone stirring and said, 'Go now. I think Nyanya's up.'

'You're not angry?' he asked.

I shook my head in denial.

'Will you still marry me, whenever it's all right?'

I nodded assent. 'Now go.' And I pushed him off.

He rose and put the sailor cap drolly over one ear. Then he formally took off my cloak. I formally gave him my hand. But before he could kiss it, Nyanya burst in.

As her mouth dropped open, I threw myself on her. 'Be silent ... for God's sake ... nothing happened ... absolutely nothing ... I give you my word ... Nyanichka ... be good.'

The little woman pushed me away and tilted her head in a ruffled white nightcap. 'That's a fine business, my Prince, visiting your betrothed at such an hour, in such a place, and in such a costume too.' She looked him up and down with broad irony.

'I know, I've made a fool of myself, Nyanya ... it will never happen again I swear ... I beg you to forget it, for the sake of your Princess, if not for mine,' he stammered.

'Well, we'll see ... it'll depend.' On your future behaviour, her stern look warned.

A whistle sounded under the window. 'It's for me ... it's time ... goodbye,' and Stevie rushed out on the balcony and over the side.

My hands at my breast, I held my breath until I heard the faint sound of oars moving away from the pier.

'He's safe.' I undid my dressing gown and handed it to my nurse. 'Tomorrow, I wish to go back to Petersburg. Tell Dunya to pack my things. Now go to bed, Nyanichka dear.'

Nyanya was not about to be dismissed without the satisfaction of a good scold.

I cut her short. 'Don't say anything. It's not needed. I know myself what can be done, and what cannot.'

I lay awake through the night, reliving the scene, feeling the strength of the arms that had lifted me like a doll, and the softness of the glossy hair and rosy warm cheeks. I had been abandoned and shameless in those arms. Beneath the vestal was a wild gypsy woman, kindred to the child Tanya who had wrecked her father's chance for happiness with Diana, who would have killed her rival. Not all my penances and good deeds could smother that mocking presence. If I did not keep the gypsy in check, she would triumph. Then what would I be but yet another sensuous woman at the mercy of a man? Even Stevie would not love me long. It must not be. I steeled myself for a long struggle.

While I was absorbed in first love, the war nobody expected or wanted galloped inexorably nearer. The system of alliances – between Austria-Hungary and Germany on the one hand, Serbia, Russia and France on the other – had been set in a motion difficult to arrest once certain postures had been adopted and 'national honour' staked. Even more irreversible was the machinery of 'defence' – no state would admit aggression.

Father, who knew Russia's weakness first-hand, urged patience and conciliation in the face of Austria's intent, abetted by Germany, to chastise Russia's ally, Serbia, for the assassination of Archduke Ferdinand. At the extraordinary council at Krasnoye on 25 July 1914, held under the presidency of the Tsar to deal with the insulting Austrian ultimatum to the Serbians, Father dissented from the decision to mobilize eight Russian army corps on the Austrian frontier.

'Austria means to annex Serbia, it's clear,' said Grandmaman after Father had given us a brief account of the session. 'Russia won't stand for it. And rightly so.' Grandmaman underlined the words with a tap of her cane.

We were sitting, after supper, *en famille* with the Veslawskis and Stevie in that same silk-panelled blue drawing room now made memorable by his declaration of love. This time Vera Kirilovna and Casimir were present. The talk was political. Love, which filled my being, seemed to have gone out of the world.

'Russia is in no position, Maman, to play protector to a brother Slav,' Father said. 'We cannot fight the Austrians, the Germans and most likely the Turks, all at once. We can only negotiate and pray the Austrians will calm down.'

'But what has gotten into the old Emperor Franz Josef?' Vera Kirilovna asked in that special tone of intimacy mingled with respect she reserved for royalty. 'He did not even love his nephew, the Archduke Ferdinand. He never forgave him his morganatic marriage to a Hungarian countess.'

'Or his liberal tendencies,' Father said. 'God knows what mad dream of restoring the Holy Roman Empire has possessed that foggy old mind! There are firebrands about Franz Josef, that's clear. And Prussia is egging them on.'

'It's only a show of teeth. Austria-Hungary is a tottering empire,' Uncle Stan observed with seeming indifference. 'It wants to make an example of Serbia for the benefit of its restless minorities. This is a Balkan, not a European crisis, and it ought to be left alone.'

'I couldn't agree with you more, Stan,' said Father. 'But there are hot heads on our general staff, too, who are burning to make good our humiliation at the hands of the Japanese.'

'Surely the Tsar is not on their side.' Aunt Sophie spoke with her usual soft deliberation, but I sensed her anxiety, different from a man's, which I shared.

'No, if His Majesty could follow his own counsel, he would avoid war at any cost. And, d'you know' – Father lowered his voice imperceptibly – 'Grishka has cabled from Siberia that war would be disastrous for Russia. I'm inclined to believe him for once.' Father surprised us by this reference to Rasputin.

'Rubbish!' declared Grandmaman. 'You are a born pessimist, Pierre. War, if it is forced upon us, will galvanize Russia. It will end this revolutionary nonsense. Our workers have never been better off, yet here they are, striking! War will unite us. War will stiffen the backbone of this soft society.'

'It will, if it's short and successful. But for that, our leadership would need to be as strong and decisive as you, Maman.' Father gave a sadly subtle little smile.

'Let us not speak of war,' Aunt Sophie said, and I heard her inner shudder. 'It's too fearful to contemplate. Can't England do something to avert catastrophe, Pierre?'

'It can let the world know at once that it will stand by Russia and France,' Father replied. 'Sazonov, Paléologue and I have been urging it on Sir George Buchanan.'

'I'll speak to Sir George also,' said Uncle Stan. 'But I'm afraid England will not intervene until it feels its own national interest threatened.'

'By then it may be too late!' Father tossed up his hand.

'Well, if war must come, why can't Russia pull itself together?' Uncle Stan said.

How ready men are to think the unthinkable! I thought. And Stevie? I looked at his set face, then at Casimir's, which was almost identically set. Yes, thought I, they are ready. They are eager to be 'men'.

'Since 1905, England and France have pumped millions into Russia's economy,' continued Uncle Stan. 'Industrialization has been rapid. Russians are splendid engineers. I was very impressed with the Sikorsky factory.'

'It's quite a place,' said Stevie, and 'I'll say, sir,' echoed Casimir, and reddened.

How fierce and funny they both are, I thought tenderly. I must get Stevie to teach me to fly. But Father was speaking again and we hung on his words.

'Russia,' he was saying, 'could be rich and powerful, the first nation on earth. It has the resources. It has the genius. It has the heart. But somehow, they do not come together. There is a fatal something at the core, a self-destructive force. I can't put it any more clearly.'

'I understand,' I said. That dark force was in me too. Perhaps it was within all human beings, and war was its expression and release. I felt, suddenly, that war could not be avoided. And as we looked at one another, I saw that everyone else felt it too.

Notices of the partial mobilization were posted on official buildings the next day and crowds gathered outside the headquarters of the newspapers *Novoye Vremya* and the *Gazette*.

Serbia humbly accepted all but the most outrageous of the Austrian demands and offered to submit the dispute to the International Tribunal at The Hague. Its offer was rejected and on 28 July Austria-Hungary declared war on Serbia. Belgrade, the capital, was bombed on the twenty-ninth.

The Tsar, on his own initiative, Father told us, cabled a personal appeal to 'Cousin Willie' – Kaiser Wilhelm – to restrain his Austrian ally, Emperor Franz Josef. The Kaiser cabled back a plea to 'Cousin Nicky' to halt further Russian mobilization. The cousins had hunted together during exchanges of state visits and had long corresponded about petty military matters – styles of uniform, decorations, etc. – dear to them both. Neither believed the other would go to war.

His Majesty, with Father's support, did countermand the general decree of mobilization. But the Foreign Minister, Sazonov, the War Minister, General Sukhomlinov, and the chief of the general staff, General Yanushkevich, prevailed on the changeable Tsar to rescind the countermanding order.

On 1 August the German ambassador, Count Pourtalès, delivered to Sazonov his country's declaration of war and burst into tears. World War I had begun.

On 2 August Nicholas and Alexandra assisted at a solemn *Te Deum* at the Winter Palace. The Tsar repeated the oath sworn by his forefather, Alexander I, at the time of the Napoleonic invasion, that he would not make peace so long as a single enemy soldier remained on Russian soil.

After blessing Grand Duke Nikolay Nikolayevich, the newly appointed Commander in Chief, the Emperor and Empress with their children passed through the St George gallery. It was thronged with nobles in court dress eager to pledge their loyalty to the sovereigns so long estranged from them. Before my imposing grandmother, leader of the high society that scorned her, Alexandra stopped, as if in pleading. Grandmaman's direct gaze was not critical but fierce with loyalty. Alexandra in her jewels and stiff brocade passed on. This time her rigid and suffering countenance did not provoke dislike. Rather, it appeared the reflection of a common painful emotion.

The Tsar's grave and calm bearing, the serenity of his handsome face, the light of faith in his mild eyes, stirred his most caustic detractors. Not a soul remained unmoved at His Majesty's passage. I inclined myself before my sovereign and godfather with glad reverence and love, catching the ecstatic mood.

Raising my eyes, I met those of my namesake, which rested on me long and eloquently.

For God, for country, for the Tsar. I repeated inwardly the Russian soldier's oath. *Za Boga, za rodinu, za Tsaria.* For these I would lay down my life, oh my dearest Tanik, my look said.

I know, her eyes replied.

As the crowd surged forward behind the sovereigns – the masters of ceremony could barely hold it back – Tatyana Nikolayevna managed to press my hand. Her slender fingers were as cold as mine. Never had we shared an unspoken emotion so totally. More than ever today, I felt, we were one.

After making their way through the packed gallery the sovereigns reached the balcony on the Winter Palace Square. The vast square was black with a crowd bearing flags and religious banners. They came without organization or prompting. Among them were those same factory workers on strike before the posting of the mobilization decree. These ten thousand people, at the sight of their sovereigns, fell to their knees and sang, 'God Keep the Tsar'. This powerful people's voice, heard by the nobles within, added to the solemnity of the occasion. Russia was one: monarch, nobility and folk united in the common cause of Slav against Teuton. The Russian Empire was at its zenith.

The fine regiments of the Guard marched through the rectilinear *prospekts* of Sankt Petersburg – rechristened in Russian, Petrograd – to the cheers of the crowd, the blessings of older women, the kisses of the young, and the tears of all. Trains carried them to East Prussia and the black bogs of Soldaur and Tännenberg. The highways west trembled with the day-long passage of soldiers in flat caps and belted overblouses, their overcoats wrapped around their shoulders like tyre tubes. In their wake rumbled the artillery, the baggage and ambulance trains, the field kitchens and supply wagons, with some lorries of English or French make and horse-drawn vehicles of all Russian types.

While the army marched west, daily processions carried holy images, pictures of the Tsar, French, English and Russian flags through the capital. A crowd also sacked the German embassy. Patriotic sentiment gave rise to the Russification of German-sounding names, the suspicion of all persons of German descent, and persecution in the war zone of Jews, who were suspected *ipso facto* of being spies. The sale of alcoholic beverages was forbidden by imperial decree.

The grandees, still fired by the scene in the Winter Palace, converted their residences into hospitals. Their daughters enrolled in war nurses' training. Grandmaman at once began converting our *osobnyak*. She also lent her talent for organization to the Red Cross. Here, as elsewhere, sublime intention vied with sublime chaos.

Merchants hung out flags and raised prices. The best emotions and the basest were displayed; the highest aspirations and most selfish. But, for a time, the best and the highest generally prevailed.

Father had begged the Tsar to relieve him of his post as *de facto* minister without portfolio, in which he now felt ineffectual. The Commander in Chief had given him a cavalry corps to command. In the first week of August, he entrained with his troops for Galicia.

A few days later, the Veslawskis departed in turn. The Tsar had told Uncle Stan what the Poles would soon learn in the manifesto of Grand Duke Nikolay Nikolayevich – that their country's autonomy upon victory over the common enemy was assured. Uncle pledged himself to recruit a volunteer regiment from squires and men of his region. The Tsar gave his permission for the reactivation of the Veslawski lancers, with the family escutcheon as regimental insignia, under the command of Uncle Stan. Stefan and Casimir were to serve with the regiment and train in the garrison barracks of Veslawow, the new regimental headquarters. Aunt Sophie was ordering supplies for the conversion of the Veslawski palace into a hospital. There I was to join her after my eighteenth birthday.

Grandmaman's hospital would not be ready for several months so I began my training as a Red Cross nurse in the Hospital Marie.

11

At the end of August 1914, the youths of the Guard regiments who had ridden so smartly through the *prospekts* of Petrograd began returning as casualties in hospital trains. The girls in organdie dresses and flowered hats who had cheered them off waited at the station in the grey uniform and white veil of the volunteer war nurse.

By September, enthusiasm had given way to sadness and doubt. The capture of Lemberg in Galicia on 2 September 1914, could not make up for the disaster of Soldau and Tännenberg, in which the proud Imperial Guard, flower of the Russian army and nobility, was destroyed. Many survived only to perish in the Battle of the Mazurian Lakes. Igor's gifted brother, Oleg Constantinovich, was mortally wounded. Igor himself nearly lost his life trying to pull his own horse out of the marsh.

The entire imperial family buried its feuds to mourn the young poet-prince. Grandmaman grieved with Grand Duke Constantine as if Oleg had been her own kin. For me, the lonely death of my childhood playmate on the way home in a hospital train was my first personal loss of the war.

How changed, how newly mature and melancholy was my namesake's pretty face above the candle she held during the long funeral rite. Did she grieve solely for the gentle kinsman whom she had known less than I, or did she mourn the girlhood that had gone by without leaving her with a soldier-prince of her own to worry and dream about?

At the end of September, the Turks closed the Dardanelles, the only year-round supply route for French and British arms. In November, Turkey declared war and Russia found itself fighting on two fronts. By then, the army's stock of weapons and ammunition was already short.

At year's end, our push into Galicia was halted. The Germans had retaken East Prussia. Orders were issued to front commanders to spare ammunition. In Petrograd, peasant recruits drilled without rifles on the Champ de Mars and the Winter Palace Square. Rumours of treason in high places and graft in the War Ministry swelled the popular anger over the munitions shortage. The communion of the nation with its sovereigns had been short-lived.

For me, this was a period of profound transformation. I emerged from total self-centredness, and became an adult. My prior existence up to the eve of war now appeared a child's game. One had no longer any right to a private life. Even love, that jealous, possessive passion I had experienced first for Father, then for Stefan, receded before the universal suffering. Not that I loved Stefan less; I loved him better and more selflessly. But another kind of love was needed for all who suffered, be they Russian, German, Austrian, Jew. I could not feel that love, but I could substitute devotion for it. Henceforth, my allegiance could not be to Russia first or to my sovereign, to my class, or even my own family. My allegiance was owed first to those who needed me most.

As grand-daughter of the patroness and board chairman of the Hospital Marie, I would have been spared the lowly tasks assigned trainees – tasks considered too nasty for well-bred women were performed by medical orderlies – *sanitars*. But both Grandmaman and I insisted I be treated like anyone else.

I made beds with the regulation 'hospital corners', bathed the patients and carried bedpans during the rush of cases brought in from a train. The body and its functions did not repel me. What repelled me was the violence done to it by the instruments of war. I saw Stevie in every mangled young officer I tended and my flesh and soul rebelled.

As I was capable and not squeamish, I was soon assisting at dressings. I took deep breaths the first time I cut away a bandage caked with ten days' pus from a young cavalryman's back. I did not retch, like other novices, at the stench of gas gangrene. I watched. I asked questions. I learned quickly to insert drainage tubes and give injections.

I learned to stand for the matron and the doctor. My upbringing had prepared me for the hierarchy and discipline of the hospital, my familiarity with military life for inefficiency and inordinate attention to trivia. I obeyed unnecessary orders so long as they were not harmful and was punctilious about trifling details. I was cheerful with the patients when my heart was breaking. I was pleasant to the most unpleasant of the staff. My attitude won me acceptance even faster than my capability and I did not stay more than two months in a subordinate position.

When the charge nurse came down with the winter 'flu, I took her place at the head of the lofty long ward. I kept the patients' charts, dispensed medicines from a locked cupboard, and gave orders to nurses older than I. To have been surrounded by attendants since babyhood proved to be of some use. It taught me to command without seeming to and to win consent.

Busy and needed as I felt, Christmas was soon upon me. I had a week's leave and was returning from a visit to our summer dacha, now converted into a soldiers' convalescent home, when I saw a gentleman in spectacles with a black goatee walking with quick little steps down the quay of the Big Neva on Vassily Island. I ordered my sleigh to stop and called to him. Professor Holveg turned around irritably, then flashed his unexpectedly pleasant smile.

'Professor, how have you been?' I asked, as my former tutor got under the bearskin rug beside me.

'How can anyone be these days, Tatyana Petrovna? Is there anything an intelligent and thinking person can derive satisfaction from in a period of mass lunacy and stupidity such as this war?'

'I know you've been working very hard, Professor. His Majesty has spoken highly of your work.'

'Yes, I contribute my share to the slaughter. As a subject of the Tsar I have no choice.'

'I thought you had rather liked His Majesty after your audience.'

'I confess I was attracted by the Tsar's modesty and simple manner. But I can't reconcile this image of a kindly, if not very intelligent man, with the monstrous treatment of the Jewish population in the war zone. Thousands deported on twenty-four-hour notice in cattle cars, summary executions of so-called spies, the turning away of Jewish wounded from hospitals.'

'Professor, no!'

'Tatyana Petrovna, yes! I'm chairman of a committee for Jewish relief, even though, in principle, I detest committees ... I know what I'm talking about.'

'But how perfectly dreadful! I'll mention it at Tsarskoye. I'm certain His Majesty doesn't know. It's only the more backward of the police and military who do these horrible things.'

'I'm sorry, Tatyana Petrovna. As Tsar-autocrat, Nicholas II must be held responsible for Russia's crimes.'

'Bureaucrats rule Russia, Papa says, not the Tsar.'

'He has the power to choose his servants. He seems to prefer the most venal and incompetent.'

I had heard similar words in my own circle. 'His Majesty believes he is an autocrat by the will of God,' I said without conviction. I doubted God concerned Himself with forms of government.

'Autocracy in the twentieth century is an anachronism. A tsar who hasn't the intellect to comprehend this has no business ruling a modern state.'

I did not care to hear my sovereign and godfather called stupid.

'I see I'm guilty of *lèse majesté*,' Professor Holveg observed, and leaned forward to tap Gerazim's back.

'Don't, Professor.' I laid a hand on his arm. 'I know you're not as dreadful as you sound. But if I didn't, I'd think you were advocating revolution.'

'I don't advocate anything, Tatyana Petrovna. I merely draw logical conclusions from my observations. I conclude that tsarism must fall.'

'But what can replace it, Professor, except something awful?'

'True enough, Tatyana Petrovna. The alternative might be chaos or communism. But that merely testifies to the backwardness of the people, which tsarism has perpetuated.'

I had often heard the Russian people called backward. But to me the people meant Nyanya, Fyodor, Gerazim and others like them whom I had known since childhood. And even though they could not read, they could make comments quite as sarcastic and shrewd as those of Professor Holveg. But the Professor did not know or love his Russian servants. Did he love his mother's people, I wondered?

'I don't love Jews any more than any other race,' he answered. 'But they have a right to justice and equality. If this is denied them, their vengeance may some day be terrible. There may be no absolute justice in this world, Tatyana Petrovna, but there is a rather crude and constant law of retribution.'

'I believe it,' I said. 'And I also believe there *is* absolute justice.'

'I hope you never have reason not to.' He smiled and went on to inquire in German about my nursing work.

'I like work. It makes me feel a real person' – real as opposed to a made-up one, a daughter of the nobility. 'I'm learning a lot, though not nearly as much as I'd like. Nursing is pretty elementary.'

'So is medicine, although surgery should make great strides. War is an enormous incentive to technological ingenuity.' The Professor's sarcasm concealed indignation. But his was a cerebral anger. He had not witnessed as I had the agony of mutilation, the dread of surgery, the terror of death.

'I think it's vile!' I retorted. 'I can't find any justification or reason for this wholesale torture and slaughter.' I turned to my former mentor in wide-eyed dismay.

'I can't either, Tatyana Petrovna,' he said in a different tone. '*Es ist ein Unsinn*. It is senseless.'

What a good friend he is! How freely we can talk! I thought. Then, 'Aren't you afraid to speak German in public, *Herr Professor*?' I asked. '*Es ist doch verboten*.'

'Ridiculous! Bach and Beethoven will be banned next, like vodka, by imperial *ukaze*. Nationalism is as absurd as autocracy, and even more dangerous. As long as it exists, war will be inevitable. Most discouraging. But it's been delightful to see you.' We had turned into the Quai Anglais and my companion stepped off.

'It's been wonderful meeting you, Professor,' I said, as he tipped his black astrakhan cap. 'God keep you.'

With Grandmaman's approval, our business administrator sent a large cheque to Professor Holveg's committee for Jewish relief. And on my very next visit to Tsarskoye, I told Tatyana Nikolayevna and Olga of the outrages reported by my former tutor.

'This is intolerable!' Olga's eyes blazed. 'I'll speak to Papa at once!'

'No, Olichka, wait.' Tatyana Nikolayevna restrained her impulsive sister. 'Let's speak to Mummsy first. Papa . . . has the entire war to think about.'

Was there, in Tanik's hesitancy, a veiled allusion to her father's way of averting his gaze from imperial Russia's uglier aspects? Had not my father often referred to our sovereign's curious indifference in the face of catastrophe – the coronation disaster, Port Arthur and Tsushima, 'Bloody Sunday' – his fatalistic resignation to the sufferings of his subjects? It was an aspect of the Tsar so contrary to the benign picture he presented to his children that it was impossible Tanik should suspect it. But, intuitive as she was, she guessed her mother would be the one to respond from the heart.

The Empress did lash out against the wartime persecution of minorities. Even 'Friedrichsy' – the venerable and devoted Minister of the Court, who was of German-Baltic descent – was not exempt from malicious attacks. Alexandra promised to look into the shocking treatment of Jewish war wounded personally, and to refer the other instances to His Majesty.

Olga kissed her and my less expansive Tanik cried, 'Mummsy, you *are* wonderful!'

Once again, I could only agree wholeheartedly.

After the New Year, 1915, I was able to transfer to our own hospital. Here I could not be denied the wish – Grandmaman called it a whim – to try my hand as a surgical nurse. I liked the aseptic cleanliness, the hushed quiet of the operating room. I liked to handle the shiny instruments, so precise, that fit so well in the cupped palm: instruments made to relieve, not inflict pain. While I handed them to the surgeon, I observed and asked questions. My anatomy studies proved useful and I began to feel I was acquiring more than elementary knowledge, the kind that would serve me as a surgeon.

(I was not sure how the future Rex Poloniae would react to having a surgeon wife, and I did not mention it in my letters to Stevie. The issue would resolve itself when the time came.)

My experience in the operating room impressed on me the importance of anaesthesia. I decided I could do most good at the front as a nurse-anaesthetist – since Stevie had finished his accelerated officer's training, I was determined to join him at the front. The chief anaesthetist, an older university professor well acquainted with Alexis Holveg, took an interest in me and agreed to train me. Under his guidance, if the operation was uncomplicated, I learned to give nitrous-oxide induction, followed by the anaesthetic of choice – ethyl chloride, chloroform or ether. I learned when and how much oxygen to administer. My patients did not struggle through the first stage of anaesthesia, so the surgeons liked me to work for them.

In the hospital hierarchy, surgical nurses ranked highest. To have a chit of a girl given responsibilities and recognition in preference to senior personnel would normally have led to open resentment and friction. Shortsighted as I was, I was made aware of my unusual situation by an incident with a young substitute surgeon from Sweden – Russian surgeons his age had all been called up.

In the course of the *débridement* of a hip wound under local anaesthesia, the patient asked for water. It was my duty to monitor the patient and keep him calm. I felt his agitation and asked to give him a sip of water. But the surgeon said, 'He can wait. We'll be done in a few minutes.'

I looked at my patient. He repeated, 'Water!' and there was anguish in his gaze. I thought 'a few minutes' might seem very long from his perspective. 'With your permission, Doctor,' I said, and gave the patient a sip through a straw.

The wound cleaned and closed, and the patient taken back to the ward, as I was tidying up, I overheard the surgeon say in English to a staff doctor outside the operating room, 'That cheeky young thing with the big eyes, I want her disciplined! Do you know her name?'

'Tatyana Petrovna, Princess Silomirskaya, my dear fellow. Her grandmama pays our salaries.'

'Oh,' said the martinet. And I neither heard nor saw him again.

'You were kind to give me water,' my post-operative patient said when I visited him. 'I hope you didn't get in trouble on my account.'

The patients knew me only as Sister Tatyana.

'Not a bit of it.' I smiled.

I felt I had been in the right and would have defied that surgeon again, in any hospital. Still, I became conscious of the falsehood of my position and all the more eager for 'real' war work.

When off duty, I attended lectures and films on the treatment and care of war wounds with the medical staff, studied my *materia medica*, wrote to Stevie and Father, and played the piano with new depth – it was a way of channelling my turbulent feelings and senses. Another necessary outlet was exercise. I astonished the hospital and household staffs by skipping rope in the courtyard and realized a childhood wish: I had a snowball fight with Mitka, the yard porter's son, who had not quite reached military age. At every opportunity I escaped with Fyodor to the woods of our dacha across the bay to ride and shoot. Fyodor was too tall for the army. And with so much of the help called up, he had become indispensable to Grandmaman.

Although it was a brilliant season, I seldom went out, except to a concert. Entertaining in our residence, on the third storey set aside for our private use, was now limited to our intimate circle. My presence was no longer required at Grandmaman's 'at home' day, but I did join her, along with Vera Kirilovna and Zinaida Mikhailovna, in an occasional game of bridge.

My former *éducatrice* no longer treated me like a child, although her every glance and gesture made patent her disapproval of my unaristocratic ways. She now wore brown and grey instead of amber and beige and covered her opulent autumnal bloom with a suitable cloak of gravity. She referred constantly to the 'gallant bravery' and 'dedication of our fighting men' of her former imperial mistress, Marie Fyodorovna, a dedication and gallantry far superior, we understood, to that of the reigning Empress.

Zinaida's only thought was for her scapegrace son at the front. She jumped whenever the telephone rang and expected a telegram announcing Kolenka's death every time a footman brought Grandmaman a message. She no longer demurred when Vera Kirilovna began her underhanded attacks on Alexandra.

Grandmaman, according to her mood, took no notice, added a sarcastic comment of her own, or told Vera Kirilovna to shut up.

'Here we are, "the Petrograd bridge players",' Vera Kirilovna quoted Alexandra's very phrase – I marvelled at how she managed to know all that was said and done in the remoteness of Tsarskoye Selo – 'and two of us' – she meant Grandmaman and herself – 'born Muscovites into the bargain! That makes us part of "the *clique de Moscou*" as well.' She quoted another pet phrase. 'Aren't you worried, dear Anna Vladimirovna, that "that man"' – a significant pause – 'might stick pins into our effigies and obliterate us?'

'Hmmmph,' said Grandmaman, trumping Vera Kirilovna's ace. There was no telling if she was angered or amused.

'I don't know what man you are referring to,' said Zinaida Mikhailovna with a distracted look at the door.

'The Siberian sorcerer. How can you be so naïve? Do pay attention to the game, Zinaida. I'm so sorry, but your finesse did not work.' Vera Kirilovna covered and took my card in turn.

'Tatyana Petrovna likes to pretend "that man" does not exist. I must have distracted her,' she observed to Grandmaman.

'Shut up and play, Vera Kirilovna,' the latter barked in Russian.

Another time, after the prefatory remarks about that '*true* Russian patriot', and that '*real* friend of our brave fighting men, Her Most Gracious Majesty, Marie Fyodorovna', Vera Kirilovna said, 'Now that Kokovtsov has fallen for daring to speak out against "that man" to His Majesty's face' – she referred to the dismissal of the Prime Minister – 'one can expect our beloved commander in chief to be relieved. Grand Duke Nikolay Nikolayevich has never concealed his contempt for "that man". A certain "high lady"' – Alexandra, we understood – 'has lately begun to detest him even more, if possible, than our own dear Marie Pavlovna. I was ever so sorry to miss her visit to our hospital today. Did you greet Her Imperial Highness, Tatyana Petrovna?'

'I was busy in the operating room,' said I, without looking up from my hand. I liked Marie Pavlovna well enough. But benevolent visits by high personages made me uncomfortable. I suspected they did more for the personage's self-esteem than for the morale of the wounded.

'Yes, of course, you work terribly hard. We all admire your high-mindedness. Forgive an old courtier's love of gossip, dear child.' Vera Kirilovna smiled ingratiatingly.

'The commander in chief dismissed!' Zinaida Mikhailovna had mounted a campaign to get her son appointed to the general staff. On behalf of Kolenka, that mother-mouse could move mountains.

'Nikolay Nikolayevich may not be a brilliant tactician' – the Generalissimo may not be very bright, was what Grandmaman meant – 'but he's enormously popular. My son won't like this latest bit of news. Pierre was already upset over the Kokovtsov affair. Imagine, in time of war, having an octogenarian for prime minister. And an arch-conservative, an enemy of the Duma in the bargain!'

'Ah, but Monsieur Goremykin, who is a very shrewd old gentleman, is on the best terms with "that man",' Vera Kirilovna purred. 'What better recommendation can there be for office?'

I remembered Father's prediction that ministerial appointments would be made according to the degree of adherence to Alexandra's seer.

'Are you quite sure, Vera Kirilovna, that His Imperial Highness

Nikolay Nikolayevich is to be replaced?' Zinaida Mikhailovna was furrowed with worry.

'His Majesty still trusts him. But Nikolay Nikolayevich has powerful enemies, and not at court alone. The War Minister hates our beloved commander in chief to such an extent that evil tongues are saying he is purposefully withholding munitions from the western front to bring disgrace on his generalship.'

'Lord God of mine, how is that possible?' Zinaida Mikhailovna exclaimed in Russian.

Both Grandmaman and I laid down our cards and stared at Vera Kirilovna.

'Well, look out, Vera Kirilovna,' Grandmaman growled. 'Such terrible statements are not lightly made.'

'*I* do not make them.' Vera Kirilovna lifted a proud chin. 'But you must admit, my very dear Anna Vladimirovna, that the munitions shortage is a national scandal. Is it any wonder it gives rise to the most far-fetched suppositions?'

'Sukhomlinov ought to be hung.' Grandmaman was aroused. 'Pierre did his utmost to get that gambler and lecher dismissed. Much good it did! Whose turn is it to play?'

'Mine, Grandmaman.' I had feared for her blood pressure and was relieved to see her calm down.

'One does wonder what His Majesty can be thinking of, keeping such an incompetent minister of war,' Zinaida Mikhailovna murmured.

'Constantinople, *chère* Zinaida. His Majesty dreams of adding Constantinople to the imperial crown.' Vera Kirilovna had the answer ready. 'While our gallant troops lack rifles and shells, our sovereign makes grandiose plans for the future peace Russia will impose on Europe. Marie Pavlovna had it from Monsieur Paléologue after his last audience with His Majesty. The French ambassador tells Her Imperial Highness everything.'

'Enough babbling, Vera Kirilovna. Play!'

I saw that the murky waters of intrigue, through which my former *éducatrice* swam like a fish, were polluted beyond anything I had sensed in girlhood. I was filled with even greater scorn for a social order that permitted war, that glorified suffering, and lied about war's squalor and senselessness. I might have sympathized with revolutionaries had they not been themselves peddlers of violence and of another kind of falsehood. Yes, falsehood was in all the words and speeches for and against war. Falsehood was at the very heart of things! Better to dress a gangrenous wound, better to drain pus or hold a basin to a patient's mouth to vomit in than go about like Vera Kirilovna, scented and smiling among liars!

However much I became aware of the grave shortcomings of our government and its supreme rulers, I succumbed afresh none the less to the charm of the Tsar's family on each visit to Tsarskoye.

In contrast to the dismay and discontent prevailing in Petrograd, the familial circle in the Alexander Palace was in the best of spirits that winter. Aleksey Nikolayevich was far into his tenth year, a year considered critical for haemophiliacs since most did not live beyond it. He seemed as well as he was impetuous and handsome. He had his comical donkey, his cocker and his cat to amuse him. He was allowed to play with the sons of Derevenko, one of his two sailor-nurses. These, besides his sisters, were his only companions. The exclusion of his own cousins, the sons of the Tsar's sister Grand Duchess Xenia, who lived nearby, was taken as proof of Alexandra's jealous mistrust of the imperial family. It reinforced the dislike, if not the hatred, in which she was held once more by its members.

Relieved of her obsessive preoccupation with the Tsarevich's health, Alexandra now displayed a new energy. While the younger children had their lessons with tutors, the Empress with her two elder daughters worked every morning in her hospital in town. Her determination inspired respect in the staff, if not in the general public, which rightly thought an empress had more important things to do.

Olga and Tatyana Nikolayevna were also busy with their respective committees for the relief of refugees. The make-believe infatuations with their dancing partners on the imperial yacht were now far in the pre-war past. Prince Carol of Rumania had not been able to win Olga. It would have taken a more compelling figure to loosen the bond of love and loyalty that tied her and her siblings to their parents. They were a world unto themselves, dependent only on one another for their emotional needs. Yet, I sometimes wondered about my namesake.

The beauty of the family could not boast a single rejected suitor. The only society ball Tatyana Nikolayevna had attended was my graduation ball. Not that she confessed to me a longing for romance. After all, the times called for selflessness and sacrifice. I was a professional nurse, she and her sister were volunteers. We had all three become acquainted with pain, disfigurement and death. Boys did not enter into our conversation.

My romance with Stefan, however, was on another level. Mysterious, fraught with obstacles, it was probably the only secret the sisters kept from their parents.

'What have you heard from Stefan?' was always their first whispered question when we had a rare moment in private.

Olga's tone would be teasing and curious, but Tanik followed my romantic involvement with intensity.

I was now maid-of-honour to Tatyana Nikolayevna, a function more honorific than actual, since I had more crucial responsibilities than to wait on royalty. We treated it rather as a joke. To the credit of the family, in my eyes at least, no one cared a whit about etiquette.

The lake in the park of the palace, where the Grand Duchesses liked to row, was frozen, so we skated instead. I soon raced around as of old, Vera Kirilovna not being there to restrain me – she had become *persona non grata* at Tsarskoye by dint of flaunting her loyalty to Marie Fyodorovna. Fourteen-year-old Anastasia tried to emulate me and took no end of spills. Aleksey watched enviously from the bank under the eye of Derevenko or Nagorny. Skating was far too dangerous for him.

'Gosh, Tata, you are colossal!' he said with a blush when I unlaced my skates.

I took his mittened hand and all six of us ran in to tea in Alexandra's mauve boudoir with the portrait of Marie Antoinette. The knick-knacks that filled it reflected the taste of the former Princess Alix, brought up at Queen Victoria's court, the icons the fervour of the Empress Alexandra's conversion. We gathered about the chaise longue on which she lay after her prescribed afternoon rest, and had a cosy tea. I managed to overlook Anya Vyrubova, who was ensconced more than ever in the bosom of the Tsar's family since the railway accident that had left her a cripple. That she had recovered at all was attributed to the miraculous intervention of Rasputin. Her personality was so vapid that I found it difficult to remember her intimate association with 'that man' of sinister repute. It was easier, as Vera Kirilovna said, to pretend he did not exist. It was easy to forget, in the midst of this handsome and close-knit, model first family, that the picture of health and sanity it conveyed was as illusory as the pink glow in Aleksey's cheeks and more false than any high-society scene.

At the end of May, I celebrated my eighteenth birthday with my namesake at Tsarskoye – over were the days of spring at Livadia, the Tsar's palace in the Crimea, of summer at Peterhof followed by the cruise in the Finnish fjords and by autumn shoots at Bialowieza and Spala. Tatyana Nikolayevna tried to dissuade me from going to Poland.

Taking me aside after the modest festivities for our joint birthday, she said, as we strolled in the Chinese garden, 'Tata, in spite of the communiqués – "our valiant and victorious armies are shortening their supply lines and so on" – Papa has admitted that things are looking bad for us in central Poland. Veslawa – I looked it up especially on his war map – is now directly in the line of the Austro-German advance. It may soon fall to the enemy. It's awfully dangerous.'

'You, Tanik, talking about danger?' I looked at my namesake, willowy in the white lace dress she had worn for the photographers, yet as fearless, I knew, as she was feminine. 'You surprise me.'

'You're right.' She gave her pixie smile. 'I can never pretend to you. My real reason ... it's not easy to say ... I don't want to hurt you, Tata ... I know how much in love you are ...' She stopped and faced me on the path.

I faltered. 'Does His Majesty suspect about me and Stevie? Is he angry?'

'No, no, Papa has no suspicion. But I warned you from the beginning, Tata. Prince Stefan is a Pole, a Veslawski. His family led two rebellions against us. How can we depend on his allegiance? The Polish situation is such a muddle.'

Polish autonomy is threatened, I thought. 'Tanik, what do you know exactly? What have you heard?'

'I've not heard, I don't know anything exactly. Olga is more *au courant* than I – but even she can't put her finger on it. Yet we both agree there's a change in the air, a different mood from that of last summer, in the Winter Palace, remember?'

How could I forget that exalted moment when I had felt one with my sovereigns, my people, and my previous friend? Now, as then, her hand reached for mine and clasped it tight.

'I'll always remember, Tanik.' Whatever happened, no matter how rudely or irrevocably the mystic union of monarch and nation was splintered, nothing and no one, no, not even Stefan, could drive a wedge between my royal namesake and me. 'And I'll always remain loyal to you and Russia,' I added hotly.

'I never doubted that.' Another smile slid my way from underneath the broad-brimmed hat. 'I just don't want you to be unhappy.'

We rejoined the imperial family, the suite and the handful of convalescing officers from Alexandra's hospital who had been invited. There was no mention of retreat, of munitions shortage, of an impending shake-up of the high command, of the change in the wind Tatyana Nikolayevna had alluded to that boded ill for my love. But I was newly conscious of the unreality underlying the life and outlook of Russia's rulers.

My departure for the war zone now met with the opposition of Grandmaman. But seeing my resolve, Tanik – my true friend – discarded her role of reasonable adviser and joined me in my petition to His Majesty. I also appealed to Grand Duchess Marie Pavlovna. At the tactful urging of both my godparents, Grandmaman grudgingly withdrew her objection.

At the beginning of June, I packed my kit bag: a change of uniform, a rubber basin and gloves, a toilet case, the New Testament in suede cover with a gold clasp and our embossed arms given me by Grandmaman for my first communion, *A Sportsman's Sketches* by Turgenev, a box of cartridges and a pearl-handled revolver engraved with my initials and crest, an eighteenth-birthday gift from Father. I said goodbye to Bobby – faithful companion of my Polish holidays – and to a weeping Nyanya. Accompanied by an older nurse, I left the Warsaw Station in a modest *wagon-lit* compartment since our private railroad car had been placed, for the duration, at the disposal of the War Ministry.

12

Veslawow had been just north of a German thrust across the Vistula the previous November. The German army had come within ten *versts* of Lublin. But as I rode, that spring of 1915, from the station along the main avenue lined with the stately limes and through the City Hall Square, I saw no sign of war.

How pleasingly familiar were the baroque façades! How my Polish half quickened on that drive to my childhood stronghold, seat of my beloved lord! And straight upon that proud and joyous thought came my namesake's tender warning: 'Prince Stefan is a Pole, a Veslawski . . . the Polish situation is such a muddle . . . I just don't want you to be unhappy.'

'I'll always remain loyal to Russia!' I had sworn readily under her spell. But, if I were faced with a choice between Russia and Stefan, what *would* I do?

I felt cold in my warm uniform. It was an unthinkable choice. I swept it to the mental back closet for the inconceivable and irreconcilable, the closet next to that larger one already full of the incomprehensible and cruel.

At the end of the climb to the Veslawa plateau, the car rolled on to the sandy driveway and the palace with its crenellated keep and ivied arcades rose at the far end of the pond. In the park, men in grey dressing gowns sat on stone benches or hobbled down the alleys accompanied by nurses in white veils. Ambulance lorries marked with a large red cross stood in the court of honour.

Great-Aunt Catherine, tall and frail in lilac, met me on the portico with Aunt Sophie in nurse's dress.

'Our Tanyussia a sister of mercy! How proud my little angel would have been!' cooed the old lady.

After I had bathed and changed into the fresh uniform laid out in a former maid's room on the third storey, now occupied by the Swiss hospital staff of fifty, Aunt Sophie took me through the wards below. But for a small dining room and sitting room, the entire ground floor had been converted into wards, each with its own dispensary and bathroom. It was more luxurious than our own hospital, supposedly the most modern in Petrograd. The beds, on wide roller casters, could be wheeled into surgery, sparing the patient the agony of being moved on and off the stretcher. My professional eye approved the excellent lighting and the array of cylinders of inhalation gases in the operating room, the former pantry. The X-ray room had the latest machines. Everywhere reigned order, quiet and cleanliness – the last our only protection as yet against infection. I felt at ease and in my element.

In the former schoolroom off the library, however, a shock awaited me. Here lay a dozen boy amputees, wards of the lancers, the Veslawski escutcheon sewed on their gowns.

'Are you going to give us a bath?' they greeted me. 'Are you a princess too?' 'Can you play dominoes?' 'What colour is your hair?'

I promised to come back without my head covering, and tell them stories. But once outside, I looked at Aunt in anguished disbelief.

'A school was shelled at Sandomierz,' she said. 'Caring for children is the most difficult part of nursing. You'll get used to it in time.'

I did not think I would ever get used to the sight of little boys with missing arms and legs. But in the morning I was all the readier to scrub for work. To do something concrete and positive was the only way to make the horror bearable.

All through June and July the Austro-Germans under von Mackensen, with the support of artillery barrages that pulverized the Russian trenches, continued their advance north between the rivers Vistula, Bug and San. By the middle of July the distant boom of cannon could be heard and from the palace towers after dark, shell bursts could be seen on the horizon.

One afternoon in the third week of July the sound of a troop of horses brought all who could walk out on the galleries.

A nurse ran into the operating room, where Aunt Sophie was assisting in the rush of fresh cases from the front. 'It's the Lord Prince, Your Serene Ladyship!'

Aunt removed mask and gloves and asked the surgeon to excuse us. We had just finished a case. We hastened into the central vestibule. Uncle Stan walked in with the gait of a sleepwalker, followed by three staff officers even more stupefied than he. All four were covered with red dust.

'How is it you're still here, Sophie?' Uncle Stan asked in English with weary exasperation. 'The Germans are at Jozefow. They may be here any day.'

'We're safe, as you see.' She laid a hand on his arm and looked anxiously into his drawn face. 'Come in and rest, my lord.'

'I can't . . . I need coffee . . . must get things organized.' But he let Aunt Sophie lead him off after acknowledging my presence with a nod and a laconic, 'Stevie's with the men, outside.'

I went out on the portico and saw a strange scene. All about the court of honour and on the grassy borders of the pond, men and horses lay or stood as though under a spell. The animals stretched their necks, spread their forelegs, shook themselves violently and buckled their knees to roll – saddle and full pack still on their back. Yet others tugged at the reins and strained to drink from the pond. The men sprawled on the grass or leaned against their mounts. Many had handkerchiefs tied about their mouths against the dust. Some had bandages about the head or hands.

Among these torpid figures a few officers moved with energy. I made my way to the most energetic, a very tall, broad-shouldered young lieutenant who was lifting a sergeant to his feet by the collar and saying fiercely into his face, 'Sir Sergeant, if you don't march your men to the village and bivouac on the cow pasture at once, I'll have your stripes, word of a Veslawski.'

'*Tak, panie poruczniku*, yes, Sir Lieutenant.' The sergeant began rousing his men.

'Sir Lieutenant,' I said diffidently.

Stevie turned around and looked at me exactly as his father had looked at his mother, with displeasure. 'You . . . here?'

I was crestfallen. 'Is there anything I can do, Stevie?'

'You can bring buckets of water to wake up these mules!' And he took no further notice of me.

The squadrons were at last marched off to bivouac. By dusk their fires glowed cheerfully about the palace grounds. The colours were marched to headquarters in the palace cellars and squadron captains rode up to report to their colonel. Stevie was assigned to staff duty and came to report after dark. Aunt Sophie and I met him in the vestibule. She opened her arms in a graceful maternal gesture, but he did not embrace her.

She understood his reticence. 'I've seen you even dirtier.'

His head dropped and a brown lock of hair fell into his eye as it used to when he was a boy. She drew his head down, kissed his unshaven cheeks and murmured childhood endearments.

He held her about the shoulders and repeated in English and Polish, 'Mother, *Matka*, Mummy, *Mamussia*.'

The fighting man had lapsed into childishness. I was moved and piqued. Will he ever love me as much as he loves his mother? I wondered. And I remembered his curt reception.

'Have you quarrelled?' my perceptive aunt asked.

'I was beastly to Tanya.'

'Oh, no, you were busy.' All was well.

Stevie returned my smile. Then he tottered like a drunkard and yawned uncontrollably.

'Come, Stevie boy, to bed.' Aunt Sophie took his arm.

'I must report to the Colonel.'

'Your father is in bed already. Tanyussia, take his other arm. Adam!' she called to the red-haired batman who lay snoring on his lieutenant's bags.

Adam was up with a start, thinking himself a valet still. 'Her Serene Ladyship desires?' Then, recollecting his new duties, he shouldered the bags.

We marched Stevie upstairs. Having put him to bed, Aunt looked in on me.

'Is he asleep?' I asked.

'Like a baby. I said his prayers for him.'

'Auntie, did you notice, his hair is curly again?'

'Yes, poor Stevie, he hates it so.' She smiled, then looked grave. I knew that she too was thinking of the strong young body that might be fearfully maimed.

'Auntie, Mother, what does it all mean? Why must there be war?'

'I don't know, child. Women don't understand war. It's unbearable, yet it must be borne. I suppose that's life: a trial of strength, a test of valour. Now go to sleep. The day after tomorrow, we must evacuate.'

'Don't you find it awful to leave Veslawa to the enemy?'

'Yes. That too is war, and must be borne. But tonight my Stan is home. And nothing seems quite so bad.'

This, then, is life? I mused in the dark after Aunt had kissed me and gone. A trial of strength, a test of valour.

Stevie had met his test on the battlefield. Mine had not yet come. It would come soon, in the field hospital. That was my arena.

And after the war, when we were married? He would fight on for his people's welfare – their freedom had been promised them by the Tsar. Tanik's father could not go back on his word!

I would continue to fight against pain and death. There was plenty of work for us both. We would have children, of course – help would not be lacking to raise them. We would experience life at its most joyful as well as its saddest. We would be complete beings. We would be real, not made-up persons. We would be equal. We would belong in the twentieth century. The madness of war would pass. Its very horror would render war obsolete. It would be the best age the world had seen yet.

In the meantime, there were the boy amputees who must be evacuated tomorrow. Veslawa must be left to the enemy. It was senseless, it was awful, yet it had to be borne. And when one bore it by the side of the man one loved, nothing seemed quite so bad.

Early next morning riders set off to all neighbouring villages to summon the elders to the palace on the morrow. Foraging parties were sent out, the horses tended to, and the men given leave to say goodbye to their families. Wounded were evacuated and fresh casualties loaded directly on to the hospital train standing on a siding at Veslawow Station to take them to the Catholic Hospital at Minsk. There Aunt Sophie and I, supposedly, would arrive later.

As I drove in the ambulance lorry with the graver casualties, past silent townspeople lining the sidewalk, I formulated my plan. At the last minute, I would let Aunt Sophie go on without me and attach myself to the ambulance unit of the Veslawski lancers. From a dispatch received by Uncle the previous night, which he had communicated to us in part at breakfast, I knew that he and his adjutants were to attend the meeting of Father's general staff at corps headquarters on the afternoon of the following day. Although Uncle did not divulge its location, I knew it was no more than an hour's ride south.

In his dispatch, Father also added confidentially: 'All civilians under my jurisdiction are urged not to panic and flee. I will oppose the scorched-earth policy dreamed up by our tacticians at GHQ. We have no right to scorch Polish earth. Nor is it to our advantage. Roads flooded with refugees impede the army's orderly retreat. Refugee hordes create a health hazard, lower morale, and pose the threat of social unrest. The Germans have behaved correctly in occupied territory. The stories of atrocities are false. Use your prestige and influence, Stan, to spare your people at least, and especially the Jews, the sufferings I am powerless to prevent elsewhere.'

At noon, a proclamation by Prince Stanislaw was read in the City Hall Square. It urged the population not to panic and flee but remain in their homes, preparing a shelter against shelling in the cellar or garden, with a store of provisions and water. Shopkeepers were forbidden to charge exorbitant prices and lancers were posted to prevent looting. Townspeople hid their valuables and spent the last of their currency.

In mid-afternoon, the novel sight of aircraft brought everyone out into the street. They were two German Fokker monoplanes of the type hitherto used in reconnaissance, which were evidently trying to bomb the rail point. The single explosive each pilot dropped out of the cockpit by hand fell wide of the mark. No one was hurt. A machine gun was mounted on the station's roof but the aeroplanes did not return. Children took pieces of the bomb casing for souvenirs. Parental supervision was lax and they ran about as on holiday. It was again very hot.

In the palace, last-minute packing of valuables – most had been stored in secret underground vaults – was in furious progress. Aunt Sophie dismayed the majordomo by bidding him uncrate the silver and china needed for the night's farewell banquet. She ordered the best wines brought up from the cellar and a menu of *chlodnik* – the cold Polish soup of greens with cream – carp, partridge, a side of roast beef, cheeses and fresh berries. She put on a gown of white brocade and the coronet of the Veslawski princesses worn only on state occasions. She lent me one of her Parisian gowns, of white chiffon *à la grecque*, which fit with two small tucks at the bust.

'You're a fine nurse, Tanyussia, but remember, you're a woman first,' said Aunt. 'And a woman likes to be beautiful for her man.'

I did not think a Parisian gown could make me beautiful, and I did not want to admit to being a woman first. But this was no time to contradict Aunt Sophie.

In my borrowed dress, my hair wound with borrowed pearls on top of my head, I went down with Aunt into the vestibule, where a spruced-up Stevie stood waiting.

Pinned on his khaki tunic were the crosses of St Anne and St Stanislaw he had already earned in just six months of battle. His boots shone, his hair lay flat as a helmet, and his shaved cheeks were again baby-smooth. He offered me his arm to pass through the enfilade of reception rooms now stripped of tapestries, portraits and chandeliers, in which the last beds were being dismantled for shipping.

In the smaller dining room adjoining the banquet hall, the Regency table had been set with gold-bordered Venetian plates, and silver candelabra lit. The Canalettos on the walls were gone, but the roses in the garden beyond the loggia were there unchanged. The boom of cannon might have been taken for distant thunder and the glow of fires on the horizon for the setting sun.

At the head of the table, Aunt Sophie in brocade gown and coronet, presided regally over the officers of Uncle Stan's staff and the members of the household. Uncle, at the opposite end, told political jokes with his normal, sad-hound air. Elsewhere, the conversation in French was about the theatre still drawing crowds in Warsaw, the latest French novel and the newest Italian film. Discussion then turned to the Petersburg gossip about the recent impeachment of the War Minister, General Sukhomlinov. This topic attracted general attention.

'The charge of negligence and incompetence is alleged to have been a cover-up for more serious accusations,' said Casimir's father, Sir Casimir Paszek. 'Only the Tsar's protection saves Sukhomlinov from being tried.'

'Yes, we know the War Minister was dear to His Majesty.' Uncle Stan treated this monstrous subject as lightly as any other. 'Personally, I don't believe him guilty of treason. But that he was guilty of taking bribes should not surprise us. A fat old man needs a lot of money to keep a pretty young wife happy.'

Lust again, possessing the possessors of power, I thought. And because of an old man's lechery, our men lack ammunition and rifles to defend themselves. How can the Tsar excuse such a man? He and his kind deserve to be shot. I grew stern. Then I remembered that ugly thoughts spoiled my face, and Father's other injunction, not to judge in haste. Sukhomlinov may be innocent. I have nothing to say about that, or anything being discussed. Stevie is such a brilliant talker. Will he think me provincial and gauche? I glanced up at him across the table. No, he seems happy just to have me here.

After the fruit and cheese, Uncle rose, and so did all the men. He lifted his glass to Aunt and said, in Polish this time, 'We thank the Serene Princess our beloved wife for this evening of peace in the midst of war. Several years may pass before we are gathered here again under this roof, in a similar harmonious and handsome setting. Some of us may never see another such gathering. But that it will again take place in its essentials, I have no doubt. Our palace has stood through invasion by Turk, Swede and Prussian and through Russian repression of two insurrections. It will stand through this last invasion. As our palace and our family have endured, so have our people, who have given us their trust.

'We have been promised by His Imperial Majesty the Tsar through our Commander in Chief, Grand Duke Nicholas, full autonomy within the Russian Empire once we have won the war. So long as the Teuton menaces us to the west we must make common cause with our brother Slav. We ask only to be treated as full brothers, not as stepbrothers to be kept in correctional school under police rule. His Majesty the Emperor gave me his word on it a year ago. And I in turn make this pledge to you now, and to those officers not present here who have joined me of their free will: after victory, freedom. I shall not return unless I keep this pledge. And if death prevents me, my son Stefan shall fulfil it.'

'I swear it!' Stevie cried.

'To victory then, and to our country's unification and freedom,' said Uncle Stan dispassionately, and drank.

The women also stood for the toast. It was a solemn and exalted moment.

Uncle then walked around the table to kiss Aunt's hand. He was followed by each member of the household in order of precedence and each officer in order of seniority. This ritual courtesy performed, Aunt Sophie suggested Great-Aunt Catherine step out into the garden with Tanyussia and Stevie.

After a short walk, the old lady sat down on a stone bench under a rose arbour to rest. 'Go on with your walk, my little ones, go on.'

Stevie took my hand and drew me down to the terraced gardens on the other side of the hedge of limes bordering the turf.

'It's not right to leave Great-Aunt Catherine,' I protested.

'You silly, why d'you think Mummy sent us out with her? Grandmother isn't as unromantic as you.' Then, sniffing, 'Perfume, for once, not chloroform,' Stevie said. 'Well, I suppose I may be thankful for the stuff one of these days.'

'Don't!' I begged.

'Why, would it upset you to see me with an arm or leg blown off, or both? Would it startle you to see my brain exposed or my intestines spilling out? There was a fellow like that walking around the battlefield with his intestines in both hands.' He went on with these ghastly descriptions, exactly as he had described tortures as a boy, meanwhile observing the effect.

It was tremendous. 'Stop, I can't bear it!' I covered my ears.

'And I thought you were such a cold-blooded thing who enjoyed cutting people up! Would you really cry if I were killed? Would you put fresh flowers on my grave every day as Grandmother does on Grandfather's?'

With a moan I sank down on the top step of the stairs connecting the terraces.

Stevie sat down a few steps below and looked up at me, hugely pleased. Underneath the smooth helmet of hair was the boy with curly locks who loved to tease and torment me.

'You're horrid,' I said. 'You're as revulsive as ever.' I used the childhood word.

'Am I really? Do you truly loathe me, Tatyana mine?' he asked in another deep and beautiful voice. 'Tell me.'

'I . . . absolutely loathe you.'

'Say it once more, just this way.'

My hands about my knees, I looked into his face, so full of boyish malice a moment ago, so tender and humble now.

'May I kiss your lovely little feet?' He seized my ankles.

'My feet aren't little, they're big, and there's nothing lovely about them.' I tugged in vain at his hands.

'Everything about you is lovely, my Tatyana.' He dropped light kisses on my legs. 'You're wearing Mummy's dress. I can smell it. It smells even more delicious on you.'

'Stevie, stop it!' I beat down on his head. When this made no impression, I pulled it back by the hair.

'You may pull my hair. Pain becomes pleasure inflicted by your hand.'

My hands flew off his head and he caught them. 'May I at least kiss your hands?'

I pulled away, bracing my back against the stone balustrade of the stairs.

'It won't do to pull, let me have them nicely, nice now, not so stiff, that's better, a little more,' he said, in a tone so insistent and tender that I could not help but obey.

I went limp and leaned against the balustrade. How easily he had robbed me again of my will! I was ready for anything . . .

To my chagrin, all he did was to kiss my hands and rise, pulling me up. He put an arm about my shoulder, I put mine around his waist, and we walked slowly around the edge of the uppermost terrace, the sound of our steps very clear on the fine gravel and sand. The scent of roses and flowering limes was strong. The first stars had appeared in the sky and the first glow-worms in the grass. Grasshoppers and frogs were tuning up for the nightly summer concert, war or no war. The peace and coolness of twilight banished the hot and uneasy languor on the steps.

I laid my head on Stevie's shoulder and he said softly, 'It's good, Tanya, ah?'

'Yes, wonderful.'

'Tanya, d'you love Veslawa?'

'Better than any place on earth.'

'We'll come back as soon as this stupid war's over and be married, Tsar or no Tsar. And I never want to leave Veslawa again.'

'You don't like playing war any more, Stevie?'

'It's no fun at all.'

'Tell me what it's like.'

'It's waiting hours for you don't know what, you don't know who, you don't know why – being filthy dirty – sloshing through mud to the waist – getting frostbite and dysentery – marching an entire day to be told to fall back at night – digging a position to abandon it.'

'And the battle?'

'You can be in the middle of it and not even know it. When the bugle blows the charge you're wild for a moment, then machine guns start popping all around. If you get over the barbed wire alive and land on top of the enemy you slash away with your sabre and that's rather satisfying as long as you don't look at the faces of the chaps under you. But it's over in a flash. Around you everything's a gory mess and you wonder what the devil's the sense of it.'

'Are you ever afraid?'

'Not before the charge. But afterwards, it makes me feel queasy. If I'm ever crippled, I'll kill myself.' He seized my arms and turned me towards him. 'I want to be whole, for you.'

'You will be,' I said weakly – what a strong grip he had! 'And give me fine sons.'

'How many sons?' He smiled and walked on.

'Peter, Stefan, Stanislaw and Aleksey. And four girls, Sophie, Tatyana, Anna and Catherine ... You don't want so many children?' I asked as he looked astonished.

'I'd love it. But what about you? Mother nearly died having me alone.'

'You were awfully large.'

'Yes, I was a real monstro. So you're not afraid of having babies?'

I thought childbirth a natural physiological process. 'You know, Stevie, I used to not want children, but recently, I've begun to think about it.'

'So have I,' said he.

I did not tell him the rest of my fantasy, how we would both work and be equal and so on. There would be time enough, and it did not seem as urgent somehow, or even real, in the dreamlike dusk, in the rose garden of the beautiful palace where we had played as children, and where we now saw our children at play. My pre-war vision of life as noble and beautiful as a legend spread before me and I heard again that stirring music of fife and strings, with a triumphant pealing of bells. Stevie raised his hand as in a polonaise and I placed mine over his. Slowly and solemnly, hand over hand, we returned to the arbour where Great-Aunt Catherine sat in frail and aged dignity, holding a white rose.

'White, pure and luminous as you.' She handed it to me. 'I picked it for you.'

'Thank you, Aunt Catherine, it is lovely.' I tucked it in my hair and we sat down on either side of the old lady.

'My roses, who'll look after them now?' she went on as if to herself. 'And who'll put flowers on my little angel's grave? No, I cannot.'

'Cannot what, Grandmother?' Stevie asked.

'Leave Veslawa. I must stay.'

'Aunt Catherine!' I cried, and, 'Father will never permit it,' Stevie said.

'A mother does not ask her son's permission. Please, don't say anything. I will speak, when the moment is right.' She put her transparent, blue-veined hand over each of ours. 'My dearest ones, I am eighty-five years old. I may never see you again. But I know you will be very happy, as I was with my little angel.' Stevie and I exchanged a look at this touching fiction. 'And if I do not live to see it, you two will see his dreams for our beloved country realized.'

She rose and walked towards the rear terrace, leaning on us as though to feel our young strength. At the head of the great staircase we stopped for a moment to look down on the turf unrolling its velvet carpet between the lime trees in white bloom.

Great-Aunt recalled the Harvest Festival night on which I had gone to sleep on my fierce great-uncle's lap. 'How he loved you,' she said. 'There'll be no festival this year, for the first time since we returned from exile. Our poor people, what sufferings await them!'

Sadly, she nodded, then turned towards the palace. The storey-high French windows down the length of the vast façade were all shuttered. As we passed into the marble vestibule now empty of tapestries and armoured knights, I felt the dismal silence and emptiness of the great structure. All thirty of us still remaining attended a service in the chapel. The chaplain then heard the Veslawskis' confession and we spent a half-hour in family intimacy in Aunt Sophie's sitting room before retiring.

The following morning the village elders summoned by Uncle Stan began to arrive, some after travelling half the night. As their high-wheeled, boat-shaped carts drove into the court of honour, platoons of Veslawski lancers passed them riding south, towards the front. Uncle received each elder for a few minutes alone in his study and at noon they were all invited to share the family's last meal, served in the servants' refectory from the regimental field kitchen. Aunt Sophie, in grey habit and white headdress and bib embroidered with the red cross, presided as serenely at the long table covered with an oil cloth and set with tin plates as she had over the banquet the previous night.

At the end of the meal Uncle Stan rose to say a few words of farewell, promised the victorious return of the lancers and a redistribution of his lands among his people. The elder longest in office answered with renewed pledges of allegiance to the Veslawski family.

When the cheers called for by the elder had died down, Great-Aunt Catherine raised her hands to command attention and said in her sweet, elderly quaver, 'Gentlemen elders, in the name of my husband, your late Prince Leon, I thank you for your pledge of loyalty to his son and mine. My son's duty as a soldier prevents him from staying with his people in this time of trial. I am only a woman and far along in years, and I cannot presume to take his place. But go back and tell our people I am staying here, in our palace, and will look after their interests, insofar as I am able with the help of Our Lord Jesus Christ.'

There was a stir among the elders. Their spokesman then made the old lady a deep bow.

'Blessed be Your Serene Ladyship in the name of Jesus Christ,' he said, and the elders, repeating his words, bowed all together.

'Mother, what you're proposing is out of the question,' Uncle Stan said softly in English.

'Gentlemen elders,' he began but Great-Aunt Catherine said, 'Stan, I command you to be silent.'

'The Lord protect you,' finished Uncle Stan in Polish to the elders, who filed out. 'Sophie' – he then appealed to his wife, his own great authority failing him at this unwonted show of authority on the part of his mother – 'will you please explain to Mother this notion of hers is absurd?'

'I don't think it absurd,' said Aunt Sophie, coming to stand at Princess Catherine's side. 'And I believe I'd do the same, in Mother's place.'

'So would I!' I moved to the other side of Great-Aunt so that the three of us faced my uncle in common resolve.

The chaplain, the palace physician, the majordomo, the master of ceremonies and a half-dozen personal servants now expressed their wish to remain with the Dowager Princess. Uncle Stan looked around at them, stood with a fine finger to his drooping moustache, then, with an elegant gesture of helplessness, gave his consent. We all followed him out on to the portico.

In the court of honour stood a mounted platoon of lancers, colours to the fore, an ambulance wagon with a white canvas top painted with a red cross, and an open carriage with an armed soldier on the box beside Tomasz the coachman. After embracing Princess Catherine, my aunt and I got into the carriage and sat putting on our grey cotton gloves, I with hasty hands, Aunt Sophie as steadily as though she were going on an ordinary voyage.

'Well, little son, it's time,' Princess Catherine said.

Uncle Stan bent his head heavily and long. Holding it, his mother kissed his forehead, then made the sign of the cross.

Turning to the chaplain, Uncle Stan received his blessing on bent knee, then he lightly descended the portico steps and as lightly mounted the bay thoroughbred his orderly held for him. The officers of his staff mounted in turn, and the aide-de-camp attached to Aunt Sophie took his place in the carriage facing us. The chaplain made a large sign of the cross in the air and Uncle Stan gave the order to march.

The colours moved forward, followed by Uncle Stan between Stevie and a staff major, the carriage with Aunt Sophie and me, the platoon three abreast, and at the tail end of the caravan the ambulance wagon with its white top. The villagers lined the border of lawn down the length of the pond, the women pressing their aprons to their eyes, the old men bowing, caps to their chest, the children jumping up and down and waving. All able-bodied men had joined the regiment. Aunt inclined her head in a graceful and stately greeting, which I did my best to imitate. As the caravan, colours to the fore, rounded the far end of the pond and headed into the woods, I looked back at the palace, framed between towering trees. On the portico I could make out a knot of people, in front of them the frail figure of Princess Catherine in her lilac dress and of the chaplain in his black cassock. Then they were lost in a blur of tears.

The City Hall Square was densely packed when our caravan rode up. A motorcar waited by the covered well to transfer Aunt and me from the carriage. Uncle Stan briefly addressed the crowd from horseback, announcing that his mother was staying on and urging once more that everyone do the same.

As he dismounted to help Aunt Sophie into the car, a grey-bearded Jew in a black caftan pushed past the crowd and threw himself at Uncle's feet. 'Serene and Mighty Lord Protector of our people, we hear that elsewhere Russian soldiers have sent our people east in cars not fit for cattle. Some have died on the way. Others have not been heard from again. Oh Mighty Lord, save us and our little ones in the name of the Lord Jehovah.'

'There will be no forced evacuation of any of our people.' Uncle Stan spoke with the British accent that became particularly noticeable when he was under stress. 'I have the word of the Russian corps commander, General Prince Silomirsky. The Princess my mother will remain to look after you, Jew and gentile alike. She will do all she can to ease your common plight. You must help one another now, during these cruel times. If we survive them, we shall be free! Goodbye. God keep you, Ibraim.' Uncle Stan extended his hand.

Ibraim took it in both of his, then kissed it tearfully. He made Aunt a deep bow and would have kissed the hem of her habit had she not forestalled him by stepping back gracefully, even as she smiled and spoke kindly words of farewell. Ibraim withdrew.

Aunt Sophie kissed Stefan and gave her husband her hand. Her great pallor alone betrayed her emotion. A soldier at attention held open the door of the motorcar and she took her place in the corner, waiting for me to make my adieus in turn.

I had no intention of returning with Aunt to the civilian rear. 'Uncle Stan,' I said rapidly, 'I'm not going with Aunt Sophie. I'm going to join Father at the front and work as a field nurse.'

'This is no time for childish nonsense, miss. The front's no place for a girl of eighteen,' he said in his most chilling tones.

'If Princess Catherine, who is eighty-five, can stay in the war zone, so can a girl of eighteen.'

Visibly shaken, Uncle looked as always in domestic dilemmas to his wife. 'You're keeping everyone waiting, Princess,' she said coolly.

'Forgive me, Aunt. But I'm not going.' And I moved away from the car door.

In the next moment I was horrified at my defiance. But Aunt Sophie motioned the aide to join her. The crowd parted for the slow passage of the car. Graciously inclining her head to left and right, she drove eastward out of the square. Like my great-aunt I had chosen the moment well. If their life depended on it, no Veslawski, prince or princess, would make a public scene.

'We'll see what General Prince Silomirsky has to say about this,' Uncle said to me frigidly. And, to Stevie, 'Take Tanya to the ambulance wagon and detail two men from the colour platoon to escort her to corps headquarters. You know the route. You'll report to me there with the staff. Dismissed.'

Stevie saluted and, taking me firmly by the arm, he cleared a passage through the crowd to the ambulance wagon.

'Pluck up, sweet,' he said and helped me up beside the driver.

The column of lancers moved on. Stevie mounted the chestnut thoroughbred Adam held for him and rode at a parade trot beside the wagon. We rode down the tree-lined boulevard between weeping and waving crowds. The sky darkened, a gust of wind sent lime petals to the ground and the townspeople home to close windows left open in the heat.

The first large drops fell on the outskirts of town, where cobblestone gave way to sand. The Vistula was no longer a silvery sheet under the sun but all rippled and grey. The summer squall quickly obliterated the sandy islets.

I was partly sheltered under the canvas top of the wagon and declined the driver's offer to let me inside. He snapped a black leather apron over my legs and gave me a piece of waterproof canvas to hold over my head.

The rain bothered Stevie no more than his horse, but he dismounted to put on his khaki raincoat. In this capelike affair, with a hood over his cap, he truly looked a legendary warrior-prince.

'It's fun, Stevie, ah?' I cried, as he smiled up at me.

'Great fun,' he answered.

But as sand turned to mud and slowed down the wagon, he said, 'The Colonel will have my epaulets if I'm late for staff meeting. I'll see you at corps HQ.'

And with a comical pout of regret, touching his hand to his cap, he trotted ahead, Adam at his side. Once far enough so that mud from his horse's hooves would not fly into my face, he put his big chestnut into a gallop and he and Adam were soon out of sight between the row of tossing poplars stretching along the riverbank.

I no longer felt so adventurous and bold, jolting along in the rain and mud, and I began to have misgivings about my headstrong act. But soon the rain stopped and wet poplar leaves gleamed like lacquer in the sun before it set, shedding a golden glow over the river and the fresh puddles on the road. The air was fresh and cool, with a scent of mushrooms and woodsmoke. My spirits rose again. I was off to war, to share it with my father and my beloved and keep both my childhood oaths, to my mother before her death and to my blood brother in the dungeon cell.

13

As the ambulance wagon neared the front, the road grew more and more congested with troops and transport that slowed the horses to a walk and caused the driver to swear profanely, always begging my pardon. A column of Austrian prisoners in blue uniforms passed under light guard. The faces of prisoners and guards alike reflected neither animosity nor resentment but simply the tedium of the muddy march. It was followed by a column of Russian infantry in khaki, with faces broader and more bearded than those of the Austrians.

At sight of me there were smiles and cries of 'Ey, Little Sister!'

A soldier raised a light hand from which a grimy bandage had slipped. 'Sister, help!' he called.

The ambulance wagon was caught in the press of traffic. Taking the soldier inside, I put a fresh dressing and bandage over the hand, from which three fingers had been freshly amputated.

'You've been fighting with this?' I wondered.

'And why not? I'm left-handed.'

'How is it over there?' I asked, looking in the direction of the boom of artillery.

'*Kasha* – a mess,' he answered gaily. 'I most sincerely thank you, sweet Little Sister,' and he ran at a dogtrot after his column.

I could soon see for myself. The wagon shortly came on military police directing traffic away from the riverbank, which was being shelled by the Austro-Germans from the other side. The road east was narrower and much rougher than the relatively wide and smooth road along the river. It ran through a wood and I had my first sight of trees stripped of leaves by shelling, looking like the seared and blackened skeletons of a forest fire. Here and there a fir had been felled to make roadblocks and trench cover. The road led through this scarred and sodden landscape into a village with a wide, unpaved central street congested with troops and transport of all arms. Peasant women in white head scarves calmly looked on from their doorsills. In the village elder's large two-storey wooden house with a shale roof – a sign of affluence – Father's corps headquarters were located.

The lancers assigned to my escort left me at the door and the sentry let me pass. In the central room of the house there was a clatter of typewriter and telegraph, a ringing of telephones, and a great going back and forth of adjutants. One of these informed me His Serene Highness was in a staff meeting and I must wait. I sat down on a bench against the wall. I was wet and I suddenly realized that I had left my kit bag in the car with Aunt Sophie. I had no change of clothes.

You're crazy, I addressed myself. Always were and always will be. Nobody needs you here, not even Stevie. And Papa will be furious and pack you off to Grandmaman right away. It will serve you right, stupid.

A group of divisional and regimental commanders with their staffs now came out of the back room. I saw the insignia of infantry, artillery and engineers as well as cavalry. Father's success in maintaining an orderly retreat, and the brilliant rear-guard action of his cavalry, had extended his command over three divisions.

After another wait, I was told to enter. In a rustic dining room, Father and Uncle Stan stood by a window, watching me silently. Stevie, by the table, was stuffing papers into his saddlebag with an absorption that clearly meant he wanted no responsibility in my adventure.

Father raised a finger and beckoned. 'Well, come here,' he said in Russian, in the mock-threatening tone he had used to me as a little girl when I had been naughty.

I flew across the room and at his broad chest. 'Papa, hold me, hold me hard!' – words I had spoken since I was old enough to talk.

He held me hard and long, then said, 'Well, it's good to see you, little girl, even if it's only to say goodbye.'

'Papa, you can't send me back. I promised Mother I would never leave you. I'm a surgical nurse, I can be more useful in a field hospital than at the rear. I want to share the war, with you, with Stevie.' I looked at my cousin, scowling jealously by the table, then back at Father's beautiful broad face. 'I beg you, Papa, let me stay.'

'It's mad. You've no conception what it's like . . . But I expect the only way you'll believe me is by seeing for yourself.'

I pressed myself to his chest again, then I had to turn from his shoulder to catch a sneeze with a fingertip. Father produced a fine monogrammed handkerchief and held it to my nose.

'No handkerchief.' He shook his head. 'No dry clothes either?'

'I left my kit bag behind, with Aunt Sophie.'

'I see. And you want to be a field nurse!' Father looked at Uncle, who was not nearly so indulgent a parent.

'Uncle Stan,' I appealed, 'are you angry at me still?'

'You're not my responsibility any more.' Then, 'Lieutenant' – Uncle turned to Stevie – 'those orders were to be delivered with all dispatch.'

'Yes, sir.' Stevie saluted smartly and left.

Calling his peasant hostess, Father asked her to look after me and find me a bed. I followed her upstairs, where she helped me into a holiday dress of her daughter's. In striped wool skirt and an embroidered blouse with beads, a silk kerchief on my damp hair, I dined with Father and his staff. Again, I felt adventurous and gay. When I was in bed in the attic under a goose-filled eiderdown, indispensable part of a peasant girl's dowry, Father came in to kiss me goodnight. He sat on my bed answering questions, mainly about the military prowess of Lieutenant Prince Veslawski. But suddenly I was oppressed by the unnatural stillness. The sound of cannonade, to which I had become so accustomed in a few hours' time that I scarcely noticed it, had ceased.

'Has the shelling stopped for the night?' I asked.

'It always lets up at this hour. The enemy will start up again in a while. We'll have to sit and listen until morning.'

'But why can't we answer, Papa? Don't we have the guns?'

'We have the guns, but not the shells. That's why, you see, we've been retreating, because Russian flesh is pitted against German steel. Not even Russian flesh can take this sort of punishment,' said Father bitterly.

'But why haven't we shells, Papa? Is General Sukhomlinov at fault?'

'It's not that fat lisping fool alone who is to blame, guilty of criminal negligence as he is. It's poor transport and distribution. It's the whole state of affairs in great Mother Russia. How can such a man and others of his ilk, you'll ask, be allowed to make such a monstrous muddle? Because efficiency and organization are something to look down upon, our worthy patriots say. They're German, un-Russian. Everything will come out somehow. The important thing is that Masha's second cousin from Tambov be transferred from the front to a safe town garrison and Misha's uncle from Saratov receive an army contract – that's the sort of business our War Ministry has been concerned with! Petty nepotism reigns from the lowest echelons of government to the highest and most august, where it's at its worst, through the intermediary of Anya Vyrubova and . . . you know whom I mean.' Father could no longer bring himself to say the name of Rasputin. 'As for Russia's destiny, the great God looks after that.' He fell silent and tapped his knee with fingers now bare of all but his signet ring.

'Papa' – I watched him anxiously – 'you don't think we're going to lose the war?'

'No, of course not. Sukhomlinov's successor, General Polivanov, is a good man. We may retreat, but we won't surrender. Now go to sleep.' He blessed and kissed me.

'Papa' – I held him back – 'tomorrow . . . would you take me to see the battle?'

'The battle?' he repeated, as though I'd said not 'battle' but 'rattle'.

'Yes, so I know what it's like. So I can share everything with you, and Stevie.'

'Very well, I'll take you,' he said, as though humouring a child. 'Since you want to be a field nurse, you may as well see it all.'

I was up at daybreak and into my uniform, which had dried overnight. As I was called to the kitchen for breakfast, there was my kit bag with its precious contents intact. Father had sent a staff courier after it on a motorcycle. 'A scandalous waste of petrol!' he responded with a little smile to my astonished gratitude.

After breakfast with the staff, I set off in a motorcar with Father and two adjutants on an inspection of the sector.

The day was again hot and the roads had dried, although large puddles still gleamed in the sun. The front extended from the banks of the Vistula, defended to the south against an enemy crossing on the Russian flank, in an almost straight line north along the Lublin-Cholm sector. After driving a *verst* or two along the road through the gently rolling, wooded landscape of the Carpathian foothills, our open motor turned into a field and headed down a slope.

Cutting straight across my field of vision at the bottom of this slope was a black wall of smoke, with here and there a flash of flame and puffs of white, black and yellow smoke bursting above. Halfway downslope the car made another left turn and bumped along the hillside on its high wheels. At divisional headquarters, a former gamekeeper's lodge at the edge of a wood, we stopped. The wood was stripped and charred by shellfire. The front wall of the low stone cottage showed a large hole. Behind the back wall, under an overhanging ledge camouflaged with branches, the divisional staff was seated at telephones about a long rustic table.

I was shocked to see soldiers lounging on the ground but Father said, 'This isn't the parade field. Soldiers at the front stand on their feet as little as possible.'

But as he got out of the car, the men sprang to attention. The staff officers also stood up and saluted.

'At ease, gentlemen,' Father said. And, to the small and angry-looking divisional commander, 'My daughter, Tatyana Petrovna, is curious to see a battle. So far she doesn't find it exciting enough.'

'I'm afraid I don't understand it very well,' I said.

The general commanding the division spread a military map on the table and pointed to the sector with a pencil. 'The battle disposition is very simple. X regiment is left, in that wood you see, N in the bottom in the middle, Y on the right, M in reserve. The division holds an eight-*verst* front. A cavalry division and a rifle brigade hold the second line.'

As he finished speaking, an officer looked up from a telephone and said, 'Your Excellency, Y telephone does not answer.'

This produced a silence. All eyes were on the small commander. He looked around the table, tapped his pencil on the map, glared at Father, then, flushing a fiery red, said, 'Call out the reserves.'

The order was telephoned to M regiment in reserve and an officer dispatched to see it carried out. Another officer was sent to report on Y regiment, whose telephone did not answer.

Then the real battle is going to be at M regiment, I thought, and looked hopefully at Father. He helped me back into the car and we skirted the edge of the wood, following the divisional staff officer on his motorcycle.

Another two *versts* beyond, we came on the reserve regiment, four thousand men in khaki ranged on three sides of a field. Over an icon placed on an altar of crossed bayonets in the centre of the field, a bearded Russian priest in stiff golden mantle read a service. As I looked at the men I recognized the pale, drawn face and glassy look that became more pronounced the closer we got to the battle zone – the face of fear. The divisional staff officer who had preceded us was talking to the colonel.

The cry 'Reserves forward!' rang out and the men broke into a run.

The priest held up the icon in his left hand and with the right blessed the men with a jewelled crucifix. The soldiers whose rifles had formed the altar seized them as they ran past.

Father and I joined the colonel of the regiment behind a shack at the edge of the wood, protected with sandbags and camouflaged with branches. Here the scene of telephones and staff officers was repeated, though this time everyone sat on the ground. Instead of regiments, battalions were now reporting and companies were manoeuvred by telephone, held in reserve or called forward. The real battle then was still further, with the battalions.

'Still not exciting enough?' Father asked. 'Come, we should be able at least to watch the action. Let's find a vantage spot.' And taking my arm, he walked rapidly downhill.

The adjutants exchanged glances, then followed.

The noise of artillery was now painful and the acrid smell of smoke and cordite unpleasantly strong. As a high whistle passed overhead, Father pulled me to one side and against a tree, covering me with his body. A six-inch shell struck the field to the left uphill from us, showering us with earth. The adjutants were knocked off their feet, but stood up unhurt, dusting off their impeccable uniforms.

'It's a stray shot. The enemy will soon correct his range,' Father said to the adjutants with barely perceptible irony. And, to me, 'Well, now that you've had your baptism of fire, we can turn back.'

'Papa, you said we would see the action!'

'Yes, hmmm. I didn't expect it would be quite so close. However ...' He took my arm again in a steel grip and strode on downhill, the adjutants following.

Some 500 yards below, a line of birch and willow trees along a stream that criss-crossed the field obscured our view of the battle line. Holding up my skirt with one hand, I gave the other to Father to leap over the stream, swollen with the previous day's rain.

In a dugout by the stream, in the midst of half a dozen telephones that he picked up one after the other as though playing some childish game, sat the battalion commander, a major.

Father stopped and looked through his field glasses. Then he handed them over, and I had my first sight of infantry going into action.

A staggered line of men crept downward, advancing like a green snake with a sideways movement of its coils. Some men crawled, some crept on their knees. A few, the officers, walked upright. White, black and yellow bursts dotted the field and at times smoke obscured it completely. The green line speeded its snaky descent. I heard a great shout, the 'raaaah' of a single 'hurrah'. Then the cannonade ceased and was followed by the crackling of rifle and machine-gun fire. Again smoke obscured the field. Where it lifted, I could see stretcher-bearers in white moving in and out of the smoke. The trench itself, where the actual fighting took place, lay in the smoke that blanketed the ravine at the bottom of the hill.

'It's going all right?' Father asked the major, who continued to play his telephone game.

'The trench has been taken, Your Excellency.'

'What are your losses?'

'Two companies aren't reporting.'

Father and the battalion commander were silent.

So the battle is over, I thought. Could this scene I had witnessed – orderly and staged like a stylized battle painting – result in death and dismemberment, cause agonies of body and mind?

In answer to my thoughts, a young private came running up the slope like one demented.

Father's towering figure blocked his path. 'Soldier, where are you off to?'

The private drew himself up at attention and stared ahead mutely.

'Discarding your rifle and running away under fire is a court-martial offence. It's better to face the enemy than a firing squad.'

'I wasn't issued a rifle, Your Excellency.'

Father blanched. Then he said in the same tone of calm authority,

'Pick one up from the field, soldier. Now walk back down the hill, counting your paces, until you rejoin your comrades. Dismissed.'

The young private saluted, turned about, and marched stiffly down the hill.

Out of the smoke hiding the slope, there now came walking wounded, some supported by one or two unhurt comrades, some limping, some with an arm or wrist hanging at an unnatural angle, some with bloody faces, smashed noses and jaws. At sight of me they stopped and looked up hopefully.

'I have no bandages or medicines.' I felt guilty and miserable. 'You must go to the dressing station.'

'Ah, they haven't time,' one of the men answered without rancour and walked on.

I looked at Father reproachfully. 'Papa, why can't these men be treated at once?'

'And why must men be sent into battle without a rifle?' he replied.

'But it's awful,' I said. 'It's a horror!'

This, then, was the battle – a nightmare, a horror, senseless and insensate. The generals knew it. The soldiers knew it. Yet they went into battle and only one out of four thousand had run away. What was it that made them go? It could not be hatred for the enemy unseen behind the smoke, nor could it be love for the far-off motherland or a tsar even more remote.

Father answered that question. 'Training and discipline, discipline and training.'

He congratulated the battalion commander on the splendid attack of his men and promised to mention it to the commander in chief. We retraced our steps up the hill. Father helped me back across the same stream between birches and willow trees, where a soldier now lay face-down on the bank as if to drink. I knew by his doll-like slackness that he would never catch up with the rest of his wounded comrades who had passed us by.

I was reminded of the first dead animal, a wolf, I had seen at a hunt when I was small, and how I had wondered then where his soul had gone to. Now, looking at the soldier's corpse, I asked myself that question again. I made the sign of the cross.

'*Strashno?* Is it fearful?' Father asked in Russian.

'No, not fearful. *Naprasno*,' I replied. 'It's a waste.'

Father nodded in silence.

We climbed on, overtaking the wounded, and returned to the regimental point where the motorcar awaited us. Father congratulated the colonel and shook hands. We then retraced our bumpy way by car to divisional headquarters.

As we drove, Father spread a military map on his knees and pointed out a spot to his adjutants. 'I believe there's a gap in the enemy line here which our cavalry can exploit. I want a night patrol sent out.'

The order relayed and congratulations extended at divisional headquarters, Father said, as he climbed back into the motor, 'Now back to headquarters. I have work to do.'

I reminded him to leave me at the field hospital.

'What, haven't you had enough yet?'

I only looked stubborn. He directed the driver to the field hospital.

Just beyond divisional headquarters a small column marched uphill in good order, colours to the fore. This was all that was left of Y regiment, whose telephone had not answered. Father ordered the car stopped and, as the column came abreast, he stood up and saluted. The men marched smartly, eyes right, as if on review. As the last row passed, he sat down heavily and his eyes again expressed bitter anguish. Five hundred yards further, we reached the field hospital.

14

The six wagons of the hospital unit stood in a semicircle by the roadside. On the ground, wounded lay on stretchers in rows under grey-green coats, their faces the same colour as the coats. Still more wounded were brought up through the charred and leafless wood. The less injured sat against tree trunks or lay propped on an elbow, smoking or chewing sunflower seeds. *Sanitars* in long white gowns carried stretchers up and down the steps at either end of the wagons. From within came an occasional 'aaaah' of protest or a burst of 'ah-ah-ah-ah', whereupon the wounded on the ground began to moan.

It was near noon and hot. The sweetish stench of stale blood was overpowering.

Father observed the dismal scene with an anguished gaze and said in a voice without authority, 'Tanichka, I can't permit it. You can be as useful elsewhere. All this is unnecessary . . . impossible!'

'Papa dearest, don't worry, I must!' And I put a hand on the car door. I wanted it opened quickly, before my resolution deserted me.

The Cossack by the driver came around to open it, the adjutants stepped down, keeping their eyes above the level of the scene, and helped me out. Papa remained in the motorcar.

Between the rows of wounded now came a portly, middle-aged nurse in a bloodstained and dirty apron, with a round face of peasant stock and an air of placid competence. She looked me over critically during Father's introduction, even while she dropped a small curtsy.

'I've had nine months of training,' I said hastily, 'six of them under Professor Sobolev, head of anaesthesiology at the University of Petrograd.'

Father pleaded with the head nurse to turn me down. 'She's just eighteen, an only child, dear to our sovereign. This is unnecessary . . . impossible.'

'Don't worry about your little daughter, Your Excellency. Nothing terrible will happen.' She decided I would do.

'Yefim!' Father called the Cossack over. 'You'll remain with the ambulance unit and guard the young Princess with your life. I'll send over your horse and field pack.'

'With my life, Your Excellency.' The black-browed Circassian saluted, straight as an arrow, seized his long rifle and my kit bag, and stepped back.

'God keep you.' Father made the sign of the cross over me as I stood on tiptoe to kiss his cheek. 'Send word with Yefim the moment you've had enough. Look after my daughter,' he said to the head nurse. 'You'll be well recompensed.' He motioned the adjutants back into the car. It drove off in a cloud of red dust.

Followed by Yefim, I passed with Nurse Marfa Antonovna between the rows of stretchers. The moans grew.

'Sisters, for God's sake, have mercy!' Cries arose on either side.

'Soon, soon. Be patient a little longer, my sweethearts,' Nurse Marfa answered cheerfully. And, as I slowed down, 'Not your business, Your Highness. This way.'

In the wagon reserved for the personnel, the eight nurses of the unit had their cramped quarters behind a blanket partition. Here Yefim deposited my kit bag, in the space left vacant by a nurse who had been killed during the last phase of the retreat.

Marfa Antonovna concluded her terse account of my predecessor's end, which left me undaunted. 'Stay close to the unit and you'll be safe. Wagon three, right of centre, is the operating room. The latrines are behind the staff wagon. Report as soon as you've changed. Your Highness knows how to dress herself?'

'I can manage, thank you.'

To dress alone was nothing. To use the latrines took courage. In ten minutes I was inside the operating wagon, scrubbing my hands in hot water poured from a kettle by a *sanitar*. Water boiled on the wood stoves in back of the wagon served to sterilize the instruments. There were no sterile sheets to drape the patients in. Neither the surgeons nor their assistants working over the four operating tables wore masks. All were incredibly unkempt and bloody. They worked with astonishing speed, with a crude, if not cruel, competence.

The absence of aseptic conditions under which I had so rigorously trained, the lack of X-ray or laboratory, the single oxygen tank for the use of all anaesthetists and no sign of cylinders containing anaesthetic gases; this scene of haste and gore, so foreign to my conception and experience, almost paralysed me.

'Why is Your Highness dawdling?' Nurse Marfa appeared beside me. 'We haven't time to be so particular. Your table is number one. They're clearing it now.' She gave me her mask for protection from the fumes and hung a stethoscope about my neck. 'You know how to give ether anaesthesia?'

I nodded as I slipped on my trembling hands the rubber gloves from my kit bag.

She indicated the anaesthetist's stool and handed me a Blair cone and an ether bottle. 'Well, God be with you,' she said, and I was on my own.

Ether, simplest and safest to use, was the only anaesthetic available. It was also the most unpleasant. Yet there was no induction with nitrous oxide, not even time to prepare and calm the patient. It hardly seemed necessary, I saw. Terrorized and subdued, they stared into the faces of the nurses and *sanitars* who handled them like parcels, swiftly and impersonally.

Can it be that I, too, will become a crude and competent medical machine without compassion? I thought as I placed the cone over the mouth and nose of my first case, an abdominal wound, and told him to breathe deeply, steadily. Can I stay in this hell? Can I face the horror without the apparatus of formal surgery? Yes, I understood. The sterile conditions, the shining cleanliness and perfect order, even the hierarchy and pettiness of the well-run hospital, had protected me from the naked reality of suffering, even as military pomp and apparel shield the soldier from the reality of battle. Now the abomination was unveiled. I wallowed in blood and excrement. No, I shall drown! It is unnecessary, impossible. Papa was right, I concluded as I dripped ether on to the cone, talking quietly to my patient to speed him through his struggle against suffocation.

Wasn't this what you wanted, Tanya? another voice within me spoke back. This *is* reality. There is no falsehood, no posturing here. This is your trial of strength, your test of valour. And if the soldier can go into the trench where you can't follow; if he can experience pain and terror even more immediately than you who only minister to it, why can't you do your job like the others? What makes you want to shirk it now that it is no longer clean and tidy? You have been playing nurse until now, Tanya. You had grown-ups to watch over you, to keep you from wearing yourself out or making a mistake. Now, if you give too much ether, your patient will die. Pay attention to your job, Tanya. Watch your patient's pupils, his colour, respiration, muscle tone. Check his heart rate. Be ready for oxygen if he should start to turn blue. I became absorbed.

As my attention shifted from the general horror beyond comprehension to the specific task within my competence, my helplessness and dread went away.

At nightfall, I left my post for a short respite. In the clearing, dimly lit by the flame of smudge pots, rows of wounded lay as they had in the morning. Still more were brought up through the dark wood, the white gowns of the bearers flitting between the black trunks.

I looked into a wagon lit by kerosene lamps where white-capped *sanitars* moved among the men bedded down in the straw. The charge nurse supervised the ward from beside a medicine chest at one end. There was only room for the gravest casualties in the wagons. The rest were laid out in the clearing under clean grey-green blankets until they could be evacuated.

Impotence and horror washed over me afresh. No, it's impossible, I thought. I must get away. And, swift as a black arrow, Yefim materialized before me.

'Your Highness desires?'

Take me to Father! was my inner cry. But all I said was, 'Something hot to drink.'

He brought me a bowl of cabbage soup with a slice of black bread, and a glass of tea. While I sat on a wagon step eating, a bay mare with a fine head in a halter came up and nudged Yefim.

'You don't tie up your horse?' I wondered.

'I hand-raised her from a colt. She keeps me company.' Yefim's downward-slanting eyebrows and moustache lifted as he smiled, and his face grew naïvely gentle.

'Do you miss your comrades?' I asked.

'This is easy duty, as long as one doesn't think too much.' He glanced about the dismal scene. 'This helps too.' He produced a harmonica. 'If Your Highness permits?'

I nodded. 'Please.'

He cradled the instrument against his mouth and began to play a haunting air on a half-tone scale, an air of the steppe full of longing for its limitless space, freedom and purity. The mare pricked up her ears. All were silent.

I fell into a reverie in which I galloped with Stevie across the steppe. But suddenly he was thrown by an exploding shell . . . I came to with a start, stroked the mare's neck, and returned to the operating wagon.

All night long the work went on without stop. The operations averaged no more than fifteen minutes, as in the days before anaesthesia when speed was imperative. The chief surgeon, Dr Kornev, a greying man in his fifties, had been professor of surgery at Moscow University. His work was brilliant. He moved from one table to the other, taking the most serious cases. While I watched him almost as closely as I did my patient, Nurse Marfa kept a corner of her eye on the young princess come to the front for thrills. Between midnight and morning, the surgeons and nurses took a four-hour rest in two shifts. I asked Marfa Antonovna to give someone else my turn.

'It will be the same all day tomorrow and all night long again,' the older woman advised, not unkindly. 'Your Highness had better rest.'

'Thank you, but I don't need to as yet.'

'Well, all right. But look out! I don't want Your Highness out on the floor in the middle of an operation.'

I had never fainted and did not suppose I ever would.

By morning I was groggy and staggered out of the wagon. But a cup of hot coffee and a bowl of kasha, accompanied by a quick inner prayer, restored me.

Towards noon, I had just finished a case and was sponging my face in a little water – that, too, was growing scarce – when I heard a commotion outside.

Nurse Marfa went to the door, where a *sanitar* reported, 'There's some kind of Pole making a scandal. Wants us to take care of his prince right away.'

'I speak Polish,' I said, as my heart sank. 'Perhaps I can help.'

At the foot of the wagon steps, Stevie's batman, Adam, was giving his opinion in fluent Russian of Russian field hospitals and all things Russian to the *sanitars* blocking his way. I felt ice-cold and quickly leaned against the side of the wagon.

Adam saw me and cried in Polish, 'Your Serene Ladyship, make them take care of my Lord Prince!'

'Where is he hit?' I managed to ask.

'The thigh. He is bleeding and weak, like an infant.'

I told the *sanitars* to follow Adam, went to see that a table was readied, and made bold to ask Dr Kornev to look at the next case, my relative. Soon the *sanitars* carried Stevie in, Adam holding his head, which would not fit on the stretcher.

Stevie lay very pale and still, terrified like every man brought to this place of horror and hope. With frightened eyes, he watched the flash of surgical instruments over the inert body on the table next to him, and the *sanitar* carrying out a bloody basin of debris and flesh.

I bent over to shield him from these fearful sights. Laying a hand on his cheek, I said in a voice I tried to make calm and reassuring, 'Don't be frightened, Stevie. You won't feel any pain.'

'I've really got it this time.' Then, craning in the old way, 'Will you still love me when they cut off my leg?' he asked.

'It won't be cut off. Close your eyes and try to relax. It'll be over soon.'

And I stepped aside for the *sanitars* to wash and paint him with iodoform. But as the surgeon, in a gown stained like a butcher's, bent over the wound, Stevie called, 'Tanya!'

'I'm here,' I said, and I put the ether cone over his mouth and nose.

'Don't let them cut it off, don't let them, don't . . .' he went on crying, while I told him to take a big breath, another big one, until his cries and struggles ceased.

I looked from Stevie's sightless open eyes to the face of the surgeon probing the wound and going, 'Aha, aha' to himself in a satisfied tone.

'It's close to the groin.' Dr Kornev answered my unspoken question. 'It'd be safer to amputate. If sepsis develops . . .' He shook his head eloquently.

Yes, I thought, if blood poisoning spreads through the lymph glands in the groin, it will be the end.

And, aloud, 'I think he'd rather be dead than a cripple, Doctor,' I said.

'Mmmmm.' The surgeon directed his attention to the wound. Then again, 'Aha, aha,' in a tone of satisfaction as he made the incision.

He did not amputate.

What a marvellous person Dr Kornev is! I thought. How could I ever think him a machine? Stevie will be all right, he will be whole. To me it makes no difference. Crippled or disfigured, I would love him all the same. But he would be like a horse with a broken leg. He would rather be shot. And I continued to drip ether on to the cone over the face of my beloved, now so dreadfully yet sweetly in my power.

When the wound had been bandaged and the leg splinted, and I had heard the heart pump strong and steady, I slipped my stethoscope and mask over my neck and stood over my unconscious cousin, alone by the table. His hair was curly once more and a damp lock fell over one eye. The full mouth was half open. The usually rosy cheeks were without colour and the circles dark and deep under the eyes. He looked very young in his utter abandon, no older than eighteen. My tenderness and sense of power grew.

It is usually I who feel weak when Stevie looks at me a certain way or speaks in a certain voice. But now it is he who is helpless and at my mercy, I thought, and my hands went to his head of their own accord. I held it, feeling it heavy and inert. I wiggled it. 'I can do anything I want with you, Stevie, even kiss you,' I murmured and bent down.

I kissed his lips long and hard, crushing their velvety softness, tasting his tongue, drinking his breath. Eyes closed, hands about his head, I knew not where I was, who I was, or what I was doing.

My next recollection was finding myself on my pallet in my cubicle.

Marfa Antonovna held smelling salts to my nose.

'I warned Your Highness you'd be out on the floor if you didn't rest. I've been at this business a long time. I know what I'm talking about. Don't be ashamed,' she continued, as I started guiltily. 'It happens to our doctors too. You're a brave girl and a fine sister of mercy. After a sleep and a meal, you'll be as good as new.' She tucked a coarse blanket about my neck.

'Please let me up, Marfa Antonovna.'

Nurse Marfa pushed me down with a broad hand. 'Dr Kornev wants you to rest. Strict orders. Be so good as to lie down, Your Highness.'

'But I must check on my last case. His respiration was poor . . . I had . . . to breathe into his mouth . . . He is my first cousin, Stefan Veslawski. I *must* see him.'

She relented. 'Well, all right, my little dove. But have some tea and a biscuit at least.'

After gulping a glass of tea with a biscuit by the outdoor stove, I went into the wagon for the wounded officers.

At the very end of the narrow aisle between the double row of wounded lay Stevie, filling the aisle with his great length. He stirred and moved his lips. I squatted down beside him. He retched as I held a basin to his chin. Then I wiped his face and mouth with a wet cloth and he lay back with his eyes closed. He looked like the eight-year-old boy languishing on a dungeon pallet after a cruel whipping.

'I'm thirsty,' he complained in that same boy's voice.

I put a glass straw between his lips. 'Only a sip or you'll be sick again.'

He sucked at the straw, then looked up at me attentively. 'Is it still there?'

'All there.' I knew he meant his leg.

He smiled with childish relief. 'I'm a lucky dog! If Kim hadn't dragged me into a shell hole in time, I'd have been blown up. And I threatened him with court-martial for disobeying my order to ride on.'

I said an inward prayer of thanks. Bless Casimir. Then, as Stevie frowned, 'I'll get you something for the pain right away,' I said. 'Count to twenty, slowly, and I'll be back.'

I crossed the wagon, controlling my haste. The charge nurse said morphine was in short supply. It must be saved for the most serious cases.

'If you don't give me morphine for this officer, Sister, the noise he'll make will be heard in the enemy lines,' I said. 'He has a voice like an organ. I know him.'

One man's cries could start off a wagonful of wounded and turn it into hell. I got my morphine.

'You're a brave boy, Stevie. This'll make you feel better right away.' I rubbed a spot on his arm with alcohol and stuck the needle in. I pulled on the plunger to make sure I had not entered a vein, and injected the morphine. He watched me a little nervously, but, as the drug quickly took effect, his features relaxed.

'There, it's passed.' I stroked his head. 'Now go to sleep. I'll look in on you again as soon as I can.'

'I'm still thirsty.'

I gave him another sip through the straw.

'I'm going to throw up again.'

I placed the basin by his head. 'Anything else you need, call a *sanitar*.' I tried to rise but he caught my wrist. Weak as he was, he was still very strong. 'Stevie, let me go.'

'Will you give a poor wounded fellow a kiss?'

The memory of the kiss he did not remember made me blush. He looked hugely pleased.

'If you'll let go my wrist.' He released me and I kissed him lightly on the lips. They tasted of vomit, as well as ether, but their softness was enough to make me feel giddy all over again. 'Bye-bye, Stevie.' I wrenched myself away.

At the foot of the wagon steps, Adam ran up to me. I told him to go in to his master.

On the way to the operating wagon, I was stopped by a good-looking young cornet with the insignia of the Veslawski lancers. 'Tanya, how's Stevie?' he asked in perfect English.

'He's all right so far, Kim.' For it was Casimir, come for news of his best friend. 'You may go in and see him.'

Casimir looked about the clearing and made a face like Stefan's. 'This isn't a jolly place, is it?'

'No. But the surgery was the best. Tell Uncle Stan, and tell him also to send an ambulance at once. If Stevie doesn't get away from this filth, infection could set in ... and he could die,' I finished with an effort.

'I'll report to the Colonel as soon as I've said hello to Stevie. Lucky for him you're here!' Casimir pressed my hand.

I detained him. 'Kim, wait a bit. Tell me how it happened.'

'It was the worst piece of luck, Tanya. A night patrol had

confirmed a gap in the enemy line' – the gap Father's experienced eye had detected on our inspection the previous day. 'We were ordered to make a sortie simultaneously with a diversionary thrust by the infantry. The diversion worked. We met little resistance. We were on top of the battery before the Austrians knew what was happening. It was mayhem. Then, on the way back, inside our lines, shells started dropping. We couldn't believe Stevie was hit. The whole platoon stopped, under fire. Stevie swore at us from the ground to get the . . . out of there . . .'

'You disobeyed him, I know, to save his life.'

'Oh, that.' Casimir reddened. 'You'd have done the same. Stevie'll get the St George for today's action.' Then, 'You look all in.' He observed me with concern.

'I'll bear up.' I forced a smile and went back to work.

Every half-hour or so, I looked in on my cousin. He was not comfortable once the first dose of morphine had worn off and he could have no more. But he knew others were worse off and it would have been unsporting to act spoiled.

Before the sun set, a motor ambulance came for him with a doctor and a nurse. I showed the bearers to his pallet and gave him the good news.

'I don't want any special treatment,' he said.

'The future Rex Poloniae is a very special person.'

Stevie sulked regally. 'Are you coming with me?'

I shook my head in denial.

'But I *need* you!'

'You'll have the best care in the world. Others need me more.'

He tried to seize my wrist, but he was strapped on to an especially long stretcher and carried out. When he saw the wounded lying by the roadside awaiting evacuation, he demanded that the ambulance take a full load.

I told the *sanitars* to put three more casualties in the ambulance.

I countered the objections of the immaculate English nurse, at once detesting her blue-eyed handsomeness. 'Princess Veslawska would want it this way.' I then described to the Swiss doctor the *débridement* of Stevie's wound and the post-operative course.

'You've been very helpful, Sister.' The doctor kept a sober face. 'I believe I'll be able to handle it.'

I was too tired to be vexed. I made the sign of the cross over Stevie and laid a hand along his pale unshaven cheek.

'Kiss Auntie for me. Ask her to forgive my rudeness in Veslawow. Be a good patient. God bless you.' I turned away to keep from bursting into tears.

Why am I crying? I wondered as I watched the ambulance drive off in a red cloud. Still, the tears fell salty on my cracked lips. I'm happy Stevie is gone. He will be well now, he will be whole.

Turning back towards the clearing, I saw the same dismal scene: the charred trees strafed and leafless, the bloody orderlies going among the bloody men on the bloody ground. To the right, a heap of bandages burned with a sickening stench, making the eyes smart. To the left, standing nose to rump, the horses of the unit swished their tails and tossed their heads at the flies. It was still hot and sultry. Each passing vehicle raised a cloud of dust that settled on the trees, the wagon tops, the wounded, the ground.

I came here yesterday, I thought, and it was like this then, and it will be like this tomorrow, and there's no end in sight.

15

When it grew dark and smudge pots were lit about the clearing, Dr Kornev ordered me to bed.

As I slept heavily on my pallet, the wagon shook with a prolonged rumble. The withdrawal from the sector had begun. All through the night, artillery, baggage train, field kitchens, mounted machine-gun sections, ambulance wagons, cavalry detachments and infantry columns passed the unit, heading north-east.

At dawn, I was no sooner dressed and braced for the day's work than an open motorcar with a Russian flag drew up and Yefim reported, 'General Prince Silomirsky to see Your Highness.'

I ran to the car, Nurse Marfa panting after, and flung myself at Father's broad chest.

'Well, little girl, have you had enough?' He lifted my chin. 'Are you ready to come with me and join Stefan?' And, as I said no with my head, 'To stay is dangerous.' He addressed Marfa Antonovna as much as me. 'Your unit must remain with the rear guard. Two infantry regiments, a sappers' battalion, a Cossack detachment and the Veslawski lancers are all that stand between you and the enemy. They are picked troops. They know theirs is the responsibility to protect the retreat. But the hazards of war are unpredictable. You could be captured. You could be heavily shelled. How can I allow my daughter to take such unnecessary risks?'

'That's for Your Excellency to decide,' Marfa Antonovna said. 'But we have come to depend on Tatyana Petrovna. She will be missed.'

'Papa,' I pleaded. 'I was brought up to have no fear of danger and to take risks. I am a descendant of Rurik, I am the godchild of the Tsar. In my place, wouldn't Tatyana Nikolayevna stay? And what would she think of me if I fled? Anyway,' I added, 'the Veslawski lancers are protecting us. We'll be safe.'

The all-powerful corps commander was powerless against his daughter. 'Young Lomatov-Moskovsky, our kinsman, commands the sappers' battalion. He'll take special care of you too. Well, Tanichka' – Father bent to kiss me – 'may God watch over you.' He blessed me and was gone.

Daylight only brought more wounded, more fatigue, less water, fewer drugs. We worked on, growing more crude, more callous, more vindictive against this sea of misery that our unit alone was expected to allay. The surgeons were sharp with the nurses, the nurses sharp with the *sanitars*, the *sanitars* sharp with the wounded.

I tried not to become sharp. I was so young and new at this business, it was easier for me than for the others. I gave my place as anaesthetist to the portly head nurse so she could sit down, and took over Marfa Antonovna's duties. I took charge of the operating room. I scheduled cases according to their urgency, gave orders to the nurses and *sanitars*, rationed the medical supplies, kept the operating room logbook. I told the surgeons how often and how long to rest.

When Dr Kornev sat down suddenly on a stool, put his grey head in his hands, and began to sob, I laid a hand on his shoulder and talked to him until he regained his composure. Then I ordered him to bed in my turn. In his state of hallucinatory fatigue, he too, like the others, obeyed.

In between my administrative duties, when a surgeon was short of an assistant, I held retractors, sponged blood and sutured the final layers of the wound. My practice in surgical needlework served me well.

All that I ever learned I drew on then. Even more useful than my nine months of training were hours of standing on my feet in church service and court ceremony since I was a small child, Grandmaman's stern schooling, Vera Kirilovna's instruction in self-possession and posture, war games and practice in stoicism with Stevie, my secret studies in anatomy, Tanik's example in renunciation and fortitude, and above all, Aunt Sophie's words: 'War is unbearable, yet it must be borne. I suppose that's life: a trial of strength, a test of valour.'

'Lord, give me strength,' I repeated like an incantation, and my strength grew with the demands made upon it.

Two more days went by. Each passing vehicle took on its load of wounded. They were placed on baggage wagons, on gun carriages, in springless peasant carts, in every empty seat. Even though the agonies of the journey would be such that many would beg to die by the roadside, their only fear now was of being left behind to fall into enemy hands. Everyone understood this and made room. Should a driver try to ignore a nurse's summons to halt, his way was blocked by the vehicles ahead. Curses rained on him. He took his load of wounded and was thankful for his life.

On the morning of the third day of withdrawal, I was supervising the evacuation, with Yefim's help, when a closed carriage approached. At the summons to halt, a lady put out a charming head under a large hat with ostrich plumes to ask what the delay was. She refused the request to take on wounded and produced a special pass from corps headquarters, signed by the commander.

At this she would ordinarily have been allowed to proceed. But I strode up to the carriage and said in French, 'I'm certain Madame will be so kind as to share her comfortable carriage with a few of these unfortunate men.'

'Share my carriage! I see, Mademoiselle, you come from a good family but you haven't been taught manners. I consider your request insolent.'

'Then, Madame, if you don't care to share your carriage, you won't mind sitting on the box beside the coachman. Or perhaps you would prefer to walk?' And I ordered Yefim to clear the carriage.

'General Prince Silomirsky is a personal friend of mine,' the lady said as she descended, followed by a frightened French maid. 'I shall report this outrage to him.'

'Please do, Madame.' My anger swelled at the suspicion the lady was Father's mistress. 'And be sure to tell him his daughter was responsible.'

The lady made a movement of fright, then quickly climbed up beside the coachman. The maid followed less gracefully. The wounded were loaded and the elegant equipage drove off.

A soldier stopped. 'Eh, Little Sister, you showed her good and proper, the damned aristocrat, and with feathers in her hat too!'

He had addressed me by the familiar 'thou'. Yefim's brows contracted. He sprang on the insolent soldier and seized him by the scruff of his overblouse. 'That's the Serene Princess Silomirskaya you're talking to!'

'Yefim, leave him be. It's all right,' I said to the soldier, and he dogtrotted after his column.

The incident struck me disagreeably. I no longer trusted my hot temper and stuck to my task in the operating wagon.

Our work went on until the last moment. Three of the wagons were already gone, including the one reserved for the personnel, which had been loaded with wounded. Then at long last we were free to go and the equipment stacked in less than the ten minutes I was told it took to set it up.

'Glory to you, Lord,' Marfa Antonovna exclaimed, and made the sign of the cross.

All the personnel, even the senior surgeon, who was not religious, crossed themselves. The driver stuck in his head and asked if the horses could be hitched.

'Yes, quickly, what are you yawning about?' Nurse Marfa yelled, expressing what everyone felt – that it must end now, the nightmare, the horror, this very moment, or it might never end.

Shells now began bursting close by, flinging dirt over the wagon top. The horses were brought, neighing in fright – the lower part of the wood was on fire. At last the wagon rolled on to the road. And the moment it began to move, the surgeons, nurses, *sanitars*, who had laid down over their coats on the wooden floor still stained with fresh blood, these sixteen people, as though rocked in a cradle, were instantly and stuporously asleep.

I felt a sudden revulsion for the fetid wagon. Climbing out front, I squeezed between the driver and Yefim, my cape thrown over the gown that had become stained and bloody like everyone else's. It was twilight and the horizon glowed red with the double light of a setting sun and burning fields. Between the pall of black smoke and a band of black clouds above, the sky was molten. Against this backdrop, forests and fields were aflame – the scorched-earth policy was officially in force, and even Father could no longer stave off its execution. Dusk was as hot as day.

I was chilled from nervousness and fatigue. I wrapped myself in my cape and let my head fall on Yefim's shoulder.

I awoke to a pleasant sensation of coolness on my face. It was raining and Yefim put a rain cape over me. Night had fallen. Lanterns swung from the tail of the wagon ahead. The horses of our wagon moved to a slow trot, their harness squeaking and jingling. Yefim's mare in full saddle and pack trotted lightly beside the wagon, the end of her halter rope in his hand. I knew that all about me hooves and feet were tramping but I could not think why. Nor did it matter greatly. Yefim's shoulder was broad and strong, like Father's and Stevie's. I felt safe against it. I woke up again as the wagon passed through the village where, only a week ago, I had spent the night. Now only a few Jews, like ravens in their black caftans, peered from behind the chimneys that stood alone amidst crumbling walls. I looked about uncomprehendingly and went back to sleep.

Our field-hospital unit passed through Lublin on 28 July 1915, two days ahead of General von Mackensen's Austro-Germans. Here we were caught in the general exodus from this city of a hundred thousand. The scene was one of indescribable confusion: wagons hastily loaded with bedding and cooking utensils; cows, pigs, goats, geese driven through the streets; looters dragging sacks from burning storehouses and granaries. Those who fled were too afraid to notice the looters, the looters too greedy to feel fear.

The panic of departure abated as soon as the refugees joined the eastward retreat. Like mountain streams rushing into a broad river they were absorbed into its flow and moved patiently, uncomplainingly, in a dogged stupor. The river bore troops and civilians, peasants in flat caps and high boots driving their stock, carts piled high with bedding and hung with pots, women in white kerchiefs on foot, a bundle tied to a stick slung over their shoulder, prim ladies in straw boaters carrying open parasols.

I rode sideways on Yefim's mare, while he walked alongside. Two schoolteachers, middle-aged ladies, had our seats beside the driver. In the wagon, the wounded, mercilessly jostled, moaned and begged for water. A young recruit with a stomach wound cried piteously.

I dismounted to give him an injection of morphine.

'Forgive me, Little Sister, but it hurts so frightfully,' he apologized.

'It will pass in a minute. You'll be home soon.'

'Home,' he said. 'That will be a wonder! Mother will make cabbage pie. Do you like cabbage pie, Sister?'

'Very much,' I lied. 'We'll all be having cabbage pie soon.'

As I mounted again, a very tall, almost effete young officer on a dust-covered horse forced his way through the marchers and rode up alongside.

'Tanya, are you all right?' he asked in perfect English. 'I've had a devil of a time getting through this mob!'

'L-M!' It was my second cousin, Prince Lomatov-Moskovsky, of the Rurik line, whom we called simply L-M. 'Father told me you were with the rear guard.'

'Yes, we sappers have the dubious honour of being the rear of the rear guard. You're looking fit, I'm relieved to see, if a bit bedraggled.' L-M rested his dark and arresting Byzantine's eyes on my grimy person. Then he smiled. 'When I saw you last, you were wearing a rose velvet court dress. It was in the St George gallery in the Winter Palace at the beginning of the war. You looked ... transfigured.'

'I felt transfigured. What a contrast!' I gazed at the wretched scene.

'*C'est la guerre*,' said my companion. 'Look out!'

At the cry, 'Make way, make way!' and the blare of a horn, the human river divided for the passage of a staff car. Confusion ensued. A cow stepped on a child's foot. A horse broke its traces and headed into the field. The turbulent river eddied, swirled, then flowed on placidly once more.

My kinsman pulled out a notebook. 'Well, at least,' he observed between scribbles, 'you've been spared the sight of Jews hanging from tree limbs. Your father forbids such "patriotic" excesses.'

'It's unspeakable!' Disbelief mingled with outrage. 'And did you say, "*c'est la guerre*" to that too?' I asked.

'No. Not at first. But it's odd, you know, how quickly one grows used to the unspeakable. I suppose it's all part of total war. I wonder what Tolstoy's Prince André would have said, he who was so opposed to a gentleman's war.'

'Prince André thought war would only end when it became equally hideous for all.'

'I doubt that. People have an extraordinary tolerance for hideousness, if not a downright appetite.'

Was L-M such a cynic, or was it a pose? I considered my Russian kinsman with new interest. A couple of years older than Stevie, he had taken a first in history at Oxford and returned to Petrograd on the eve of war to fascinate more than one society girl with his aloofness and poise. I had found him insufferably conceited. Now, still elegant in his dusty grey tunic, he seemed more substantial. He had been in the trenches. He had seen the ultimate horror of which I remained as ignorant as my namesake was of the ordeal of the retreat.

I tried to cheer myself up. 'Well, at least the war won't have been a complete waste if it brings freedom to the Poles.'

'They'll have to wrest it for themselves.'

'And the Tsar's pledge of autonomy, the manifesto of Grand Duke Nicholas?'

'A political ploy to ensure the Poles' allegiance.'

'I don't believe it! His Majesty could never be guilty of such duplicity.'

L-M glanced down at me. 'Sorry. I forgot you're practically one of the dynasty. It was a tactless remark.' He offered me a drink of water from his canteen.

I realized how thirsty I was. I found myself dreaming about Tsarskoye, dwelling in that oasis of family closeness and peace.

L-M broke in on my reverie. 'It's odd to think of you being so close to the Tsar's daughters. You're such an original girl, and they, well, frankly, they seem quite conventional.'

'They've no chance to be anything else. They're absolutely genuine . . . and good!'

'They're lucky to have you for a friend.' L-M smiled with his eyes in a kindly way reminiscent of Father's.

I smiled back and we rode on in cosy comradeship.

At every narrow bridge over the many streams of the Lublin uplands, the human flow, bottled up, churned angrily. Military transport drivers shouted civilians off the road, then fell to quarrelling over right-of-way among themselves. A field kitchen and a gun carriage rushed together on to a bridge. The field kitchen overturned noisily. The gun carriage was forced off the road with angry cries: 'Ah, what's it good for? There is no ammunition. But we've still got to fill our stomachs!'

Urging his horse forward and brandishing his riding crop, L-M restored order with a few dry commands. The field kitchen was righted. The river flowed on.

L-M again made notes. Then, 'Mutiny and desertion are in the air,' he remarked dispassionately. 'The Russian soldier is rife for revolutionary propaganda. If we're beaten, it will be 1905 all over again, but on a grand scale.'

I had a vision of Tanik, standing willowy in white lace in the Chinese Garden at Tsarskoye, and of an angry populace approaching like a thundercloud. Would the cordon of galloping Cossacks that ringed the Alexander Palace night and day be sufficient to protect her and her loved ones?

'We won't be beaten!' I said. 'We can't be!'

Tempers fray as the day wears on and heat adds its burden on the marchers. Civilians and soldiers alike are felled by heat stroke. The wounded who cannot make it home to mother's cabbage pie are buried by the roadside, a short service read over the grave by a priest, and a crude wooden cross erected. Dead animals are left to rot. Their maggoty carcasses, alongside abandoned household goods, broken-down carts and carriages, will line the road, between burning fields, for the advancing Austro-Germans.

L-M left me at twilight to rejoin his men while my hospital unit camped in a wood. The gypsylike scene about campfires suggested the eve of Harvest Festival rather than flight before an invader. This recurrence of peaceful and even cheerful activity in the midst of war and destruction no longer struck me as incongruous. I saw that L-M was right, human beings were supremely adaptable. And at least this struggle with the physical and prosaic kept one from grasping the vaster tragedy of war. So my main preoccupation was with my state of filth, my one desire for a hot bath.

This was soon realized. Even as the horses were being unhitched from the ambulance wagons, three officers rode up, one of them silver-haired and Olympian. Father's face was no longer fresh and rosy, but its lofty beauty had never struck me more.

He anticipated my first question. 'Stefan is safely in his mother's care in the Catholic Hospital at Minsk. Casimir is due for lieutenant's epaulets. The Veslawski lancers have surpassed themselves. Your presence with the rear guard inspires them.' Father regarded me teasingly, but also with new pride. 'Oh, and there's a letter for you from Tsarskoye.'

I rode in a borrowed cart to his field headquarters, set up in a tent. Soaking blissfully in hot water in a portable tub, I read the two-page letter from my namesake delivered by imperial courier.

Attached was a homemade greeting card. On the cover was a pencil sketch by Olga of me in nurse's uniform alighting from a field ambulance. Inside, Tatyana Nikolayevna had written: 'We admire you. We envy you. We miss you.' Marie and Anastasia had each added a line, Aleksey a row of kisses for Tata. At the bottom were the words in the Tsar's even hand, 'Our prayers are with you and our brave men. God bless and protect you, my godchild.' From Alexandra, not a word. The absence of her approval added a sting to my joy.

After my bath, I slipped on a clean linen shirt of Father's and, sitting cross-legged on my camp cot, managed to write to Stevie and my friends at Tsarskoye before falling asleep. I did not mention Stevie to my namesake, knowing that this letter would be shown and eagerly discussed.

Before reveille, Simyon, Father's faithful orderly, served us breakfast *à deux* as in Smolny Institute days. Father had dictated his dispositions for the day's action during the night and we had half an hour to ourselves.

'Tell me about the field hospital,' he said. 'But first, I have an apology to extend on the part of Lady Antoinette for her selfishness towards the wounded. She bears you no ill will.'

'How good of her!' said I.

Father looked at me askance. 'Lady Antoinette put her manor at our disposal for a headquarters this winter. I was indebted to her.'

So she was Papa's mistress, I thought.

Father's expression plainly said, 'You should never have ugly thoughts. They spoil your lovely little face.'

'Did she tell you,' I could not resist adding, 'that a soldier called her a "damned aristocrat"?' And, as Father frowned, 'L-M says there's mutiny in the air.' I related the race between the field kitchen and the gun carriage and my kinsman's pessimistic reflections.

'Mutiny's always in the air at the front,' Father said. 'That is why discipline must be maintained at any cost. As for revolution, that's been in the air since you were born. The best way to avoid it is to win the war. That's our job.' He crinkled his eyes in a smile of enormous tenderness and not a little pride. 'Now then, tell me quickly about the rest of your experience.'

I did. 'It's strange, Papa,' I concluded. 'At first everything at the front seemed a horror, a nightmare, I could not wait for it to end. But now I miss the unit. I feel I belong, awful as it is.'

'Yes, that's the way a soldier feels towards his comrades. I abhor war, you know it. Yet I've never felt useful except in active command.'

Father spoke to me as to a comrade-in-arms, an equal. For the first time, I was no longer a little girl in his eyes. I had won recognition and compelled admiration from the person in the world whose approval mattered most. It was a moment of triumph.

'So you feel you must go back to the unit?' Father asked. 'And Stefan? He will not like it, I very much fear.'

Father gave his subtle little smile and I felt he did not mind Stefan's discomfiture one bit. So Papa is jealous too, I thought, and smiled inwardly to myself. Then I remembered the kiss, the velvety feel of Stevie's lips, the strength of his grip on my wrist. It was not approval I wanted from Stevie, it was him. Even Father's approval paled beside that desire. I underwent a momentary struggle. Being near Stevie won't be the same as having him, I thought. That is impossible at present. Being near will only make it harder. At least, at the front, there isn't time for idle longing. At the front, I can be strong and useful, and not just a woman in love.

'I've written to Stevie, Papa.' I voiced my decision. 'I've tried to explain that if his leg was whole and his wound healing, it was because I had been there to assist Dr Kornev. And how many others like him might be crippled if I were not? He'll understand.'

'In time,' said Father. 'He will in time. I'll send both your letters along with my dispatch to GHQ.'

We returned to my unit and were met beside the ambulance wagons by the senior surgeon and the head nurse.

'Your daughter has conquered our hearts,' Marfa Antonovna told Father.

Dr Kornev said, 'A remarkably able nurse, your daughter, Prince, a real surgical talent. When she finishes her medical studies, I will be happy to recommend her.'

'She thought of it,' Father said. 'But now, I believe, she has other plans.' He looked at me a little uncertainly.

'I'm going to be a surgeon and have eight children,' I said rashly.

My fastidious father looked appalled at both prospects.

'Eight children *and* a surgical career?' Dr Kornev exclaimed.

'Well, well, that's quite an ambition! You know, Prince, I believe Tatyana Petrovna is capable of fulfilling it,' he added as he observed me in turn with paternal pride. 'I have a daughter too, somewhat older than Tatyana Petrovna. But she only thinks of dresses and parties. Her mother spoiled her rotten. Well, Prince, I suppose you'll be sending us more work?'

'I'm afraid so, Doctor.'

Again our unit made its semicircle in a clearing by a stream. Again the medical stocks replenished in Lublin ran low and we had not enough drugs, not enough water, not enough rest, and no other choice but to hang on. Nightly, Yefim's harmonica brought a whiff of the steppe to our encampment. Whenever I felt on the verge of collapse, Father appeared with his adjutants and took me to his field headquarters for a bath, a good night's rest and a breakfast chat. Each time I scribbled off a letter to Stefan and one to Tanik. The knowledge that Father was protecting our rear and watching over us every moment renewed my strength and made me feel safe.

All through August the unit stayed in the rear, leaving just ahead of L-M's sappers, who blew up the last bridges and railway junctions. Warsaw had been occupied on 5 August. The Germans and Austrians advanced in the north, in the centre, in the south, trying in vain to encircle and cut off the retreating Russians. Stolidly, uncomplainingly, the rear guard held positions hastily dug after a forced march, and stubbornly, in a somnolent stupor, the main body of the army flowed eastward, slowed but not stemmed by the refugees. I could always look forward on the move to the bracing company of L-M. Russian endurance was still equal, in his words, to the confusion and inefficiency that had created these inhuman hardships.

At the end of August our unit passed through the smouldering ruins of Brest-Litovsk. We loaded our wounded on to the last hospital train before the rails were torn up. At the edge of the Pripet marshes, where reeds grew to the height of trees, we made our circle by the light of smudge pots. Along causeways crossing the treacherous marsh, along the road skirting the virgin forest more fearful in its fastness than German guns, along the three rail lines east – the stream of humanity, soldier and civilian, flowed ever more slowly, with ever greater difficulty, but without once being dammed up or cut off.

By the end of September, all the fortress-towns, Lutsk, Grodno, Brest-Litovsk, Kovno and Vilna, had fallen. All Poland was in the hands of the Central Powers. More than a million men had died on either side. The advance had cost the Austro-Germans dearly. The Russian retreat never became a rout.

Yet the commander in chief, Grand Duke Nikolay Nikolayevich, latest target of Alexandra's animosity, was made the scapegoat for the army's reverses and transferred to a secondary command in the Caucasus. At Alexandra's urging, his place as generalissimo was taken by the Emperor in person.

Father thought this more dangerous for Russia than the loss of Poland. Although the actual command was in the able hands of the chief of staff, General Alexeiev, Father foresaw that with the Emperor at the Stavka – the Russian GHQ, now moved from Baranovichi to Mogilev – Alexandra would be free to rule the empire from Tsarskoye Selo.

In the first week of October my field-hospital unit rolled into Minsk, where it was inactivated and its personnel given its first leave in a year. Yefim rejoined his detachment. It was all the same to him, he said, where he was assigned, as long as he had his mare to keep him company, and his harmonica. After parting from my comrades-in-arms in the confidence that their expressions of respect were not for my rank alone, I was driven to the Catholic Hospital now administered by Aunt Sophie, and fell into her forgiving arms.

16

As soon as I had cleaned up, Aunt took me to see Stevie. His room adjoined her apartment at the rear of the hospital, overlooking the park.

At our knock, he answered, 'Come in,' in a bored tone. But as we entered, he quickly put down the book he had been reading and watched me wordlessly, with fierce intensity. I advanced slowly, also in silence, to the armchair by the window, in which he sat in a dressing gown, the wounded leg stretched on a hassock, a cane at his side.

'Look who I've brought, Stevie,' Aunt Sophie said. And, as I looked at her, 'He does look ferocious, our Stevie boy, but he's still shaky on his feet.' Aunt smiled with gentle humour and left.

Stevie finds me strange and unattractive. He no longer loves me, was my interpretation of his silence.

I sat down beside him. He was no longer fresh and rosy like a baby out of the bath, nor smooth and sleek like a fine hunter. He was thin, pale and irritable, like a boy too long in bed.

'What were you reading?' I asked, my mouth dry, in order to hear him say something.

'Gibbon's *Decline and Fall of the Roman Empire*. It's very instructive. I can't read novels any more.'

'Neither can I.' Literature, once more trustworthy than life, had been outdistanced by galloping reality. And love? Had it, too, gone the way of literature?

'I've had lots of time to read.' Stevie spoke in a clipped tone unlike his own. 'Especially since your letters were so brief.'

'Stevie, how could I write long letters? I hadn't time!'

'Naturally. You had time for the lowliest private in the Russian army but none for your intended husband.'

'That's not true!' But I could not say truthfully, I thought of you always, when I had thought of nothing, in the field hospital, beyond the unimaginable effort of every moment. As for the days spent with L-M, days that would have been dismal otherwise, I had better pass them over for the present. Stevie was jealous enough already!

'I hope,' he continued in the same vein, 'being a beastly heroine makes you happy.'

'I haven't been heroic. Casimir, yes, and you.'

'I?'

'Papa said your capture of the Austrian battery was brilliant. You'll get the St George for it.'

'My horse ought to have the medal, not I. He was going like an express train and we were on top of the battery before I knew it. Heroism is bunkum!'

'Then why call me a heroine?'

'The newspapers call you one. The Tsar, they say, is going to decorate you.'

'Oh no, it wouldn't be fair to the rest of the unit! I did no more than anyone else!'

'What possessed you to do it in the first place?'

What indeed? Sadly, I realized that I could share none of the past two critical months with Stevie. Not only had war, real war as fought by men, eluded me, but the adventure undertaken to draw me closer to my blood brother and beloved had apparently only served to estrange us.

'You ought to see yourself!' Stevie went on relentlessly. 'Thin as a scarecrow, your complexion awful, and those eyes that shine with a light like a fanatic's!'

'I know I'm not beautiful. I never was to begin with, and I haven't had time for my appearance. But if that's all you ever saw in me, I'm certain you'll find a great many girls who'll suit you much better,' I said, and rose to go.

At the door, I met up with my cousin's English nurse, who was not thin as a scarecrow and whose blue eyes held nothing but their very blue colour. I said, 'How d'you do,' very coolly, and, crossing the hall, knocked on the door of Aunt's study.

Aunt Sophie excused her secretary.

'It's finished, Auntie,' I said. 'Stevie no longer loves me. He called me a beastly heroine. He said I looked like a scarecrow and that my complexion was awful . . .' I was ready to cry.

'What a rude boy!' said Aunt. 'And how miserable he must feel now. Come here, child.' Taking my hands in hers, she went on.

'Stevie is jealous of every wounded man you tend, of your father, of the Grand Duchess Tatyana, of your every thought and feeling that is not about him. He's had two months to brood on his jealousy' – Aunt Sophie laid stress on 'two months', and I thought, Poor Stevie, with nothing to do but read and brood. Oh, I have been cruel!

'My Stan is the same,' Aunt went on. 'After an absence, the more anxious he has been to see me, the more disagreeable and difficult he is when we meet.'

'But how do you handle it?'

'I coax him around. Men need a good deal of coaxing, Tanyussia, and Veslawski men more than any. They're so very proud. They can be butter in our hands. But we must melt before they will. Are you too proud to, child?'

I could feel myself melting already.

The English nurse now came in to report that His Lordship was tense, his temperature was slightly elevated, and he did not wish his supper. Would my lady care to take His Lordship's tray in to him?

'I will if I may,' I said.

Aunt smilingly inclined her head and the nurse went out.

'Auntie' – I turned back at the door – 'do you think it wrong of me to have stayed with the field hospital after Stevie was wounded?'

'I confess I thought it selfish at first. But looking at it objectively, it's better for you to be free now, while you can, than to wish you were after you're married.'

'Can't one be married and free?'

'Not in the same way, child. Not in the same way.'

I had suspected as much.

At my entrance, Stevie did not turn his head but continued to gaze at the yellowing beeches and limes of the park.

I set the tray down on a low table beside his chair and said, 'Stevie, I've brought you supper.'

'I'm not hungry,' he pouted.

I understood he wanted coaxing. I sat down facing him, tucked a linen napkin with the Veslawski monogram into his dressing gown, and offered him a spoonful of soup. He took it, and another, and a third, never taking his eyes off me. Soon the sulky baby began to look like a baby after his bottle, sated and content.

When it came to the chicken à la Kiev, he took the fork from me and held it to my mouth.

'You first. You're much too thin.'

'Like a scarecrow?' I asked, taking the tasty morsel. It was doubly delicious from his hand.

'Who said you look like a scarecrow?' he asked, after a bite. 'Tell me the man and I'll chop him up with my sabre.'

'Oh, no, you mustn't!'

'Why not, the coarse and insolent fellow!'

'Because he is, he will be . . . my husband.'

We finished the dish in rapt silence. Then I pushed the table aside and sank down on the floor, letting my hand lie in Stevie's. The yellow light of the late autumn afternoon had dimmed. Only a faint glow lingered on the white walls and white hospital furniture. My eyes went to the crucifix over the bed and I made a silent prayer of thanks for having found Stevie well and whole.

Stevie stroked my hair and face as he watched me. 'You don't mind becoming a Catholic?'

'Not at all.' I loved the rich Greek-Orthodox ritual, but Catholicism seemed a more universal religion.

'Tanya,' he went on, 'have you ever thought of taking vows?'

'How could I?' I was astonished. Wilful, vengeful, jealous, proud and lustful as I was. 'I'm far too sinful.'

'Good,' he said. 'I like you sinful. Remember, I fell in love with the little girl who played naughty doctor games, not with the field-nurse heroine.'

'Will you stop calling me a heroine?'

'I don't object in principle to heroines. Several Veslawski princesses have been heroines. But first, they have been wives of Veslawski men.' He held my wrist as he spoke.

I felt an exquisite shock.

How fierce and solemn he looks, I thought. If one can't be married and free, at least it will be glorious to surrender one's freedom to Stefan Veslawski. I laid my flaming cheek on his hand.

'When you are my wife,' he continued, 'who will come first, your father or I?'

'You will!' I said unhesitatingly, under the spell of his fierceness.

'The lowliest wounded private or I?'

'You, my lord.' I kissed the palm of his hand. Having asserted my independence, I now enjoyed the taste of abnegation.

'Tatyana, my beloved, my own.' He spoke in the deep voice of Slavic resonance, like Father's, which made my name the most beautiful-sounding of all. 'My chaste little nun, my brave little nurse, my sweet little sister, my naughty playmate, my humble mistress, my proud princess, I shall love and honour you as well and better than Father does Mother. I shall make you the happiest of women!' He gazed afar, as if into the future, and I, too, tried to picture our happiness.

Instead of a legendary vision, a realistic one arose. Now was the time – there might not be another – to tell Stevie all. 'Stevie, after the war, let's not go back to Veslawa right off, not until the children are born. Let's live in Warsaw, or London. You can finish your university studies and I'll go to medical school.'

'Medical school?' He lifted my chin.

'Stevie, you know I've always wanted to be a surgeon. I could be a very good one. Dr Kornev, the senior surgeon at the field hospital, said so.' I felt how childish I sounded.

Stevie released my chin. 'I don't doubt you could. And d'you know what I'd rather be than anything? An opera singer. Seriously. I have the voice and the acting ability. My coach told me. If I weren't Stefan Veslawski, that's what I'd study for. But I am Stefan Veslawski, and there's no running away from that role.'

It was a definitive statement, but it did not silence me. 'Suppose,' I persisted, 'the world were so changed after the war that being Prince Veslawski no longer meant very much.'

'As long as there is a Poland, it'll mean something. And Poland has existed for ten centuries. As for the world changing' – he glanced at *The Decline and Fall of the Roman Empire* – 'that's nothing new either. We'll adapt and we'll survive. Perhaps, in a world of rapid change, we who have survived for ten centuries will acquire more importance rather than less.'

I could not argue with Stevie. I felt as dominated by his worldly knowledge and political maturity as I was by the hands that tilted my face. It was easier to yield. It was strangely appealing.

'Well?' he said comically.

'Nothing.'

He bent down to kiss me. Then, 'Now what?' He stopped as I stiffened.

'Stevie, I'm afraid . . .'

'Afraid? You? Oh, I see.' He smiled indulgently. 'It's natural. I should be afraid of you' – he moved my head back and forth – 'my chaste huntress, my terrible Artemis. You might metamorphose me into a laurel tree.'

'No, you've got it wrong! I'm not afraid of *that*' – I could not say 'sex' – 'not with you. I'm afraid, on the contrary, that we shouldn't be able to stop, once we started.'

'D'you think I can't control myself? I'm no longer the raw youth who tried to abduct you. A war, and a wound, make one mature in a hurry. You're far too precious to endanger our future for the sake of a temporary satisfaction. There'll be time enough. Now will you trust me?'

I closed my eyes. This time my head was inert in his hands, my mouth obedient to his. And again time stopped. Past and future, war, peace, everything ceased to matter.

In the moment my breath failed, Stevie released me. He lay back against the chair, his face pale and weary once more.

'Stevie, are you all right?' I jumped to my feet.

He opened his eyes. 'Oh, it's not going to be easy,' he murmured. 'Don't fuss,' he added as I closed my hand on his pulse. 'Leave me now.'

I picked up the tray and went out.

'I see Stevie has his appetite back,' Aunt Sophie remarked as we passed each other in the hall. I did not tell her how I had helped clean up the plate.

After my visit, Stevie asked to be moved to an officers' convalescent ward. Aunt Sophie agreed upon his promise that he would not turn the ward into a riot or ruin his fellow officers at cards. I understood that he did not want to be tempted by privacy.

I was also eager within a few days to set to work. Work was my safeguard against the temptations that assailed me. The hospital was old, and not nearly so well appointed as ours in Petrograd, or Aunt Sophie's at Veslawa. The beds were iron and the thin mattresses of dried grass. The equipment was neither new nor shiny. Still, after the field hospital, to work again under aseptic conditions, with scrubbed hands, properly masked and gowned, using sterile instruments and linens, seemed to me a marvel. I had also gained new respect for the nursing profession. In my former striving for medical heights, I had viewed nurses as little better than doctors' servants. I saw now that a good nurse was just as valuable as a physician, and the patient's recovery as dependent on her care and insight, if not more. My ambition to become a surgeon was clearly incompatible with my future role as Princess Veslawska. But I could continue to practise my nursing skill, if only in an administrative capacity, like Aunt Sophie.

This compromise was surprisingly easy to accept so long as I saw Stevie daily. His presence put an end to all questing, all questions. His mood was greatly improved and he was able to hobble about ever more quickly, although he liked to lean on my shoulder, instead of a cane, and exaggerate his limp. There was a piano in the recreation hall, and I fell upon it. Soon Stevie limped in to listen. And, one evening, he brought sheets of music. I accompanied him in operatic arias, and songs by Fauré and Rachmaninov. Whenever Stevie sang, an audience gathered. The entire hospital seemed to fall under a spell. And life's vision, which had become all jagged and strident like a cubist painting, would smooth out again briefly into harmonious contours in softly glowing colours.

In the middle of October 1915, the Tsar passed through Minsk with the Tsarevich. The town was headquarters of the western front, and a review was held in grand style, the sun breaking through the clouds true to army tradition that the sun always shines when the Emperor reviews the troops. Father had come from the south-western front for a conference of the general staff and was in His Majesty's suite. Against the panorama of the plain and the massed body of men, the Tsar looked thinner, older and smaller than I remembered him. There was a vagueness in his gaze, a hesitancy in his gesture. And I thought how different he was from Father, whose melancholy had been cured by active duty. Not for Father the calm family life in which the Tsar had basked. For the first time I guessed how unequal was Russia's ruler to his crushing task.

But as our field unit was cited for bravery and the Tsar pinned the cross of St Anne on my breast, looking straight into my eyes as of old, I could not help the pounding of my heart. I felt renewed loyalty for my sovereign and fresh affection for eleven-year-old Aleksey, erect and soldierly in his long soldier's overcoat. The boy's beautiful blue-grey eyes were fastened on mine, and his fair face flushed.

Steve also received the decoration he had deprecated. By tacit agreement we did not exchange congratulations. Beside the magnet that drew us together, what did a bit of painted metal on a ribbon mean?

Before the end of the month the Empress and her two eldest daughters, after visiting the Tsar at the Stavka, came to Minsk and the Catholic Hospital. While Aunt showed Alexandra and Olga Nikolayevna through the wards, I remained alone with my namesake in a small sitting room off the entrance vestibule.

'Tata, darling, we're all so proud of you! We simply devoured your letters! Papa thinks you're splendid and Aleksey blushes every time you're mentioned.' Tatyana Nikolayevna drew me down on a couch and continued to hold my hands.

'Why proud of me?' I looked tenderly into my friend's face. I found it charming, even under a rather unbecoming round hat of grey wool. 'Everyone's talking about your refugee committee.'

'Oh yes.' Tatyana Nikolayevna laughed and sat back. 'I've become frightfully efficient. But actually,' she went on with new earnestness, 'we accomplish so little. We've been visiting some of these wretches with Mummsy. It's pitiful!'

'I know,' I said. We were silent a moment, communicating without words our new perspective of life's jagged ugliness. As I observed my friend more closely, I noticed a hardening of her features, an expression not unlike her mother's. Under her reserve, I suspected, she hid a passionate nature inherited from her mother. Dammed up, that passion would turn Tatyana Nikolayevna into a premature old maid, just as Olga's intelligence, unused, would sour her too in time. And what might I become without Stevie?

'Tell me, Tata, about the field hospital and the retreat. Wasn't it awful?' The Grand Duchess spoke first.

'Yes and no. It's difficult to describe the front' – impossible to someone in the rear. Nevertheless I tried. I found myself telling about Stevie's wound, the anaesthesia, the kiss ...

'Tata, you didn't!' My friend watched me wide-eyed. 'Did no one see you?'

'I don't think so. Not even Stevie knows. You're the only one, Tanik, I'd ever tell.'

'I won't tell. Not even Olga.' Tatyana Nikolayevna understood. 'And have you kissed since?'

'Just once. It's better like this. The other way ... is almost unbearable.' Could Tanik know what I meant, she who had never even held hands with a man?

'Yes, I can see how it would be.'

She knew! She was closer, dearer to me than ever! 'We kissed after our first quarrel.' I relished my confession as much as she relished hearing it. 'Stevie had called me a beastly heroine, and thin as a scarecrow.'

'Well, you are a bit scrawny. But as long as Stefan loves you ...' My friend gave me a sidelong glance.

'I'm not sure, Tanik. I'm never sure. I always wonder why he should love me. I'm not beautiful like you, or clever like Olga, or good like Marie.' I wanted to be sophisticated in the eyes of the world and good in the eye of God. But these two contradictory goals, so naturally and imperceptibly blended in Aunt Sophie, seemed impossible for me to achieve. 'When Stevie and I are together, we don't know what to say. But when we're away from each other, we're utterly wretched.'

'Then, being in love still means being miserable?' Smiling, the Grand Duchess laid her hand in mine.

'Yes. You have a feeling of anguish, here.' I pressed her hand to my diaphragm. 'Tanik ... I'm frightened about the future.'

'I'm frightened too at times.' Tatyana Nikolayevna thoughtfully folded her hands, and her fine features took on that prematurely prim and hard expression. 'And Mummsy's forever having premonitions. She thinks she has such bad luck. And, d'you know, *he*' – my namesake was too tactful to mention her mother's friend by name to the daughter of Prince Silomirsky, his archenemy – 'has predicted our end. But Papa always says there's no use in worrying. "The Lord's will be done."' She quoted in Russian the Tsar's favourite saying.

I recalled Father's impatience at the Emperor's passive dependence on the Heavenly Will. More disconcerting still was His Majesty's habit of falling back on that Will whenever his own imperial will was contested. But to my friend I said, 'You miss your father, Tanik, since His Majesty is at the Stavka?'

'Dreadfully, Mummsy especially. She writes to him morning and afternoon and cables him besides. If a letter doesn't come from him one day she's simply frantic. We all tease her about it. Poor Mummsy is so unwell. Her heart is enlarged and she's short of breath. She has to be carried upstairs. But she still insists on working mornings at the hospital, even though she has so much else on her shoulders. Now that Papa keeps Boysy with him at the Stavka, we all miss the little pest. Schwibzik's quite lost without him.'

The mischievous Schwibzik – Grand Duchess Anastasia – was closest in age to the Tsarevich. I smiled as I recalled their squabbles. We chatted happily of good old times at Tsarskoye, until the entrance of Alexandra with the Grand Duchess Olga Nikolayevna and Aunt Sophie. Olga Nikolayevna wore a plain costume of grey wool and the Empress a similar dowdy outfit, with a stiff-brimmed boater that made her look even more like a schoolmistress.

'Princess Veslawska tells me you're becoming quite a competent nurse, Tata,' Her Majesty said to me in English. 'But I hope that in future you'll be content to do your duty without attracting so much public notice.'

I blushed and bowed my head. Tatyana Nikolayevna tried to cover her embarrassment with a haughty air of displeasure. Olga's blue eyes blazed.

Stepping up to me, she embraced me warmly. 'I think you were brave, Tata. I think you were fine!'

Alexandra flushed in patches. 'Being brave's not so very difficult. If one is well born, *ça va de soi*, it's a matter of course. What's difficult is to do one's duty in obscurity, with God alone as judge. Even as a child, Tata, you were always given to excesses. I trust you'll now begin to learn not only nursing, but moderation and modesty as well.'

'I shall try, Your Majesty.' I kept my eyes low. What the Empress said was true. But I only hated her the more at this moment.

Aunt, whose manner towards the Russian Empress, for all its customary gracious dignity, suggested distance rather than deference, now smiled on me encouragingly and said, 'It will come with maturity, Madame, I'm certain. Would Your Majesty care for a cup of tea before resuming your journey?'

Alexandra declined. 'Thank you, Princess, we'd best be off.'

We followed her into the entrance vestibule, where the hospital staff stood in a semicircle. Their attitudes reflected the malaise and strain that the Empress created on such visits despite her good intentions. Alexandra herself seemed at a loss for words.

Aunt broke the awkward silence by saying, with a graceful inclination of the head, 'In the name of our patients and our staff, I thank Your Imperial Majesty and Your Imperial Highnesses for honouring us with your visit.'

'You have a very well-run institution, Princess. Thank you for your time and courtesy.' Alexandra stiffly extended her hand.

Aunt did not kiss it, after the Russian custom. She held it lightly as she made an easy curtsy, imitated much less gracefully by the nurses present, while the doctors bowed. I was invited to accompany the visitors to the station. The passage of the imperial motor brought no cheers from the passersby. Behind it, fingers were pointed and the words, now common wherever the Empress went, were heard on all sides, '*Nyemka yedet, Nyemka yedet*. There goes the German woman.' The people, in its ferocious simplicity, had found a culprit for the army's reverses: '*Nyemka*', the German woman.

Alexandra's visit left a painful impression. Not only did I feel newly sorry for Olga and Tatyana Nikolayevna's blighted young lives but I was worried, as well as hurt, by the Empress's unexpected animosity. I knew that the success of Polish autonomy depended in great part on Alexandra's feelings towards the people most interested in this cause. I had displeased the jealous Empress by drawing to myself the attention reserved for her own family. She already disliked Father. If the Veslawskis, too, incurred her displeasure, the Polish cause was as good as lost.

Stevie's departure for a desk assignment in the quartermaster department in Rovno made November a dull month beset by nagging anxieties over our future. These were somewhat relieved when, a week before the Catholic Christmas, I was urgently summoned to Tsarskoye Selo to nurse the Tsarevich, stricken with his most severe attack of haemophilia since Spala.

17

By the time I arrived at Tsarskoye Selo in the early afternoon of 19 December 1915, after travelling overnight in a *wagon-lit* compartment, the crisis had passed. In the children's apartments at the Alexander Palace, Aleksey was asleep, propped up on pillows. The devoted Nagorny, his sailor-nurse, who had held him up all during the harrowing twenty-four-hour journey home from Mogilev, was able to rest. The blood vessel that had burst in the boy's nose from too hard a sneeze and caused the near-fatal haemorrhage, had been cauterized on the previous night. The bleeding had stopped, but the patient had to be kept still for fear it might start up again. I was to make him comfortable and keep him calm. The attending physician – there were three on the case – would change the plugs in his nose with extreme care as needed. All this Dr Botkin told me when I entered the sickroom.

The purple circles about his closed eyes were all the colour in the boy's face. His pulse was thin and irregular. Weak as he was, it would not be difficult to keep him still. The Tsarevich was most in danger when he was well. A hot temper and a natural rebelliousness against the restraints of illness made him court disaster.

'It seems a rather simple case at this stage,' I said, after I had read the chart.

'For you, Tatyana Petrovna, it would be, after being in charge of a field hospital.' Dr Botkin's round eyes behind round-rimmed gold spectacles regarded me in fond wonder. 'But you always were a strong-minded girl. What a row you raised when we tried to cut your hair, the time you had typhoid fever. You remember?'

I could not recall it without blushing.

Dr Botkin smiled as he stroked his thinning beard. 'Now go and see your friends. Their Imperial Highnesses are expecting you eagerly. We'll call you when Aleksey Nikolayevich awakens.'

What a good, plain man, Botkin, not like a court physician at all! He's straight out of a Chekhov play, I thought, as a palace runner in the picturesque livery of the reign of Empress Elizabeth showed me to the playroom.

Both fireplaces blazed in the familiar room with the green-and-yellow frieze of peacocks, with tall windows on the park, its frozen lakes and snowy islands. The four Grand Duchesses made an attractive tableau about a fireplace. Anastasia, the only one still in sailor dress, played on the floor with Tatyana's bulldog – the Tsarevich's cocker would not leave his door. All four girls rose and surrounded me. Marie, who was beginning to look quite handsome, was still shy and slow. Anastasia would have bombarded me with questions. But Olga Nikolayevna said, 'It's time for you and Marie to return to your lessons. Mummsy's resting after being up all night with Boysy, and *I'm* in charge. *Allez-vous-en.* Go!' She waved an imperious hand.

'*Vite!*' Tatyana Nikolayevna seconded her sister.

'For that, we won't sign ourselves OTMA any more.' The sisters had formed an anagram with the first letters of their names. 'We'll be MA *tout court* from now on,' Anastasia shot back. And, seizing Marie by the hand, she strode out.

We smiled. Then Olga looked grave, Tatyana pensive. They led me to a seat by the fireplace.

After an exchange of eager inquiries, Olga Nikolayevna said, 'It's such a relief to have you here, Tata. Aleksey should get better right away. Perhaps *he* won't need to come any more.'

It was the first time Olga Nikolayevna had openly expressed her dislike of her mother's friend, although I had guessed at it by her manner.

'Father Grigory at the palace?' I, too, mentioned Rasputin for the first time.

'He came to pray with Mummsy yesterday. She believes his prayers saved Boysy's life!'

'Whether they did or not, he brought Mummsy peace of mind.' Tatyana Nikolayevna assumed the pinched air of displeasure she had unconsciously copied from her mother.

'Did you actually see him?' I asked Olga Nikolayevna. The man all Russia talked about was a mystery figure to me, and, I liked to think, to my friends.

'We met at the door of Mummsy's boudoir as he was leaving. He made me a bow to the floor, like a peasant. With Papa and Mummsy, he's positively rude. But with me, because I avoid him, he's unctuous. His eyes are very blue and deep-set. They look right into you. He has Mummsy under a spell.'

'If Mummsy trusts him, he can't be evil.' Tatyana Nikolayevna looked even more aloof. 'I wish you wouldn't criticize Mummsy's friend.'

'Oh, you're so blindly devoted to her, you can't see the harm she is doing to herself and Papa!' Olga was undaunted.

'Mummsy's under such a strain!' Tatyana Nikolayevna's voice rang with passionate tenderness. 'With Papa at the Stavka, unwell as she is, she's trying to run the government. It's beyond human strength!'

'*He* runs the government,' said her forthright sister. 'It's quite intolerable, really. I don't understand why Papa doesn't put a stop to it.'

'None of us understands it,' I dared murmur.

We looked at one another in silence.

'But what can we do? What can anyone do?' cried Olga.

'We can each do our job from day to day. And try to be kind,' Tatyana Nikolayevna enjoined.

'You are an example to us all.' Olga smiled with engaging candour. And we began to talk of lighter matters.

I thought either one of them, Olga Nikolayevna with her incisiveness and courage, Tatyana with her self-control and tact, would have made a better heir to the throne than their sickly and turbulent brother. That stupidly discriminatory law passed early in the nineteenth century, which barred women from accession, was at the root of the Rasputin phenomenon and the decadence of our court.

After tea in Alexandra's boudoir with the Tsar, the children and the indispensable Annushka – Anya Vyrubova – who fawned on me sickeningly, I was called to the sickroom.

Aleksey was still in a state of prostration, but he recognized me nevertheless and clung to my hand tenaciously. It was not easy for someone as active as I to sit immobile for hours. Prayer came to my aid. A new clarity and calm followed the long period of concentration. I slept deeply when Nagorny relieved me, and awoke refreshed.

On the second day, Aleksey was willing to eat a little if I fed him. He not only wanted to hold my hand, but I had to tell him stories.

I drew on Jules Verne and H. G. Wells, adding my own unorthodox twists.

In another day, Aleksey was able to talk, and I asked him, after I had taken his afternoon temperature and arranged his pillows, how he liked being with his father at the Stavka.

'I like it well enough,' he said. 'Zubrovka' – his cat – 'is lots of fun. But I didn't like the casualty station we visited. It smelled bad, and the wounded groaned most dreadfully. It gave me nightmares.'

I thought it a mistake on the part of the Tsar to subject a nervous and highly impressionable eleven-year-old to such a shock, especially one as sheltered from reality as Aleksey Nikolayevich had been until then.

'Papa says I must be strong,' Aleksey went on. 'I want to be strong, like Peter the Great. But everybody babies me so, even Papa. I'm "Boysy" and "Little Treasure". I can't bear to be babied. All the girls do it. You're the only one who doesn't, Tata.'

'I'm not family. And I'm a professional nurse. One never babies the sick.'

'You're different.' Aleksey played with my hand. 'I like you a lot, Tata. I called for you, when I was so sick. I won't let them send you away.'

'Who would send me away?' I asked, although I could guess.

'*You* know . . . Father Grigory. I don't want him to come and see me. He isn't clean. He's just a dirty *mujik*,' he added in Russian.

'There's nothing wrong with being a *mujik*.' I remembered how I had associated dirt with the lower classes at that age. 'If peasants aren't always clean, it's because they haven't the means to wash. And Father Grigory won't need to come any more, since you're getting well.'

'I hope not! But why are *mujiks* so humble?' Aleksey's volatile mind did not dwell long on his mother's friend. 'When a deputation comes to see Papa, they kneel. Why does Papa let them? It embarrasses me horribly.'

'I'm sure His Majesty doesn't care for it. But it's an old custom he finds difficult to break with.'

Aleksey switched back to idiomatic English. 'Well, I'd soon chuck it. And no majestying. Just plain sir, and ma'am, like Uncle George and Queen Mary.' The boy called his father's cousin 'Uncle'.

I thought Papa would be glad to know that the Tsarevich took the English king and queen for his models. 'You'll make a modern monarch,' I said.

'A modern monarch. I like the way it sounds. Say it again.'

'A modern monarch.' And I made His Imperial Highness a face.

Aleksey laughed.

My principal duty, besides keeping him still and comfortable, was to make Aleksey laugh. And Olga Nikolayevna was bold enough to say, by the end of the week, when Nagorny carried the boy out of the sickroom into his mother's boudoir for tea, 'Tata making him laugh is what has made Boysy well.'

The very next day, Alexandra thanked me in her driest manner for my able care, and gave me permission to return to my 'more pressing duties'.

I went to say goodbye to Aleksey.

As I came down from the children's floor, I was met at the foot of the private staircase by a palace runner and asked into the Tsar's study. I was surprised – the children never entered – but I followed with timidity. The Tsar had always treated me with the warmest affection, like a daughter.

At the far end of the corridor, beyond the office of the aide-de-camp on duty, the Ethiopian footman who stood guard outside the Tsar's study opened the door. The room was of modest size, soberly furnished in dark woods and leather, with a meticulously tidy desk top and family busts and portraits on a low bookcase. The Tsar sat by the single window, smoking. He motioned me to the armchair facing his across a low table and, after a few words about the Tsarevich, asked me to tell him in detail about my experiences with the field hospital.

I told them as candidly as I would have told Father. Though I glossed over my cousin's wound, I took the opportunity to stress the gallant rearguard action of the Veslawski lancers.

'A splendid regiment,' the Tsar agreed. 'Go on.'

When I had done, 'Dreadful, dreadful!' His soft voice rang with heartfelt compassion. Then, 'But we must beat the Germans, no matter what the cost,' he added.

What if, thought I, instead of letting their armies fight till they had no blood left to spill, the warring governments got together to negotiate peace? If soldiers in the line could fraternize between battles, why couldn't the commanders in chief who issued battle orders from the safety of general headquarters order a cease-fire?

The Tsar looked out of the window dreamily. 'Ah, if you only knew, Tanichka' – he turned back to me and spoke Russian – 'how much I envy your father. To be in command of one's own loyal troops, facing a known enemy. I . . . I can count on one hand the servants I can trust. And my unseen enemies are everywhere. But it's all in God's hands.' He put out his cigarette, stroked his sideburn with the back of his right hand, and murmured, '"Oh my Father, if this cup may not pass me by except I drink it, Thy Will be done."'

I felt a pang of mingled sympathy and dread: sympathy for this sensitive, gentle man unwittingly responsible for the sufferings of millions, dread for my loved ones and my country governed in time of peril by a hollow figure of authority.

'Well, Tanichka' – the Tsar collected himself and rose – 'we must both be on our way. I would take you as far as the Stavka in my train, but I know Anna Vladimirovna will want to see you. Thank you for everything. You're a fine girl.' He embraced me, and I left.

I thought I was dismissed from the palace. But when I was packed and ready to leave, I was recalled to the imperial apartments. There, in the presence of her daughters, Alexandra hung about my neck a medallion with the portrait of the Tsarevich set in jewels, and gave me a kiss.

Anastasia clapped her hands. Marie blushed crimson. Olga Nikolayevna hugged me. But no one was better pleased, I felt, looking into her sloe eyes, than the reserved Tatyana.

The Tsar was right. I could not go back to Minsk without visiting Grandmaman.

In the course of my brief stay in Petrograd, we attended a gala benefit performance of *Boris Godunov* with Chaliapin in the title role. Grandmaman would not let me go in uniform. Nyanya, who pronounced my hair 'some kind of yellow string', brushed it mercilessly. As I was helped into my unaccustomed finery, I felt like an actress being costumed for the role of princess.

In the orchestra pit at the Marinsky Theatre, I spied Professor Holveg in stiff shirt-front and coat-tails. He came for Chaliapin, I thought, and smiled. He hates formal dress, although it makes him look distinguished in spite of himself. Ah, he sees me too. Delighted, I nodded and smiled.

Grandmaman noticed it, and trained her opera glass on the scientist. He turned his head towards the stage and did not glance at me again.

I was too engrossed in the opera – my favourite – to dwell on the Professor. How thrilled Stevie would be to hear Chaliapin, was my thought. And what a pity he can't be an opera star, any more than Father could have been a painter, or I can become a surgeon. But these personal disappointments were trivial beside the great drama of madness, private and universal, unfolding on the stage.

The opera over on the Simpleton's plaint, 'Weep, Russian folk, weep!' I had difficulty being civil on the way out to the friends and acquaintances who crowded about Grandmaman and Zinaida Mikhailovna – fortunately, Vera Kirilovna was not in our party. Unable to withstand the rigours of Grandmaman's wartime regime, she had fled with Bobby to our Crimean estate – both suffered from rheumatism and the cold.

As I was being looked over by the society curious who exclaimed over my 'heroic war work', I glimpsed Professor Holveg in the crush. 'I must disappear for a moment,' I whispered to Zinaida Mikhailovna, and sent Fyodor to catch the scientist.

We met in a corner of the downstairs foyer.

He kissed my hand. 'Tatyana Petrovna. To see you again on this night of all nights . . . I'm overwhelmed.'

'It was overwhelming!' I thought he must have meant the opera alone. 'And you know, it never seemed so real, so close before.'

He understood. 'Yes. Since we last met, we have indeed come closer to that sixteenth century we used to regard as barbaric. I fear we may come much closer yet. Only this twentieth-century Time of Troubles will dwarf its predecessor.'

'I believe you now. I've just spent a week at Tsarskoye, in the Alexander Palace.' No more needed to be said.

We had so much else to talk about. But Fyodor signalled the approach of Grandmaman.

'Tatyana Petrovna,' the Professor said hurriedly, 'you have my address. Please feel free to contact me in case of need. I have friends on both sides of the political spectrum.'

'Thank you. God bless you.' I slipped away.

On the drive home in Grandmaman's Delauney, I sat silent in my corner, watching the gulf fog swirl yellow about the streetlights. I thought of the Professor's words, and of the Time of Troubles that had followed the reign of Boris Godunov. I thought of the young son and heir of Tsar Boris and of his daughter, both put to death by his successor. And was there not another tragic opera in the making at Tsarskoye – a vacillating yet stubborn tsar dependent on his unbalanced but determined wife, who leaned in turn on a cunning peasant with mysterious powers? Or were all three being used by a clique of venal opportunists? Was it no grand opera but a shabby melodrama? Whatever the case, the vacuum at the top could only be filled by the cruel and the unscrupulous. Grandmaman was right. There could not be, in Russia, a state of things sensible and moderate.

In the remaining days I spent in Petrograd, I went with Grandmaman to the Marble Palace to pay a visit of condolence to the widow of Grand Duke Constantine. Shattered by the death of Oleg, his favourite son, the Grand Duke had died less than a year later. In the foyer of rose marble with the tall amphoras in which we used to hide as children, the familiar shadow passed over me, as if that palace too had the mark of Greek tragedy upon it.

More cheerful was the informal visit to our *osobnyak* of that faithful family friend, Grand Duchess Marie Pavlovna. She too wanted to know about my experience in the field. I was more reticent than with the Tsar. She was a civilian who would not understand.

'You are too modest, dear child,' said Marie Pavlovna. 'Bravery coupled with modesty is positively awesome. It will frighten away all suitors, Anna Vladimirovna, don't you agree?'

'That wouldn't be a bad thing.' Grandmaman glowered. Better no suitor than a Stefan Veslawski, I understood.

I would not satisfy Her Imperial Highness's curiosity about my stay at Tsarskoye either.

'Well, Their Majesties have at least one loyal subject at court who is neither a fool nor a crook,' was Marie Pavlovna's comment.

In every member of the dynasty I sensed exasperated rage, exacerbated by helplessness, at the crowned heads become unworthy of their trust.

*

I found the lights, luxury and elegance of the capital strange after the drabness of the war zone. The civilian mind had become alien to me. The contrast between our own palatial Admiralty quarter and the squalid refugee settlements by the Warsaw and Nicholas stations was so shocking that I was glad to leave. Grandmaman accompanied me, attended as ever by Zinaida Mikhailovna. Nyanya had to come along too, having declared that I might be splendid at caring for others but incapable of caring for myself.

What a joyful surprise to be greeted at the station in Minsk by Father and Uncle Stan, Stevie and Casimir, all come up from the south-western front on Christmas leave!

After Grandmaman had been settled in Aunt Sophie's own apartment in a wing of the hospital, and presents opened, the family group spent the evening in Aunt Sophie's monastically furnished sitting room. Zinaida Mikhailovna had rushed on to Mogilev on a flurried visit to son Kolenka, promoted adjutant to the chief of staff, General Alexeiev, thanks to maternal effort. There being no outsiders – Casimir was practically family – I could relate fully my illuminating visit to Tsarskoye.

It produced a strong impression.

'One hears so many rumours,' Aunt Sophie said. 'But here we have it from an unimpeachable source. Russia's sovereigns are on the verge of a nervous breakdown.'

'It makes me even more pessimistic for our cause' – the cause of Polish autonomy, Uncle did not need to add. 'Wielopolski, Potocki, Zamoyski' – the names, hoary with history, of the Polish grandees, dropped from Uncle's lips with clipped, British matter-of-factness – 'all our friends seriously doubt the Tsar will keep his pledge.'

'Is there no way to apply pressure on His Majesty?' Aunt asked. 'Or does it merely make him more obstinate?'

'Nicholas will yield to pressure every time,' answered Father. 'But the problem is, he yields in the end to the pressure that is strongest – his wife's. And the Empress has been adamantly opposed to any change in the *status quo*. She, at least, has the virtue of consistency.'

'She should be put in a convent,' Grandmaman stated. 'For life.'

'Nikolay Nikolayevich did advocate it loudly.' Father gave his subtle little smile at mention of the unsubtle ex-commander in chief.

'All the Romanovs are fed up with her,' said Grandmaman. 'Her own sister won't go near her as long as she dotes on her false prophet.'

Alexandra's sister, Grand Duchess Elizaveta, had taken the vows after the assassination in 1905 of her husband, Grand Duke Sergey. Beautiful and pious, she was one of my girlhood models.

'Why not dispatch Rasputin?' Stevie suggested. 'It would be an act of patriotism.'

Casimir looked at him admiringly, I in some shock.

'It may come to that.' Uncle Stan remained imperturbable.

'It might do more harm than good,' Father said. 'Grishka the martyr could be even more powerful than Grishka the prophet. Besides, he is only a tool.'

Rasputin a tool? It had occurred to me after *Boris Godunov*. 'Whose tool, Papa?' I asked.

'Of those bureaucrats and reactionaries who would rather see Russia perish than progress. Beletsky, the former chief of the secret police, is one. Monsignor Pitirim, the Metropolitan of Petrograd, is another. There is also that notorious anti-Semite, the former minister of justice, Shcheglovitov, a worthy successor of that late influential nobleman whose name I blush to recall.'

'Prince Meschersky,' Uncle elaborated, 'publisher of that reactionary rag *Grajdanin*.'

'Which Nicholas read faithfully. This clique shrewdly exploits the deepest wishes and beliefs of Nicholas and Alexandra, using Grishka to reinforce them. So you see' – Father threw up his hand – 'it's quite hopeless.'

'Nonsense!' Grandmaman gave a rap of her cane. 'Russian defeatism makes it hopeless, that's what. It's no sort of talk to hold in front of young people, Pierre. We have vigorous leaders in the Duma. Under our good Prince Lvov, the Zemstvo union has performed miracles in support of the war effort.' Like most progressive landowners, Grandmaman was a great partisan of the *zemstvos* – elected local councils with a measure of autonomy. 'Between them and Polivanov – an able and honest war minister at last,' she continued, 'we have almost made good the munitions shortage. We have fine generals and lionhearted troops. We only need to hang on till victory. Our sovereign is a patriot. He must be brought to his senses!'

'*Bravo, Maman!*' Father smiled.

Uncle said he would get in touch with the French and English ambassadors. 'Let their governments put pressure on Nicholas. They have strongly supported our cause.' And on this the discussion ended.

A part of me, the active, decisive one, agreed with Grandmaman. A nurse could not be defeatist. But another, the imaginative, religious me, thought Father right and the situation hopeless.

Everyone, whether at the bottom or at the top, was the tool of someone else. No one person, or group, or nation, was responsible for the war. No one would take the responsibility to stop it. It was like an immense machine with innumerable meshing cogs, which, once set in motion – nobody knew by whom – could only run down of its own accord. If it was so, life was absurd, war a grisly joke.

I could not accept this. My Christian ethic revolted. If no single individual was responsible, then all must be. Humanity bore the collective guilt for war. It was no use blaming a monarch, a president, a country or, like the Communists, an entire class. The seeds of evil and violence were within each of us. And only one of two attitudes was possible: universal detestation or universal compassion.

These pressing questions were discussed in Aunt Sophie's sitting room again. But politics and pessimism were set aside for the dinner in celebration of the new year 1916. The long table in the staff dining room had been set with Belvedere plates, crystal, and silver from the Veslawski palace. I wore a fitted dress of red velvet trimmed with ermine and my hair long as Stevie liked.

Stevie sat across the table from me, no longer thin and sickly but strong and sleek again. Casimir, by his side, looked almost as vibrant. We three now had the added bond of war comradeship. I also found Casimir newly interesting since Stevie had told me about his 'reputation' – much better deserved, Stevie claimed, than his own. Stevie surmised it had something to do with Casimir's mother having run off with a lover.

Father, at my side, observed my glow of love with wistful and tender pride. Uncle Stan, in his reserved way, basked in the radiant presence of Aunt Sophie. Even Grandmaman looked on approvingly. The only one missing was Great-Aunt Catherine. Uncle, amidst a solemn silence, relayed the news brought from Poland through the enemy lines by a Jewish courier:

The district of Veslawow had been spared the general devastation. The palace was headquarters for a German prince and his staff. The Prince extended every courtesy to his aged hostess, which she did not reciprocate. Princess Catherine communicated with the conqueror through an intermediary and only left her apartment to carry the daily flowers to her husband's grave, which had become a place of pilgrimage for their people. Their people were not well off but better off by far than those who had fled, or been driven to flight. The palace stood, as it had through eight centuries and four invasions, its keep intact, its great limes unscarred.

'I am keeping it all safe for my son and for his son and for his son's children,' was Great-Aunt's message. Uncle repeated it in a voice calm in spite of emotion, and looked at his son.

Stevie looked at me and I knew that he, too, saw in the preservation of the ancestral Veslawski home a wonderful portent, the assurance of the family's succession through our sons, the triumph of love and life over war and death.

18

The morning after New Year's dinner, we all went our separate ways. Accompanied by Zinaida Mikhailovna, still aglow from seeing Kolenka, Grandmaman took the train to Petrograd. Nyanya and I accompanied Father and Uncle Stan, Stevie and Casimir on their return journey south. I was assigned to a field hospital less than an hour's drive away, in the vicinity of Rovno, an old and pretty little town set among gardens. Nyanya remained at Father's headquarters to take care of me properly when I had leave.

Papa had just been transferred from the command of cavalry, which had become obsolete in trench warfare, to that of a three-divisional infantry corps, and I accompanied him on the first inspection of his new troops.

Standing in an open car, we drove slowly past the ranks massed in the snow. The sun shone, as it had earlier for the Tsar. The weapons, cleaned and polished, glittered. Flags and regimental pennants flew. Drums rolled. Bugles repeated a fanfare all along a review route. I perceived the fearful beauty of war, and the hold that it could have on men's minds.

Sixty thousand men roared their 'hurrah' for their new commander. I thought Father in his white fur *papakha* the very reincarnation of the Varyngian Prince Rurik, our forbear. Never had I been more proud to be his daughter. I stood as erect in my nurse's cape as if I had a book on my head, and tried to observe every face as Father did. I was glad of my medal now. It showed the soldiers I was one of them. Until now, I had been a weak patriot. But as I looked at the round, open Russian faces rapt upon us, I said to myself, There is no kinder, warmer, more generous, great-hearted people on earth, and loved them with a passion.

A few days later I accompanied Stevie and Aunt Sophie to Uncle Stan's regimental base further south in the Strypa River sector. The Veslawski lancers had polished their sabres and their horses' hooves as they would not have for the Emperor. They too were so gallant,

I loved them also with a passion. The inspection over, Stevie was surrounded by the men of his platoon. I recognized several of the boys of his village company, and they called me 'Little Lady Tanyussia', as in the past. So we were all acting out our childhood games: I my game of nurse, the boys of the company and their Sir Lieutenant their game of war.

After the review, Stevie and I spent our last afternoon of leave together. Stevie kept his arm about me when we walked, my hand in his when we sat. Our mutually imposed chastity created a strain, and we were often at a loss for words. But there was poignant pleasure in it. We were not ordinary lovers. We were cast in a legendary mould. And the consummation of our love would be the more sweet and lasting for having been postponed.

Thereafter, we saw each other only on liberty. Stevie was assigned to an intelligence unit to decode enemy messages. I worked in the operating room of a well-equipped hospital train on a railroad siding behind the front line. Horse-drawn ambulance wagons and the crude conditions attending them were a thing of the past, even as ammunition was no longer critically scarce. It was not so much rifles that were now lacking as the men to fire them. Yet the soldiers were much less patient and good-humoured than during the terrible retreat. They wanted to go home, to Mama's cabbage pie, to wife and sweetheart, to a warm stove, a dry house. They were beginning to wonder how much longer they must stay away from home and why.

I understood their feelings well. Again and again I asked myself as the *sanitars* laid a shattered body on the operating table the moment it had been washed of another's blood: How long must it go on, this horror of massacre and mutilation? A half a million men have perished at Verdun. The British and French expeditionary corps has finally evacuated Gallipoli after hideous losses – Russia will not get Constantinople, it's clear. Outside of the Tsar and a handful of archpatriots, how real was that dream anyway? Serbia? The Serbian army is routed. Serbia, over whom the war was fought, is no more. Then what is it for? No one can possibly benefit from the war. It cannot be a trial God sends us. It will not bring mankind closer to God. On the contrary, the only way to bear the butchery is to become hard and insensitive. Our good-natured Russian lads are growing bitter, not against Germans and Austrians, their fellow sufferers, but against those they hold responsible, their officers and their commander in chief, the Tsar. It will take more training and discipline than ever to send them into the trenches. But in fact, I saw there was not more of it, but less.

There was enough of discipline still in the summer of 1916, however, for General Brusilov to mount his big offensive in June.

June-July-August 1916 saw some of the bloodiest fighting of the war. The army's advance over a 300-mile front showed Russia was a power still to be reckoned with. It stopped the Austrian attack on Italy, induced Rumania to finally declare war on the Central Powers, and forced the Germans to bring up fifteen divisions from the western front. It proved a Pyrrhic victory, however. The Russian army suffered a million casualties before the Tsar called a halt to the offensive in October. Its reserves were depleted, the soldiers' morale irreparably damaged.

Father's corps, which spearheaded the southern prong of the push into Galicia, suffered heavy casualties. So did the Veslawski lancers. Casimir lost his father, the former administrator of Veslawa, and Stevie several men of his boyhood company. He himself had clamoured to be allowed back on active duty. By the end of August, the momentum of the offensive had spent itself. To my immense relief, the lancers were withdrawn from the front line for garrison duty.

While the earth shook with the thunder of artillery under my hospital train, and Stevie again led his platoon in reckless feats, political events, decisive for our future, were taking place in the rear.

In July, the long-awaited definitive announcement on Polish autonomy had been expected from the Emperor's headquarters at Mogilev. Vigorously prodded by the ambassadors of the Entente Powers – Buchanan and Paléologue – Sazonov, the Foreign Minister, pressed the Polish decision on the Tsar. The Tsar, as Father had predicted, yielded, and was especially gracious to Sazonov – a bad sign, said Father. The Tsar was always most gracious to a minister before he dismissed him.

Father's political intuition proved correct. Even as an announcement was forthcoming, the 'great guns', as Alexandra's letters were known at the Stavka, went into action. Then, the Empress arrived at Mogilev in person. The announcement was not made. Instead, before the end of the month, Sazonov was 'permitted to resign on grounds of ill health'. Stürmer, the inept and unpopular prime minister who had succeeded the aged Goremykin upon the same qualification – loyalty to Rasputin – became foreign minister as well. Once again Alexandra's passionate maternal determination to pass on the empire intact to her son prevailed over the Emperor's more statesmanlike impulse.

With Sazonov went the last liberal on the Council of Ministers. Already General Polivanov – the minister of war who had more than made up for the calamitous, if not criminal, administration of his predecessor, Sukhomlinov – had been dismissed early in April for his excellent rapport with the Duma and the *zemstvos*. Grandmaman had stormed and Father had been deeply dejected. The Emperor's about-face in the Polish question – now tabled indefinitely – was the final blow. It confirmed the absolute ascendancy of Alexandra, which was soon to prove fatal. For me the consequences were immediate.

In the middle of August, a staff motorcar sent by Father drove me to his headquarters, a Polish manor with a pillared portico and pitched tin roof in a grove of oaks and limes. Although not in the Kingdom of Poland proper – now under enemy occupation – this border district in the province of Volhynia had belonged to Poland before partition and still had a large proportion of Polish farmers and landowners. Here I found Aunt, Uncle and Stevie. I took Casimir's absence as a sign that a crucial family council was impending.

After an early dinner with Father's staff, the family withdrew alone to a veranda in an angle of the manor. Simyon served us iced tea and left. Aunt and I sat in wicker chairs, Uncle Stan at her side. She looked cool and elegant in a print chiffon. I felt hot and unattractive in uniform. Father, facing me, tapped restlessly on the arm of his chair. Stevie stood scowling into the glass of the veranda, which reflected the stormy grey-green light of the wood.

I had been lost in the exquisite misery that my cousin's nearness always produced. But as ice clinked in tall glasses and mosquitoes and bees made more than their usual hum, I grew aware of the silence, and its oppressiveness. I looked up at Uncle anxiously. Clearly, he had something important to impart.

'As I told you on my way to Mogilev, Pierre, I put little hope in my audience with the Tsar,' he began at last. 'Briefly, His Majesty told me that although he agreed in principle to *some* form of autonomy for the Kingdom of Poland, he was unable to commit himself on particulars until the day of victory over the Central Powers.'

A silence greeted this declaration.

Uncle Stan continued in languid exasperation, 'I reminded His Majesty that many Poles, my own lancers included, had enlisted in the Russian army on the strength of the pledge implied in the manifesto of Grand Duke Nicholas. His Majesty replied that the first concern of Poles and Russians alike ought to be to push the war to a speedy and victorious conclusion and that he would lend consideration to the claims of those who had loyally contributed to this end. Imagine, Pierre, lend consideration to *our* claims, when it is our country which has been the battleground of this war, a war for which it had no responsibility and in which it has no stake.

'I did not disguise my reaction to this condescension. His Majesty at once hastened to praise the record of my regiment and assured me its services would not be forgotten. I further reminded His Majesty that my efforts, and those of the Polish nobles who trusted the Russian crown to restore our constitution and autonomy, had largely prevented the spread of insurrection during the troubles of 1905. I could not guarantee to do the same, once central Poland was freed from enemy occupation, unless the autonomy of the kingdom was assured.

'At mention of 1905, His Majesty looked uneasy. He was caught off guard and could not find words to reply at once. At last he said, "I thank you for your loyalty, Prince. You have my personal admiration and sympathy. I can only repeat that I have the welfare of the Polish people at heart. But they must be patient."

'I saw I could expect nothing further from Nicholas. I had already spoken to the French attaché at the Stavka and to General Alexeiev. You know that Russia, between now and December, has agreed on French insistence to send five brigades of ten thousand men to France. The attaché assured me France would be proud to welcome the Veslawski lancers, and Alexeiev left it up to His Majesty.

'I now came to a decision. "Sire," I said, "in token of the gratitude you have been pleased to express, allow me to transfer my regiment to a brigade assigned to France, or I cannot vouch for its morale any longer."

'"Once in France, will you fight under Polish or Russian colours?" His Majesty asked.

'"Sire, my first concern is, like yours, victory over the Central Powers. My men can contribute towards it best at the side of our French allies. They will do so as soldiers of Your Majesty's army."

'"And after victory?" he persisted.

'"Sire," I replied, "if you will not commit yourself on the status of my country until the day of victory, I beg to be allowed the same privilege in regard to my troops."'

'Good for you, sir!' Stevie cried, and Aunt added softly, 'Well said, Stan.'

'And so?' Father showed some impatience at this display of Polish pride. 'Did His Majesty agree?'

'The request to transfer my troops to France was granted.'

I let out an 'ah!' of despair, but Stevie cried joyously, 'When do we leave, sir?'

'I'm authorized by His Majesty to make up our losses from Poles in other cavalry units who wish to join us and proceed to Murmansk with dispatch, there to join up with the second of the Russian brigades to leave for France. We embark in the middle of September.'

'I'm glad for you, Stan.' Father had mastered his momentary exasperation. 'God knows what may happen here!'

Uncle resumed his account. 'I believe the Romanov dynasty is doomed. The atmosphere in Petrograd is seditious. Fantastic rumours fly about the Empress and Rasputin. The court has lost all prestige, the ministers the confidence of the Duma. The opposition is up in arms. Food is scarce, typhus and cholera spreading, the mood of industrial workers ugly. The peasantry has been bled white for no reason it can understand. Russia can't take another year of war and the Central Powers aren't half finished.

'Had the Tsar been loyal to us, had he restored our constitution and civil liberties as implied in the Grand Duke's manifesto, I'd have been loyal to him to the end. Poles are notoriously loyal to lost causes,' added Uncle with irony and concluded, 'I've served the Russian Empire well and faithfully, though my father called me unworthy of our Piast ancestors. My father warned me on his deathbed not to trust the word of Nicholas II any more than the word of Nicholas I. He was right. I no longer feel under any obligation to the Russian Empire, other than as a soldier of its army. Once the war is over I'll seek my country's unification and independence of all foreign powers by any and all possible means.'

Stevie rushed to his father and wrung his hand. 'Right you are, sir! We don't want autonomy under the imperial eagles! We want sovereignty under our own! Mother,' he cried, 'we're off to France! The legions will march again!' He looked challengingly about the veranda. As our eyes met, he rushed to me and seized my icy hands. 'My sweet, I've not forgotten you. We can be married now, as soon as you're converted to our faith. We'll honeymoon on the Basque coast –'

'Before you go honeymooning on the Basque coast, sir, shouldn't you speak to Prince Silomirsky? You're not yet married, nor even formally engaged,' came Uncle Stan's not so chilly reminder.

'Uncle Peter, you'll allow Tanya to come with us and be married in France?' Stevie cried, still holding my hand.

Father nodded. 'Of course, of course.'

His tone was heartbreaking.

'Papa, how can I leave you?' I asked desolately.

'You must! Stan's right. The Romanovs are doomed. Veslawskis need not remain loyal, but Silomirskys must. I will be doomed with my sovereign and so would you, my darling, who are so close to his family. I did not raise you to see you destroyed. I know your devotion to me and bless you. But if you truly want to make me happy, you will make your own life, and give me grandchildren whom God grant I may know after the war.'

The selfless words, spoken in Father's resonant voice, stirred me to tears. I turned to Aunt Sophie in my unbearable dilemma and distress.

'Poor child,' said my understanding aunt, 'what a cruel choice! But your father's right, Tanyussia. The young cannot sacrifice themselves for the old. The future has precedence over the past. You must come with us.'

'Auntie, Mother, how can I? Ah, God what am I to do?' I cried.

Stevie dropped my cold hand grown inert in his, stepped away, and looked at me sombrely. I stood up, put my hands over the bands of my nurse's headdress, and looked at each of the four people waiting for me to decide my fate. I knew I could not long control my distraction and despair.

'Aunt, Uncle, Papa, excuse me, I must be alone a moment to think,' I murmured, and ran out.

The wood was oppressively still. The thump-thump of artillery had ceased, as it did towards the end of every day, before the resumption of the night barrage. Thunder rolled in the distance. Although it was stiflingly hot, I was cold and shivering. Having run until my throat hurt, I fell against the broad trunk of an oak, pressing myself to it and digging my nails into the bark. And as I lay against it, I fancied the stout trunk to be the broad chest of my father, himself a fine oak of ancient lineage, deeply rooted in the soil of his land.

Papa says he is doomed, and it's true, I see it in his face, even as I know when a wounded man is going to die, I thought. So is our sovereign and his son, my beautiful Aleksey, and his daughter, my best friend. And I'm to run away so as not to be doomed with them. I'm to be happy and live in beautiful Veslawa while they lie in imperial Russia's ruins. But how could I be happy if they were destroyed? How could I face myself, knowing I had run away? Yet, if I let Stevie go to France, I may never see him again. I may lose him forever. I may never know happiness. No, I can't be happy either way and so happiness is not paramount – it's not even relevant to the problem, as Professor Holveg would say. What matters is, who needs me most, Papa or Stevie?

Stevie is twenty-one years old, beloved of his men and his people. He has his father to protect him, his mother to nurse him if he's ill. But if Papa were ill or wounded, who would care for him? Grandmaman is over seventy. Papa is all alone. Even our sovereign, who once loved him, is estranged from him because of that awful Rasputin. Papa has protected and spoiled me all my life and now that he is in danger, is it not my turn to be by him when everyone else abandons him? Was it not because of me that he did not marry Diana, that he has no one to look after him in his old age except me? If I stay by him, perhaps he need not be doomed. And if he is doomed, isn't it right for me to share his fate? Would Tanik leave her father the Tsar? Would her sisters or brother? No, they would not.

Oh, but why should I stay to be doomed, another voice countered,

I who am young and in love? Father has lived and loved. I have not. The young must not sacrifice themselves to the old, Aunt said, and Papa does not ask it. He himself married a Pole. But, in marrying him, Mother became Russian. If I marry Stevie, I will become a Pole. Didn't Uncle Stan say that when war ends he would seek his country's independence by any and all possible means? The Romanovs may fall, but Russia will not. Unless they are under one sceptre, Russia and Poland will fight. Stevie is such a fierce patriot, if I became his wife, I – a descendant of Rurik – might have to turn against Father, against the very soldiers I have nursed. Wasn't our betrothal put off not to imperil the cause of Polish autonomy? Wasn't our marriage contingent upon its success? And now that the cause is lost, how could our marriage succeed? No, it's impossible, Nyanya was right. I cannot bear a son to a Pole to fight Russians.

And yet, when Stevie's hands are on me, and he speaks to me in that especially deep and beautiful voice, he can make me do anything, forget everyone. I could be happy with him. No, not happy, but oblivious. If I stay, I'll be wretched. But, at least, I'll have done my duty. And how long would I be blissful, knowing I had run away? I did not run away from my field unit during the retreat. Yes, it's clear now. Just as Stevie belongs to his platoon, this is where I belong, with my Russian comrades-in-arms. So long as we're at war my post is here, by my father, at the front. It's settled.

I felt calm again and pushed myself away from the tree. But the calm of my decision was the acceptance of the grave. I was not ready to die and sorrow overcame me. I fell back against the trunk, my forehead on my bent arm, biting my lip not to weep. I heard then the quick approach of a long and lithe step, and knew that my cousin stood beside me. Pillowing my cheek on the trunk, I half turned to look at him. A rain cape was over his shoulders and his face was like that of the coming storm.

'Well, what will it be?' he said harshly. 'Russia or Poland? Your father or I? Why do I ask?' he continued bitterly as I was silent. 'I knew it beforehand. You've always loved your father more than me and always will. I asked you in Minsk who would come first in your life when we were married, your father or I, and you said, on your knees, that I would. But your promise was worth no more than that of the Tsar your godfather, or any Russian's.'

He turned the knife in the wound with the truth of his accusation. Long before that I had sworn a blood-brother oath to follow him everywhere in war and peace. But I had also sworn an oath of allegiance to the Tsar my sovereign. And I could not keep both.

'If you must hurt me, say what you want. But it won't change my decision, dreadful though it is,' I said. And I braced myself against the oak to endure whatever Stevie seemed determined to inflict in revenge for his pain.

'I'm not so sure I can't change it.' He pinned me to the tree. 'You weren't afraid of hurting me when you let me be evacuated from the field hospital. Why should I be afraid of hurting you?'

I looked at him wordlessly while tears rolled down my cheeks. Already, between his hands, with his fierce masculine face close to mine, I felt my dreadful resolution weakening.

Oh, kiss me till I'm senseless, and carry me off, the other Tanya mutely pleaded. Don't be taken in by my brave front. I may hate you for it later. I may hate myself. But I'm ready to defy my nobler self. Help me to! Sweep away my strong and cogent reasons! Let me be your mistress, nothing more!

My brimming eyes tried to say what my tongue could not. But he did not understand their language.

His expression of cruel anger turned to shame. 'My sweet, my own, have I made you cry? Have I been such a beast?' Tenderly, he wiped my eyes with his handkerchief. 'I'm not worth your precious tears.'

'You are, you are!'

'Am I really? And will you still cry when I'm gone or forget me the moment I'm out of sight?'

'Never! But you'll forget me. You've had girls before and you'll have them again. You'll find one much prettier than I . . . and marry her.' At the thought, my self-control deserted me. I turned my face to the oak and burst into sobs.

'Come, if you must lean against something, lean against me,' Stevie said.

He took me gently in his arms. I continued to sob. But as I lay against his chest, a well-known sensation of safety, triumph and bliss, known first in Father's arms, came to me from early childhood. I laid my palms flat on his chest to feel more of this strong and comforting manly surface, and my sobs ceased. I closed my eyes and pretended, as I used to with Papa, that I would go to sleep against Stevie's chest and be entirely and forever at peace.

'Listen to me, my Tatyana,' Stefan said, after I had grown quiet. 'I've had girls, it's true, as any normal man will, and I can't swear not to have others. But they've never mattered and never will. As long as you'll wait for me, I'll wait for you, one year, or two, or ten, and I'll take no one but you to Veslawa as my bride. That is my word, word of a Veslawski. If there is revolution in Russia, and you're caught in it, I'll come for you. Wait for me, and never lose faith.' He held my chin and bobbed my head up and down in his hand. Then he bent to kiss me.

He had no sooner put his lips to mine than the clouds burst and rain fell in torrents. He pulled his rain cape over my head and went on kissing me. When we were as breathless as we were wet, we broke away and headed at a run towards the manor house, holding the cape over our heads. The rain sizzled among the leaves, a welcome coolness descended on the hot earth, and there rose from it a fragrance of mushrooms and damp leaves.

Looking at the drops running down Stevie's face, I remembered how he had ridden in the rain beside my ambulance wagon. The night of our first Harvest Festival dance, our blood oath in the dungeon cell, our embrace in a stale sickbed, the girl playing nurse in earnest with the soldier boy in the fetid wagon of the field hospital – all our sweet and poignant moments came back to me as we ran hand in hand through the park. And when we returned to the veranda, where Father and the Veslawskis awaited us, though we told them we had agreed to part for now, we both knew that neither time, distance nor revolution could sever our lifelong ties, no, nothing whatsoever except death.

In the first week of September 1916, on a flat plain behind the south-western front, a train stood by a goods platform near a low warehouse shed. The last three squadrons of Veslawski lancers were entraining and with them their colonel, Prince Stanislaw, his wife and son, and his son's friend, Lieutenant Casimir Paszek. A group of local Polish landowners, some French officers attached to headquarters and several Allied war correspondents were seeing them off.

After making their adieus to this group, Aunt and Uncle joined Father and me. Casimir, very stern and soldierly, shook hands and boarded the train. Stevie, standing at attention, reported to his father that the men and horses were all aboard.

'Well, it's time,' Aunt Sophie said. She wore a smart grey travelling suit, with a veil over her straw boater. 'Stevie, kiss Tanya goodbye.'

Stevie and I stood rigid before one another.

Ah no, I thought, this is preposterous! I can't remain on the platform while Stevie goes on the train. Something must be done to stop it! But I could do nothing.

Stevie's face expressed the same helpless desperation. Neither of us spoke. He bent down and kissed my forehead. I placed my hands flat on his chest and looked into his fierce, not at all comical face with the dear funny monkey ears and amber eyes.

'Bye-bye, Stevie,' I brought out and pushed myself away with a tremendous effort.

While Father embraced my cousin, Uncle Stan took me by the shoulders. 'Remember our motto: "*Nunquam dīmitto*" – I never give up. Never give up, Tanyussia, never lose hope. Be true to our son as he is to you. We'll be expecting you, Daughter.' His sad long face was noble and strong, his drooping moustache tickled my cheek as he kissed me.

I turned last to Aunt. I had a dreadful premonition I would never see her again. It is my mother who is leaving me now, I thought, and I'll never have another.

This was almost as awful as parting from my beloved. I fell into Aunt Sophie's arms, and the self-mastery in which I had been schooled since childhood now failed me. 'Auntie, Mother, I can't! I haven't the strength!' I moaned childishly.

'Yes, you do, Tanyussia. And you'll have more, as you need it. The Lord keep you and grant we may have you with us soon. Be brave, child.'

I could not be brave. I lay as though insensible, my head on Aunt's shoulder, and could not move.

'Pierre, take her,' she said.

Father took me by the shoulders and put his strong arm under mine. I saw movement before my eyes and heard sounds that had no relation to me. A head like Aunt Sophie's was making a stately inclination out of a train window. The very tall, stony-looking young officer who had stood by the train door was now gone.

A bugler blew the departure, threw the horn on his back, and jumped into an open wagon. The train moved slowly. Horses passed me, nostrils red and distended in desperate whinnies. On the platform, gentlemen waved hats, ladies handkerchiefs. Officers and troopers waved caps from the train. Then there was nothing under a hazy sky, nothing in all that flat landscape between the low sheds and the woods but empty track. A dreadful execution had taken place. I had been torn asunder by a train, between lover and mother to one side, father and country to the other.

Father led me down the platform to the waiting staff car and helped me in. I sat in a stupor throughout the hot and dusty drive. In an hour we reached the pillared façade of the manor house – Father's headquarters, I dimly recollected. Father took me up to the vaguely familiar room overlooking a great beech, where I must have stayed before, and handed me over to Nyanya.

After she had helped me out of my uniform and sat me down at the dressing table to brush my hair, the pallid face with the huge eyes that stared back at me in the looking glass seemed that of a madwoman. I hid against Nyanya's dried-up bosom. And here, in the earliest place of confession and release, the ache that lay like a heavy stone below my ribs poured itself out in a storm of tears.

'There, there,' Nyanya soothed, 'he's not dead, your lover, only gone for a little while! You'll be together again soon. God is merciful. Everything will come out all right.'

When I was in bed, having refused supper, Father came in.

'My dearest, my poor little daughter!' He sat down on the bed and took me in his arms. 'We'll send you after your Stefan tomorrow. There's still time.'

'No, no, it's all right.' I clung to his broad neck. 'I'll stay with you, Papa, I'll stay.'

'My brave little one!' He stroked my hair, sodden with tears. 'It won't be so bad, you'll see. The war can't last much longer and we'll go to France together, to meet your love, from the Crimea, on our yacht. And when I have leave, we'll go to Alubek and swim and ride along the Black Sea coast as we used to, and read Pushkin together. How will that be?'

I put my palms to his face and thought, Truly, it won't be so bad. I have Papa still. And it will be like the first years of childhood when I had not two loves, which divided me so cruelly, but one alone.

PART THREE

REVOLUTION

1916–1918

19

After the Veslawskis' departure, Uncle Stan's predictions approached their fulfilment with a rapidity and impetus that stunned even those who prophesied the empire's collapse.

At the Stavka, the Tsar busied himself with military trivia – decorations, inspections, petty matters of equipment – which lowered his prestige with the general staff more and more. Meanwhile, the real business of government was conducted at Tsarskoye by a bizarre triumvirate: the Empress, her Prime Minister Stürmer and Rasputin.

In the forlorn hope of shaking his sovereign out of his apathy, Father went to Mogilev in October, taking me with him.

Not only did His Majesty seem glad to see me, he clearly did not want to be left alone with Father. I was shocked by his listlessness. Only when he spoke of his children did his face light up in the old way. At first his conversation was inconsequential. Only on the second day of our visit, when we went walking *à trois* after breakfast, did he confess: 'It's so comforting, Pierre, having you and Tata here. Family visits have become a trial. Lately, everyone scolds me: for being too soft, for being too unyielding, for not halting the Brusilov offensive sooner, for not prosecuting the war more vigorously. Mama, even Alix, treats me like a child. I am still Tsar!' His voice grew firmer, 'I bear the final responsibility!'

'Quite so, Sire,' Father said. 'Your Majesty only needs to let everyone know it unequivocally.' Everyone, including your own wife, the meddlesome Alix, I understood him to mean.

'That is what Alix rubs into me.' The Tsar either ignored or did not grasp the implication. He hastened to change the subject. 'How the girls must miss you, Tata! Would you like to come home to Tsarskoye with me for Christmas, if your father has no objection?'

'Oh Papa!' I looked at Father pleadingly.

I knew he was not pleased, but he said of course, it would be a joy and an honour.

'I'll write to Alix about it at once,' said His Majesty.

At lunch with the general staff I could not help contrasting the outward deference of the high-ranking military with the disdain many of them felt now, I suspected, towards the Tsar, their commander in chief. Afterwards, I begged to be allowed to visit the wounded. His Majesty could not refuse such a request, and Father had at last the opportunity for a private audience.

'It's no use,' Father commented on our prompt return journey to Rovno. 'No one can make His Majesty understand the reality, let alone the gravity of the situation. None but his beloved Alix can reach him. And you know what sort of advice she gives, poor lady! She has swallowed the sentimental view of Russia as a nation of pious peasants who adore their Little Father Tsar – *Batiushka Tsar*. It would be ludicrous were it not tragic!'

'His Majesty seemed on the verge of nervous exhaustion,' I said. 'His thoughts wandered, his concentration was poor.'

'Yes, and so was his memory, which used to be excellent. Small wonder there are rumours he is drugged.'

'Perhaps a holiday will do him good.'

My spirits lifted at the thought of embracing my namesake. Her letters had sustained me since Stevie's departure, the slowest, saddest months in my life.

'You are so brave and loyal,' she had written on hearing of my renunciation. 'I don't know if I would have had the strength to do as you did. But I'm sure, in the end, it was wise.'

'Was it wise?' I wrote back. 'I no longer know. I only know that not at any time since Mother's death and Father's flight to the Far East have I felt so forlorn and alone!'

'You are not alone, Tata,' she had answered at once, 'you have us! You have your father and your work.'

My work, yes. It continued to absorb me. Yet, in the hours off duty, sadness overwhelmed me. True, Stevie was safe for the time being. Because of their fluency in several languages, he and Casimir were now liaison officers between the Allied commands. But they could be transferred any day. Stevie could be killed in battle like Lord Beresford, our cousin from Kent, and so many others.

'Must an entire generation be wiped out,' I wrote to my namesake, 'before the slaughter ends?'

Then, too, the adventurous part of war was over, for me as for the fighting man. There was no movement, no advance or retreat: only a murderous contest over several hundred yards of ground pockmarked with shell holes, strewn with rotting corpses. Trench warfare and the repair of shattered bodies had both become routine. As the weapons grew more sophisticated and hideous, surgical technique and prosthetic devices improved correspondingly. 'The mind functions automatically. The heart withers. Oh Tanik,' I wrote, 'I feel myself dying alive.'

I was not to share my sorrow with Tatyana Nikolayevna and Olga in person. In a letter thanking Father and me for our visit to GHQ and transmitting warm greetings from the Empress and the children, His Majesty made no further mention of my accompanying him to Tsarskoye at Christmas.

I took it as yet another rebuff characteristic of Alexandra's seesawing attitude – she'd been so kind when we'd last parted, it was time for a slap. I felt the familiar surge of rage, but Father said, 'You may be sure Grishka is at fault. He doesn't want Silomirsky's daughter emancipating the Grand Duchesses and the Tsarevich from his tutelage.'

'What tutelage, Papa? If they humour Rasputin, it's only for their mother's sake. Olga won't even do that. I wish,' I added, 'Tanik were as independent.'

Father startled me. 'And I wish you weren't so attached to Her Imperial Highness. Henceforth, your close association can only be harmful. I'm vastly relieved that you're not going.'

I swallowed my disappointment.

The pain of double separation, from Stevie and my friend, was made still keener by the farewell call L-M paid to Father's headquarters. He was leaving for Murmansk with the last Russian brigade destined for service in France.

'If you run into Prince Veslawski, my cousin, and his friend, Sir Casimir Paszek, give them my love,' I managed to say.

'I'm likely to be assigned to liaison too.' I felt sure L-M would take this new chapter of his war experience as he had the retreat, observing the incongruous and the unspeakable alike out of Byzantine eyes and noting it all down for a future historical work.

'I've made up my mind to send Tanya to France as well,' Father, without warning, declared. And, as I did not know whether to feel delight or dismay, 'I have a month's leave due after the New Year.

We'll go to Petrograd and arrange your passage, yours and my mother's.'

'Then we may see each other again soon.' L-M did not question his superior officer and elder.

I made only a weak protest.

My kinsman gone, the tragicomedy of imperial government played on, with a buffoon added to the cast: the unbalanced Protopopov as minister of the interior. His appointment aroused derision and indignation. In the Duma, the leader of the liberal Cadet party, Miliukov, attacked the government and asked, 'Is this folly or is this treason?'

This brought a peevish letter from my namesake complaining about the unfairness shown her mother. 'Mummsy is so misunderstood,' wrote Tatyana Nikolayevna. 'She's only trying to help Papa, to make him be strong for Boysy's sake and Russia's, and everyone abuses her, and her friend.' Was this uncharacteristic allusion to Rasputin prompted by the Empress? 'She feels,' continued my namesake, 'the storm of criticism against her friend is only a pretext for attacking her. You know I personally have no great liking for him, and Olga can't bear him, but he *is* a support to Mummsy, the only support, beside Annushka's, she can depend on.'

Oh Tanik, I thought, how blind you are! How can you take your mother's part so uncritically? But then, how could you do otherwise, you who have been by her side, inseparable, all your life? You have no other perspective from which to judge her.

I felt immense pity and tenderness. But I began to sense that if we did not perish in the coming hurricane together, our paths must inevitably diverge.

Early in December, at the instigation of Alexandra, Protopopov forbade the meeting in Moscow of the popular Union of Zemstvos – Russia's most democratic institution – whose president, Prince Lvov, was a dear old friend of Grandmaman's. The United Congress of the Nobility, meeting in Petrograd in the same month, passed an unprecedented motion of censure against the Tsar.

In her weekly letter from Petrograd, Grandmaman railed against the government's attack on the *zemstvos*. 'I am beginning to lose faith in Russia's miraculous capacity to rebound,' she concluded. 'Unless Alexandra is removed, she will lead Russia into chaos and horror such as only our motherland can give birth to.'

'Mother sees it coming too, at last.' Father dropped the letter he had been reading aloud and covered his eyes with his hand. 'Ah, what a vision!' Then, rousing himself, he reiterated his decision to pack us off to France.

But Rasputin's assassination on 17 December 1916, forced him to postpone his plans.

Wrote Grandmaman from Petrograd:

I advise you not to show your nose around here for a while. Alexandra is convinced you had a part in the demise of her friend and would like nothing better than to dispatch you, if not to the other world, at least to the farthest corner of this one. Marie Pavlovna had all the Romanovs over to write a petition to the Tsar to lift Dimitry's sentence of banishment.

Twenty-five-year-old Grand Duke Dimitry, it transpired, had been the accomplice of young Prince Yusupov in Rasputin's assassination, together with the older Purishkevich, Rightist leader in the Duma.

The petition was returned by His Majesty unread. 'It is given to no one to occupy himself with murder,' was his only reply.

The Romanovs are furious at the snub. There is discussion of a palace coup to depose the Emperor and place the Tsarevich on the throne with Nikolay Nikolayevich, our former commander in chief, as regent. I quite agree with Marie Pavlovna and the rest of the imperial family that if Alexandra will not stay in the nursery where she belongs, the only place for her is the nunnery. However, I fear all this is mere talk. I fear the old order will not be overthrown from above, but from below.

The Bolsheviks have been inundating the workers' quarters with leaflets. The Petrograd garrison – which is much too large and idle – is heavily propagandized. You remember that a regiment refused to fire on rioting strikers a couple of months ago, and Cossacks had to be called to restore order. Food shortages continue, due to the unusually harsh winter, which has blocked transport, and to the usual incompetence of our administration.

But to return to the Rasputin affair. Since his body was fished out of the frozen Neva by the secret police a few days after his demise and taken to Tsarskoye Selo, Their Majesties remain in complete isolation in the Alexander Palace. His Majesty has postponed his return to the Stavka to help Alexandra bear her loss. They will see no one but Anya Vyrubova, who is as disconsolate as her imperial mistress. The Emperor plays billiards and his favourite dominoes, goes for walks with his daughters, and builds his son a snow fort. All very touching, but I am reminded of a Roman emperor who played the fiddle while Rome burned.

'It's as I feared,' Father commented. 'Rasputin's death has drawn Nicholas and Alexandra even closer. They have severed their last ties with the world. Ah, those hotheads!' He shook his head. 'However, had I been Dimitry's age and Yusupov's, who knows what I might not have done!'

Predictably, Tatyana Nikolayevna's response echoed her mother's bereavement and shock. 'We pray for Mummsy's friend and visit his grave with Annushka every day. The blow has drawn the family even closer. There seems no one out there who cares. How could any good come of such a wicked and cruel deed?' Her letter ended with these words: 'I fear Father Grigory was right. His death, he predicted, would mean our fall. Oh my Tata, dearest friend! Prince Silomirsky is right to want to send you to France. Go, go to your Stefan before our ruin brings you down!'

This selfless wish rekindled my devotion and my conflict. Could I abandon my namesake and my sovereign when they were in danger? Could I abandon Father?

I tried to remonstrate with him when he returned to the subject of my departure to France.

He came back with an asperity that revealed his exasperation with our sovereigns and his own helplessness. 'You are a minor and under my military command. You'll do as you're told.'

After delaying our journey for a fortnight on Grandmaman's advice, in mid-January of the new year Father resumed his preparations for a month's absence. He had given full powers to his second-in-command when he was stricken by a severe case of hepatitis, then epidemic among the troops.

I came alive. I took charge of his apartment in a wing of the manor, had the telephone removed from his room, and forbade the delivery of newspapers and dispatches that excited him. Nyanya and Simyon, who helped nurse Father, executed my orders with relish. I stopped feeling sorry for myself. Since Father needed me, my sacrifice was justified.

News of the Revolution, which came first in a telegram from Grandmaman, did not greatly startle me. I had been expecting it, I realized, not only these past months but for years. General Brusilov's call to Father, which I intercepted, shook me more. The southern-army commander wanted Father's concurrence in the general staff's consensus that the Emperor must abdicate.

I had concealed Grandmaman's cable from Father. In this case again, medical consideration overrode political. I told General Brusilov that Father had a high fever, and a matter so grave as the Emperor's abdication might cause fatal excitement. But I begged the general to keep me informed, which he did.

The Emperor's subsequent abdication left me numb. My sovereign and godfather had been as much a part of my life as Father and Grandmaman. I could not conceive what course Russia's destiny, or mine, would take, except that it must be frightful. And my heart ached for my namesake, her sisters and brother, yes, even for proud passionate Alexandra, who had been defeated in the end by her own husband's weakness.

I sat down immediately to write to Tatyana Nikolayevna. If I had been stunned by the abdication, what of her who had lived exclusively in the small, magic circle of her father's power? Of the world beyond, she knew nothing. She was unprepared, untrained to meet it. What could her future hold? And what if she had no future? In that case, neither had I! Eyes full of tears, I poured out my love and unwavering allegiance.

The letter describing her state of mind at the momentous news was late in arriving, brief and unemotional. 'We are all five of us ill with the measles. It is quite ridiculous at Olga's age and mine. Mummsy nurses us as much as her poor heart allows. How we wish we had Tata here! The young ones and Aleksey have been clamouring for you, but Olga and I will not hear of your coming. God knows how long we will be at liberty. The mood in Petrograd is very ugly, and everyone has deserted us, the regiments of the Guard, even our own Cossacks.' The pampered Cossacks of the Emperor's escort! For shame, I thought. 'They've all rushed to pledge loyalty to the Revolution! The police alone made a stand. Many have been killed, some quite barbarously. It's all so much beyond our comprehension, we hardly know how to react! Being ill is almost a relief. We try to put on a cheerful face for Mummsy's sake, and so does she for ours. We await Papa's return. With him here, we can face anything. Your ever-loving friend and blood sister forever, Tanik, Tatyana Romanova.'

The signature, Tatyana Romanova, was most telling of all. How simply and without fuss had my namesake renounced the ringing title Grand Duchess of Russia! In truth, it had never meant much to her. It had only served to imprison her. Now it might serve to condemn her.

In the early days of March, by the old Russian calendar, I was sitting at Father's bedside around midnight when the night nurse who was to relieve me came into the room. 'General Maysky has just returned from Petrograd and asks to report to His Excellency,' she whispered.

I went into the sitting room next door, where the General stood vigorously erect, his arched black eyebrows knitted over his falcon beak of a nose. Boris Maysky was of middle stature and pencil-slim, a forty-year-old bachelor whose only family had been the Silomirskys and service to that family his life's career.

He bowed with military precision over my hand and asked in French, in a voice unexpectedly soft and melodic, 'How is the Prince your father, Tatyana Petrovna?'

'Papa is better at last, Boris Andreyevich. You may see him tomorrow morning. What news have you of Grandmaman?'

'Anna Vladimirovna was arrested. But she has been released unharmed.'

'Arrested? Dear God!' The word *revolution*, with which I had imagined I was familiar, suddenly acquired concrete meaning. 'Please sit down and tell me about it, Boris Andreyevich.'

He declined a seat and said tersely, 'Anna Vladimirovna was seized by the mob which sacked the Silomirsky *osobnyak* on the night of 25 February. She was taken to the Palais Tauride, where the Petrograd Soviet of Workers and Soldiers was in session, but released the next morning. For the moment she is safe under the protection of Prince Lvov, who is now head of the Provisional Government, as you probably know already, Tatyana Petrovna.'

'Provisional Government?' I turned around at the sound of another deep and melodic voice. 'But His Majesty the Emperor? What has become of our sovereign?'

Father, a yellow silk robe trimmed with mink thrown on his broad shoulders, stood in the doorway. Simyon and the night nurse followed him with respectful remonstrances.

I rushed to his side. 'Papa, you must go back to bed!'

He ignored my appeal. Supporting himself on my shoulder, he advanced slowly towards his chief of staff. 'Boris, speak quickly!' he commanded. 'Where is His Majesty?'

'His Majesty, after his abdication, was brought back to Mogilev until the road to Petrograd could be cleared.'

'Nicholas has abdicated!' Father let his silver head fall on his chest.

Simyon and I helped him into an armchair. He remained with head bowed, as though in obeisance to the fallen monarch.

'My unhappy sovereign,' he said at last in the native tongue he reverted to in moments of profound emotion, 'my poor friend! But, was there no other way?'

'His Majesty,' General Maysky answered, 'apparently did not realize the gravity of the revolutionary crisis . . .'

'Revolutionary crisis!' Father murmured. 'I'm all at sea.'

Boris Maysky looked at me. Then, as I nodded, he related with the crispness so at variance with his voice, 'It began with bread riots in Petrograd and assaults on the police. The troops that were called out to quell the disorders fraternized with the mob. In short order, Petrograd was festooned with red flags. Police were hunted down and murdered. So were officers who resisted sporting a red rosette. In Moscow, it was the same picture.

'When Duma President Rodzianko cabled that only the immediate formation of a popular cabinet and the granting of full legislative powers to the Duma could save the dynasty, His Majesty ordered the Duma dissolved. The Duma ignored the decree. By the time His Majesty was at last ready to make concessions, it was too late. General Alexeiev, after consultation with the army commanders, advised His Majesty to abdicate.'

'How could he?' Father struck the arm of his chair with the flat of his palm. 'Doesn't Alexeiev realize the army will go to pieces now? Why wasn't I consulted?'

'General Brusilov did try to reach you, Papa. I told him you were too ill to be disturbed.'

Father frowned at me. Then, to his aide, 'Go on, Boris.'

'His Majesty had started for Petrograd, but the line was in the hands of insurgents beyond Pskov. Guchkov and Shulgin, the delegates from the Duma, received the Emperor's act of abdication in his train on the night of 2 March 1917. His Majesty's composure was remarkable. He did not betray the slightest emotion.'

'Yes, that's his way,' Father observed. 'It is all characteristic of Nicholas. Make no concessions to the bitter end, then throw it all up at once and let the Lord's will be done. Well, perhaps it was for the best after all. With a good regent until Aleksey's majority, Russia may yet be saved.'

'His Majesty, not wishing to be parted from his sick son, abdicated in favour of his brother Grand Duke Michael,' General Maysky stated. As Father gazed, dumbfounded, at the speaker, the latter continued. 'Under pressure from Kerensky, the new minister of justice and deputy of the Petrograd Soviet – the real power of the day – His Imperial Highness refused the crown pending the election of a constituent assembly.'

Father again brought his palm down on the arm of his chair. 'Mikhail Alexandrovich! Naturally he would refuse if he met opposition. He is even weaker than his brother. But how could Nicholas do such a thing? He had no legal right to abdicate on his brother's behalf. The whole act of abdication is invalid! We'll march on Petrograd, proclaim Nikolay Nikolayevich regent. The army at the front is still loyal. I'll lead it if no one else will. Shall I sit by while Russia goes to the devil – I, descendant of Rurik and Vladimir? Daughter, help me, I must get well!' He raised himself but fell back.

I put a hand on his shoulder to keep him from rising again. 'Of course you'll get well soon, *Papochka*. Come, we'll help you back to bed now.'

In bed, Father tossed even under sedation, knotting his sheet and repeating, 'Is it possible everything will go to the devil now? Is my beloved country to be put to the fire and sword for the crimes and follies of its rulers? Will no one come forth to save it?'

I increased the sedation and left him sleeping fitfully. Then I returned to Boris Maysky and asked him to send a telegram to Grandmaman through General Brusilov's headquarters, and another to the Empress nursing her sick children at Tsarskoye. I expressed our warmest wishes for their recovery. I dared not say more.

Father suffered a relapse and ran a high fever again for several days. He remained ignorant of the Tsar's arrest *en route* to Tsarskoye, and of the escalation of events crisply reported by Boris Maysky.

The Empress and the children had also been placed under arrest and were guarded in the Alexander Palace by the soldiers of the revolutionary Petrograd Soviet. Count Friedrichs, the aged minister of the court, and Anya Vyrubova had joined the former war minister, Sukhomlinov, and other former colleagues of his, less culpable if not more capable, in the Fortress of Petropavlovsk. Sukhomlinov and Protopopov had narrowly escaped lynching. Grand Duke Nikolay Nikolayevich, whom the Tsar upon abdication had once more appointed commander in chief, had arrived at Mogilev GHQ after a triumphal journey from the Caucasus only to be told by the Provisional Government his services were no longer needed.

No sooner had the Grand Duke headed back to the Caucasus than Father, too, was relieved of his command. Along with the termination order from the Stavka, the courier delivered a sealed letter from Grandmaman. There was no word from Tanik. How I fretted at her silence!

This is how Grandmaman described her experience of the Revolution in Petrograd:

I had a few friends to dinner on 25 February. We knew the situation was becoming serious. Our honourable but inept prime minister, the good Prince Golitsin – could no better replacement be found for Stürmer, Trepov, et al? – called the cabinet into extraordinary session at the Palais Marie. Our benighted sovereign was away, of course. His Majesty could not have chosen a worse moment to return to the Stavka. The mob was on the rampage, the Guard regiments were mutinous.

In the middle of the Nesselrode Pudding – Anatole had surpassed himself – we heard shooting on the Quai Anglais followed by a roar of voices in the courtyard. The majordomo ran in crying, 'Your Highness, the mob is breaking down the doors.' I asked my guests to keep calm and had them shown out on the side street through the cellars. All begged me to come away but I went instead to meet the mob.

When I appeared at the head of the portrait gallery, the rioters stopped dead in their tracks. In the silence I said our house was now a hospital and asked them to leave quietly and not disturb the wounded. They started to go when some bold fellow, a tipsy-looking soldier, steps forward and asks where is my son, the traitor and enemy of the people.

'My son is at the front where you ought to be,' I answer, and several voices begin to shout: 'Down with the war!' – 'Shut up, old woman!' – 'Down with the Tsar!' Then my bold fellow states that since I cannot surrender my son, I must be arrested in his stead.

So I was dragged out to a motorcar where some more bold fellows almost sat on top of me, seventy-three-year-old menace of a woman that I am, and taken to the Palais Tauride. I spent the night on a chair leaning against a column about which a soldier rode circles on a bicycle. Others, in a litter of leaflets and cigarette butts, sprawled on the divans or the floor. Heroines of the Revolution with cigarettes stuck in the corner of their mouths were typing and rushing about with messages. Even during a revolution, in Russia, women do most of the work. All night long prisoners like myself were being dragged in, some much more mauled than I. None of us had any idea why we were wanted or what would be done with us.

In the morning I was hauled before the Petrograd Soviet of Workers and Soldiers, which had been sitting all night. I was told that I was known to have been unfriendly to the *ex-Tsaritsa* now deposed by the people and if I would now give my opinion of her for the record I could go home unmolested.

I replied that, as the descendant of sovereign grand princes of Russia, it had been my privilege to criticize the Empress if I so chose, and it was also my privilege by the same token not to make any statements to impertinent fellows like them. Whereupon I was taken back into the foyer and greeted with shouts of: 'To the fortress!' – 'Shoot her!' – 'Down with the enemy and exploiter of the people!' and more of the same.

'Well, Anna Vladimirovna,' I said to myself, 'your hour has come,' when all of a sudden a workman jumps on a chair and begins to shout that I am no enemy of the people, I am its friend. Then he tells how I had supported his family for a year after he was injured on the job. Other workmen promptly came forward in my defence, and, in conclusion, I received an ovation! I was lifted on to the shoulders of the crowd and carried home in triumph. So that after leaving the house with several soldiers sitting on top of me, I returned to it sitting on top of the soldiers.

So much for this misadventure. As for the rest, the house has been rather badly smashed up, and your precious paintings damaged, Pierre, but not beyond repair. The hospital has become an insane asylum. The soldiers tried to murder the officers, and we closed the officers' wards, spiriting the officers away to the embassies as corpses. Both personnel and patients have formed soviets and are equally unmanageable. The patients no longer obey the doctors. They get up when they should be in bed, lie in bed when they should be up, refuse medicine if it tastes bad or because it doesn't taste bad enough. The orderlies won't change the linen. The only nurses still maintaining our former standards of care are the volunteers of good families. Our poor directress has been reviled and forced to witness obscenities.

I called the ambulatory patients together and told them we were dismissing them within twenty-four hours and closing the hospital as soon as we found room for the bed cases. The announcement was greeted with fist-raising and spitting but I held firm. And to think that all our care was free, that we gave each man a new suit of clothes and travelling money when he left, that we cared for their families, sent them to our villa for convalescence, had them taken to the theatre and the ballet. I know full well that gratitude sticks in a human throat and I have never expected it of any human being, but such ingratitude is not easy to swallow either. I also know our Russian people to be capable of any baseness, as they are of nobility and greatness. But, I confess, all this is beyond me.

Our carriages and motorcars have been confiscated and I don't leave the house, but I'm told the streets are littered and filthy, couples are behaving shamefully in public, there is complete licentiousness and *laisser-aller*. At home I am well cared for. The servants naturally formed soviets and proceeded to hold a meeting whenever I rang to decide who would answer, if at all. I summoned them and informed them I was not about to change my ways at my age and that those who did not like my ways could leave. We have six devoted personal servants left. Until your return, I am guarded by a dozen citizen soldiers on orders of the Petrograd Soviet – *it* is the real power of the day, make no mistake. The soldiers don't molest me, as I am also under the protection of my good friend Prince Lvov, our present head of state – if 'state' it can still be called. I beg you, I entreat you, I command you, do not return. Go to Alubek and I will join you there as soon as things calm down. If you will not think of yourself, think of your daughter. The Lord keep you both in these trying times. *Maman*.

Father and I were both moved by this brave letter and tacitly agreed we could not go south and leave Grandmaman in Petrograd as hostage to fickle mobs and citizen soldiers. I was secretly resolved as well to gain admittance to the prisoners at Tsarskoye. I could not long endure being cut off from my namesake at a time when she needed me most!

During the remainder of March, although superficial calm returned to Petrograd and Moscow, the phenomenal growth of revolution, whose birth had been hailed by Liberals as well as Leftists, hurled Russia on a course beyond anyone's control.

Army Order No. 1, the first edict issued by the Petrograd Soviet, granted soldiers the right to form committees, elect officers and question orders. The response to this heady declaration was the wholesale demotion, and not infrequent massacre, of officers.

Officers were no longer an aristocratic caste nor were they, in the main, particularly harsh. They were massacred because they represented the training and discipline that compelled the soldier to stay in the trench. The soldier did not want to stay in the trench – the soldier wanted to go home – and the officer was in his way.

Army Order No. 1 was felt at Father's former headquarters soon enough. We barricaded ourselves in the manor, where his staff was joined by officers from his corps now fleeing for their lives. The fugitives brought accounts of atrocities committed by citizen soldiers against their fellow officers.

Meanwhile the superintendent of the estate – a property of distant maternal relatives of mine – feared a peasant revolt. Peasants in sheepskin jackets and caps formed sullen groups at the park gates by day. At night we could see neighbouring manors aflame. The 'red rooster' was again abroad.

In Petrograd, on the contrary, according to Grandmaman's rare but still regular letters, things did seem to calm down. There had been a gigantic funeral, without benefit of clergy, for the 'victims', some two hundred of them, of the Revolution. Socialists the world over were flocking to Petrograd to witness the dawn of the new day. Political prisoners had returned from Siberia in triumph. So had the exiled Bolshevik leader, Vladimir Lenin, courtesy of Field Marshal von Hindenburg, who had provided him passage through Germany in a sealed train.

'From the Finland Station, where a delirious crowd greeted the hero's return,' wrote Grandmaman early in April,

> Monsieur Lenin was driven on top of an armoured car to Bolshevik headquarters in the town residence of Kshesinskaya, our *prima ballerina assoluta* and darling of grand dukes. Her house, by the way, was sacked even more thoroughly than ours in the heyday of our 'bloodless' revolution.
>
> The day after Vladimir Lenin's arrival, the Petrograd Soviet of Workers and Soldiers was treated by him to several hours' harangue, which was reprinted in the Bolshevik newspaper, *Pravda*, in full. How those revolutionary fellows love to talk! His reception, I gather, was mixed. But I would not dismiss Monsieur Lenin as lightly as some of our friends in the new government do. He wants to end the bourgeois-capitalist war, the bourgeois-capitalist provisional government, the Duma, and the reactionary institution of private property. Unlike our gentlemen liberals, he is resolute, ruthless and unencumbered by old-fashioned notions of 'duty' and 'honour'. He is

outrageous enough to appeal to the demons that have been unleashed in the Russian folk.

'There is no time to lose,' Father said in response to this news, 'if one is to stop the demoralization of the army before the Bolsheviks finish the job. America's entry into the war guarantees the victory of the Entente. Russia is not only honour-bound to continue the struggle, but her survival as a great power is at stake.'

Unlike Father, I was something of a pacifist. The stated aim of the Petrograd Soviet, 'Peace without annexation or indemnities', seemed to me reasonable and fair. The only way to prevent future wars was for the victor *not* to exact vengeance. None the less, I found desertion repugnant. Nor could I conceive of a beaten Russia suing for peace. I, too, I suddenly realized, was still caught up in the old-fashioned code of duty and honour. All of us were, except the Bolsheviks.

By mid-April, Papa felt well enough to undertake the journey to Petrograd via Mogilev, where he meant to stop at the Stavka to urge stern measures, like those taken against mutinous soldiers in France, to halt the army's disintegration. Accompanied by Boris Maysky, two dozen of his most devoted officers and the faithful Simyon, we set out, all of us armed except for Nyanya, in two lorries bristling with gun muzzles.

20

My sickroom isolation had hardly prepared me for the wild spectacle that awaited us at the railroad station in Rovno!

Soldiers with rifles and fixed bayonets, their khaki greatcoats beribonned with cartridge belts and red scarves, their fur bonnets and flat caps adorned with red rosettes and worn rakishly at the back of the head or over one ear, thronged the platform. When a train, like a caterpillar crawling with ants, came in with men hanging on to the roofs, engine, steps, those who did not want to get off gave battle to those who wanted to get on.

'Lord have mercy!' Nyanya viewed the scene with fearless contempt. '*Suma soshli* – they've gone mad!'

Protected by Father and his officers drawn up in a phalanx around us, I stared at the mob scene unmoved, even when several bodies rolled off the roofs to lie untended beside the track. Only when a soldier ran out in front of a departing train, could not gain a footing, and was run over, did a cry escape me.

Father turned me towards his shoulder. 'Don't look and don't move,' he ordered.

The stationmaster now ran up to him. 'Your Excellency, try to reason with the men, for God's sake! I cannot give them all trains! I'll kill myself if those devils don't kill me first. And what will become then of the wife and the little children?'

'Before you kill yourself, friend, let me know when you have a train for Moscow. And here's for the wife and the little children.' Father gave the stationmaster a handful of gold roubles.

After several hours' wait, the stationmaster reported a train was due for Moscow. We stormed a coach without casualties, taking it over for ourselves and posting a submachine gun at each end. The car was fourth-class, with wooden benches, and a shelf for baggage running along the top. The deserters who still lay on the shelf were disarmed and allowed to remain there. The train crawled, stopped for hours in the middle of nowhere, or gave bursts of speed that cruelly jolted us. Since train engineers were sometimes forced at gunpoint to exceed safe speeds, railway wrecks added to the delays of travel in revolutionary times.

At the first stop, Nyanya and I were ordered under the bench. While the men defended the coach from assault by would-be passengers, I kept my revolver cocked and ready in my hand.

Nyanya crossed herself and muttered, 'Lord God of mine, such frights at my age! And how tight it is under here, a regular coffin.'

We both refused to hide at the next stop. I pleaded for a rifle and took careful aim to scare off the assailants without wounding them. I had kept up my marksmanship first in the park, then in the cellar of Father's manor headquarters.

Less exciting were other discomforts: lice, fleas and the lack of toilet and water. Drinking water we had in our canteens. The men went to one end of the car and urinated out of the window. Nyanya and I managed with that invaluable rubber basin from my kit bag.

We kept our spirits up with singing, storytelling and jokes, and at the end of two days and a night – it took that long to cover 600 *versts* – we reached the Mogilev junction.

Father expected to be met by friends from the Stavka. Instead, he was received by a detachment of Red soldiers under the command of one Comrade Citizen Bedlov, a representative of the Petrograd Soviet.

'Piotr Alexandrovich Silomirsky? I have the honour to inform Your ex-Excellency that you are under arrest,' Bedlov said. 'And you also, ex-General Boris Andreyevich Maysky.'

Father's officers offered to make short work of the Soviet comrade and his men, but Father reminded them Anna Vladimirovna was hostage in Petrograd. He surrendered his sword and pistol and, thanking his officers for their loyalty, parted with them calmly. Boris Maysky also gave up his weapons. I had slipped my revolver in my bosom – the rifle I had left behind – and I was not searched. Simyon declared he would accompany his Prince to prison if necessary, and the five of us, including Nyanya, were led off to the station's first-class dining room.

Since the initial news of the Tsar's abdication, my acquaintance with revolution had progressed through a series of shocks for which I had no adequate response. So now I could not say what I felt exactly. Disbelief, dismay, anxiety, anger, pride? There was some of each, and overall a sense of unreality heightened by sleeplessness. I was thirsty. I itched. *That* was real. The rest was hallucination.

In the dining room, Bedlov ordered tea. He put strawberry preserve into his glass and sucked on the bun that he dunked.

'Awfully good strawberry jam!' He closed one of his small green eyes with a look of sensuous satisfaction. 'Try putting some in your tea, Your ex-Excellency. Don't be embarrassed. Try!'

Father sipped his tea in contemptuous silence. I did likewise, even as I observed our chatty captor.

Bedlov was in his early thirties, small and stocky, with a smooth-shaven face of Mongolian cast and black hair cut straight at the neck like a peasant's. His eyes, bright as jade, rested on me with sensuous satisfaction, as though I were awfully good strawberry preserve. He inspired in me not merely repugnance but puzzlement. This was my first encounter with that new breed – *Homo sovieticus* – which was coming to power in Russia, a species sprung not from native soil or tradition or any source recognizably Russian but from a foreign ideology.

After a two-hour wait, during which my growing repugnance was accompanied, I came to admit, by fear, we resumed our journey, this time in a first-class coach with plush seats.

How different was this leg of the journey from the preceding! We were much more comfortable now but how much more dispirited! Until Mogilev, we had navigated the maelstrom of revolution like skilful pilots. Relying on our own discipline and daring, we could still imagine ourselves masters of our destiny. Henceforth, like the Tsar and my namesake, Father and I were captives. The Petrograd Soviet, an upstart power with a hypnotic spell over the populace, had laid its paw on us. What they wanted us for, what they would do with us, we had no idea. Any danger or privation was bearable so long as one was free. To be a prisoner was profoundly humiliating, even degrading. It had robbed me of courage for the first time in my life. How, without freedom, did one keep one's sense of self? Yet, there must be a way.

Looking at Father and Boris Maysky, I saw that they were very much themselves still. They are soldiers, I thought, and capture is one of the hazards of war. A prisoner of war does not give information to the enemy. A prisoner of war tries to escape. Yes, that is what they are thinking now, how to escape. And why shouldn't we? The main thing is to remain calm and resolute, to give no comfort to the enemy. I turned my gaze from the endless landscape to look haughtily at Comrade Bedlov.

Father's fleeting smile showed me he understood I had taken heart, and approved.

'Your ex-Excellency's daughter has spirit.' Bedlov approved also. 'And she's not been insensitive, in the past, to the injustices of the old order. Why don't you come over to our side, Tatyana Petrovna, the side of the people?' he coaxed. 'You're really one of us at heart.'

That my iconoclasm should be known to Bedlov, and he should think me capable of betraying my kin and kind – who were now the oppressed – made me crimson with shame.

'I have nothing whatever in common with you,' said I.

'*Jalko* – what a pity!' Bedlov cocked his head at me. 'But you may change your mind. Under the present circumstances, it would be . . . realistic.'

I looked out of the window once more to avoid conversing with our captor. The more familiar Bedlov became, the more frightening. His very way of sucking air through his teeth as he spoke had a sinister sound.

'Enough! Leave her be,' Father said in a choked voice. 'She has not turned twenty yet.'

'As you please,' Bedlov responded with false bonhomie – his good humour, too, was chilling – and began softly to whistle 'The Marseillaise'.

The following day, after sitting up all night under our captor's half-closed eye, we reached Petrograd before noon.

The Nikolayevsky Station, like every station on our journey, was overrun with mobs of deserters. A disciplined detail of Red guards in high sheepskin caps was drawn up on the platform to greet Comrade Bedlov and his dangerous prisoner. We learned later of the rumour that General Prince Silomirsky, on his march to the capital to overthrow the Provisional Government and restore the Tsar, had been intercepted and captured by the heroic Comrade Bedlov.

As two guards of our travel escort opened the door and stepped down, rifles at the ready, the deserters forgot for a moment their all-absorbing preoccupation, going home.

All eyes turned to the coach. When Father appeared on the top step, the white fur *papakha* on his silver head, the only sound in the stillness was the hissing escape of steam from beneath the train's wheels. He stood there as though in the reviewing stand, and I expected to hear from the impressionable crowd the mighty 'hurrah' Father had always wrung from his troops. But instead, a jeering voice called familiarly, 'Is it *thou, Prince*?'

'I, General Prince Silomirsky,' his answer rang back, and without looking down, he slowly descended the steps.

'Lookit what a proud one!' – 'Show us a fist, comrade!' – 'Put on a red ribbon!' – 'He despises us simple soldiers!' – 'He wants to lead us back to the slaughter!' – 'He wants to put his playmate Nikolenka back on the throne!' – 'He wants to crush our revolution!' – 'We won't let him, we'll crush him first!' – 'Yes, crush him!' – 'Spit on him!' – 'Let him have it!'

Spitting, fist-shaking, catcalls accompanied the jeers. Then caps, tins of army rations, canteens began to fly. I saw Father hemmed in by the guards, who swayed with the shoving of the mob.

I turned to Bedlov. 'They're going to murder Father if you don't stop them!'

'That wouldn't fit our plans at all,' Bedlov drawled. 'Comrades!' He drew his pistol and fired twice into the air. 'Comrades,' he shouted, 'I am with you in your hatred of this oppressor of the people and accomplice of Bloody Nikolay. Only let me take him to the fortress and bring him to trial for his crimes.'

'Hurrah! To the fortress! Long live the Revolution! Down with the generals! Down with the princes! It's the noose for them all!' The mob now pressed on to the exit, carrying along the prisoners and their guard.

My descent with Nyanya attracted little notice.

In front of the station stood two closed cars, a soldier with an automatic rifle stretched over each mudguard. In the first vehicle, Father with his guards, General Maysky and Simyon were joined by Bedlov. It sped away at once.

I was shoved into the backseat of the second car between two soldiers. Nyanya was secured between the driver and a soldier and used her elbows on them until she was comfortable. We drove off down the Nevsky Prospekt.

I stared out of the window, dazed by the aftershock of the scene just witnessed, racked with anguish over Father's fate in the fortress.

The crowd on the sidewalks sporting red rosettes, armbands, scarves; shop windows smashed or boarded up; dirty snow piled along the gutters; paper litter, neglect and shabbiness in place of elegance, order and luxury – all this was part of recent events so alien I had no emotion with which to respond. But when we drove down the Admiralty Quay and the smell of sea and tar came pungently on a warm spring breeze, the return to the familiar and dear moved me as the unfamiliar, however horrible, could not. My eyes burned with tears and only the thought of Grandmaman helped me control myself.

We turned shortly into the carriage entrance of our *osobnyak*. A red flag now flew above the house instead of the red-and-white flag of mercy. The courtyard was strewn with papers and broken bottles. The Silomirsky arms above the double-panelled, mahogany entrance door had been splattered and chipped. No Swiss doorman stood in the entrance hall, halberd in hand. No footman in livery rushed forward to take my cape. The rose carpet of the central vestibule and grand staircase was filthy and torn. On the first storey the rose marble columns of the foyer had been soiled, the family escutcheons on the wrought-iron balustrade knocked down and red streamers draped over it. The doors to the former grand ballroom, converted into a hospital ward, were padlocked. The enfilade of reception rooms through which I passed between my guards, Nyanya following behind under similar protection, showed increasing evidence of the sacking. Draperies were torn, satin upholstery slashed, the works of great masters daubed with ink, chandeliers and mirrors shot to bits, porphyry vases overturned and smashed, obscenities scribbled on the frescoes and whiskers added to nymphs. It was unpleasant, but unimportant beside Father's capture, wreckage left by the hurricane of revolution. When life and sanity were imperilled, what did objects matter?

The guards deposited us on the floor above, in the anteroom of Grandmaman's apartment in the wing overlooking the Quai Anglais, where lounged six guards armed to the teeth. I knew it would not do to go in to Grandmaman unannounced so I knocked on the double doors to the inner rooms.

'Who is there?' a big voice responded.

'Fyodor, it's me, Tatyana. Let me in.'

The doors were unlocked and flung open. The giant in clean

livery stood aside stiffly to let me pass, keeping his eyes straight ahead.

I rose on tiptoe to kiss him on the cheek. 'Fyodor dear, how glad I am to see you!'

He coloured to the roots of his now grey-blond hair, even while his childlike features remained impassive. Then, having locked the doors after Nyanya, he preceded me to Grandmaman's sitting room.

'Her Most Serene Highness, Tatyana Petrovna,' he called at the door in his stentorian voice.

Lousy, filthy, exhausted, on the verge of tears, I still drew myself up and went in.

Handsome and stately Petrograd was sadly changed, our handsome and stately house was sadly changed, all Russia was changed, but Grandmaman was just the same. She sat in her usual rose-and-silver Empire armchair surrounded by photographs of Father and me at all ages and in all attires, Zinaida Mikhailovna plump and self-effacing at her side. Only her toy poodle was missing. She was buttoned up to the neck in black. Her carriage was as erect as ever, her grey hair as carefully waved even without the help of her French hairdresser – vanished along with our Polish chef, the great Anatole, on the night of the sacking. Her gaze was still disconcertingly direct. The soulful depths of her beautiful brown eyes, like Nyanya's lively dark ones, held comprehension and acceptance of man's capacity for evil.

'You're well, child?' she asked as I curtsied and kissed her hand. She held my face in her wide, strong hand to observe me better. Then, evidently satisfied, she turned to my nurse, giving her both hands to kiss. 'Well, Nyanya, how do you like the doings of our people these days?'

'Foo, the devils! You won't find worse in the whole world,' answered the woman of the people. 'It's a sorrow and a shame! They nearly tore my Prince to pieces before our eyes at the Nikolayevsky Station when we arrived, but the Lord was merciful. He was spared!' Nyanya crossed herself.

'Papa has been taken to the Fortress of Petropavlovsk,' I said, 'with Boris Andreyevich and Simyon. Bedlov ... this member of the Petrograd Soviet who arrested us ... said they would try him ... and shoot him.'

'Nonsense! The arrest was *pro forma*, to appease the Petrograd Soviet. Kerensky, the Minister of Justice, has promised to send my son home before dark.'

I was so overjoyed that, like Nyanya, I kissed both Grandmaman's hands. Then, 'Grandmaman, I must see Tanik and the others!' My obsession over the fate of my captive namesake again became uppermost. 'Please ask Mr Kerensky to get me a pass to the Alexander Palace.'

'In good time, my girl, in good time. Tatyana Nikolayevna can wait.'

Grandmaman's tone was cool – like Father, I sensed, she would now prefer me to forget my intimacy with the Tsar's daughters. To mollify her I inquired after Toby, her poodle.

'I let Marie Pavlovna take him to the Caucasus, to Kislovodsk – she needed to take the cure. I had no one any longer to walk or bathe him, and he became very nervous after the sacking. Marie Pavlovna is crazy about him. Toby will be as happy with her as your Bobby is with Vera Kirilovna at Alubek.'

'How are Her Imperial Highness and Vera Kirilovna?' I dared not inquire right away after my friends at Tsarskoye.

'Marie Pavlovna was very low, quite broken in health and spirits. Vera Kirilovna is well – busy, no doubt, plotting the restoration of the monarchy. And Marie Fyodorovna is at Livadia next door, so our kinswoman is in ecstasy.'

'It's a relief to know Her Imperial Majesty is safe out of the soviets' reach,' Zinaida Mikhailovna said, while I could not help smiling at the thought of my former *éducatrice* reunited with her imperial patroness. 'But how the poor lady must suffer for her son!' Zinaida's maternal sympathy went out to the mother of the captive Tsar.

'Are His Majesty and the family very badly treated at Tsarskoye?' I put in as the familiar ring of anguish tightened about my heart.

'They're not abused. But I don't imagine they're enjoying themselves any more than we. Enough chatting for now. Fyodor!' Grandmaman gave two taps of her cane, and he appeared. 'You will accompany Tatyana Petrovna to her rooms. Don't let her take a step in the house without you. Tanya, wash your hair carefully and scrub with vinegar – I expect you're lousy. Your Dunya's still with us. We'll send you a luncheon tray. Take a good long nap after lunch. I'll see you at tea. Five o'clock as usual.'

Washed, fed and rested, I felt not only human again but cheerful when I returned to Grandmaman's sitting room. And, as the lights went on – 'It's a marvel, the electricity works,' Grandmaman remarked – in strode Father with Boris Maysky.

'*Maman chérie, vous êtes formidable!* You're magnificent!' Father kissed Grandmaman's hand and cheek.

'Kerensky kept his promise. Now go and change, both of you, and we'll have dinner and talk.'

An hour later, as we sat down at a round table in her sitting room, with Simyon serving a still excellent meal, 'Tell us, Pierre, was it very terrible at the fortress?' asked Grandmaman. Exactly in the same tone she had formerly inquired whether the sitting of the Council of Empire had been very boring.

'Not very,' Father answered likewise, 'although I hear some of the ex-ministers are having a bad time of it in the Trubetskoy bastion.'

'If you mean Sukhomlinov, Protopopov, and company, they deserve it,' declared Grandmaman.

'No doubt. But why torment Anya Vyrubova? You know I could not bear the insipid creature while she was Alexandra's favourite. But to accuse that poor, credulous cripple of sinister intrigues and treason is as stupid as it is cruel.'

'That must be hard on Her Majesty,' I said, recalling Alexandra's incomprehensible infatuation with Annushka.

'Oddly enough, it seems Alexandra repudiated her bosom friend,' said Grandmaman.

'How typical of royal caprice!' Father observed. 'Alexandra needed a scapegoat. Anya was made for the part.'

'I think, perhaps, Her Majesty herself was to blame for her own misfortunes,' ventured Zinaida.

'We were all to blame.' Grandmaman would honour fallen majesty, though it had deserved to fall.

'Anna Vladimirovna, if it's not being indiscreet, could you tell us how you got Mr Kerensky to release us from the fortress?' Boris Maysky now inquired.

'Yes, Maman, do tell us of your connivance with that revolutionary firebrand. That Prince Lvov eats out of your hand is one thing – he is one of us. But Alexander Kerensky!'

'Young Mr Kerensky' – anyone under fifty was young to Grandmaman – 'who is as dashing as he is eloquent, has been involved in a liaison with a girl of noble family, one known to us all. The brother was about to challenge Kerensky to a duel. There was going to be a proper scandal. I managed to hush it up. The girl is devoted to me. And Mr Kerensky, to his credit, has acknowledged his debt of gratitude.'

'Only half acknowledged, I should say, since the Prince, and I with him, remain under house arrest,' said Boris Maysky.

'Kerensky cannot defy the Petrograd Soviet as yet to the extent of freeing you. He needs its cooperation to continue the war. But he will, as soon as the Provisional Government is solidly established, he will, Boris Andreyevich, have no fear.'

'A very ambitious and brilliant politician, young Mr Kerensky,' said Zinaida Mikhailovna. 'He is quite the man of the hour. I wonder if he could make use of Kolenka.' Zinaida's thoughts still ran in that single direction.

'Kerensky is a fool or a dreamer if he thinks he can work peaceably with a Bolshevik-controlled soviet,' Father said.

'He's a bit of both,' Grandmaman conceded. 'But the Bolsheviks don't control the Petrograd Soviet as yet. And their following throughout the country is small. When the Constituent Assembly meets, there's a good chance they'll be roundly defeated.'

'*Chère Maman*, always an optimist!' Father smiled a little sadly. 'I fear Monsieur Kerensky has not taken the measure of Comrade Bedlov and his ilk as we have had the opportunity to.' And Father related our journey and capture with his usual storytelling skill. In conclusion he said, 'I also learned today at the fortress, from a former colleague of his, that Bedlov had been an informer for the Okhrana. So, apparently, was Monsieur Lenin's right hand, Comrade Stalin. Charm and oratory will not outwit those fellows!'

'Well, perhaps it's healthier to have the crooks and criminals out in the open, rather than working for the secret police.' Grandmaman persisted in her optimism.

It was contagious, and we finished the evening in animated talk, ignoring the shouts and laughter of our guards. At ten o'clock the family, with our attendants and servants, were mustered for curfew roll call in the music room.

The corporal of the guard called the servants first. Last of all he demanded, 'Comrade Silomirsky, are you here?' He used the familiar form of address.

'Present,' answered Father resonantly. 'And in the future' – he took a step towards the corporal – 'you and your men will remove your caps in the presence of ladies and officers.' As the corporal made no move, he advanced on him. 'Off with your cap,' he said, striking it off.

All the guards whisked off their caps.

'*Mon Dieu*, I thought they would massacre us,' murmured Zinaida Mikhailovna as we saw Grandmaman to her rooms.

'They can massacre us any time they choose,' she responded. 'But they're less likely to if they respect us. Ah, had Russia had men like my son among its leaders, we wouldn't have come to this! Our lions turned out to be lambs, to be meekly led to the slaughter. Well, Tatyana, off to bed. Do you still have the revolver your father gave you?'

'I do.'

'Keep it under your pillow just in case.' She gave me her hand to kiss and passed it over my hair in a rare caress.

I went to bed in my old suite of rooms, which Nyanya and Dunya, my maid, now shared. Fyodor was to sleep in the anteroom, as in my early childhood.

So began my life in post-revolutionary Petrograd. And this period too, like war nursing for all its drama, soon became commonplace. I could neither grasp the import of the new epoch I witnessed emerging, nor its danger.

21

Although Father and Boris Maysky were confined to the second-storey private apartments and only allowed to take the air in the inner court, Grandmaman and I could circulate freely so long as we reported for evening roll call. I begged Grandmaman once more to use all her influence with Mr Kerensky that I might be allowed as an exceptional favour to visit 'Colonel Romanov' and his family. Seeing I would not be deterred, she spoke to the Minister of Justice. Early in May, I received the necessary pass. Accompanied by Fyodor, I took the train to Tsarskoye Selo. Fyodor wore knee-high boots and a Russian blouse and cap, I my nurse's uniform. He was to walk beside me and not highness me ever.

The railway line reserved for the imperial family and members of the court, on which I had travelled in Vera Kirilovna's company, now served the crowds of the curious going to gape at the diverting spectacle of imprisoned royalty. At the Alexandrovsk Station in Tsarskoye Selo there was no imperial motorcar or carriage with scarlet-caped footmen to take me to the palace. We walked rapidly the distance of less than a mile across the wooded town dominated by the 'Old Palace' of Catherine I. As I neared the low, wrought-iron gate to the grounds of the newer Alexander Palace, I saw from the street a scene as extraordinary and inconceivable as any I had yet witnessed since the Revolution.

The Emperor and his daughters, in full sight of the spectators gaping over the gate, were at work in a vegetable garden. Olga Nikolayevna spaded beside her father. Tatyana Nikolayevna, grown thin, and Marie, grown large since I had last seen them, were pulling a roller over freshly seeded ground. Sixteen-year-old Anastasia trundled a wheelbarrow with comical application. All four Grand Duchesses wore round woollen caps and plain black skirts. Aleksey was not in sight.

The Tsar, as usual, was in colonel's uniform, but he looked greatly altered. His complexion was sallow. The serenity and mildness were gone from his handsome face. Its expression made me feel anger and shame.

Alexandra, in a flowered hat, a black band about her neck, sat in a wheelchair. Her heart must be worse. Her legs are swollen, I thought. She looked older, more matronly but also less rigid and forbidding. Her fingers, which were never idle, flew over her needlework. From time to time she looked up at her husband, who put down his spade and smiled.

The Empress, like the Tsar, seemed oblivious of the guards who dogged his steps with rifles low. To me they were all too visible. I advanced towards the railing with a pounding heart.

'Look at the auntie sitting there,' remarked a woman with a little girl by the hand. 'They say she had poisoned candy sent to children who refused Rasputin's blessing. And her daughters, simple and decent to look at, but the way they carried on with that Rasputin, the tales one hears ...'

'You evidently think those are fine tales for your little girl, my good lady,' I said. 'And you, worthy citizens' – I turned to the rest of the curious – 'have you nothing better to do than to catch flies with your mouths open?'

A boy at once shut his mouth.

'Now go, all of you! Fyodor, keep the gate clear until I return!'

I showed my pass to the sergeant at the gate with a trembling hand. He wore the St George medal of the fifth class, so I said, 'Civilians are no-good loafers. It's a wonder you put up with that nuisance.'

'What's to be done? You can't keep them away,' he said, and unlocked the gate.

The Grand Duchesses left off gardening and converged on me.

The Tsar put down his shovel. Quickly covering the three strides that etiquette prescribed, he seized me by the arms, forestalling my obeisance, and kissed me on both cheeks. 'Tata dear, it's good to see you,' he greeted me in English. 'The girls were wondering when you'd come.'

'I've been waiting for the authorization, Sir, ever since we returned to Petrograd.'

'Ah yes, of course.' That new expression I could not define was intensified. The Tsar glanced at the railing behind which Fyodor paced alone, ominous of bulk, impassive of mien. 'Why did you make a fuss at the gate?' he asked in his soft voice.

I coloured. 'I'm sorry, Sir. It was just that those people ...'

'They don't bother us. You mustn't let them bother you either.' Then, accompanied by his daughters all talking to me at once, he brought me before Alexandra's chair. 'I told you, Sunny, Tata would come as soon as she could.'

'It's very good of you, Tata.' The Empress spoke in her familiar stiff and awkward manner as I made my obeisance. 'We haven't many visitors these days.'

I presented Grandmaman's and Father's homage, which he was unable to present in person.

'Yes, we heard Prince Silomirsky was under house arrest,' Alexandra said. 'I hope he's having a better time of it than dear old Friedrichsy. The poor old man is shockingly treated, even in hospital.' She made no mention of her former favourite. So Anya Vyrubova had indeed been cast aside, at least for the present.

I told the Empress I'd ask Grandmaman to speak to Prince Lvov about Count Friedrichs, the former Minister of the Court, once the butt of the Grand Duchesses' childhood pranks.

Alexandra made a few more inquiries about Petrograd acquaintances. Then, with an attempt at her former humorous self-deprecation, 'But you haven't come to sit with an invalid old lady, Tata,' she said.

This brought the inevitable protests: 'Oh Mummsy!' from her daughters, and 'Oh come, Sunny!' from her husband, together with a heartfelt, 'Your Majesty!' on my part.

'But I *am* an invalid old lady.' The Empress smiled. 'I know you'd much rather talk to our Tatyana. And don't forget to say hello to Sunbeam. I don't see him ... Well, he can't be far. *A quelque chose malheur est bon* – it's an ill wind that blows no good. At least we're now assured of proper surveillance for our son.' With a brief look she acknowledged the guards, until now seemingly invisible.

Alexandra's lighthearted tone could not disguise her bitterness. Of all her family, I guessed, the proud Empress found their present situation most galling.

'You two run along,' the Tsar said to Tatyana Nikolayevna and me. 'I need a strong back to help spade this last row.' He looked at his two youngest daughters.

'I think my back is strongest, Papa,' Marie said with a shy smile.

Olga Nikolayevna handed over her spade and began slowly wheeling her mother. She, once the most rebellious of the four, seemed to have become reconciled to her mother and her lot.

Anastasia followed Marie. After watching her start to dig, she seized the shovel. 'Not this way, clumsy,' she cried, and began spading away with furious vigour and speed.

As my namesake and I headed for the lake, two guards at our heels, I saw the Tsar remonstrating with his wilful youngest daughter.

'Poor Marie,' Tatyana Nikolayevna said in English, taking my arm, 'we're still cruel to her. It's a family habit. But she's really been splendid. When Olga and I were at our worst with the measles, she went out with Mummsy to talk to the Red soldiers, during the disorders.'

'You did not mention disorders in your letter,' I reproached her.

'They weren't serious, just a few rowdies demanding to see us for fear Boysy had been spirited away. They calmed right down when they heard we were sick. I didn't want to worry you over a trifling incident.'

That was my darling Tanik! 'Your letter was so calm, it surprised me. Later, I understood.' For the inconceivable, there were no ready emotions. 'How did you hear of His Majesty's abdication?'

'Grand Duke Paul brought us the news. Mummsy simply wouldn't believe it at first. She tried to persuade herself and us that it was a false rumour. Even when we were placed under house arrest, she was absolutely unshaken. Then, when Papa was brought home under guard, we all went to pieces. But that's passed, there's no point in talking about it. Tell me how it was with you.'

I related the effect of the Revolution on our lives. I tried to make our journey from Rovno to Petrograd sound comical, and the Grand Duchess laughed. But when I described Father's reception at the Nicholas Station, I shuddered at the recollection.

'How awful!' Tatyana Nikolayevna pressed my arm. 'And Prince Silomirsky was so popular with the troops! You know, what's happened to the army has been hardest of all for Papa to bear. He's said, had he known it'd turn out this way, he'd never have abdicated. He did it so there'd be no dissension in the country in wartime, because he felt the most important thing was to win the war, and now he's afraid the Provisional Government might agree to a separate peace. He has no thought for himself at all, his only worry is whether he did right for our country . . . and he's called a traitor, and all sorts of dreadful things.'

'Don't speak of it. It's too unfair and contemptible!'

We had reached the boundary of the area of the park to which the imperial prisoners were restricted. We sat down by the bridge to 'the children's island', as we called it.

'Still nervous, Tata?' The Grand Duchess took my icy hand in hers.

'It's passing. D'you know what I was thinking just now?' As children, we had played at guessing each other's thoughts.

The Grand Duchess concentrated with childlike seriousness. 'Gathering mushrooms at Bialowieza,' she said at last, correctly. 'D'you remember what I called the tame deer?'

'"The pretty creatures".' We smiled at one another. 'Oh Tanik, it's so good to be together again!' I cried. 'If only Papa and I could join the suite,' I blurted out without thinking how Alexandra, or Father, would react.

'I'll speak to Mummsy. We'll all go to England together. You can marry your Stefan, and the four of us will be your bridesmaids!'

'Tanik!' I gazed into her face, which had grown from mere prettiness to a finer beauty. 'Tanik, beloved friend,' I said in Russian.

Tatyana Nikolayevna smiled wistfully. Then, putting a hand to her round wool cap, she asked in casual English, 'How d'you like this elegant *pot de chambre* I'm wearing?'

'It looks well on you. And I like you better without the curls on your forehead.'

'I haven't any curls left. The five of us were shaved after the measles. We're as bald as Tartars. We had our photograph taken and we all whisked off our caps before it was snapped. Mummsy thought it a bad omen. But you know she's forever seeing omens! And after all, things aren't so bad, Ortipo, are they?' The bulldog, who had joined us, put his big snuffly head in her lap. 'So long as we can remain together, nothing's *really* bad, and if Tata comes, it'll be colossal! Wouldn't Boysy be glad though? Ortipo, where's Boysy? Where's Aleksey?'

The bulldog did not know.

'Oh, you look funny!' cried his mistress, and I said, 'One mustn't laugh at dogs, Tanik. They're very sensitive.'

I received a mock-penitent look. 'I'm sorry if I offended you, Ortipo, I'm *dread*fully sorry. Let me get up now.'

I had risen in the same instant. 'With your permission, Tanik, I'll go and look for your brother.'

'Do, and I'll talk to Mummsy in the meantime. But Anna Vladimirovna – what will she do if you and Prince Silomirsky join us?'

I could not imagine Grandmaman leaving Russia. 'She can either go to Alubek, where Vera Kirilovna has been looking after the estate, or to Marie Pavlovna in Kislovodsk. Her Imperial Highness has been urging Grandmaman to come.'

'Then there's no obstacle.' And the Grand Duchess joined Mlle Schneider, the court reader, who had been sent to look for her.

I cut through the park along the boundary marked by the presence of a guard at every few paces. I found Aleksey in tears. The guards had confiscated his toy rifle.

Nagorny, his sailor-nurse, tried to comfort him. 'It's not worth your sorrow, Aleksey Nikolayevich. I'll make you a real bow and arrow much finer than a toy rifle.'

Seeing me, the boy crimsoned. 'Hello, Tata,' he said, and avoided my eyes.

Aleksey, in his thirteenth year, had spurted in height. He still wore the belted overblouse and flat cap of an army private, as he had by his father's side all through the war. Fair-skinned and slender, he was more beautiful than his sisters at that age. His dark eyes held a new resentment: this hurt was even harder to comprehend and accept than physical pain.

'Nagorny's right. A toy isn't worth making a fuss about,' I said in English as Aleksey leaned his forehead against a rock. 'Weren't you taught a prince doesn't cry over trifles?'

'I'm not a prince anymore.'

'If you're born a prince, you remain one no matter what. And you must always behave like one, as your father does.'

Aleksey stopped sniffling. He cast a wrathful look at the guards surrounding us at rifle-point, faces screwed up in an effort to understand the foreign tongue. 'Papa is so polite,' he said, 'and they, they're so rude! At Easter, he kissed all the men of the guard.

Every night, at roll call, he shakes hands with the officers. The other night, one of them refused his hand ... How can ... how can Papa be so humble?'

So that was the real source of the boy's shame: doubt in the father he had believed all-powerful. 'What did His Majesty do when the officer refused his hand?'

'He said, "Ah, I'm sorry," and looked at him in such an odd way.'

'As though he were sorry for him?'

'Perhaps ...' The boy considered this.

'It's not your father who was humiliated by the insult, but the man who committed it. His Majesty is above pride. That's very different from being without.'

'I am not without pride! I don't care about that old rifle! I don't care what anybody does to me! I don't care about *them*!' Aleksey stuck out his tongue.

The guards fell to muttering among themselves.

'Tata, make them a face. Make them one of your really horrid faces.' And, as I hesitated, 'I command you,' he added.

So I bowed to imperial command.

Aleksey laughed immoderately.

'Aleksey Nikolayevich, let's go back, for God's sake!' Nagorny pleaded.

'*Poshli* – let's go,' the boy said cockily in Russian and offered me his arm. 'Tata' – he looked up at me with his old air of lively adoration – 'it'd be such fun to have you with us.'

'Perhaps you will.'

We joined the rest of the family. Olga and Anastasia were quarrelling over the privilege of wheeling their mother in. My namesake's expression told me her plea had been unsuccessful.

Alexandra bade Anastasia show Aleksey the beetle she had caught. The two youngest gone, she said to me, 'Tatyana has asked to have you, her favourite maid of honour, in attendance. It would make all the children happy. But I cannot ask you to share our probable fate.'

The three Grand Duchesses and I looked at the Empress gravely.

'But Mummsy,' said my namesake, 'we'll all be going to England soon.'

'We may never leave Russia alive.'

There was another, heavier silence.

Tatyana Nikolayevna was again first to break it. 'Oh Mummsy, you're being too gloomy! Papa says Uncle George will surely get us out.'

'Your father does not know the world.' Alexandra looked on each of her three eldest in turn. 'My darlings, I didn't mean to frighten you. You're all big girls now, even you, my brave Marie – I can't hide anything from you. I know you'll help me keep it from the little ones.'

'We shan't be afraid so long as we remain together,' said Olga.

'Yes, that's the main thing,' Tatyana Nikolayevna assented. 'Of course it'd be splendid to have Tata, but not if there's the slightest chance we mightn't get away. She has someone very important waiting in France.'

She has told them about Stefan, I thought. But what was my happiness at such a moment? 'Your Majesty,' I said, 'whatever lies ahead, whatever the hardships, or worse, that Your Majesty fears, both Father and I would be honoured to share them.'

Alexandra's still handsome features stiffened disagreeably and she said in her former schoolmistressish tone, 'Still dramatic, aren't you, Tata? I've sometimes wondered if your true vocation were not the stage, rather than medicine. Come, girls, push. It's time to go in.'

With head bowed and heart aching, I stood aside for the passage of Alexandra wheeled by Olga and Marie. Both girls looked at me comfortingly.

Don't mind Mummsy, it's only her way. She loves you, and so do we all, said their gaze.

In the entrance semicircle of the palace, the prisoners were checked off by the commander of the guard. I was allowed to accompany the former sovereigns into the wing of apartments that they were now restricted to, and make my goodbyes in private. As I stood in the Empress's Victorian boudoir once again, the blood pounded in my face and chest while my hands turned to ice.

Alexandra in her wheelchair, her flowered hat in her lap, a finger to her temple in a handsome pose, sat under the familiar portrait of Marie Antoinette and the Dauphin. On either side stood her husband and her son.

The four Grand Duchesses clustered around me.

I had come to cheer them, and it was they who were trying to give me courage. Even Anastasia vigorously squeezed my hands and nodded in comical earnest. Marie's tear-filled eyes were even more blue and beautiful. Olga's face was full of lively intelligence while Tatyana Nikolayevna's, as she embraced me, expressed that strength of character called forth by her recent experience.

Aleksey now came forward manfully. He shook my hand, then flung himself about my neck. 'I love you, Tata,' he whispered.

'I love you too. Be brave, look after your mother and sisters.'

Alexandra's rigid manner helped hold back my tears.

'I'll see you to the door, Tata,' the Tsar said.

He was not in time to forestall my low curtsy.

'Come, Tata, that's not necessary. You know I've never cared for that sort of thing, especially now.' His Majesty raised and kissed me. 'Give your father a big hug for me. Tell him we pray for his release every day. The Lord keep you, my godchild,' he finished in Russian and blessed me with a slow and stately gesture.

There came a loud knock on the door and the officer on guard duty entered to take Colonel Romanov to his quarters. The Emperor was allowed to see his family only at meals and during exercise period.

'Right away,' he answered. 'Only allow me to take leave of my wife.'

I flung the officer of the guard a look of contempt and turned quickly down the hall. There was no master of ceremonies in gold braid to escort me through the familiar enfilade of reception rooms. I passed no runner in Empress Elizabeth costume bearing a message from Their Imperial Majesties to some exalted member of the Court. Gone were the gold braid, the pomp and ceremony, the sumptuous tiaras and stiff brocades. The crowd that had knelt before its sovereigns in the Winter Palace Square only three years before now jeered at them over a gate.

How could such a change have come about in three short years, I asked myself? Had the pomp and ceremony of empire lost its magic in the glare of this inhuman age I had seen born in the travail of modern war? Had the Russian people outgrown its faith in monarchy, even as children outgrow their belief in fairy tales, as Professor Holveg had once said? Or had Russia's sovereigns brought about their own downfall?

Whatever the causes of their downfall and however grave their fault, it was now, in their cruel adversity and humiliation, that Nicholas and Alexandra had achieved true stature. And for this the world would honour them as it had not honoured them as emperor and empress.

Fyodor was still keeping the curious at bay as I came out. Without a backward look at the crowd again collecting at the gate, I headed rapidly towards the station, the chill of late afternoon cooling my flaming cheeks.

My behaviour at the gate and towards Aleksey's guards was duly reported and my requests to visit the Alexander Palace henceforth denied. The letters I wrote to my namesake remained unanswered. The Tsar and his family were refused passage to England by the Petrograd Soviet. The British government was sincerely sorry. But it did not pursue the matter. In the harsh light of the newborn age, the fate of another monarch gone the way of so many monarchs in the course of history was not worth making a fuss about.

22

After my visit to the Alexander Palace, I found myself chafing at the routine of captivity that my elders in the Silomirsky household had adapted to with surprising ease.

Pending his appearance before the 'Extraordinary Commission of Inquiry into the acts of ministers and important personages of the former imperial government', Father remained under house arrest.

Grandmaman did not leave the house. Garage and stables were both empty, and she was not about to go out on foot at her age, she declared. I soon found that she could keep Father company much better than I. I could not savour their witty anecdotes and characterizations out of a bygone era. I still awaited the fulfilment of my legendary love, and did not understand then that for Father and Grandmaman life's significance lay not in its passions but its refinements. For the first time I felt estranged from Father, and doubted the justification of my cruel separation from Stefan.

In my need for companionship, I thought of Professor Holveg. Father encouraged me to look him up. I sent him a message with Fyodor and we met in Solovyev Garden on Vassily Island, near his flat, the very next day.

He was dressed with care and not without elegance and carried a bouquet of spring flowers.

'In the old days, when the Silomirsky *osobnyak* was full of flowers, these would have been superfluous,' he said in French. 'But I thought, under the present circumstances, you might enjoy them.'

'How very thoughtful!' I smelled the fragrant bouquet and looked at the Professor fondly as we sat down on a bench by the water. His black goatee was more precisely trimmed than ever, his cuffs very white about his fine wrists. Exact and gentlemanly, he looked more like a Polish than a Russian scholar. He was a welcome contrast to the prevailing sloppiness.

'How is your mother, Professor? Is she still in Warsaw?'

His mother was well in Warsaw, he was well enough at the university. 'And your father? How does the Prince bear house arrest?'

'Quite well, actually. He is writing his memoirs. He paints. He expects to be released soon.'

'I hope so! Now tell me about yourself,' the Professor urged, 'from the night we last met at the opera – such an unforgettable night! You were on your way back to Minsk. Did the Revolution surprise you there?'

'No, we were at Father's headquarters near Rovno.' I poured out my heart and mind – well, not altogether, since I did not mention Stefan. For I suddenly understood Alexis Holveg loved me, had loved me, perhaps, as long ago as our tutor–pupil days. I would not give him false hope. But I was afraid to discourage him for good, and lose him. Whatever he meant to me, I knew the moment I laid eyes on him again that he was important and precious.

'Now I'm at loose ends,' I concluded. 'Practising the piano and posing for Father hardly fills my day. Yet I can't commit myself to a nursing position, even if anyone dared hire me.'

'Are you continuing your medical studies on your own?'

'No, not even that. The future is too uncertain.'

'On the contrary, the future is open to you. There are no longer any obstacles to your becoming a physician. This passivity, Tatyana Petrovna, is quite unlike you. Do you need books?'

'The medical library of our former hospital is intact.' I felt myself coming back to life.

'Excellent! You can begin to read some physiology and pharmacology. And I am at your disposal, if you would like to go to the theatre, a concert, or simply for a walk. The street, these days, is an instructive spectacle.'

'I may take a lot of your time,' I warned him.

'You can never take enough of my time, Tatyana Petrovna.'

'Dear Professor Holveg!' I said, even though his last words had not been spoken in a professorial tone.

'Please do not call me Professor any longer. It makes me feel, not fourteen, but forty years your elder.'

'Then I'll call you Alexis, if I may. Aleksey Alekseyevich is too cumbersome.' And too Russian, I thought. Alexis Holveg was not

Russian or Polish, Jewish or German. His was a universal mind, a mind for that new world I had once envisioned, but which turned out so different in reality!

'I'm not only idle, I'm confused,' I reflected aloud. 'I can't help but endorse most of the programme of the Petrograd Soviet: peace without annexations or indemnities, self-government for national minorities, the abolition of anti-Jewish statutes, distribution of land to the peasants, equality for women. All this seems just and necessary. Why, then, are the results so disastrous?'

'They're not as disastrous yet as they could be. The breakdown of administration in a country the size of Russia was bound to be attended by disorder. But if this disorder can be exploited by a group of fanatical ideologues, then there is no hope for a free society.'

'One does hear more and more about Lenin and the Bolsheviks. Do you think they might come to power?'

'They have a simple and forceful platform – land, peace, and bread – which corresponds to the basic desires of the masses. They have a simple and forceful programme – direct action – which the masses can respond to. They have an able and forceful leadership, which the Provisional Government lacks. There are excellent liberal men in the government, but, so long as it is pledged to continue an unpopular war, its position will remain tenuous.'

'What do you think of Kerensky? Is he not forceful?' I asked a touch ironically. Kerensky was an all-too-zealous servant of the Petrograd Soviet in its persecution of the Tsar.

'He is very good at giving that impression. I don't doubt *he* believes in his ability to save the country "with honour". But the Bolsheviks are more realistic.'

'Yes. "Realistic" is a favourite adjective of Comrade Bedlov.' The recollection sent a chill through me.

'You're cold, Tatyana Petrovna. I will walk you home.'

We discussed, as we walked, that new free society of which we both dreamed.

'What is needed,' stated Alexis Holveg, 'is universal education, to eliminate superstition and prejudice, to base human conduct on knowledge and experimentation in place of tradition and dogma, to develop in every modern child the spirit of scepticism and free scientific inquiry.'

I smiled at his long words. We reached the Quai Anglais, where a group of seamen held a political discussion on a landing stage by their moored boats. 'Well, this is certainly the day for the spirit of free inquiry,' I remarked.

Alexis pronounced it an encouraging phenomenon.

'It's also a fine pretext for loafing.' I found myself echoing Grandmaman. 'My grandmother always said the Russian people were the laziest and most undisciplined in the world. She also said they could be capable of savage cruelty. I used to think the people good, and close to God, as Tolstoy does. Now I don't know what to think.'

'They are called, for good reason, *tiemnyi liud* – the folk in darkness,' Alexis said. 'Whether deliberately or through negligence, the Russian folk have been kept in darkness. Today, we see the result.'

'Yes.' I looked up at the colonnade of my great house. 'And we who kept it in darkness, whether deliberately or through negligence, we will be called to account.'

'That is a simplification, Tatyana Petrovna. Yesterday's ruling class was no more homogeneous than today's proletariat. You, as an individual, bear no guilt for Russia's plight.' He held my hand and his black eyes flashed behind his spectacles.

'Thank you, Alexis.' How well he knew me! Better than Papa, far better than Stevie! It was a relief. It was a novel thrill.

We fixed a rendezvous for the very next day.

Both Father and Grandmaman were pleased that I should renew acquaintance with Professor Holveg. With a smile, Grandmaman recalled the episode of the skeleton.

'What trifles one used to get upset about!' she remarked.

Father encouraged me to read in the medical library. I was surprised and touched by this belated recognition of my former burning ambition. Little did I know that Grandmaman, too clever to put forth her own biased objections to my Polish-Catholic cousin, had successfully played on Father's abnormal dread of childbearing and on his unacknowledged jealousy. He thought a revival of interest in my medical career the best antidote to my infatuation for Stefan.

The next day, and many a day thereafter, I enjoyed the uncommon experience of seeing the city on foot. Accompanied by Fyodor and

Alexis Holveg, I not only walked along the quays but ventured on to the crowded *prospekts* as well. The mood on the boulevards was more earnest than festive.

We met continual processions of workmen, women students, veterans and war wounded, racial minorities and political parties of all shades. The slogan 'All Power to the Soviets' recurred on the banners. Even more frequent were the words 'Down with the War'. At every street corner there was also an orator mounted on a bench or box, who gathered about him an attentive audience of young recruits, sailors, workmen, office girls and tradespeople. Most speakers had the native gift of colourful expression and held their audience. But the same people, I noticed, listened just as earnestly to speakers expounding opposite views. What they thought, if anything, was hard to guess.

One afternoon, on the Gorokhovaya, my attention was caught by a virulent orator in a black leather jacket. I stopped with Alexis at the edge of the crowd to listen.

'Will the Provisional Government give you land?' shouted the speaker, a Georgian by his looks and accent. 'It will not, because the Provisional Government is run by landowners and bourgeois capitalists. Will the Provisional Government put an end to the imperialistic war? It will not, because war makes the factory owner rich. The Provisional Government will not make peace. The Provisional Government will not give you land. Only the Soviets will give you land and peace. Lenin will give you land and peace. All power to the Soviets! Hurrah for Lenin!'

The response, I saw, was mild. The words 'land and peace' everyone understood, but what was this 'capitalist-imperialist-bourgeois' business and who was this Lenin fellow? The orator apparently sensed these doubts, for he launched into a tirade against the war. Then, pointing at me, he cried, 'Here is a sister of mercy. She can tell you about the war. Were you at the front, Sister?'

'Yes, I was at the front,' I answered and added unthinkingly, 'Where were you?'

Consternation, curiosity. 'Yes, where *have* you been all these years?' asked a soldier on crutches.

'I've been among the ranks of persecuted revolutionaries, preparing the coming victory of the proletariat,' blustered the speaker under his black moustache, which moved in ludicrous fashion.

The words, the moustache, excited derision. 'Listen how big he talks! Lookit, what fine black whiskers! He dyes them, most likely.' And, as the speaker raised his voice, 'Enough, brother, you're a bore! Step down. Give the sister of mercy a chance to have her say.'

Before Alexis could drag me away, the speaker had been hauled down and I hoisted on the box. I saw the open, friendly faces of the people looking up at me and said colloquially, 'Friends, I'm just a simple Russian girl who hasn't learned any long words from the Germans like the gentleman with the black whiskers' – laughter – 'so I won't make a long speech. I'm not acquainted with this Mr Lenin and I can't tell you what sort of person he is. But I've heard that he came to our country in a sealed train the Germans let through because it was to their advantage that Mr Lenin come to Petrograd. And what's to the advantage of the Germans can never be to the advantage of us Russians, to my mind. That's all I have to say.'

I would have jumped down but the Georgian speaker, who had been conferring with a fellow agitator in the crowd, suddenly planted himself in front of me, spreading his arms wide and crying, 'You're a fine bunch of free citizens, lads, when you pick on one of your fellow revolutionaries and listen instead to the dearest little friend of the daughters of the ex-Tsar, Bloody Nikolay!'

'Yes, it's she, the Serene Princess Silomirskaya. I've seen her photograph. I recognize her now. Her father's under arrest.' Voices arose. The faces turned up to me were no longer friendly but hostile. I recalled the scene at the Nicholas Station on our arrival and my head swam.

Alexis was signalling me to keep quiet. But I mastered my fright and said in the same cocky tone, 'If this is a gathering of free citizens I suppose I've a right to say my piece. But I'll gladly step down for the citizen with the black whiskers, if anybody still wants to listen to him.' And I looked for a free spot to jump down.

My bold speech divided opinion. A part of the crowd continued to rumble menacingly, while others said, 'Ah, let her go! She's one of us. She talks our language. She nursed our soldiers in the front line. She's done us no harm.'

Just then Fyodor loomed before the Georgian who blocked my escape, seized him by the lapels of his leather jacket, and sent him flying. Then he announced, 'If anybody lays a finger on the Princess, I'll smash his face in.'

The threat was momentarily effective. At the same time Alexis, wielding his cane, forced his way through the crowd, which fell back before his fury. 'Will you leave this girl alone? I am Professor Holveg of the University of Petrograd and the Academy of Sciences. I will not have my student molested!' He gave me his hand and I jumped down. Then he flagged a horse cab and hustled me into it, Fyodor following.

I sat back limp, my eyes closed, grateful for the jolting of the carriage on the cobblestones and the light May wind on my face. How good it is to be alive! I thought and smiled at my escort. How gallantly he had behaved! 'Thank you, Alexis, for your timely intervention.'

'There's no need to, Tatyana Petrovna. But I trust, in the future, you will be less imprudent. In these times, one must learn to be anonymous in order to survive.'

'That won't be easy,' I said, 'for either of us.'

He smiled in turn. Then he said, 'I think we had better avoid the centre of town for a while. I will fetch you in a cab from now on.'

'It's an unnecessary expense. If you're not afraid of compromising yourself, why don't you come to the house? Father and Grandmaman would be delighted to see you.'

'I'm not afraid' – I'm not afraid of anything where you're concerned, his eyes said – 'but if I'm to be of use to you, should matters take a turn for the worse, I should not be associated too closely with your family. I'm already suspect in some quarters as a former imperial tutor. I would like to maintain my position as a detached scientist, although, personally speaking, it's obviously impossible...'

'I think you're wise.' I pretended not to notice his confusion. It amused and touched me. It flattered me as well. I was somewhat in awe of his scientific genius.

Alexis Holveg, the pioneer in radioactivity, was my creature, I thought as he dropped me off. As a woman and an aristocrat, I felt no compunction in using him. But as a Christian, on my prayer stool that night, and in the confessional the next morning, I asked God to forgive my duplicity.

Just as I concealed from Professor Holveg my true relationship with Stefan, so I disguised to my cousin under an ironic tone my growing attachment to Alexis. A fortnight after our first meeting, I was writing to France:

I still walk every afternoon with Professor Holveg and my faithful Fyodor. We stick to the Quai Anglais after my bad moment with the Georgian orator on the Gorokhovaya. Yesterday evening, I had another close brush with citizen soldiers, the elite of the republican era. The Professor had invited me to the ballet. Papa thought it would be a pleasant change. Dearest Papa, he's always thinking of distractions so I won't be too depressed, and I do my best, for his sake, not to show how hard my separation from you is – you don't know how hard!

I felt in one of my reckless moods and decided to dress up for the event. Nyanya and Dunya helped me. We were as excited as country girls. I put on a black taffeta gown with a bouffant skirt, an emerald necklace and pendants from Mother's collection, the smallest black satin slippers I could squeeze my big feet into, long white gloves, and a black velvet cloak lined with ermine. I thought, I am going with Stevie to the Paris Opéra and I imagined it down to the smallest detail.

My head full of these fantasies, I sailed past our gawking guards, Fyodor in a royal-blue coat, white silk scarf and astrakhan cap behind me, and so down the soiled grand staircase into the vestibule where the Professor stood waiting. He looked taken aback at my appearance. He excused himself for wearing a dark suit.

'The ballet isn't what it used to be,' he said. 'It might be safer for you to change.'

I said it was too much bother and added meanly, 'But if you're afraid to take me, I'll be quite happy to stay home.'

'I went through quite a bit of trouble and expense to find this motor cab,' he said. Soviet soldiery has requisitioned almost all motor vehicles. 'Let us go.'

How right the Professor was! The Marinsky Theatre was unrecognizable. Fyodor stayed by the cab to guard it against seizure – the Professor, dear man, had hired it for the evening. An usher in a shabby grey jacket showed us to our seats in the orchestra pit. The floor was littered with cigarette butts and papers. The eagles above the imperial boxes had been torn down. In the boxes, their caps at the usual tipsy angle, lolled sailors and soldiers, chewing sunflower seeds and smoking cheap cigarettes.

You don't know the shock it gave me. I remembered the Marinsky in 1913 during the tercentenary celebrations: the blue velvet draperies and yellow escutcheons, the entire orchestra pit – court officials in scarlet coats and white elkskin breeches, Guardsmen in dress uniform – rising and turning as one man at the entrance of our sovereigns! I remembered – with such a sinking heart for I'm completely cut off from her – my stately promenade with Tanik between the rows of Chevaliers Gardes. I had thought then all that pomp and glitter superfluous and silly, yet, in retrospect, how stately and splendid it seems!

The ballet was as beautiful and disciplined as ever and I said to myself, From now on in Russia, beauty and elegance will exist only on the stage, in the world of make-believe, while everyday existence becomes increasingly shabby and drab. My own elegance seemed out of place. Disgust seized me, and at the end of the first act of *Swan Lake*, I asked the Professor to take me home.

In the foyer, our way was blocked by a dozen soldiers, armed with the rifles they now carry everywhere, like boys playing pirate. They started to throw insults at me and my 'dirty little imperial girl friend' – Tatyana Nikolayevna. The Professor protested furiously to no avail. Who do you think rescued me? Six Polish officers. The Polish units formed since the Revolution are among the few still maintaining discipline. My rescuers threw the citizen soldiers down the stairs and escorted me out to the cab with sabres drawn. I thanked them in the name of the Veslawski family, and they kissed my hand as only Poles know how. I could have hugged them all. On the way home, Professor Holveg lectured me again on the need for anonymity in the new Russia.

He was quite rightly annoyed at my recklessness and extravagance. Our *soirée manquée* had cost him a fortune! He's such a dear, absolutely devoted, yet I can't help taunting him. I *do* have enormous respect for his intelligence and achievements, and he *has* been an absolute godsend these dull, dismal days without you, my darling.

Papa and Grandmaman were surprised to see me home so early. I told them of my rescue by the Poles, and remarked on the difference between the Polish and Russian characters.

'Why is it Poles are at their best in adversity, whereas we Russians seem to go to pieces?' I asked.

I was afraid Grandmaman might take this badly – you know how patriotic she is – but she agreed. 'Yes, there is a flaw in the Russian character. It runs through every class of society. It is some strange weakness, a lack of fibre, of loyalty. The people are full of superstition, not faith, of submission, not respect for authority, and above all of greed. In times of weak leadership, it flourishes.'

Professor Holveg says that the Bolsheviks are cleverly exploiting the popular greed. He fears they may succeed. I have never known him to be wrong, but still it's too awful to contemplate. It is all so vast, so confused, so much beyond my grasp! Like Papa and our friends I drift along from day to day, thinking about my daily tasks and always, every minute, every second about you, my darling Stevie, my brother, my lord.

After the fiasco of our gala night out, I half expected Alexis to reject my next scheme, to return to Tsarskoye without official permission in his company and try to toss a message to my friends over the palace gate. That he agreed was proof positive – if any were still needed – of his bondage.

The curious were less numerous, but otherwise the scene was almost the same, the Tsar and his two youngest daughters gardening, Alexandra knitting in her wheelchair. Olga and Tatyana Nikolayevna were not in sight, nor was Aleksey. Again, I felt the heat in my face and the pounding of my heart. Marie and Anastasia had their backs turned as they hoed and raked. As I waited to catch their attention, the Tsar straightened to rest on his spade and saw me first. He frowned and quickly shook his head from side to side. 'Don't, Tata,' his gesture clearly said, 'don't try to communicate with us.' It was a command and I turned away, the ball of yarn wrapped around my message crumpled in my sweating palm. Why must all my attempts be abortive? My intrepid old self rebelled at my passivity. I, too, had become a victim.

'I hope this is the last of your escapades,' Alexis said severely as we boarded the suburban train back to Petrograd – I could hardly hold back my tears. He relented as he dropped me off at home. 'Well, at least they'll know you tried. And now you must cut your last tie with the former Grand Duchess your namesake. Not only your life, Tatyana Petrovna, but your father's, may depend on it.'

How could I cut all ties with my other self? Yet I knew that, for Father's sake, I must. My former sovereign himself commanded me to.

While our household awaited Father's summons before the tribunal, and his subsequent release, the rest of the nation drifted on the revolutionary current. The Provisional Government tried to steer an honourable course. The death penalty was re-established for desertion under fire. Alexander Kerensky, now minister of war as well as justice, travelled up and down the front to rally the troops, but his fiery oratory, which electrified Petrograd audiences, was lost on the peasant soldiers.

A Death Battalion and a Battalion of Knights of St George were formed to inspire the soldiers, a Women's Battalion to shame them. The men would neither be inspired nor shamed.

The offensive Kerensky mounted on the south-western front ended in retreat in July. Miliukov and the other Cadet ministers resigned, and the Bolsheviks took advantage of the cabinet crisis to attempt a coup. Once again machine-gun and rifle fire spattered on the *prospekts*. But the Cossack lancers who would not defend their emperor charged the insurgents and saved the day for the Provisional Government. To the Cossacks' dismay, however, the ringleaders of the insurrection – Messieurs Lenin, Trotsky, and company – were not taken to the fortress but allowed to escape thanks to the misguided magnanimity of Mr Kerensky.

In protest, Prince Lvov resigned with his entire cabinet. He took leave of Grandmaman a much thinner, older, baffled and disheartened man. That eminently sane and able administrator, who had performed marvels as president of the Zemstvo Union – a democratic body composed of men of goodwill – had been helpless against the prevailing hysteria.

Alexander Kerensky now became president of the Provisional Government. The new president, as vain as he was idealistic, took his role as Saviour of the Country seriously and strove valiantly to be all things to all people: to honour Russia's pledge to her allies, to put down uprisings but avoid bloodshed, to be a hero to peasants and workmen, and to protect the legitimate interests of industrialists and landowners as well.

Russia, meanwhile, was disintegrating. The Ukrainians, the Georgians, the Cossacks of the Kuban and the Don, the Siberians and the Mongol tribes, each demanded autonomy. The front had broken down, industry had broken down, administration had ceased to exist. The flood of paper roubles – popularly known as *kerenki* – fed inflation. The government so powerless against the progress of anarchy was all the more diligent in prosecuting its predecessors.

At the end of July, Father was called to testify before the Extraordinary Commission of Inquiry sitting in the Winter Palace. The former war minister, Sukhomlinov, had been sentenced to death, but Anya Vyrubova had been found too stupid to be capable of intrigue, and set free. The witnesses' all-too-frequent readiness to put the entire blame on the hapless ex-Emperor was profoundly distasteful to Father. His unwillingness to answer intimate or leading questions about his childhood playmate, friend and sovereign, Nicholas II, did not help his defence.

The Petrograd Soviet again demanded he be taken to the fortress. Out of regard for Grandmaman and thanks to the intercession of the French embassy prompted by Veslawski influence in France, Kerensky had him remanded into the custody of his guards and returned a prisoner in his own house.

The information, conveyed by relatives of members of the suite imprisoned at Tsarskoye, that the Tsar and his family were to be transferred to a distant location moved me to plead with Grandmaman once more. 'Won't you try to find out from Mr Kerensky why they are being sent away and where?' I begged. 'It's driving me mad not to know!'

'The former sovereigns are being sent away to Tobolsk for their safety,' Grandmaman reported grudgingly a few days later. 'The children have been given the choice to join their grandmother at Livadia. They have refused.'

They had refused! They had spurned the chance of safety – their last chance perhaps – in order to stay near their parents. I recalled my namesake's words. 'So long as we can remain together, nothing's *really* bad.' They could not have done otherwise. But Tobolsk! It was in the Urals, in western Siberia. They would be beyond reach, beyond rescue!

'Boris Andreyevich, you're so resourceful and clever.' I took the General aside. 'Can't you think of a plan to rescue Their Majesties? What about ambushing their train? Surely you know some officers who would undertake it. I'll speak to them.'

'Tatyana Petrovna,' he said, 'I know several dozen men who would unhesitatingly risk their lives to save your father. We shall have need of them. But not even he could ask them to risk all for Nicholas and Alexandra. They – forgive me for being so blunt – have dug their own grave.'

23

The change in government shook us out of our inertia. We hid gold coins and jewellery that had been left carelessly unlocked in the past. Nyanya sewed a quantity of each into the bodice and hem of her *sarafan*. I made a pouch with straps for my revolver to fit securely in my bosom, and a soft cartridge belt. I now wore both, day and night. Grandmaman transferred a large sum of money to Vera Kirilovna in the Crimea, where we hoped to make our escape. And as a first step towards the latter, we planned Boris Maysky's escape.

To raise money, we persuaded Father to part with his art collection. Under the pretext of repairing the damage of the sacking, his dealer came and took the cartload away. The dealer was a Jew from Odessa for whom Father had obtained permission to reside in the capital with his large family. He readily agreed to hold the money obtained from the quick, covert sale of the works abroad, and to disburse it to General Maysky or his emissaries on presentation of the identifying code. The General himself made up the code with imaginative relish.

Underneath his trenchant exterior, Boris Andreyevich Maysky had a supple and resourceful mind. An excellent mimic, he adopted disguises with the facility of an actor. Once out in the world, he would be hard to recapture. But how to get him out safely?

Providentially, Zinaida's son, Kolenka the adjutant, who had managed to steer clear of combat if not of gambling debts, happened to be in Petrograd, hard-pressed for funds. Wearing a red rosette and a red scarf for good measure, he called on his doting parent. For a sum, as well as for the sport of it, he agreed to trade uniforms with Boris Maysky.

Boris Maysky, hands in his pockets, feet turned out, swaggered out of the house armed with Kolenka's pistols, which were duly returned when he signed out. Kolenka, keeping his face and voice low, reported 'present' at evening roll call. Fyodor and Simyon then conveyed him in a woodbin down to the cellar, where I led him along the underground passage to the side door I had used in my own flight from home ten years ago. While I chatted with the guard posted at the door, Kolenka slipped away.

In the morning, before roll call, I went out to the guards and told them General Maysky had escaped during the night.

'We'll all be in trouble unless we can think of a scheme to cover it up.'

The corporal said, 'I have to report it. There's no other way.'

'They'll demote you, for sure,' a guard pointed out. 'And they'll have us cleaning latrines.'

'Say he was shot trying to escape,' I suggested.

'And his body?' countered the corporal. '"Where, then, is his body, comrades?" they'll ask.'

'He ran across the street and down to the river. You shot him on the embankment. He fell in and the Neva carried off his corpse.'

'It's a good yarn. But will they believe it?'

'How can they disprove it?'

The yarn was adopted, rehearsed, reported and apparently accepted.

Shortly thereafter, however, our lax and friendly guards were replaced by a less sentimental, more bolshevized lot. They restricted Father's outdoor exercise and took away his painting materials. They stationed a guard in his room round the clock. They watched him even when he went to the toilet, causing his fastidious nature acute distress. They forbade him to take his meals with us and only let us see him during evening roll call.

Neither were Grandmaman and I spared the new guards' vigilance. They searched our rooms at odd hours, so we took to sleeping fully dressed. They forbade us to leave the house. The servants were searched for messages each time they went in and out.

I managed to send Alexis a note through the courier from the French embassy who came under diplomatic immunity to bring me Stefan's letters and take my letters to him. Professor Holveg was denied admittance.

The family administrator was also met by fixed bayonets but stood his ground. If the guards wanted to eat at their prisoners' expense, they had better let him bring the necessary funds!

The administrator brought alarming news. In the face of ludicrous worker demands, factory managers were resigning one after another. Estate superintendents reported pillage and land seizure by the peasants.

'Give them the land,' said Grandmaman. 'Let them enjoy it while they still can, before it's taken away from them. Pierre, do you agree?'

Father, bodyguard at his back, had been allowed to attend. With his approval and mine, Grandmaman ordered all our lands distributed with the exception of Alubek, in the Crimea, and our suburban dacha. The factories were ordered closed. The machine works in Petrograd were still operating on war orders after a fashion. But, only the day before, the manager had escaped lynching by trading places with his chauffeur. He asked for severance pay so he could take his family to the United States. Grandmaman consented to this request, too.

Father now lifted his head and declared, 'All this is idle talk. Our property, like our liberty, is out of our hands. What matters now is for you and Tatyana to leave Russia without delay. Basil Zakharovich' – he addressed the administrator – 'have the necessary funds ready and deposited with the French embassy –'

But Grandmaman interrupted, 'Tatyana can go abroad any time. But I warn you, Pierre, I have not the slightest intention of leaving you alone in Petrograd, to be dispatched to the fortress the moment I'm gone. *N'en parlons plus*. Have another cup of tea, Basil Zakharovich, before you go.'

I said I was not leaving either. I had already let pass the opportunity to go to England with my Veslawski aunt, her Russian diplomat-husband, and their children. I was fortified in my renewed determination by the example of the Tsar's children. If Tanik and her sisters and brother would rather follow their parents into Siberian exile and oblivion than flee to their grandmother's side in the Crimea, I could do no less!

Grandmaman was shattered by the administrator's visit.

'Who'll run the hospitals and the schools? Who'll see that the crops are rotated and the soil is not overworked?' she asked. 'Who'll protect the peasants from speculators and crooks?'

I expressed surprise that she should still care.

'If your child behaves like a criminal, will you love it less? When my people behave like lunatics and criminals, will I not suffer, rather, and ask how am I at fault? Yes,' she reiterated, 'we are at fault – sovereigns, grand dukes, princes, priests. We did not set the people an example. We did not give it ideals. We did not prepare it for war. We are responsible for our country's breakdown.'

I was not sure. War, as I had known it, explained today's insanity better than anything.

'Our expiation will be hard,' sighed Grandmaman. 'I only pray that God will give me time . . .' 'To expiate my sins,' I understood.

With her drop in spirits, Grandmaman's health failed. Her blood pressure rose alarmingly. The doctor, whom I was allowed to summon, prescribed strict bed rest. Between Nyanya, Zinaida, and myself, we managed to make the patient comply.

Grandmaman took to her bed in the early part of September 1917. The Germans had just captured Riga, and Petrograd feared a German advance. At this critical juncture, the rumour that General Kornilov, the commander in chief, was marching on the capital to seize power and restore order, raised the hue and cry of counter-revolution. Again, the Bolsheviks profited from dissension in the government. For the first time, they acquired the majority in the Petrograd Soviet.

In the Silomirsky *osobnyak*, another new contingent of guards relieved those comrades who had allowed Father access to his sick mother.

The corporal elected by the new guards was a short, thin, sway-backed and supple young fellow who strutted about like a bantam rooster. He had a crest of black hair that he combed and pomaded painstakingly, and was as exacting of his men's discipline as of his own appearance. He subjected the guards to political lectures, forbade drunkenness and allowed no relaxation in the surveillance of prisoners. Father was again relegated to his apartment. Simyon was forbidden to wait on him and compelled to serve the guards instead. The family priest was warned off the premises on pain of death.

Grandmaman sorely missed him. On the last Sunday in September, she announced that she was going to the chapel to light a candle to our ancestor, St Vladimir. I could not dissuade her. As for Zinaida Mikhailovna, she was too cowed by this resurgence of autocratic spirit in her mistress to even try. We helped Grandmaman dress. The guards let us pass, only barring Fyodor's way. We made our silent descent through the great soiled house to the chapel off the entrance vestibule. At first the guard on duty would not allow us in. Then, with a nervous look up the grand staircase, he consented, for just a minute.

No sooner had Grandmaman lighted a candle to her patron saint than the bantam corporal, hands on his pistol holders, strutted in. The young guards on either side of him carried rifles with fixed bayonets. Their bland faces were uneasy.

'If you have come to worship, we bid you welcome,' Grandmaman said. 'But I must ask you to remove your caps and leave your weapons at the door.'

The corporal, followed more hesitantly by his men, continued to advance.

'We feed and house you and in return you persecute us and deny us even the comfort of a priest. Have the decency at least not to desecrate the house of God,' Grandmaman went on still calmly.

'How you talk, old woman! What's it to us, your house of God? It's a house, like any house. I'll bring my pistols or spit in it, if I like.' The corporal spat a mouthful of sunflower seeds on the face of St Vladimir.

Zinaida Mikhailovna crossed herself.

'*Allons-nous en*, Grandmaman – come away.' I laid a hand on her arm.

Erect against the gold-and-brown apostles ranged along the apse, Grandmaman did not move. 'Beware of what you do, not to us, but to your souls,' she said in a voice especially deep and ringing.

'You don't frighten me with your big voice, old woman, nor you, miss, with your big eyes,' said the little corporal. 'It's not you who give the orders around here, it's me. And I've decided you're not to come here any more, and all this' – tossing up his chin at the chapel – 'will be smashed. Go to it, men!'

'Stay!' cried Grandmaman as the soldiers hesitantly raised their rifle butts.

Their young faces reflected even greater unease and they lowered their rifles. But the little corporal, crying, 'What are you, afraid of an old woman? Here's the way,' emptied his pistols into the icon of St Vladimir on which he had spat.

The soldiers fell to.

Zinaida Mikhailovna hid her face in her hands. Grandmaman continued to stand erect, the candle steady in her extended hand. She did not heed my pleas to come away. Her face grew dusky, her stance more rigid. When rifle butts and boots attacked the central door of the iconostasis, the candle dropped from her hand. With a cry, Grandmaman fell heavily at my feet. Zinaida Mikhailovna threw herself down on her knees beside her mistress, screaming piercingly.

The corporal raised a pistol and would have struck her, but I leaped at him and held his arm with all my strength. 'Stop! You've already killed the Princess, my grandmother. Isn't that enough?'

I was more than a head taller than he. He must have felt embarrassed at his size, for he turned on his heel and strutted out, followed by the soldiers with lowered gaze.

I told the companion to hold her breath, which put an end to her screams, and to fetch Fyodor. Attracted by the noise of firing, the footman was already on his way, after overpowering the guards, who had tried to stop him. He lifted my large grandmother with ease and carried her up to her apartment, where he laid her still unconscious on her brass bed.

When Grandmaman came to, she was paralysed on the right side. Half of her face was fixed and frozen. Her left eye retained its great beauty and vivacity and expressed what her tongue could not. I moved my camp bed into her room. Her eye continually sought me out. On all others who came near, it frowned with effort or exasperation. But on me it rested, first with hope and entreaty, then peacefully, after I had answered its plea with the assurance that I was there beside her, that I was not going anywhere.

Three weeks went by without change.

One evening in the second half of October, Grandmaman suddenly improved. Her face regained its mobility and she was able to speak intelligibly, if slowly and with effort.

'I'm sorry I was angry about your wish to study medicine,' she said. 'You have a gift ... Alexandra was right, it is God's gift. In the future, to be a princess will no longer mean anything. To be a physician will be very fine.'

I thought being a Princess Veslawska might still mean something. 'I don't think I can marry Stefan and practise medicine.' I heard myself say words that no longer sounded real. None of my dreams was real any longer.

Grandmaman frowned. 'The Poles will profit by our country's misfortunes. They hate us, and always will. It's not right for you to marry a Pole ...'

'Why should the Poles hate us, Grandmaman, if we let them be free? It's just prejudice and narrow nationalism, and unchristian besides.'

'You're right... I'm a bad Christian... proud... narrow-minded ... full of prejudice. I've lived ... by the code of my world ... not God's. Now this world ... has ended. It is too late ... for me to change ... '

'It's not too late, Grandmaman. Your sins will be forgiven.' I spoke softly, reassuringly, until her face again expressed hopefulness and peace.

That same night, Grandmaman had another stroke. Although she groaned deeply from time to time in her comatose state, she felt no pain. The doctor doubted she would rally. I asked the guards to let me send for a priest.

After the desecration of the chapel, they had held an election and demoted the bantam corporal. He had left in a fury threatening to report them all as counter-revolutionaries to the Petrograd Soviet. For fear of being accused of counter-revolutionary heresy, the newly elected corporal outdid his predecessor in vigilance. But he granted my request for a priest. He also allowed Father to see his dying mother.

Zinaida Mikhailovna, Nyanya, Simyon and the half-dozen servants remaining all pressed into Grandmaman's room. The guards in the anteroom ceased their usual noise.

When the last sacraments had been administered, Grandmaman opened her eyes and rested them on Father standing by her head, a guard at his back.

'Petya, forgive me,' she said clearly in Russian.

'Forgive? Why? I thank and honour you.' And bending the knee, he laid his forehead on her hand.

'Petya, listen to me. When your time comes to follow me, soon perhaps, don't be afraid. I know now, all terrors, all agonies come to an end. The Lord is merciful.'

These were her last words. She sank back into a coma, but her face retained its beatific expression, which death sealed a few hours later.

Grandmaman's body was laid out in the foyer – the chapel having been smashed – and the Silomirsky *osobnyak* opened to the public by special government order. Mourners from all ranks of society filed past her bier all day long. The highest came to pay tribute to the dying aristocracy Anna Vladimirovna had represented and led in its greatness and narrowness, piety and pride. The lowliest came to pay tribute to one who, they now remembered, had truly been their friend.

Father in field uniform, his face newly lined and sallow in its silver frame, stood at attention beside the coffin between two soldiers, who were relieved every hour like a guard of honour, the revolutionary soldier being disinclined to stay long on his feet.

Wearing black crêpe with a veil to the floor, I accepted condolences from government officials, the diplomatic corps, the few members of the dynasty still in the capital, and those friends and acquaintances remaining in Petrograd. Among the latter, Alexis Holveg held my hand longest, his black eyes resting on me most intently. To him as to everyone, Grandmaman's features set in stern beatitude seemed to say, 'All terrors, all agonies come to an end. The Lord is merciful.'

In my brief low-voiced exchanges with the Romanovs present at the ceremony, I learned that, according to smuggled missives, my friend and her family led a simple healthy life in the compound of the governor's residence at Tobolsk. The Tsar had organized classes. Aleksey was well and growing tall. The children participated in outdoor projects with their father. They were isolated but well treated. I took hope.

Grandmaman was buried in the family crypt in the Church of the Annunciation in the Convent of St Alexander Nevsky on 23 October by the old Russian calendar. The wind blew bitter cold and snow fell thickly, but the Neva had not yet frozen.

With Nyanya and Fyodor, I left the house for the first time in almost three months to attend the funeral. Father was not allowed to go. The mourners were much fewer, but Alexis Holveg was there again. This time he pressed into my hand a message for Father from Boris Maysky. This he asked me to send home with Fyodor.

'Tatyana Petrovna, don't go back to your house! This may be your last opportunity to escape. Your father himself would want it. Flee to the Crimea while you can,' he pleaded.

'Thank you for your concern, Alexis, and for the message,' I said. 'But I must deliver it in person.'

Directly after the funeral, Zinaida Mikhailovna, overcome with grief, left for Alubek with Kolenka.

Having spent the sum earned by helping Boris Maysky escape, he had come to his mother again for money. Also, wily opportunist that he was, he sensed Mr Kerensky's days in office were numbered and he was ready to try his fortune in more congenial territory.

As Grandmaman's heiress, I had the administrator give Zinaida enough money for the trip in addition to the legacy left her by her late mistress. I warned her, quite in vain, not to let her son hold it for her. I also gave her a letter to my namesake with a note to Marie Fyodorovna, begging Her Imperial Majesty, if she could do so without danger, to transmit it to the prisoners at Tobolsk.

The administrator then drove me back with Nyanya and Fyodor to my house, now more than ever dismally empty, dirty, and mournful. Father's guards had not expected me back. So astonished were they to see me, in my mourning veils, that they allowed me free access to Father's apartment.

I stayed up with Father until two o'clock in the morning, his night guard remaining mercifully out of sight behind the open doors. I showed him Boris Maysky's note, which promised a prompt rescue. I had a long cry against his broad shoulder and he stroked my hair with his beautiful big hand, murmuring the childhood words of comfort and endearment, and making me blow my nose into his monogrammed batiste handkerchief. I poured out my longing for that other broad shoulder of my cousin and beloved. Father, in turn, confessed his foolish fears, abetted by Grandmaman, of my becoming a mother, and his even more shameful jealousy. How could he have allowed me to remain in Russia for his sake?

'I am so weak,' he said, 'so weak!'

But Boris Maysky could be depended upon, and we would soon be on our way to France.

I wanted to believe him. For all my grief at Grandmaman's death, I was happy in our renewed closeness. And when I said, as I kissed Father goodnight, that I was glad I had stayed by him, truly I was.

24

While Petrograd paid my grandmother its last tribute, in a room in my former school, the Smolny Institute, the emergency Military Revolutionary Committee under the chairmanship of Vladimir Lenin made ready to level the crumbling society that Mr Kerensky had so frantically and ineffectually striven to shore up. Kerensky's measures to counter a coup were inadequate and belated. The Bolsheviks controlled the garrison. The Cossacks were wavering. Only the military cadets and women soldiers were willing to fight for the Provisional Government.

On 24 October, sitting with Father by the window, we saw the Bolshevik cruiser *Aurora* head upstream to anchor in front of the Winter Palace. Again we stayed up late, wrapped in our sable-lined cloaks against the cold of the unheated room. While we slept, Red soldiers seized all rail stations, bridges, power plants, telegraph and telephone offices, and when we awakened on the morning of 25 October 1917, the Bolsheviks were in virtual control of Petrograd.

Kronstadt sailors surrounded the Marie Palace and dissolved the pre-parliament in session there. Mr Kerensky raced out of town in an American automobile in search of reliable troops. The ministers took refuge in the Winter Palace, defended by young cadets and a detachment of the Women's Battalion.

At five o'clock in the afternoon, the Bolsheviks attacked. At nightfall, sitting by the window once again, Father and I saw the flashes of the *Aurora*'s guns. By the time we went to bed at three a.m., the boy soldiers and women soldiers had been overcome. The victorious Bolsheviks had sacked the Winter Palace, dragged off the ministers to the fortress, and lynched the Deputy War Minister, Prince Tumanov, in Kerensky's stead. Tumanov's dismembered body was thrown into the Neva, not far from the spot where, less than a year ago, Rasputin's corpse had been found.

Even while these glorious deeds were in progress, Vladimir Lenin proclaimed the dawn of world revolution to the opening session of the second All-Russian Congress of Soviets. Private property and ownership of land were abolished. The dictatorship of the proletariat had arrived!

At daybreak, Bolshevik troops paraded through the great square of the Winter Palace where the tsars had reviewed the regiments of the Guard and where, seven months earlier, these same regiments had sworn allegiance to the republican revolution now come to its end, as finally and irrevocably as the autocratic empire it had overthrown.

The sound of boots and shouts in the hall awakened me with a start on the morning of 26 October. Pulling on a black dress over the underwear and petticoat in which I now slept, I ran into Father's apartment. Four unfamiliar soldiers in sheepskin bonnets were ransacking his rooms. Fortunately, I had concealed his memoirs in Grandmaman's secret wall safe.

In Father's dressing room I found the bantam corporal I knew only too well. He wore a high fur cap to enhance his inadequate stature and looked even more truculent. Simyon, his round face very red, helped Father into his tunic with shaking hands.

As Father buttoned himself with composure, the little corporal gestured with his pistols. 'Hurry up! There's no need to primp where you're going.'

'Where are you taking my father?' I demanded.

'Where he should have been long ago,' he answered.

Father made me a sign in the looking glass to keep quiet. Simyon handed him his white fur *papakha*, but the little corporal objected. Instead, Father put on a flat cap with a visor. Simyon helped him into his overcoat.

Father then slipped off the last of his ancestral rings – the others had gone into the safe with his memoirs – and handed it to Simyon. 'Here's in memory of me. Thank you, thank you for everything, Simyon. *Paka* – farewell.'

The orderly dropped on one knee, kissing Father's hand and begging to be taken along.

'He'll have no need of a valet where he's going,' the corporal observed. 'Foo, what a dog.'

'Dog yourself!' Simyon would have sprung on the corporal, who lifted his pistols.

I feared he would empty them into Simyon's stomach as casually as into the icon of St Vladimir, but Father pulled Simyon aside in time. 'Be still!' he ordered.

With his pistols, the corporal motioned Father to move on. In the anteroom, the servants pressed behind the soldiers to bid Father farewell.

The soldiers shoved them aside, only to be shoved aside in turn by a little old woman in a blue headdress and quilted jacket.

'My nursling, my Petya, my Prince' – she threw herself at Father – 'that was put to my breast when my own baby died . . . is that what I nursed you for? Is that why I raised you?' Nyanya turned on the Reds. 'Foo, good-for-nothing swine, God will punish you if the people don't.'

'Nyanichka, be calm. Thank you for everything, look after Tatyana. Don't grieve.' Father embraced his old nurse.

Again, the servants tried to break through, but were shoved out of the door. Father asked to say goodbye to me alone.

'No. You've kept us waiting long enough,' answered the corporal.

Father took me by the shoulders and said in English, 'Everything we have left is in your name; you can draw what you need at the bank. Basil Zakharovich will help you. As soon as the streets are quiet, go to the French embassy. Uncle Stan has your passage arranged. Don't delay! The most that you can do for me now is to get away safely yourself. Promise you will!'

'I'll be safe, Papa, don't worry.' I steeled myself to appear calm.

'Enough of that foreign chatter. Let's go!' the corporal urged.

'Well, *Dochenka*,' Father said in Russian, 'it's time. Be strong.' Meaning, be brave, have hope and remember nothing is so bad as it seems. Then he drew me to his chest.

As I pressed myself to Father, I felt him strong and broad as an oak that might be felled, but never bent. I had grown up under its protective shelter. Who would protect me now?

'Papa, hold me, hold me hard.' I murmured the childhood words.

Father held me hard, then he kissed the top of my head and released me. 'The Lord keep you.' He blessed me.

'The Lord be with you,' I answered solemnly. There was no one else. And what trials did He reserve for Father?

'Enough or we'll take the girl too,' the corporal said.

Father drew away hastily. The soldiers surrounded him and he was gone.

Left alone, I went to the window and leaned my forehead against the cold pane. Two army lorries turned out of our *podiezd* into the quay and headed towards the fortress, leaving tyre tracks in the lightly falling snow. Traffic was slight. No processions passed with banners to celebrate the Bolshevik victory, no seamen sat by their boats discussing the dawn of world revolution. Only a few cars sped by, a soldier with rifle at the ready lying on each mudguard. Long floes of thin ice floated upriver like ghostly hulls. The sky was low and grey. I gazed at this bleak scene, frozen in helpless despair. I could not cry. I could not even pray.

The sound of weeping and soft murmuring roused me. The servants had approached, waiting for orders and guidance from their new mistress.

I roused myself, 'Good friends, thank you for staying by us this long. I don't know what will happen next, but in the meantime we'll continue as before. The streets may not be safe for several days. Do we have enough provisions?'

Agafia the cook said we had.

'Are the Red soldiers gone?'

'All of them, Your Highness, God be praised.'

'Well, at least we won't have to worry about feeding them any more.' I made a pretence of cheerfulness.

They smiled broadly, in the popular confidence that everything would work out, and, having received my instructions, they left.

After my breakfast had been served, a street urchin in sheepskin jacket and cap was shown into Grandmaman's former sitting room with an important message he would only deliver to me in private.

'I am to tell you . . . patience!' he said importantly when we were alone.

'Patience, I see. Who gave you the message?'

He described a workman with a nose like this and eyebrows like that – a vivid portrait of Boris Andreyevich Maysky.

'Where is that workman now?'

'And how would I know? He caught me on the Galernaya, gave me this' – the boy showed a gold rouble – 'and up and vanished. Like a bird. And he looks like a bird too.'

That was General Maysky all right. I gave the boy a handful of *tenuchki*, the soft caramels of which Zinaida Mikhailovna had been so fond.

'You can have more if you'll take a message for me and bring me the answer,' I said, and wrote in German on the back of a caramel wrapping, 'Papa arrested, find out where.'

I wrapped a caramel in it and told the boy to take it to Professor Holveg's flat on Vassily Island right away. 'Can you remember the address?'

'*Can* I!'

From the window I saw him skip past a picket of Red Guards on the Nicholas Bridge.

I stayed home for the next three days waiting in vain for his message. The quay was ominously quiet. Unlike Moscow, where fighting raged for a week, and other provincial capitals, once-turbulent Petrograd had been silenced.

On the night of 29 October I heard firing again. This was the insurrection of the cadets in the Paul, Vladimir and Engineering colleges, in expectation of Kerensky's reinforcements from Gachina. The reinforcements did not materialize and the rising was savagely put down. The leaders were thrown from the college roofs and their heads raised on bayonets; the remainder were arrested. A few managed to escape, and early the next morning, three wounded cadets made their way to the Silomirsky *osobnyak*. With Simyon's help, I dressed their wounds. Nyanya got rid of the soldiers hunting the escapees.

We were not bothered again, and a week after the Bolshevik coup, I felt it safe to send the cook to market.

Agafia heard me out respectfully, but did not move.

'Well, what is it, Agafia?' I asked.

'Your Serene Highness, my little dove, forgive me, but it's not as in the old time, when the name of our house was enough and they settled the accounts in the office by the month. Without money, Princess my sweet, not one rotten cabbage leaf you'll buy, not one bag of gritty buckwheat.'

I was confronted for the first time in my life with that mysterious commodity – money.

'How much do you think you'll need?' I tried to look wise.

'Lord God of mine, everything is so dear now, so dear!'

After some more doleful comparisons between the old time and the new, the cook mentioned a meaningless amount that I did not have in any case. I gave her what I did have, told her to manage, and said confidently I would go to the bank.

Leaving my wounded cadets in Simyon's care – like me, he was overjoyed to have someone to look after – I started out with Fyodor.

The bank was on the Quai Anglais itself. I had not gone halfway, however, when I was challenged by a picket of Red Guards, in a variety of civilian attire but uniformly armed with automatic rifles, who stood warming themselves at a street-corner bonfire.

I had no pass and was promptly hustled with Fyodor into a motorcar requisitioned on the spot together with its chauffeur. With an armed Red Guard standing on each runningboard we tore down the quays around the bend of the river to the Smolny Institute, along the route I had taken as a schoolgirl.

Between the broad columns of the neo-Grecian entrance, machine-guns and cannon now pointed. The familiar corridors were no longer white and immaculately polished, but muddy and littered with leaflets, cigarette butts, soldiers' gear and stacked rifles.

Fyodor and I were taken into a former classroom full of prisoners seized, like me, at street corners. There I found several aristocratic acquaintances relating their capture to one another with amusing detail in English or French, and was greeted by them affectionately. When I explained I had been on the way to the bank, throats were delicately cleared. Princess Palitsin took me by the hands and, drawing me on to a bench gently explained to me the facts of life under the Bolshevik regime.

'Why don't you come and stay with us, my dear,' she concluded. 'Sergey' – her husband, the former most-secret councillor of state – 'has had a brilliant idea. He's going to send our majordomo on behalf of our servants' soviet to obtain raises for them. In that way we'll all manage until the Constituent Assembly meets. These Bolsheviks are mere adventurers. They can't possibly last.'

Everyone shared these hopeful sentiments.

I was too young and earnest to adopt the worldly tone considered good form in my set, no matter how bad the circumstances. I thanked the Princess for her offer of hospitality but said I must stay home, at least until I found out where my father was imprisoned. I did not think it wise to mention the cadets. The news of Father's arrest was taken seriously enough – a few pessimists wondered if it was the beginning of a Red terror – and I received expressions of sympathy on all sides.

Princess Palitsin rested lovely light blue eyes on me. 'Remember, my dear, you're not alone in this,' she said. 'We're all hangman's bait – *gibier de potence*. You will call on us if you need anything, won't you?'

Although there was little comfort in the Princess's gallows humour, I did feel less alone and helpless for her kind offer.

In an hour, Fyodor and I were called into another classroom where a Bolshevik official and a mannish-looking woman stenographer sat behind a table.

'We could use a fine fellow like you in the Red Guard,' the official said to Fyodor.

'He's deaf and dumb, he'll do you little good,' I quickly interposed.

'What's your name?' the official shouted.

Fyodor's face remained blank. The official fired a bullet past his ear. Fyodor did not blink. A pass was made out for him.

I was interrogated next. Had I heard from ex-General Maysky?

He had been shot trying to escape, so far as I knew, said I.

Had I received any communication from the ex-Grand Duchess Tatyana?

I had not.

What was my relationship with Professor Alexis Holveg?

He was a former tutor and an old friend.

When had I last seen and heard from him?

Not since my grandmother's funeral.

Did I know that the possession of weapons was now illegal and had I any to declare?

I was a nurse. I did not possess weapons, I lied boldly.

At last I was fingerprinted, issued a temporary pass to be renewed weekly, and told I could go.

Once outside, I broke into a cold sweat. What if I had been searched and my revolver found? And what of Alexis? Had I endangered him by our association? Must I give it up? He and Boris Maysky were my only hope for saving Father. Alexis was more than that. He was the last link with my old self, the self that thought, strove, quested – that was so much more than hangman's bait. I needed him as never before.

As I stood in the hall where I had walked with my classmates in pairs behind our class matron, protected, not persecuted, by a benevolent authority, a wild idea came to me. I went up the muddy stairs to the first storey, where the President of the Council of People's Commissars and new head of the Soviet state had his offices. I walked down the corridor more hesitantly and, seeing an open door, I stepped into a large room where a dozen women secretaries were typing away and carrying messages in a blue cloud of cigarette smoke.

'What do you want? How did you get here?' asked a mannish matron who seemed to be in charge.

'I would like to speak to ... Mr Lenin,' I brought out.

The head secretary looked at me as the grand mistress of the imperial court might have looked at some peasant girl asking to see the Tsar. 'Comrade Lenin is busy. What is your business with him?'

'I have ... no business. I only wanted to ask to be allowed to see Father. He was arrested a week ago. I have no other family ...' I am entirely alone and lost, my face said.

'If your father was arrested, it is a matter for the People's Commissar for Justice,' the secretary said less raspingly. She took notepad and pencil in hand. 'I will refer you to him. What is your name?'

'Tatyana ... Silomirskaya.'

The head secretary slowly put down the pad. Then she turned to the other secretaries, who had all ceased typing, and said, 'Comrades, my little doves, look who has deigned to come and call on Comrade Lenin ... the Serene Princess Tatyana Silomirskaya *in* person. What an honour!'

All present burst into laughter.

I went quickly out of the room and building, turning up my mink collar to avoid recognition. I was glad of the icy wind on my flaming cheeks and the needles of fine snow stinging my tear-filled eyes. Preceded by Fyodor, who cut the wind for me with his broad back, I walked the long distance home along the river, which was beginning to freeze, showing my pass to every picket of Red Guards stamping their feet about bonfires. It was afternoon and already dark. Bursts of firing and drunken singing echoed down the deserted *prospekts*.

As I came alongside the majestic façade of my house, I saw a workman pasting notices on the wall. The notices stated that by order of the Soviet People's Commissar for Internal Affairs the building was now the property of the Soviet state. I understood I no longer had a house.

'Where am I to live?' I said to the workman, who stared at me with open curiosity.

'And what's it to me where you live?' he answered sensibly. Then, with a wink, as he picked up his bucket, 'And anyway, who's to know?'

I let myself into the vast entrance vestibule with my key. It was cold and silent as the tomb. In my apartment, I found a note and a purse filled with gold roubles that had been delivered on the part of Basil Zakharovich, the family administrator. The note said that my bank funds had been frozen by the Soviet government and advised me to seek asylum at the French embassy. Basil Zakharovich himself was leaving the country with his family and could do nothing more for me.

During my absence there had also come a Bolshevik official with the order to vacate the premises of the Soviet state, Agafia had been unable to obtain credit at the market, the janitor had been unable to order coal, the telephones could not be connected, running water and electricity were cut.

I gathered the servants about me and told them I could no longer afford their services. 'I cannot even feed or house you,' I said, as they denied wanting pay. 'You'd best return to your native villages. Perhaps life will be easier for you there.'

I distributed gold roubles among them, and they covered my hands with kisses and tears. Only Nyanya, Fyodor and Simyon were to remain.

The following morning, when the servants had set off with their bundles on their backs, I moved into the stable, taking over the quarters of the former head groom. The wounded cadets, together with a supply of linen, instruments and medicines from the former hospital stores, as well as jewellery, gold and Father's manuscript – all that was most precious – were also transferred. Rugs, blankets and fur-lined cloaks were brought in preparation for the cold, and a small stove lit. In the attic room that I was to share with Nyanya, an icon corner was dedicated and a wick lit in a red *lampada* before my favourite medieval icon of the Saviour on the Cross. Photographs of my family, of Stefan, and the Tsar's children were placed on the furniture of painted pine. *A Sportsman's Sketches* and a dozen favourite books in several languages were arranged on a shelf. I was ready to start life under the new regime.

25

Once settled in my stable quarters, my first concern was to find Father. At the French embassy, where I brought my letters to Stefan, I received a money cable from the Veslawskis and was advised to make it last. The embassy's funds were being curtailed and the staff was preparing to leave in expectation of the separate peace the new government was pledged to sign.

The embassy's first secretary was very courteous, very kind. But he would not undertake to discover Father's whereabouts, much less intercede on his behalf. As for the family of the former Tsar, the new regime had 'other cats to whip – *d'autres chats à fouetter*,' said *Monsieur le secrétaire*. No, he did not expect the conditions of their captivity to worsen for the present. As for the future, who could say? He concluded with a Gallic shrug.

Since my interrogation at Smolny, I was afraid to send another message to Professor Holveg. To my surprise as well as joy, I found a note from him on my return from the French embassy, inviting me to come and see him in his office at the university to discuss my study plans.

At the appointed time, I took my manual of pharmacology and some notepaper along. His secretary, a matron of the old school in a pince-nez, showed me to his office with all the deference due the head of the chemistry department and one of Europe's greatest scientists.

'Ah, Tatyana Petrovna, very glad to see you.' Alexis greeted me like a student and shook my hand. Then, having shut the door, he kissed and held my hand as he looked at me hungrily, and with sudden timidity. 'I have been quite frantic about you,' he confessed in French. 'But you are safe and well?'

'Yes. Have you news of Father?'

'He is in the Trubetskoy bastion, in the Petropavlovsk Fortress.'

'The Trubetskoy bastion!' The very name made me quake. 'Is he ... is he being mistreated?'

'No. He is only held incommunicado. But I think I can arrange for you to visit him. Sit down, Tatyana Petrovna, please.' He helped me into the chair in front of his desk. 'Your hands are so cold! Try to be calm. Shall I send for some tea?'

'Thank you, no. Only tell me everything quickly. How is it you're not afraid to receive me openly? I was beginning to feel a pariah.'

'The Soviet government' – the Professor sat down behind his desk – 'is far more awake to the importance of science in the modern age than its imperial predecessor. It is willing to overlook my former "tsarist" connections. Moreover, the new commissar for education, Lunacharsky, a man of culture, is a friend of mine. I have spoken to him about you at some length, and he is sympathetic. He will do his best to ease the Prince's imprisonment, as well as obtain permission for you to visit him. Is there any special request you would like me to make on your father's behalf?'

'If he could paint . . . no, that would be impractical. Father was writing his memoirs. He felt an urgent need to finish them. If only he could be allowed to!'

'I will mention it. Now that's settled, tell me about yourself.'

I told Alexis all that had befallen me since Grandmaman's funeral, omitting, however, my concealment of the wounded cadets. He was risking enough for me as it was! While I talked, I observed my surroundings: the desk with tidy piles of files and without personal mementos; the bust of Mendeleyev, the great chemist; the lithographs of Bach and Beethoven on the wall; a globe of the Copernican universe; books from floor to ceiling – the office of a universal scholar and music lover, a man of taste and sensibility. What had he in common with a Bedlov, a Stalin, a Lenin?

'Alexis,' I said when I was done with my story, 'do you really mean to cooperate with the new regime?'

'It will depend. If it honours the Constituent Assembly after it convenes, if it respects civil liberties, I think it has great possibilities for science – possibilities unequalled elsewhere, except, perhaps, in North America.'

'But isn't communism fundamentally alien to you?'

'How shall I say? All governments, all societies are alien to me, Tatyana Petrovna, as, I believe, they are to you . . .'

'Yes.' I looked at Alexis gratefully. He knew me. He made me

feel I did more than merely exist. 'Only some are more alien than others. I can't see you adapting to Soviet society any more than I can see myself.'

'Perhaps not. But in the meantime, I will pretend I can, so that I can help you. And, Tatyana Petrovna, if you can take the advice of your old professor, it would be useful for you to pretend that you can adapt too.'

'I?' I sat upright. 'What are you suggesting?'

'Tatyana Petrovna, this isn't the time to be proud. The Prince your father can't help it, and it may well be his undoing. But you have a life ahead, a vocation, a career. If the Soviets believe that you can be converted, if they believe *I* can help convert you, we will be so much freer to meet.' And, as I continued to sit stiff and disbelieving, 'It does not commit or compromise you in any way. In a totalitarian state, one must learn not only to be anonymous but to dissimulate. I am learning it for your sake. I believe you capable of learning too.' He shot me one of his searing, all-seeing looks.

Yes, I was capable of dissimulation! I could hide my cadets from him, I could hide my true feelings for Stefan. Gone was my youthful candour, my adherence to absolutes of right and wrong. I too had become a smiling liar.

'I am,' I said.

His answering smile, startlingly frank and agreeable, made him look young, even handsome.

'Alexis' – I was emboldened to bring up the forbidden subject – 'I'm terribly worried about Tatyana Nikolayevna and the others. What are the Bolsheviks going to do to them?'

'The Bolsheviks are busy consolidating their power. The Romanovs are their least concern at the moment,' he answered, rather like the First Secretary of the French embassy. 'The Romanovs are of little concern to anyone, Tatyana Petrovna, except you. They are past history.' He rose and saw me to the door. 'I don't think it prudent to prolong our interview.'

'Alexis, just one more favour, a small one. You used to be friendly with Dr Botkin, the former court physician. He's with the sovereigns ... with the prisoners at Tobolsk. He has a daughter who used to live in Petrograd. Perhaps she has some contact with him. I'm afraid to look her up.'

He answered by asking, 'Is there anything I can do for *you personally* before you go? You do have enough money to live on?'

I tried to look wise about that still mysterious necessity. 'Oh yes! What I miss most is my piano. I daren't go into the main house, and it'd be too cold to play in any case. It's such a pity, that fine Bechstein grand going to waste. Could you use it, Alexis?'

'I have my own Steinway. But the university might. That gives me an idea.' He flashed me a conspiratorial glance – how happy he was to have become indispensable – and opened the door wide. 'I expect a report from you at the same time next week,' he said in Russian.

'I'll do my best to have it ready, Professor,' said I, and passed through the secretary's office and out of the corridor into the courtyard without attracting a glance.

Within a week, I received a notification to appear at Petropavlovsk Fortress. I took along underwear, food and writing materials. In the visiting room facing an inner court in the infamous Trubetskoy bastion, I was told to sit down at one end of a long table.

Father appeared between two guards, and sat down at the other end. In field uniform without his medals, he looked a little more sallow and careworn, but not too greatly altered. Only his eyes gazed into some unfathomable distance that separated us even more than the length of the table.

'Why haven't you left Petrograd?' he said severely in English.

'I can't leave you.' It was beyond my will.

'You must. I command you!'

'Speak Russian, prisoner,' ordered a guard.

'I brought you writing materials,' I said in Russian, 'for your memoirs. Do you have light?'

Father nodded. He even smiled his gay little smile. He had not died inwardly as I had feared. I was his connection with his vibrant old self, even as Alexis was mine.

In five minutes, the visit was over. Yet, slight and unsatisfactory as this contact was, it gave my life purpose and meaning during the next four months.

I never overcame my trepidation at the prospect of those torturous moments. While Nyanya laundered the underwear I brought home, I tried to press it. I nearly cried when I burned a hole in an undershirt – my pent-up feelings would give way over such trifles – and Simyon took over the chore.

At the end of the first month, I had the joy of receiving a chapter of Father's memoirs, written now in Russian instead of English. I began copying it on the typewriter I had managed to salvage before the Soviets came and carried away everything useful. The hours spent learning to type shortened the day. Thanks to Alexis, I was also able to practise on my own piano in a music room at the university.

Before long, however, the money sent by the Veslawskis was inadequate to feed my household and the wounded and to bring food parcels to Father. No one would hire the ex-Princess Silomirskaya. So I took to going to the ragpickers' market with linens and silverware.

I stood behind a rented table in the driving snow, among erect ladies in mink bonnets and caps. When I sold my wares to wives of Bolshevik commissars, I could buy herring or potatoes on the black market to supplement the rations that my third, or lowest-category, food card, entitled me to as a member of the proscribed class.

Standing in the cold, I developed chilblains on my hands and feet. I could barely write my weekly letter to Stefan, to whom I had less and less to say. (I had given up writing to my namesake long ago.) I could no longer type or play the piano.

At this point Alexis demanded a full accounting. I confessed the needs of my cadets.

'Tatyana Petrovna, you are reckless, headstrong, thoughtless and irresponsible!' he burst out. 'There is a third prerequisite for survival in a totalitarian state: one does not take unnecessary risks,' he added. I continued to look at him meekly while he paced with quick, nervous steps. Then, 'You must get rid of the cadets.' He came to a stop before me. 'There are Jews who sell false papers, not far from the ragpickers' market. It will be expensive.'

'I can sell jewellery.'

'Do it then. And I must insist you let me provide the food parcels for your father from now on.'

That I could not refuse. Nor could I turn down his offer to get Father's memoirs typed.

In exchange for papers for my cadets, I sold the emerald necklace I had worn on my disastrous night out to the ballet. By Christmas they were well enough to head south to the Don, where General Alexeiev, joined by other army commanders, was forming the Volunteer Army. Composed of Cossacks and fugitive officers, it was to become the nucleus of the future White Army. Alexis was greatly relieved to know my cadets were gone.

Happily for me, a young Polish officer now came to the back door one night, with a broken arm that I set with Simyon's help. The Polish units formed after the fall of the Tsar had resisted bolshevization, and their members had gone into hiding. The officer kissed my hand on bended knee when he left. Soon another came sent by the first, and so on in steady succession.

I saw Stefan and Casimir in all these young Poles and defied my protector's admonitions. After I had overcome my surprise at his show of authority, I held my ground in the knowledge that I had Alexis in my power.

The hayloft and grain bins in which I myself had hidden as a child made excellent places of concealment during the periodic searches of my stable quarters. Otherwise the Bolsheviks seemed satisfied for the time being to have the former Princess Silomirskaya reduced to living in the stable of her *osobnyak*.

During this relatively benign interim, while the Bolsheviks consolidated their power in the face of Socialist opposition and dissension within their own ranks, Father's status remained unchanged. Then, after the first of the year 1918, when I took the last instalment of the memoirs to Alexis, he examined it closely and said, 'The erasures are more careful and consistent this time. I believe there may be a message concealed underneath.'

As Alexis erased the lines thickly crossed out in pencil, the message in Polish, written in ink in Russian characters, emerged over many pages.

Tanyussia, dearest daughter,

These may be the last papers you will receive from me. I fear I will not be here much longer, though where I am to be moved, I have no idea. It has been intimated that I will not be as comfortable. I have not been, according to Comrade Bedlov, 'realistic' – i.e., I have refused to cooperate by incriminating my former sovereign in the ways that he asks. They have tried to persuade me nicely. They have shown me films of pogroms, famines, hard-labour camps and other such lamentable aspects of the old order. They have shown me the evidence against Sukhomlinov and reminded me again and again – as if it were necessary – of our hideous losses because of the munitions shortage. They have tried to make me feel guilty and ashamed – as if I were not already – of the black side of tsarist Russia. They have offered me redemption through confession! They have held out the promise of rehabilitation and release.

Worse yet, they have told me that you, my darling daughter, are making progress in your conversion to their creed! They put great hopes in you as a contributor to their future society! Needless to say, I do not believe a word of it, any more than you'll believe any lies they may tell you about me. I keep my sanity through prayer, the memory of my mother, and the thought of you, my brave Tatyana. You have done nobly by me. You have done enough. When peace is finally signed – and what a dishonourable peace for Russia it is – the Allied embassies will close. You must leave *now*, before it is too late. I will soon be taken out of your reach in any event. When my captors finally realize they can make no use of me, they will execute me. I am prepared for it. I have lived my life. It is yours, yours alone that matters now. I thank and bless you.

Papa

I made the sign of the cross. 'God have mercy!' I murmured in Russian mechanically. For there was no mercy to be hoped for, not in this life! Cold and nausea, the symptoms of that hitherto unknown disease – fear – assailed me.

'Tatyana Petrovna, are you all right?' Alexis, who had been leaning over my shoulder, laid a hand on it lightly.

I glanced up at him wet-eyed. 'What will they do to Father next?'

'Shoot him, Tatyana Petrovna, as he says. It is the most merciful eventuality. I, in the Prince's place, would be a terrified wreck. But he will face it calmly, I'm sure. You must obey him and leave.'

'But the Constituent Assembly convenes this month! You said yourself, Alexis, the Bolsheviks may be overthrown!'

'I said there was a slim chance. I would not stake your life on that chance. Your life, Tatyana Petrovna, is as precious to me as to your father.'

His right hand, which rested on the desk, closed over mine. It was as soft as it was white, the hand of an intellectual, a man ill at ease with love, not used to expressing it. His awkwardness was touching, his hand comforting. I swallowed my tears.

'If I leave, what will you do, Alexis?'

'I will follow.' He amended his bold declaration. 'If you will allow me.'

Now is the time to tell Alexis about Stefan, I thought, even as I continued to finger lovingly the manuscript we had painstakingly deciphered. These pages might be the last in Father's handwriting that I would ever hold in my hands. And I pictured him writing at a rude desk by the light of a naked bulb in a felt-padded stone cell of the Trubetskoy bastion, stopping to listen to the fortress chimes, the only sound in the gravelike stillness. Beside that haunting reality, what Stefan meant to me now seemed a girlish dream! My confession could wait.

Father's communication made me desperate for contact with Boris Maysky. But how to get hold of my street-urchin Mercury? I took the risk of sending Simyon to the art dealer who held the escape funds. A neighbour told Simyon the dealer had fled to Odessa after the banks had been nationalized in December. I was doubly desperate now. Then suddenly, on my name day, came congratulations from the birdman and an invitation to walk down the Liteiny Prospekt.

In the busiest part of town at the busiest time of day, Boris Maysky materialized long enough to tell me that Father's officers were preparing to free him in transit from the fortress. And yes, the art dealer's money had been placed with people of confidence before his departure. There was an underground network of communication and mutual help, I realized with joy. It was another of the ways to survive in a totalitarian state, one that appealed to me more than being anonymous, learning to dissimulate, or taking no unnecessary risk.

'There is also the Constituent Assembly,' I said to Boris.

'There is indeed!' He winked under his workman's cap, jumped on to the crowded steps of a tram, and vanished.

Not only my hopes but those of all Petrograd resided in the Constituent Assembly, the first universally elected body in Russian history.

When the delegates met in the Palais Tauride, former seat of the Duma, on 18 January 1918, the Bolsheviks had barely a fourth of the votes on the floor. But Kronstadt sailors – the praetorian guard of the new regime – filled the galleries, drowned out anti-Bolshevik resolutions with their din, then descended into the chamber to order its first and only sitting closed.

The people did not rise up against the outrage. They were too numbed, too weary of words, too confused. They bowed to the Soviet power – *Sovietskaya Vlast*.

The Bolsheviks now turned their energy to the peace negotiations at Brest-Litovsk. German territorial demands, which included the Ukraine, were too much for Trotsky, the Commissar for Foreign Affairs and chief delegate to the peace conference. But in the face of a fresh German offensive, he yielded in the end to Lenin's insistence on peace at any price. Even before the treaty was signed on 3 March 1918, the staffs of the Allied embassies had left.

A space was held for me on the diplomatic train until the last moment. With the train went the typed manuscript and the original of Father's memoirs, my correspondence with Tatyana Nikolayevna, my last letter to Stefan, and my last chance to leave Petrograd openly.

In February, my visits to Father were cut down to every other week. I was forbidden to bring a food parcel in the interval and writing materials at any time. They are starting to punish Father for his refusal to cooperate, I thought, and felt sick at heart.

In March, at the usual morning hour, I entered the vast, walled enclosure surmounted by the gold spire of the Petropavlovsk Cathedral – once such an inspiring Petrine landmark. When I passed through the succession of inner courtyards guarded by gun turrets, to the last of the six polygonal bastions, the Trubetskoy, I felt even more oppressed than usual. I presented my pass for the seventh time only to be told the prisoner's visiting privileges had been cancelled.

The next morning, as Fyodor fetched water from our courtyard well, a snowball rebounded at his feet. Inside the snow-coated rubber ball was a message in French, in Boris Maysky's handwriting. 'Prince S. moved unexpectedly, by night, under heavy escort. Cheka suspicious. Watch yourself! New plan under way. Courage!'

My last Pole in hiding had been sent south with forged papers in anticipation of my flight. I warned Nyanya to be on the lookout and repaired to the headquarters of the Cheka, the dread new counter-revolutionary police, for a renewal of my visitor's pass. It was denied.

In quest of Father's whereabouts, I tramped from the House of Detention on the Shpalernaya to Viborg Prison, to be met everywhere with uniformly coarse indifference. The government had moved to Moscow, and it was no use even attempting to see Comrade Lenin. Nor could Alexis give me any information either.

In the forlorn hope of running into Boris Maysky, I went up and down the Nevsky and Liteiny *prospekts*. No idle crowds gathered about a street-corner orator. Instead, the passersby hurried along, fearful of armed robbery, an inspection of papers by the Cheka, or a labour roundup.

Along with others of bourgeois appearance – *burjouy* in popular parlance – I was caught in such a roundup and set to shovelling snow. My frostbitten hands could barely lift the shovel. We were rescued by a passing German officer from a war reparations commission. Since the separate peace, German military were in evidence even in non-occupied territory. He clicked his heels to me gallantly and I thanked him, although I disliked being beholden to a conqueror. After this incident, I avoided the centre of town.

With the thaw, my chilblains healed, but now came another ordeal. To put down 'counter-revolution' – i.e., the growth of the White resistance movement – Comrade Trotsky had formed the Red Army, one that brooked no egalitarian nonsense such as soldiers' committees and election of officers. In addition, all other able-bodied civilians were to be conscripted into the labour force.

Fyodor remained deaf and dumb. Nyanya was too old and cross. Simyon did not show himself out of doors. But on one of my weekly reports to the Cheka, I was enrolled, this time in a gang of women streetcleaners. During the week in which I helped clear snow, my hands were cruelly blistered. The women knew who I was and did their best, for all their sarcasm, to lighten my work. For a day of heavy toil, I received a pittance.

Nyanya rubbed my aching legs and back at night.

'Lord God of mine, how low have we sunk!' she muttered.

Alexis was equally distraught. Since the weather had warmed, we had decided to meet in Solovyev Garden, and he arrived, as he had the previous spring, bearing a bouquet. The flowers were not as fresh, he was not as elegant, but his emotion was just as tremulous.

'Ah, if you only would!' he exclaimed after he had heard the wry report of my experience. 'But no, it's unthinkable.'

'If I would only what, Alexis?'

'If you would only be my wife, I could spare you all this needless suffering! But . . . how could you love me?'

I thought, I could love you, Alexis, if I did not love another. I could love you even while I loved that other, in quite another way.

I said, 'I could love you, Alexis, if circumstances were different. But I can't ask you to compromise your career, your life, by tying yourself to hangman's bait. You have too much to give the world to take such unnecessary risks.' I paraphrased his earlier words.

'You mean more to me than all the world, Tatyana Petrovna. But, for the present, you may be right. My life and career aside, you are too frantic over your father to make an intelligent decision in such a serious matter.'

I smiled. Love, for Alexis Holveg, must be based on an intelligent decision.

He took my hand. 'I have written to Lunacharsky. I have talked to Maxim Gorky. I am exerting all my influence to discover your father's whereabouts. When he is found and freed – maybe by death, Tatyana Petrovna, you must prepare yourself – you will be free to think about your own life.'

Then, thought I, I might be free again to dream about Stefan!

I had made no commitment to Alexis. Nor had he asked for one. Time would undo the tangle. The danger, the hardship of existence excused my duplicity, absolved me of responsibility.

May came and Alexis still knew nothing about Father. But he startled me by saying that Dr Botkin's daughter had received an Easter card from Tobolsk signed by Alexandra and all five children. 'I must also tell you,' he added, 'that Nicholas and Alexandra have since been moved further east, to Ekaterinburg, with some of the children. The others are to follow. Ekaterinburg has a strong Bolshevik soviet. It's likely their imprisonment will become more rigorous.'

'Dear God!' To be jeered at by the very crowds that had knelt before them, to be banished and forgotten had not been enough! What else lay in store?

Carrying a double burden of anxiety and desperation, I made my weekly report to the special police on the Gorokhovaya. In answer to my usual plea for news, I was taken up to the third floor where Comrade Uritsky, the chief of the Petrograd Cheka, had his office. I was led into a former dining room, with peeling wallpaper, a portrait of Lenin, torn mesh curtains, and high-backed chairs with torn seats around a long mahogany table.

At first I walked about, then I stopped at one of the long windows overlooking a dingy courtyard. Hands loosely joined at my waist, head high, I adopted the court pose taught me by Vera Kirilovna, which always helped preserve my self-possession. Thus I stood when in came a personage who filled me with instant repugnance and dread.

'Tatyana Petrovna, I'm very glad to renew our acquaintance.' Comrade Bedlov proffered his hand. Then, as I did not stir, 'Comrade Uritsky has asked me to see what I could do for you. Will you sit down? No? You don't mind if I do.'

He found a dining chair with a seat that was whole and settled his stocky peasant form sideways, resting his pudgy hand on the table.

'Where is my father?' I said. 'When can I see him?'

'Tatyana Petrovna' – Bedlov held up a pudgy index finger – 'be realistic. Is this the tone to take when one comes to beg a favour? It is a favour, or isn't it?'

I lowered my eyes and said softly, 'I would be most grateful for news of my father.'

'That's much better. Ex-Prince Silomirsky is, for the time being, in Kronstadt Maritime Prison. As for your being allowed to visit him, that will depend.'

I was stunned. Kronstadt, where prisoners were taken from Petrograd to be shot! Kronstadt, den of those ferocious sailors! 'You say whether I can visit my father will depend ... on what?'

'Well, for instance, on whether you can tell us where we can find ex-General Maysky, your father's ex-chief of staff, or any others of his former officers we are most anxious to get in touch with.'

'General Maysky was shot last summer trying to escape.'

'A very convenient story! I am not so simple a soldier, Tatyana Petrovna, as to believe it.'

'Then you are surely not so simple as to believe I would know where to find Boris Maysky if he were alive.' I managed to control my voice, but not the heat that rose to my cheeks.

'A good point, Tatyana Petrovna.' Bedlov's eyes grew smaller and greener, and I felt like a mouse between a cat's paws.

'I wonder,' purred the cat, 'whether you could resist persuasion as well as the ex-prince, your father. I think you had better sit down, Tatyana Petrovna,' he added as icy cold succeeded my fiery flush. 'Sit down, don't be embarrassed.'

I fell into the chair he pulled out for me.

'I'll open a window. It is stuffy in here.' He opened a window wide, then went back to his seat.

I put my face down on the table until my access of faintness and terror abated. 'Are you torturing Father?' I brought out.

'Torturing? Tatyana Petrovna, we are not so primitive. I speak of psychological persuasion.'

'What are you trying to persuade my father to say?'

'The Soviet power intends to bring the ex-Tsar Nikolay Romanov before a revolutionary tribunal to answer for his crimes. We merely want your father, as first general aide-de-camp and chief military adviser of the aforesaid Nikolay Romanov, to admit the ex-Tsar's role in provoking the war, for the purpose of diverting popular discontent with his regime. That war, as you know from personal experience, Tatyana Petrovna, caused untold sufferings to the Russian people and their proletarian brothers in all belligerent nations.'

'That is a lie!' I interrupted his smug oratory. 'Our sovereign did everything in his power to avert war. He even cancelled the mobilization orders against the advice of the chief of staff. And even if you could "persuade" Father into such an admission, no real twentieth-century court would accept testimony obtained by your methods.' I had remembered that in this very building, there were known to be cells so cramped that the prisoner could not lie down and had to keep his mouth to the small aperture in the door in order to get air.

'The testimony would indeed be worthless were it not heartfelt,' said Bedlov. 'We still hope to persuade the ex-prince, with the help of the secret protocols we have shown him, and your encouragement, Tatyana Petrovna, to testify freely before a revolutionary people's court. Once again, I appeal for your cooperation in your father's name. A fine gentleman, truly. I would be pleased to bring him the comfort of his daughter's visits, as well as restore his other privileges.'

'Suppose I did convince Father to do as you ask. What would happen to him?'

'That will depend on the sentence of the court. But there is no question that you, Tatyana Petrovna, would be rehabilitated in our eyes. Soviet society would welcome you. You are the kind of woman it needs.'

'So that I can be put to clean the streets?'

'An unfortunate error, Tatyana Petrovna. You will have all facilities to become a physician and surgeon. Comrade Lunacharsky, no less, has your interest at heart.'

'That is very good of him.'

'You should be more respectful of our commissar for education. He has undertaken to erase illiteracy among the Russian masses. Is that not a worthy goal?'

'It is,' I said, while I thought, You are teaching the people to read so that you can stuff them with propaganda.

'You see, we are building the kind of society you desire, Tatyana Petrovna.' Comrade Bedlov fairly beamed. '"From each according to his abilities, to each according to his needs," Karl Marx has said. Would you, a sister of mercy, not agree with that aim?'

'I do. I agree, in theory, with many of your aims. Only I can't reconcile them with the Cheka.' I did not mention the dissolution of the Constituent Assembly.

'A temporary counter-revolutionary measure. When the White forces – backed and supported by world capitalism and imperialism – are defeated, and the German and Austrian empires collapse under the revolutionary tide that must sweep Europe, Russia will know a flowering of science and the arts, a freedom and abundance such as the world has never seen!' Bedlov sat up straighter as he waxed eloquent.

Does he really believe his Bolshevik credo, or is it merely a police ruse to win me over? I wondered. I suspected it was both. The high officials of the tsarist Okhrana -- humble predecessor of the Cheka – were, no doubt, believers in their reactionary creed.

'I pray you are right as to the latter,' I said with sincerity, and rose. 'I should like to give your proposal some thought. In the meantime, may I send a letter and a food parcel to Father?'

'You may bring the parcel in person, Tatyana Petrovna, as soon as we are assured of your support. But I will gladly convey a verbal message. What shall I say to your father?'

'Say I love him and hope to see him soon.' I could no longer bear the sight of Bedlov. 'Am I free to go?'

He stood up and again extended his hand. This time I shook it. Father, forgive me, I do it for you, I whispered inwardly. Then I quickly went out of the room.

The moment I was home, I scrubbed my hands as if I had a surgical case. Then I fell weeping into Nyanya's arms. I wept in rage and humiliation, in black helplessness and despair. 'It can't go on like this, Nyanya! Someone must take pity, someone must help! Are we wholly at the mercy of these devils, Papa and I?'

Yes, we are, I answered myself, we and thousands like us. We are nobody special any more. Now is our real trial of strength, our test of valour. For there is no one to watch us, whether we fail or pass, but God.

26

I spent the next twenty-four hours, after my interview with Bedlov, in a near-frenzy, unable to eat or sleep. I recalled the tales told of the interrogation methods of the Cheka and of the atrocities committed by Kronstadt sailors. I imagined my friends at the mercy of Ekaterinburg's fanatical soviet. And I heard the Empress, on my final visit to Tsarskoye, say in that sombre, arresting tone: 'We may never leave Russia alive.'

Would we never get out of Russia alive, Tanik, Father and I? Would they break us, before they killed us, until we begged for death?

Alexis was alarmed when I came to our rendezvous the next day. This time it was in the zoological gardens adjacent to Petropavlovsk Fortress. I could not speak coherently at first. But after he had held my hand and talked to me softly, I grew calm enough to relate my confrontation with Bedlov.

'Tatyana Petrovna, I'm sure your father's position is not as desperate as you were led to believe,' he said when I was done. 'It is merely a police trick to force your compliance.'

'But how can I comply? Father would only despise me for it! What am I to do?'

'First you must eat, sleep and become rational again. You have some barbiturates, don't you, in your medical stores?' I nodded. 'Then take some. You know the dose. Second, we will get word to your father.'

'Yes, to let him know he has not been abandoned and forgotten. But how?'

'The newly appointed medical supervisor of prisons for the Petrograd area is a former university student of mine. I will ask him to do all he can.'

'Bless you, Alexis!' Tears came to my eyes. 'You have become so dear to me, so close. What would I do without you?'

He looked at me oddly, as if he would temper emotion with

caution. I was clearly in no state to make intelligent decisions in love, said that look.

'*Allons, calmez-vous.* You are wrought up.' He patted my hand. 'Shall we walk a bit?'

He offered me his arm. I was warmed by its pressure as we walked through the unkempt garden bordered by the *cronwerk* – the outer fortification – of the fortress I had come to know so well and that seemed now, in retrospect, almost a refuge. Father had not been tormented there, in his felt-padded cell. I thought how, bit by bit over the past year, I had lowered my expectations, until a once-dreaded prison became a monastic retreat! And how much lower had I to sink until I touched the bedrock of reality?

A week later, when I met Alexis at another spot in the zoological gardens, I saw at once that he had grave news.

'I have a letter for you,' he said after I had sat down beside him on a bench, 'but before you read it, Tatyana Petrovna' – he laid his hand over my icy one – 'you must know that what it refers to is past. The doctor, my former student, has had the Prince moved to a large cell with a window on the gulf, and the interrogations have been stopped on medical order.'

'Interrogations! So they did torture Father.' I felt faint.

'Not exactly. They would not physically harm a witness of the Prince's stature whom they wanted to produce in court. He should recover completely from his mistreatment, according to my medical friend. Shall I read you the letter, Tatyana Petrovna?'

'No, I'll manage.' I took the letter in a trembling hand.

I read the small pencilled scrawl, in English, on a medical form:

Dearest daughter, my Tatyana,

I write these lines in haste to warn you not to come here, whatever subterfuge they use to induce you to. I have not signed any lies. I will not make any false confession in court. My only fear is that I might say something inadvertently, out of exhaustion. I cannot stand up straight or stretch out full length in my cell. They will not let me sleep. The electric light is on night and day. Every five minutes, a guard shines a flashlight on me through the judas. It is driving me mad. I went on a hunger strike and was threatened with force-feeding. The interrogations are almost a relief. At least, they sharpen my mind. I don't hope for escape, only release through death. I implore you again, flee Russia – you have friends who will help you – then let the world know what this accursed regime has done to me, to our unhappy nation! God keep you, my darling.

Papa

'Dear God!' I moaned. 'How can we be sure, Alexis, they will not torment Father again?'

'My friend was emphatic that the Prince would not survive further mistreatment. And both Maxim Gorky and Lunacharsky have interceded on his behalf with Felix Dzerzhinsky himself.'

The Pole, Dzerzhinsky, founder and head of the Cheka, another renegade country squire like Lenin, as coldly cruel as he was refined and handsome! 'Then, they may let Father go?' I grasped at the straw.

'Tatyana Petrovna' – Alexis looked at me sadly – 'why won't you do as your father bids and let me arrange your escape? I will get papers for you as my wife and Nyanya as your mother.'

'Would you leave Russia for my sake?'

'Not for your sake alone. I find life in a police state abhorrent.'

'I'm glad. But I haven't yet given up hope. We have friends, Alexis, working to free Father. I should hear from them any moment.'

'Your escape, by whatever means, is my prime concern,' said Alexis nobly.

He waved aside my thanks irritably, and I parted from him eager for solitude and prayer.

Home in my stable, I spent many hours on my knees before my favourite icon of the Saviour. And, next morning, as if in answer to my pleas, here was my street urchin with a coded message from Boris Maysky. 'We are infiltrating Kronstadt Prison,' it read. 'Hope and patience!'

I made the boy wait and wrote on a thin scrap of paper easy to swallow. 'My brave father, my sweet martyr, your release is coming. Hold on! T.' I folded it in a larger piece of paper on which I wrote, 'Get this to Father in the name of God!' This I slipped inside the lining of the boy's cap with the injunction to deliver it to Professor Holveg at his flat in person, before he went to his lecture.

May and June went by in a feverish state of alternating hope and despair, made all the more poignant by the balminess of the short northern spring and the dismal deterioration of the deserted capital.

On my twenty-first birthday – mine and my namesake's, of whom there was no more word – Nyanya recalled the birth of the two Tatyanas. That solemn event no longer bore any relation to me or Tanik. Her father's days were numbered and she too existed in a numbness of terror shot through with wild flashes of hope. But was there hope for the prisoners at Ekaterinburg?

Alexis, when I pressed him, agreed that the White insurgents in Siberia were making progress with the aid of the Czechs. Earlier he had explained how a Czech army, 300,000 strong, which had fought on the Russian front, had refused to lay down its arms at the conclusion of the separate peace of Brest-Litovsk. Resolved to make its roundabout way home through Vladivostok, it had commandeered the Trans-Siberian Railway. Attacked and blocked in its progress by the Bolsheviks, it had made common cause with the White forces under Admiral Kolchak. The Czechs were only one of the many bizarre and disparate elements to form the ever-shifting patchwork pattern of the emerging Civil War.

'I'm afraid, though,' Alexis now added, 'that the advance of the Whites may endanger the former Tsar and his family even more. The Bolsheviks will not want to risk his liberation.'

'You mean that they will shoot him first.' I contemplated the prospect as I did Father's fate and mine, numbly. 'Unless' – hope surged unaccountably – 'unless the Whites seize the town by surprise.'

I clung to that hope while I awaited word from General Maysky. In the latter part of June, there came at last a warning to stand by. I girded my revolver and cartridge belt, sewed jewels into the hem of my skirt, told Fyodor and Simyon to arm themselves with knives and be ready. At last, in the beginning of July, I received an address on Vassily Island where we were to proceed one by one without arousing suspicion on the night of 10 July 1918.

On the afternoon of the ninth, I went to meet Alexis for the last time in Solovyev Garden. He had another sealed letter from Father, delivered to the medical supervisor of prisons on his monthly visit and forwarded by the latter to his former professor. Inside the envelope was a sheet of paper written without haste, in Russian this time.

Dochenka,

I thank you for your sweet words of comfort. My trials have not been renewed since I was moved from the Hole thanks to the merciful intercession of the good doctor who will see that this last letter of mine reaches you. I am left in peace and am even shown little kindnesses which bring me exquisite pleasure. My cell is clean and quiet. Already I have no memory and no resentment of my ordeal. Do not exaggerate that ordeal, dearest. I suffered far more when your mother died. Thanks to my recent trials, I have at last expiated my guilt for her wanton death, which haunted me always and made me melancholy in the midst of good fortune.

In these final days of my life, I feel deeply at peace. The faith which had been mere form is now revealed to me in all its strength and beauty, as it was to you long ago, when you were still a child. You remember Mother's words to me before she died, 'Petya, when your time comes, soon perhaps, don't be afraid. All terrors, all agonies come to an end. The Lord is merciful.' The terrors and agonies are ended for me now. My only sorrow is for my unhappy country in the cruel hands of men like Bedlov and for all my friends now at their mercy, among them my poor sovereign. My only desire is to know that you are on your way to your beloved, who will soon make you forget these dreadful times you bore so bravely for my sake. I feel deeply this will come to pass and so I succeed in banishing from me these anxieties for your safety which alone disturb my rest. I ask you to similarly banish such anxieties about me from your thoughts. Nor must you feel regret if things do not come to pass as your sweet words assured me. Be content my death is honourable and does not disgrace our ancient Russian name.

I kiss you, my sweet daughter, and press you long and tenderly to my heart. Of all the honours heaped upon me, of all the loyal friendships shown me, of all the loves once lavished on me with little return, of all the things men so ardently desire and that I had in abundance without striving for them, my greatest reward in life was a daughter's love. This has remained with me when all else vanished, and this I will carry with me into the beyond. The light of your marvellous eyes falls on this page as I write, and I am well in it. The great God keep you, my Tatyana. Farewell.

Your Papa

I sat long gazing at the letter, its words blurred beyond recognition by my tears. Without showing it to Alexis – the reference to my beloved could not be explained now – I folded it and slipped it into my bosom next to the revolver.

'Papa is at peace,' I said. 'He awaits his death. Are they going to execute him?'

'Yes. And you with him, Tatyana Petrovna, if you don't get away at once. I had the false papers ready for that eventuality.' He reached inside his coat.

'Alexis, you didn't! They must have cost a fortune!'

'That's immaterial now.'

'But my escape has already been arranged, Alexis, to coincide with Father's rescue. I came to say goodbye.'

Poor Alexis faltered. 'I'm ... very, very happy for you.' How wretched he looked! 'I can only pray that it goes well ... and that I may see you again in happier circumstances ...'

'I'm sure we will meet again.' Weren't our lives curiously, inextricably bound? 'Though how, where, when, who can say? Will you leave yourself right away?'

'There is no emergency for me. I will wait till Poland is freed of German occupation. The war cannot last much longer. You can find me through Warsaw University, if I don't find you first.'

'I wish you a safe journey, happiness, fame, everything that you deserve, dear Alexis. And thank you, thank you for all you've done, all you've meant to me.' Now, in the moment of parting, I realized how much! I looked into those vivid eyes, so fiery behind the scholarly spectacles, then I leaned over and kissed Alexis on both cheeks, after the Russian custom.

The tip of his goatee fairly quivered with emotion.

'Tatyana Petrovna ...' He jumped to his feet as I rose.

But I turned away and quickly walked out of the park.

Fyodor joined me at the garden gate and we started for the Nikolayevsky Bridge. Barely had we reached it when a street urchin came skipping towards us. His wide nose was turned up, his round face lively and comical. As I drew up with him, he put out his hand and said, 'Put a *kopeyka* in my hand, miss, and I'll tell you a story. Only walk the other way.'

I put some coins in his hand and turned back towards Vassily Island. 'Well, what's your story?'

'There came some sailors to the Silomirsky *osobnyak*,' he related, 'straight into the stables, where they found Simyon and a little old woman.

'"Where is your mistress, the ex-Princess Silomirskaya?" they say.

'"And what is it you want with her?" she asks.

'One of the sailors laughs. "Tomorrow at dawn, she and her Papa are going to be shot. Now tell us where she is or we'll cook you over a slow fire." And he takes hold of the old woman.

'"She's not here and where she is I don't know and it's nothing to me anyway. Take your dirty paws off me!" So he does and the sailors go all through the big house smashing things, and at last they drive away and take Simyon with them.

'And the old woman says to me, "Run and watch for the Princess on the island side of Nikolayevsky Bridge and tell her not to come home. We are watched."'

'An entertaining tale,' I said. 'Can you find the birdman?'

'I think so.'

'Then go and tell him the story, every word, and add that I'll be at the "place of marvels". You'll remember?'

'The place of marvels.' He turned up an impudent face.

I kissed him and he skipped away, whistling. I continued to walk north across the island.

'Fyodor,' I said, 'turn back slowly and bring Nyanya at dusk to this house on Maly Prospekt.' I gave him the address Boris Maysky had indicated. 'They'll expect you. They'll put you ashore at the Silomirsky dacha. I'll be waiting by the birch wood, the secret cove where I used to hide when I was little. Remember?'

'I remember, Tatyana Petrovna.'

'Good. If you're stopped, you're deaf and dumb. Let Nyanya talk. Go now.' The giant's face, which could so admirably express an absolute blank, reflected stolid resistance.

'Go!' I repeated, and he obeyed.

I continued on my way to the rendezvous house. The small white house in the vicinity of the cemetery of Smolensk stood at the edge of a field, at the bottom of a garden with lilac bushes and a picket fence.

Uncertain of my reception ahead of the appointed time, I went cautiously around to the back door. But the motherly, middle-aged lady of the house who let me in behaved as though I had been expected to tea. Her husband, a former quartermaster in Father's cavalry corps in Galicia, now worked for a Soviet commissariat of supply. I was offered real tea with black bread and jam. My hostess then helped me into a peasant dress of coarse print cotton, padded my bust, blackened a tooth, and tied a kerchief low over my forehead, hiding my hair.

After sunset, a fisherman came to lead me through the deserted woods and fields of the island's west end. A fishing trawler was moored at a solitary wooden pier. I boarded it and hid in the tiny cabin.

We had not sailed more than fifteen minutes when the motor idled and the boat swayed in the swell of a larger one. I heard a hail and, very clearly, 'Comrade fisherman, we're looking for a girl, twenty-one years old, tall, thin, a blonde, the ex-Princess Silomirskaya, wanted as an enemy of the Soviet People's Republic. Anyone assisting her escape will be shot.'

'And right too,' came the ringing reply. 'I'll keep my eyes open, comrade.'

Another hour and a quarter later, the boat stopped again, the hatch was opened, and I was helped out of the cabin. I gave the seaman my watch in payment, told him to expect more business that night, and, taking off my shoes, I let myself overboard. Quickly, I waded into the sheltered cove on the Silomirsky estate along the Gulf of Finland, a *verst* north of our villa on its exposed knoll.

I climbed on to the bank and hid in a marshy growth, spreading out my skirt wet at the hem and breathing deeply the cleansing sea air. The cove was still and eerie in the white light of the summer solstice. The leaves of a great oak growing on the very shore hung motionless over the softly lapping water. This was the oak of fairy tale in my childhood world of make-believe, and I heard Father's beautiful voice reciting the opening lines of Pushkin's *Ruslan and Liudmila*:

On the sea shore grows an oak.
A golden chain is fastened to it.
And on this chain a learned cat
Night and day goes round about.
Turn he right, a song he'll sing you,
Turn he left, a tale he'll tell.
It is a place of marvels . . .

'The place of marvels,' I had called it as a child, a place with hidden paths and prints of beasts unheard, unseen. Thirty warriors young and fair might well step out of the deep, or would it be the

Red sailors come to shoot me and Father at dawn? Was this to be my last night on earth, and would I never again feel Stevie's lips velvety-soft against mine? Only three summers ago I had been confident in the realization of my legendary vision of love and life. I had planed like a bird of rare plumage above the ordinary world. And now I was a hunted bird, with glazed eye and racing heart, hiding from the Red bloodhounds in the marsh.

Papa, Papa, I thought, will they free you in time? Shall we take you to the Basque coast, where you will grow strong again and forget your torments as you watch your grandchildren play on the beach? Or is this letter folded against my heart your farewell to me? And how beautiful that letter is!

I took it out and reread it in the glow of the northern night till I knew it by heart. How I wished Tanik could share it! Where was she now? Was she a fugitive too? Had she been freed in the nick of time? Closing my eyes, I almost sensed her calm, strong presence.

Sweet and poignant sadness banished fear as girlhood memories unrolled before my mind's eye. Every close and happy moment with Father from the beginning of the war to the eve of his arrest came back vividly as well. The shore was silent. Further south, the Neva estuary, I knew, no longer reflected the jewelled lights of pleasure steamers. No sound of accordion, no laughter would come from the Soviet patrol boats that nightly swept the Bay of Kronstadt with their searchlights. I spread out Father's letter, pressed it with both hands to my breast, leaned my head against the trunk of an elm, and dozed off.

I awakened with a start at the sound of a motor idling. I recognized with relief the fishing trawler that had brought me. As it pulled away, Fyodor waded into the cove, carrying my old nurse, small as a child in his arms.

'Lord God of mine, such doings, such excitement in my old age,' puffed Nyanya as Fyodor set her down. 'Praise God you're safe, my love.'

'You have the jewels?' I asked.

Nyanya patted the bodice and skirt of her *sarafan*. 'Here they are. I brought something even better.'

The spry old woman produced bread and sausage, which I

devoured. Then we crawled into the brush and crouched on the marshy ground to await our rescuers.

At dawn the sound of cannon on our left, in the direction of Kronstadt Fortress, sent my heart racing. Before long, a motor launch circled about the cove and sputtered to a stop under the overhanging growth. Half a dozen Red sailors jumped out of it, and I froze. But then I recognized the falcon beak and flying eyebrows of Boris Andreyevich Maysky. I leaped up and made my way through the undergrowth towards him. My joy and relief vanished as I looked at his face. His eyebrows met in a furious frown over his beak of a nose. His gaunt cheeks worked.

'You were too late?' I understood.

'Yes. We were only in time to free Simyon ... we brought the Prince your father to you ... for burial.'

Four of the false sailors now waded ashore, carrying something long and heavy in a canvas. A weeping Simyon followed. General Maysky directed them to a flat grassy spot out of sight of the shore. Here they laid down their burden and opened the canvas.

I approached slowly and looked down on my dead father. His great body was emaciated and aged, his silver hair now white as chalk. Yet he lay erect. Small brown spots showed on his tunic where the bullets had penetrated. The wind stirred the full white beard on his gaunt chest. His features in austere repose expressed, like those of my grandmother set in stern beatitude, her final words to him: 'All terrors, all agonies come to an end. The Lord is merciful.'

Slowly and gravely I made the sign of the cross and sank to my knees by Father's shoulder, gazing into his face. Simyon, weeping ever more bitterly, fell to his knees by Father's legs, and Nyanya threw herself over them, clasping and kissing them. Boris Maysky gave terse orders to camouflage the boat and dig the grave in all haste. Fyodor joined the gravediggers. I remained alone with my old nurse and the orderly.

'Tell me how it was, Simyon,' I said quietly. 'Did you see Father before he was shot?'

'I spent the night wih him, Your Highness.' Simyon swallowed his sobs. 'First they put me in another cell, but I begged and begged until they let me in to him. He was weak, lying on his pallet, and grown so thin since I last had seen him! His liver was bothering him again.'

'"Simyon, you too!" he cried when he saw me. "And Princess Tatyana, my daughter?"

'I told him what had happened.

'"Praise God!" he said. "Nyanya will have warned her. She will be safe."

'Then he was calm and comforted me. He talked about Your Highness when you were a little girl, and sometimes about our sovereign and then about the battles we had been in together, but always again about you. He did not sleep, but he was calm and without fear. At dawn some Bolshevik sailors came into the cell. Their officer read from a paper that my Prince had been found guilty of crimes against the Soviet people and was sentenced to be shot by order of ... order of ... the Presidium of the All-Russian Extraordinary Commission for Counter-revolution – in one word, Cheka. They love long names, these Bolsheviki!

'"It's you who are the criminals," I said, and they would have struck me, only my Prince stopped them.

'One of them stayed then to help me dress my Prince. So weak he was, he could hardly stand. They let him wear his uniform – it was much too big on him now – and the crosses of St George and St Andrew as he asked. I combed out his beard and his hair, white like an old man's it had become. Then the sailors came for us again. They laid my Prince on a stretcher and one of them said it'd be easier to shoot him right there, but their officer said Comrade Bedlov liked things done according to the rules.

'They carried him out into the yard, I following with my hands tied behind my back. They tied my Prince to a post. He asked them not to put the sack on his head, and they did not. They could not look at his face, the sailors, so beautiful and sad it was, like Our Saviour's on the cross, and the sailors were nervous – not even Reds like such murdering business.

'"Well, Simyon, be brave," my Prince said to me. "See you in a little while."

'I stood with my hands tied beside the firing squad, looking at my Prince. And when I heard the volley and saw him sink into the ropes and his head fall on his breast, I felt as though I'd been hit by twenty bullets in the chest. It was all the same what anyone did to me now, all the same, but instead of the sack being put on my head, I heard shouts and firing and His Excellency General Maysky is cutting me loose.

'I ran to my Prince. Some of the Reds who shot him helped me cut him down. I slung him over my back – I felt as strong as Fyodor – and carried him out of the fortress. All around us there was firing. The prisoners in the common cells were turned loose. They locked the guards in, they took the commander of the fortress hostage. Sirens were wailing. Such bedlam it was, the Reds did not know who to chase! So we found ourselves in a boat and the guns of the fortress firing over us, but it was all the same to me now, all the same ...' He finished in a heart-rending voice and fell to sobbing once more.

Nyanya, clutching Father's legs, joined her sobs to Simyon's.

I did not cry. A solemn stillness filled me, wherein each sound was acutely perceived: the gravediggers' shovels striking a stone, the scurryings of polecat and squirrel in the wood, birds chirping in the branches, the tide lapping against the shore, the seagulls' plaint.

'Nyanya, why do you cry?' I asked. 'Papa is well, Papa is with Our Lord. Be still a little.'

'How can I not weep when my heart is breaking?' she answered. 'But we will leave you to yourself if our noise disturbs you. Come, Simyon, let us leave the Princess.'

'Stay.' I was ashamed. 'You loved him too. We will pray for him together.'

I began to pray softly, Nyanya and Simyon adding their deeper-voiced responses, until General Maysky returned to say the grave was ready.

Once more I gazed at Father's face. Then I bent and kissed him on the forehead. 'Sleep peacefully, *Papochka*,' I murmured. And I felt a compelling desire to stretch out beside him and never get up. But, before I could, General Maysky had lifted me up. He led me out of sight while the body was lowered in the canvas into the grave.

When the grave was covered, the dozen officers in sailor disguise lined up in two ranks on either side. At its foot, where a birch grew in the shade of an oak, knelt Simyon, Fyodor and Nyanya. I advanced to the head of the grave and asked Boris Maysky to say a few words.

He removed his cap and, holding it to his chest, said in the soft and melodic voice that belied his cutting manner, 'We commend to You, Lord, the soul of General Prince Silomirsky, who died for the honour of his sovereign and the motherland. When our time comes to join him, may we do it in a manner worthy of our Prince and Commander. Amen.'

For fear of detection, no salute was fired. The officers presented arms. Then, one by one, they came up to me. Gravely and without tears, I extended my hand and thanked each of them in turn for his loyalty to my father. One last long and solemn moment we stood in tribute to the dead, then we considered the business of life.

General Maysky took charge. He checked my revolver and led me to a growth of blackberry bushes. Here I was to remain concealed until nightfall, when we would make our run for Finland, where the other boatload of Father's officers had preceded us. Simyon was to cover me while Fyodor stayed by Nyanya. Boris Andreyevich then left to post his men as sentries. In case of attack they were to use firearms only as a last resort. All had knives ready.

I crouched in the bushes, my revolver in my hand. As the sun rose high, I became hot and uncomfortable. I ate blackberries, brushed the flies from my face and the ants from my legs, and grew somnolent. The fears, hopes, sorrows of the past month merged into the overwhelming wish for sleep. I curled up on the ground, one hand under my cheek, the other clasped about my revolver, and slept.

I slept stuporously, and the heat of day abated; a cooling wind blew from the gulf. Still I slept on and did not stir when I heard, as in a dream, the prearranged warning whistle, the grunts and scufflings of a hand-to-hand fight, and the purring of a motor launch. With a start, I opened my eyes to see a genuine Red sailor raising a bayonet over me. The hand with the revolver was below my breast. I pointed it into his glistening, red face with long whiskers and bared teeth like the fangs of a seal, and fired. His rifle dropped from his hands and his body, twisting, sank on top of mine, splattering me with blood. I pushed it off with the strength of revulsion and got to my feet. But in the moment I straightened, I felt the violent pain of a blow at the back of my head. I grew nauseated and dizzy and a great lassitude overcame me, into which I gratefully sank. I was dying, and soon I would be laid by Father's side to sleep forever peacefully in his grave.

27

My first sensation when I regained consciousness was regret. What a pity I'm not dead, I thought. As in the illness of my tenth year, I tried to go back to sleep in the hope I might die yet. Headache and nausea prevented me and I opened my eyes.

I lay prone in a cellar. From a narrow opening high in the wall, milky light filtered down, and a face bent over me, with flying eyebrows and a beak for a nose.

'Tatyana Petrovna, how do you feel?' The falcon spoke.

I remembered the revolting sensation of a heavy weight on my body. I pushed myself up on my palms, felt violent pain, and vomited.

Nyanya held up a pan. She wiped my face and said to the General, who changed my bloody compress, 'You mustn't question her, Your Excellency. It makes her ill.'

'Nyanya,' I said.

'You see, Your Excellency, she knows me. Yes, my love, what is it?'

'I want my bed. I want my papa.'

'Soon, soon, go to sleep,' crooned Nyanya, but Boris Maysky said, 'Don't encourage her. She must be made to remember! Tatyana Petrovna, who am I?'

'Boris Andreyevich Maysky. Did I fall off a horse?'

'No, you did not fall off a horse, Tatyana Petrovna. You were struck with a rifle butt on the back of the head. Simyon killed the Red who wounded you. The launch was surrounded and we could not get you out. The rest of our men escaped. Fyodor carried you to the cellar of your villa. He and Simyon are with us. We'll hide in the cellar until we can get away. Do you understand what I'm saying, Tatyana Petrovna?'

'I don't want to leave. I want to wait for Papa.'

'Tatyana Petrovna' – Boris Andreyevich pressed his hand down on my shoulder – 'your father is dead, shot by the Bolsheviks. We buried him under your eyes. You're not a baby girl, you are twenty-one years old. You've had a great shock and a blow on the head, but now you must come back to reality.'

'If the Lord in His mercy wants to spare our Princess the knowledge of her father's death,' Nyanya said, 'who are we to know better, Your Excellency? He will clear her mind as He has clouded it, when He sees fit.'

Simyon was ready to make his new master comfortable. Sheets and bedding had been brought from upstairs, stores of preserves and tins discovered in a storage room, rainwater in a cistern. A blanket partition was hung between my quarters and the men's. The men altered the door to the cellar to make it open from the inside only and camouflaged it with cases and barrels. Simyon and Fyodor took turns as sentinels in the campanile of the villa, whence all approaches to the estate by land and water could be watched.

The day passed without alarm, but at dusk Fyodor reported a launch heading for our pier from the direction of Kronstadt. The cellar door was pulled to after him, and General Maysky placed himself by me to smother any outcry. Nyanya told me pirates were attacking the villa and we must be very quiet.

When the tramp of feet and the sound of voices just beyond the wall died away, General Maysky said, 'Tatyana Petrovna, this was no game. Those pirates were Reds, looking for us. They killed your father and they'll kill us unless we keep our wits about us.'

'It's not true. Papa will come home soon!'

'Oh God!' Maysky groaned. 'And there's no getting a doctor! Still, I've seen concussion cases with amnesia at the front; there's not much to be done except rest.'

For more than a month I lay ill on the cellar floor. As the pain and nausea subsided, General Maysky thought I might recover faster if I had some fresh air. While Simyon kept a lookout in the campanile and General Maysky stood guard, Fyodor carried me into the now unkempt garden, where a wild growth of brambles and grasses concealed me. He accepted my childish state as naturally as did Nyanya and Simyon. The educated General Maysky alone persisted in bringing back my memory. Whenever he prodded me, I screamed in my sleep.

In my nightmares I was pursued by a man with the Mongolian

features of Bedlov, but with the moustaches and fangs of a seal. I ran through a city that was both Warsaw and Petrograd, until I saw a scholarly gentleman walking ahead of me with quick little steps. 'Alexis,' I called, 'it's me, Tanya!' He turned around. He was not Alexis, he was Bedlov the Seal.

I fled from him into a vast hall filled on one side with ladies in jewel-studded *kakoshniks*, on the other with court officials in white breeches and scarlet coats. The doors opened, and in walked my sovereign in a mantle of yellow velvet and ermine, carrying sceptre and orb. I was seized with gladness and reverence. At last I was safe. But as I rose from my obeisance and looked into my sovereign's face, I saw not the mild and handsome features of my godfather the Tsar but the malignant green eyes and yellow fangs of Bedlov the Seal.

At the end of August, Boris Maysky resolved to go to Petrograd to arrange our escape. All our motorboats had been confiscated, but he found a leaky rowboat that he repaired with Simyon's help. The General had grown a moustache and beard that disguised his face. Dusty old seamen's oilskins were found in the boathouse.

I gave Boris Andreyevich my hand to kiss like a polite little princess, and he bent his head long over it. 'If anything goes wrong with us, God keep you, Tatyana Petrovna.'

Boris Maysky and Simyon did not return. Two weeks went by, and Nyanya ceased to expect them.

September passed. October brought frost. The tins were empty. Fyodor picked berries and nuts, fished and hunted. To save cartridges for self-defence and avoid making noise, he fashioned a bow and arrow. The wild ducks he shot we roasted over stones, fanning away the smoke not to betray our presence. He chopped wood for the coming winter. Nyanya sewed quilting and blankets into winter clothes. She gave me light housekeeping tasks.

Dim memories weighed on my consciousness, as foul and oppressive as the recollection of a dead body on top of mine. I struggled to clear the haze, panicked not to know my full identity, and fell into a stupor.

'Oh Lord my God,' Nyanya prayed, 'I know you wish to spare my Princess greater grief than she could bear, and I will care for her according to Your Will. But I am seventy years old and soon my own mind may be that of a child. Then who will look after her, Lord?'

She was certain the Lord would do what was necessary in good time, she told me during her later detailed account of these 'lost' months. But she began urging Him to make haste.

In the middle of October, Fyodor, as usual, made a tour of the grounds before barricading the cellar for the night. He returned with a man in his grasp and set him down in front of Nyanya, whose greater intelligence he acknowledged.

'I would have killed him only he claims he is a White and Her Highness will know him,' he stated calmly.

'Even if she does, she may not remember,' said Nyanya. 'Who are you?' she asked the stranger.

'Naval Lieutenant Baron Niessen, former ensign on the imperial yacht the *Standard.* I am now in the White Guard. I bring Tatyana Petrovna a letter from the late Grand Duchess Tatyana Nikolayevna.'

'Late? How? The Grand Duchess is dead?'

'Yes. Murdered by the Bolsheviki. With our sovereign and all his family.'

'Lord God of mine, what horrors!' Nyanya crossed herself. 'When my Princess hears this she may lose what little of her mind she has left. But, if it's God's Will . . . We bid Your Honour welcome. Fyodor, give His Honour something to eat and drink while I fetch the Princess.'

She stepped behind the blanket partition, where I lay dozing. 'A White officer has come, my love, to bring you news of the Grand Duchess Tatyana Nikolayevna.'

'Tatyana Nikolayevna?' I started up.

I remembered dancing class at the Winter Palace as if it were yesterday. I looked down at my coarse cotton dress, bleached a faded blue by repeated washings in rainwater. How did I come to wear such a dress? 'Give me my shoes,' I said.

Nyanya rushed to hand me my only pair.

I smoothed my hair, parted in tresses, and pulled the blanket aside.

There rose from the table an unshaven youngish man in a tattered sailor's vest, with a caked bandage about his head and a fair moustache in need of trimming. He bowed in a military manner over my hand.

'Won't you sit down?' I said to him in English and sat down at the table, putting my hands in my lap and crossing my bare ankles as I had been taught.

'I was hoping you'd remember me, Princess.' He introduced himself. 'I was at your graduation ball in 1914.'

There had been nothing memorable about Baron Niessen. Of an old Baltic family long prominent in the imperial navy, he had been chosen for duty on the *Standard* for his good English and good manners.

'Perhaps you don't recognize me because of the bandage,' he continued. 'I'm afraid it's rather a messy job. I wasn't able to get a doctor.'

I examined the bandage attentively. 'How did you hurt your head?'

'I was hiding underwater from a Bolshie patrol. The tip of a propeller blade caught me on the side. It's not important, Princess. I bring you a letter from –'

'Not now.' I concentrated on the bandage. 'I need scissors, alcohol, sterile gauze . . .'

Nyanya stared, then crossed herself with a muttered prayer of thanks. 'And where am I to find them, Princess mine?' she asked.

I took in my surroundings. 'Sit still.' I put a hand on the officer's shoulder. 'Water and a clean cloth will do, then.'

I soaked the caked bandage until it was loose enough to come off. Telling Fyodor to hold up the candle, I held the wounded man's head to the light.

'It's a deep cut. It ought to be disinfected and sutured. Nyanya, where are we?'

'The cellar of the Silomirsky dacha, my soul. We are hiding here from the Bolsheviki –'

'Later, later. Wait, let me think. The villa. We had a convalescent soldiers' home here. There is a dispensary. There must be medical supplies. We'll go and look.'

Over Nyanya's protests, I went, Fyodor lighting the way. I took my time to wander through all that ghostly, uninhabited space. Some of the rooms were disturbingly familiar, as if I had visited them in a past life. Here I had slept as a child, with a teddy bear in my arms. There, a seventeen-year-old girl in love, I had listened to the lapping waters of the gulf. In love with whom? How long ago?

I felt a headache coming and quickly found the dispensary on the ground floor.

I returned to the cellar with the needed supplies in an enamel basin. Fyodor held up the candle while I cleaned and sutured the wound with fingers that had not forgotten their skill. Then, exhausted by prolonged attention, I told Baron Niessen I would hear his news the following day and went to bed.

All night long I tossed, straining to shake off the curtain of oblivion still clouding my consciousness. At dawn, I slept at last and, upon awakening, remembered everything in a flash, including my final meeting with Alexis, the street urchin's warning, the boat crossing to the secret cove. But frown and shake my head as I would, what had happened on shore, how I had ended up in this cellar, were still behind the curtain.

I went outdoors for my morning toilette, broke the ice that had formed over the water cistern, and found the cold morning air on my skin a delight. A flight of wild ducks passed overhead, heading south. I looked at my image.

'Stevie would say you look like a scarecrow all right, Skinny-ninny,' I addressed it fondly. It was no beauty, but it was me.

I combed my tresses carefully, put on my shoes even though they pinched, and went out to meet my officer guest for a breakfast of water, berries and the remains of a wild rabbit, served on rose, gold-bordered china from upstairs.

Baron Niessen was also shaven, his moustache trimmed with care. But if he was no longer self-conscious about his appearance, he seemed even more nervous, and bit his lip continually. I asked him for his message.

He took a folded paper from inside his sailor's vest, and placed it wordlessly before me.

I carried it to the dim light of the barred window. The letters danced before my eyes, no longer accustomed to reading, then steadied at last. I recognized the bold, angular handwriting of my namesake.

I read in English,

Dearest Tata,

My blood sister, my only friend, wherever you are I pray this letter reaches you with all my tenderest love, and wishes from all of us for your safety and happiness. Thank you for your letter with the sad news of Anna Vladimirovna's death.

So Marie Fyodorovna did forward my letter – bless Her Imperial Majesty!

It reached us through our rare and precious contacts with Anmama, just before we left Tobolsk. Here in Ekaterinburg, there have been no more letters of any kind. I'm sure you wrote many more, as I did to you. Papa told us you even tried to see us again at Tsarskoye. He guessed that you wanted to toss us a message and warned you off. He did not fear reprisal for us but for you and Prince Silomirsky. It was also for your sake that Mummsy sounded unkind on your last visit. I've tried repeatedly to let you know, so that you would not carry any bitter memories after she's gone. Even if Mummsy was unjust to you at times, she has always loved you at bottom. She proved it that day at Tsarskoye when she so brusquely rejected your sweet offer to join us. I was a bit resentful at first, but now I'm ever so grateful.

The governor's house in Tobolsk wasn't at all bad. There was no staring at us over the high wooden fence – everything in Siberia is made of wood. Nor was anyone interested in us over there. It was comfortable and peaceful. Olga and I read a lot. The little ones studied with Aleksey's faithful Gilliard. Odd, isn't it, that a Swiss should remain loyal to us, when so few Russians did? Papa sawed wood for the stoves, and played dominoes, of course. For Christmas, Mummsy made beautiful cards in Church Slavonic. Strange to say, we were content. We never regretted for a moment our decision to stay together come what may. But ever since we joined Papa and Mummsy in the house of the merchant Ipatiev in Ekaterinburg, life has become more and more unpleasant.

We are still allowed on the roof for brief periods and that's how we happened to see Baron Niessen in disguise in the street. Aleksey will throw this letter to him inside a ball of yarn. Niessen's presence makes Papa hopeful someone's working to free us. Botkin has heard a White army is approaching. He is the only one of the suite left to us. Papa makes up tales of escape that Sunbeam finds very exciting – poor Aleksey has been unwell again. He badly misses Nagorny. His other sailor-nurse, Derevenko, you know, went over to the Reds. And how we spoiled him! But never mind that now. We all do our best to cheer Aleksey. Mummsy is wonderful. She seems to grow stronger every day. I'm afraid, though, she was quite right about what awaits us. We no longer have any illusions.

Darling Tata, I'm afraid I'm very dull and can't think of any fine last words. I'm sorry we won't be bridesmaids at your wedding, but I know you'll be just as happy with your Stefan. We pray for your father every day and for all who suffer for their loyalty to us. Brest-Litovsk was bitter for Papa. But he still has faith in the Russian people. Surely some good must come of all this evil that now seems so senseless. I kiss you, my precious friend, and ask you to remember always your Tanik, Tatyana Romanova

I read the letter through twice. Then, turning to the officer standing tight-lipped by the table, 'Where is Tatyana Nikolayevna now?' I asked.

'Her Imperial Highness is dead.'

'Tatyana Nikolayevna dead?' Had I not expected it? Had I not felt her fearless presence on the night of my escape to the dacha and known then she was ready? 'When did it happen?'

'On the night of 16 July 1918, in the cellar of Ipatiev's house in Ekaterinburg.'

'And the others?'

'Murdered all.'

'Not the little ones ... not Anastasia and Aleksey?' For that, I was unprepared.

'All. Shot, bayoneted, then dismembered and burned.'

'No, it's impossible, what are you saying?' I cried. 'I thought I'd lost my mind and found it, but *this* is madness!'

I fell into a chair, putting my throbbing head in my hands. Nyanya held me about the shoulders.

'It's true, all true,' Baron Niessen said, in Russian this time. 'I know it sounds unbelievable but it's true. After Ekaterinburg fell to the White forces under Admiral Kolchak, I saw the cellar in Ipatiev's house: the blood, the bullets, the marks of bayonets. I heard a Lett soldier, one of the murdering squad, tell us how it was done. All of them herded into the cellar, our sovereign with the Tsarevich in his arms, Her Majesty and the Grand Duchesses, Dr Botkin, three servants, shot down without warning. The rest of the suite, Prince Dolgorukov, Countess Hendrikov, Mlle Schneider, shot in prison, even Nagorny, a simple sailor. The conditions in Ipatiev's house were barbarous. The doors of the Grand Duchesses' room were taken out. The guards were lewd and insolent. Nagorny was taken from the Tsarevich. No humiliation was spared them. Yet they were steadfast and stoical to the end.'

So Tanik too had touched the bedrock of reality! 'Nyanya, did you hear?' I looked up. 'They murdered Tatyana Nikolayevna, and Aleksey, a sick boy not quite fourteen, and funny Schwibzik Anastasia, and clever Olga, and good Marie, and our sovereign, my godfather, and Alexandra Fyodorovna, and Dr Botkin who took care of me when I was ill . . . First they humiliated and insulted them, then they shot, bayoneted, dismembered and burned them . . . Ah no!' I looked wildly about the cellar. 'It's only another nightmare and when I awake, Boris Andreyevich will be here. He'll explain what happened since I fled to the dacha. Nyanya' – I put my arms about her – 'where is Boris Andreyevich?'

'He left with Simyon two months ago and never came back.'

'And Papa? Is Papa dead?'

Nyanya stroked my hair. 'He is, my soul. The Bolsheviki shot him, in Kronstadt Prison at dawn, 10 July it was.'

10 July, only six days before the murder of his sovereign and boyhood friend! The last fold of the curtain of oblivion was drawn back. 'We buried Papa under an oak tree nearby, before the Reds landed . . .'

Nyanya held me as I shuddered. 'That's how it was, yes.'

That's how it was and it could not be changed. The tortured and maimed could not be made whole again. The dead could not be resurrected. The living must carry their dreadful load of memories, the hideous vision must be faced, the unbearable must be borne. The test of life is to be endured to the end, even as Papa and Tanik endured theirs.

I was silent a long time, collecting myself. At last I said to my guest, 'Thank you for bringing me the letter from Tatyana Nikolayevna, Baron. Did you come all the way from Ekaterinburg just to deliver it?'

'I'm acting as courier for Admiral Kolchak, the Supreme Commander in Siberia, and General Denikin, who now leads the former Volunteer Army in the south. I'm carrying messages from them to Archangel, where the British and Americans have landed several thousand troops in support of the anti-Bolshevik government in the north. General Denikin heard from your father's officers who escaped and were interned in Sweden that you might still be hiding at your dacha. It wasn't greatly out of the way.'

'Then there is full-scale civil war?'

'Yes. General Denikin only awaits Allied reinforcements and supplies to mount an offensive.'

'Is there hope of the Bolsheviks' overthrow?' My leaden spirits lightened a little.

'There is hope, Princess. We cling to that hope.'

More war, I thought, more hatred, more horror. And what could come of it but horror and hatred tenfold? Yet the human spirit would not be quelled. The Communists had underestimated its force. 'We must hope!' I echoed. 'We have no choice. Have you, by chance, heard anything about General Maysky, my father's chief of staff?'

'Nothing, Princess, I'm sorry.'

'And the Great War? Is it over yet?'

'Not since I last heard. But the Central Powers are near collapse. It's a matter of a few months, perhaps weeks.'

He agreed to remain at the dacha until I could remove his stitches.

During Baron Niessen's stay, Fyodor took the White officer's boat on mysterious night expeditions, from which he brought rifles, cartridge belts, tins of meat, biscuits and several Red Army uniforms, overcoats and boots. The laconic giant did not say how he obtained this loot, but clearly it was without qualms. To Fyodor, Reds were as fair game as rabbit or polecat.

During Fyodor's absence, Baron Niessen stood watch. He helped us move from the unheatable cellar of the main villa to the gamekeeper's deserted cottage in the nearby wood, where Father had begun his ill-fated affair with Diana.

His presence had a more crucial function. It helped stabilize my still shaky mental state and strengthened my will to live. If it was still unbearable to talk about Father, I found it a relief while we worked to be able to talk about my namesake to someone who had known her relatively well. In bittersweet sorrow, I listened to Niessen's innocuous anecdotes of pre-war life on the *Standard* – the dances and games on board, the picnics ashore under the pines, the receptions for visitors of state. That life of royal pomp, privilege and propriety so appropriate to the Edwardian era would look like a puppet play, I thought, to those who survived the Great War. And so it would to me, had I not known the flesh-and-blood actors intimately.

'If it's too painful,' I said to my companion during a pause as we fetched another load, 'you needn't go on, Baron.'

'No, on the contrary, it makes it easier. I've been obsessed by the memory of that bloody cellar in Ekaterinburg. I'd rather envision the girls in their white hats and dresses, skipping and twirling on deck, with smiling faces and long hair flying.'

'Tatyana Nikolayevna was the best dancer.' I held back tears.

'Yes, and Marie the worst. Luckily, Tatyana Nikolayevna usually chose me for her partner.'

'Did you . . . were you a little bit in love with her?' I hazarded. I would have liked to endow her memory with one anonymous passion.

'I? Not in the least. For all their simplicity, the Grand Duchesses were inaccessible. They were a precious symbol, no more. As a symbol, one could love and honour our sovereign and his children. As people, they were attractive and appealing, but nothing out of the ordinary. You, Tatyana Petrovna, on the other hand, are of another mould. There isn't your like, I believe, in all the world.' He stopped to regard me over the box he carried.

Exaltation lent new distinction to the pale, conventionally pleasing face under the bandage. Was Niessen falling in love? Or was it simply a natural arousal caused by his proximity to a young woman on this deserted shore?

'I'm glad, Baron.' I was determined not to encourage him. 'There is still someone to whom our sovereign and his children are precious. In Petrograd, since the Revolution, I'd met only bitterness and resentment towards Their Majesties.'

'It was understandable. But that will pass, now that they're dead. And the more the Bolsheviks show their true colours, the better the Tsar's rule will look in comparison.'

'Can the Bolsheviks get any worse?'

'The Red terror didn't begin in earnest till you fled Petrograd, Tatyana Petrovna. Since Uritsky, the chief of the Petrograd Cheka, was assassinated, and Lenin himself wounded in an assassination attempt this past summer, executions have been wholesale.'

'Lenin wounded? By a White?'

'No, a Social Revolutionary, a young woman. The Communist dictatorship is hateful to a large segment of the Left. The Bolsheviks are beset on every side.'

'That's good for our cause!'

'It ought to be. But our cause has its own dissensions and chaos to deal with. One positive aspect is that the Bolsheviks' disarray has enabled you to survive undetected within thirty *versts* of Petrograd.'

'They must think I escaped with Father's officers after the prison break.' I evaded my companion's intense look. 'In any case, who would dream I would be hiding on my own dacha?'

Niessen gave a short laugh. 'That does take nerve. True,' he reflected, 'the suburban trains no longer run, the factories to the north have closed, the villages and summer cottages have been deserted. Still, Tatyana Petrovna, don't count on being safe. The Bolsheviks, if they hang on, are going to hunt out and eradicate every one of their class enemies.' He set down his load inside the cottage. 'They must not find you, Tatyana Petrovna. You ... you *must* survive.'

'I intend to.'

He offered to arrange my escape but I said, 'Only get word to Stefan Veslawski, my cousin, who is like a brother to me. His family is extremely influential both in Great Britain and France. He'll have greater means at his disposal for our rescue than you.'

'I'll do whatever you ask.'

This promise Niessen reiterated when he left at the end of ten days, after I had removed his stitches.

28

Our visitor gone, my old nurse, my middle-aged footman and I waited on the deserted shore for word from Stefan. The nearness of Father's grave, at which I prayed every day, was comforting and drew me to this spot. I thought it fitting that he should lie buried where Mother, whom he had so adored, had died. I felt close to them both and loved them in death as I hadn't in life, with a pure filial love free from selfish need and jealousy.

As snow fell, the woods were beautiful and still. Wearing a Red Army overcoat, a sheepskin bonnet and lined boots with several pairs of wool socks, rifle slung over my shoulder like a guerrilla partisan, I tramped about checking the traps Fyodor set out; game was the mainstay of our diet.

Once, Fyodor returned from one of his mysterious night expeditions with a bag of badly threshed buckwheat. The gruel we made, after grinding it in a homemade press, tasted heavenly, though it pricked the tongue and left sores in my mouth. We had plenty of firewood to keep the tile stove in the central room of the gamekeeper's cottage going by day. At night we slept fully dressed on the benches, Fyodor and I sharing the watch.

As the cold deepened, again I suffered from chilblains on my hands and feet. I grew numb, in mind as well as body, and this state was not entirely unpleasant. My torment over Father's agony at Kronstadt, my shock at the murder of the Tsar's family, these had given way to a feeling akin to homesickness – sad and gnawing, but not unbearable.

A veil lay over my life since the Revolution, which made me see it as if from afar, without emotion. My relationship with Alexis, so vivid and necessary at the time, was as hazy as the rest. I rejected Nyanya's suggestion that we turn to him for help.

'We haven't the right to endanger a stranger,' I said.

She looked at me oddly, and did not bring Alexis up again.

In this condition, instead of making plans, I dwelt in romantic daydreams, reliving my love in all its exquisite misery, imagining passionate embraces and caresses.

The most common daydream was this: some morning, when I lay weak from cold and hunger on my bench, a deep and resonant voice would ring out through the cottage and Stevie would bend over me his full rosy cheeks, his dear funny monkey ears fiery red from the cold, and his amber eyes as adoring and good as my absent setter's. Then he would lift me, wrapped in a sable cloak, and off we would fly to safety in a swift troika.

This fantasy came to acquire reality, and when, in November, the bay froze, making it possible to cross on foot, I said to myself, Why should I seek help in Petrograd? *He'll* come soon enough and rescue us. It was our childhood pact, it was his promise to me before we parted. If he does not come, it's because he is dead. And if Stevie's dead, then there's no point in going anywhere, no point in anything any more.

I did not voice my thoughts to Nyanya for fear of a frightful scolding. But the wise old woman, seeing that I took no action, grew cranky and complained of toothache. I applied hot compresses, fed her aspirin, and at last I said, 'It must be an abscess in the root. We must get you to a dentist.'

'Why worry about my tooth,' said Nyanya, 'when you're prepared to let us perish in this freezing wilderness? Death will soon put an end to my terrible pain.'

'Don't say that, Nyanichka darling! We'll find a dentist for you. We'll get false papers and escape.'

I thought I could obtain the papers from my former Jewish contacts. To this end, Nyanya wanted to send me to Petrograd with Fyodor. I wanted to go alone; Fyodor did not want to stay. Nyanya held a private conference with him, and in the end we decided to go all three.

Accordingly, in the morning of the next day, we started out by the shortest and safest route, across the ice. It was pitch-black and snowing. Nyanya was bundled in a coat fashioned out of a quilt, and held a wool blanket over her head and shoulders. I wore a Red Army overcoat, a Scotch plaid carriage shawl on my head, and mittens made out of a quilt. If we were stopped, I was to pass as Nyanya's daughter, Tamara Yegorovna from Pskov province, fleeing the rigours of German occupation and come to Petrograd to look for my father, a machinist in the former Putilov works. Fyodor was to keep at a distance from us and be deaf and dumb.

With the aid of a compass found in the boathouse, we headed south-east for Vassily Island, where I planned to look up the kind people who had helped me escape to the dacha. Walking was slow in the snow, in the dark. The former passage to the north shore was no longer cleared and snowdrifts delayed our progress. Nyanya had to stop frequently to rest. At last Fyodor carried her, only setting her down when we came, some four or five hours later, to the wooded deserted west end of the island. Here we met woodcutters with a sledge and pretended to be gathering firewood also. Our strange attire attracted little notice. Women commonly wore men's clothing in the new Communist equality of the sexes and everyone wore whatever could be found.

At the house with the garden on Maly Prospekt, the picket fence and wooden porches had been torn down for firewood. There was no one there. When I went to a neighbour's back door to inquire about my former acquaintances, an old woman said hurriedly, 'Don't know, don't know,' and slammed the door in my face.

Nyanya suggested we look up Professor Holveg. When I again refused to endanger him, she motioned to Fyodor, who waited across the street, to go on ahead. We had agreed earlier, should this first stop be fruitless, to head separately for the ragpickers' market, where Fyodor would await us while I looked up my contacts nearby.

We started south, Nyanya and I, along one of the numbered avenues that crossed the wide *prospekts*. The once-bustling academic and commercial quarter was empty and desolate. Streetlamps were not lit – electricity was cut off for most of the day for lack of coal. The sidewalk, uncleared of snow, was littered with refuse. A rare army lorry or official motorcar drove by. In the arcaded entranceways, women in shawls rummaged in trashbins. Passing a bakery queue, I stopped instinctively over a prostrate woman and saw she was a corpse.

'How can you . . . why doesn't someone take her away?' I said to the women standing so indifferently about the dead one.

'It happens every day, what's there to look at? Where is it you come from, my girl, that such sights surprise you?'

'From my village in Pskov province,' I said and quickly walked past the line of staring shoppers.

'One would say *you're* fresh from the village the way you gawk,' Nyanya threw at the curious, and, to me, once out of their hearing, 'You had better not talk to anyone, my soul. You look little enough like a peasant girl with your fine face, but once you open your mouth, you wouldn't fool the village idiot.'

I drew my shawl over the lower part of my face, keeping my eyes low and seeing only the snowy sidewalk.

As we started up the incline of the Nikolayevsky Bridge, Nyanya suddenly exclaimed, 'Look, look, my love, it's he, the Professor, God be praised!'

The small gentleman in a fur-lined overcoat and astrakhan cap slowed down at this very moment and looked over his shoulder. He stopped for me to catch up on my tired legs. I put out my hand. 'Have you a *kopeyka* for Tamara Yegorovna from Pskov province, kind sir?'

His black eyes flashed behind his steel spectacles, his little beard quivered so that the snowflakes on its tip were shaken off. 'Tatya ... Tamara ... I could hardly believe it when your footman told me, but it is you!'

'Fyodor!' I looked at Nyanya reproachfully as we walked on. 'It was not I who sent him after you, Alexis. But I am awfully glad to see you!' The old impression of familiarity and fondness, amusement and admiration, which our meetings had always evoked, returned with a vivid pang. But the recollections it brought up were painful, and I gratefully let the veil of distance and indifference slide back over them.

'I'm happy to see you also, Tatya ... Tamara, even under such unhappy circumstances. May I ask what you're doing in Petrograd?'

'I'm on the way to get papers, from those Jews we used to know by the Moscow Gate. We've been hiding on our summer dacha ... it's such a long way ... Nyanya's tired ... I don't see how we'll manage.' I looked at the scientist in dismay.

'Whatever we decide, we can't stay here.' He took my arm.

I had stopped by the chapel of St Nicholas, guardian of the bridge. On my left I could see the low walls of Petropavlovsk Fortress with the angel on its golden spire soaring into the sombre sky. To the right, imperial palaces and aristocratic residences lined the granite quays.

A leaden desolation seized me at the sight of the stately colonnade of my former home, the snowcapped row of Grecian statuary along the roof. I stared at the third-storey windows of my rooms. 'Is anyone living there now?'

'It is now a Soviet housing commission, Tatya . . . We must move on. I know an illegal tearoom near my flat where one can eat without food cards. A bowl of hot soup will do you good.'

I continued to gaze before me motionless, now in the direction of the Winter Palace, where, as a child, I had been taken to dancing lessons every Saturday. 'Alexis, is it true, what I heard happened at Ekaterinburg?'

'I'm afraid it's true, Tatya . . . Tamara.'

'Why did they have to kill Anastasia and Aleksey? He was not quite fourteen.'

'He was the rightful heir to the throne.'

'The Tsar had named his brother, Mikhail Alexandrovich, to succeed him.'

'Grand Duke Michael was also shot, even earlier at Perm, in the Urals. His English secretary was killed with him.'

'And your pupils, Costia and Igor Constantinovich?' I persisted in hearing the full litany of horrors.

'The Princes Ioann, Igor and Constantine, together with the Empress's sister, Grand Duchess Elizabeth, Grand Duke Sergey Mikhailovich, and the son of Grand Duke Paul, Vladimir Paley, were put to death by the Bolsheviks at Alapayevsk, near Ekaterinburg, shortly after the Tsar and his family, in an even more horrible manner. They were thrown down a mineshaft and stoned, then left to die of hunger and their wounds.'

Beautiful Elizaveta Fyodorovna, the nun, whom I so admired, bold and gay Igor Constantinovich, my childhood playmate and intended – all those people whose lives had been so intimately bound with mine were gone, after suffering indignity and torture. And how was it I had been spared?

I voiced my revulsion at all I saw and heard. 'I have no right to be alive.'

'That remark is unworthy of an intelligent person, Tatya . . .' the scientist said crossly. 'Now come!'

He pulled my arm but I resisted, my eyes still fastened on the façade of my house. I noticed then three officers heading in our direction along the bridge. The two on the outside wore peaked, medieval-looking hoods with the red star, emblem of the Red Army. The one in the middle wore a particularly high sheepskin cap. They stopped alongside us. One of the taller officers said to the Professor respectfully, 'Is that woman bothering you, Comrade Commissar?'

'She's not bothering me. I like her, do you understand?' Alexis replied.

'We understand.' The Red Army officer winked broadly and would have gone on, when his short swaybacked companion in the tall fur cap suddenly exclaimed, 'I know that girl! She's the ex-Princess Tatyana Silomirskaya!'

'Lord God of mine, the things people will think up, my Tamara a princess! Why, we've just come from Pskov province.' Nyanya gave out our story in a spate. 'This kind sir took pity on us, strangers in the big city. Times were a mother wouldn't let her daughter talk to a stranger, but what's one to do now?'

'She's no Tamara from Pskov and you're not her mother,' the short officer jeered. 'I know who she is all right. You don't fool me for a minute, old woman.'

I knew who he was, too, that former corporal of our guards. Faint with fear, I pulled the shawl over my face.

My accuser turned to his companions, but they avoided looking at me. 'Ah what's it to us who she is? We're not chekists! The devil take her!' they said and pulled their comrade along.

We watched them argue and separate. The Red officer who had recognized me retraced his steps across the bridge in the direction of Cheka headquarters. In the meantime, Fyodor had come into sight, on the sidewalk opposite. At a sign from Nyanya, he crossed over to us.

She pointed to the informer. 'He has gone to denounce the Princess. We'll wait for you behind the empty house on Maly Prospekt where we stopped earlier today.'

Fyodor started out after the informer, like a giant after Tom Thumb.

Alexis took us to a nearby house where a faculty wife ran an illegal tearoom for students and professors. He introduced us as out-of-town relatives and took us up wooden back stairs to a cold room full of shabby scholars in hats and overcoats. We were given a table by the wall and served weak tea without sugar, a herring, and a hard slice of black bread. Nyanya fell to ravenously, dipping her bread in the tea and sucking on it with relish – her supposed toothache had vanished at the appearance of Alexis. I almost broke a tooth on the hard crust and put it down, feeling like a child forbidden to touch cake.

Alexis broke the bread, put a piece in a spoon, dipped it, and handed it to me.

'Under the circumstances, Tatyana Petrovna, it's permissible.' He smiled his never-more-startling youthful and agreeable smile.

The waves of fear, loathing and desolation that had assailed me on the Nikolayevsky Bridge had passed, leaving me as limp emotionally as I was physically, and glad to be taken in hand. I pushed the shawl off my face, enjoying the warmth of the tea, and smiled back. 'You don't know how wonderful it is to talk freely again, Alexis. Tell me how you've managed since I last saw you.'

'Later. Tell me about yourself first. We're safe here,' he added as I looked around. And, as I was silent, '*Pravda* reported your father's execution,' he continued. 'The prison riot and break at Kronstadt on the same day was hushed up, although it was common knowledge here in Petrograd. A manhunt went on for days, but I was confident you had escaped abroad. Why didn't you?'

'We were trapped at the dacha, after we buried Father.' I spoke with reluctance. My head was beginning to throb.

'And you remained there all this time? It's beyond belief! Why didn't you try to reach me? I still have those false papers I obtained for you and Nyanya as my wife and mother-in-law.'

'It all seemed so long ago. I was well at the dacha, I was near Father.'

'Tatyana Petrovna, your attachment to your father while he lived was touching and admirable, but after his death! It's abnormal!'

I looked at Alexis. I no longer felt so close to him. I wondered what I was doing here, in this strange place. I wanted to be back at the dacha, tramping the white woods, weaving my romantic fantasies.

'Tatyana Petrovna.' He seared me with his gaze. 'You have been ill.'

'I had a concussion from a rifle blow. I was amnesic for nearly three months. I'm quite normal now,' I said.

Was it not normal to be indifferent to all but physical sensation to find consolation in daydreams? Did not most people live that way, half asleep, and was not Alexis, with his intensity, his ever-active intelligence, his undaunted curiosity, the exception?

'No, Tatyana Petrovna' – he shook his head – 'you're not yourself. Small wonder!' He reached hesitantly for my hand, then held it firmly as I did not withdraw it. 'When I think of what you've gone through in this past year! But you'll recover. You'll start life anew, away from this charnel house that Russia has become. Now, for our escape –'

'Alexis, wait.' I was still loath to tell him about Stefan. 'First tell me how you are doing.'

'You can't imagine how low we've fallen at the university. Cold, hunger, typhus and the Cheka, that's what Russia's best brains are thinking of these days. I live in my overcoat. I have no electricity in my flat. I found some kerosene to light a lamp in my laboratory, and we somehow keep our research going, my graduate students and I. Since Poland became free, I've been waiting for the end of the semester to cross over, with or without permission. I have a false passport ready for the second eventuality.'

'Poland is free! Then the war is over at last?' Stevie was safe, Stevie was on his way!

'Yes, the armistice was signed on 11 November 1918, more than six weeks ago. Tatyana Petrovna' – he took my hand in both of his – 'I must insist that you consider your present danger. I am ready to leave. I only need a few days to make final arrangements.'

'It's so kind of you, Alexis, but there's no need for you to take such risks. We're quite safe at the dacha. We'll wait.'

'Wait for what, Tatyana Petrovna?'

'For my cousin, Prince Veslawski, to come for us. You see,' I continued as Alexis looked amazed, 'we were raised like brother and sister, and we made a pact when we were children that we would come to each other's aid, wherever we were. I know Stefan will keep it.' I found myself unable to say more.

'Tatyana Petrovna, you're even more naïve than I thought! You've no conception of practical matters – it's a miracle you've survived this long! How could your cousin come for you, all the way from France?'

'Baron Niessen came all the way from Siberia to bring me a last letter from Tatyana Nikolayevna. There is an underground network. There are anti-Bolshevik forces in the north and in the south.'

'There are anti-Bolshevik forces in Estonia, too, Whites fighting by the side of the Estonians for that country's independence. But unless you have the money and the contacts, there's no getting through the lines. Supposing your cousin managed to find you, how would he get you out?'

'Across the border to Finland.'

'The Finns have closed the border to refugees since their civil war ended in the spring. They want nothing to do with Russians, Red or White.'

'Then we'll cross into Estonia. You don't know Stevie ... my cousin Stefan. Nothing's impossible for him.'

'Tatyana Petrovna, I'm afraid it is,' said Alexis gravely. 'I hope this news won't be too much of a shock on top of everything else, but, for your survival's sake, I feel I must tell you the truth: Stefan Veslawski is dead.'

'Stefan? Dead? I don't believe it!'

'I saw it in the newspapers just before the end of hostilities. He was killed in the Argonne offensive at the end of September.'

'Killed!' I echoed.

Lord Beresford had been killed, millions of splendid young men had been killed, and why not Stevie? He was no more immortal than Father, than the Tsar. That I had survived was the miracle, as Alexis said. Only it was no miracle. It was a mistake.

Again I felt detestation and revulsion towards all I saw and heard, and above all towards myself. I turned hot, then cold. A deep torpor enveloped me.

When it lifted, I was no longer sitting at a table but lying on a bed in quite a different room. The proprietress of the tearoom held smelling salts to my nose. I understood I had fainted, a common enough occurrence these days.

Alexis now bent over me. He lifted my head and held a thimble of vodka to my lips. His face was no longer familiar and dear. A bit more of this, and he would turn into Bedlov the Seal.

I set my teeth and pushed his hand away. 'Alexis, look after Nyanya and Fyodor. Let the Reds find me here. Save yourself.'

'Tatyana Petrovna, you know I have very little patience with the

Slav spirit of martyrdom. You must make an effort! Have a drop of vodka.'

'Leave me be,' I said with exasperation.

Alexis jumped off the bed and muttered as he paced, tugging at his goatee, 'What a stupid situation! How can a supposedly intelligent man find himself in such a stupid situation!'

It was Nyanya's turn to scold to no avail.

At last the proprietress said that if the Communists found someone without papers in her flat she was done for.

At once I got up and apologized for causing her inconvenience. Alexis saw us down to the street.

'I have nowhere to hide you. Wait for me at the dacha,' he said to Nyanya. 'I'll come and fetch you as soon as I can. Look after your mistress.'

'The Lord answered my prayers and sent Your Honour. We'll wait.' Nyanya blessed him.

Fyodor awaited us at the appointed place. 'That little Red devil ... there won't be another peep out of him,' he reported laconically.

We retraced our route of the morning across the ice, but when we had gone halfway I stopped and said to Fyodor, 'Carry Nyanya back to the dacha. Wait for the Professor. Leave me here. Did you hear? Go on, both of you.'

My old nurse began to mutter furiously. I sank down on to a snowdrift. I was eager to be left alone, all alone, for good.

Fyodor picked me up. 'When Your Highness was a little girl and wouldn't come when she was called, it was Fyodor who carried you in.'

'Fyodor, how dare you! Put me down this minute! Fyodor, *please*, I'll walk. Carry Nyanya instead. Fyo – dor!' In vain, I wriggled and beat my fists on his huge chest.

He walked on impassive, carrying me with ease and waiting from time to time for my old nurse to catch up. I ceased my struggle at last, laid my head against his chest, and closed my eyes. Dozing off, I fancied it was Stevie's chest I lay against, that he had come for me as I knew he would, that he was carrying me to his swift sledge. But when I awakened as we stepped ashore and felt my footman's shaggy, snow-flecked beard tickling my forehead, I thought, No, Stevie did not come for me, Stevie could not come because, because he's dead. He was killed, my brother, he is dead, my Stevie monkey ears, my warrior-prince, my lord. Papa is dead, Tanik is dead, Aleksey the Tsarevich is dead, Prince Igor is dead, they are all dead, all. I could live on without them but without Stevie I cannot live, I *will* not live. It's too boring and repulsive, this world of the dead. I can't bear to look on it any more.

The gamekeeper's cottage was dark and freezing when we returned. Fyodor fired the stove. Nyanya got me into bed on my bench, piling on rugs and blankets, for I shivered so hard that my teeth chattered. She could not get me to eat or drink. I was deaf to her rebukes and exhortations.

I had turned my face to the wall in the expectation of death.

Outside, wolves howled, a blizzard raged along the banks of the frozen estuary. In the gamekeeper's cottage where, once upon a time, gypsies had entertained Father's foreign guests, there was no sign of life. Exhausted from the day's excursion, Nyanya snored with open mouth. Fyodor, who had strangled a man a few hours before, slept with placid countenance by the door, rifle at his cheek. Only I did not sleep. I lay in a frozen stupor, and when the quilt slipped off me I made no move to cover myself. Instead, I welcomed the cold's embrace.

Towards morning, I felt a stabbing pain in my chest and a violent chill. When Nyanya awoke later than usual and found me shivering under a single blanket, she let out a cry and stoked the embers in the stove. By evening I was delirious and sucked greedily at the icicles she put to my cracked lips.

Nyanya spent the night sitting up beside me, with the stove burning in spite of the danger of detection. At dawn she sent Fyodor after Professor Holveg. He was back at nightfall with Alexis and a horse and sledge.

Alexis helped Nyanya dress me in the woollen clothes he had brought and made me swallow a sleeping powder with aspirin in hot tea. I took him for Dr Botkin, the murdered court physician, and meekly allowed him to handle me. Fyodor then carried me out through the wood to the long, broad sledge with a curved yoke standing in the driveway before the villa's pillared portico. Icicles hung from the horse's shaggy belly and long fetlocks. The coachman's eyebrows and moustache were hoary with frost. Fyodor laid me on the straw-covered floor of the sledge and Nyanya lay down beside me, pulling a bearskin over us both.

What followed I observed without comprehension or reaction, or it never could have happened.

Alexis handed Fyodor a packet of roubles and an envelope. 'Here is a letter of recommendation to a friend of mine.' He gave him the name and address. 'He'll find you work and get you identification papers. You'll be safe with him. Goodbye.'

Fyodor fingered the money and envelope wonderingly.

'Put it away before you lose it,' said Alexis irritably, and, holding his overcoat, prepared to climb into the sledge.

'Your Honour' – Fyodor understood at last what I did not – 'take me with you. I can carry Her Highness. I can drive horses and an automobile too. I can hunt. I am strong. You can find use for me. Let me go with Tatyana Petrovna for God's sake!'

'I haven't papers for you. You're too big, too well known. You'd give the Princess away. I'm sorry, I'm terribly sorry, but it's impossible.'

The face of the giant, which could so admirably express nothing, now expressed absolute desperation.

'You, Pelageya, speak to His Honour,' he addressed my old nurse, who watched him, sitting up, out of wise dark eyes.

'Couldn't we take him?' she ventured.

Alexis cut her short. 'Impossible, altogether impossible.'

Fyodor went over to my side of the sledge. 'Tatyana Petrovna, have mercy! I carried you in my arms when you were a little girl. I played the balalaika for you when you cried. You wouldn't leave your Fyodor behind, would you? Tell His Honour, for God's sake!'

No, I would not leave my Fyodor behind, not for anything or anyone in the world. But I did not know I was being taken away.

'I'm thirsty, cold, it's hard to breathe!' I thrashed and tried to push an oppressive weight off my chest. And in the childlike face with snowy whiskers and beard, I saw not Fyodor but Bedlov the Seal. I averted my eyes in terror, and Nyanya, crooning, covered me to the chin. Then the old woman rested on Fyodor those eyes, so very Russian, which could comprehend and accept every horror, injustice, baseness and sorrow.

'The Lord keep and have mercy on you, my poor friend,' she said rapidly as she made the sign of the cross over him. Then she threw herself down under the bearskin rug beside me.

Alexis was already settled in the sledge.

'Well then, are we ready?' he shrilled at the coachman from the narrow seat in which he sat like a furious, furry ball, a knitted scarf wrapped about his face, his fur-lined cap pulled down to his eyebrows.

The coachman turned his padded bulk towards his passenger and blew a white cloud from his bearded mouth. 'Your Honour had best lie down too. The wind cuts.'

'Don't worry about it. Drive on.'

The coachman shook the reins and chirruped to his little dove. The shaggy horse broke into a shuffling trot and the runners squeaked on the fresh snow as the sledge slid down the slope of the elevation on which the villa stood and on to the ice of Kronstadt Bay, heading for the opposite shore.

How many times since have I pictured that night of my flight from Petrograd, when I left behind not only the grave of my father and the place of my birth but a living man whose fate has haunted me since.

I see the scene still. It is dark, cold and snowing. On the wooded shore of a frozen bay where once the sound of gypsy singing, of balalaika and accordion was heard, hungry wolves prowl. In front of a white villa with colonnaded galleries and a high campanile, in the middle of an empty driveway stands a bearded giant of a man. An envelope has fallen from one hand and paper roubles spill out of the other, eddying and whirling like flakes of the slowly falling snow.

And from this spot there arises a howl that I, in my delirium, clearly heard: the howl, not of a hungry wolf but of a man, a man of the people, abandoned, like all his people, and betrayed.

PART FOUR

THE PATH OF NO RETURN

1919–1922

29

Of my three-month journey from the northern to the southern shore of western Russia, I retained the impression of different kinds of painful motion and of a succession of ceilings and skies.

Night and day, sleeping and waking, reality and fantasy blended into one another. I knew I was delirious. But delirium, I felt, only sharpened my mental powers, even as it heightened my physical perceptions. And though I had no precise knowledge of time or place, my very being perceived the chaotic and satanic nature of the time and of the place.

Eventually, I perceived that I was stationary, that the lofty ceiling was beautifully painted, and an odour of jasmine and lilac came from an open air window.

My journey is ended, I thought. I have crossed the most fearful places, I have gone through fire, ice and suffocation, and now I'm to be well at last. I have come from the northern wastes to the Garden of Perpetual Spring where all are children again.

Tanik and her sisters awaited me there in white middy dresses and straw hats. Aleksey leaped from rock to rock. Igor Constantinovich with his brothers followed their leader, Sir Lieutenant Stevie-levie monkey ears. 'Come on, Tanya, this way!' he called joyously. But the way to the Garden eluded me. I opened my eyes and saw instead a nurse in a white veil.

She turned to the doctor. 'The Princess is awake.'

'Tatyana Petrovna, you have a visitor,' he said. Then, in French, to a small and slim older lady all in black, who held herself like a tall and imposing person. 'Only a moment, Madame, please.'

'Tata, do you know me?' the lady asked in English, laying a hand on my cheek.

'Your Imperial Majesty.' I kissed the small hand.

It accepted the homage, then laid itself again on my cheek.

'How changed she is!' Marie Fyodorovna spoke in her slow, attractively slurred speech. 'Tata dear, I know you're tired after your long journey and I must let you rest, but tell me ... have you heard from Tatyana?'

'Yes, I've heard from Tatyana Nikolayevna, Your Majesty.'

'Have you really? Where is she?'

'She's in a lovely place, Your Majesty ...'

'A lovely place!' The voice quickened. 'What sort of place?'

I wanted to describe the Garden but could not find the words. Tears rolled down my cheeks, startling the little hand.

'The Princess is delirious, Madame,' the doctor said.

'Yes, so I see.' The Dowager Empress stroked my face and hair. 'My grand-daughter always corresponded with her. I had hoped she might have a letter.'

'I have a letter, Your Majesty.' I put my hand to my breast. 'Where is it? Who took it? I want it back!'

The nurse at once handed me the leather pouch containing the last letters from Father, from Stefan and from my namesake, which had been taken off my neck.

'May I see the letter?' Marie Fyodorovna's little hand reached for it.

'It is for me alone, Your Majesty.' I held the pouch to my breast. Tanik would never have forgiven me for showing her grandmother such a letter. 'We *never* show one another's letters.'

The little hand betrayed impatience but restrained itself. 'Yes, of course, that's quite right. But you do have a letter! Tatyana *is* alive. I've never believed these ... these rumours. Get well quickly, Tata dear. I'll come and see you again when you're better.' The hand caressed my cheek and was gone.

I tried to find my way back to the Garden. But it was still so far, so high, and I was short of breath ...

Faces materialize out of the haze: the doctor's, the nurse's, Nyanya's. Alexis, holding his little beard, stands at the foot of the bed.

'After all that Tatyana Petrovna has survived, bitter cold, primitive conditions, danger!' His voice rings with angry precision. 'How can she die now?'

And the doctor replies, 'We often see patients with pneumonia who survive the winter only to succumb in spring. Tatyana Petrovna has an iron constitution, like all the Silomirskys. But, in this case, there is a psychological factor . . . The patient has no will to live.'

Now the smell of incense mingles with the scent of lilac and jasmine, and I hear a priest praying to the Lord in a deep monotone to save and have mercy on the sinner Tatyana Petrovna – the Serene Princess beloved of all Russia – save and have mercy, Lord, on her soul.

So I *am* dead, I think, and see myself lying on my bier dressed in white like a bride, tall candles about me and lilies at my head. I feel no sorrow but only haste to set out for the Garden. Instead, I wander in a grey void without end.

'Speak to me, Lord,' I cry, 'show me the way!'

There is no answer.

'Is this what I am condemned to? Better to go through fire, ice and suffocation than be cast out into the void!'

I was lying in bed. The priest had gone. Only the odour of incense still lingered. Instead of a solemn chant, I heard a dog whimpering close by. Without opening my eyes, I felt along the silk coverlet until my hand rested on a no less silky, but living surface. It was warm, it was loving. The whimpering became a joyful squeal. My hand was nudged, then licked. Bobby! I thought.

And as hard as I had wished to die, I began to wish to live. I wished with all my might. I fought for every rasping breath. At long last, exhausted by my struggle, I fell into a profound and dreamless sleep.

I awakened bathed in sweat. I felt a delicious sleepy languor. 'Nyanya,' I said, 'I want my chocolate in bed.'

Instead of scolding me for such lazy habits, Nyanya beamed. 'Right away, my love, right away.' She spoke to the sister on duty, then fell to kissing my face, shoulders, and hands. 'Glory to You, Lord, you have come back to us, my love! We said farewell to you last night. The priest gave you the sacraments and all the churches in Yalta held services for you. The Lord heard our prayers!' She crossed herself fervently.

Shortly after, as I lay in a fresh gown in a freshly made bed, sipping delicious hot chocolate from a spoon, I looked at the sunlight streaming into the French window open on a balcony and said, 'Nyanya, I feel I'm at Alubek, by the Black Sea.'

'You are, my love, you are.'

'Then Bobby was really in my room?'

'He would not be kept out, old and weak as he is, and the doctor said it did not matter in any case – you would not survive the night.'

'Let him in again.'

'He is covered with sores. He sheds and he smells . . .'

'He is alive. He is warm and loving. Let him in!' I was Princess Silomirskaya once more and mistress in my own house.

Nyanya relayed my wish, then returned to the bedside. 'They have gone to Vera Kirilovna's apartment to fetch Bobby. Her Ladyship is sleeping after praying for you late last night.'

'Vera Kirilovna, of course.' The name conjured up the pre-revolutionary past, as well as its violent ending. 'We're safe from the Bolshevik?'

'We are, praise God!' Nyanya did not add for how long.

I looked down on myself next and missed the tresses to my waist.

Nyanya expressed the popular belief. 'We cut your hair, my love, because it was too hard to take care of and took your strength.'

'But Stefan likes it long –' I broke off as I remembered the impossible: Stefan was no more.

Nyanya looked at me with those dark eyes, so very Russian, which saw and accepted the human condition.

My delicious languor upon awakening to life had vanished. It's a dull, grey, boring, and repulsive world I have come back to, I thought, but it's still better than nothingness.

'I'm glad you cut my hair,' I said. 'I'll always keep it short, in memory of *him*. And in memory of the Grand Duchess Tatyana Nikolayevna, I make a vow never to wear jewels again.'

'With eyes like yours you need no jewels,' Nyanya said and gave her place to the doctor, who pronounced me out of danger. In a few weeks, he assured me, with proper food and care, I should be completely well.

Then Bobby was brought at last. My once-sleek and bounding setter waddled up to the bed and put one paw on the cover. Half blind and mangy old dog that he had become, he was still a finer and more welcome sight than the beautiful phantoms of my unattainable Garden of Paradise!

'*Chère, chère enfant*, you have been returned to us. It's a miracle!'

Vera Kirilovna laid her rosy cheek against mine and settled by the bedside her scented, hennaed and manicured person. 'Her Imperial Majesty has been so concerned. She came over from Livadia at once. You were still delirious.'

'I remember. Marie Fyodorovna asked to see the letter I received from . . . from Ekaterinburg.'

Vera Kirilovna assumed an air both mournful and reverent. 'Her Majesty refuses to believe in the massacre. She is indomitable. Under the Bolsheviks, when she was under house arrest, she was an example to us all. It's shameful to admit, but after four months of Red terror we welcomed the Germans as saviours! I must say, they behaved decently.'

'Have you heard from Marie Pavlovna?' I wondered if my godmother, the best of the dynasty, had survived.

'Her Imperial Highness, with her sons Boris and Andrey Vladimirovich, were last known to be hiding in the Caucasus. They escaped the Bolsheviks just in time. The region around Kislovodsk was the scene of atrocities surpassed only by the sailors of the Black Sea Fleet in our own Crimean ports. I'll spare you the details . . .' Vera Kirilovna's measured society voice quivered.

'Please.' Red sailors made me think of Father at Kronstadt. Controlling myself in turn, I said, 'I pray Marie Pavlovna is safe. Poor Toby, though.' It was unlikely that Grandmaman's poodle had survived. 'Bobby at least has lived out his life in comfort.' I stroked the old setter, who sat up on hearing his name. 'Thanks to you, Vera Kirilovna.'

'Dear child, it was a pleasure to care for him.' No task was too onerous for the last of the Silomirskys, her expression said.

I accepted the unspoken homage with amused irony. Weak and ill as I was, I indulged the forgotten luxury of royal treatment, though I would not take it seriously. I knew it could not last!

'How did you and Zinaida Mikhailovna manage under the Bolsheviks?' I asked.

'Quite well, actually, thanks to Kolenka. He appointed himself my jailer and assured the Bolsheviks that I was properly mistreated. He organized our servants into a soviet, and they kept us fed and cared for. Fortunately, they are Moslem and immune to Bolshevik propaganda. He's a clever rogue, Kolenka.'

'Yes. I must thank him. Were you able to keep the hospital pavilion open and our war wounded cared for?'

'We were, by taking German wounded in exchange for supplies. Poor young men! Some of them would be better off dead.' Vera Kirilovna laid her plump hand over my emaciated one and observed a compassionate silence.

I understood it to refer to Stefan. 'Perhaps *he* is better off dead,' I said. 'He was so afraid of being a cripple.'

'It was a terrible thing, terrible. The Prince was so young, only twenty-four, already a full major and a hero, and such an attractive, such an interesting young man! And to think that he was here, in this very house, only three months ago. Destiny is cruel!'

'Three months ago?' I seized the Countess's hands. 'Vera Kirilovna, what are you saying?'

'He came here looking for you. I saw him myself.'

'Then, he is alive, his death was a false report! Where is he now?'

'My poor child, I did not mean to arouse false hopes. Professor Holveg asked me not to mention it for the present; news of your cousin's purported death had upset you greatly in Petrograd. He'll be furious at me. He doesn't like me very well, I'm afraid –'

'Vera Kirilovna, don't torture me!' No sooner had I composed myself to accept the unacceptable, no sooner was I steeled to bear the worst – Stevie's death – than I was wrenched and racked all over again. 'Tell me what you know!'

'Dear child, I beg you, calm yourself – excitement is bad for you. Since I've already said too much, I will say all. The first report of your cousin's death was false. Prince Stanislaw, his father, was killed in the Argonne, not Prince Stefan, and some newspaper dispatches reported it wrong. Prince Stefan landed in Odessa with the Polish legionnaires of the Allied expeditionary force on 18 December 1918. He obtained leave to look for you. He came here first, hoping to find you. I had to tell him we had little hope you had survived. He refused to believe it and said he was going to Petrograd, where you had last been seen alive on your dacha. Kolenka furnished him with a false passport; he keeps several handy.

'Prince Stefan started north on the first of the year. Within a week of his leaving Odessa, his body was found in the hills by Polish troops. He was buried with military honours, and a day of mourning was proclaimed in his country.'

'His body was found,' I repeated as Vera Kirilovna was silent. If Stefan would not believe me dead, why should I believe him dead either? And, aloud, 'How do they know it was his body?' I added.

'His own men brought it back, dear child. He was definitely identified, I'm afraid.'

'How was he killed?'

'Shot in the head,' answered Vera Kirilovna promptly, too promptly. 'He did not suffer, as so many others have, at the hands of Grigoriev's bandits.'

She is keeping something from me, I thought.

Vera Kirilovna drew herself up. 'You can ask Professor Holveg if you doubt me. He heard about it from the Poles who took you into Odessa.'

Could it be true, I thought? Not fallen on the field of battle but slain by bandits, wantonly, stupidly lured to his death by the thought of saving me!

'It was such a shock' – I heard Vera Kirilovna's voice through the din in my ears – 'to have seen him so full of life, so strong and confident barely a fortnight before, and now, to think you missed each other by only three months . . . what a cruel irony! Dear child, Princess, are you conscious?'

Slowly, I reopened my eyes. Yes, I was conscious. I would no longer faint of shock, attempt to die of grief, or lose the memory of what could not be borne.

'Poor Aunt Sophie,' I said, after sipping the water Vera Kirilovna eagerly handed me, 'to lose both husband and son within a few months. Her loss is greater than mine.'

'Princess Veslawska was spared that sorrow, dear child. She did not survive her husband by more than a few weeks. She died of the Spanish grippe which has been raging in Europe.'

'Aunt Sophie too! I knew, when the Veslawskis left for France, I would never see her again.'

Aunt's gentle maternal visage rose before me as I had seen it last on a train siding behind the south-western front, in that awful moment before I felt torn asunder. Gone too, the wise and gracious lady I had called by the name sweetest of any to a child, who would have guided me in the roles of mother and wife she had filled so well – gone like all my loved ones, all before their time! I alone had a life still ahead, a lifetime to mourn them.

'Dear child' – Countess Liline now spoke with genuine feeling – 'I know how much you loved the Princess your aunt, I understand how lonely you must feel. But you still have many friends and admirers who are ready to risk their lives for you. And, if it's not presumptuous, I would like you to think of me as a mother.'

'Dear Vera Kirilovna, thank you,' I answered with corresponding feeling.

I would not judge that incorrigible courtier again after the lessons of the past two years. They had taught me the importance of Father's warning against righteousness, for I had experienced Marxist righteousness to the fullest.

'Vera Kirilovna,' I added as she kissed my cheek and rose, 'you're the only one besides Nyanya and Boris Maysky to know all that Stefan meant to me. I would like it to remain that way. You haven't told Professor Holveg, have you?'

'I haven't hidden from him that you loved the Prince like a brother,' said Vera Kirilovna, holding high the bust of a former lady-in-waiting schooled in discretion and tact. 'And, now that we're on the subject, I must put you on your guard against Professor Holveg. He is very possessive, very protective towards you, almost as if – it's quite ludicrous, really – as if he considered himself your husband. You must be firm, dear child. You must make him keep his distance.'

'His distance? You speak as if he were an inferior!'

'Oh I know he's extremely intelligent, even cultured. But he's not one of *us*.'

One of us, the ruling class, who delivered Russia to the Bolsheviks! 'Thank goodness for that!' I said. 'Please ask Professor Holveg to come up and see me right away.'

'Dear child, you're all wrought up. You must rest first.' Countess Liline rose in a rare fluster.

'It's you, Vera Kirilovna, who are being possessive and protective,' I remarked, not unkindly. 'I wish to see him right away.'

'As you wish,' she complied.

In a short while, after the nurse had taken my temperature and made me comfortable, Alexis sat down by the bedside all prickly and quivery with emotion. 'I can't tell you how happy I am to see you out of danger, Tatyana Petrovna.'

'Alexis.' I looked at him tenderly. In spite of his ill-fitting and baggy suit, he still wore the mathematically trim goatee and air of the scientist who leaves nothing to chance. It was such a familiar and welcome figure, the same that I had sensed close by all during the months of travel and delirium. It had hovered over me like a wizard's, keeping danger at bay. 'Dear Alexis, how can I thank you?'

'Please, don't mention it. It's past, forgotten . . .'

'I have such a hazy recollection of our journey. I thought we were going to Poland.'

'Fighting was so heavy on the Lithuanian border, I decided to go south to the Ukraine. We tried to cross over in Podolia, where we could take refuge in a Jewish settlement if necessary. That did not succeed either. And so, after zigzagging all over the map and encountering the most absurd adventures, here we are in the Crimea instead.'

'I want to hear all about it. But first, what did you learn about my cousin Stefan's death?' And, as Alexis squirmed in his chair, 'Vera Kirilovna said you could confirm her report,' I prodded.

'Vera Kirilovna!' Alexis seemed relieved to vent his feelings. 'She might have kept quiet until you were stronger.'

'I am strong enough. What do you know, Alexis?'

'The bandits captured and robbed your cousin, that's all. Then they shot him with the rest of their prisoners. An idiotic and wanton death worthy of this idiotic and wanton civil war. I deeply regret it. But you had accepted Prince Stefan's death before. You can accept it again. Your task now is to live!' Behind his spectacles, his dark eyes flashed with the old fire.

'I know that, Alexis. Life can't be shirked, but it seems so dull, so . . . pointless.' Even as I spoke, I realized I was not only self-pitying but cruel. Had not Alexis reason to think that he could give my life a new purpose? Had I not tacitly encouraged that belief?

'How can you say such a thing, Tatyana Petrovna? There is knowledge, there is great music, there is beauty in nature, in art.' Tactfully, Alexis did not bring up any personal claim.

I looked out the window. Through the long muslin curtains and the stone balustrade of the balcony, the sea was as blue as the sky of the painted ceiling. Yes, Alubek was heartbreakingly beautiful. But was not the world's beauty a mockery and a burden?

'So long as we have a functioning mind, life cannot be pointless and dull,' Alexis continued.

But I, I functioned more with my heart than with my mind! And my heart, without Stevie, was only half alive.

'Would you like me to leave, Tatyana Petrovna?' Alexis asked.

'No.' I needed his presence. He was the only one left! 'Tell me about our odyssey. I have the impression I spent some time in a hospital.'

'Yes,' Alexis eagerly began, 'after leaving Petrograd, we remained over six weeks in Pskov, in a hospital run by a former student of mine. You needed oxygen and were in no condition to travel. Before you could recover, the city health commissar became curious. We put you on a hospital train bound for the Baltic front, only to be taken off at the border and rerouted to Smolensk. From there to Kiev via Kursk, we made the railway journey in a confiscated private coach – it could have been yours, Tatyana Petrovna – at the invitation of the wife of a Red Army general who was a former university colleague.

'In Kiev, thanks to her good offices, I obtained a safe-conduct to the border of Polish Galicia and an exit permit. I thought we were safe – but the countryside was not.'

Alexis recrossed his legs and from force of habit tugged at the absent crease of his comically large trousers.

'The Bolsheviks,' he continued, 'had only recently defeated the forces of the separatist government – the Rada – set up with German help. Ukrainian partisans were still active. They blew up the bridge over the Bug. As our train halted at the river, they attacked and captured it.

'As Joseph Goldstein, the Jewish health commissar of my false passport, I was going to be castrated and hung from the nearest tree. How I gave thanks to my mother for having me baptized! When the partisans saw I had not been circumcised, they believed that my passport was only a disguise and let us go free, after robbing me of most of my possessions.'

'Not your violin,' I interposed, 'your precious Stradivarius?'

'Thank goodness not! Our partisans did not realize how valuable it was. But they took all my clothes, even my toilet articles. Vera

Kirilovna has kindly fitted me out with whatever she could find.' With a rueful gesture, Alexis indicated his suit.

'She did very well.' I smiled. 'What happened after that?'

'Some peasants took us to their village, where I hired a *tarantas*. After a day's jolting in that springless buggy, you begged me to let you die by the road. Our horse went lame in the middle of the steppe. Luckily we were found by a party of Don Cossacks. They slung you between two horses and put *me* in the saddle. It was my first experience on horseback and, I pray, my last.'

I could not help smiling again at the thought of Alexis emerging out of the maelstrom of civil war intact, if not impeccable.

Alexis chuckled, then continued: 'Their chief had served under your father in Poland, so this *ataman* treated us royally. He put us up in his tent and gave us an escort to Odessa. Before we could reach it, however, we were attacked by a party of Grigoriev's bandits, who were blockading the city. Our Cossacks vanished and the bandits prepared to make short work of us. Had you not been ill and possibly contagious, I shudder to think what they might not have done to you!

'Luckily, their chief spoke with a strong German accent, so I appealed to him in that language. It happened that he was a German army deserter, born in the grand duchy of Allensee. Once again I was thankful for my noble parentage. I made myself known as the son of the last duke. We received an escort through the lines and were left in no-man's-land.

'Nyanya and I carried your stretcher with a white flag until we were challenged by a Polish sentry of the Allied expeditionary force. Here I became Aleksey Holveg of Warsaw, escorting a kin of the Veslawskis. The Poles took you to their field station, and from there an ambulance brought us in comfort to Odessa.'

'Poor Alexis!' I wondered at his courage. 'You had a worse time of it than I. Then were our troubles over?'

'Not yet. General d'Anselme, the French commander in chief, had ordered the town evacuated and it was chaos. The French were only interested in saving their own skins. Those refugees they did take on were treated shamefully. In contrast the British were correct, even kind. But the ships they sent were inadequate for the overflow of refugees. Again, the Poles came to our rescue. Their commander put some husky legionnaires at our disposal and they got us on board a fishing vessel with sabres drawn. You can't imagine the scenes that took place in the harbour: refugees fighting each other, jumping into the sea. Thousands were left behind sitting on their bundles on the dock! It was pitiful.

'Our vessel made for Yalta, where I telephoned Alubek. What a novelty to find telephones in order! I had not a rouble left of any kind of currency and precious few of your jewels. Nyanya was chary of relinquishing them all along, you may be sure. Countess Liline sent an ambulance for you and had me fetched in a car with a chauffeur. I thought myself back in the grand old days. You were greeted triumphantly, though you were too ill to care. You gave us all a bad fright, Tatyana Petrovna, but that's passed too ... I'm going, Sister.' He rose as the nurse entered to end the visit.

I detained him. 'Alexis, wait a moment, there's one more thing. You've made no mention of Fyodor. Where is he?'

Alexis fingered his goatee uneasily. 'Tatyana Petrovna, I deeply regret that it was impossible to bring him.'

'Impossible to bring him? Then ... you left Fyodor all alone at the dacha?'

'I could not get false papers for him too. To revalidate the papers I had obtained for you and Nyanya earlier was difficult enough in the short time I had. Also, he was too well known as your footman, impossible to disguise, huge as he was. We were stopped in Peterhof by a Communist militiawoman – he'd have given you away at once. I left him a sum of money and the address of a faculty friend, on good terms with the Bolsheviks, who promised to look after him. It was all I could do, Tatyana Petrovna.'

I looked at my rescuer in disbelief, dismay, yes, even with dislike. 'Alexis, how *could* you? It was monstrous, inhuman!'

'But ... there was no other way to save you, Tatyana Petrovna!'

'I did not ask to be saved! I asked you only to look after Nyanya and Fyodor. What right had you to take it upon yourself to rescue me and not him?'

The nurse again asked the visitor to leave.

Alexis stood looking down on me sadly. 'I did what I thought best for you, Tatyana Petrovna. Forgive me if I presumed to consider myself a friend, more than a friend perhaps ... at least the only one in a position to help.' He faltered, then concluded with dignity, 'After I have seen you safely out of Russia and discharged what was to me, until this moment, a sacred trust, I shall withdraw from your life, as I now will from this room, with your permission.' He bowed and walked stiffly to the door.

My anger turned to shame. It was not Alexis's fault that he did not understand what Fyodor meant to me, I thought. He was not carried in a footman's arms as a child. It was my fault Fyodor was abandoned, mine alone. I had been a coward. I wished to be forever rid of care and sorrow. I would not eat, I would not stir in the cold, and in my delirium I could not say, 'If Fyodor cannot come, then I must stay; my life cannot be saved at the expense of his.'

'Sister,' I said, 'please recall Professor Holveg for a moment.' I was not only ashamed, I was afraid I had alienated Alexis by my ingratitude when I needed him as never before!

'Alexis,' I said when he stood over me once more, 'I am unworthy of your devotion, but I thank you. For that, and all you did for Father, I shall be indebted to you for life. Can you forgive me?'

I put out my hand and he clasped it in both of his. 'There's no need to thank me, or to apologize. You can best repay me by getting well. And I hope you will never again yield to those morbid, fatalistic tendencies which nearly killed you.'

'I'm not proud of them, Alexis.'

'Under the circumstances, they were understandable. You're not yet twenty-two. You're intelligent and capable. There is nothing now to prevent your studying medicine. I'll be happy to help you, if you'll allow me ...'

I was happy to be led and helped. I smiled. Alexis kissed my hand in a fluster and fled.

The next day I saw Zinaida Mikhailovna – like Vera Kirilovna, she was newly respectful towards Grandmaman's successor, however penniless I might be. I also thanked Kolenka for preserving Alubek from the ravages of Bolshevik rule. On hearing that he was joining the White Volunteers, I asked him to make inquiries after Boris Maysky.

He saluted. 'I hear and obey, Tatyana Petrovna.' And, to his mother, who begged him not to sign up, 'I speak foreign languages, I can be useful to our cause,' said he jauntily.

I was sure Zinaida Mikhailovna need not be alarmed. Kolenka could look after himself.

They were my last visitors. The Dowager Empress did not come to see me again. It was the second week of April and the Bolsheviks were overrunning the Crimean peninsula. All had but one thought: flight.

Once more, the British rose to the occasion. The battleship HMS *Marlborough* came for Russia's Dowager Empress, sister to England's queen mother, Alexandra. Marie Fyodorovna refused to go on board with her family until every refugee, imperial or otherwise, had been safely evacuated. The British sent more ships to Yalta to take them on.

A launch was dispatched to Alubek for me and a small suite. I in turn refused to leave until my entire household had been evacuated. This included all who had fled here from our far-flung holdings, the wounded, and all tenants and servants who wished to leave. I was spared the painful necessity of leaving Bobby behind – he would not have passed British quarantine. He had died peacefully in his sleep by my bed during the night.

All my people were taken aboard the British transport anchored in the beautiful bay where our yacht the *Helena* had once flown the blue-and-gold Silomirsky colours. Alexis, Vera Kirilovna, Zinaida Mikhailovna and Nyanya went with me in the last launch. Besides packing sheets and blankets with my light luggage, Nyanya had stuffed her own bundle with down pillows and as much of our monogrammed gold service as she could carry. Alexis had one small suitcase and his violin, Zinaida two ample suitcases, and Vera Kirilovna two huge trunks.

As my stretcher was lifted up the ship's side, I had a final glimpse of the tall cypresses lining the coastal road that wound and climbed through our park. It was here that Boris Maysky had taught me to ride. From here also I had been driven to the Tsar's palace at Livadia to play with Tatyana Nikolayevna and Olga. Now the apple orchards were in full bloom about the Moorish roof of our villa. For the last time, a breeze brought me the scents and sounds of childhood springs.

The ship's captain welcomed me aboard. Through the open porthole of my stateroom I heard the band of the HMS *Marlborough* play our anthem, 'God Keep the Tsar', as the warship passed us on the port side. It seemed a fitting requiem to imperial Russia and to my loved ones, sleeping in the soil of our native land.

30

For the next five weeks, while I recuperated in the British military hospital in Constantinople, Alexis, the academician, played the violin in a nightclub where Russian princes waited on tables. Nyanya kept house for him – badly – and feuded with the Turks, Jews and Greeks of their working-class district in Galata. Countess Liline taught French to upper-class Turkish girls in the hills of Pera. Zinaida Mikhailovna worked as a pastry cook.

Upon my discharge as a patient, I joined the nursing staff in return for room, board and clothing. On my twenty-second birthday, 28 May 1919, the hospital staff gave a party, and all four of my little family came. Zinaida Mikhailovna brought the cake she had baked, Vera Kirilovna a Byzantine icon out of her trunks, Alexis flowers and a leather-bound copy of *A Sportsman's Sketches*. The celebration over, and all the guests but Alexis and Nyanya gone, he attempted to discuss future plans. He had written to major European universities for a position, as well as to the Radium Institute in Paris. The latter was his first choice.

'As soon as I receive an offer – and I've no doubt I will – I will apply for a visa. Fortunately, I can get a Polish passport. You and Nyanya, for the time being, will need a Nansen passport – a passport without nationality issued to émigrés,' he explained as I looked blank.

'I know. Alexis, please, I can't yet put my mind to practicalities.'

'But you need one to get your French visa. It takes six weeks, and is expensive besides.'

I excused myself. 'First let me get used to working again.' The truth was, I was not ready to go so far from Russia.

Alexis reassured me. 'There is no urgency. Would you like to live in Paris?'

'Oh, it's all the same to me where I live,' I said, and added, as his face fell, 'so long as you're there, Alexis.' Wherever he went, it seemed, Nyanya and I must follow; he was in charge of our lives.

He flashed his unexpectedly youthful smile, started to speak, became flustered, and broke off.

I put aside further thought of a future that Alexis anticipated so eagerly, and which, for me, had no reality. I applied myself to my job, little as it challenged my skill. Having no credentials, no international publications like Alexis Holveg, I was assigned the lowliest nursing tasks. Still, it was better than cleaning streets. And there was always the opportunity to observe and learn. Being around the sick made me forget temporarily my emotional emptiness and sense of loss. Nor did I feel as alien in a hospital. Like the laboratory for Alexis, any hospital was home to me.

I asked to be assigned to the ward of most severely burned and mutilated casualties. I tended the purulent flesh that brought a nervous hastiness to hands more experienced than mine, and looked the pitiable horror squarely in the face. Only by accepting and consecrating myself to its relief could I atone for being alive and well, while Stevie had died for my sake and through my thoughtlessness Fyodor had been abandoned.

Through the Swedish embassy, Alexis had sent an urgent message to the friend in Leningrad who had promised to help Fyodor. I allowed myself to be comforted by the thought that Fyodor had found a protector. I began to await with pleasure my weekly outings with Alexis. On those fine summer days the Bosphorus was a deep blue between gentle green hillocks. Slender blue-white minarets soared into the sky as we walked streets so narrow it seemed one could jump across from balcony to balcony. The old brown houses, clustered together, looked like old women gossiping. Alexis pointed out the exquisite detail of the arabesques decorating the tiny arched windows, at once rigorous and flowing like the ornamentation in Bach's music.

I was more fascinated by the crowd: uniforms of many nations mingling with native men in red fezzes and veiled women with magnificent, speaking eyes. We visited the Blue Mosque, tiled all in blue and richly carpeted, the lofty basilica of Hagia Sophia where my Byzantine ancestors had been crowned, and the palaces of the deposed Sultan Abdul Hamid II. While Alexis, out of his seemingly inexhaustible store of knowledge, re-created both Byzantium and the Ottoman Empire, Arabian fairy tales came back to me from childhood.

I told Alexis how I had played Moslem princess as a little girl. I preferred to talk about early childhood, about the time before death entered my life. In contrast Alexis was reticent about his first years in Warsaw when his beautiful young mother, whom he adored, supported them by taking in laundry that he delivered to the houses of the rich and great. Imbued with hurt pride, she had taught him to mistrust emotion and to be guided by intelligence.

'Until recently,' he said, 'experience proved my mother right.'

'She may well be,' I mused. Had I not learned how changeable my own feelings were? 'But intelligence does not help me very much either.'

'You have not yet learned to apply it to life, Tatyana Petrovna, or to the emotions.'

'Is there such a thing as intelligent emotion?'

'I like to think there is, Tatyana Petrovna, and that I am experiencing it as I walk with you.' Alexis placed his free hand over my arm as it rested on his.

The gesture, delicate yet self-assured, bespoke more experience with women than Alexis would hitherto admit.

'Have you never been in love, Alexis?' I asked. 'When you were young,' I added as he looked at me in reproachful surprise.

'When I was your age' – he smiled a touch ironically at being considered 'old' – 'I was madly in love with the sister of a fellow university student. I saw her frequently at my friend's house for about a year without declaring myself. Then one day, I learned she was engaged to another student. I was stunned, quite literally, into insensibility. I spent forty-eight hours in a kind of stupor, after which I awoke sane. I learned from it two things: one, love is indeed possession, as the poets say, and two, it is an emotional luxury.'

'And now? Do you still think so?'

'Yes and no. I still believe love a luxury. But life without luxury, I've discovered, is only bearable under conditions of primitive survival.'

It was cleverly put. Alexis was never boring.

'For me, love is an essential emotion, not a luxury,' I rejoined. But there were different kinds and degrees of love, and it was no simple matter. 'Did you ever again have more than a platonic love?' I asked.

'Love, in the sense in which I spoke of earlier, no. I have had sporadic affairs. In retrospect, they always seemed a waste of time and money. I never dreamed that I would want to marry, that this could become an absorbing goal!' He pressed his hand more firmly over my arm.

I rather enjoyed the pressure. I liked this courtship by innuendo, which did not commit me. And so, between the huddled houses and lofty minarets, the babel of tongues, the influx of military personnel and refugees, I came during the next three months to know Constantinople as well as the simple, forthright heart ruled by the great and complex mind of my opposite – my guide. He could read my mind like a book. But he could not guess the convolutions of my heart!

Less enticing was Constantinople by night. One heard sporadic shooting and read of assassinations in the morning paper. When I went, in the company of two English nurses, to hear Alexis play in his nightclub by the waterfront, I was shocked to see a swarm of very young Russian prostitutes. Those girls looked no older than twelve or thirteen! At the approach of a policeman, they would disperse, then come flocking back like birds.

Alexis's playing was a revelation. In place of the precise and elegant Polish gentleman scholar was a brother to the frenzied Jewish fiddlers on Harvest Festival night at Veslawa. All the passion that betrayed itself in the flash of his black eyes was there in his gypsy music. I was spellbound. It made me understand fully for the first time the depth and fire of his love. It was frightening, as well as flattering. I was compelled to leave the nightclub suddenly so as not to burst into tears. Once back in my hospital room I wept for the first time in more than a year, wept for all the dead young men of Europe and Asia, and for him with whom my love lay buried.

I finally asked Alexis again to tell me the details of Stefan's death as told him by the Poles in Odessa.

My cousin, he said, had been shot in the head with two other captives. His seal ring with the ancestral eagle of the royal Piasts had been recovered from one of his captors, who had described him unmistakably.

'Shot in the head how?' I persisted. 'Were his features recognizable?'

'He was shot dead, isn't that enough?' Alexis retorted.

I had the impression that, like Vera Kirilovna, he was keeping something back. I determined to find out all I could about Stevie's death for myself. The opportunity presented itself before summer's end.

The Russian civil war, in its capricious ebb and flow, had taken a more favourable turn for the southern White Army at the same time as Admiral Kolchak, deserted by the Czechs, was falling back in Siberia. The Crimea had been liberated in mid-June. General Denikin's forces were also pushing northward into the Ukraine, capturing Kharkov in July. Russian refugees subsisting in camps or as menials in Constantinople began to dream of going home.

None was more anxious than Zinaida Mikhailovna, pining over her pastry board for her son. In August, Kolenka, once more an adjutant safely behind the lines, invited her to join him in Taganrog, on the Sea of Azov, where General Denikin had moved his headquarters.

'Tell Her Highness, Tatyana Petrovna,' he added in a postscript, 'that General Maysky is here in Taganrog. He is in isolation in a typhus hospital. Also please transmit respectful greetings from naval Lieutenant Baron Niessen and from her kinsman Captain Prince Lomatov-Moskovsky. We are hers to command.'

Baron Niessen and L-M in Taganrog! Boris Andreyevich Maysky alive! All three had survived unthinkable perils. It renewed my secret hope that Stefan might surface too, in some unexpected part of the world, after he had long been thought dead. In any case, I had to see Boris Andreyevich, and at GHQ in Taganrog, I might discover the truth about Stevie's purported murder. In my surge of purposefulness I no longer needed to cling to Alexis. Rather, my dependency irked me.

Zinaida Mikhailovna sold an heirloom and took the first available boat, promising to find accommodations for us all. I plotted to follow her.

Vera Kirilovna pronounced herself eager to accompany me. She was thoroughly sick of teaching French to Turkish girls. But I met only opposition from both Alexis and Nyanya.

'When will you stop making noble gestures, Tatyana Petrovna?' said he. 'What can you do for Boris Maysky by visiting him? You cannot take him out of quarantine. If he recovers and leaves Russia, we can help him settle abroad. A trip to Taganrog at this juncture will only be an unnecessary risk and expense.' And, as I reiterated my intention – I suddenly chafed at his protectiveness and possessiveness. 'Have you thought how you will finance this expedition?' he queried.

I had assumed that Nyanya would part with one of the jewels still embedded in the hem of her *sarafan*. But she would not even sell a gold spoon salvaged from Alubek! What neither Bolsheviks nor bandits could extort from her, I could not hope to obtain, even though, by rights, it was mine. Fortunately, however, Vera Kirilovna was ready to part with more valuables from her trunks.

When Alexis saw there was no stopping me, he said, 'Since you will do as you please – *vous en ferez à votre guise* – get the proper vaccinations at least.'

This Vera Kirilovna and I duly did: against typhus, cholera and smallpox. As an added precaution, I packed the special, tight-fitting, one-piece suit the British now issued nurses on typhus wards to protect them against lice. I took a month's leave from the hospital and we booked passage on a British ship in the third week of August.

In the interim, Alexis had received the hoped-for invitation from the Radium Institute in Paris and applied for his visa. His plan was to leave ahead of me and find me an apartment and a job.

He reiterated this intention as he saw me off with Vera Kirilovna at the boat and added, 'It's important for you to be financially independent.'

It's important for you to have your complete freedom, I understood he meant, and was thankful. Was not the freedom he granted me the very thing that bound me to him?

'You've been wonderful as ever, Alexis.' I felt ashamed of my rebelliousness. 'Be patient with Nyanya.'

Nyanya had consented to stay behind at his urging and mine. I feared for her safety in the midst of civil war and Alexis, I suspected, wanted to keep her as hostage.

'We understand each other, Nyanya and I,' he reassured me.

Remarkably well, I thought. She had become his chief ally! 'Well, God keep you both until my return.' I gave Alexis my hand.

He pressed it firmly with his smaller one and said, 'I will wait for you one month. If you're not back at the end of September, I will leave for Paris as scheduled, and you'll be forced to handle visa formalities on your own.'

I understood I was free to follow my fancy but, contrary to previous experience, Alexis would no longer shield me from the consequence: having to manage without him in an alien world beset with practicalities. It was an effective threat.

'I'll be back in time,' I promised, and added truthfully, 'I shall miss you, Alexis.'

The boat was packed with volunteers from Russian refugee camps, among them several young women going to nurse or fight with the White Army. When they learned from Vera Kirilovna that I had been in charge of a field hospital, they pressed me with questions. I had the novel and curious experience of being looked up to as an older, as well as more experienced woman.

'I hope I'm assigned to your unit,' one of my admirers cried.

I said, somewhat shamefacedly, that I had personal reasons for going to Taganrog. They looked disappointed.

I, too, felt cheated. I envied their enthusiasm. Naïve they might be, but they had a purpose. They wanted to serve something greater than themselves. So had I, once. And why shouldn't I again?

Torn between eagerness and anxiety, I waited along the crowded rail for the first sight of my native land: the majestic blue arc of the Caucasus range. Even more poignant, if less awesome, was the Crimean coastline on our left before we crossed the isthmus into the Sea of Azov and its quieter waters. At its furthest, north-east end, was Taganrog.

Zinaida Mikhailovna and Kolenka were not alone to greet our ship. Also on the dock were L-M and Baron Niessen, the latter with a huge bouquet. Underneath his threadbare uniform, I saw the tattered seaman whose wound had jolted me out of amnesia. L-M's presence too aroused mixed emotion: the pain of remembrance – how vividly our days on the march during the retreat of '15 came back to me – the joy of being welcomed by a family member and friend. In comparison with the adventurous and giddy young crowd on the ship, both men had the sober, seasoned look of veterans. And what a contrast with Alexis! Could that small scholar really have been my anchor and my salvation? Had I truly promised him I would return in a month?

Vera Kirilovna fell upon L-M – one of our blood, one of *us*!

'You have not been out of my thoughts since I left you at the dacha,' Niessen blurted out. 'I did get word to your Veslawski cousin as you asked.'

'I am indebted to you for it,' I said sadly. That word had lured Stevie to his end! 'He was killed, you know, after he landed in Odessa.'

'I know. L-M was with the Allied expeditionary corps. I'm terribly sorry. L-M also served with Prince Stefan in '17, on the Somme.'

I turned to my kinsman. 'Did you get to know Stefan Veslawski well?'

'Not as well as I would have liked. I'll never forget his voice. He used to entertain us with his singing at liaison. But I see that's a painful subject.' L-M's Byzantine eyes rested on me with kindly detachment.

'Yes. Still, I want to hear more once we're settled.'

'In that case, there's someone in Taganrog who knew him longer than I, an English cousin –'

'Not Lord Andrew?'

'The same. His older brother, Lord Beresford, was killed in action in France. Young Andrew's attached to the British military Mission here. Shall I bring him over tonight?'

I was suddenly afraid to meet so close a kin of Stevie's. 'Let me get my bearings first. I may have to stay in the typhus hospital to nurse General Maysky.'

'God forbid!' Niessen cried. 'It's a dreadful place.'

'It is, Tatyana Petrovna, it is,' Zinaida Mikhailovna interposed timidly.

'All the more reason to do what I can.' I could not deal with L-M's kindliness and Niessen's intensity all at once either. So much attention on all sides was overwhelming.

'Tatyana Petrovna, perhaps you'll decide to join up after all,' called one of my shipboard admirers as the nurse-volunteers passed by, with flirtatious glances at L-M and Niessen.

'Perhaps I will,' I replied. 'I've been thinking during the crossing that I should volunteer,' I said to my companions as we followed slowly behind the girls.

'Splendid idea!' said Niessen. 'I wouldn't have expected less of you.'

'Don't rush it, Tanya,' L-M observed. 'Our advance looks impressive on the map, but victory's by no means certain.'

'I sometimes wonder, L-M, if you even consider it desirable.' Niessen spoke with nervous irritability.

'You will make careless remarks, Prince,' admonished Kolenka. 'Counter-espionage will get you yet.'

'Counter-espionage?' I looked at my escorts.

'An essential arm of our movement. I must warn you, Tanya,' said my kinsman, 'aristocrats are suspect *ipso facto*.'

As before, I did not know how much pose there was behind L-M's world view.

'You're joking surely. *Vous faites de l'esprit, cher prince.*' Vera Kirilovna was resolutely ingratiating.

'Not in the least, Countess. Oh, there's a high-society circle in Taganrog, which will welcome you with fanfare, but the White Army itself is largely democratic.'

'So much the better!' said I.

We had reached the low sheds at the end of the wharf. Bounded on one side by low coastal hills, the flat little seaport town on the edge of the steppe, where our beloved Chekhov was born, presented an unprepossessing vista after Constantinople's Golden Horn. L-M and Niessen rode off. Kolenka whisked us through customs and medical inspection, then showed us to a staff motorcar 'guaranteed deloused'.

Our lodgings were in the house of a grain merchant where Kolenka and another adjutant were billeted. The merchant, who had already yielded the room of his grown daughter to Zinaida Mikhailovna, had now ceded his son's room and the conjugal bedroom to accommodate Vera Kirilovna and me.

This Kolenka told us as he drove us, flags flying and horn blaring, down the wide and straight main street, one of the few that was paved. It was as crowded as Constantinople with Allied uniforms. With a start, I recognized the four-square Polish *czapka* on two superb officers, next to whom the White Volunteers looked shabby indeed.

I reproached Kolenka. 'It was not necessary to dislodge our hosts. I can sleep in any old corner.'

'I'll sleep in an attic, too, as long as it's clean.' Vera Kirilovna would not be outdone in abnegation.

'Don't worry, Your Ladyships. Our merchant is so terrified of the Bolsheviks, he'll gladly make any sacrifice for our cause.'

We were greeted with a low bow and curtsy by the dignified merchant pair on the wide front porch of their white, wooden house. Each spouse so vied with the other in lavishing attention upon me that I suspected Kolenka of touting me as a royal personage.

My spacious bedroom with a fireplace and an icon corner overlooked the vegetable garden and orchard of the substantial Russian provincial home. A young peasant maid waited on me. The meal we were served, seasoned with fresh dill, was a fine repast by local standards. Best of all, the drawing room had a piano, not too badly out of tune.

'And Your Highness will have a horse to ride,' said Kolenka. 'She shall find that nothing is too good in our White headquarters for the daughter of General Prince Silomirsky.'

I reminded Kolenka I had come, not for a vacation, but to visit General Maysky.

'That has been arranged, Tatyana Petrovna. You need only present your inoculation certificate at the hospital. However, if you want my advice, don't go. We have such a jolly little town here: cinemas, theatre, weekly symphonic concerts, parties, "at home" days, a cosmopolitan society. Since Kiev was liberated, everyone is jubilant. Why visit such a depressing place?'

Vera Kirilovna approved. 'Very sensible advice' – with a glance at me that meant: But I know good sense is wasted on you.

'Yes, do listen to Kolenka, Tatyana Petrovna dearest,' Zinaida Mikhailovna urged.

I silenced my well-wishers. 'Enough said. Kolenka, I desire an interview with General Denikin. Can you arrange that too?'

'I hear and obey, Your Highness.' Kolenka smartly clicked his heels and saluted, took a bonbon out of his mother's hand to pop into his own mouth, wagged his finger at her and drove off with a roar.

Early the next day I presented my inoculation certificate and anti-typhus suit at the isolation hospital on the outskirts of town and was given a visitor's permit. (Everything required a permit in Taganrog, I quickly learned. To cut through the paperwork, even bribery and connections were insufficient. It took no less than a rogue like Kolenka.)

The hospital was so overcrowded that the sick lay on pallets in the corridors. In the wards, there was hardly room to step between the cots. Fortunately, in the officers' ward where Boris Maysky lay, there were beds.

He was awake, but gave no sign of recognition.

I laid my hand on his shoulder and said, 'Boris Andreyevich dear, it's me, Tatyana.'

His listless gaze fastened on mine, his arched eyebrows joined over his beak of a nose. 'Tatyana Petrovna, is it really you? I'm not delirious still? I heard you had escaped to Constantinople. And now you're here?'

'I came to see you, Boris Andreyevich, to thank you, to help you get well.' I fluffed his pillow, tidied his covers.

'What a light touch you have! I'm so happy I've lived to see you again!' He pressed my hand to his lips. 'Now then, sit down and tell me your odyssey.'

I told him all that I remembered, calmly, with detachment. That was an earlier me, I thought with relief, one that cannot disturb us any longer.

'What an ordeal!' Boris Andreyevich said when I was done. 'But the main thing is that you're well, you're safe. I was frantic with worry about you. I got money, papers in Petrograd.' He was eager to tell his story in turn.

'There's no hurry, Boris Andreyevich, don't tire yourself.' He was pale and sweating, his melodious voice strained.

'No, I must. From Petrograd I followed the Neva upstream to contacts in the country, for provisions and a motorboat.' He spoke in a whisper. 'On the way back, we were attacked by river pirates, Simyon and I, robbed, left naked on a bank. Reds conscripted us to dig trenches on the Archangel front. Americans rescued us. We just missed Baron Niessen. Heard you were at the dacha, asking about me. I had frostbite, lost three toes, spent all winter in hospital in Archangel. In spring, we took a British ship, sailed all around Europe, landed in Novorossiisk. I was greeted as the "hero of Kronstadt". Attempt to rescue Prince Silomirsky called one of the most glorious deeds of anti-Bolshevik resistance.' He paused, out of breath, then continued telegraphically, 'Fought in liberation of Crimea. Landed here in July. Caught spotted typhus. Put away. Forgotten. No matter. Now I can die in peace.'

'You won't die, Boris Andreyevich! I'll get you out and care for you properly . . .'

'No one leaves here except for the burial pit, Tatyana Petrovna. It's not a bad way to go. There are worse, far worse . . .'

I understood that if it was already so difficult to visit a patient in isolation, to take him out would be impossible indeed.

'You won't go to the burial pit, Boris Andreyevich, I promise you that, at least. You will have the full military honours that had been due Father.'

Boris Andreyevich smiled weakly.

'But in the meantime,' I continued, 'I can bring you food and help nurse you. Patients do recover from typhus with proper care.'

'When they are young, Tatyana Petrovna. Don't expose yourself by visiting me again. I need very little food, and I have the best possible care. Look, there he comes now, my angel from heaven.' He pointed to the white-gowned *sanitar* who approached us, beaming.

'Simyon!' I cried.

Simyon fell over the hands I put out to him and covered them with kisses. 'Glory to you, Lord, here's a joy for His Excellency!'

'Simyon, dear Simyon, God bless your good heart!' I looked tenderly on the rude angel ministering to forgotten heroes on this fetid ward and I thought: Angels are made, not in heaven, but in hell.

I spent the day at the bedside, talking to Simyon when Boris Andreyevich tired, reminiscing about Father, resurrecting him in memory. In the evening, Boris Maysky began to thrash. The ward was filled with the sound of creaking beds, of moans and mutterings. They would reach a paroxysm during the night, turning the gentlest of the sick into raving maniacs, to leave them prostrate, with a wisp of pulse, at dawn.

As I rose to go, promising to be back in the morning, the stare of the officer in the bed adjoining detained me.

'It's you,' he muttered. 'I did not kill you. I'm so relieved!'

'His Honour shot a Red Army nurse, in the heat of battle, God save his soul!' Simyon explained. 'His conscience torments him when the fever comes on.'

'You were so young, so blonde, a slip of a girl,' the officer continued. 'You ran up and down the bank wringing your hands. I had you in my sights. I pulled the trigger . . . it was so easy! Why? I was not myself. But you lived! Praise God!' Tears ran down his gaunt cheeks.

'God has been merciful and now Your Honour can rest,' said Simyon, wiping the officer's face.

Shaken, I quickly left the ward.

The head doctor, a middle-aged man with a cropped head like a German officer's, told me there was no taking a patient out of isolation, not even by decree of the Supreme Ruler himself. (Sarcastic references to Admiral Kolchak were common in General Denikin's camp.) 'However, since you're wearing that suit, you may visit the patient again. Unfortunately, such innovations are beyond our means.'

'Surely your British allies could supply you with suits!'

'The British do not even send us up-to-date military matériel, not to speak of medical supplies! Any more questions?'

'One last one. What is your mortality, doctor?'

'Ninety-nine per cent. This is a pesthouse, Princess, not a hospital. I don't need to remind you to shower and scrub with green soap before you leave. Good-day.'

As I left the hospital, I thought of the White officer turned killer, of Boris Andreyevich the forgotten hero, of Simyon, content in his obscure, saintly service. I thought of my country sinking into dark ages, of human savagery springing from and adding to the horrors of famine and pestilence. I saw that the feverish activity in this provincial backwater was like the illusive flush of health on a consumptive cheek.

I guessed the physical wretchedness and moral corruption underlying the frantic pursuit for pleasure and profit in this White headquarters. Yet, as I neared the lighted centre full of motorcars and carriages, of officers mounted and on foot, of women in wide-brimmed hats and light summer gowns, this town in the free play of folly seemed sick, perhaps, but not moribund like Russia under Red rule. Laughter could still be heard. Newspapers of all shades and provenance could be bought openly. The priest walked about freely in his cassock. It was not all drab, fearful and desolate.

I stopped in a church full of women praying for their men at the front. I placed a candle in front of St Vladimir, our family patron, and as I knelt to pray, the idea, born of my shipboard encounter with the nurse-volunteers, became a resolve: I must enlist in the White forces as a nurse.

I know how to stop a haemorrhage. I can clean and suture a wound. I can reduce a simple fracture, and a complex one if I have to. I can ease pain without drugs. I don't know how, but I have that gift. I am a war nurse whose skill is being wasted. Is it not my duty to aid the only movement still fighting – with what meagre means – to save my country from the Red blight? Will I not be closer to Stefan, be he dead or alive, on Russian soil? And if the Reds should kill me, as that White officer killed a Red Army nurse, won't it be a fitting tribute to him who died for me?

But what of Alexis? said another voice. He expects you back. Nyanya is with him. What of her?

Alexis will take care of Nyanya, the first voice answered. He will get used to my absence. I am only an emotional luxury, after all. He will be great and famous without me just the same.

Stop a moment, that second voice said, before you throw away the protection, tenderness, companionship he offers. Will you trade a child – you know you want a child – a calm professional life, the means to fulfil your medical ambition, all that for a field hospital, for the risk of death, perhaps worse?

I cannot picture the life you speak of, retorted my other self. Peace, the future, safety, comfort, a normal life, these words have no meaning for me any longer. Do I deserve them? Do I want them even? War, sacrifice, privation is all I know. In their midst, I can perhaps learn to serve my fellow man as Simyon does with no hope of reward on earth. Then, when I die, I might find the way to the Garden.

I was back at the isolation hospital early the next morning to tell Boris Maysky of my decision to volunteer with the White forces.

'Don't, Tatyana Petrovna, I beg you!' He roused himself from prostration. 'Conditions are worse, believe me, than in 1915. If the Reds capture a field hospital, they give no quarter to either wounded or personnel. Those who die quickly are lucky. God forbid you should fall into their hands! For your father's sake, if not for mine, give it up!'

'If Father were alive, wouldn't he fight with the Whites, and wouldn't I be at his side?'

'He would protect you. No one else will. You may think we Whites still cling to honour, honesty, *noblesse oblige*. But precious few of us do. On our side, there is only hatred and despair; on the side of the Reds, hatred and fear.'

'Despair! Why not hope?'

'Hope is superficial, ephemeral; despair, deep and enduring.'

That I could understand. 'And fear, why fear on the Red side?'

'Fear of punitive detachments. Very effective. No humanity in either camp. Leave Russia, Tatyana Petrovna, begin a new life!'

His emotion shook me, but not my purpose.

'I have something for you,' he said as I remained silent. 'Simyon,' he called, 'my pistols.'

From under the bed, Simyon pulled out a trunk and lifted a fine pair of pistols, kept oiled and shining.

'I was going to leave them both to Simyon,' Boris Maysky said, 'but now I will divide them between you. You no longer still have your revolver, Tatyana Petrovna?'

'It was confiscated in the hospital at Pskov.'

'Then you need a weapon. This one is much heavier. Show me how you will hold it.'

I turned sideways, put my left hand on my right shoulder, and rested the hand with the pistol on my raised elbow and forearm to steady it.

'Very good. Practise using it. Only be sure to get a permit at once, or you may be arrested as a spy.'

'A spy? We're not in Bolshevik territory.'

'Suspicion, counter-espionage are rife on the White side too. It's inevitable in wartime.'

I recalled L-M's warning. 'I'll apply for a permit right away. And I'll treasure the gift, Boris Andreyevich.'

He nodded and closed his eyes, exhausted.

I helped Simyon bathe his master and make his bed. He was very weak, and I feared he would not survive another night. His wardmate of the previous day had already succumbed after receiving the sacraments.

'Peacefully,' Simyon beamed. 'So peacefully in the Lord's forgiveness His Honour went.'

As I rose to go, Boris Maysky started out of his stupor. 'Remember what I used to say when I taught you to ride, Tatyana Petrovna?'

'Light hand, strong seat, heel down, head up. I'll never forget it. God be with you, Boris Andreyevich.' I bent to put a farewell kiss on his forehead.

'Simyon,' I said as he accompanied me, pistol and cartridge box in their leather case under his arm, 'will you come with me after Boris Andreyevich dies?'

'Thank you, Tatyana Petrovna, but I am needed here to care for Their Honours. And, should the Reds come, they know I will not leave them to their mercies.' He patted the pistol case. 'I have promised.'

My head reeled. 'But you, Simyon, what will become of you?'

'I'm a man of the people. What do the Reds want with me? I will save myself, if God wills.'

'I have a kinsman with the general staff.' I gave him the name of L-M. 'He will help you. Goodbye, Simyon. God reward you.'

He handed me the pistol case and I marched straight to the doctor's office.

'General Maysky appears to be terminal,' I said. 'Have any arrangements been made for his funeral?'

'That is up to the military authorities.' The doctor looked more exasperated with me than ever. 'We report the deaths. If the body is not called for within twenty-four hours, it is removed with the others.'

'Removed where?'

'To a mass grave.'

The doctor's callousness, his cropped head revolted me. He obviously hated aristocrats.

'In the case of officers, it has not happened yet,' added the doctor unexpectedly, whether out of sympathy or fear I might make trouble I could not say.

I appealed for his cooperation. 'I'm sure, Doctor, like all who serve our cause, you too would like to see General Maysky rendered full military honours.'

On an impulse, I left the hospital by a back door, in time to observe long, sheeted grey bundles being loaded into a truck.

From the pesthouse to the burial pit, as in medieval times, I thought, riveted by the sight.

The truck door slammed. 'What do you want?' the driver asked rudely.

I shook my head and walked away.

I reiterated my promise as I clutched my precious gift. 'They will not toss you into a truck to dump you into a mass grave, Boris Andreyevich.'

That night, when Kolenka asked after Boris Maysky, I said that he was dying. 'I trust,' I added, 'he will receive the final honours due him. I and my friends would take it as a personal insult if he did not.' This, I knew, would reach the right ears.

I also asked my factotum to register my pistol and get me a permit. It was too big to slip into a pocket or between my breasts, but a pouch with a strap, carried over one shoulder, should be easy to make.

'That, Tatyana Petrovna, will take money.' For the first time, Kolenka hedged about a 'royal' request.

'I will cable Constantinople.' I was already uncomfortable about accepting the hospitality of our hosts. I would word it in such a way that Alexis and Nyanya could not deny me.

'Kolenka, shame on you!' Zinaida Mikhailovna unpinned a gold watch from her maternal bosom. 'Pawn this and get the permit for Her Serene Highness.'

'How am I to pawn it when the Jews fled at our coming?' Kolenka dangled the bauble appreciatively.

'It's an ill wind that blows no good,' remarked Vera Kirilovna.

'It's my impression,' said I, 'the gentiles are profiteering nicely in this town without any help.'

'True, Tatyana Petrovna, true.' Kolenka was his jaunty self again. 'People will put up with anything so long as they're free to make profits. If only the Reds would understand this, they would have us! But on their side, profits can only be made on the black market. As a result, life is even more expensive – if you can call it life.'

'How you babble, Kolenka!' Vera Kirilovna gave him an imperious look. 'Do what you must to get the permit without fuss – *sans chichis*,' she added in French.

'At your orders, Your Ladyships.' Before I could ask him to, he dropped the watch into his mother's hand and gave her a kiss. 'If you'll excuse me, General Denikin, our *ad*mirable commander in chief, is a slave driver – I'm ready to drop. I'll take your pistol now, Tatyana Petrovna, not to wake you in the morning.'

'Darling Kolenka!' Zinaida gazed after him adoringly.

Next morning, when I called at the hospital, Boris Maysky was dead.

Two days later, he lay among flowers in an open casket in full uniform with all his decorations, surrounded by a guard of honour. The high command and all the military missions, as well as the society ladies of Taganrog, came to honour not only the 'hero of Kronstadt', but the memory of the man whom he had endeavoured to save.

The ceremony was as stirring as only a Russian military funeral could be and I realized that my fears had been vain.

In honouring its high-ranking dead – and there were more and more of them – the White movement lifted itself, ever so briefly, out of the morass into which it was sinking even as it strained for victory. Death and despair were its banners. In the church, and in the solemn march to the burial site, to drum roll and the slow stamp of feet, their banners waved with a mournful grandeur, unsoiled by cruelty.

31

DEEPEST SYMPATHY FOR GENERAL MAYSKY STOP WHAT IS KEEPING YOU IN TAGANROG?

ALEXIS

WAITING TO SEE GENERAL DENIKIN STOP PLEASE SEND MONEY

TATYANA

EXPECT MY ARRIVAL SHORTLY WITH NYANYA

ALEXIS

'What shall I do, Vera Kirilovna?' I asked on receipt of this startling telegram. 'Nyanya can share my room, but where will we put Alexis?'

'If he insists on coming, Professor Holveg can fend for himself,' said she. 'I hope you don't intend to make him welcome. What a nuisance the man is!'

'Alexis saved my life. He can never be a nuisance,' I reminded my kinswoman.

I was both touched and irritated by my rescuer's zeal. Obviously he would demand an accounting. I could explain that I wanted to ask General Denikin for a report on Stefan's death. But how could I confront Alexis with my resolve to join up as a war nurse? It was a decision taken on my own that excluded him from my life, at least for the duration. It required, I learned at the recruiting office, General Denikin's approval, and gave me a double reason for seeing the commander in chief. And in the interim, my life was full.

Immediately after the funeral, L-M had brought Lord Andrew to me. One glance at his eager young face with the trim chestnut moustache – the same colour as Stevie's – told me that Beresford's brother was innocent of war.

'Tanya, by golly, fancy meeting you in Russia in this godforsaken hole after all these years!' Lord Andrew exclaimed. 'You used to be a perfect bore as a girl, but now you've had all sorts of adventures ... I hope you'll tell us about them.'

'Tanya wanted to talk about your Veslawski cousin,' L-M put in thoughtfully.

Lord Andrew was happy to reminisce about Beresford's close friend and hero.

'I can't quite believe he's dead.' I felt free, among family, to voice my obsession.

'I don't blame you,' Lord Andrew agreed. 'Stevie's not the sort to fall into a bandit trap.'

'Indeed, my dear Andrew,' L-M rejoined. 'I know his death is officially accepted. But if I wanted to cross Russia incognito, what better way than to give myself out as dead?'

My heart leaped.

The week before the arrival of Alexis flew by. I practised the piano. Niessen, L-M and Lord Andrew accompanied me on horseback along the beaches or the steppe. To ride alone was unsafe according to my escorts, as well as unsuitable according to Vera Kirilovna. Kolenka, on his motorcar errands, taught me to drive along the dusty back roads.

From my escorts I learned a good deal about what Lord Andrew called the White Russian Wonderland.

'The main thing to have in the White camp,' L-M instructed me as we set off on horseback in the rare absence of Niessen, 'is an "orientation". Are you a liberal Cadet, a Social Democrat? Are you a partisan of General Denikin – that simple Russian soldier, as our ladies call him – or do you support his rival, the Commander of the Army of the Caucasus, General Baron Wrangel? Are you – God forbid – a tsarist?'

'And what is your orientation?' I asked.

'I'm a student of history. I have none,' L-M replied. 'That's even more suspect than having the wrong kind.'

I laughed. 'Then I shall be suspect too.'

'You're too much of a wit for your own good, L-M. But we'll give you asylum if you get in trouble,' Lord Andrew gaily reassured his friend.

'That's very kind of you, Andrew,' responded L-M. 'The French would as soon turn me over to the Bolsheviks.'

'Yes.' I remembered tales of French conduct during the evacuation from Odessa. 'I hope, Andrew, there is unanimity of views in the British Mission at least.'

'Not by a long shot. General Thompson, our chief, is all for crushing the Bolshies. Winston Churchill is 100 per cent behind him. But partisans of Lloyd George think we should drag our feet, let Reds and Whites bleed each other to death so we won't have a strong Russia to contend with. Am I right, L-M?'

'Absolutely,' said the latter. 'A weak Russia is in the short-term interest of her allies. Look at what's happened. The British have annexed Batum. Rumania has Bessarabia. The Poles are grabbing not only Polish-speaking Galicia but Volhynia, which is preponderantly Russian. And if the Ukrainians don't stop them, they'll claim the Ukraine as well.'

'The Russo-Polish conflict again! How depressing!' I said.

'They're as bad as the English and the Irish,' said Lord Andrew. 'But perhaps there's hope. A Polish delegation's due in Taganrog soon. I'm to act as interpreter. You're surprised, aren't you?' He caught my look. 'I did absorb enough Polish from my mother to speak it tolerably.'

'There's more to Lord Andrew than meets the eye,' L-M said.

That glimpse of the Veslawski in Lord Andrew made me feel closer to him. He had Stevie's hair, his straight nose. I began to see in him a younger, anglicized Stevie. And my conviction grew that Stevie lived.

Baron Niessen was back with us the next day. I suspected that his mounting irritability with my Russian kinsman was not only politically motivated.

'Niessen finds our foursome irksome.' L-M verified my guess. 'Shall we leave him a clear field?' he asked as we rode ahead.

'Please don't. I'm not ready for his attentions.'

'Very well. I admire Niessen, even if I like to taunt him. I envy him rather.'

'Envy him?'

'Yes, for being capable of passion and hatred.'

'Is that desirable?'

'It helps one feel alive.'

I understood all too well.

Meanwhile Vera Kirilovna, having quickly judged L-M passionless, encouraged Baron Niessen as an antidote to Alexis. My plan to become a war nurse she called romanticism. I could be more useful to the Whites, she maintained, in other ways. To that end she began to hold teas and receptions at which she deplored the factional strife in the holy cause against bolshevism. Only the monarchy could unite the Whites under a common aegis. And was I not like a sister to the late daughters of our beloved Tsar? In honouring me one paid homage to the imperial martyrs, one laid the ground for the restoration of the dynasty.

Whenever I tried to evade a social engagement, Vera Kirilovna would say, 'Oh, but you must see General K. He was so devoted to the Prince your father.' Or, 'Dear child, you know Baroness V. was such an admirer of Anna Vladimirovna. You can't refuse to say a few words to her.'

For these occasions, Vera Kirilovna had outfitted me in a couple of dresses borrowed from our hostess's daughter. With the help of Zinaida – the only one of us with domestic skills – these had been divested of provincial frills and taken in at the bust and waist. At first I had protested. But our plump and attractive hostess pressed them on me with tears in her eyes. Neither would she accept money for her hospitality.

'*Nye nado, nye nado* – it's not necessary, Your Highness,' she begged, pink with embarrassment. 'If the Bolsheviki come, they will grab everything. Should we escape, God willing, what use will money be? Enjoy what we have with us, enjoy it while we have it to share.'

I thanked and embraced her. She smelled of lavender and lilac. She was as clean and tidy in her person as in her housekeeping. Both she and her merchant husband were God-fearing, upright, hardworking. And these, I thought, were the bloated bourgeois exploiters of the people, the class enemy depicted in Communist propaganda.

It took Alexis no time at all to size up my situation in Taganrog. Upon his arrival, he was put up at the Hotel Europa as a guest of the Ministry of War. I had feared unnecessarily for his frail, scholarly person in this military town. On the basis of his war work for the imperial government, he had been hired as a consultant on high explosives. He had paid for his own boat fare and Nyanya's.

He even offered me a sum that I refused. But I could not refuse to see him face-to-face.

'I see I have become superfluous,' said Alexis at the end of our first evening together, when we were alone – Nyanya had deserted me on the pretext of old age and fatigue. 'You are surrounded by cavaliers. You are treated like a royal princess. You do exactly as you please. I'm the old professor who comes to spoil the fun.'

'What fun, Alexis?' I toyed with my napkin while he walked with quick little steps about the dining table where we had just sat and talked Russian-style over tea, with my hosts and my 'suite', as Alexis dubbed it. His reproach stung me. I had enjoyed my cavaliers, the sense of freedom and adventure I missed around Alexis. But as for my social obligations . . . 'It doesn't amuse me at all to be put on display by Vera Kirilovna. It's not only tedious, it's painful.'

'She is insufferable! Your kinsman now, of the historic double name, he's quite another matter, highly intelligent, sensitive, reasonable. As for that Byronic baron, the Baltic one, he never took his eyes off you. May I ask, Tatyana Petrovna – I think I have a right to – whether you reciprocate his feelings?'

Poor Alexis, a prey to jealousy, that unintelligent emotion! 'No, Alexis, not in the least. Niessen is a link with Tatyana Nikolayevna. I appreciate his genuine devotion to our late sovereign's family, a devotion which Vera Kirilovna's crowd merely professes.'

'Snobs, speculators, your Taganrog crawls with them as it does with lice.' Alexis summed up the White headquarters not inaccurately. 'Will you tell me your real reason for staying on?'

'I am waiting to ask General Denikin for a report on the death of Stefan.'

'If you must have it, it can be sent. You have some other scheme in mind.'

I could hide the truth no longer. 'I need General Denikin's approval to join the army as a field nurse.'

Even as I confessed, I realized the enormity of my defiance. I had dismissed Alexis from my mind all too lightly. The moment he had reappeared he had reestablished his dominion over me. Yet had I not defied Stefan? Had I not defied Father? Was I not older, stronger, and would I yield to Alexis now? Resolutely, I lifted my head.

'Tatyana Petrovna, you are out of your mind!' came the predictable explosion. 'The White movement is reactionary, retrograde, antisemitic, narrowly militaristic. It has all the faults of the old regime and none of its virtues. I did not bring you all the way across Russia at great expense and peril to see you throw yourself away on a false and futile cause!'

I rose and paced in turn. 'I appreciate the risks you took for me, Alexis, and I'd gladly repay the expense if I could. But it doesn't give you the right to dictate my life, to make me go against my conscience . . . to ask me to neglect my duty . . .' I could not maintain my righteous stance.

'You have no duty to the Whites. It's a romantic fantasy, nothing more. And as for what you call your conscience, in this instance, if you examine it, you might see that it's rather the product of your upbringing. It's time you freed yourself from the past, Tatyana Petrovna. I say it not for my sake alone, but for yours.' He stopped beside me as I leaned on the piano to avoid his gaze. His little hand fluttered up to my shoulder, then fluttered down again. 'Fall in love with your Baltic baron, or with any worthy young man – I can accept that – but don't, don't sacrifice your life!'

'Dear Alexis!' I was deeply moved. 'There is no young man now living worthy of greater love than you.' If I survived, and Stefan did not reappear, who but Alexis could lead me into that future I could no longer envision?

Alexis kissed my hand fervently. 'I'll go now. All I ask is that you *think* before you act, that you investigate all aspects so that you can make an intelligent, not an emotional decision.'

Alexis was kept busy on his mission and I did not see him again until the symphony concert.

The soloist in the second Rachmaninov piano concerto was the famous Russian pianist Genady Roslov, a recipient in the past of Grandmaman's largesse. I remembered visiting his home in Petrograd years before. With the enthusiastic approval of my hosts, I invited him to a small party. My hostess prepared *zakusky* and Zinaida Mikhailovna made *kisyel* – a fruit compote of raspberries from the garden. The concert was packed, in spite of the danger of contagion, with an enthusiastic and surprisingly elegant public. Afterward, Alexis and my cavaliers came back with Genady Roslov. Kolenka, who preferred young men himself, nevertheless returned with several young women for his friends.

'I remember your visit to Petrograd seven years ago,' Genady Roslov said, once I had greeted both my younger guests and those 'devoted to my family' whom Vera Kirilovna slipped in. 'My mother made us scrub our faces and wear our best clothes as if we were going to church. I was so intimidated! Then I saw you were shy, and felt at ease.'

I was shy because he was poor and I was embarrassed, I thought. 'You showed me how to play a difficult passage in the Mozart C minor sonata.'

'In the adagio!' He hummed it. 'Quite devilish, Mozart! And do you still play the piano, Tatyana Petrovna?'

'There's nothing I love better. I fear it won't be possible, though, after I volunteer.'

'Must you really?' He looked genuinely unhappy.

'It's insane,' Alexis said. 'Perhaps you can talk her out of it, maestro. I've given up.'

'The daughter of General Prince Silomirsky could do no less,' Niessen challenged.

Alexis picked up the gauntlet. 'Tatyana Petrovna is more than the daughter of General Prince Silomirsky, more than the friend of the late Grand Duchess Tatyana. She is a person in her own right, with her own abilities and aspirations.'

I came between the disputants. 'Professor Holveg is referring to my old ambition to study medicine. Serving as a field nurse will only postpone it.' And I led Alexis and my guest of honour to a corner out of reach of Niessen's barbs where they settled, like old friends, into a lively conversation.

'We talked mainly about you,' said the pianist later, after Alexis had been button-holed by a high-ranking officer in the monarchist camp.

'Oh? I should have thought you'd have many interests in common.'

'We do, and many friends. My elder sister was a student of Professor Holveg at the University of Petrograd. She was infatuated with him as I recall. Most of his female students were.'

'I'm not surprised.' Alexis had never hinted at his popularity. He seemed to want to repel, rather than charm, yet I could testify to his odd magnetism.

'His lectures were mobbed.' My celebrated guest delighted in another's fame. 'And to think you had him as your tutor!'

'Yes. I'm afraid I didn't realize at the time what a great privilege it was.'

'We took so many things for granted in the old days. If we never take anything for granted again,' concluded Genady Roslov with engaging modesty, 'it may be the most useful lesson the Revolution will have taught us.'

'Don't take the love of Alexis Holveg for granted,' were the words I heard behind the spoken ones.

The subject of my volunteering came up again before the close of the evening, when Kolenka had taken his young ladies home and Vera Kirilovna's 'people who count' had also left.

The old servant couple had gone to bed at sundown – servants were now few and respected. I dismissed the young maid and the weary daughter of the house, who had been helping serve the honoured guests. We carried our iced tea and drinks to the open porch that ran around the lower storey, and set them down beside an oil lamp on a table overlooking the watered garden. The moonless sky was starry, the air fragrant with mint and the more distant scent of mowed hay. After the chalky taste left by months of dry heat and pervasive dust, the freshness was a balm.

In a silk Spanish shawl borrowed from Vera Kirilovna, I sat down in a rocking chair opposite Genady Roslov in white dinner jacket and black tie, sitting forward as if on a piano bench beside his glass of tea. Alexis, in a tropical suit of acceptable cut bought with his nightclub earnings, paced the length of the porch, driven by emotion, I suspected, as much as by his racing mind. My officer-cavaliers also remained on their feet. Lord Andrew's well-pressed dress uniform was a dazzling white beside L-M's and Niessen's clean but shabby tunics. As soon as Vera Kirilovna left, both unbuttoned their collars with the veteran's disdain of formality. Taking advantage of the royal role she had foisted on me, I had graciously excused her from prolonging the fatigue of the evening.

'What a splendid museum specimen, the Countess!' exclaimed Lord Andrew. 'She should be kept under glass! May I, Tanya?' He lit a cigarette after we all declined to join him.

'Can't afford the habit,' said L-M.

'Too jittery already,' said Baron Niessen.

Like Genady Roslov, I did not want to stain my hands with nicotine. Alexis neither smoked nor drank.

'We're all museum specimens, we Russian aristocrats, my dear Andrew,' L-M then remarked. 'Only it won't be a glass case for us. Instead, we'll be consigned, in Comrade Trotsky's phrase, to the dustbin of history.'

'Give me an honourable grave,' said Niessen. 'For a White Russian officer it's the only acceptable alternative to victory.'

'Must you always be so grim, Niessen? This is a party for Mr Roslov after all,' Lord Andrew reminded his fellow naval officer. He was careful to blow his smoke away from us, into the garden.

'Oh, I do not mind.' Genady Roslov spoke with the diffidence that even a famous Russian of the old school still felt in the presence of aristocrats. The imperial government had sent him to England and France during the war to play for the troops, and he spoke both English and French passably. 'I am not so gay myself since I heard Tatyana Petrovna wants to be a White Army nurse.'

'It is a depressing thought, rather,' Lord Andrew agreed. 'I should think you'd have had enough hardship and danger, Tanya, by now.'

'Perhaps not.' L-M, resting his back against the white porch rail, watched me as I rocked in my chair with affected carelessness. 'Perhaps that's just what Tanya does want.'

'Precisely,' Alexis agreed cuttingly. 'It's that Slav spirit of self-sacrifice –'

'Isn't it a noble spirit?' Niessen was a sabre to Alexis's dagger.

'On the other hand,' L-M went on, to my relief, 'if she is volunteering from idealistic and patriotic motives, I would suggest she give it more careful thought.'

'Just what do you mean by that?' Niessen rounded on L-M next.

'I will tell you in a moment. Let's examine the question coolly – we are among trusted friends, are we not? Everything is topsy-turvy. We, the Whites, are forced to accept Allied intervention at the price of Russia's dismemberment. The Bolsheviks, who are supposed to be internationalists, are actually fighting to unite Russia. They, not we, will restore her greatness.'

'What kind of greatness?' Niessen countered. 'The greatness of a tyranny with undreamed-of means of mass control, is that what you, a Rurik prince, desire for Russia?'

I spoke up for my kinsman. 'I'm sure not.'

'My dear chap, I resent the imputation that we are helping you out of imperialistic motives,' said Lord Andrew facetiously.

Alexis also came to L-M's defence. 'I agree with Prince Lomatov-Moskovsky. Should the Whites win, Russia might well be ruled by warlords, like China since her revolution.'

'You would rather see Russia ruled by the Cheka, Professor?' Niessen's voice was so taut I expected it to crack.

'I abhor the Cheka, Baron, as I do any instrument of oppression.' Alexis switched to fluent French then back to textbook English. 'I merely would like Tatyana Petrovna to see that this Russian civil war is not a mass movement, not a popular cause on either Red side or White, but simply a contest of armies led by Red or White generals.'

'Don't forget the Greens,' interjected L-M.

'Greens?' Lord Andrew cried. 'There you go joking again!'

'I'm not joking. The Greens are peasant partisans of the bandit Makhno, some twenty thousand strong it's rumoured. They're not far away either, my dear Andrew.'

'I believe you.' Lord Andrew laughed.

Alexis seized his little beard in sign of alarm. Genady dabbed at his brow and frowned into the cosy, overgrown garden as if bandits lurked behind the indistinct shape of cherry, pear and apple tree.

I tried to ignore the insects and look the picture of composure.

Alexis, swatting at a mosquito with his handkerchief, gave me an exasperated glance. 'Reds, Whites, Greens, not to speak of Cossacks, Czechs and God only knows who else, what alternative do they offer the people? Armies requisition, conscript, plunder, commit atrocities. Where is your "noble spirit", Baron? What does an idealistic young woman like Tatyana Petrovna have to do with any of it? Can you picture it, maestro?'

'What you say is true, Aleksey Alekseyevich, but it is too abstract,' Genady Roslov replied in his deliberate way, as if careful not to offend. 'There must be some less intellectual reason to discourage Tatyana Petrovna from her intention.'

'Well, for one' – L-M shifted his weight, then leaned back against the rail once more with casual elegance – 'she might be forced to witness conduct unbecoming officers and gentlemen, to put it mildly.'

'I've already been warned by General Maysky,' I said. '"No humanity on either side," were almost his final words to me.'

'What humanity can one expect?' Niessen waved off a mosquito with a flick of the wrist. 'Your own family and your sovereign's have been brutally murdered. You liberate a town and find a wasteland; mutilated corpses in the cellars of the local Cheka; other victims heaped, some still breathing, in a mass grave. You're animated by hatred. You're half starved and ragged. Your only pleasure, your only relief is vengeance. It takes crack regiments like those composed entirely of officers to maintain discipline under such conditions. You're a general's daughter, Tatyana Petrovna. You can understand,' Niessen appealed.

He wanted approval, whereas Alexis wanted me to agree with him rationally. Alexis had never held a rifle. He had not shot a man dead as I had. I granted Niessen's wish. 'Yes, I can see how one might become intoxicated with vengeance.'

Niessen appeared to relax a little, while Alexis, after glaring at me, resumed his pacing.

'That's the difference between your civil war and our Great War.' Lord Andrew was serious for a change. 'We on the western front killed without emotion or rancour, like automatons. We were turned into killing machines. I'm not sure that's any better.'

'It's not,' I said. 'Either way, war is horrible.'

'It was always my feeling,' Genady Roslov said in his slow English as he sipped the last of his tea reflectively. 'I absolutely could not participate in the general enthusiasm at the beginning of the war in 1914. Of course, I was mainly afraid for my hands, in case I would be drafted.'

'Lucky for us you weren't!' Lord Andrew spoke for all of us.

Clearly, the young pianist, with his unmistakable civilian softness and vulnerability, aroused neither disrespect nor resentment among the officers. Roslov was modest about his prodigious talent. Like Alexis, he had the independence of judgement and breadth of vision that mastery of a universal language confers – science in the case of Alexis, music in his. What Genady said was spontaneous, original and just. I liked him enormously.

'You see' – he put down his empty glass – 'I don't understand anything about our world any more. I only know this. I live. I own these hands' – he held them up – 'nothing else. They can earn my living and give a few hours of joy and forgetfulness to my listeners. It is a big enough goal for my little life.'

'It's a beautiful goal,' I said, and thought: I, too, have hands which can earn my independence and give respite from pain, however brief, to my fellow sufferers on earth. Aloud, I added, 'My hands are also skilful, in a different way. I simply want to use them where they're needed most.'

I realized, as I spoke, that my left hand had been tying surgical knots in the long fringes of my shawl.

I was the more startled to hear Alexis say, 'You could use your hands best by becoming a surgeon as you once dreamed, Tatyana Petrovna' – he paused in his pacing – 'before something, or *some*one in this unreal town caused you to change your course.'

I feared Niessen would not let the allusion pass. But once again L-M skilfully veered the discussion away from the personal.

'I don't think, Baron,' he said, 'to get back to your argument, we can excuse our cruelty on the pretext of just revenge. Our cause is handicapped already by the lack of a new historical vision. Fallacious as it may be, Communism has that advantage. We must have moral rectitude on our side. We can't afford to dirty our hands with pillage, pogroms, stripping and beating of prisoners of war, and the like.'

'The high command does its utmost to curb these excesses. But at least with us, reprisal is swift and savage. It is not a policy of terror, as with the Bolsheviks,' Niessen was quick to retort.

'Is it a policy or an expression of terror?' Delicately, L-M brushed a mosquito off his sleeve.

'You're being provocative!' Niessen turned even paler in the soft half-light.

'You're not leaving?' Lord Andrew looked distressed.

'I'm going to fetch another drink, with Tatyana Petrovna's permission. Can I get anyone anything?'

'I'll get my own,' Lord Andrew followed Niessen indoors.

The level of tension dropped noticeably. I listened to the squeak of the rocking chair, Alexis's short step, the whir of moths around the lamp, and, farther off, the intermittent barking of dogs and the incessant song of grasshoppers – peaceful sounds all.

'How quiet it is!' L-M expressed my thought. 'I haven't got used to it yet, after two years of thunder on the western front. Over there, artillery barrages seldom let up.'

'I would grow deaf.' The pianist lifted his hands to his ears.

'Many did. Still, *odnako*,' mused L-M in Russian, 'there is nothing quite like our southern Russian night, ah, Professor?'

'True.' Irritation had gone out of Alexis's voice.

'Do you love Russia, Alexis?' I asked as he drew near. I felt free, in Niessen's absence, to call him by his first name. After all, Alexis had grown up in Warsaw, taken his doctorate at Göttingen, done his earliest research in Paris. 'You've spent more than half your life abroad.'

'I have spent enough of it here. Who would not love the Russian earth? It is so vast, so abundant, so beautifully described by her writers and poets! The potential for human development is unparalleled. But what has become of it, I ask you?'

'Father said something similar once,' I murmured.

Evidently Alexis did not hear. 'Did you know' – he turned to L-M – 'that Jewish officers in the White Volunteer Army were asked to resign their commissions?'

'General Denikin did it for their protection, much against his will. It's really too bad,' L-M commented with typical understatement.

I could not look at Alexis and busied myself untying the knots I had made in the fringes of Vera Kirilovna's shawl. I was glad to see Kolenka return with Lord Andrew and Niessen, all three with drinks in hand. Now, perhaps, we could talk of lighter matters. But Genady Roslov wanted to continue our political discussion.

'That was very interesting, Prince, your earlier remark about the Red terror.' He lifted his face to L-M. 'Bolshevik fear and suspiciousness pass all normal limits. What is your explanation?'

'The Bolsheviks, it seems to me,' L-M obliged, 'have good reason to be terrified. A small clique seizes power in a vast country and maintains itself by propaganda and brute force. As a predictable result, it has a civil war on its hands. Foreign powers soon intervene and your upstart government is now beset by external as well as internal enemies. Quite naturally, its paranoia knows no bounds.'

'What would you have us and our allies do?' Niessen asked. 'Lay down our arms? I'm afraid you haven't understood the nature of Marxist-Leninism.'

'I'm not sure the Bolsheviks do either. All I'm saying, really' –

L-M responded to our surprise after a pause – 'is that it doesn't help to create a mythical Red monster. If it becomes a reality, the entire world may not be able to grapple with it.'

'Very well put, Prince. Excellently put.' From beyond the circle of light came the precise voice of Alexis.

'You're right.' I, too, was struck by L-M's words. 'There must be an end, not to resistance – human dignity must be preserved at all costs – but to hatred and violence.'

'This discussion is treasonous,' Kolenka said. 'I hope there are no counter-espionage agents listening.' He peered underneath the table and around the corner before taking a cigarette from Lord Andrew with relish.

'What you said about creating a reality in the mind, Prince. I once had a similar thought.' Genady Roslov's tone reflected the growing excitement. We had forgotten the insects. We did not want to miss a word. 'When the Revolution broke out in 1917, I was in Moscow. I saw a boy of not more than twelve leading a platoon of policemen, some forty big, strong men, to prison. I thought then, One day we believe the policeman has power over us, and the next we no longer do. The policeman does not believe it either and lets himself be led to prison by a boy. I understood then that revolution happens in the mind.'

'Revolution happens in the mind . . . That's very good too.' Alexis stepped back into the circle of light.

'Such an incident could only happen in a free society like Russia's before 1917,' scoffed Niessen. 'All the change of mind in the world won't shake off Bolshevik rule.'

'It might,' Alexis insisted, 'if Bolshevik rule were allowed to take its course. Counter-revolution and foreign intervention will only strengthen the Bolsheviks in the long run.'

'Professor, have a care!' cried Kolenka.

'You're saying, if I understand you correctly, Professor, that if we offer no resistance we are less likely to be crushed?' Niessen queried.

L-M spoke in my stead. 'It is an odd sort of logic, but a part of me agrees with Professor Holveg.'

'Both your points of view are convincing.' Genady Roslov regarded the heated antagonists quizzically. Then, 'I have been thinking something completely irrelevant,' he added.

'Tell us, maestro,' I urged before the conversation could turn dangerous again.

'Here we are on a porch in late summer in a provincial Russian town, conversing like characters in a Chekhov play. And the familiar emotions from which they suffered, thwarted love, thwarted ambition, now seem – how shall I say it? – manufactured. I see now that in the past I suffered in the main from manufactured emotions.' Genady looked with appealing shyness from me to Alexis to the four officers.

'So here we are instead talking about war and Communism, and from some perspective up there' – L-M glanced up at the sky – 'it may be just as insignificant.'

'Or as urgent,' Lord Andrew's eager young voice rang out. 'Logically, they're one and the same. Speaking for myself, Mr Roslov, I, in this moment, am my entire reality.'

'I agree with His Lordship.' Kolenka was eager to show off his fluency in English. 'I may be absolutely insignificant in the grand scheme of things, I may even be insignificant in the ordinary scheme – nevertheless, my own well-being is always important and urgent. I think this is true of the most exceptional people, like Professor Holveg and Maestro Roslov, and the most average, like myself. Alone, the Bolsheviks refuse to accept this universal fact. That is why,' concluded Kolenka, 'they have to kill so many people.'

'Let's have no more talk of killing,' I enjoined, glancing at Kolenka with sympathy. In Taganrog's atmosphere of sectarian passions his selfish pragmatism was almost a relief.

There was a silence loud with emotion. What were Alexis and Niessen thinking? How strange that both men, antipodal as they were, should be in love with me! And I could not love either one. Like L-M, I was incapable of passion. I watched the shooting stars, listened to the trilling insects of the steppe – earth's perennial summer fiddlers sawing away as jubilantly here, in the midst of civil war, as at Veslawa during the retreat of 1915. I felt a sharp pang.

'Oh where, oh where have you departed,
My golden days of youth and Spring?'

I started at hearing Pushkin's familiar verses sung behind me *sotto voce*. How aptly they expressed my thought! How that soft baritone recalled another velvety, unforgettable man's voice!

'"What fate awaits me on the morrow?"' Baron Niessen continued to sing Lensky's aria from Tchaikovsky's *Eugene Onegin*.

'What fate awaits us indeed!' echoed L-M matter-of-factly.

I rose to put an end to the evening.

'What are your plans after Taganrog?' I asked Genady Roslov as I saw my guests to the front door. 'Will you leave Russia?'

'I may be forced to. I go next to play in Batum, then I am invited to stay in Tiflis with friends.' He mentioned Georgia's foremost princely family. 'But who knows how long Georgia will remain an independent republic?'

'L-M seems to have hit it off with Professor Holveg much better than I,' Niessen remarked under his breath while Alexis and my kinsman exchanged warm farewells. 'I did not like his familiarity towards you, Tatyana Petrovna.'

'Oh, he's such an old friend, and I owe him so much. And one can't apply conventional standards to great scientists.'

'Great scientists don't intimidate me.' Then, 'Forgive my irritability, Tatyana Petrovna.' Niessen softened his tone. 'I used to be rather like Lord Andrew, without sense of the tragic. Now, I fear, I have no other.'

'I understand. I am close to it myself. That's why I must *act*.'

'Yes, action is our only salvation. Unless ...' His restless gaze devoured me. 'Another time.' He kissed my hand with military correctness as L-M approached to take his leave in turn.

'I return to Constantinople by the early boat tomorrow,' Alexis said curtly while Kolenka escorted my musical guest to the car. 'I will come for Nyanya. I also have your ticket, should you wish to use it.'

I did not know what to say. But Alexis, with a stiff little bow, had turned and left.

Nyanya was in bed but she got up to brush my hair after I had undressed. 'Well, and how did your party go, my little dove?' she asked.

'All right. Genady Roslov and Alexis like each other ever so much.' I told her all that Genady had related.

'Oh he's a great scholar for sure, Aleksey Alekseyevich, but I wouldn't put too much stock in his genius if I didn't know how greatly he loved you,' Nyanya declared.

'What's so special about that?' I asked with false blitheness – I was far from taking any man's love for granted. 'Baron Niessen loves me too.'

'And what of that? He finds a young princess hiding on a deserted shore. She cares for his wound. What young man wouldn't fall in love? But Aleksey Alekseyevich now, a real man, a mature one, how he nursed you when you were ill! How gentle he was and never took advantage of your helplessness! How he braved every danger, every hardship, always putting you first . . . That kind of love one should treasure and not despise. That kind of love a woman will find only once in her life.'

'I don't despise it, Nyanya. It has been life-saving to me. But can't you understand, I don't believe Stefan is dead. I feel he is *here*, in Russia somewhere – I have sensed it ever since I came to Taganrog – and I will not leave till I find him or his bones.'

'You will destroy yourself . . . Well, there's no stopping you.' Nyanya looked darkly at my reflection. 'Only I won't stay to watch it.'

'You can't stay, Nyanya. God knows where I'll be assigned. Vera Kirilovna will look after you if you don't want to leave with Alexis tomorrow.'

'I thank Her Excellency but I would rather go with Aleksey Alekseyevich. We will console each other for your hard heart.'

There was no doing the right thing! I went to bed wretched, and came down sleepless early the next morning to a stiff and smart Alexis in his one tropical suit and straw boater. Nyanya followed with her bundle.

'You still persist in your crazy scheme?' he asked.

Again, pride choked me, anxiety paralysed me. I could not bear to see him go. But I would not beg him to stay.

'Very well. Here's money for your temporary needs.' He laid a sheaf of Kerensky roubles on the vestibule table. 'They're worthless outside White Russia. I will proceed with my original intention to go to Paris in three weeks and begin my work at the Radium Institute. My work . . .' He hesitated. Then, 'I have that at least,' he added with the old conviction.

'How lucky you are, Alexis!' I had no such clear and uncompromising imperative.

He looked at me long. 'So it was all for nothing, all for nothing!' he remarked as if to himself, called to Nyanya to follow, and was gone.

32

The departure of Alexis left me dazed. Again, as at each critical turning point in my life, I experienced separation as severance, abandonment, rejection. It was not I who had sent Alexis away, but he who had deserted me. At the same time, I also felt in the wrong, unworthy, bent on a sacrifice no one appreciated. I saw Taganrog society through the eyes of Alexis, with all its petty hierarchies and false gaiety – the triumph of trivia in the midst of tragedy. I became exasperated at Vera Kirilovna. I would neither make nor accept social calls.

While I sulked and stewed in the imminent expectation of my interview with General Denikin, the dreaded Makhno and his bandit army made an unscheduled appearance in the hills north-west of town. I loaded my pistol. Vera Kirilovna took special care of her toilette and covered her pallor with rouge. Zinaida Mikhailovna was too terrified of us to whimper. The household alternately rushed about hiding valuables and packing for emergency evacuation on Allied ships.

For supper my cavaliers appeared along with Kolenka.

'Taganrog is practically denuded of troops,' L-M observed with his usual detachment.

'General Thompson, the chief of our mission, has been drilling the foreign section.' Lord Andrew was full of boyish excitement. 'Some of our navy men had never sat a horse. What a sight!' He laughed as L-M chuckled.

'I'd be amused too, if there were not women in danger.' Baron Niessen looked at me. 'Makhno is even worse than the Bolsheviks in that respect.'

'Who is this Makhno?' I had my pistol. I felt safe.

'An anarchist bandit, a sort of modern-day Robin Hood, as colourful as he is sanguinary,' said L-M. 'His motto is, "Hang a Red, a Jew, and a *Pan*" – a landowner.'

'Then what does he want with us?'

'We, my dear Tanya, are the landowners.'

'I don't see that any of you Whites owns anything any more,' Lord Andrew remarked.

'We don't. But Red propaganda,' L-M explained, 'which is much more thorough and effective than ours, has managed to smear us with that label.'

'What d'you mean, *smear* us?' came Baron Niessen's instant challenge.

'In the eyes of the peasantry, my dear fellow. Unfortunately, our excellent and scrupulous General Denikin would like to postpone agrarian reform until victory and the convening of a constituent assembly. In the meantime, landowners have been promised compensation – one must uphold the principle of private property, if only for the sake of our allies, who are here, let's not forget, in defence of capitalism. And so we lose a badly needed opportunity for popular support.'

'You don't think,' retorted Baron Niessen, 'our peasants so naïve as to believe Bolshevik promises of land any longer?'

'Our peasants are by no means naïve. The proof is they distrust us and the Reds equally. They'll sooner follow a Makhno.'

'I'll sooner take the Bolshies.' Kolenka was no longer jaunty. 'Cleverness may help you out with them. With Makhno, nothing will.'

'It's a perfect madhouse, Russia.' Lord Andrew summed up the feeling prevailing in the foreign missions.

Overnight, the bandit army vanished, and Taganrog resumed its pretence of normality.

The next exciting event was the arrival, on 13 September, of a Polish delegation under the auspices of the International Red Cross. Headed by General Karnicki, the delegation's real purpose, which quickly became common knowledge, was to discuss an accord between Polish and White armies.

Vera Kirilovna immediately plotted a reception for General Karnicki. For this once, I made no objection. It would be an opportunity to talk about Stefan. But before the reception took place, I was fetched by Kolenka to General Denikin's office.

The commander in chief was a rather small, average-looking man of middle age. He rose and shook my hand, expressed regret at being unable to attend General Maysky's funeral, then sat down at his desk and said in the tone of a busy executive, 'I have before me your application for service in the White Volunteer Army as a field nurse. While I appreciate your interest in our cause, I must deny it.'

Had he heard of Vera Kirilovna's monarchist machinations? Or did he feel the resentment common among officers of the general staff risen through the ranks, like himself and Alexeiev, towards the highborn General Prince Silomirsky?

'No one as closely associated with the late family of Tsar Nicholas II as you are in the popular mind may be accepted in our ranks,' General Denikin continued. 'I have turned down similar requests from members of the deposed dynasty.' He was more than brisk; he was brusque.

My first thought was: Alexis has won. My second: Russia no longer needs me. My third: It's out of my hands.

'I'm very sorry that you cannot use me,' I said. 'I'd hoped to be able to do my small part in the cause that offers the only hope for saving our unhappy country.'

General Denikin's tone changed. 'I believe you, Tatyana Petrovna.'

As he looked me straight in the eye, I liked the openness and integrity I read in his pleasant bearded face. He reminded me of the Tsar, without the polish and the aura of majesty. He was certainly a man after the Tsar's heart.

After a moment's deliberation the General rose and went to stand before a wall map of Russia. 'However, there is something you can do for us which would be even more valuable than your services in the field.'

A line of movable white flags crossing the Ukraine north of Kiev showed the most recent advance of the White Army in its impetuous drive on Moscow. With a pointer, General Denikin indicated a line across Podolia from the Rumanian border to Zhitomir. 'This sector is held by Polish troops, forty thousand strong and in fine fighting trim, equipped by the French. They are confining themselves to a holding action. If we can persuade them to attack in coordination with our offensive, its success is assured. Your father had influence with the Poles. Will you speak with General Karnicki?'

'The General has been invited to a reception at the house where

I am lodging. May I ask how Your Excellency stands with the Polish delegation?'

'Our talks have been cordial but non-committal so far. The Poles, in return for an accord, want to exact territorial guarantees in regard to eastern Galicia, as a start. Eventually, their claims will include Volhynia, and other border provinces which were Polish centuries ago. *Ot morza do morza* – from sea to sea,' he quoted in Polish, 'that is the true extent of the new Poland's ambition.'

I thought it was no different from Russia's. Most of her wars had been fought for that dream.

'And is it Your Excellency's impression that the Poles fear a White Russian state would not respect its new-won independence?'

'They have no reason to fear us,' General Denikin declared. 'We are not expansionist, nor imperialist. Our goal is Russia One and Indivisible. We recognize the Polish state in principle, of course. But its final frontiers cannot be settled until the convening of the Constituent Assembly, which alone can speak for the Russian people.'

How very like the Tsar General Denikin was! Just so had Nicholas II spoken to Uncle Stan. I knew it would be useless to explain to General Denikin that, from a Polish viewpoint, neither a tsar nor a constituent assembly had any right to decide Poland's affairs.

'If Stanislaw Veslawski, my uncle, were alive,' I said, 'I'm certain you would have found in him a strong ally. His only son, Stefan, was also reported killed, on Russian soil –'

'I have asked for the report of the investigation made by the Poles and the French.' General Denikin was quick to get the point. 'I was informed you wanted corroboration of that tragic accident.'

'Your Excellency, is it possible it was not Stefan who was murdered, but someone who resembled him?'

'Anything is possible in civil war, Tatyana Petrovna. Witness the escape of your father's officers from Kronstadt. That was as inconceivable a feat as the rescue, the previous year, of General Kornilov from captivity in Petrograd.' He paused, started to glance at his watch, drew himself up, and asked, 'Is there anything more I can do for you?'

'If I may presume on your time, since I'm to speak with the Polish gentlemen, could Your Excellency give me an idea of the relative strength of the opposing camps?' I eyed the wall map with the curiosity about military dispositions I had acquired from campaigning with Father.

'Gladly.' With his pointer, General Denikin outlined the boundary of Soviet-occupied territory west of the Urals. Then, 'Our forces and those of our allies are thinly spread out, here in the far northern wilderness.' He pointed first to Archangel province, next to a vast region below Murmansk. 'Our allies, the Americans especially, are on the point of abandoning the enterprise. Here in the north-west, on the contrary' – the pointer moved west of Petrograd – 'General Yudenich is advancing with his army. If the Estonians don't betray him, and the British don't withdraw their support, he may capture Petrograd.

'We, in the meantime, are pushing by forced marches towards Moscow, not to be caught by the cold – our troops are woefully ill-equipped against the cold. We must also make speed because the Cossack, who fights with us, does not like long campaigns. He likes to go home to his *stanitsa* laden with booty as quick as he can. We must also beware of bandits and anarchists in our rear.'

'Like Makhno,' I said. 'He had my good hosts in a fine panic.'

'You see how unpredictable and precarious our situation is.' General Denikin did not permit himself a smile.

'And the Bolsheviks? They look surrounded.'

'Thinly surrounded by armies that can make no contact with one another.' The tip of the pointer moved across the Urals. 'If you can imagine that a telegram from our Siberian army headquarters in Omsk has to go through London or Paris to reach us!

'Now, as to Bolshevik strength. They have interior lines of communication and an industrial base. Their military discipline is enforced by punitive detachments. Their tactics have been improved by advisers from the former German general staff. But the Bolsheviks too suffer from hunger, disease, demoralization. They too are strained to the limit. At this point, any one factor can tip the balance. That is why, you see, Polish intervention is so crucial.'

'I will do my best.'

'I thank you in the name of the Motherland.'

The Motherland – *Rodina*. Once again, I had none.

General Denikin seemed to understand. 'What plans will you make now, Tatyana Petrovna?'

'I don't know, Your Excellency.'

It depended on the outcome of my talk with the Poles. It depended on the report about Stefan. I was not quite ready to turn my life over to Alexis, tempting as that now seemed.

General Denikin shook my hand.

'I wish you success with all my heart,' I said and went away even more confused and unhappy than I had come.

I dressed with some care to receive my Polish guests. True to my vow, in memory of my imperial namesake, I refused the offer of Vera Kirilovna's rope of pearls. I wore instead a small golden cross on a chain that I had bought from a refugee in Taganrog.

'Won't you wear the ribbon of St Catherine I found for you, on this occasion at least?' Vera Kirilovna pleaded. 'You are entitled to it as a princess of the first rank.'

On this occasion, I agreed to let her drape the ribbon over one shoulder and across my breast. Lastly, I slipped into my one pair of sandals with a small heel. Short hair and the tall, boyish figure were becoming fashionable. I no longer felt unattractive.

'You look stunning, Tanya,' Lord Andrew complimented me while Vera Kirilovna greeted the General and his aides in her turn. 'Pity Baron Niessen's not here.'

L-M smiled. 'He has been ordered, in fact, to stay away. Niessen's no diplomat.' L-M represented the foreign relations section at my reception, and knew my intent to woo General Karnicki.

The head of the Polish delegation was much more martial and magnificent than our General Denikin. His ADCs outshone the Russian adjutants correspondingly. Polish gallantry was still nonpareil. I was both amused and saddened.

After a suitable interval, I took General Karnicki aside on the porch.

He expressed his sympathy for the death of my father, 'a friend of Poland, a rare Russian'.

'Yes,' said I, 'and his loss was followed in the same year by that of my Veslawski aunt and uncle. How glad and proud they would have been to see their beloved country granted independence!'

'They will be missed in its reconstruction, and their son Stefan even more. *Polskie Państwo*' – the Polish Lorddom was how Poles again referred to their country – 'has need of such splendid young men.'

I mastered the pain that shot through me. 'Would Your Excellency know anything of Stefan's comrade, Sir Casimir Paszek?'

'Major Casimir Paszek, who hasn't heard of his bravery! He's now at the front, facing the Red Army.'

This gave me the opening I needed. 'Your forces, I'm sure, represent a formidable barrier to Soviet expansion. But would it not be to Poland's advantage to coordinate its thrust with the southern White Army's offensive, and put an end, once and for all, to the Communist threat?'

'Poland is in no danger from Communism.' The General dropped his gallant manner to become the blunt military man. 'Poles love freedom far too much.'

'That I well know. But the Soviets, contrary to their stated aims, have not been exactly respectful of their neighbours' freedom. They tried to subvert Finland. Only General Yudenich's army and the Estonians keep them from overrunning the Baltic states. Are you not afraid, should the Bolsheviks defeat the Whites, that they might turn on Poland next?'

'We are prepared for that eventuality. But what guarantee do we have that a White Russian government will respect our frontiers any better than a Red?'

'If I may speak from personal experience, *Pan General*, no White Russian government can be as great a threat to Poland, and the entire free world, as the Soviet People's Republic.'

'We will be wary of both,' said General Karnicki.

He views Poland as a great power on a par with Russia, I thought with growing exasperation. I gave no sign of it but continued calmly, 'Is there no way the provisional White government can reassure you of its friendliness towards the new Poland?'

'We have asked for guarantees regarding eastern Galicia. They have been denied.'

How foolish of General Denikin, I thought, not to placate Polish pride! I spoke with deliberation. 'The commander in chief is no politician. He does not feel competent to make political decisions. For these, he relies on the Constituent Assembly which is to be convened immediately upon victory. But it's my impression he is as scrupulously honest as he is stubborn. I would take his word against that of Comrade Trotsky any day.'

The General gave me a quick glance, then closed himself up even more. He suspects me of knowing some secret, flashed through my mind. Can it be that the Poles are planning to conclude an accord with the Reds?

'We would be fools to take the Bolsheviks at their word,' said the General.

'Especially,' I pressed on, 'since Comrade Trotsky and company, unlike General Denikin, will promise anything, then break their word when it suits them. Marxists have a saying: "The end justifies the means." For a people with a strong tradition of loyalty and honour like the Poles, this may be difficult to conceive.'

'We have dealt with treachery before,' General Karnicki said.

Yes, and are not past dealing in it yourself, I thought, as my conviction grew that an agreement with the Bolsheviks was under consideration, if not already signed.

'I'm sure Poland's new leaders are as able as they are brave.' I concluded our fruitless talk, and we rejoined the party.

It ended with smiles and civilities. Vera Kirilovna notwithstanding, I swore this would be my last social event in Taganrog. L-M and Lord Andrew returned after escorting His Polish Excellency to his car. One look at my face told them I had achieved nothing.

'General Thompson will be roaring mad,' said Lord Andrew. 'We want the Poles to join up with the Whites and smash the Bolshies, but they're too bloody suspicious of one another. They'd rather be gobbled up by the Reds one at a time.'

'And that's exactly what will happen,' L-M observed.

'Unless General Denikin can be persuaded to accede to Polish demands, I have the feeling they'll go back and make peace with the Bolsheviks,' I said.

General Karnicki was not a Veslawski. Poland's leaders too were a new breed, arrant nationalists like their counterparts in the infant nations spawned by the Treaty of Versailles, or, for that matter, like the Italians, the Greeks, and the French.

L-M broke in on my thoughts. 'General Denikin won't budge. He's too staunch a patriot.'

I was suddenly sick of patriotism, be it Russian or Polish. 'Nothing has changed since 1914. Nothing has been learned.'

'Nothing,' L-M agreed, 'except that instead of tsars and kaisers and their noblemen-diplomats who more or less observed international proprieties and honoured treaties, Europe's new leaders will be vulgar demagogues. They will learn the art of propaganda from the Bolsheviks. They too will manipulate the masses. Instead of "The People's Liberation", "National Greatness" will be their slogan.'

'That will mean more war.' My mind flew to Alexis, the small scientist who towered over nationalistic and ideological divisions. With him one might retain sanity in a mad world.

'Assuredly.' L-M contemplated both past and future wars with cool curiosity.

'Bosh!' cried Lord Andrew. 'You enjoy upsetting people, L-M. Why don't you go to England, Tanya, to Lansdale? The family will welcome you with open arms.'

'Thank you, Andrew.' I was touched. But it was Nyanya's arms I wanted to fall into, Alexis whom I longed to see.

I asked L-M to cable him that I had been turned down by the White Army. Would he advise the British military hospital to please keep my position open as I would probably return to Constantinople soon?

Now, only anticipation of the investigation into Stefan's supposed death still kept me in Taganrog.

33

Three days before my scheduled departure for Constantinople, as I returned with Lord Andrew and Baron Niessen from my morning ride, I found L-M waiting for me with a briefcase.

He took from it a dossier and said, 'General Denikin has asked me to convey this to you personally, Tanya, along with his thanks for your efforts with the Polish delegation. Would you like us to remain while you read the report?' he added as I stood stock-still, unable to reach for the file.

I looked around at the three faces bent on me. Even Lord Andrew's was grave and solemn, as it must have been when the telegram came with news of his brother Beresford's death in action.

'Thank you,' I said. 'I would rather read it alone.' And grasping the dossier decisively, I went up to my room and locked the door.

I laid the thick envelope containing the report marked 'confidential' on the writing desk by the corner window overlooking the garden, unfastened the clasp, and slowly removed the sheaf of papers and photographs. Then I got up and walked about, taking deep breaths to quiet my racing heart. Finally I sat down at the desk. Laying aside the medical report and the photographs – I could not face these yet – I began to read the verbal account, taken down in Russian and translated into Polish, of the chief eyewitness. He was a twenty-two-year-old Ukrainian peasant, a former corporal and deserter from the Galician front who had fled from Red Army recruiters and joined up with Grigoriev's bandits.

On the 12 January 1919, our scouts spotted a food and forage convoy under White Army escort heading north from Odessa between the Dniester and the Bug. Two hundred of us were dispatched to ambush it. We circled around to cut the convoy off as it veered eastward, and took cover behind the cliffs at a crossing of the Bug. We watched the Whites coming, slow and unaware of danger. There was a strapping young fellow with them, a civilian sitting next to the driver of the foremost wagon, leading them in song. His voice was like a deacon's, rich and deep, with such a sweet note ... It made me long for my village and another life than a bandit's. I'd have let the convoy pass, had I been in command. But our chief – he was one of our toughest – gave the order to attack as soon as they'd crossed the bridge.

They were fifty armed and mounted men to our two hundred. Their machine gun jammed, and we captured it first off. We took some casualties but we had automatic rifles stolen from the French. We had them covered. They surrendered. We disarmed and tied the prisoners' hands behind them, loaded their horses and ours with sacks of grain and potatoes, and headed back to our camp across the Dniester, leading the prisoners on their horses. The *pan* with the fine voice we put on a dray horse. We did not bother with the drivers. They got a bullet between the eyes.

When we started to climb our heights, slippery from the rain, it got hard for the horses, loaded as they were. Our *ataman* – our chief – calls a halt just beyond the river in a small field bounded by a wood and sheltered from the bridge. He assigns twenty of us to help him dispose of the prisoners and load their horses with booty. And he orders the main body of our men to continue the march.

Our chief sets up the machine gun. Me, I don't have much stomach for cold-blooded killing – in the battle, it's different, one gets excited, one forgets – and I say, 'Why don't we give them a chance to join us, *pan ataman*, the Ukrainian lads at least?' And I say a prayer that my singer can speak our dialect.

'Well, why not, it will save ammunition,' says my chief. 'You test them out. And if they escape, it'll be your neck.'

So I go around and talk to them, and about fifteen are from our region, as I suspected, and we accept them.

'Take me too, you'll be well recompensed,' whispers my singer, but the chief, it turns out, has other plans for him and the two officers in charge of the convoy.

He has them led aside and with the machine gun he mows down the two dozen remaining prisoners. Like wheat in a field they lie down one on top of another, without a sound.

Now my chief is getting excited. Drawing blood does that to him. He takes a swig of vodka from his flask. His eyes get even shinier and he says, 'Let's have some fun, lads, with these three fine fellows. You men, prove to us your loyalty.' And he orders our new recruits to dig three man-size pits.

'Oh dear God, no!' I put my hands to my head, got up, and paced the room distractedly, stared out the window at the apple tree. But the truth, however horrible, had to be faced. I read on.

While the pits are being dug – it goes fast in the wet, sandy soil – the two White officers suddenly declare that they're not Whites, they're Reds. They went over to the Volunteer Army when the Cossacks took them prisoner, to escape a beating. And one of them still keeps his Red Army tag, it turns out, in a secret pocket, with his service papers. He's a major, no less, and he hints that he will get our band a reprieve if we let him and his comrade go free, when the Soviet power reconquers the south. 'Soon now,' he says, 'our army's on the way.'

'You son-of-a-whore,' says my chief. 'Do you think a Bolshevik dearer to me than a White?' And he orders all three men stripped.

The two officers struggle and scream like demons, but my singer, he is absolutely calm and quiet.

His passport, which my chief gives me to read out loud, says that he is from Saratov, a horse buyer for the White Army. His outer dress is like a country trader's but his linen, that's of the finest quality! Between his shirt and undershirt are more identity papers. On these he's a trader in grain from Orel, in the Red zone, with a safe-conduct from the Soviet commissariat of supply.

Well, brother, I say to myself, you're a spy! Whether for the Reds or the Whites or both, I don't want to know, and I tell the chief these second, secret papers are purchase orders for horses.

We continue to search him. In one boot we find a knife, in the other a small revolver. Around his naked waist is a wide cloth belt with cartridges and gold roubles sewn into it. And in between the gold is sewn a ring, a gold ring with a seal and an eagle's head, like a king's!

'Some horse buyer you are!' says my chief to him in Russian. 'You're a proper bandit, is what you are! You robbed some rich prince, you did.'

'I am myself a prince,' my singer replies, 'and you will get many more gold roubles for my ransom if you will send word to the French. I give you my word you will not be pursued if you let me and these two officers live.'

'And what are these Reds to you,' says my chief, 'a prince?'

'My fellow men,' he answers in a way that gives me a turn.

'*Chudak* – you're an odd one!' laughs my chief as he tries the ring first on one hand, then the other. He likes gold, my chief. Next to blood and vodka, he likes it best of all.

'I'll tell you what I'll do,' he says at last. 'I'll bury you and your Red *fellow men* up to the neck, *then* send word to the Frenchies. And if they find you alive, they can have you without ransom!' And he bursts out laughing.

So in they go, each into his pit, the Reds still carrying on like madmen, the prince without resistance. My chief is in a kind of trance over the ring, and he's gathered up the roubles too. Our lads are eyeing them and muttering among themselves. Finally the boldest of them speaks up. 'There are twenty pieces there, just enough to divide evenly among us. You keep the ring, *pan ataman*, and give us the gold.'

'What, you sons of dogs!' he says. While they're quarrelling, our recruits quietly untie their horses and off they ride!

'After them!' cries my chief, pocketing the roubles, and we give pursuit.

'Pan ataman,' I say as we gallop along, 'should we leave those three back there alive? What if Cossacks should find them and get our description? They'll invent a worse execution for us!'

I don't actually believe anyone will find them, except foxes and vultures, but I'm sorely sorry for the singing prince. I would like him put out of his misery.

'You're a smart one,' says my chief. 'It's not for nothing you learned to read. You keep after the traitors. I'll catch up with you.' And he turns back with his second.

I hear shots and in a little bit my chief and his second come galloping back. 'We shut them up for good,' my chief says. He's very merry - he has kept all the roubles for himself. 'I'm afraid, though, by the time they find their prince,' he adds, 'the Frenchies won't know him any more.' And he and his second have a good laugh.

Well, they did not have the last laugh in this adventure. We lost our fugitive recruits as evening came on, and made camp. We planned to go back in the morning and retrieve our booty. Instead, we were surprised by Polish legionnaires.

My chief and his second were killed in the attack. With the Poles were our fugitives, who had ridden into French and Polish positions the night before and told everything. The Poles made me lead them to the scene of the massacre. A flock of vultures flew away at our coming. The corpses still lay in the field, only they had been stripped, during the night, either by peasants or some of our own bandits. The sacks of grain and potatoes were all gone. The three heads were still there, sticking out of the ground, well, what was left of them, between the bullets and the vultures . . .

I broke off with a cry.

There was a soft knock at the door.

'Tatyana Petrovna, dearest, you have not had breakfast yet,' came Zinaida Mikhailovna's voice timidly. 'May we bring you something?'

'I don't want anything. Leave me alone!' My voice sounded unlike my own.

It can't be! Left alone, I paced up and down. I kissed Stevie when he was wounded, still under narcosis. He kissed me, in the hospital in Minsk, and in the wood, in the rain, before we parted. His lips were so full, so velvety-soft . . . And the vultures feasted on them, they put their foul beaks in his mouth, they picked out his eyes . . . No, I will go mad!

Later in the day – I had lost all sense of time – I returned to the terrible report I had demanded to see! The bandit corporal's account had been corroborated by his fellow bandits and their prisoner-fugitives. He had been reprieved from execution and sent to a labour battalion.

The medical report confirmed instant death by shooting from two bullets fired at close range with a pistol through the top of the cranium. The victim's chest and lungs were unusually developed, like a singer's. He had a scar several years old, from a penetrating wound in the left thigh. A photograph showed the covered body, too large to fit on a stretcher, as it was brought to the Polish legionnaires' outpost near Odessa. Other photographs showed the military honours rendered Major Prince Veslawski by French, Polish and White troops, and the casket being shipped to France with a military guard.

Although a day of mourning had been proclaimed in Poland in Stefan's memory, the Dowager Princess Catherine refused to believe her grandson dead and to accept his body in the Veslawski family crypt. Out of regard for the revered old lady and at the request of the Veslawski kin in Poland, France and England, the investigation of his murder had been kept confidential and no sensational details given to the press.

Appended to the report was a note by General Denikin. 'My friend, General Ruszky, was buried alive by the Bolsheviks, after indignity and torture. The noblest men come to the most ignoble ends in these cruel times. Be thankful young Prince Stefan did not suffer long. I have sent his description to our field commanders, but I fear this report must be accepted as final. Please believe me ever at your disposal, Anton Denikin.'

'I fear this report must be accepted as final,' wrote General Denikin. I put it back in its envelope, tied the clasp, and sat staring at it. This report was final. I too had to accept it. But how, without losing my mind?

With a trembling hand, I wrote General Denikin a note of thanks. Then I jumped up and turned my back on the testimony on the desk. But the scene of horror rose before me all the same. Anywhere I turned in the room, it lurked, waiting to spring.

Day waned, night fell. Vera Kirilovna knocked on the door and was repulsed. Mechanically, I undressed and bathed, took a sedative, and got into bed.

I dreamt that I was walking along a country lane, when I met a horse and wagon laden with boxes. 'What have you got there?' I asked the driver. He opened the box. It contained a body severed from its head.

I awoke in a cold sweat, only to sleep and dream again, this time of a peasant procession carrying sacks. I took them for sacks of grain and potatoes at first but when the peasants set them down at my feet, I knew they held living victims suffering in silence – their vocal cords had been cut. I started awake, pulling at my hair roots sodden with perspiration.

When exhaustion and the drug overcame me once more, I found myself going down into the cellar of a hospital. Here were bandaged, burned and misshapen human forms even more ghastly than those I had seen in reality. I sensed their mute pleading. I felt helpless, useless, at fault.

I sat up, wide awake. Night's horrors were worse than day's! My mind could conjure a worse hell than war and revolution combined!

My girlhood vision of society as a cesspool below a flowery surface surged up and was superseded by one far worse: the world as an ocean of blood in which humanity drowned . . .

I leaped out of bed and washed my face in cold water in the porcelain basin on my dresser. By the light of the half-moon, the face that I lifted stared back, haggard, in the mirror. Is that really me? I wondered, and my eye fell on my pistol.

I took it up, cocked and caressed it. If I could not exorcise these visions, I could not live! This would be taking the direct route to damnation, I well knew. But better emptiness than insanity!

I put my elbows on the dresser, and watched myself slowly lift the pistol to my mouth. It was swift, sure death. How easy! Blow out my brains from below, as Stevie's had been from above . . . Stevie . . .

I laid the weapon down. How well he died, I thought. Like a stoic, a true prince! And if Stevie could die quietly, with a last thought for his fellow men, why can't I get on quietly with the business of living, and think more about others than about myself?

If his death teaches me that, then I can look on it, not as a horror, but an example.

I felt a deep peace, a great calm and detachment as when Father had been laid into his grave. I wanted to be outdoors, imagine myself from some point amidst the multitude of stars looking down on my puny pain. I threw my nurse's cape over my shoulders – the nights were turning cool – picked up my pistol, and went down to the back porch.

As I leaned against a rail post, drinking deep draughts of the clean, cool air, I discerned a man's figure moving below. I lifted my pistol . . .

'Tatyana Petrovna, don't shoot,' came a familiar voice in English, and Baron Niessen, a rifle under his arm, appeared on the side steps.

I was glad to put down my weapon. 'Baron, what are you doing here at night, with a rifle?'

Wrapping my cape about my nightgown, I dropped down on the top step.

Baron Niessen took off his cap and sat down on a step below, rifle at his feet. 'I was keeping watch. We caught a Red spy yesterday disguised as a woman. He came to Taganrog to spy on you. I was afraid the Bolsheviks might send agents to assassinate or kidnap you. They don't like anyone to escape their clutches. And there is nothing they fear as much as a figure that might unite and inspire the White movement.'

'I, unite the White movement?'

'Why not? You're such a magnificent woman, Tatyana Petrovna, a warrior-princess like your ancestor Olga, who nailed Rurik's shields on the gates of Constantinople. You could lead our armies to victory! Did you never dream of altering the course of history? I did, when I plotted to rescue our sovereign's family.'

'Yes, when I was ten years old. I imagined myself another Joan of Arc. Only, I haven't heard voices.'

'Well, perhaps it's for the best. I could not bear to see you burn.' Niessen's voice took on another kind of urgency. 'But neither can I bear to see you leave Russia.'

'There is nothing more for me to do here. And I must work. Like Genady Roslov, I need to use my hands.'

'Such wonderful hands! I have never forgotten their touch. May I?' He reached for them, put them to his lips. Then, 'Tanya, I've been mad about you since we were together at your dacha,' he rushed on. 'To talk of marriage is meaningless in these times, but let me love you. Let us find in each other's arms, if not salvation, at least forgetfulness and respite.' He clasped my waist and pressed his head against it.

'Niessey!' I called him by the pet name the imperial family had given him on the *Standard*.

I let my fingers caress his hair and feel the scar of the wound they had sutured. I was attracted. I was stirred. Alexis had never affected me like this! Yes, I would like to obliterate my nightmares in these strong, ardent arms! But afterward, what?

It would either be a casual affair, or I would become tied to another condemned man. I had already lost one who was also noble and brave, passionate and young. I would rather take his opposite, a man of peace, of a vision beyond nationalities that encompassed the globe. With Alexis, I might re-create a reality without hatred of others or of self, a world of 'intelligent emotion', calm and tender.

'Niessey, I'm touched, I'm tempted,' I said. 'But I must go back to Constantinople. I owe it to Professor Holveg.'

'You're not going to marry him.' Niessen released me.

'Yes.'

'But it's all wrong! Your ages, backgrounds, temperaments are incompatible. Would you marry out of gratitude?'

'Not gratitude alone. We have shared so much together, Alexis and I. He knows me better than anyone. I trust him.'

'But you don't love him! Tanya' – Niessen seized me by the arms and pulled me up – 'I could make you love. Let me prove it to you. Just once!' And he began to kiss my throat.

My momentary excitement could not be rekindled, and he quickly sensed it. 'Forgive me.' He released me. 'I wish you and Alexis Holveg happiness.' His voice broke.

'Oh Niessey!' I felt deeply sad. 'I don't hope for happiness. That would be extravagant. I'll be content to find a purpose and peace of mind.'

'Then you'll be more fortunate than I.' He shouldered his rifle.

Dawn was breaking and I was overcome with fatigue. I left him at his watch and went up to bed.

*

When I came down to breakfast the following morning and greeted the household in my normal manner, there was a palpable release from tension. I calmly handed L-M, who came with Lord Andrew to inquire after me, the confidential report to take back to General Denikin.

Emboldened, Vera Kirilovna tried to persuade me to accompany her on a side trip to Anapa. Here, in this fishing village on the Black Sea, Grand Duchess Marie Pavlovna and her sons had come to rest after a six-month flight across the Caucasus. Here they remained to follow the White Army's progress towards Moscow.

'Dear child,' Vera Kirilovna reminded me when I proved obdurate, 'not only is Her Imperial Highness your godmother, but she was Anna Vladimirovna's closest friend. You owe her a visit on both counts.'

'I owe it to Professor Holveg to return to Constantinople as soon as possible. You can explain that my leave of absence from the hospital is almost up.'

Vera Kirilovna was shocked speechless. Professor Holveg to come before royalty! Then, recovering her breath, 'Very well, if you must,' she acceded. 'But do nothing rash until I join you. I'll be back in Constantinople in ten days.'

If my godmother's robust sense of humour had survived her ordeal, Marie Pavlovna might be amused to find Vera Kirilovna her incorrigible old self. At any other time, I would have gone to Anapa gladly. But now I was hastening to new loyalties and duties, and I dared not delay.

L-M and Lord Andrew were among those who came to see me off at the boat.

'Poor Niessen's too heartbroken,' my kinsman said.

I asked him to help Simyon to safety, should the emergency arise.

'I'll do all I can, if evacuation doesn't again turn into a general *sauve-qui-peut* – an each-for-himself stampede like Odessa in the spring.'

I gave the rest of the money Alexis had left me to Vera Kirilovna to use on her royal visit. I embraced Zinaida Mikhailovna and my hostess, who were in tears, and entreated Kolenka to care for them both.

'We shall miss you, Tanya,' said Lord Andrew as we shook hands

He was not nearly as foolish a young man as he had seemed at our first meeting – was it really less than a month ago? I had changed even more than he.

Don't look back, I said to myself as I went up the gangplank. Never look back again.

I was never so glad to spy Alexis's perfect triangle of a goatee, above the roses he held at the dock in Constantinople! As for Alexis, he was ecstatic; all the more so since Vera Kirilovna was not in attendance. After dropping off my kit bag at the hospital, I allowed him to take me back, for the first time, to his tiny flat in Galata, where Nyanya (who slept in the kitchen) greeted me with tearful kisses.

'I was afraid you would not come back,' she said. 'I was afraid you would invent another reason to stay over there.'

Alexis ordered a true Turkish feast from a neighbouring restaurant. Afterwards, he demonstrated the fine art of brewing Turkish coffee.

I admired the deft precision of his gestures. 'You would have made a first-rate surgeon, Alexis.'

He denied any such ambition. 'But I did consider the violin as a profession. I never dreamt I would support myself one day by playing in a nightclub!' Then, 'I have prepared a surprise for you, Tatyana Petrovna,' he added. 'Stay there, I'll clear up. If I remained in Constantinople much longer, I too would be forced to learn to sit cross-legged on a divan. You do it so gracefully, Tatyana Petrovna.' He could not look at me enough.

I enjoyed being waited on. It was my last night of hospital leave. Alexis had managed to transform his quarters with the aid of *kilims* and other native decorations. The decor showed a sure aesthetic touch, which I appreciated the more so since I felt deficient in it.

Alexis returned from the kitchen, laid down his glasses, and took up his Stradivarius to play the surprise: Bach's 'Chaconne in D minor', which he had practised in my absence.

Again, as in the nightclub, I was moved to tears. Only now, in Bach's sublime music, Alexis's passion was under the control of a lofty intelligence. And I envisioned the starry multitudes above the steppe, from whose perspective our earthly trials dwindled into insignificance. All will pass, I thought, but this music will soar on to the farthest reaches of the universe, to the Source.

'Alexis,' I said when he had sat down, bespectacled once more, by my side, 'you know how to move me to my depths. I feel so cosy here, so removed from the terrors, the tragedies that are taking place over there.' I would not say 'in Russia'.

'So you should be. So you will be, if I have my say. Tatyana Petrovna' – he rose and seized the tip of his goatee – 'I was going to wait till Paris, till you had a position and your independence, to bring up the subject, but a decision can help you through the visa formalities –' He broke off, made the turn of the small room, and stopped resolutely before me once more. 'Before the Revolution, I would not have presumed . . . I know I'm no handsome and dashing young man . . . I will never be wealthy . . . but I do have a name and future in my field . . . what I'm trying to say is –'

'I know what you're trying to say, Alexis' – I gazed up at him affectionately – 'and I accept.'

Before leaving for Paris, where he promised to find us an apartment by the time Nyanya and I arrived, Alexis took me to the French consulate. As Princess Silomirskaya, I would have had to join the queue of Russian refugees outside the commissariat's doors. These were guarded by a Senegalese soldier armed, of all things, with a *knut* – I had never seen that cruel whip in Russia. However, as the fiancée of the celebrated Polish scientist Alexis Holveg, I was received with Gallic courtesy. It was my initiation into the two aspects of French officialdom, the brutal and the polished.

Alexis was less successful in tracing Fyodor. No one of that description had contacted him, wrote the friend in Leningrad. The friend regretted that he could not pursue the matter. We understood that he was being watched. We could think of nothing more to do for the present.

In the middle of October, Nyanya and I saw Alexis off on the *Orient Express*. He had paid the rent so she could remain in his flat while I lived at the British hospital until we joined him.

'The Lord bless you for your kindness, Aleksey Alekseyevich,' said the old woman as he kissed her on the cheeks three times. 'In my old age, it's a load off my shoulders to know my Princess will have a good husband to love and protect her.'

How easily had Nyanya accepted Alexis as my future husband, I thought, as if it had been predetermined long ago! As for me, I found it suddenly strange.

'Tatyana Petrovna,' said Alexis as he took my hand, 'please consider yourself entirely free, during these next six weeks, to change your mind about our engagement. You have no obligation to me of any sort. I would feel ashamed to have rushed you . . .'

'You did not rush me, Alexis.' How perceptive he was, and how tactful! 'And I am much too proud of my ring' – I placed my left hand over his – 'to give it back.'

He kissed my hands – he had been as correct and formal since our engagement as before – his dark eyes flashed revealingly, and he mounted the steps of his second-class coach. He had spent almost the last of his pay as a nightclub entertainer on my engagement ring, a small pearl in a gold-leaf setting, and could not afford to travel first-class.

I took Nyanya back to Galata. I was worried how she would manage alone amid 'heathens', as she called Moslems, Greeks and Jews indiscriminately, but that problem was soon solved by the arrival of Vera Kirilovna from Anapa.

Vera Kirilovna was all too glad to find room for herself and her trunks gratis, and grandly offered to share the one room with Nyanya. The latter, however, was content to sleep in the kitchen.

Having settled Vera Kirilovna and heard the full account of her visit with Marie Pavlovna – 'Her Imperial Highness is so altered, so aged!' she said in that mournful and reverent note reserved for fallen royalty – I asked her what plans she would make now that I was engaged to be married.

'Engaged to be married?' In her self-centred recital, Vera Kirilovna had failed to notice my ring. Then, 'You haven't accepted Professor Holveg?'

'I have.'

Vera Kirilovna's bosom lifted expressively. 'I see. He took advantage of my absence to propose. I wonder he had the presumption. He has no rank, no fortune. His mother was a Jewish laundress. His father's family disowned him . . .'

'Vera Kirilovna, I must ask you not to speak disrespectfully of my future husband. I admire him. I owe him my life.'

'I appreciate fully what Professor Holveg has done for you, dear child,' she rejoined with dignity, 'but others would have done as much and it gives him no special rights. I must tell you, moreover, that your marriage to a person of his origin would be badly received – *serait mal vu*.'

'Badly received by *whom*, Vera Kirilovna?'

'By all those of our Russian refugee colony who are devoted to you, who see in you not only a descendant of Rurik, but one who had the rare, indeed the unique privilege of being intimate with the murdered family of our sovereign ... one who was like a sister to his daughters, murdered, with the Tsarevich their brother, at the command of a Jew – Yurovsky – on orders of another Jew – Sverdlov – a people so intimately connected with bolshevism it can only be accursed to all who loved our sovereign and his family.' Vera Kirilovna folded her plump, manicured hands below her waist and stood by the single tiny arched window, bust held high.

I too folded my hands in the court pose she herself had taught me and said, 'I believe I am more sensitive to the horrible outrage committed against our sovereigns and their children, Vera Kirilovna, than any of those who now profess their love and devotion. You know as well as I do that these same people did nothing but criticize Nicholas and Alexandra during their reign and did not lift a finger for them after their downfall. The few who were really devoted to the Tsar are not alive to boast about it or they are fighting to the death.' I thought of Baron Niessen, and his figure too took on a tragic aura. 'I owe my survival to Alexandra Fyodorovna, who would not let me share the fate she foresaw for herself and her family.

'As for cursing the Jews for the crimes of bolshevism, that I call presumption, Vera Kirilovna. God alone can pass judgement on an entire people. Jews in southern Russia are already suffering for the association of a minority with bolshevism. So will any group whose members, however few, support an evil cause. Those are the workings of that Higher Justice we ignore, again and again, at our terrible peril.'

Yes, I thought, the crimes conceived by the human mind, wherever they be committed, must, in the end, be accounted for by all of humankind.

Having spoken with force and passion, I fell silent. Then, as Vera

Kirilovna stood speechless, I went on in a calmer and more worldly tone, 'As for our colony's possible disapproval of my marriage to Professor Holveg because of his maternal origin, that would be absurd! Alexis Holveg is a scientist of international repute. He enjoyed the friendship, as well as the esteem of Grand Duke Constantine and others in the imperial family. The Tsar thought highly of him. And were our sovereign here now, he would be the first to ridicule your pretensions. He was Colonel Romanov when I saw him last, digging a vegetable garden. We would all do better to cultivate vegetable gardens after his example, rather than titles and distinctions which have become meaningless!'

Vera Kirilovna bent her head in decorous acceptance of the rebuke. 'As ever, you make me feel small and petty, dear child. We exiles have our faults ... we are only human, too human. Perhaps we are wrong to cling to titles and distinctions which you call meaningless, but they are all we have left. We are not all twenty-two like you. You may wish to forget you are the Serene Princess Silomirskaya but we cannot. I believe it entails certain responsibilities and obligations that your grandmother, your father, and our late sovereign your godfather would have expected you to fulfil.'

It was my turn to bow my head. 'I won't forget who I am, Vera Kirilovna, or my responsibilities to our people in exile. My marriage to Professor Holveg will not keep me from fulfilling them, I promise. Forgive me for lecturing you.'

Countess Liline smiled maternally and extended her hands, into which I put mine. 'I deserved it, dear child. But before you set the date for your wedding, I ask you to think carefully, to wait a few months more, until you are fully recovered from your terrible experiences. Professor Holveg is a support to you now, but how much do you have in common otherwise? Remember that marriage is a great step, the greatest you will ever take. An engagement can always be broken. Divorce is a much more serious matter. I speak from my greater experience of life. You are so young and innocent still. I do want to see you happy.'

I saw she was genuinely moved and I embraced her. But I felt quite old and wise enough to face confidently this greatest step of my life.

*

Vera Kirilovna was too subtle to openly criticize Alexis to me again. Whatever she continued to think privately, she was glad enough to be taken by Alexis Holveg's fiancée to the French commissariat as her aunt and be spared the humiliation of queuing up with the other refugees. There were, among the latter, some of those same exalted members of our colony whose disapproval of my forthcoming marriage so weighed with Vera Kirilovna. It was one of those small social ironies that relieved for me briefly the bleak picture of exile.

After Vera Kirilovna had applied for her French visa and all three of us, with Nyanya, had booked passage for 1 December on the strength of our Nansen passports on a ship to Marseilles, there was nothing to do but wait.

The wait was not made easier by the disheartening news from Russia. Upon the return from Taganrog of their delegation, the Poles had signed a truce with the Bolsheviks, freeing the Red divisions in Podolia to attack the southern White Army's flank. At the same time Makhno rose up in Denikin's rear, forcing the recall of troops from the Moscow front. Thus, after capturing Orel and coming within a hundred *versts* of the capital, the White Army, at the very peak of its success, began to fall back.

In October too, General Yudenich's north-western army took Gachina and came within thirty-five *versts* of Petrograd. But, unable to cut the railroad, without the support of the British fleet or the Estonians, who only cared to consolidate their border, he too was beaten back.

In Siberia, Admiral Kolchak's retreat culminated in the capture of Omsk by the Bolsheviks on 14 November. And so began the epic trek of the Siberian armies to Trans-Baikalia.

The Czechs held on grimly to the Trans-Siberian Railway, bent on reaching Vladivostok with their enormous booty and resolved to let all others, military and civilian, perish. The fleeing White armies slogged over 3,000 kilometres of snowy forests and plains, harassed by enemies on all sides.

No less harrowing was the flight of the Ural and Orenburg Cossacks through the Caspian steppe to Persia. These were not armies alone that retreated but their families and entire populations, risking death rather than capture, extermination or enslavement by the Bolsheviks.

Russia's tragedy was still far from being played out. But my own, I believed, was drawing to a close. On 1 December 1919, I left Constantinople without regret, having someone, and something, to look forward to after all.

34

Nearly three years had gone by since the Russian revolution of February 1917. What had begun as a trickle of expatriates had swelled to a flood of refugees. Eastward it flowed into Manchurian Kharbin and Chinese Shanghai. It even reached as far as the United States and Canada via Vladivostok. Westward, through Turkey and Rumania, it spilled into the European capitals. Most of this westward wave came to rest on Parisian shores, which, if not exactly hospitable, permitted the exiles to establish their own colony, with its churches, schools and customs.

By 10 December 1919, I would not have thought the landing in Paris of one more shipwrecked aristocrat likely to cause much of a stir. I was all the more surprised to be greeted by the press at the Gare de Lyon on my arrival with Vera Kirilovna and Nyanya from Marseilles.

'When did you last see the family of the late tsar?' 'Do you believe any of them survived?' 'Did you receive a letter from the Grand Duchess Tatyana from Ekaterinburg?' 'Are you going to publish your father's memoirs?' 'How did you hide from the Bolsheviks after Prince Silomirsky was shot?' 'Did he have a part in Rasputin's assassination?' 'Was your father marching on Petrograd to overthrow the Provisional Government when he was arrested by the Soviets?'

A barrage of questions and the flash of cameras assaulted me as I stepped down from our second-class compartment. I still wore the uniform of a British war nurse given to me at the hospital in Constantinople. Helpless, I looked for Alexis. Why wasn't he there to meet us?

'If you would be good enough to all stop talking at once, messieurs, perhaps Her Serene Highness will be able to make a statement,' Vera Kirilovna interposed to my relief.

In the ensuing hush, I said haltingly, 'I thank you, gentlemen of the press, for your interest, which I did not know I merited. I wish to express my gratitude to the French government and nation for offering me asylum, as it has to so many of our exiles. As for questions touching on my father or the murdered family of our sovereign, I regret I cannot answer them at present. They are not only distasteful, but painful . . .'

The reporters looked somewhat abashed, but they were not about to let me off that easily.

'Your Highness, we don't mean to be indiscreet, yet in the interest of history, would you mind telling us –'

Vera Kirilovna cut them short. 'That's all, gentlemen. Be so good as to let Her Highness by.'

The reporters began to make way. Then, 'Is it true,' a provocative voice rang out, 'Prince Silomirsky admitted the belligerent attitude of the Tsar in the Sarajevo affair, which led to the outbreak of the Great War?'

The challenge, no doubt from a Leftist newspaper, made me lift my head. 'My father was mistreated, but he made no false confession. That is a calumny, like so many others . . .'

I thought I would collapse, when a small gentleman in a black bowler came up, flashing a cane and very black eyes. 'Have you no shame? Will you let the Princess by?' Seizing my arm, Alexis propelled me past the press. 'Go on, go on, leave the Princess alone. No delicacy, no tact, free press, fine thing!' he sputtered.

'I was delayed in traffic,' he apologized as he led me to a taxi that looked like a veteran of the Battle of the Marne, and settled me in its musty interior with Vera Kirilovna. He and Nyanya took the folding seats, while Vera Kirilovna's trunks were piled on top and at the back of the venerable vehicle. My slight baggage with Nyanya's – *kilims* and Turkish hangings included – went in the front seat beside the driver.

We rattled off down the Left Bank along the Seine towards the apartment Alexis had found us in Passy. He was staying in a cheap hotel nearby.

'Dear Professor, I will not impose long on your hospitality, have no fear,' Vera Kirilovna hastened to reassure him. 'I will look for a position at once. I may not be able to do anything myself, but I'm very good at directing others. And, if need be, I have enough valuables to enable me to live in a modest *pension* for a good long while.'

'We will call on my Veslawski relatives, Vera Kirilovna,' I said. 'They should be able to help.'

'Your relatives you must call on, of course,' Alexis allowed, 'but you'll have little time, Tatyana Petrovna, for a social life.' The remark was clearly for Vera Kirilovna's benefit. 'As soon as we're married, you must begin to study for your baccalaureate in July in order to qualify for university entrance. I've also found an opening for a part-time nurse, in the private surgical clinic of a Polish doctor, within walking distance of our apartment. He took my word for your qualifications.'

'*Mon Dieu*, Professor, give Tatyana Petrovna a chance to catch her breath,' Vera Kirilovna observed. 'Work, study, marriage, all at one blow! Surely you must allow some time for wedding preparations, announcements . . .'

But I was relieved to find my life arranged and my duties prescribed. 'We don't want a formal wedding, do we, Alexis,' I stated confidently, knowing his dislike of ceremony. 'Let's get married as simply and quickly as possible.'

'Nothing could make me happier, Tatyana Petrovna,' my fiancé said, and glowed for the rest of the bumpy drive.

The apartment we were to share with Nyanya, once married, consisted of a dining room, kitchen, bedroom, bathroom, and a separate *cabinet de toilette* with thunderous plumbing. The whole looked out on an inner court with a plane tree.

'I chose it for the plane tree,' Alexis said uneasily. 'When it comes into leaf next spring, it will be beautiful. And next year, when I get the professorship at the Collège de France I have been nearly promised, we can move to a larger flat. For the present, on my salary as a research associate, this was the best I could do.'

'You did splendidly, Alexis,' I said.

'Nyanya can sleep on this.' He indicated the divan in the dining room. 'And you can begin to practise tomorrow.' He tapped the Pleyel upright across from the divan. 'With this' – showing the metronome – 'and this' – opening the music on the stand.

'Czerny *études*, how dreadful!'

I felt like a schoolgirl obedient to her dear teacher. So this, I thought, would be married life, at least until I myself became a professional woman. Well, I had always been a prize pupil. And school was a much easier, safer life than the terrifying one beyond.

During the following week, I applied with Alexis for our marriage licence. For fear the press would hound us, he bribed the clerk in the marriage bureau not to publish the banns. Our marriage was to be as secret as it was swift.

Alexis also helped me obtain my identity card and work permit. Then I was interviewed by the Polish surgeon to whom Alexis had spoken and was hired as of the first of the year to work half a night shift in his clinic. I would be caring for the acute post-operative cases.

With the help of the *kilims* and hangings, the apartment began to look cosy. As for Vera Kirilovna, she found a position in short order as companion to Mrs Williamson, a wealthy American dowager who had rented the Veslawski town residence for the winter, in the absence of its owners.

I was relieved on calling, together with Vera Kirilovna, at the Veslawski *hôtel particulier* in the Faubourg St Germain, to find my relatives away in their villa at Biarritz. To find myself, at the invitation of Mrs Williamson, in the familiar, tastefully luxurious setting of my golden girlhood was bad enough without having to speak about the deaths of Uncle Stan, Aunt Sophie and Stefan.

Fear of the past also made me ask Vera Kirilovna to call at the Quai d'Orsay, the French Foreign Office, with a letter asking for the return of Father's memoirs and the letters of Tatyana Nikolayevna, which had been entrusted to French embassy officials on their departure from Petrograd. When the sealed parcel was delivered, I gave it to Alexis unopened to keep in his laboratory safe.

Less than two weeks after my arrival in Paris, on 22 December 1919, Alexis and I were married in a civil ceremony in the *mairie* of Passy. With the proceeds from one of my last remaining jewels, Vera Kirilovna had procured for me a short, smart dress of white crepe with a fox-trimmed jacket, and satin shoes with pointed toes that pinched painfully. She was one of our witnesses, a fellow scientist of Alexis's at the institute the other. Nyanya had stayed home to make mysterious preparations. Much to the disappointment of Mrs Williamson, Alexis and I refused her kind offer of a party. But we did accept her dinner invitation at Maxim's.

Alexis overcame his nervousness and delighted our jolly hostess with stories collected in Constantinople of the Middle Eastern folk hero Hoja.

'Oh my dear Princess, your husband is the cleverest, most amusing man I have ever met!' declared Mrs Williamson, her heavy jowls shaking with laughter.

I too was rather impressed. Alexis had so many, and such unexpected sides!

After he had dropped off his American mistress and her new Russian companion, Vera Kirilovna, at home, Mrs Williamson's chauffeur drove us in turn to our apartment.

Nyanya now took charge. First she sent my husband into the bathroom to get ready. After he had emerged, combed and scented, without his glasses, in pyjamas and silk dressing gown bought with his supplemental earnings as a gypsy violinist in a Russian restaurant, she bade him wait in the dining room until she called.

In the bedroom, the odour of incense lingered; Nyanya had had the bridal chamber blessed by a Russian priest. The bed was made sumptuous by the monogrammed sheets and satin eiderdown she had carried away from Alubek, and there were the down pillows side by side – for us refugees, unheard-of luxury! As I stared at the bed, I was struck by the enormity of the step I had taken!

In a stupor, at Nyanya's command, I bathed in turn and slipped on the white silk nightgown Vera Kirilovna had chosen, as she had the rest of my trousseau. Nyanya then sat me down at the dressing table to brush my hair.

'Nyanya' – I seized her by the arms – 'Nyanya, what have I done? Alexis is dear and close to me as a friend, a teacher, a protector, but I don't *love* him. How can I be his wife?'

'Don't be afraid, my soul. Your husband loves you enough for two. He will know how to make you love him in time.'

'Nyanya, Nyanya,' I went on, unheeding, 'I was to be married in the Veslawski palace chapel, in a beautiful and solemn wedding, with all the bells of the province pealing. Our sovereign's daughters were to have been my bridesmaids . . .'

'Well and it's better this way than that your ashes should lie in a Siberian wood as theirs do.'

'Not better, worse . . . far worse!'

'It's a sin to think such thoughts,' my old nurse said. 'Get down on your knees and beg the Lord's forgiveness, lest He punish you with barrenness.'

I knelt before my single icon of the Mother and Child, softly illumined by the *lampada*'s red glow. But even as I murmured my prayers and crossed myself piously for Nyanya's benefit, Stefan rose fearfully before me.

But you're dead, Stevie, my warrior-prince, my lord, I told his image. The vultures picked out your amber eyes. Their foul beaks feasted on your soft lips, which I kissed. Why do you rise up out of the earth to torment me tonight? Must you haunt me my life long? *Is* it wicked of me to turn to one who will love and protect me since you no longer can?

And my cousin's beautiful voice answered, I am not dead a year and you have forgotten your troth. You are ready to lie in another man's arms, to let him take what was rightfully mine, this man you don't love and will deceive as lightly as you have deceived me. No, I shall not leave you in peace, until you hate this man whom you call husband and any child you bear him in betrayal of our love.

I hid my face in my hands and cowered by the bed. 'Nyanya' – I clasped her legs – 'have pity, tell Alexis I'm unwell.'

Nyanya would not hear anything. She got me into bed, straightened the covers, blessed me, and throwing open the door, she told Alexis in a solemn tone that his bride awaited him.

He did not come in immediately, but paced nervously back and forth. Then, 'What do you think Nyanya,' he asked, 'my beard, should I shave it off? Maybe Tatyana Petrovna, my wife, doesn't find it attractive.'

'If she finds you attractive, she'll like you with the beard, and if she doesn't, shaving it off won't help,' was her retort.

There was a silence. Then my husband said, 'Nyanya, I hadn't time to speak to my wife about it. Do you think she wants a child?'

'And what else did you marry her for? What else, if not a child, will bring a dimple into her cheek again, and a look other than of sadness into those beautiful eyes? Well, go in to her, Aleksey Alekseyevich, and may God bless you with a son this night.'

After my initial panic, I accepted married intimacy with ease. Alexis brought to it the sensitivity and intelligence that had won me, as well as the fiery romanticism I associated with his gypsy violin playing. If it was not the divine rapture I had imagined in my fantasies about Stefan, there was sweet solace in physical closeness, an affirmation of living warmth and caring in the face of indifferent, cold death.

Two months after the wedding, I told my husband I was expecting a baby around 1 October 1920. Alexis was very moved. He went out and got himself a third job, this one as consultant with a chemical firm, so that I could give up my night hours at the clinic. This I was glad to do. But once into my fourth month, I began to feel so healthy that keeping our small apartment clean, preparing our frugal meals, practising the piano and studying for the baccalaureate did not begin to use up my energy. I cast about for something to do.

Spring of 1920 saw the rout of General Denikin's southern White Army and the flight into Rumania of all but a remnant fighting under General Baron Wrangel. Even earlier, in February, Admiral Kolchak, betrayed by his one-time allies the Czechs, had been turned over to the Bolsheviks and shot. General Yudenich and his north-western army had been beaten back into Estonia and interned by the Estonians, their former allies. The last of the White forces in the extreme north of Russia had embarked on the ships of the Allied expeditionary corps in March, thus ending that futile attempt at encirclement of the Bolsheviks. Foreign intervention, half-hearted at best, had collapsed under the pressure of war weariness at home, mistrust of the White movement, and underestimation of Soviet expansionist aims. Alone, General Wrangel still received French aid for the sake of France's ally, Poland, which, after a three-month truce, had reopened hostilities and was now waging full-scale war with its Soviet neighbour.

White retreat swept more refugees into France, among them Grand Duchess Marie Pavlovna, who died shortly after her arrival. A thinner and even more timid Zinaida Mikhailovna along with an impenitent Kolenka were also washed on the Parisian beach, as was my kinsman, L-M, after narrowly escaping internment in Rumania. Less fortunate were my Taganrog hosts. Although urged by Kolenka to leave in plenty of time, they had delayed because of a pending grain deal. Kolenka suspected they had been stranded along with thousands of other refugees in Taganrog. For every fugitive safely washed ashore, more than one was swept up by the Red tide. It did not bear thinking about.

Simyon was another who remained behind, as orderly to Baron Niessen. The latter, as one might expect, had joined Wrangel's diehards.

'I'm sure Niessen and Simyon talk about you endlessly,' said L-M, who brought me the news. 'It must be a comfort to them both.' He rested his Byzantine eyes on me with that gentle detachment of one who observes the human tragicomedy from an extraterrestrial perspective.

There was no running away from the past. In keeping with my promise to Vera Kirilovna not to forget my responsibilities to the Russian colony, I conceived a centre of information and assistance for our refugees. Vera Kirilovna took up the idea enthusiastically, and by mid-May, the Russian Refugee Centre was operating with a volunteer staff in a mansion in Passy lent us by the émigrée wife of a French industrialist. This was the modest beginning of the Silomirsky Foundation. Besides what it owed to backers like Mrs Williamson and other generous Americans, a great deal of its success is due to Vera Kirilovna. Whatever her failings, there was never her equal for pulling strings to get things done.

I also learned that in the Paris *beau monde* Madame Holveg elicited only polite response whereas, to Princess Silomirskaya, the doors of the rich and the influential were open. I became quite cynical about this too, and the more meaningless my former rank, the more shamelessly I used it to help our cause. For this reason I had my maiden name printed on my letterhead as president of the Russian Centre.

I began spending every afternoon in my office, in spite of my husband's initial objections. For though I still obeyed him in my academic studies and piano practice, when it came to what Vera Kirilovna loftily called 'our duty to our people in exile', my moral imperative was stronger than his intellectual authority. He resigned himself to the centre as he did to our ever-widening circle of friends, among whom were émigré bachelors like L-M badly in need of a meal.

Alexis also gave up trying to make me grasp the 'concept of economy', which I found even more difficult than Newton's binome. ('How can you call binomial expansion a bore, Tatyana Petrovna?'

My husband was shocked. 'Why, it has endless possibilities!') He took over the budgeting as well as the marketing – he was saving money to bring his mother from Poland – and gave me just enough money to buy the evening newspaper and take a taxi home should I need to. I walked for the exercise. On the way, the money went into the cap of the *grand blessé de guerre* with stumps for legs, who sat on the sidewalk on a board fitted with rollers.

However busy I might be, I made sure my husband had a healthy diet and enough rest. I brought him his tea after supper, made an effort to understand his research. I accompanied his violin on the piano. I treated him on the one hand like a great scientist, on the other like an eccentric, beloved uncle. I was affectionate, if not passionate, in bed. It made Alexis flash his surprisingly youthful smile more and more often.

'I had thought the fire in the blood was dead,' he said. 'But you make me feel young again. I'm full of scientific inspiration.' And he went on to explain, pacing about the bed while I drank my morning chocolate, the emerging theory of a new kind of atomic physics and chemistry sprung from the discovery of radioactivity.

According to this theory, the nucleus of the atom was held together by enormous forces. The atom with its electrons was spinning like the earth and the galaxies. 'You see, Tatyana Petrovna, we now know that there is no such thing as a solid object. Everything is in motion. Everything diffuses. The physical world is a continuous flux. It is a concept as revolutionary as the Copernican theory of the universe, and it will have as profound an effect on human affairs. Perhaps, perhaps, it will bring man to the realization that he is one species on one planet, a unique manifestation in this solar system, possibly in the universe, and that his highest duty is to preserve and cherish this species and its habitat.' He took my empty cup resting on my large abdomen and regarded me with proud joy. 'Our child, Tatyana Petrovna, may witness this.'

'I want it more than anything!' Only, I thought, for a scientific revolution to work such a change, there was needed also a corresponding transformation of the human heart.

Except in the moment of abandon, Alexis continued to call me by my patronymic, and I addressed him by the French *vous*. The formality in which I had been raised had left its indelible mark. Fortunately, Alexis was both meticulous and reserved.

I, on my part, was up and dressed before him, and never showed myself in dressing gown and slippers outside our 'private apartments', as he called our bedroom. While I expected him to observe palace courtesy and decorum in our small flat, he exacted of me application in my studies and strict tempi in my piano practice. He knew when to impose himself and when to yield. I thought myself lucky. Only sometimes, when I pored over my textbooks, would I look up at the plane tree in leaf and a wild longing would possess me to gallop beside Stevie behind a yelping pack of hounds, through the woods of Veslawa ...

On a beautiful day at the end of May, when plane trees and horse chestnuts were in bloom, I went as usual on my way home from the Russian Refugee Centre to the tobacco shop on the corner of our street for the evening paper. My uphill walk had made me ravenously hungry. My head swam and I had to steady myself on the counter.

The proprietress behind the cash register was a stout woman in a coarse grey sweater who wore tiny earrings and usually knitted something coarse and grey. But of late she had taken to knitting something soft and blue for *la petite dame russe*, as she called me.

The proprietress asked about the object of her knitting. '*Alors, la petite dame, il va bien, le petit?*'

'I think he is hungry,' I answered, as the baby bumped around.

'Well, he has to be given something to eat.' She laid on top of the newspaper a chocolate *bouchée* wrapped in tin foil. 'Here, I give it to him. And there's your newspaper. It looks like the war's going badly for Poland.'

Both Alexis and I closely followed the Polish–Soviet conflict. The Poles' audacious capture of Kiev earlier in the month had roused the Red Army's spirit, and it had fallen with all its might and fury upon the invaders.

I glanced at the headlines.

'POLES RETREATING', I read, and directly below, in equally large type, 'STEFAN VESLAWSKI FOUND ALIVE'.

'*Ma petite dame*, what's the matter, you're not well?' I heard the proprietress say.

Next I lay on a tile floor sprinkled with sawdust. The proprietress of the tobacco shop squatted beside me, tapping my cheeks and explaining to the customers, 'She was hungry. It's her condition. She has to be taken home. *Monsieur le professeur Aulveg* is her husband, *au numéro 27 bis*.'

'Ah oui, les russes,' said the sympathetic onlookers. A taxi driver who had walked over from his stand offered the use of his cab.

I was hoisted into the car by two workmen who had been drinking apéritifs at the café next door. The proprietress of the tobacco shop accompanied me. At the door of my apartment house I was still in no condition to walk up three steep flights. The cabdriver and the concierge made a chair of their hands and took me up, to be met for their pains by Nyanya's flood of abusive Russian. The driver wanted no money and left. The proprietress stayed on to look after me until the return home of Alexis, whom she called at the laboratory.

'It was the hunger, it's her condition,' she explained all over again.

'It's this senseless overwork I've been protesting against,' he raged when she had gone, pacing about the divan in the dining room where I lay. 'I must insist you cease your work at the centre at once. I'll speak to your doctor. You have no sense of moderation, no common sense at all. I can't trust you out of my sight. You're not fit to be about in the street.'

What a ridiculous, angry little man he is, I thought as I looked at Alexis, and why is he so shrill? And, aloud, 'Lower your voice, Alexis, please. The window is open.'

He sat down on the divan beside me and put a hand over my wrist. 'Forgive my brusque tongue, dearest, but I worry about you so. Are you better? Shall I call your doctor?'

'It's not necessary . . . Did you bring a newspaper?'

'You usually buy it, Tatyana Petrovna.'

'I had this . . . hunger spell when I stopped to get it. I wondered what news there was from Poland.'

'I'll go down and buy a newspaper right away. No, don't move. I'll prepare dinner. Or better still, I'll order it at the café. What would you like, roast chicken, beefsteak?' Since my pregnancy, I took great interest in food. But I answered in exasperation, 'Anything you like . . . please go!'

He returned in great excitement. 'Tatyana Petrovna, here is news that will make you feel better! Just imagine, your cousin Stefan

Veslawski was found alive by Polish troops, in a peasant hut in the Ukraine, just recovered from typhus. All Poland is celebrating. He rode into Lublin at the head of the Veslawski lancers! The crowd almost pulled him off his horse – here are photographs.' He sat down beside me on the divan and spread them out.

Dim as my vision was, I distinguished a tall horseman in the four-cornered Polish cap riding ahead of a column of lancers in a crowded street hung with flags. Girls lifted their hands to his saddle. The same tall officer was making a speech on a tribune draped with the Polish flag, then bending the knee to receive the command of the Veslawski lancers and the regimental standard from Marshal Pilsudski, the Polish commander in chief.

'Tatyana Petrovna, aren't you happy?' Alexis asked, as I remained speechless.

'Yes, of course. But it's so strange, I can't quite believe it. I was so certain that he was dead. I read the report of his murder, I saw photographs of his body. You know I was certain of it,' I repeated.

'Everyone was certain. And he hasn't said what he did during the sixteen months he was in hiding. Perhaps he'll tell you when you see him.'

'Me? Why should he tell me? What makes you think I'll even see him?'

'But why not? You told me yourself he was like your brother. Why are you acting so strangely, Tatyana Petrovna? You seem angry, instead of glad.'

He had spoken the last words in Russian and Nyanya, who had picked up the newspaper and was looking at the photographs on the front page, said to him, 'It's her condition, Aleksey Alekseyevich. A woman in her condition can act in all kinds of strange ways. Don't worry about it, she'll feel better after she eats.'

'Dinner is being sent up. I'll set the table,' Alexis said.

I offered to do it, got up from the divan, and did it all wrong. My husband watched me smilingly, obviously touched to see me weak, capricious and inefficient.

Why does he look at me so tenderly? I thought. Why isn't he cruel and horrid so I'd have a reason to hate him as I do?

I set a service for fish. He put an arm about me and took the hand that held the fish knife. 'I told you I ordered beefsteak, Tatyana Petrovna.'

I jumped away. 'You know I don't care for that sort of familiarity, Alexis,' I flung the words at him. 'I'm not hungry.' And I fled into the bedroom.

In a few minutes Nyanya knocked on the door and entered I was sitting at the dressing table, looking at myself with loathing.

'You can say what you want, you can scold and lecture all you like, but I hate him, I can't bear for him to touch me. His voice exasperates me. Everything about him exasperates me. I can't help it, it's beyond me,' I greeted Nyanya with a tirade. 'And he is my husband, this man I loathe, I couldn't wait to marry him. I wouldn't listen to Vera Kirilovna. And now I'm pregnant, and it's too late, it can't be undone. I'm going to have a child by this stranger and if it's a boy he'll be his father's son and a stranger to me too.'

'Unhappy babe,' Nyanya said gravely, 'that's denied a mother's love even before it's born. Sinful you are, my Princess, like a spoiled child in your bad temper and shameless in your passion. Would you rather your poor cousin had been dead than be cheated of your pleasure with him?'

I looked no longer defiantly but with dread into those wise dark eyes that saw and understood human baseness and folly.

'Would you hurt your poor husband who wishes you only good?' Nyanya continued. 'Would you punish your child as yet unborn? His birth will be hard and your milk will dry up in your breast if you bear him in such hatred and wickedness.'

Her words shamed me. 'You're right, Nyanya, I *am* wicked. How can I have such terrible thoughts, against my husband, against my child?' I put my hands over my large abdomen, which had so repelled me only a moment before. 'He is bumping around again. Feel.' I placed the wrinkled rough hand under my ribs. 'I love him, Nyanya, really I do, and I'll try to love his father, I'll try to be good to him, I promise. And I'm happy he is alive, my Stefan, and whole. I'm happy the vultures did not pick out his eyes. I'm happy he has been returned to his people. I'm glad he will give a woman fine sons. I thank God for sparing him. I thank Him on my knees.'

I went down on my knees, clasping my nurse about the waist and bowing my head.

Nyanya kissed and stroked my head while she said, 'Yes, bad you are, my love, but not all bad, and so young still, so young to have known so much suffering and so little joy. And I see your trials aren't ended yet, they're only beginning. Well, it's the Lord's Will. They're ringing at the door. Let's go and eat.'

I went in to my husband meekly, begged his pardon for my ill temper, brought him his tea after lunch, fussed over him as though he, not I, were expecting a baby in four months. My momentary aversion had passed entirely. I felt as fond of him as ever.

Alexis protested delightedly and begged me to take care of myself more. I promised to lighten my workload and to let him fetch me at the centre and walk me home.

A week later, a French officer on the staff of General Weygand was shown into my office at the Russian Refugee Centre. He had a letter from Colonel Prince Veslawski.

'The Prince has heard of your work at the centre, Princess, but he does not have your private address,' he said. 'He asked me to inquire after your comfort and to tell you an account has been opened for you with the Guarantee Trust Bank. He will come to Paris immediately upon the cessation of hostilities. I am returning at once to Poland and will be happy to take whatever message and letters you may have for Prince Veslawski. I shall wait next door while you prepare them.'

I asked him to remain and opened my cousin's letter. It was hastily scrawled in mixed English and Polish. 'Tanya-panya, Skinny-ninny, Tanyussia, Tatyana, my beloved, little sister, sweetheart, wife, I shall soon be coming for you to take you home. Grandmother and all my people await you. Make haste to be converted to our faith so we can be married at once. I warn you I can't wait much longer to make you mine. Our nightmare has ended, our ordeal is over. I shall make you forget it ever was. I shall love you fiercely, tenderly, humbly, and better than any woman was ever loved. Until then I place a kiss on your beautiful lids and on each of your hands, most respectfully in adoration your Stevie-levie monkey ears, Stefan your husband.'

I sat a long, torturing moment contemplating this letter. Then I wrote rapidly in Polish on centre stationery: 'Praise be Jesus Christ Our Lord you are safe. I am married to Professor Alexis Holveg and expecting his child in four months. Do not write me again or try to see me. Forgive me if you can. I will always grieve over your parents' death. Convey my respects and tenderest love to Princess

Catherine, my warm greetings to Casimir. I pray every day for the success of your forces over the enemy. Thank you for the bank account but I need nothing. Our Saviour and the Mother of God protect and keep you, my brother.'

I signed and sealed the letter, stood up and handed it to the French officer, who could not disguise his astonishment at my pregnant form. 'Please give this letter to Colonel Prince Veslawski, *Monsieur le commandant*, together with my best wishes and those of Professor Holveg, my husband. Thank you for your trouble. What news have you of the Polish–Soviet front?'

'Not very good at the moment, Madame. But France will not allow her ally to be conquered once more. We will stop the Bolshevik hordes.'

'Is there hope for the forces of General Baron Wrangel in southern Russia?'

'We're sending them equipment, Madame. But that, I fear, is a lost cause.'

Life resumed its decorous and disciplined course in our household. I studied with fresh application and in July, after three days of written examinations at the science faculty of the Sorbonne and an oral test a week later, I passed my baccalaureate and qualified for university entrance. Alexis was prouder of my feat than I; my medical career seemed suddenly to have become more urgent to him than to me!

Pregnancy and childbirth had become my primary concern. As I grew more encumbered and clumsy, I fell into an indolent, contemplative state not unlike the languor of first love. I found myself daydreaming about my confinement, not as it would be in an impersonal Paris clinic, but as the solemn and joyful event it would have been in the Veslawski palace. At such moments, as when the baby moved around, I would drop whatever task I had in hand and smile secretively to myself. Then Nyanya would also put down her darning sock and assume an air of supreme solemnity, as though I were about to bring forth an heir to the imperial throne.

In August 1920, the Red Army was defeated in the Battle of Warsaw and thrown back in disorder towards the border. The Veslawski lancers, who had spearheaded the attack that broke the siege of the capital, were in hard pursuit. The front dispatches I read avidly described the terror inspired by the lancers' young colonel in the Red ranks.

'He spares neither himself nor his men,' wrote one correspondent, 'he seems to be everywhere at once. He takes no prisoners and shuns no risk. He is never seen to smile. He rides his chestnut horse with a set face at the head of every charge and at sight of this terrible figure on his huge mount the Reds throw down their rifles and run.'

35

In September, my mother-in-law arrived from Warsaw for my confinement and was put up at a modest hotel nearby. To my surprise, Sarah Holveg was a tall and portly lady with defiant bearing, whose black eyes burned like her son's. Unlike her son, she had decidedly Semitic features.

She came prepared to detest me. For my part, I showed her the consideration inculcated in me from infancy towards all elder relatives however crotchety. Nyanya had strict orders to stay in the kitchen during my mother-in-law's visits. I ignored my nurse's mutterings against that insolent, godless Jewess, as I did her imprecations against that dirty, crooked, godless French. My mother-in-law, in contrast, gave her frank opinion of me to my husband the moment I left the room.

'So,' I could not help overhearing, 'all your life you hated aristocrats and now you marry a princess, and fourteen years younger than you in the bargain. She did not marry you out of love, that anybody can see. Then why did she marry you?'

'Mother, I forbid you to criticize my wife.' My husband's voice took on a shrill note.

'So, now she has turned you against your own mother already.'

'My wife is incapable of such a thing. She has never said one word against you. It's you who are prejudiced, who are behaving illogically, in a manner unworthy of an intelligent person . . .'

'So, now my son calls me stupid.'

I returned to find Alexis tugging in impotent fury at his goatee.

I knew his mother exasperated him. He told me how much he disliked her loud voice after my soft speech. He confessed his dread of what my highborn friends might think of her. On the one hand he forbade anti-semitic remarks in his laboratory, on the other he looked in the mirror every morning to see if his nose was beginning with the years to look Jewish, like hers. He was himself behaving illogically, in a manner unworthy of an intelligent person.

At last, however, my deference and my pregnancy broke down my mother-in-law's defences. She became motherly and would not allow me to wait on her. She insisted I lie down with my feet up and took over the cooking, to the vast improvement of our fare.

Sarah Holveg now spoke often of her son's hard childhood and his determination to rise above it and show up his paternal, ducal family.

'He has not much strength in his hands, my Sasha,' she said of Alexis, 'but a strong mind, that he has. Whatever he decides to do, he will. A gypsy woman told me when he was an infant that he would marry one as highborn as an emperor's daughter and become one of the most famous men of his time. The prophecy also warned,' she added, 'that he would meet a violent end when he was fifty years old.'

I only smiled at my mother-in-law's superstitious belief.

On the subject of religion, however, despite differences in observance, my mother-in-law and I were in agreement. She deplored her son's agnosticism. Had she done wrong to raise him in his father's Lutheran faith, in the hope that his rights would someday be recognized?

'When I sent him to Sunday school the pastor asked me to keep him home because he disturbed the class with his questions,' she said, and I could not help smiling. 'But perhaps he will see it is not right to raise his child in godlessness.'

Alexis, when we discussed it, was willing for me to have full say about our child's religious upbringing. 'If he's intelligent, he'll come to his own conclusions,' he said, 'and if he isn't, it won't matter anyway.' Clearly, he'd have no use for a stupid child.

My mother-in-law wondered if the baby should not be baptized a Lutheran, in case the Allensee family might extend to him the recognition it had refused his father.

I was not much impressed by an erstwhile Prussian grand duchy and intended to christen my son in the Russian-Orthodox Church. Perhaps because I was so large, everyone agreed that it was a boy. He was to be named Peter for his maternal grandfather, Alexis for his father and paternal grandfather.

'And he should be a clever one,' said Nyanya, 'with his father such a learned man and his mother stuffing her head with all that mathematics and science while she carried him.'

By the end of September I could not sleep comfortably in any position. I could not bend over. My deliverance from Peter Alexis could not come soon enough.

On the evening of 30 September labour began. At midnight, Alexis called a cab and took me with Nyanya to the maternity clinic.

After my obstetrician had come and gone, Alexis was allowed to see me. I was sitting up in bed in a hospital gown, with the red, glistening, enlarged and distorted face of a woman in labour. I saw my husband was wrenched with pity and queasiness. I felt sorry for him and told him to go home until the baby was born. The child was in a faulty position and labour was expected to be long. A cot was placed for Nyanya in my private room.

Stevie would have been with me through labour, I thought, as Uncle Stan was with Aunt Sophie, and it would have been a labour of love.

By the end of the second day of labour, Nyanya was in a fury.

'Idiots, stupid French, horse doctors!' she muttered. 'They do nothing to help her, they only torture her more. My poor darling, she is so brave and patient, and that scientist husband of hers not even here.'

Alexis did come once or twice, but I would not let him in.

'How is my wife, Nyanya? Is she suffering frightfully?' I heard him whisper at the door.

'She's suffering, and hard, but this isn't the worst kind of suffering there is, nor will she remember it even,' my wise nurse answered. 'Go home, Aleksey Alekseyevich, you're no use to her here. It will be over soon.'

Alexis left and Nyanya returned to my side. She wiped my face, gave me a piece of ice to suck on since I could not have fluids, and held my hands through the contractions. As night wore on, I felt I was coming to the limit of my endurance.

Oh my God, I thought, it's so long! When will it end? Aunt Sophie, Mother, help me! Stevie, brother, my lord, where are you, I'm all alone!

In my distraction, I imagined for a moment he was there and experienced a moment of ecstasy and exultation through my agony. Then my mind cleared. I understood he was not there, he whom I would have loved in my pain.

It can't go on much longer, it must end soon! I gritted my teeth not to cry out. Then I was afraid for my child.

The obstetrician laughed at my fears. He appeared very pleased with the progress of labour and even more with himself. I wished for a midwife, for my own home. This artificial, antiseptic environment presided over by men was all wrong. A woman should feel triumphant giving birth, not humiliated and dehumanized.

When I become a physician and deliver a child, I'll do it differently, I thought.

At last, in the late-night hours, I was taken to the delivery room. At seven o'clock on the morning of 3 October 1920, my son was born by breech delivery. I knew his weight, length, and that he was without forceps mark or blemish, questions I asked over and over again as I came out of the light anaesthetic, but I was wheeled back to my room without having seen him.

At nine o'clock, Alexis came to visit me with his mother.

Alexis sat down at the bedside quivering with emotion. 'Tatyana Petrovna, forgive me.' He kissed my hand repeatedly. 'I was horrified that you had such a hard time. Our boy is splendid I thank you.'

'Oh it wasn't that bad, was it, Nyanya?'

Crying with joy, she covered my face, shoulders, and arms with kisses. 'No, not bad, my love, only a little slow.' She nodded at Alexis, as though to say, You see, I told you she would not even remember.

My mother-in-law approached in turn.

I asked her how Alexis had borne the ordeal.

'Terribly.' She smiled, and one could guess how beautiful she had once been. 'I thought he would pull out his beard. But now he is the happiest, proudest father in the world! Peter Alexis looks exactly like Sasha when he was born, only Sasha was not so long.'

On hearing this, I demanded to see my son. A nurse brought him swaddled in a cotton blanket and laid him inside the crook of my arm. He was profoundly asleep, with an air at once disdainful and austere. I jiggled him to wake him. He opened his wandering eyes of an indefinite blue and looked about as did Alexis when he mounted the lecture platform. Why did all you people come here to bother me? said that look. Don't you know I have something much more interesting and urgent to do?

How like his father he is, I thought, disappointed. But as I stroked the soft fuzz on the hot little head and placed my finger into the tiny hand that closed fiercely about it in the grasping reflex, I was blissfully penetrated and enveloped by this warmth and softness. I had never known anything so delicious.

Alexis had again come near, holding the point of his goatee perplexedly.

I showed him Peter's hand with the long fingers and rosy, translucent nails.

'Exquisite,' marvelled my husband, 'so tiny and so perfectly formed. To think that I have a son! It makes me feel strong and inadequate at the same time. It's incredible, fantastic ...' Clearly he saw infinite possibilities there, as in the expansion of the binome.

Peter now turned crimson and let out a powerful hunger cry.

'What a voice he has, what a voice!' Nyanya was ecstatic. 'And how he wriggles! He's strong, my Petya, and born feet-first too. He'll be someone out of the ordinary to be sure.' She held out her hands.

'Take him,' I said.

Before the nurse could object, Nyanya had Peter against her shoulder, her hand firmly at the back of his head. He was very comfortable there, for he instantly ceased his bellows and fell into profound, austere sleep, a disdainful nose on her shoulder. The triumphant and possessive look she cast on everyone, myself included, made it clear that no one but she would raise this child.

During the day, mountains of flowers were delivered, and, late in the evening, a telegram came from Poland. WELL DONE. YOUR BROTHER, it read. My elation fell.

On the following morning, Alexis was appalled to find me in tears. 'Tatyana Petrovna, what is wrong, what has happened? Am I at fault?'

'No, no, of course not. Only, I was thinking of Papa ... how happy he would have been to see Petya.' The words spoken, I did begin to think of Father, and my tears flowed afresh.

Alexis patted my hand comfortingly, to no avail. I was equally irritated by my mother-in-law and by everyone but Nyanya. Poor Alexis did not know what to make of this phenomenon, known to obstetricians as postpartum depression. But on the third day Peter had his first meal.

The moment my milk began to flow my tears ceased, and I became entirely absorbed in the marvellous development and incredible growth of my son from feeding to feeding and hour to hour.

Alexis could not grasp what was so extraordinary about a creature whose intelligence had not yet begun to function. He was more excited by the confirmation of a full professorship at the Sorbonne.

'I'm so glad for you, Alexis,' I said.

He was hurt by my apparent indifference to his career, while I was hurt by his supposed indifference to his son.

He excused himself weakly. 'But, he's always sleeping, and he looks like all the others.'

'What, Peter Alexis like all the others, his own son?' His mother and I both pounced on him.

On the sixth day postpartum I had ventured on to the balcony overlooking an inner garden, when a discreet knock made me leap back into bed. I said, *'Entrez,'* rather breathlessly, and in walked Countess Liline, chic, rosy, perfumed and fulsomely feminine.

'You have been up,' she said reproachfully.

'But it's so stupid to lie in bed when I feel perfectly well. I'm ready to go home, but my doctor won't hear of it. I'm so glad you came, Vera Kirilovna, I'm so bored! How did you get by the head nurse? She's a terror.'

Visits had been restricted to the immediate family. Reporters had not been allowed.

Vera Kirilovna's expression implied that no head nurse was a match for a lady-in-waiting to the former Dowager Empress of Russia.

She settled herself at the bedside, opened her camel coat with a lynx collar, and stripped off her doeskin gloves. 'How well you look, dear child. A woman is at the height of her beauty after she has her first baby. But this is also the time when her beauty can be spoiled if it's neglected. Your doctor is quite right not to want you to go home yet. That dreadful apartment, with those stairs and the lack of air, is quite unsuitable.

'But,' she continued, 'Mrs Williamson has gone home to the United States for six weeks and left me her house and servants to use as my own.' Since the return in September of Stefan's aunt and her family, Vera Kirilovna and her employer had moved to Neuilly, on the edge of the Bois de Boulogne. 'We have a garden. Professor Holveg can visit you every day. His mother can keep house for him. Nyanya, of course, will be with us. Under those conditions, I'm certain your doctor will let you go.'

'Oh, Vera Kirilovna, it sounds marvellous! But what about the bother and expense?'

'As to the expense, Mrs Williamson has given me *carte blanche*. She wants you to be treated, she said, like the princess you are. And how can it be a bother? It can only be a joy, to someone who has not had a daughter, or a grandchild of her own.'

'I'll have to speak to my husband . . .' Alexis was still not fond of my kinswoman.

Vera Kirilovna dismissed this obstacle too. Then she dutifully inquired after Peter Alexis.

'He almost pushes me off the bed when I nurse.' I was glad to supply the details. 'And he has such a voice! I can hear it from the nursery. It's like a bell. His eyes are beginning to focus. He has such an intense, intelligent look, as if he already understood everything.'

Vera Kirilovna smiled in fond indulgence at these maternal delusions. The head nurse who was a terror then appeared, and my visitor, laying her cheek against mine, collected her coat and gloves without haste, and left.

Alexis was at first reluctant to agree to Vera Kirilovna's proposal. 'She'll have you and the baby holding day-long receptions for delegations of well-wishers, Tatyana Petrovna. It will be no rest. But it's true that our apartment is unsuitable. I'm looking for a much larger one. You're going to have a maid to do the housework, Tatyana Petrovna. And I won't need to play violin in a Russian restaurant in order to pay for it.' He looked at me in a plea for a little of the attention lavished on his son.

'You've done wonderfully, Alexis,' I said with feeling.

He was ready at once to agree to let me stay at Mrs Williamson's house.

A few days later, my ten-day-old son and I were discharged from the clinic. When Alexis went to settle the clinic bill, for which he had borrowed on his expected raise, he was informed it had been taken care of by someone who wished to remain anonymous. He assumed it was one of the Russian Refugee Centre's rich patrons, a supposition Countess Liline seconded.

'Vera Kirilovna, I believe you know who paid the bill,' I said to her in private later.

'Dear child,' she answered, 'there might be any number of people who would welcome the opportunity to express their admiration and appreciation.'

My spacious room in Mrs Williamson's attractive Directoire villa opened on to the garden through French windows, ceiling-high. Furnished in white-and-gilt Louis-Quinze period, it had antique silk curtains and a painted bed with a blue satin bedspread. Peter's cradle was draped to the floor in satin to match. He had an immense and impractical layette, the gift of feminine friends, and I a closet full of elegant robes and tea gowns.

'Dear child,' Vera Kirilovna reassured me, 'you know I bring customers to exclusive shops. I have arrangements. I can permit myself these small extravagances for my own pleasure.'

Besides Mrs Williamson's butler, maid and cook, a Swiss nurse had been hired to look after my son. Nyanya immediately cut the latter's task in half. She put on a white kerchief and uniform and did everything except suckle the infant.

'Go on, go on, you'll spoil your fine robe, Princess mine,' said Nyanya when I wanted to help bathe the baby. Or, 'What do you think, I can't change a diaper?' she demanded if I tried to assist.

I suggested that the diaper should not be pinned so tight. Nyanya only pinned it tighter. She handled Peter firmly and vigorously, rather like a package, but still in some way mysteriously agreeable, for as he began to differentiate between the various persons with whom he came in contact, he made plain his preference for Nyanya. And at the hour of his father's visit he chose to have his daily fit.

Alexis's ears were painfully affected. 'Why does he cry all the time?' he asked. He refused to believe that the child only cried the moment he walked in the door.

My son did not cry long, because Nyanya lifted him, all hot and hiccupy, out of his cradle and carried him to her rocking corner, even though the Swiss baby nurse said a baby must be allowed to cry. Nyanya also brought him to me whenever his bell-like tones told her he was hungry, regardless of whether it was the exact hour prescribed by the pediatrician. The Swiss nurse said Madame must wait another half-hour, but the bell-like tones aroused some mysterious physiological response, and I could not wait either.

I hastily lay down on my silken bed. After some confusion due to rage, Peter clamped down on the breast and pulled away, eyes closed, fists rapturously clenched, toenails working into my side fuzzy head warm and soft against my arm. A delicious languor stole over me. I dropped off to sleep with my son.

'I'm so lazy, it's not right,' I said to my old nurse when I awoke to find the baby asleep on his stomach in his cradle.

'Yes, it's right, my love. It's the way it's meant to be,' Nyanya rejoined.

I believed her. After years of privation, torment and sorrow, I was content to be without care, to feel soft fabrics against my skin, to doze off when I nursed, to live in a languid, physical present like the summer of first love. And in this state, my sweet and guilty fancies increasingly turned to *him*, the lover and husband of my dreams, now also the dream-father of my son.

On 12 October 1920, Poland signed an armistice with the Soviet Union and my mother-in-law announced that she was going home to Warsaw.

The poor lady, I fear, had been sadly disillusioned by the turn of events. The butler who opened the door for her clearly made her feel she ought to come in by the kitchen entrance. Vera Kirilovna was perfectly correct towards her, and had even, at my request, shown her the sights and shops. But none of her high-society friends was ever around when my mother-in-law called. 'Professor Holveg, the celebrated scientist and academician, tutor to the martyred sons of our late beloved Grand Duke Constantine,' in Vera Kirilovna's words, was one thing, but Madame Holveg *mère*, *née* Goldstein, with unmistakably Semitic nose and accent, was quite another.

My mother-in-law sensed this very well. Had historical circumstances been different, I've no doubt she would have made quite as fine a lady-in-waiting to a queen of Judea as had Vera Kirilovna to an empress of Russia. She held her bosom high. She blazed defiance out of coal-black eyes. I remained as deferent as before. But the differences in our backgrounds, which my mother-in-law had overlooked in a two-room apartment without servants, became painfully apparent in my elegant new surroundings.

When I said dutifully, on hearing of her departure, that I had hoped she would settle in Paris, she answered that her son would have enough difficulties in his marriage without her adding to them. Her brother Nathan Goldstein had prospered in the United States and she had decided to join him there in a few months. I suspected Alexis was even more relieved than I at this announcement. In the first days of November he put his mother on the train. She emigrated to the United States early in 1921.

With the departure of Sarah Holveg, Vera Kirilovna felt free to open the house to the delegations of well-wishers my husband anticipated. I received these in the afternoon. In the morning I dictated an international correspondence to my secretary from the centre. Our new apartment was to be ready in mid-November. A maid had already been hired. But as I neared the end of my six-week laying-in, I became prey to mixed emotions. On the one hand, I felt guilty about my luxurious surroundings and my idleness. On the other, I was not eager to resume married life.

The lime trees bordering the lawn shed their shrivelled leaves, and as I awakened in my silken bed, in a room not unlike Aunt Sophie's, I imagined myself at Veslawa. Soon, I fancied, *he* would come from his room through his private passage, rosy and smooth-shaven, strong and glossy like a thoroughbred hunter and as nice to stroke . . .

On one of my last mornings in Mrs Williamson's house, Vera Kirilovna entered my room with a mysterious and excited air to say my secretary had a cold and could not come.

I wanted to take the baby to the Bois, but Vera Kirilovna said the weather was much too nasty.

'It might rain any moment. The house is so cold,' she added, 'you can wear your velvet gown.'

At her insistence, which seemed odd, I put on the most luxurious of my *robes d'intérieur*, of ruby velvet trimmed with ermine at the neck, cuffs and hem. It fell to the floor in a circlet like a small train.

'You look beautiful,' Vera Kirilovna pronounced. 'Your figure has filled out, it is more feminine. Your skin has a new bloom. You need only a little powder on the nose – there. Now just a touch of lipstick to bring out the glow in your eyes – you are perfect!'

'Why do I need powder and lipstick at ten o'clock in the morning if no one's coming, Vera Kirilovna?' I asked in growing bewilderment.

She looked even more mysteriously excited. As the doorbell rang, she excused herself and went out.

My room was at the back of the house, on the side opposite the entrance vestibule. I could not hear words, but the resonance of that masculine voice sent my heart into a gallop. I went to the French window, clasping the cold bronze handle and staring at the leaves dancing wildly on the lawn.

I did not turn towards Vera Kirilovna as she re-entered.

'There is a visitor here to see you, dear child,' she announced in a portentous tone.

'A visitor? At this hour? Who can it be?'

'Someone . . . of importance.'

'I'm not in the habit of receiving people whose name and business I do not know, however important they may be.' Then, as Vera Kirilovna remained silent, 'It is Prince Stefan? I will not see him,' I stated.

'Dear child, the Prince your cousin has come a very long way. I don't believe he'll be dismissed so easily.'

'Vera Kirilovna, how could you!' I exclaimed, pacing about and twisting my hands. 'Oh, what am I to do?'

'Dear child' – her tone was maternal – 'I desire only your happiness. We shall expect you in the library.'

Left alone, I put my cold hands to my burning cheeks. 'Lord, I can't, I haven't the strength. Spare me, save me!' I murmured. Then, as no help came, I said firmly, 'Well, it can't be helped,' drew myself up, and walked with outward calm into the vestibule.

Through the open door of the drawing room I caught sight of a Polish uniform and started. It was only an aide of Stefan's. The butler told me *Madame la comtesse* awaited me in the library. He threw open the double doors and I went in.

36

The library formed the angle of the house on the street side, hidden by curtains of rose damask drawn across the French windows. Two Regency settees and a wingback armchair made a conversation group before the marble fireplace in which a log burned. A pair of table lamps cast a soft light. The wind sang in the chimney, the fire crackled, light household sounds did not disturb the hush. The clock on the mantel chimed half past ten.

Stefan stood in front of the fireplace, facing the doors by which I had entered. He was in cavalry uniform, booted and belted. The French Croix de Guerre was pinned to his khaki tunic, the Polish Cross of *virtuti militari* to his gold-braided collar. He seemed even taller, broader and stronger than I remembered, as well as much older. The large monkey ears were the same but they no longer looked boyish and comical, because his head, once covered with curly locks and later with a helmet of chestnut hair, was now entirely bald. This lent a newly barbaric air to the baby-smooth face with the full pouting lips and cheeks.

I remained by the door and said softly, with a formal inclination of the head, *'Mon cousin.'*

He bowed slightly and said likewise, *'Ma cousine.'* His expression, as he watched me, was vindictive and cruel.

Countess Liline went to the French doors that closed off the library from the drawing room. '*Cher prince, chère enfant*, if you'll permit, I have some household matters to attend to. I shall leave you for a moment.'

'Vera Kirilovna, please remain,' I said.

'We don't wish to detain you, Countess,' said my cousin.

With a pout of regret, my hostess went through the double doors into the dining room, closing them behind her.

I took a few steps in the direction of the dining room, then of the vestibule, stopped, and, with the pounding heart and glazed eye of a trapped bird, turned at last to face my captor.

Stefan had observed my every move with the same sombre, fixed gaze.

'Do I really look such a terror now?' he asked in English, as he passed his hand with the heraldic ring of the Veslawski princes over his bald dome.

'Oh no ... only it was strange at first,' I stammered. With both hands, I steadied myself on the winged back of the armchair.

'Typhus. I lost so much of my hair I shave off the little that's left.'

'Ah yes, I heard. I ... I'm very sorry.'

'You seem to be.'

'Your parents' death ...'

'You already expressed suitable sympathy in your note. I haven't come all the way from Poland to exchange formalities.'

'Why have you come? I asked you never to see me again.'

'I wanted to hear you say it to my face. I found it hard to believe you could dismiss me so lightly from your life with a few lines.'

'Not lightly.' I bowed my head over the armchair, while my fingers played with the cording. 'But I thought it would be easier for you, for us both.'

'It would have been easier, no doubt, for you if I hadn't been discovered in the Ukraine by our troops. It would have spared you embarrassment at your treachery.'

'Treachery!' I lifted a flaming face. 'I thought you dead!'

'You thought me dead! You *heard* I was dead and you promptly believed it. You couldn't even wait a year before marrying. You must have been in a hurry to be rid of me!'

'It's not true! I wouldn't believe it at first. I went to Taganrog to see General Denikin. He sent me the dossier. I read the eyewitness report. I saw the photographs. When I think of it, I shudder.' I was, in fact, seized with a long shudder.

As I looked at my cousin's bald, barbaric head, it seemed to me to be rising up out of the ground like the vision of horror conjured by the report of his murder – the vision that had almost driven me to take my own life. I covered my face in my hands.

'It isn't one of my fondest memories either,' said Stefan, beginning to pace before the fireplace. 'But did you really think I was going to let myself be buried alive, you who knew me so well? Did you have so little faith, did you have so little love? If you hadn't already forgotten me, you'd have refused to believe every evidence, as Casimir, as Grandmother, refused to believe it, as I refused to believe the Bolsheviks had killed you. I too heard you were dead, but I crossed all Russia to find out for myself, to keep my promise, when your promise was already broken, when you'd already run off with that professor you married –'

'No, I hadn't,' I broke in. 'I didn't run off with anyone. I had pneumonia, I was acutely ill, delirious. I'd been waiting for you at the dacha, I was certain you'd come. I told Alexis nothing was impossible for you. And . . . you did come?'

I looked up at him in wonder, remembering how, in my hungry, somnolent state, I had daydreamed that he'd carry me off in a swift sledge. But his face was no longer humbly adoring as that visage of sweet fantasy; it was now hard and vengeful. Unable to bear its stare, I sank into the armchair and stared silently into the fire.

'Yes, I came,' Stefan said. 'I was wild, mad with hope. I feared nothing and no one. I'd made my way north in various disguises. I arrived in Leningrad driving a sleigh with a load of lumber for the commissariat of supply. I told the Reds I had come to fetch my bride . . . Bah! What's the use of going back over it? What does it matter now!' He pushed the fire tongs with the tip of his boot, and they went clattering down.

I started. Then, 'No, tell me, I beg you. I must know everything!' I pleaded.

'I got to Petrograd in the middle of February 1919. I drove my empty sleigh across the ice to your dacha. I went to the gamekeeper's cottage. Empty. I tramped all over the estate, into every outbuilding and boathouse. Then I searched the villa itself, from cellar to attic. It was all smashed up, broken windows, furniture, snow in the halls. At the top of the central stairs I saw an apparition, a huge gaunt fellow with a long beard. He announced me, and I recognized your footman, Fyodor. When I asked him where you were, he answered, "Her Highness has gone for a drive," and asked for my card.

'I went all through the house calling for you, Fyodor behind, asking for my card. I went into your bedroom where I attempted to abduct you on the eve of the war – I knew even then it was the only way I could have you, by force. Ah, what a fool I was not to have done it!'

'And Fyodor?' I felt the heat in my face. 'Did you take him with you?'

'I couldn't. When I tried to get him into the sleigh, he seized me by the neck, repeating, "I asked you for your card." I had a time overpowering him. Poor devil! I expect he's still there.'

'I shall never forgive Alexis for leaving him. I shall never forgive myself!' Again, I had my face in my hands. Then, by a tremendous effort of self-control, I lifted it and asked, 'I still don't understand the report of your death. It was so convincing. There were shots. Three bodies were found, shot through the head. One was exceptionally large, with a big chest, a scar ... Was the report false, then?'

'No, it was accurate as far as it went. It was merely incomplete.'

'In what way? How *did* you escape death? Or was it a miracle?' I was prepared to believe it.

'It was a miracle of sorts. But why should you care? What could the full story matter to you now?'

'I was nearly driven mad.' His unfairness roused me. 'I came within a second of blowing out my brains with my revolver ...' Of going straight to the Void, I thought, of damning my soul!

'Tanya!' His expression lost its cruel fixity. He took a step towards me, frowned, then turned back towards the fire. 'Very well, I'll tell you.' He spoke without looking at me, hands clenched behind his back. 'The moment the bandit chief ordered the pits dug, I said to myself, Keep calm, Stevie, save your breath. You're not going to be buried alive. When the chief came back with his second, after his band had decamped in pursuit of the White fugitives, I began to whistle a Ukrainian air, the only one I knew. He shot the other two wretches in the ground. Then he stopped over me, pistol in hand, as I whistled, literally, for my life.

'"Listen to his birdsong!" he said. "Maybe he can fly out of his hole!" And they galloped away.

'When darkness fell, peasants came to strip the corpses. I whistled that same air. At first, they took to their heels. Then they came back and dug me out. They took me to their village, wrapped and rubbed me until the blood flowed normally through my limbs again. They couldn't have been kinder had I been their own lost son. Odd, isn't it, the kindness one meets in the midst of civil war.' He half turned to glance at me. Then, 'Had I known how it would affect you,' he concluded, 'I'd not have gone to such lengths to pass myself off as dead.' His voice was no longer accusing.

'But, that body ...'

'That was a bit of a miracle. I told my peasant rescuers I was afraid the bandits might return and, finding my hole empty, look for me in the village. They told me then that a young deacon from their village had just come home to die. He had seen the priests martyred by the Reds in the Cathedral of Smolensk, where he sang, and it had unhinged his mind. He resolved to join his brethren in heaven, turned his face to the wall in his mother's hut, and gave up the ghost. He was about my age, a vigorous fine fellow with a singer's chest. He even had a scar on his left thigh, from a shellburst when he'd served at the front as a *sanitar*. When I saw the scar, I took it – fool that I was – as a sign from Providence.

'Well, the villagers let me have their dead deacon to fill in my hole. I loaded him on a cart, took along a pistol found on one of the bodies just stripped, buried and shot him twice through the head like the other two wretches.

'At dawn, I put on his peasant garb, which fit like my own, and went on my way, my bundle slung over my shoulder, whistling my Ukrainian air and thinking the worst was over –' Stefan broke off and clenched his hands behind his back once more.

'What happened after you went to the dacha?' I asked.

'What's the use? It's not what I came for.'

'Tell me quickly, please!'

'I was so desperate at not having found you, I grew careless. I was caught and thrown into Kronstadt Prison, a jolly place. I heard what they did to your father there ... you know I admired Uncle Peter more than any man, God rest his soul. They tried some of the same treatment on me, as a suspected White spy. When it got them nowhere, they decided it'd be a pity to shoot such a husky fellow. I was allowed to "volunteer" into the Red Army, with a political commissar from a punitive detachment at my back. They sent me all the way to the Caucasus.

'The Whites were retaking it inch by inch – mountain terrain is murderous – under the command of General Wrangel, the Black Baron they called him because of his Cossack uniform. The Cossacks made him an honorary chieftain, and he deserved it. He was the last Russian I'd ever want to fight, so I slipped away at the first opportunity.

'I avoided revealing my identity to the Whites. They were hopping mad at the Poles for signing a truce with the Bolsheviks at the very time the Whites came within striking reach of Moscow.'

'I know,' I put in. 'I pleaded with your General Karnicki to make common cause with the Whites. Of course, General Denikin, on his part, refused to make concessions. It was hopeless.'

'A provincial lot, on both sides.' Stefan made an elegant, deprecatory gesture that reminded me of Father.

'I'm glad to hear you say that! But your own story . . . you haven't finished.'

'Oh that!' I saw he was hesitant to continue talking about his odyssey. 'Well, by the end of 1919, just as the Poles resumed hostilities with the Soviets, I'd made my way beyond Kiev to a Jewish settlement in the Pale, only to be stricken with typhus. This time it was a Jewish family that took me in and saved my life. They hid me when the Bolsheviks came down, driving the southern White Army to the Black Sea. They nursed me like a son.

'That day in May when I heard Polish voices, I wept with joy. Although a skeleton and half bald, within a month I was able to sit a horse. I rode into Veslawow at the head of our lancers . . . God, what a welcome! Grandmother was standing on the palace steps . . . For a moment I expected you might be standing next to her. I had inquiries made after you. I thought surely you'd have gone to England, where my cousins at Lansdale would have welcomed you. Instead, I heard you were president of the Russian Refugee Centre in Paris. I sent you Commandant Dugard. Then, your letter.

'Tanya, you don't know what his news did to me. To come back to life . . . for that! To see this dream I'd carried through war, prison, typhus, through the death of my mother and father . . . Mother, who died in my arms, calling me her Stan, only a few weeks after the Colonel was blown to bits before my eyes . . . to see this dream shattered, to be betrayed by you, after the most agonizing year of my life, which took my youth, my health . . . to be cast aside less than a year after my purported death . . . yes, that was hard, harder than any torture I underwent at the hands of bandits or Reds!'

'If it was hard for you, wasn't it even more bitter for me, all the more so for having thrown happiness away with my own hands!' I cried with equal passion. And overcome by self-pity as well as remorse, I put my head into the angle of my chair and began to sob.

At the harsh sound of my weeping, my cousin's expression changed. He approached and began stroking my hair. 'You're crying, my sweet, I've made you cry. Forgive me . . . But if what you say is true, then it can still be remedied.'

My sobs ceased under his caress. I raised my tearful face. 'What are you saying?'

'That nothing is irreparable except death. That there's no need to throw our happiness away.'

'But I'm married! And I have a child!'

'I know you do, sweet. She's so grown up now, my Tanya-panya, she's become a mother, and I love her the better for it. Now stop making a soggy mess of Mrs Williamson's chair and come and sit here by me.' He drew me from the armchair on to one of the settees. 'You're not frightened of me any more, are you? Let me see your face. It's all wet, and so's your hankie.' He handed me a clean handkerchief from his trousers pocket. 'What a child you are still.' Tenderly, he watched me wipe my nose. 'And with short hair, like a schoolgirl.'

'It was cut during my illness. I didn't let it grow again . . . because I thought you dead.'

'Really? Well, now you can let it grow, so I can play with it. Remember how I used to pull it, and tie you up?' He passed his large and well-shaped hand with the seal ring over my hair.

'How did you get your ring back?' I said quickly.

'It was sent to Grandmother when she refused to accept the body as mine. Why do you sit so stiff?' He continued to stroke my hair.

'Don't . . . please,' I pleaded, unable to move away.

'All right. There'll be time enough.' Taking my hand, he twined my fingers with his and lightly kissed my fingertips.

I looked into the face that had been so vindictive a moment ago and was now so kind and tender. The baldness that had so startled me only added to the overall smoothness of Stevie's person. It no longer seemed, as in youth, the result of vain application, but effortlessly natural. He wore the uniform with the casual ease of his British-educated father yet with the martial dash peculiar to his countrymen. I laid my free hand on his broad chest and looked at him in childlike admiration. 'Stevie-levie monkey ears, how elegant you are!'

'You don't find me "revulsive" without hair? I'm no longer a monstro?'

'You're not revulsive in the least. I like you bald. I like you better than ever.'

'Tanya-panya, Skinny-ninny, I like you even better too. Only you're not skinny any more, you're just right, and that dress is most elegant too. You had one like it, which you wore at the New Year's dinner at Minsk, in 1916. Remember?'

'Yes. Uncle Stan told us about Great-Aunt Catherine. How is she?'

'Just the same, only a little more frail. She stayed at Veslawa all through the Red invasion. I couldn't get her to budge. Our people think her a saint. Ah, my sweet, you don't know what these years have been, what our people have gone through. The devastation, the poverty! There's so much to be done, so much to rebuild, and I'm so anxious to start! I can't wait to take you home, with your son, whom I'll make mine and heir to his share of whatever I've left, with the brothers and sisters we will give him. Do you still want eight children, love, after the hard labour you had with your first?'

'It wasn't that bad.' I was still and submissive under the beautiful resonance of his voice as I had been under his caress. 'And it wouldn't have mattered, had you been there.'

'I will be in the future. But I think one or two more children will do. Times have changed. I haven't any large estates to leave them; I've given all but Veslawa away. You'll have to take me poor as I am. But I'll raise a loan in England – I'm leaving today – we'll get things in shape again. While I'm gone, you'll start divorce proceedings. My solicitor will be in touch with you –'

'Solicitor, divorce! Stevie, wait . . .' I drew away, breathless.

He rose abruptly, scowling. 'You weren't married in the Catholic Church. I'll see to it that there's no publicity or scandal. Your husband will consent, once he learns of my prior claim. I'll speak to him.'

'No!' Alexis would discover my deceit, I thought. I would lose all esteem in his eyes.

'Wha-at? Do you love him?'

'Yes. No. Not in the way you think.' I could not bear the terrible look Stevie bent on me. 'I admire Alexis. I respect him. I trust him. I'm used to him.' He was familiar and safe, not this terrifyingly attractive, new and mature Stefan. *Him* I could not bend to my will. 'Alexis has been through so much for my sake,' I continued. 'He has done me only good. How can I hurt him?'

'You cannot hurt him, you say. But it's all right to hurt me!'

'Stevie, forgive me!' I pleaded. 'I know I've done you a great wrong. But will I make it right by doing my husband an even greater one? He was my only support during the Revolution. He helped Father. He rescued me.'

'He did not rescue you, he risked your life unnecessarily. He took advantage of your youth and naïvety. He manipulated you to gain his ends –'

'It wasn't like that at all!'

It was I who had taken advantage of Alexis's infatuation, I who had toyed with his devotion, I who lied to him about Stefan. I had allowed him to think me noble and pure, as Stevie still did. Oh, they wanted their women spotless, these gullible men. And why did we foster their delusion? Why couldn't I tell Stevie the truth? Why couldn't I tell Alexis? Because I was too proud, too vain.

'What a loyal little wife you are.' Stefan observed me bitterly. 'As loyal as you were a daughter. If only you could be as loyal to your love! But that, with you, has always come second.' He sat down again and regarded me in angry bewilderment. 'I don't understand you, Tanya.'

Did I understand myself? I saw only turmoil and contradiction – insoluble dilemma.

'Alexis is the father of my child,' I said more weakly. Stevie's proximity drained my will.

'The father of your child! I know it well. But I'm willing to be a father to him too, and a better one, I'll wager. What can he do for a boy, that scientist of yours? Can he teach him anything that's not in a book? Can he be a friend and an example, as my father was to me? Which of us can do better, he or I?' He took my hands. 'Answer me.'

I tried to pull away, but he drew me closer. 'Tatyana, look at me.'

His voice, commanding yet caressing, added to my confusion. I should have asked, Would Aunt Sophie, were she alive, tell me to leave my husband? Would Uncle Stan want Stefan to bring a divorced woman to his palace and call another man's son his own? I should have pleaded with Stevie not to exploit my weakness and seduce me into breaking the higher law of right and wrong. But I could not speak.

A force stronger than gravity bowed me down. I laid my cheek against one of the hands that held mine. With eyes closed, I let myself be drawn to that broad chest that was still the place of ultimate safety, triumph, peace. A hand whose touch was warm, gentle yet strong, tilted up my chin, and I felt upon mine those velvety lips . . .

Fantasy had not lied. There was an elemental power in those lips equal to my son's pull at my breast, a rapture, divine or satanic, that could make damnation sweet! Had the house not been full of people, it would not have ended there. I would have committed adultery on the spot. But end it did, perforce.

In the moment after that timeless interval, a reckless inspiration came to me.

'Stevie,' I murmured, 'let us disappear, go to South America, or better still, Africa, to Kenya. They need white settlers. We can buy a plantation. There'll be space, horses, big game. The natives will need medical care.' It would mean adventure, I thought, challenge, and, best of all, freedom and privacy. 'We'll change our name. No one will know who we are. No more Poland, Russia. No more Prince Veslawski and Princess Silomirskaya. Just us, and Peter, and Nyanya, of course.'

'Would you really do it?' The old boyish gleam lit up Stevie's eyes.

'Yes!' It was the only way. To flee without facing Alexis, flee from the personage I had been raised to be.

'I didn't know you were such a romantic.' Stefan mulled over the proposal. Then, getting up from the settee, he went to the French window and slightly parted the curtains. 'There are two men sitting in a car across the street, reporters without a doubt. For all my precautions, I've been followed. We'd never get away with it.' He came back to my side. 'Besides, why do we need to go to Africa to hunt big game when we have our own Polish forests? Don't you love Veslawa anymore, Tanyussia?' he added as my face fell.

Why, I thought, must life always interfere with love?

'Oh I do! But it would be going back, don't you see?' Back, I meant, into the fairy-tale world of princes and princesses, the world of pomp and privilege whose destruction I had witnessed in Russia, whose destruction must follow in Poland too.

'You still believe in a brave new world?' The gleam of daring and adventure was gone. In place of the boy Stevie sat the mature, responsible Stefan, the working prince who saw his duty clearly and without equivocation. 'Well, I don't. I believe we must make the best of the world such as it is. True, there are Poles in power today who hark back to our past greatness, who haven't seen with their own eyes the shape of the future, Soviet-style. I'm not one of them. I intend to go with modern times, with the potential good they hold. I thought you ideally suited to help me. I could never imagine another woman in Mother's place. Was I wrong?'

Was I suited to take Aunt Sophie's place? Had I ever really wanted to? 'To be a princess will no longer mean anything. To be a physician will be very fine.' Grandmaman's words on her deathbed came back to me as I gazed into the fire mutely.

'Was I wrong, Tanya?' Stefan repeated, turning my head towards him.

I went limp again. But before another kiss could rout the last vestige of reason and resistance, the vestibule doors were flung open by Nyanya, and my son's irate screams poured in from the nursery.

'Well, Princess mine, a fine business this is!' scolded Nyanya. 'Your son is half starved and blue in the face from his cries, and what are you doing, if one might ask?'

My hand went to my breasts, which became swollen and painful in automatic response to the baby's cries. I faltered. 'Stevie, I must go nurse Petya. I will try to think, and give you my answer in a while, if you can wait. Nyanya, talk to Prince Stefan. Tell him everything.' Tell him all I could not say in my defence, I entreated her silently, and rushed out.

After I had lain down and the Swiss nurse had put Peter to the breast, I reflected on my dilemma:

What was the last thing I thought of, before Nyanya erupted into the library? Yes, I wondered if I was suited to take Aunt Sophie's place. A Princess Veslawska must learn to yield graciously, to rule without seeming to, to put herself second, always, to her husband and lord. The life of a Princess Veslawska is proscribed and circumscribed to the smallest detail. She can only be free with her husband ... in bed. Ah, but for that freedom, would I not willingly exchange all others?

You would, Tanya, you know you would. Yet, wouldn't that be slavery rather than freedom, slavery to the Gypsy Tanya kept in check all these years? Once she were awakened, would Stevie discover he had married, not a replica of his mother but a jealous, tyrannical harpy?

Come now, Tanya, don't exaggerate! You can control yourself. You always have. Yes, but with Stevie I am not myself. My will, my mind, my soul are annihilated. It's not his fault. He would be the last to wish it. Yet he can't help doing it. Whereas Alexis holds up to me the strong, competent, independent *free* self that I strive for.

Oh! but what's the use of a cold, proud, unloving self? Is it not a sham? At least, Gypsy Tanya is honest. She does not care what the world thinks. Is it not better to be frankly wicked than dishonestly good? Haven't I always despised conventional morality? Didn't I know long ago that it only served to hide the cesspool that was polite society? If so, should I not follow my heart and go with Stevie?

I felt a surge of joy and wanted to get up and tell Stevie at once. But Peter was nursing greedily. I looked at my wristwatch. It was a Swiss platinum watch Alexis had given me for my twenty-third birthday. He had had it inscribed in French *'to my dearly beloved wife'*.

He paid for it by playing in the Russian restaurant, my thoughts ran on. He has worked so hard in the past year to make me comfortable. Everything he has achieved, his knowledge and eminence, the respect and affection of his students, the esteem of his colleagues, his acceptance into high society – everything cost courage and enormous effort since childhood. Nothing was given him by right of birth, nothing made easy. Yet he is as cultured and fine a gentleman as many an aristocrat, perhaps more. I and Peter Alexis are his reward and crowning pride. And how can I simply take this away from him to satisfy my passion? What right have I to take Peter from his own father? Might not my son reproach me for it later if I did?

Oh! but how shall I kiss Alexis after I have kissed Stefan? How will I lie in his puny arms when I have felt Stevie's strong embrace? Either way, it's impossible!

At this, Peter doubled up and looked ready to scream.

I'm going to give him colic if I don't calm down, I thought, and took several deep breaths to quiet myself. I succeeded in putting Stefan and Alexis out of my mind long enough for the baby to get his fill. Then, emotionally exhausted, I dozed off.

'My angel, did you have a good meal? Did it go well, my love?' asked Nyanya when she came back from the library after an hour, picking up Peter to burp him.

'He was so furious, I almost cried out when he took the breast. After a while, we both calmed down. Did you have a long talk with Prince Stefan?' I asked as I got up to dress.

'I did all the talking. He listened without a word. When I told him about your wound, and how you forgot everything when we were hiding in the cellar, he shook his head and repeated, "Poor Tanya, poor, poor Tanya!" He will not be angry with you again. He asked to see Petya.'

'I'll take him in.' I combed my hair and powdered my nose. Then, 'Nyanya,' I asked while she changed the baby's diaper, 'what shall I do?'

'You know yourself what to do, Princess mine,' she replied without glancing at me.

'No, I won't let you off that easily.' I left the dressing table and came to stand over the bed beside her. 'It's so frightfully complicated. Advise me.'

'What's complicated about it?' Nyanya took a safety pin out of her mouth and pinned the diaper tight. 'If you desert your husband, your conscience will gnaw away at you. If you stay, forbidden lust will torment you. You choose.'

I could deal with lust better than with conscience. Lust I had dealt with for a long time. And if I could not trust my emotions, if I could swing from adoration to rebellion against one and the same man, pass from one absorption to another, would it not be better to heed God's commandments?

'I'm so terribly sorry for Stefan, Nyanya.' I tried once more to justify the path of desire.

'Yes, he suffered plenty for you.' Nyanya was pitiless. 'But he's young, attractive. He'll find himself a beautiful princess, one with a fortune, as he should. He'll forget grief, he'll forget passion. He'll love you again with a pure brotherly love, as in your childhood. As for you, you'll just have to learn to deal with your own passions.'

Nyanya's every word was a blow. I wanted Stevie's happiness, yet I could not bear to contemplate it. I wanted his brotherly love, though I knew it would be torture.

I took the baby from Nyanya and was about to return to the library when Vera Kirilovna, unable to repress her curiosity any longer, came in to say that luncheon would be served in forty-five minutes. She hoped Prince Stefan would stay.

I made no response.

'I've made a point, you know, of following Polish affairs,' she went on airily. 'The Poles are already at each other's throats again, and there is talk, for the sake of unity, of a restoration of the monarchy with Marshal Pilsudski as premier.'

'Indeed?' I said.

'Prince Stefan is immensely popular,' she went on, 'the hero of the Polish–Soviet war, and he *is* the direct descendant of the Piast dynasty.'

I understood that Vera Kirilovna was willing to spend her remaining years as lady-in-waiting to the Queen of Poland, in my humble person.

To do my kinswoman justice, I believe she truly desired my happiness, just as the best of mothers desires the most prosperous and prominent marriage for her daughter. So now, as I carried my son into the library, I could imagine her asking herself, Is it a good sign she takes the baby in or a bad sign? Is it possible she could refuse the Prince: his rank, fortune, youth, and attractiveness? No, it's not humanly possible . . . or is it?

In the library, Stefan looked at me sadly, but no longer angrily. I understood he was ready to give me up if he must. But in the moment of announcing my own renunciation, words failed me.

I can't, I can't give him up again, I thought. I looked at him mutely as tears came into my eyes.

'Is it no, then?' he said.

I lowered my head and swallowed my tears.

'I can accept it better now that Nyanya has told me how much you owe Professor Holveg.' He spoke with calm dignity. 'But to ask me to renounce you altogether is beyond my present strength.

I may not see you for several years, certainly not until I'm married and have a child of my own, but I don't want to be cut off from you. I'd like to be a friend and guide to your son. Perhaps, when he's older, you'll let him come to Veslawa for a summer. I won't invite you without your husband. I'll only see you in his presence. I'll forget our former ties. We shall be first cousins, brother and sister, nothing more. Do you accept?'

'Oh yes!' I was reprieved from a sentence of death. I dropped a kiss of joy on Peter's fuzzy head. Nothing was irreparable except death, Stevie had said. And what might the future not bring?

'May I?' Stefan reached for Peter.

I handed him over. 'Be careful of his head. He works at holding it up but it's still weak.'

In my cousin's large hands, Peter looked like a doll.

Stefan held him without awkwardness, bending over to look into his sleeping face. 'What a tiny thing! You're no beauty, boy, but you look awfully pleased with yourself just the same. Wake up so I can see your eyes.'

Peter drew up his legs, worked his hands free from underneath his blue shawl, wrinkled his disdainful nose, and opened his eyes. They rested fixedly and intelligently on Stefan. Stefan blew up his cheeks. Peter's eyes almost closed, his mouth opened, and he let out a sound, between a squeal and a hiccup, but definitely expressing delight.

'He laughed, he laughed, Nyanya,' I called, and she ran in. 'Petya laughed for the first time.'

'Maybe it was something else.' She took the baby from Stefan. 'No, you're dry. Did you really laugh, my angel? Show us how you did it.'

Peter had become absorbed in blowing bubbles, even while he pulled off Nyanya's white kerchief with one hand. Stefan bent over, filled his cheeks with air, and once again Peter made that sound, part squeal, part hiccup – it was a laugh.

Vera Kirilovna now came in, and finding us all smiles she smiled also, with a happy significance. But when she learned that Baby's first laugh was the reason for the jollity, she could not repress a movement of pique. She managed to hide her disappointment at the realization that she would never be lady-in-waiting to Poland's future queen, and only asked Nyanya pointedly if it was not time to put the baby down for his nap. Obviously she considered Peter Alexis responsible for the failure of her plans.

After Nyanya had borne off the offender, Vera Kirilovna turned to my cousin. 'Will you stay to lunch, *cher prince*?'

'Thank you, Countess, but I must be going. Tanya, before I do, is there anything I can do for you?'

'The Polish government seems reluctant to grant me a passport.'

'What nonsense! I'll attend to it at once. Anything else?'

'I have a kinsman, a brilliant amateur historian. You knew him during the Great War, on the Somme. He returned to Russia at the same time as you, and escaped last spring.'

'L-M? I like him immensely. What can I do for him?'

'He's barely subsisting in Paris as a freelance journalist. He should get an advanced degree at the Sorbonne so he can teach, but he's very proud. One can't give him money outright.'

'The thing is to set up a contest with a scholarship as prize, for foreigners in France, or something of the sort. I'll give it some thought.' Stefan jotted it down in a pocket notebook. 'Is that all?'

'Our Russian Refugee Centre needs an estate, preferably near Paris, where we could establish a *maison de retraite* for our older refugees,' I was emboldened to ask.

'Well, well, you're playing philanthropist in earnest! Grandmaman would be proud of you. I'll find you an estate, dear cousin, only don't go putting my name on any donor's plaques or they'll fry me back home. Any aid I lend to a Russian cause must remain anonymous.'

'You do a great many things anonymously, *mon cousin*.' I thought of the bill at the maternity clinic.

Vera Kirilovna gave me a reproachful look. She was not only impressed with the Veslawski manner, it fairly made her burn with disappointment.

'We're not going to start keeping accounts *en famille*, are we?' Stefan retorted.

I felt petty and ungracious. 'No. There's one thing more. If there is any way of helping Fyodor . . .'

'That's the most difficult request of all. But if there is a way, it'll be done.'

I believed him implicitly. 'Please give my regards to your family in England, to Lord Andrew especially. Thank you . . . for everything.'

'There's no need. Please convey my greetings to Professor Holveg. Vera Kirilovna, if I can be of service, you know how to reach me. Tanya . . .' He turned towards me.

I gave him my hand. 'Give my love and homage to Princess Catherine. And remember me to Casimir. Is he still in the army?'

'Not much longer. He's going to put Veslawa in shape as soon as he's out.' Stefan held my hand high while he looked at me intently, kissed it, then stood aside for Vera Kirilovna to see him out.

His great voice rang out in the vestibule, then the front door closed and a car drove off. The fire had died down. The room seemed to grow smaller, colder. The clock on the mantel chimed a quarter to one with icy precision.

Motionless, I gazed at the doors through which Stefan had gone. My hands held loosely below my waist, my velvet gown falling in a circlet about me, I stood in the court pose of supreme moments of trial as well as solemnity. A gnawing emptiness filled the centre of my being, where my son had been. It swelled larger than my recently pregnant abdomen, rose to my throat. Nothing, nothing in this world could ever fill that gap!

In those few moments I felt myself growing years older. Until now, in spite of all I had undergone, I had remained a romantic young woman. Since Stefan had walked through those doors, I had relegated my woman's dreams to the realm of fantasy.

When Vera Kirilovna came back and found me in the same posture still, with the same grave gaze, she must have understood there was nothing more to say.

'A pity the Prince your cousin had to leave,' she remarked while she drew back the curtains on the deserted, windswept street. 'Such a generous, such a noble young man. A true prince. What abominable weather! It will be a cold winter, I fear.'

The butler appeared inside the French doors and announced lunch.

Vera sighed. Lifting her head with inimitable composure, she invited me to precede her into the dining room.

EPILOGUE

On 3 December 1920, when he was two months old, Peter Alexis Holveg was christened in the Russian Cathedral on the Rue Daru. Countess Liline was his godmother, and Prince Lomatov-Moskovsky, L-M, his godfather.

On this occasion, I could not deny Mrs Williamson the pleasure of giving a gala christening party in her house in Neuilly, and of showing off the court curtsies she had practised under Vera Kirilovna's instruction, to the rather startled imperial highnesses present. These included the three sons of the late Grand Duchess Marie Pavlovna, Boris, Cyril and Andrey Vladimirovich, the last now married to his former mistress and darling of imperial Russia, the famous ballerina Kshesinskaya.

The buffet supper had been prepared by no less than the former Silomirsky chef, the Pole Anatole, who had defected ignominiously when the revolutionary mob invaded our *osobnyak*. Discovered by Vera Kirilovna lording it over the kitchens of the Ritz, he had been shamed into donating his artistic gifts.

For dessert, tribute in specie as well as labour was offered joyously by Zinaida Mikhailovna, who had opened a Russian tearoom in Passy under the management of Kolenka. In spite of a choice international clientele, however, the business only just supported its owners: Zinaida Mikhailovna had the greatest scruples about charging customers, and Kolenka, who had none, could not keep money in his pocket long.

The party over, Alexis and I, with Peter Alexis asleep on Nyanya's shoulder, were driven home in Mrs Williamson's Packard to our new apartment overlooking the Trocadéro Gardens. Large and old-fashioned, with the high ceilings I craved, it was soberly but handsomely furnished in Empire style with bargains ferreted out by Vera Kirilovna. It included a Steinway baby grand, bought with the sale of my last jewel.

In this our new and, I believed, permanent home, my husband and I resumed married life much as before, but without the honeymoon glow. He was extremely busy as a full professor at the Collège de France, and very much involved in his revolutionary atomic research. I had my hands full with a child and the Russian Centre. Alexis still helped me with my science studies, while I continued to accompany his violin and to play in our chamber-music evenings once a week. He now welcomed the friends his former possessiveness would have excluded. To me, they were a godsend. Especially cherished were L-M, ever the wry aristocrat with an objective view of our common lost grandeur, and Genady Roslov.

The great pianist appeared in Paris after the forced annexation of Georgia by the Soviet Union in April 1921, with his Georgian bride, the ravishing young princess whose family guest he had been in Tiflis. Genady and Alexis became close friends, and the couple joined our intimate circle.

Another marriage across class barriers – one happy result of the Revolution – was that of Prince Gabriel of Russia, single surviving son of Grand Duke Constantine. Prince Gabriel had escaped execution thanks to his commoner wife and her intercession with Maxim Gorky. They too became habitués of the Holveg household. Gabriel Constantinovich still held his brothers' tutor in fond awe, and was full of anecdotes about Alexis at Pavlovsk.

I liked to see my successful husband surrounded by admiration and affection. He was justly proud and content. It made up, I felt, for my want of passion. He did not seem to miss it. We, and our friends, who had survived the storms of war and revolution, were grateful enough to have come into a quiet harbour. Although it offered no glorious or romantic vistas, we remained free and, at least for the present, safe.

On 1 February 1921, the Russian Refugee Centre, now rechristened the Silomirsky Foundation, celebrated the first anniversary of its founding with its first annual benefit ball. At this ball, I made the announcement that a suburban estate with a château and several pavilions had been donated to the foundation by Lady Dorothy Hadlow. Shortly after, the press reported the engagement to Stefan Veslawski of Lady Dorothy Hadlow, only surviving child and heiress of the Scottish Catholic peer, the seventeenth Duke of

Scarsbury, and Lady Maude, only daughter of an immensely wealthy Glasgow industrialist.

On the night after this news appeared, I felt an irresistible urge to pick a quarrel with Alexis and make wounding remarks. I left the house on the pretext that Vera Kirilovna had been taken ill, and spent the night with her. There I locked the door of my bedroom and gave myself up to sorrow and rage.

Nyanya's prophetic words about Stefan rang in my ears: 'He's young, attractive. He'll find himself a beautiful princess, one with a fortune, as he should. He'll forget grief. He'll forget passion ... As for you, you'll just have to learn to deal with your own passions ...'

He had forgotten! In a few short months, he had already forgotten! He had replaced me with the greatest of ease, with a Scottish noblewoman not only immensely rich but lovely – how I had stared at her newspaper photograph! For him, it had worked out for the best. As for me, I must learn to live with my own passions ... It was intolerable!

Hold on a moment, Tanya, the voice of reason spoke. It was you who jilted Stevie, you who married another man. And when he came to reassert his prior claim, you spurned him. What right have you to gnash your teeth and wail?

Be quiet. I have listened to you long enough, I flung back. I could give up Stevie because I thought I could keep his love. Without it, I cannot live.

I stormed through the night, and came down to breakfast red-eyed and with an inflamed throat. Vera Kirilovna had the tact to keep silent. When I went home from the Silomirsky Foundation at the end of the day, I had a fever.

Alexis attributed my illness to overwork, and nursed me like a father. This return to our prior roles, when he had been my rescuer and I a half-crazed fugitive, reawakened my tender gratitude and my dependency. I owed Alexis so much! I owed him not only my life but its meaning, in our son, in my medical career. If I could not offer him passion, if I could never tear Stefan out of my heart and flesh, I could none the less give my husband all the affection and devotion he so richly deserved, without any reservation.

I recovered in ten days, and was my usual composed self once more. But this time my outward calm corresponded to an inner, bittersweet tranquillity.

On 18 March 1921, the Treaty of Riga ratified the peace between Poland and the Soviet Union.

Before the summer, Great-Aunt Catherine passed away in her sleep and was laid to rest beside her 'little angel', Prince Leon, in the cemetery overlooking the Vistula at the edge of Veslawa. To the end, she refused to believe in my marriage to Alexis or Stefan's engagement to Lady Dorothy, and awaited my return as her grandson's bride.

A month after her obsequies, Stefan and Dorothy were married with pomp and splendour in the chapel of the Veslawski palace, where Stefan and I were to have become man and wife. True to his resolve, Stefan undertook to restore Veslawa to its former grandeur and rebuild the family's shipping and manufacturing fortune with the help of his wife's capital. But neither his contribution to Poland's renascent economy nor his near-legendary popularity earned him a role in the new nation's turbulent and petty political life. The loss, I felt, was Poland's more than his. This made me uneasy about its future.

Our eighteenth-century château near Fontainebleau became a retirement home for former members of our armed forces and court, their relatives and retainers – footmen, maids, wet nurses, and so on, who had followed their masters into exile. Since private rooms were not available for everyone, and quarrels of protocol arose, the court chamberlains and ladies-in-waiting preferred to share their rooms, not with their own kind, but with their Nyanyas and Fyodors, who bullied them as Nyanya did me.

In the entrance vestibule is a full-length portrait of Nicholas II in admiral's full dress. More portraits of Russian emperors and their consorts hang in the drawing rooms. Here their aging excellencies play bridge and bezique, reminisce about the grand old days, and avidly follow the news on the radio for signs of the awaited overthrow of the usurping Bolsheviks. On the wall of the *grand salon* is a life-size painting of Nicholas II on a white horse surrounded by his mounted military entourage – all the full generals *à la suite* – among them several murdered grand dukes and my Olympian father.

At my request there are no portraits of our sovereign's children. The chapel is dedicated to them and bears on its doors the Russian inscription: *'In memory of Their Imperial Highnesses, Aleksey Niko-*

layevich the Tsarevich, and his sisters Olga, Tatyana, Marie and Anastasia, murdered at Ekaterinburg on July 16, 1918.'

The Russian Civil War had come to a close at the end of 1920 with the evacuation from the Crimea of General Baron Wrangel's decimated force. In that heroic last stand, Baron Niessen earned his wish for an honourable grave. His orderly Simyon was interned in Rumania, and to bring him to France I began a battle that illustrated the petty nationalistic passions and spites of the post-war era. Eventually I succeeded, and he became caretaker of our Home, where he swapped endless tales of the Civil War, its horror and its glory, with Their Honours, the retired officers.

All attempts to find Fyodor proved futile. The dacha had burned down. Marauding bands of orphan boys – *bezpryzorny* – camped in the woods. There was a rumour, reported by a Finnish journalist, that a white-haired giant roamed the forests to the north. The peasants called him the 'Ghost of the Old Time'.

The Civil War had ended, but Russia's trials had not. As a result of the ravages of war and the ruthlessness of forced collectivization, two million people died of hunger in the once-rich Ukraine, which had fed all Europe. Many more would have perished but for the aid rendered by the Quaker Relief Committee organized by Herbert Hoover. The Soviet government, none the less, chose to remember America's part in the ill-fated expedition to Archangel during the Civil War rather than this selfless gesture.

But even the Soviet government had to relax its paranoid system of oppression when its staunchest defenders, the Kronstadt sailors, mutinied. The New Economic Policy proclaimed by Lenin gave the country a few years' respite and an ensuing flourishing of culture that was prematurely hailed in the West as the promised dawn of the New Age.

Those of us – my husband was one – who wished to believe in a peaceful world, progressively shed our illusions as America boycotted the League of Nations; as Mussolini's version of the totalitarian state came closer to reality in Italy; as France bled Germany with war reparations and occupied the Ruhr; as Germany's wildly inflationary economy collapsed; as Great Britain, so staunch on the battlefield, in peacetime grew mawkish and weak.

Watching the European scene, and remembering, we did not join in the reckless gaiety of the twenties – *les années folles*, the French called them. Our sober existence was enlivened enough by our son.

When Peter was two years old, I appointed Countess Liline to succeed me as president of the Silomirsky Foundation. With my science degree from the Sorbonne, earned by a prodigious effort the previous year, I enrolled in the faculty of medicine.

Peter, who was as gifted for mischief as for languages, led his young English nanny a merry chase through the Trocadéro Gardens and the long hall of our apartment, abetted by his ebullient cocker spaniel. The world was not large enough for Peter's curiosity, the universe did not contain so much energy. All the stages of civilization, all human history began afresh in this one small child. He was endlessly entertaining, exasperating, exhausting. He was a wonder. He ruled our life.

When my son was hurt, tired or cross, he did not go to Nanny or even to me. He climbed instead into Nyanya's lap and pressed his blond head against the dried-up bosom that had nursed his martyred grandfather.

Looking at them, I knew that for the little woman at the close of her life, as for the little boy at the beginning of his, there was neither sorrow for a fearful past nor apprehension of a threatening future, no thoughts of War, Revolution or Death. There was only the knowledge of something stronger than all three, which had triumphed over all three, and which my son did not yet know how to call by its name – Love.

889. 4074..